The Witch's Rebels

Books 4-6

The Witch's Rebels: Books 4-6

Blood Cursed
Death Untold
Rebel Reborn

ISBN-13: 978-1-948455-30-5

ALSO BY SARAH PIPER

Reverse Harem Romance

THE WITCH'S MONSTERS

Blood and Midnight

TAROT ACADEMY

Spells of Iron and Bone

Spells of Breath and Blade

Spells of Flame and Fury

Spells of Blood and Sorrow

Spells of Mist and Spirit

THE WITCH'S REBELS

Shadow Kissed

Darkness Bound

Demon Sworn

Blood Cursed

Death Untold

Rebel Reborn

M/F Romance

VAMPIRE ROYALS OF NEW YORK

Dorian & Charlotte

Dark Deception

Dark Seduction

Dark Obsession

Gabriel & Jacinda

Heart of Thorns

Heart of Fury

Heart of Flames

BLOOD CURSED

BOOK FOUR

ONE

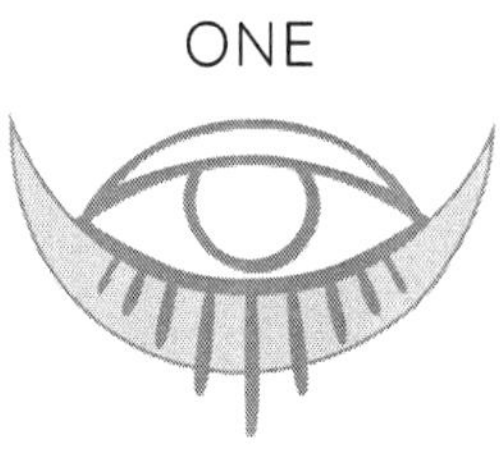

RONAN

The instant we stepped into the hell portal, I knew I'd lost her.

I was still holding her tight against my chest, but it wasn't her body that'd left us. I'd fucking *felt* it—the departure of her soul. The entirety of the woman I loved violently wrenched away as we'd tried to rescue her from the disaster blackening the skies in the Shadowrealm.

One horror after another, and yet for Gray Desario, they just kept on coming.

After what felt like a hundred years, the portal puked us out into the underground chamber beneath the Vegas desert—same spot where Darius and I had first entered. I hit the ground hard on my back, cushioning the blow for Gray.

I grunted at the impact, pain exploding along every bone-tired inch of my spine. She didn't make a sound, though.

Blinking the stars from my eyes, I laid her on the ground and checked her over, feeling her head, her limbs, anywhere that might've been hurt. She seemed okay—warm and still breathing, heart still beating, blood still pumping through her veins, blue beneath the near-translucent skin at her wrists. But her eyes were—

Wait. *Blood…*

The thought tugged hard, yanking my attention away from Gray for a split second. Just long enough for me to recognize the wet, strangled gasps emanating from the other side of the chamber, shrouded in darkness. I sucked in a deep breath. The acrid tang of copper scented the air.

Fucking hell. Gray and I had not been the first out of the portal.

He'd beat us here.

"Beaumont?" I called, rising to my feet and creeping closer to the darkness. The shapes before me emerged slowly, revealing the gruesome scene one sliver at a time. A pair of shiny black shoes came first, attached to legs that jerked and spasmed. Clenched fists, split knuckles and pale skin turning white. A chest blackened and wet with blood. A face twisted in shocked horror—a face that had once belonged to the demon thug that'd escorted us here earlier.

And then, almost unrecognizable in his violent, blood-splattered stupor, our vampire came into view, looming over the body and siphoning its blood like a starved newborn.

I stood immobilized, watching with a mix of fear and fascination as this primal beast devoured his prey. All traces of the cool, composed man I'd known and cared for had vanished, leaving in his place nothing but sharp fangs and a deep, desperate need.

It was too late to backtrack, too late to grab Gray and make a run for it. He'd already noticed my presence—I could see it in the twitch of his head, the brief but detectable pause in his wet, incessant slurping.

My eyes darted around for another exit, a weapon, a miracle, anything, but there wasn't a damn thing I could've used to our advantage. Even the darkness worked against me, given vampires' superior sight.

As if he could read my mind, the bloodsucker formerly known as Darius flicked his cold gaze up at me, not bothering to detach his mouth from the victim's throat. In his eyes I caught a glimpse of something so horrid, so animal, it would probably give me nightmares for the rest of my long damn life—assuming I made it out of here alive.

His message was clear:

Move an inch, and I'll devour you next.

I had no choice but to let him finish, and hope to fucking hell the demon guard was enough to sate him. Because if Darius came at me in his current primal, blood-drunk state, I wasn't sure I had the strength—or the heart—to fight him off. Not with Gray lying behind me, soulless and unconscious. And if I died, she'd be next —slaughtered by the very hand of the vamp she loved. The vamp I was pretty sure loved her, too.

When he finally finished his meal, he tossed aside the body like an empty sack and rose to his full height, wiping his mouth on the back of his hand, his eyes never leaving mine.

"That gentleman tasted like shite," he announced.

"That's because he's a demon," I said firmly. The skin on my arm burned at the spot where I'd allowed Darius to feed after he'd turned up wasted and half-dead at Elena's house. "Vampires despise the taste of demon blood."

Darius took a step closer, stumbling a bit, then catching himself.

"And who might you be?" he asked, his words slurring together. His eyes were glassy and dark, his lips and chin shiny with smeared blood.

Drunk, lost, and feral. Seeing him like that... It nearly broke me. The beast wobbling before me was so far removed from the Darius I'd known that my brain kept rejecting the images, desperate to convince me that it wasn't real. That we were all trapped together in some heinous nightmare, or imprisoned by another cruel trick of the Shadowrealm.

But deep down I knew the cold, hard truth. We weren't lucky enough to wake up from this. It was real. It was now. And unless I figured out a way out of here, it was going to get us all killed.

I swallowed the tight knot in my throat, forcing out my response.

"Me? Just another shite-tasting demon," I said, but it seemed I'd already lost his attention. Darius's eyes wandered past me, an unnatural grin stretching across his face.

I didn't have to turn around to know exactly where his gaze had landed.

Fear soured my gut, spiking my blood with adrenaline.

"She's spent," I hedged, stepping in front of his path as he stalked closer to Gray's form. "Not worth your effort—trust me."

Ignoring this, he sidestepped me, a blur of color that vanished before my eyes, then reappeared right next to her. He knelt down and touched her face, fingering a lock of her hair, then pressing it to his lips to inhale her scent. A low rumble of desire reverberated in his chest.

But unlike the kind of desire I'd witnessed the night we'd shared her in bed, bringing her to the edge of ecstasy in a tangle of hot limbs and endless kisses, this was different. Dangerous. This desire meant to devour her, drain her of all that remained.

Every hair on my body stood at attention, my muscles tensing for a fight. But I couldn't make a move in here. Not without risking his ire. Risking her life.

Best I could hope for was a distraction.

"We need to get out of here," I said, forcing my voice to stay calm and steady. "You killed one of hell's soldiers. More will come. Let's go."

"Without this lovely creature?" He stroked her face.

It was all I could do to keep my heart rate in check. "Dead weight. She'll only slow us down."

"I could lighten the load a bit." He leaned in close and brushed his nose along her neck, his eyes so dark they were nearly black now. I felt my own shift into blackness as my demon instincts took over. "Maybe I'll just take a little off the top."

A glint of fang, and I was on him, barreling into him with enough force to knock him halfway across the room. I'd caught him by surprise, and now I used up the very last millisecond of my advantage by slamming a fist into his face.

The force of the blow dislocated his jaw, splitting the skin over my knuckles wide open. I waited for him to retaliate, but Darius merely smiled, licking my blood from his lips as his jaw snapped back into place.

"You're right," he said smoothly, malice soaking his voice as we rose from the ground. He'd lost some of his slur, and now he towered over me, menacing and cold. "You taste like shite."

"Told you."

The two of us circled each other like wild cats fighting over a wildebeest. He was clearly toying with me, and I was still holding back. I didn't want to hurt him any more than I had to, though I suspected he had no such hangups about *my* safety.

"So there's no reason for me to let you live," he said. "Unless you can think of one?"

"We're *brothers*, asshole. Let's start with that."

Darius laughed, hollow and chilling. "A vampire and a demon? Mom and Dad must be so proud."

"Genetics has nothing to do with it."

He zipped behind me, a blur in the darkness. When he spoke again, his breath was icy at the back of my neck.

"Try again," he whispered.

I dropped into a crouch and kicked backward, hitting air.

"Is that the best you can do?" he asked, already in front of me again. Taunting. Tormenting.

"Stand still and find out." I charged, but he went blurry on me again. Every time I blinked, he vanished, then reappeared behind me. Next to me. Across the room. Again. And again. And again.

Demonic strength could do a lot of damage, but vampires were still stronger. Faster. I was outmatched, and he was enjoying the game, batting me around like a cat with a caught mouse.

Then came the cruel grin.

A chill raced down my spine.

"Whatever you're thinking," I said, holding out a hand as if that alone could stop him, "don't—"

The plea died on my lips.

He came at me full on, and his attack was torrential, like a thousand powerful fists battering my jaw, my gut, my ribs, my kidneys, everything at once. My ears rang, my mouth full of blood, the blows coming so fast my bones hadn't even had time to crack yet.

They would, though. That much was certain.

A human would've died five times over, but I was still on my feet, my body desperately trying to heal itself. I was still swinging, still clawing and scratching, still hoping for that miracle, even as the adrenaline started to fade.

"Done yet, hellspawn?" he taunted, landing another solid punch to the gut.

I gritted my teeth against a wave of excruciating pain, my entire body throbbing, bruising, bleeding, everything at once. My vision swam.

Blackness crept in around the edges, whispering promises of sweet relief as Darius continued to unleash his fury. But I couldn't give in, couldn't slide into the bliss of unconsciousness. Not like this.

As fucked up as this was, I hurt for him almost as much as I hurt for myself. There was a chance, however minute, that he would remember me. Maybe not today or tomorrow, maybe not in a year, but one day might come when his memories rushed back like a river breaking down the dam. He'd remember our friendship. And then he'd remember this moment.

And it would eat through his bones like acid. All the gut-punches in the world wouldn't come close to the pain he'd feel on that day.

I wanted to spare him. To save him, even if I couldn't save myself. Even if I couldn't save Gray.

"Darius Beaumont," I panted, holding up my hands for a momentary cease-fire. "That's your name. Listen to me. You're the most powerful vampire on the west coast. You were born in London, many years ago. You own a club in the Bay called Black Ruby. Gray is… You're bonded to her, Darius."

He stopped the violence long enough to hear my words, but none of them seemed to be sinking in.

"You've suffered memory loss," I continued, spitting out blood. It was a struggle to stay on my feet, but I had to keep talking. Had to keep trying to get through his thick skull. "The three of us just returned from the Shadowrealm. We were trying to get Gray back to her own magical realm, but we were attacked by memory eaters and had to jump into the hell portal. Now her soul's trapped in hell, and we're here trying to kill each other."

"Hmm. Charming story," he said, his tone now light and teasing. "But how will it end, I wonder? The suspense is nearly killing me. Perhaps it will kill you, too."

"The ending hasn't been written yet." I took a deep breath to regroup, hoping we still had a shot at a good one. Hell, I'd settle for one where we all walked out of here alive. Broken bones and bloody knuckles would heal. Gray's soul was trapped in hell, but it still existed, which meant we might be able to get it back. And Darius's memories? I wasn't ready to give up on them yet, either. Somewhere, maybe they existed. In this realm or another.

Shitty as things had gotten, we hadn't yet crossed the point of no return—not with any of it. There was still a glimmer of light. Of hope.

"Darius, listen to me. We can still—"

"Sorry, demon. I'm afraid your part in this tale has come to its inevitable end." He grinned again, his eyes sparkling with fresh desire as they roamed over Gray's body. "It's time for my midnight snack."

"Not a chance, brother." I wound up for another hit—anything to stall him from his end game of feeding on her—but stopped short at the strange look on his face.

Brother, the word that'd barely registered with him earlier, seemed to snag on a memory. His gaze went far away for a beat, then came back, and he cocked his head at me and narrowed his eyes. The whole thing happened in the span of two heartbeats, but I swear I saw the flicker of recognition pushing out from the depths of rage.

"Beaumont?" I called, unable to keep the hope from my voice. "Darius? Do you—"

His hand shot out and grabbed my throat, instantly choking off the words right along with my air supply. He hauled me up, my feet dangling a foot off the ground as his mouth twisted into another sick grin.

Then it went slack.

I thought he had another memory, a flash of something. But Darius gasped in pain, his eyes wide with shock. He dropped to his knees with a grunt.

Finally freed from his impossibly strong grip, I squared off with a new assailant.

I took in the sight of her, my mouth dropping open. With her short stature, wrinkled skin, and head of close-cropped white hair, she looked like she should be sitting in a rocking chair and knitting blankets, not taking out vampires outside the hell portal.

Yet there she was, still gripping the hawthorn stake she'd jammed between his shoulder blades. She shoved it in a little harder now, her mouth pressed into a grim line as Darius's head slumped forward.

Certain the vampire had been immobilized, she stepped back from him and brushed her hands together, finally meeting my eyes.

Recognition twisted my gut. My heart fucking stopped.

It was *her*.

TWO

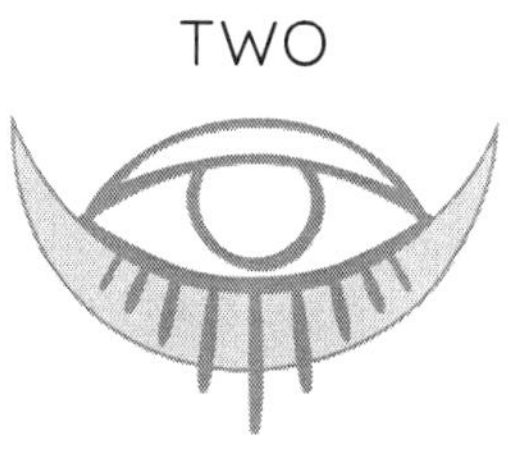

RONAN

"Deirdre Olivante," I said, hating the shape of it in my mouth. Though we'd never met before, her name had been seared into my memory for decades, the echo of it like a ticking time bomb that haunted my every step.

She looked like I'd always imagined her. Short, small-boned, and old, but tough beneath her layers of crafted sweetness, with the same intense blue eyes and sharp cheekbones as her granddaughter.

I wanted to despise her, but right now I could only be grateful.

She'd saved us. Ironic, all things considered.

"Foolish boy," Deirdre snapped, the first words she'd ever spoken to me. "Rayanne's soul is trapped in hell, and you're playing around with a vampire. I thought you were her guardian."

I said nothing. She was right. Gray—Rayanne, to her—was my charge, and I'd failed her.

Again.

But the fire smoldered out of her words quickly as she took in the sight of Gray. Kneeling beside her on the floor, Deirdre brushed her fingers across her granddaughter's forehead for the first time in more than twenty years.

"She's beautiful," Deirdre said, momentarily lost in her own world. Her voice was thick with emotion. "So grown-up. I never thought..."

She trailed off as a tear slid down her cheek. In that moment, she looked vulnerable and wounded, a woman who'd seen more than her fair share of suffering and loss.

Behind us, Darius twitched on the floor, groaning at the pain of the poison coursing through his blood. Despite the fact that he'd damn near killed me, I hated seeing him in that state. I hated seeing Gray unconscious on the floor, the grandmother she didn't remember weeping over her body.

A fresh lump lodged itself in the back of my throat.

For so many years, I'd believed the worst thing I'd ever have to face was Gray's death—the event that would trigger the official start of her contracted servitude, requiring me to deliver her straight to Sebastian.

But now here she was, very much alive, her soul trapped in his hell. Was that worse than becoming a demonic servant? An eternal slave?

Was there any chance at getting her out of either disaster? Of any of the obstacles and terrible situations she'd likely face, even if we could free her from this latest round of torments? She was a powerful Shadowborn witch. To think she'd survive this life unscathed was a ridiculous pipe dream.

I turned away, unable to look at her another minute. I didn't have the strength for this. It turned me inside out, like someone had carved me open and set all my nerves on fire. It hurt to breathe. To blink. To think.

Gray's death? It would've gutted me.

But this... This was definitely worse. She wasn't dead, just trapped, condemned to an eternity of suffering, mere seconds after we'd liberated her from the last otherworldly prison.

Deirdre sighed, and I turned back to face her, our eyes locking once again. Hers were cloudy with sadness and regret, and for a brief instant, that shared pain connected us by an invisible thread.

In another life, we might've been family.

I wondered if she was thinking the same thing. Then she got to her feet and said, "Don't just stand there moping, demon. Sebastian is certainly expecting you by now."

"Fuck Sebastian." I closed my eyes, breaking the momentary connection. "There's nothing he can do for me now. And if you think for one hot second I'm taking her anywhere near him, you're—"

"She's lost in his domain now, Ronan Vacarro. He's the *only* one who can help us get her back."

"*Us*?" I opened my eyes and looked at her again, eyeing her skeptically. "You think there's an *us* in all of this?"

She folded her arms across her chest and jutted out her chin, a look that was so very Gray, it shot a bolt of pain through my heart.

I stepped closer, staring her down. "Let me tell you what it means to be part of an us. Gray and I were an us. We had each other's backs. We cared for each other. We shared things, went through shit together, came out on the other side swinging. We didn't condemn each other to—"

"Enough!" Her eyes blazed, and she didn't back down, glaring at me as if she were the one towering over me rather than vice versa. "We've all done unspeakable things to keep her safe. Don't pretend you're above all of this. I know the truth."

"You know nothing about me, witch."

"Oh no?" Her steely gaze softened, and she reached up to touch my face, her palm soft against my cheek. "I know what you gave up for her. I know what she means to you. And," she said, her voice dropping to a whisper, "I know what haunts your dreams."

At first her touch felt kindly, like I'd always imagined a real grandmother's would. But then it turned icy cold, spreading across my jaw and into my head, boring into my skull. The feeling was like a brain freeze, like eating ice cream too fast, and everything else in me went still as she rifled through my mind—not my thoughts, I realized, but my dreams. My nightmares. I saw each one flicker and glow as she paged through them like stories in an old, dusty book.

When she finally pulled back and the warmth rushed back into my head, she was looking at me with a mixture of righteousness and pity. Compassion.

"Do that again," I warned, "and you'll… I'll…"

I pinched the bridge of my nose and shook my head, letting the words die off. I didn't have it in me to threaten her. She'd been right. We'd all done things to protect Gray. Would do them again in a heartbeat. I had no right to judge her.

In a fluid, effortless motion at complete odds with her small physical stature, she hauled Darius to his feet and yanked his arm over her shoulder, taking the bulk of his weight against her body. Darius groaned in half-hearted protest, but he leaned into her, trying to find his footing.

"I'll deal with him," she said, then nodded toward Gray. "You get Rayanne to Sebastian. I'll meet you there as soon as I can."

I looked at Darius, the blood congealing on his lips and chin. His hands trembled, his head lolling sideways as if he didn't even have the strength to hold it up. His eyes held none of their earlier viciousness.

Fucking hell, Beaumont.

Deirdre must've seen the concern in my face. Adjusting him against her body, she said, "He would have killed you both had I not intervened."

"He would've tried, maybe."

"Ronan, we don't have time. I've got him. You need to help Rayanne."

"He's not himself," I went on. "But he's… he's important to her. To both of us." I stepped closer, putting a hand on his shoulder as if he was mine to claim. "I can't let you end him, Deirdre. No matter what he's done."

She sighed loudly, her patience clearly thinning. "I'm not planning to decapitate him, demon. He needs sedation and treatment. Unless you want me to release him into the wilds of Las Vegas, I need to relocate him somewhere safe, preferably before sunrise."

Safe? I almost laughed at that. Where the hell in this city was a safe place for a powerful vampire with no memory, out of his mind with bloodlust, currently neutered by hawthorn, completely at the mercy of a pint-sized, dream-stealing, elderly witch?

"I'll find you at Sebastian's casino once the vampire is secured," she said, the sternness in her voice leaving no room for argument.

Darius groaned again, but if he had an opinion on the matter, I had no idea what the hell it was. I had to go by instinct, trusting that I knew the real Darius well enough at this point to know what he'd want.

Like me, he'd want to protect Gray at all costs. He'd want me to focus on her. To find some way to get her out of this fucking bind.

I scooped Gray into my arms, holding her tight against my chest.

For a moment, Deirdre and I stood facing each other, looking over the charges each of us held close.

These are the most important people in my life.

"I'll take care of him, Ronan," she said, a little bit of that grandmotherly tone creeping back in. "You have my word."

Her gaze dropped back to Gray, her lips pressed into a tight line. The creases between her eyes deepened with worry, and she glanced back up at me, as though she wanted me to give her the same reassurances.

But I didn't owe her a damn thing. She knew who I was. Knew that I was perpetually obligated to keep Gray safe, even if I *wasn't* in love with her so deeply my heart would never hit a steady beat without her touch again.

With my best friend—hell, my entire life—cradled in my arms, I emerged into the lonely desert night, leaving Darius in the care of the one witch I'd hoped I'd never, *ever* meet in person.

The witch who—twenty-some years ago in her own dark moment of desperation at the crossroads—had signed her name in blood on a contract with the Prince of Hell, bargaining away her granddaughter's eternal soul.

THREE

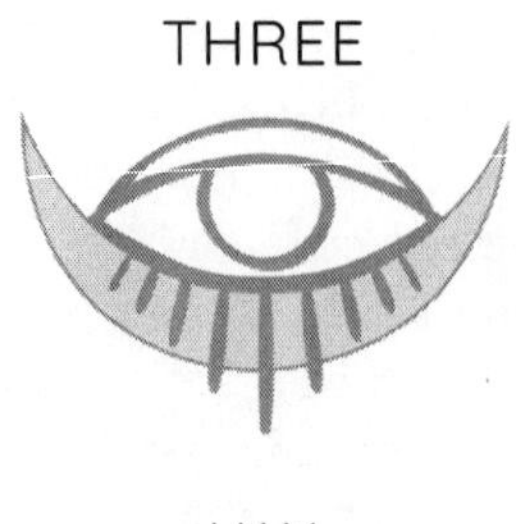

LIAM

For all the power I possessed, for all the fear my presence invoked in humans and supernaturals alike, for all the incomprehensible vastness of my very being, I could not save her.

The pain wracking my human vessel was agonizing, guilt's red-hot lava boiling in my stomach, shame blazing a new fire in my chest, regret eating a gaping hole in my heart that could only be repaired by Gray's safe return. Shifting into my shadow form would've spared me, but the pain was no less than I deserved.

I couldn't risk depleting my rapidly waning energy with another shift. Not until I made my journey into the heart of hell.

For once, I wasn't speaking in metaphor.

"Ah, my old friend, the Lord of Shadows. Welcome to Sin City." Sebastian entered the conference room with a flourish, then sat at the head of the long, sleek table, his image perfectly framed by two large paintings depicting nude women pleasuring scores of demons.

How the natural order saw fit to keep this despicable being in power was beyond even my understanding.

"My assistant tells me you requested a meeting," he continued with a smirk. "Does this mean your rendezvous in the Shadowrealm didn't go as planned?"

"Let us not pretend you don't know *exactly* how things unfolded in the Shadowrealm." My temper flared, but quickly faded under the watchful eyes of the women in the paintings. They seemed to be disappointed in me, as though I'd managed to fail them as horribly as I'd failed Gray. I could hardly blame them.

Hanging my head, I said, "I'm afraid I've… miscalculated."

"An understatement, I presume." Sebastian chuckled, removing a small silver box from his inside jacket pocket. "Cigar? Something tells me you've got a doozy of a story to tell."

The greasy demon prince held out the box, his thrill at my misfortune—*Gray's* misfortune—plainly evident. When I waved him off, he removed and lit a cigar for himself, his cheeks billowing as he puffed the thing to life.

Smoke curled around his pockmarked face. I wished I had the power to bring disease to his lungs. To cause him a very long, very painful demise.

But Sebastian was immune to the powers of Death.

"So tell me. Did the witch refuse your proposition?" he asked. "Tell you to stick it where the sun don't shine?"

"The proposition, as you call it, is no joking matter. It's a matter of her true destiny. As such, it was not something to be entered into lightly. There are many facets, many details which must be explored and debated ad nauseam. We did not have the time to fully discuss her options."

"You never even told her there *were* options." Sebastian sucked on his cigar, the end of it crackling. His eyes shone even more menacingly in the orange glow. "There's a difference."

A thousand retorts swirled in my mind, but every one of them turned to dust on my lips. Sebastian was right. I'd kept everything from her—everything that mattered. Her true choices, and what each one would've meant. Her legacy. Consequences. Information that would've altered the course of her destiny and saved a lot of lives in the process.

I'd staked everything on my ability to train her in time, to persuade her onto the right path. I was so certain, so blindly convinced she'd accept, none of the myriad other pathways spiraling out before her seemed plausible.

After all, who could refuse the call of Death? According to the scrolls in the hallowed Hall of Records, no one in a hundred thousand lifetimes had ever dared.

Then again, I was fairly certain Death had never fallen in love with his protégé, either. That was a complication I could not have foreseen.

I knew I should regret it, but I couldn't. No matter the outcome.

Even now, the remnants of our kisses on the beach in the Shadowrealm warmed me inside. I closed my eyes, allowing the moment to replay itself. I smelled the salt of the ocean, felt the grit of sand and shells beneath my back as Gray fell into my arms, her mouth warm and soft, her hair tickling my cheeks, her laughter like music I'd only just begun to remember.

If I lingered there, if I allowed myself to partake in the comforting opiate of human memory, the pain burning through my body might finally ease, ever so slightly…

"In any case," Sebastian said, wrenching me from that blissful haze, "she's in my possession now, and though I can't use her as I'd originally intended, what with her soul being trapped in hell and her body being—well, wherever that thing ended up, I'm not keen on relinquishing her. As you have failed to uphold your end of our bargain, it seems our partnership has come to its unavoidable end." He rose from the table in a cloud of smoke, the fat cigar lodged into the corner of his mouth. "Now, if that's all, I'm a very busy man, and—"

"You *must* allow me to reclaim her soul," I said, suddenly frantic. "To reunite it with her body before she dies. There's still time, Sebastian. She deserves better than lingering in hell, and you know it."

He glared at me a long moment, then said with another smirk, "The way I see it, Lord of Shadows, you should be thanking me."

"Whatever for?"

He resumed his position at the head of the table, taking another puff on the cigar. "I've spared you the ugly task of killing her yourself. This way she'll never even know about our arrangement."

"I *never* agreed to killing her. That was your term for it."

"What would you call ending her life as she knows it, then? Tearing her from the ones she loves, forcing her into a service from which she'd most certainly recoil? What would you call eliminated one's every last choice?"

"I did not sign her original contract."

"No, of course not. You merely agreed to alter the start date."

"I never should've accepted your terms." The lava inside me sputtered to life once again, burning a hot path to my throat, though I was admittedly more upset with myself than with the demon presently taunting me. "The natural order is not something to be twisted and bent to one's will, Sebastian. We must respect it at all costs, or what are we left with? What do we become but a rabble of unconscious ghouls, roaming the earth like the primordial beasts of old, tearing one another limb from limb for the pure sport of it."

"Save your philosophy, demon. You and I had a perfectly legitimate deal. You failed to deliver, ergo—"

"I am *no* demon, Prince."

"Ahh, but aren't you?" He stabbed the cigar into his ashtray, grounding it until his fingers were coated in ash. The room was hazy with smoke, and now it began to descend on us like a fog. "You've bargained with her life almost as many times as I have. And here you are at the final hour, once again begging me to make another deal."

"I've done no such thing."

"Then why are you here? To enjoy the many pleasures of my establishment?" He gestured toward a blackened window on the opposite wall. At his attention, the glass lost its smokey tint, clearing to provide a view into the adjacent room. A soft red glow emanated from the ground, just enough illumination to reveal the garish scene unfolding inside. It seemed to be a near-exact replica of the artwork on his walls, and though the almost-nude woman chained to the wall did not move as three male tormentors carried on, her haunted eyes told the story of her endless torture.

She couldn't have been more than eighteen years old. Twenty at best.

"Perhaps your human vessel is craving a bargain of the, shall we say, carnal nature?" Sebastian's eyes glinted as he drank in the sight of the woman's brutalized body, licking his lips as one of her captors tore off the last remaining scrap of fabric covering her breasts. "Violet is a client favorite. I'm told she's never refused a request, no matter how degrading or bizarre. Then again, she doesn't have much of a choice. Such is the way with the Devil's bargains."

"You are a monster," I whispered, unable to look away from Violet's pained eyes. There was nothing I could do to help her. She was a demonic servant, the details of her own bargain unknown to me. Even death couldn't save her now.

"No, I am the Prince of Hell," Sebastian bellowed suddenly. "You would be wise to remember that before wasting my time with your pathetic pleas. I am not the hero in this story, Shadow Lord. Nor have I ever pretended otherwise. So, if you'd kindly stop wasting my time, I do have other business to attend to."

His eyes glowed the same eerie shade of red as the torture room next door, cutting through the remaining blanket of smoke and reminding me *exactly* who I was dealing with.

"So be it," I finally said, resigned. He was right—I *had* come here looking for one last bargain, and now I would have it. "There's no deal I wouldn't make to save Gray's soul from Hell's grip."

"I'm very glad to hear it." At this, he snapped his fingers, and a manilla envelope appeared, thick with what could only be another contract. "The terms are rather simple, actually."

"State them plainly, Prince. I've neither the time nor the interest to parse through your fine print."

"Very well." He set the envelope on the table before him, then stroked his goatee, gazing through the window as if he were deep in thought. As if he were actually considering the options rather than simply pausing for dramatic effect and enjoying the sick view next door.

Sebastian was no fool. He'd known full well why I'd come today, and full well the terms he'd offer. Still, I let him play his games, hoping that the day would come where his confidence would so fully blind him that someone more powerful than I would slip behind his defenses and plant the trap that would usher in his final undoing.

"I will allow you to retrieve your beloved witch's soul and work your shadow magic to bring her back to life."

"At what cost?"

"No more or less than our previously arranged price. The cost of your failure. An excellent bargain for you, I do declare."

It was precisely what I expected, yet everything I most feared.

I'm so sorry, Gray.

I knew there was no room for negotiating here. Sebastian might let me bring Gray back to life, but he would not allow her to walk away from him unscathed. Not when he already had her soul in possession. He held all of the cards here, and I was out of ideas.

I had to accept. Leaving her soul to float untethered through hell was simply not an option.

"On one condition," I said. Sebastian raised an eyebrow, and I pushed on, gesturing toward the window. "Release Violet into my possession. I… I *must* have her."

He eyed me suspiciously for no more than a breath, then laughed, smug satisfaction distorting his already vile features. "Ah, so our fan favorite has tickled your fancy. She's quite remarkable, I'm told."

"You were right," I said, trying to appear both aroused and ashamed. "My human vessel does have certain… proclivities. The longer I retain this form, the more insistent those proclivities become. I will comply with your terms, and ask only that you grant me this gift of flesh as a show of good faith."

Still laughing, Sebastian slid the contract and a pen across the table. "You've got yourself a deal."

I signed quickly, and the entire envelope vanished.

"I will have Violet prepared and waiting for you in Suite 666. It's my personal favorite." He produced a keycard, and I took it without ceremony, sliding it into my pocket.

"Always a pleasure." He stuck out his hand to shake, but a sudden commotion outside the conference room door interrupted our farewell. The door crashed open, and Ronan shoved his way inside, cradling Gray in his arms.

The sight of her lifeless body… I nearly gasped.

"I'm sorry, sir." Another young woman stumbled in behind Ronan, breathless and trembling. "I tried to stop him, but he was very insistent that he see you."

"Indeed. And what have I told you about Ronan Vacarro?" he asked.

"That's R-Ronan?" She quivered, bowing her head low. "I didn't realize it was him, sir. He never said."

"Ignorance is not your savior, child."

"I know, sir. I'm very sorry."

"As am I. Now I'll have to find a new assistant." He whispered a brief incantation, and then she vanished, leaving nothing but a black wisp in her wake.

"And to what do I owe this honor?" Sebastian drawled. "What an unexpected surprise."

He couldn't hide the raw pleasure on his face as he approached Gray. Here in the flesh, after all this time, was the witch he'd been patiently stalking her entire life. Longer, even. From the moment he'd heard about the Silversbane prophecy, he'd known she was special.

Ronan and I remained silent as Sebastian looked her over, barely keeping his greed in check. With her head resting peacefully on Ronan's shoulder, Gray was warm and alive, the color high on her cheeks, her curls glossy despite her ordeal in the Shadowrealm.

But her soul was gone, just as I'd known it would be. And unless I could find it and successfully reunite the two, her body would decompose, and everything about her that had ever existed would simply cease.

A world without Gray Desario… It was incomprehensible.

Though I didn't deserve to touch her again, I reached out anyway, brushing my knuckles along her jaw. Her skin was silky-soft, but it felt wrong—a great void where before there had been vitality and warmth and pure magic.

"Do something," Ronan barked at me, ignoring Sebastian. "Fix this." His commanding voice broke into something helpless and desperate at the end, heartache soaking his every word.

"I shall do my best," I assured him, but hopelessness was contagious, and the longer I stared into his desperate eyes, the faster I felt myself slipping into the same dark oblivion.

Neither of us had the luxury of giving up or checking out.

"I see you two are already acquainted," Sebastian said. "Excellent, that saves me the trouble of introductions. Ronan, your friend and I were just having the most fascinating conversation. I understand the witch's soul is lost in hell. Can you imagine? What are the chances that my sharpest demon guardian would make the mistake of bringing a demon sworn through the hell portal?"

"We were out of options," Ronan said, his jaw tight. And swollen, I now noticed. Blood dried in the corners of his mouth, and along a deep gash above his eye.

"Well, I'm nothing if not generous," Sebastian said. "It turns out there *is* one more option. One way—and only one—to retrieve Gray's soul and reunite it with her body."

Ronan closed his eyes and took a deep breath, composing himself. "What's it gonna cost me this time?"

"Not a red cent, boy." Sebastian grinned, jerking his head toward me as he slapped a meaty hand over my shoulder. "This one's on him."

Ronan's head turned slowly, his eyes blazing with twin flames of fury and fear.

"What," he whispered, "have you done?"

I opened my mouth intending to explain, but there was no time.

And at the moment, I was severely low on courage and valor.

I nodded once, my form of an apology, then vanished without a response.

Gray's demon guardian would have his answer soon enough.

FOUR

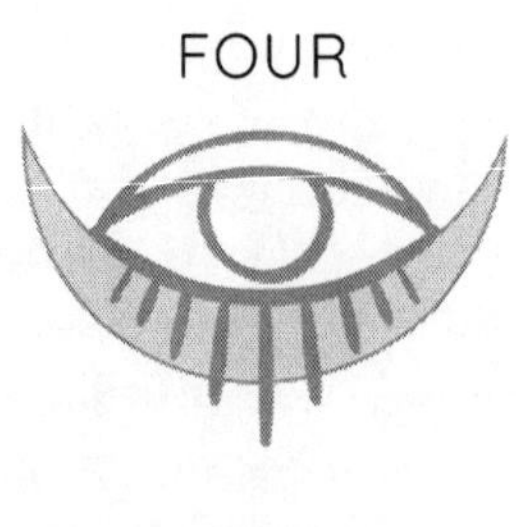

GRAY

I knelt in the bottom of a small wooden boat blackened with rot, floating on an obsidian lake. A striking orange-red sky bled across the horizon, beautiful like the dawn but for the faces looming in its dark gray clouds. They were the ghosts of hell, each mouth stretched and howling in torment, every one of them reflected endlessly in the black-mirror lake.

Their screams roared like the wind, but caused no ripples. When I reached over the side of the boat and trailed my fingers through the water, I felt nothing but air.

It was all an illusion meant to slowly drive me insane.

My predicament was neither a mystery nor a surprise. As a demon sworn witch, my chances of escaping the hell portal had been less than zero. I'd known the risks, but I'd taken them anyway; all I'd wanted was one more moment in Ronan's arms. To make him understand that I trusted him implicitly, no matter what the consequences. To leave him the parting gift of my unfaltering faith.

He'd earned it.

My eyes watered. The acrid stench of sulfur and burned flesh soaked the air, but I wasn't scared. Wasn't cold or hungry or tired or in pain. Stuck on my rickety boat in the middle of this endless yet nonexistent lake, I knew I wasn't in any real danger.

I was just… empty. Empty and alone.

Though I'd never met him, I was getting a crash course in Sebastian's precise form of cruelty. I'd no doubt that he'd crafted this version of hell specifically for me—his red-carpet welcome.

Unlike in the Shadowrealm, here I found no fire-breathing, flesh-tearing demons, or needling glass rainstorms, or Jonathan and his monstrous torments. Simply and ingeniously, the Prince of Hell had doled out the worst punishment he could've imagined for me: separating me from the ones I loved, leaving me to float helplessly on a boat that would never reach the shore while my rebels were left to fight their wars and face their demons without me. My memories would never fade, and I'd never be allowed to sleep. There would be no respite for me, no escape from the knowledge of all I'd lost. Just this boat, this lake, and all the ghosts that lived in my head. Every hour, every century. An eternity of regret.

That was his style.

But as much as I was learning about my new captor, it seemed he hadn't bothered to study up on me. If he had, he would've known that being a hostage wasn't really my strong suit. After all, Jonathan's cave prison hadn't been enough to hold me. And hadn't I managed to escape the Shadowrealm? Out of the frying pan and into the fire, maybe, but an escape nevertheless. One that should've been impossible given the fact that I'd banished an unwilling soul.

Yet Sebastian thought an unplanned side trip to Hell would stop me?

Hard pass, asshole.

I smiled, and something flickered beneath all that emptiness and despair inside. An ember of something that felt a lot like hope.

I got to my feet and climbed onto the narrow foredeck, the boat rocking but not tipping over as it probably should've. I knew my voice would never carry above the vicious howl of those ghastly clouds, but I felt the need to say my piece anyway.

"I am not your hostage," I called out. "You can burn my body, but my soul is and will always be mine. You hear me? I am *mine*. I am mine."

It started softly, but the words themselves were like a spell, magic gathering in the air before me, crackling with power, swirling into a hot wind around me that lifted my hair and gave me strength.

"I am mine. I am mine. I am mine." I repeated the words a hundred times, a thousand, a million, each time getting louder and louder until my soft calls turned into a powerful roar that echoed across the lake, drowning out the sounds of the damned, scraping my throat raw and reverberating through my bones. In one final, triumphant call, I lifted my hands to the sky, tossed my head back, and screamed, shattering the black mirror lake into dust.

"I. Am. *Mine!*"

"I want more than anything for that to be true," came a dark echo. "But there isn't enough magic in all the realms to make it so."

The magic wind surrounding me suddenly stopped, and when I brushed the hair from my face and opened my eyes, I found myself staring into the electric blue gaze of a massive white raven.

He flapped his great wings, then transformed into a pillar of smoke that roiled and churned before me, finally falling away to reveal a familiar sight.

A man with sun-streaked hair and a worn flannel shirt, gazing back at me with ancient blue eyes that swirled with all the mysteries of the universe.

My heart leaped. It felt like I'd conjured him. Like he'd heard the call of my magic across the realms, and then he'd appeared, ready to sweep me into his arms and escort me out of this terrible nightmare.

"My knight in shining flannel," I teased, unable to hold back my smile, even as fresh tears filled my eyes. "You have *no* idea how happy I am to see you."

I stretched up on my toes and kissed the corner of his mouth, wrapping my arms around his neck, but Liam didn't respond.

"Liam?" I pressed. "You… you *are* here to rescue me, right?" Why else would he have tracked me down in Hell if not to help me fight my way out? To warn me against all my crazy schemes, and then back me up as I put every single one of them into motion?

"I'm so sorry, Gray. I'm not here to… I'm… Not this time," he sputtered, sounding as scared and uncertain as a child lost in the woods. He pulled out of my embrace and looked at me, eyes flashing with a deep and endless pain. He grabbed my upper arms so tightly I was certain he'd leave bruises.

"Liam?" I whispered.

"I am here to offer you a choice." Holding me just beyond the reach of his warmth, of his now-familiar strength, he said somberly, "The very last you will likely be allowed to make."

FIVE

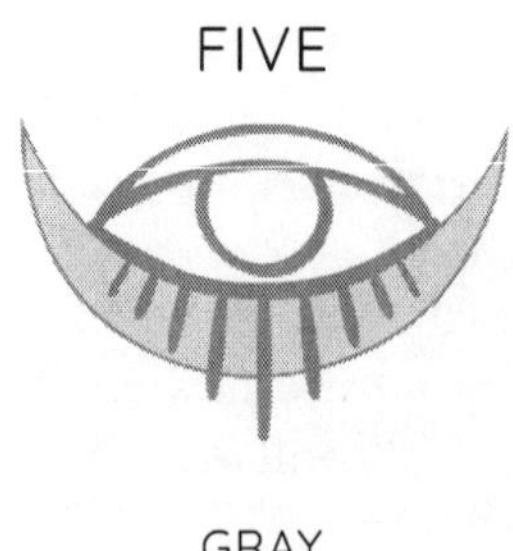

GRAY

I'd turned Hell's black lake into dust, and now our rotting little boat drifted on a sea of nothingness, our knees touching as we sat across from each other on cold, damp benches.

Minutes passed in deadly silence, time stretching before us like hours. Days. Even the ghostly clouds had drifted away, as if the trapped spirits had grown tired of waiting for Death to explain.

"Jonathan is trapped in your realm," he finally said. "I chased him through the black forest, but he eluded my capture. Something is very, very wrong with him. He's no longer part of the natural order, and therefore not subject to its rules. He didn't seem to recognize where he was, or how he'd gotten there—only that he wanted out."

"He's a hybrid now," I said. "Vampire, shifter, who knows what else. He jumped through the rune gate, and then…" I closed my eyes, my body trembling at the memory of the winged beasts that attacked us. That stole Darius's memories. "Liam, Darius lost his—"

"There's no need for you to relive that pain. I know what happened."

"Oh. Right." I opened my eyes, and he lowered his, his cheeks colored with something that looked a lot like shame, though I couldn't imagine what he had to be ashamed about. It wasn't

Liam's fault he knew all possible outcomes before they happened. That was just one of Death's many burdens.

At least, that was how I saw it. God, I couldn't imagine carrying that kind of weight.

I reached for his hand, but his own was cold beneath my touch.

"I could do nothing to help you," he said, still not meeting my eyes. "Nothing to warn you or turn back the ceaseless march of time. The attack, Ronan's decision to bring you through the hell portal, Darius's memory loss… all of those things belonged to an infinitesimal set of possibilities in an infinite sea of others. I saw those terrible events unfold, but I also saw you arriving in your magical realm to meet me as we'd planned, and returning home safely. I saw other outcomes where Ronan died, where Darius was lost in the hell portal rather than you, where you were the one whose memories were swallowed. I watched you turn on your beloved demon, stabbing him in the chest with your blade because you perceived him as a threat instead of your guardian. I saw the three of you enter your portal at the Pool of Unknowing, arriving in the magical realm unharmed together. I saw you healing Jonathan rather than attacking him, reversing the damage his twisted experiments caused his own body and urging him to relinquish his evil quest. I saw you sending Ronan and Darius home through the hell portal, only to remain behind to fight the memory eaters yourself. In one version of events, you even became Queen of the Shadowrealm, sacrificing yourself once again for all those you cared for. And I saw Jonathan escaping into the material plane, unleashing his terror on the remaining witches of Blackmoon Bay… and beyond. It wasn't until I felt the pulse of your soul in this terrible place that I knew the final, irrevocable outcome from all of those possibilities."

"So all of those things… those were all actual possibilities?" I asked, still uncertain about how it all actually worked. Still in awe.

Liam nodded, then tipped his head back, gazing up at the now cloudless sky. It'd faded from orange to the palest gray, not unlike the skies of Blackmoon Bay just before a misty rain. I could almost taste the salty air of home on my tongue.

"Each one of those scenarios was equally likely until the decision just prior to it. In all things, Gray, with each decision one makes, hundreds of other pathways branch outward. No matter how large or small the choice seems in the moment—which side of your mouth you start brushing your teeth on, whom you confide in about your deepest secrets, where you decide to live, which route you take to work, the words you speak to express yourself, the way you style your hair on a given day—you are changing your possibilities, and therefore your fate, with every one. As Death, I see all of those possibilities at once, at all times. Unless..."

"Unless?" I prodded, losing patience with his obvious stalling. He'd come here to offer me some kind of choice, and so far, all we'd done was rehash the terrors that had landed me in this rotten boat. I didn't blame him for trying to ease into it, but really, what was the point?

"Rip off the Band-Aid, Liam." I spread my hands, indicating the hellscape around us. "How much worse could things possibly get?"

Liam finally met my gaze again and took my hands, his touch gentle, his eyes filling with an emotion I recognized instantly. I was intimately familiar with it, in fact; I'd stared it down in the mirror almost every day for the last decade.

Guilt.

"I see all of those possibilities," he repeated, so softly I had to lean in to hear the rest, "unless there are truly no other options."

No.

Other.

Options.

Each of those words echoed across the black sea, hammering into me like another nail in the coffin.

"Before you came into my presence," he said, his voice ragged with an ache so deep it made my own bones hurt, "I did not know it was possible to feel such a deep well of regret."

"You... you regret meeting me?" I tried but failed to keep the hurt from my voice. I couldn't imagine my life without Liam. Or Death. Or any of the ravens or owls or smoke-and-feathers illusions he'd embodied. He'd taught me so much, but I was starting to care for him so much more than as a mentor, or even as a friend. He'd come to mean something to me I hadn't even been able to put into words yet. In the absence of those words, the sparks we'd created on the beach had felt like the closest approximation.

I'd mistakenly thought he'd felt that way about me, too.

I released his hands, but he leaned forward and grabbed mine again.

"Look at me," he whispered. "Please. I need you to look at me. To hear this as well as see it."

When I finally did as he asked, I found him in tears.

"I could *never* regret meeting you, Gray. You have been a light I neither expected nor deserved."

"Then what is it? What are you trying to tell me?"

Crushing my hands in his grip, he shook his head and said, "I have wronged you, Gray Desario. More terribly and irrevocably than you can possibly imagine. And even if your soul is cursed to be hell's immortal prisoner and I remain here at your side, and together we gaze upon the very sunset of the human race, it still would not have been enough time for me to make amends for what I've done."

SIX

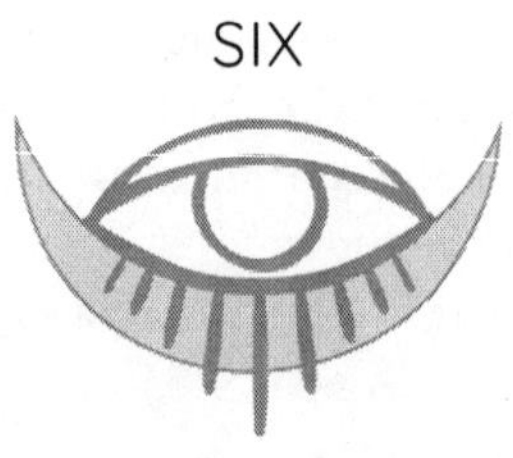

EMILIO

"The city of Blackmoon Bay has fallen under fae control," Jael said.

That was it. No small talk, no preamble. The Seelie Prince simply stepped into my sister's foyer, bringing in a gust of chilly air, and detonated the bomb.

"Explain," I said, holstering my weapon. Elena followed suit, but like me, she didn't take her eyes off him.

"The fae have taken the city," he said grimly, "though I'm loathe to call those monsters fae. Darkwinter are no kin of mine, I assure you."

At the mention of the brutal fae bloodline, a panicky buzz filled my chest, but there was no time to indulge it.

"I've been in touch with my guys at BBPD all night," I said. "No one mentioned anything about a hostage situation, especially not at the hands of Darkwinter."

"They are unaware of the circumstances." Jael lowered his eyes, almost as if he were ashamed. "Say what you will about my people, detectives, but the fae are quite subtle. No one in the Bay feels like a hostage. They are willing participants in this, thanks to the magic. *That* is the kind of power we're dealing with here."

"That's not power," I said. "That's manipulation. It's coercion. And it's against the laws of humankind as well as our own. I assume you've informed the Council?"

He met my eyes again, the shame replaced by a look of utter defeat.

The reality of the situation sunk like a stone in my gut.

The Council didn't need Jael to inform them.

"They already knew," I said.

Elena and I exchanged horrified glances. Our so-called conspiracy theories were suddenly getting a lot less theoretical.

"Talia was in the Cape tonight," I told him. "It's my belief that Darkwinter is partnering with hunters to eradicate witches in the Bay and possibly elsewhere, and I wanted the Council's help."

"Did she offer it?" he asked.

"Oh sure, Jael. Right along with a plate of cookies and a glass of warm milk." I pinched the bridge of my nose, breathing deep. Jael was probably the only fae ally we had left—I needed to cool it.

In a much calmer tone, I said, "Turns out she already knew about the Darkwinter-hunter connection. Looks like she just wanted to find out how much *I* knew. How much danger I would pose to her grand plans."

"Yes," Jael said. "She knew about Darkwinter and the hunters. It's my understanding Talia is the one who brought the parties together initially."

It made sense. Talia had always stricken me as a climber. She'd probably been in league with Darkwinter for years, keeping them on speed-dial, just waiting for a chance to make her big move with the Council. Her earlier tirade about the witches echoed in my mind, each word taking on new meaning.

The witches are a problem that should've been dealt with long ago…

The Council has not been as involved as we should've been. That is changing…

We must find a way to make the distribution of power more equitable…

"Now she's convinced the rest of the Council that *you're* the threat," Jael continued. "She insisted Blackmoon Bay needs ongoing protection from you and your associates. They agreed. Late last night, she called in her hand-picked Darkwinter Knights to secure the city."

Late last night? So, after my frantic phone call, but before tonight's meeting.

She'd played me, of course. And I'd fallen right into her trap.

"The same Darkwinter Knights," I said, "who've teamed up with hunters to build an army of supernatural freaks and biological weapons with the power to kill and enslave entire races of beings."

I gave him the quick-and-dirty rundown on the situation in Raven's Cape and the prison we were still trying to locate, doing my best to protect Gray's privacy. Jael might've shown up here with helpful intel, but that didn't make us partners. I didn't yet know if I could trust him, and it wasn't my place to share details about Gray's magic or her current predicament.

"That does sound like Darkwinter," Jael confirmed. "They've had their eye on hybrid technologies and genetic manipulation for some time, though I had no idea they'd already had some successes."

"And now they're the de facto power faction in the Bay." I clenched my fists at my sides, my hands shaking with rage. It was a major effort not to totally wolf out. Not to track Talia back to Council HQ and take out the whole traitorous lot of them.

How could they sanction this? How could they sit back and let the supernatural community tear itself apart? By the time anyone inside the Bay realized what was happening, it would be too late.

Talia, Darkwinter, the hunters… I didn't know who'd be left in power when the dust finally settled, only that it wouldn't be the people. The citizens who'd lived and worked and played and built our homes there for decades.

Human and supernatural alike, most of the Bay's residents probably had no idea the city had been occupied. Jael said there'd been no physical attack, no bombs, no guns, nothing to actually fight.

No, that wasn't Darkwinter's style. Their real attack would simply unfold without a sound, slowly and subtly as a weed. Inch by inch, hour by hour, the residents of my city would be gently—pleasantly, even—coerced into relinquishing the very last of their freedoms.

Later, when they finally snapped out of the haze and realized how miserable and desperate their lives had become, they'd get angry. The supernaturals among them would take their anger to the Council, demanding answers.

And in response, the Council would give them exactly what they needed to turn the embers of that anger into a raging inferno: a common enemy.

Our community would destroy itself from the inside out, just as Elena and I had predicted.

"Is there *anyone* on the Council who's still an ally?" Elena asked.

"I don't know," Jael said. "But for the moment, I don't believe any of them can be trusted."

"*Jesús, María, y José.* This is insane." I still couldn't believe what I was hearing. The Council was our governing body. Ignoring a few supernatural skirmishes was one thing. A rogue Council member like Talia making a power grab—that made sense, too. Happened in the human government all the time.

But sanctioning an act of war against supernaturals?

I reached for my phone, instinctively ready to call Ronan and Darius. To rally the troops. But then I remembered they were fighting another battle in the Shadowrealm, trying to find a way home for Gray.

My heart twisted to think of her again. To think of all of them out there, lost, trapped, injured, or worse… Hell. Were we ever gonna catch a break?

"How do you even know all of this?" I finally asked Jael. I needed to stay on point. Worrying about things over which I had no control wouldn't help Gray and the guys any more than it would help the Bay. "You're not part of the Council, are you?"

"No, I'm not." He held my gaze for a long time, taking his measure of me, then looked to Elena, assessing her as well. I got the feeling he was trying to decide how much he could trust us—if at all.

I couldn't blame him. I was doing the same to him.

"You said yourself you don't want an all-out war," I said. "That you're one of the few remaining fae who feels that way."

"I am."

"If that's true, then we're on the same side, Jael."

"All of us," Elena said firmly, coming to stand at my side. Her shoulder pressed against my arm, the contact so solid and reassuring I had to blink back tears. It'd been a long time since we'd presented a united front. It almost felt like we were a pack again.

She seemed to pick up on my feelings, and surprised me again by sliding her hand into mine and giving me a reassuring squeeze. I squeezed her right back.

The crises facing our communities had converged here, and maybe that was the only thing holding us together. Maybe when this was all said and done, my sister and I would go our separate ways again.

But right now, we had each other's backs. And from the grave look in Jael's eyes, it was clear we'd need all the strength and solidarity we could muster.

"Okay. It sounds like we've got a lot more ground to cover tonight," Elena said, motioning for Jael to hand over his cape. She hung it carefully in the hall closet, then shooed us into the dining room. "I'll put on fresh coffee and fix us something to eat. I don't know about you guys, but I can strategize much better on a full stomach."

As Jael and I settled into our chairs, I heard the unmistakable knock of the chef's knife against the cutting board in the kitchen, followed by the *tick-tick-tick* of the oven preheating. Despite everything, I smiled. Elena was so much like Mamá. Birthday, funeral, holiday, unexpected company, hostile fae invasion—there was no occasion that couldn't be marked with food, and no food worth preparing unless it was an outright feast.

"I hope you're hungry," I warned Jael. Then, getting right back to business, "What else can you tell me about the situation in the Bay?"

SEVEN

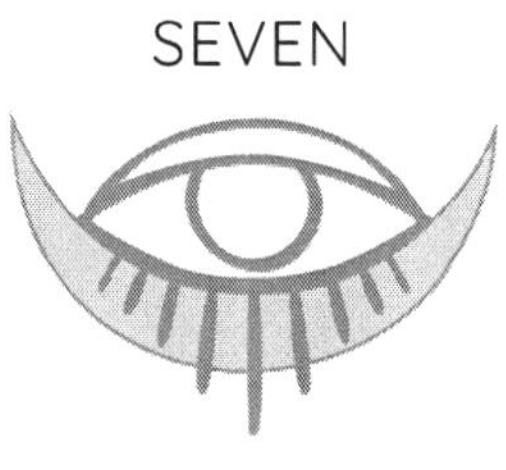

GRAY

The air rushed out of my lungs at Liam's dire words, but I forced myself to remain calm. "Tell me. Whatever it is, we'll work it out."

"It's a very long, highly complex—"

"Highlights version, Liam. Let's start there."

Liam waited a beat, then finally released my hands. He exhaled deeply and closed his eyes.

"I've told you before I'm not exactly as I seem," he said. "And that is only a modicum of my treachery. But it is where we must begin." He opened his eyes again, twin blue orbs that burned with new intensity and locked onto my gaze as if that alone could keep us from falling apart. "I was human once, Gray. A shadowborn, like you. In some respects, I'm *still* human."

Briefly, I wondered if that was the worst of it, but the fierce look in his eyes said otherwise.

I sat down on the bench and nodded for him to continue, unable to look away, to blink, to breathe.

Liam sat across from me and wove his tale. At first, each sentence came at an agonizingly slow pace, then built up, layer upon layer, finally rushing out in a deluge, so many confessions and images and beginnings and endings I could barely grasp a single thread.

"...and that is simply because Death is neither a being nor an entity," he was saying, "but an immensely honorable appointment

—one which I was supposed to offer to you. Upon your acceptance, I would then transfer my responsibilities to you and resume the mortal life I relinquished millennia ago—in a different vessel than my original, of course. Instead, I withheld that choice from you, and as a result, watched you endure untold horrors, much of which could have been avoided if only I'd been straightforward about your destiny from the onset…"

Liam babbled on about the dawn of man and witchcraft and Shadow magic and Death's great big capital-R Responsibilities on the ever-turning wheel of life, but I was lost, my head spinning as I tried in vain to keep up, my ears ringing from the impossibly loud beat of my heart. Tears gathered in my eyes, but I had no idea why I felt so sad. So lost.

Finally, after the pale sky had turned black and the obsidian sea reformed in a glassy sheet beneath us, reflecting the wrongness of a million red stars, Liam paused to take a breath.

"Say something, Gray. Please." He reached for my face, his fingers stopping just short of my cheek.

"What… what are you?" I whispered. It was the only question that came to mind. A starting point at the center of a vast labyrinth I wasn't sure I could escape.

"I am Shadowborn, like you. A human. At least, I was. As I've said, that identity becomes murky once a human dons the mantle of Death."

"But… when?" I asked, wondering if he was as old as Darius and Ronan. Did he have a life before? A family? Did he remember them? Miss them? Had they been made to believe he'd died in an accident, like Darius's family had? "How long ago were you human?"

"In terms of years, I don't know. I no longer process time the same way humans do. But I can tell you that it was so long ago, I scarcely recalled the simple joys of even *being* human. When I felt the call of your power across the realms, I knew only that the time had come for me to reclaim my humanity, live out the end of my days, and eventually find my soul's peace."

"The call of my power? How—" But my words evaporated as the realization hit. It must've been the night I'd inadvertently resurrected Bean in the alley. He'd been there—the dark raven who'd watched me touch her soul. The same one who'd appeared in Sophie's room the night she'd been murdered. He'd transformed before my eyes into the hooded figure I later learned was Death, and we'd been entangled in each other's lives ever since.

"Ah. I see you are beginning to understand." He almost sounded relieved.

He was wrong, though. I didn't understand at all. If anything, I was more confused than ever. Human? I couldn't have heard him right. "But you're… you're Death. The Great Transformer, older than time, vaster than the seas, more illuminating than a thousand and one suns."

"Yes. Death is all of those things and more. So much more. So *very* much more, in fact, that the energy of such a being cannot possibly be contained by a single entity. Boiled down to its very essence, Death is but another role. That is what I'm trying to explain."

"A role? Like a job? Liam, you're not making any sense."

"Sparing you the specifics, it happens thusly: In an ancient rite as old as existence, the mantle of Death is passed down from one Shadowborn to another of their choosing, revealed only when the time is right. It was bestowed upon me many, many centuries ago by the Shadowborn who'd held the position before me. So yes, it *is* a job. The loneliest, most difficult job one could ever be tasked with, as well as the very highest honor. To wear the cloak of shadows and balance the great scales of life is a responsibility few are ever given the opportunity to consider. None who've been called to serve have ever refused."

"*Could* they refuse?"

"Of course. To wear the mantle of Death is a choice. One that is entered into freely and fully informed, or not at all."

My head was spinning again. Of all the things Liam had ever shared with me, of all the lessons he'd imparted, this was the most baffling. "So this… this choice? It's the choice you mentioned earlier? You're saying I have to decide whether to become you? To become Death?"

A bitter laugh escaped his lips. "If only it were as simple as—"

"No," I said. I didn't even have to think about it. My life as an orphaned, Shadowborn, demon-sworn, deranged-hunter-targeted witch was a red-hot mess on the best of days, and at the moment, my prospects for getting off this hell boat were looking pretty grim, too. But my friends on the material plane were counting on me to find a way out. It was way too early to lose hope. "I don't want that life. Death. Whatever you call it. No. Final answer."

"You don't understand, Gray." Liam shook his head, his every movement weighted with sadness. "That choice is no longer before you. You see, I chose you to be my successor. I began your training. And then I neglected to give *you* the choice of accepting or declining. Now, you're here. You do not get to make that choice."

I nodded somberly. Here in hell, I didn't get to make *any* choices. That was kind of the point of this place.

"It doesn't matter," I said. "I would've said no anyway. I still would've ended up right here, and you'd have to go with your second choice either way."

"It doesn't work that way. The moment I chose you, I un-chose all others." Liam pulled his foot up onto the bench, absently picking at the laces of his boot, and I almost laughed. Dressed in a flannel shirt and dark jeans, rocking that messy blond hair, Liam looked like a regular guy. One I'd had the distinct and fairly recent pleasure of making out with—kisses I still felt tingling on my lips. Yet here we were, floating aimlessly on the black lakes of hell, talking about things that would make most people's heads explode.

And judging from the severity in his eyes, we were just getting started.

"If any chosen Shadowborn fails the training or refuses the call," he went on, "the current servant of Death is permanently bound and forced to serve for eternity. It is the risk we take when we make our selection, but I never considered it a risk. As I said, no one has ever refused before."

"Yet here I go, breaking all the rules again." I offered him a small smile and reached out to squeeze his knee. I was pissed at him for keeping me in the dark on this—it was a major revelation, to say the least, and I'd need time to fully process it later, and ask more questions and probably ignore him for a few days—but in the grand scheme of our current predicament, and everything that still waited for us on the material plane, Liam's sins of omission weren't exactly unforgivable. I had bigger battles to fight, and I was counting on Liam to stand by my side through all of them.

Besides, he'd picked me, and I'd refused. Now, he'd be stuck as the Grim Reaper for all eternity. That sounded like punishment enough.

But Liam didn't return my smile. His gaze darkened, his brow creasing with deep lines. "Yours was not a refusal as much as a… well, a different sort of complication"

"What sort of—oh." *Damn. Of course.* The labyrinth of this insane tale just branched out in a thousand new directions. "Because of Sebastian. My contract."

"I named you as my successor, unaware of your existing bond. Regardless of the strength of your power or whatever greatness I believed you capable of, as a demon sworn witch, your soul was already claimed. I couldn't move forward without the permission of your master."

The sound of the m-word made my skin crawl with revulsion. Liam had the grace to look embarrassed, but it was too late.

"So you made a deal," I snapped, getting to my feet. This was his true confession—the real source of his guilt. I turned away from him and knelt on the foredeck, gazing out across the endless black mirror beneath us, shaking my head in disbelief.

Fucking Sebastian. What *was* it about him? Why did the men I cared most about always turn to him when the chips were down?

"You made a deal," I repeated. "With the Prince of Hell."

"At the time," he said softly, "I thought—"

"Yes, I know, Liam. You thought it was the only option at the time. You and everyone else who's ever signed on Sebastian's dotted line. That's why they call it a devil's bargain." I rubbed my temples, a new headache squeezing my skull like an overripe melon. I could forgive Liam for not telling me about the Death thing. But making a deal with the Prince of Hell? After everything

I'd been through on that front with Ronan? "Just tell me what happened."

"Well, Sebastian heard my case, of course. He already knew how powerful you were—how powerful you were destined to become. And just as I'd bargained on you accepting the mantle, Sebastian had bargained on your refusal."

"Oh, I'm sure he did." I couldn't keep the sarcasm from my voice. "And the terms of this clandestine deal of the century?"

"For a small price, he agreed to grant me the opportunity to assess your magic, train you to the fullest extent that time allowed, and ultimately present this choice to you as I was meant to. If you accepted the honor, you would continue on in my stead, and I would be free to live out a mortal life, just as I'd planned."

Wow. So that's what all this had been about. Liam wanted his mortality, and he was willing to trade away mine for the privilege.

"And this so-called small price?" I asked.

"I was to bring him the soul of a woman who broke her contract years ago, and has eluded his capture ever since."

"Bring him the soul? How?"

"I would've had to take her life, Gray." He let out a deep sigh. "I'm not proud of that now. Please understand—when I made that deal, I did not think and feel as a human."

"No, that didn't happen until you became Liam Colebrook, surfing philosopher, giver of advice and spreader of knowledge, Mr. Humanity himself. Right?"

"Not... quite. It is only in your eyes that I see my human reflection. You look at me as if you truly believe I could be human. As if you truly believe I could be loved."

I didn't respond, and after a few moments of chilling silence, Liam said softly, "It's what I thought I wanted at the time, Gray. My soul was ready to move on."

"And now?" I asked, my own voice just as soft. Just as broken. I was still kneeling on the foredeck, and I couldn't bring myself to turn around and look at him. I was too afraid of what he might say. "Is that still what you want?"

"It doesn't matter. It's not possible now."

"But if it *were*, Liam. Would you want that? A mortal life?"

Liam didn't say anything for so long, I thought he'd vanished. That I'd only been imagining the feel of his heat cresting behind me, the imprint of his presence refusing to fade from my memory.

But when I finally found the courage to get back on my feet and turn around, he was standing right before me, solid and real, closing the small distance that remained. Fresh tears shone in his eyes.

"I did want that, yes," he admitted, resting his hands on my shoulders. "And I kept on wanting it, right up until—"

"Until what?" I felt my own tears gathering again, my throat tight with emotion, my heart heavy with the sting of betrayal. "Until you realized that mortals die painfully and that being the Great Transformation and the Vast Almighty Fuckwhit of Time Immemorial isn't such a bad gig after all?"

At this, he let out a small laugh, but it was hollow. I tried to look away, but he took my chin between his thumb and finger, gently tilting my face up until I had no choice but to look into his eyes.

"What I realized, little witch, was that living a mortal life would hold no joy for me if you were not living that life by my side. Everything I thought I'd wanted vanished under the bright light of your smile, and every time I heard your laugh or tasted your magic in the air or felt even the barest touch of your hair against my cheek, I swore I'd rather die a thousand deaths by your side than be human for a single day in a world that you no longer inhabited—a world where I'd spend every night dreaming that the woman I was falling in love with was curled up beside me, only to awaken to the chill of her absence and the emptiest ache a human heart could bear."

"You… you're falling in love with me?" I gasped at his words, each confession a tiny flame that surged and burned its way through my heart.

Liam smiled again, his cheeks coloring. "Another unforeseen complication, I'm afraid."

God, that smile. I wanted him to kiss me. I wanted him to take me into his arms and promise me he'd find a way out of this for both of us. To convince me that his betrayals didn't matter. That love was enough, and if we only had the chance to find our way back to each other—to grow and nurture that love—we could get past this.

But we were in hell, and hell was the place where all wishes died.

We couldn't get past this any more than I could still become Death. Not because of the secrets or even the deal with Sebastian. But because there was too much still uncovered. Unconfessed. I saw the guilt of it lingering in his eyes, felt his shame in his touch.

As if he could read my thoughts, Liam said, "I'm sorry, Gray. For all that I've done. For all that I've yet to confess. For all the ways my words and deeds will cause you more pain."

There was so much emotion, so much love in his eyes, anyone else would've melted before that gaze. But the longer Liam stared at me, the more enraged I became. It was more than the things he'd confessed, or even the secrets he still held. It was, I realized suddenly, that I'd started falling for him, too. And all along, he'd been something else—some*one* else—entirely.

Everything about us suddenly felt like a lie. Every memory was tainted. In that way, he'd stolen them from me—some of the most beautiful, meaningful moments of my life.

How could I have trusted him so easily?

Fury was lapping at my feet like a wave, and when I couldn't take another second of his intense gaze, I finally exploded, letting that fury wash right over me, sucking the last of my patience out to sea.

"In all your training and mentoring," I said, jabbing my finger into his chest, "you led me to believe it was for my own good, so I could learn to strengthen and direct my magic, to call upon my powers, to grow as a person. But it was really training camp for Death—a job that you no longer wanted. Something you called the loneliest, most difficult job ever. *That's* what you were to pass along to me."

"I would have told you in time, but—"

"No. You kept me in the dark because you made a deal with my soul and couldn't bring yourself to admit it. Meanwhile, you watched my best friend die, my other friends get kidnapped and tortured, the men I love risk their lives to save me from a Shadowrealm I banished myself to, all the while knowing you could've spared us this if only you'd been honest with me. No, I wouldn't have chosen to become Death, so all of those things would've happened anyway, just like they did. But I had a right to know there was another way, and you kept that from me."

"Gray, I—"

"All your rambling about choices and destinies and paths. All along, you were making my choices for me. I trusted you, Liam. I cared for you—more than you even realize. And when you told me things—about the realms, about my magic, about what I could do—I believed you."

I blew out a breath of air, my body shaking, my heart pounding. Somewhere along the line, I'd hopped on a roller coaster of understanding to frustration to forgiveness to anger to rage, and I still wasn't ready to step off this crazy ride. The longer we talked, the more it hurt. And the worst part was that none of this even mattered. Not if I couldn't find a way out of here. Eventually, Liam would have to leave, go back to his Death duties. And I'd be left here, alone with these feelings. With this blackness.

"I never misled you about your capabilities," he said. "You and I were only just beginning to tap into your potential. You *can* do all of those things. And more. So much more, Gray."

"Ah, but I can't. Remember?" Angry tears threatened to spill, but I eradicated them with a quick swipe. I would *not* let my emotions lead me back into his warm embrace. Not now. "I'm *here*. A permanent guest in Sebastian's playground. Banished. No better off than I was in the Shadowrealm. All that's missing is a visit from the Prince himself, come to introduce himself and gloat at his big win."

"Gray, this wasn't... Your ending up here had nothing to do with my deal." Liam's face paled, his shoulders slumping under the weight of whatever he was about to say next. "Remember, Sebastian was betting on your declining this opportunity. Per our arrangement, if I failed to properly train you or convince you to accept the honor, I... I was bound to burn your life scroll."

"My life scroll?"

"Do you recall the soul ferrier you met the night Sophie passed? The owl I entrusted with her soul?"

I nodded, the familiar sadness of Sophie's death clawing at my heart. It was a pain I'd learned to live with, but now it flared anew, as bright and strong as it had been in those first few days after her murder. For her, I did let those tears fall. They slid down my cheeks and into my mouth, the salty taste a reminder that I could still feel.

Liam cupped my face, gently catching my tears with his thumbs. I let him, desperate for the comfort, however brief it had to be.

"They take many forms," he continued. "Owls, ravens, bats. Ferriers ensure safe passage of the recently deceased to the Shadowrealm. But that is not what marks a human's death in the cosmic sense. Deep within the cosmos, at a distance beyond infinity, lies the Great Hall of Records. A library, essentially, that contains the life stories of all creatures. Their life scrolls."

"Literally," I said.

"*Quite* literally, yes." He dropped his hands, and I canted forward, already missing his touch. Liam continued speaking, pretending he hadn't noticed. "Every being is issued a blank scroll upon birth, upon which their life stories are written. Of course, what are stories but a series of choices, and as such, they are never written in permanent ink, for they are ever-changing. The only chapter that is final, immutable, is death. So, when a being dies and passes into the Shadowrealm, it is Death's responsibility to see that their scroll is burned. The burning is symbolic of the great transformation of the soul, and it's how the natural order is kept in balance. There are never more scrolls—or living beings—than intended."

In typical fashion, Liam's explanation left me more confused than ever.

"So Sebastian wanted you to… to kill me?" I asked. "Like the woman who'd escaped his capture?"

"No. He wanted me to burn your life scroll. As I said, that is a symbolic gesture—it does not literally *bring* your death. It merely *records* your death, as far as the natural order is concerned."

"But I wouldn't actually *be* dead? Just *listed* as dead on an old dusty scroll that you would then set on fire?" I closed my eyes and shook my head. Hell's atmosphere must have been screwing with my logic circuits, because clearly I was missing something. "Liam. If all Sebastian wanted was for you to record my death on paper, why wouldn't we just do that?"

"It's so much more complicated and devastating than that, Gray." He paused, his eyes electrified with pain and guilt. In a voice so low I had to read the words on his lips, he said, "Remember what your death—even on paper—actually means for him."

The full horror of Liam's deceit hit me then, all at once, like a thousand glass rainstorms pelting me from all directions. I collapsed onto the deck, all my bones turning to dust. I couldn't breathe.

Liam really had bargained away my soul. If I'd accepted his offer, I would have become Death. If I'd failed or refused, I would've been marked as "dead", a tiny loophole just big enough for the Prince of Hell to step through.

A loophole just big enough to allow him to collect on my original contract, years—decades—before it was meant to begin.

In exchange for a shot at his own mortal life, Liam had sold me into demonic slavery.

EIGHT

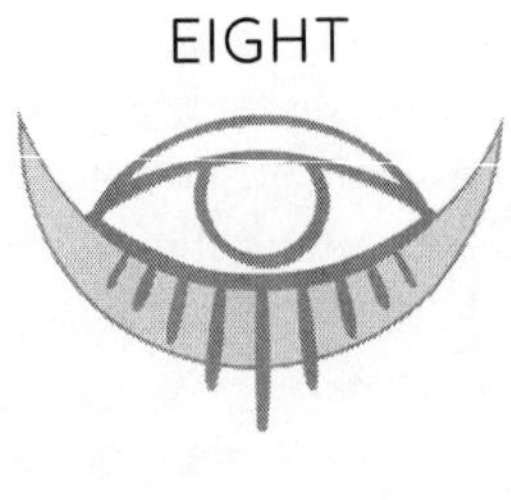

GRAY

Blurred by my tears, three women appeared on the boat behind Liam, dressed in white and carrying their silver swords, just as they had in my dream in the Shadowrealm.

We told you not to follow him, they said.

"Where is my sword?" I asked, nearly delirious with grief. "There are supposed to be four."

I was vaguely aware of Liam kneeling down on the deck before me, his warm hands wrapping around my calves, his blue eyes scanning my face, searching for signs of life. But I looked past him, reaching instead for the women.

You must seek your own sword, they said, their voices unifying into a single, shadowy echo. *Before you no longer have the strength to rise.*

They vanished in an instant, leaving their swords behind, suddenly embedded in my chest. Blood leaked from the wounds, soaking my shirt and staining the wooden slats of the boat.

"Do something," I whispered to Liam.

Tears glittered in his eyes, and he leaned forward and pressed a kiss to my temple, the scent of his skin like summer and the beach and the ocean and everything I'd come to love about him. "I'm trying, little witch. Please let me help you."

I leaned into his touch, and just as quickly as it had appeared, the dream-haze lifted. I was whole again, my mind focused, the blood no more than a nightmare receding in the dawn.

Liam pulled back, watching me intently. Waiting for me to speak.

"I don't know what to say to you," I admitted. "Part of me wants to hate you. The other part can't imagine letting you go."

"I understand." He lowered his eyes, shame coloring his cheeks once again. "I… I've utterly failed you."

"Liam, don't—"

"In guiding you through your magic without revealing my own secrets," he pushed on, "I have failed you. In withholding this choice and its ramifications from you, I have failed you. But most of all…" Liam cupped my face, each of his words a struggle that seemed to wring another drop of life from his being. "In falling in love with you, I have failed you. I wanted to keep you whole and unbroken, to hold on to the sweetness I tasted in your kiss, to believe in the fairy tale I saw in your eyes when you looked at me that day on the beach."

"Then why didn't you?" I reached up to touch his lips, soft and lush. Tiny sparks danced across his mouth, making my fingertips tingle. "Why?"

"Oh, Gray. Your heart was never mine to claim. That is why these sparks—the lightning—why it followed our every kiss. You and I… We were never supposed to exist in that way. There was no room for that possibility in the natural order. I broke it when I tried to make it so. I broke *you*."

My heartbeat sputtered, twin halves pounding very opposite rhythms. One half for the new love I'd only just begun to feel for him during our time in the Shadowrealm, fizzy and hopeful and as delicate as lace. The other half for the black rage still coursing through my blood, heating up all over again.

"Say something," he whispered. Desperate. Lonely.

"I never want to see you again." I closed my eyes. Apparently, I was a good liar, too. "Go."

Liam sighed, but he didn't make a move to leave. "I'm afraid I can't. Not until I've offered you this final choice. It is why I've come, Gray." He got to his feet, pulling me up with him. Grabbing my shoulders tight, he said, "You must hear me out. Please. It is your *only* chance at leaving this realm."

"Go," I said again. I needed him to leave. I needed him to stay. I needed him to undo all of this so we could avoid this soul-crushing pain and skip to the good part. The falling in love, learning about the universe together part. The kissing part.

"Go," I repeated.

Liam ignored me. "Now that your soul is trapped here, you are no longer free to accept the mantle of Death I was meant to bestow upon you. You are Sebastian's possession, and I am meant to continue eternally as the Great Equalizer, Lord of Shadows, Bringer of Transformation. Death."

Fresh anger welled inside, and I jerked out of his grip, shoving him hard in the chest. "You've condemned us both, all because of your stupid ego! You're supposed to be above all this human crap!"

"I am supposed to be a lot of things, Gray. As are you. Yet we keep defying those expectations at every turn." The smoldering look in his eyes brought me right back to the beach. Our kiss. The lightning. He said we broke the natural order, and maybe we did.

But in that moment, breaking the natural order had made me whole.

The part of my heart that still cared for him beat harder, and I almost reached for him again. Almost pressed my lips to the hollow of his throat where his shirt opened up, licking the salty taste from his skin. Almost felt a thousand tiny sparks exploding between us.

With every image, every fantasy, my heart started to shift, making room for the possibility of forgiveness even now. Was that what it meant to love someone? To accept their flaws and fuckups, no matter how disastrous, as long as they were willing to bare their soul in front of you? To strip everything down, admit their mistakes, apologize? Mean it? Was it enough? I had no doubts that Liam was sorry. That he'd do anything to take back his actions and heal this great rift he'd opened up between us.

But did that mean I was strong enough to cross that rift?

My heart thought so. My skin, my eyes, my body, all the places that wanted to drink him in thought so.

But in the end, my brain just couldn't be convinced.

I broke away from his fiery gaze and backed off, folding my arms across my chest to keep him from getting any closer. "What do you want, Liam?"

"There is a final choice for you here, as I mentioned on my arrival. This time, I'm giving you the options equally and honestly, as I should've done before."

"Honestly?" I laughed, but the harshness of it hurt my ears. "Well, *honest* would be a good start, coming from you."

"A good start? No, little witch." He dropped his voice to a whisper, his face falling into a look of utter devastation. "It's the end."

"Of course." I sighed. I was out of anger, out of rage. Out of patience for his melodramatic declarations. "Just… just tell me, Liam. Get to the point."

"Option one," he began, the heaviness of his words pressing on my heart before he'd even finished his sentence. "We concede to this loss. I will return to my eternal work, donning the cloak of shadows for all time, and you… remain."

"Remain what? Where?"

"Here, Gray. Exactly as you are now, only without my company." He looked out across the vast emptiness surrounding us, the black sea still wholly unbroken by land or other vessels or even a cloud on the horizon. "This moment, this place, this view, this life, these memories, endlessly haunting you."

"In other words, live out eternity trapped in the most fucked-up Groundhog Day in the universe?" I shook my head. "Hard pass."

"You might reconsider, once I've shared the rest."

A tremble rolled through my body, head to toe, but I held it together. "What's behind lucky door number two?"

"I burn your life scroll, as Sebastian intended from the moment we made our first deal."

"First. So this is part of a new deal, then?"

"It is. We have no other choice in the matter, Gray. This is his domain."

"What does he want?" I asked, though I suspected I already knew the answer.

"He'll allow me to escort your soul back to your body and reunite the two, restoring your life force. You'll be physically alive and integrated, just as you were before you entered the Shadowrealm."

"And my magic?"

"Shall be restored as well. Your power will continue to develop—to whatever extent you are allowed to continue your magical training and studies—and you will grow and age and transform as you normally would. Upon your natural death, you'll... you'll remain in his possession, per the terms of your original contract."

I closed my eyes, the last of my hope evaporating. Of course Sebastian had thought of everything. *The devil is in the details.* For the first time in my life, I was starting to understand what that actually meant.

"So that's it, then," I said. "Stay here, or start a new life as the Prince of Hell's magical plaything."

Liam had the good sense not to try to soften the harsh reality of that situation. "If you need time to consider this, I can come back—"

"Oh, I've already made my choice, Liam. But you were wrong about one thing."

"I was wrong about a great many things."

"I'm talking about the part where you said this would be the last choice I'd ever be allowed to make." I opened my eyes and glared at him. "I *guarantee* you it won't be."

Liam said nothing, but his lips held the hint of the same smile I'd caught in the Shadowrealm after I told him I wasn't giving up hope—that I'd find a way out of there, no matter how impossible it seemed.

"So what have you decided, then?" he finally asked.

I tipped my head back and looked up at the sky, gazing across the spray of red stars. They were beautiful, yet eerie. Not home. Not true.

I took a deep breath, calling up the magic from deep inside. It answered immediately, swirling in my chest, buzzing through my nerves, across my skin, into my blood, right down to my very bones. I might not be able to use it here in Hell, but this magic was a part of me, something even Sebastian couldn't take away.

I was done running from him. Done prolonging the inevitable. It was time to meet my so-called master and let him know exactly what I thought of *that* little arrangement.

Lowering my face once again, I met Liam's intense gaze with my own brand of ferocity. He flinched in surprise, and I let out a laugh.

Then, with a smile on my face and all that beautiful, dark, incredibly powerful magic racing around inside me, I made my choice.

"Burn it, Liam."

NINE

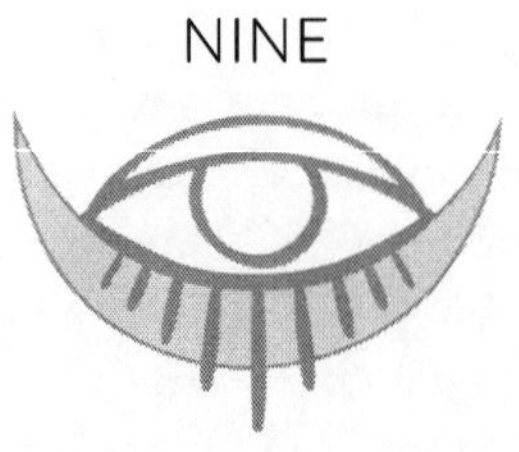

EMILIO

"All non-fae travel has been restricted," Jael said, helping himself to a second serving of Elena's *canelones de espinaca.* "Communications into and out of the Bay are glamoured. I'd advise you not to trust any reports you receive from your men or anyone else in town, and don't bother trying to warn them, either. They won't receive your messages as you intended."

I pushed my own plate away, my worries about the situation back home killing the last of my appetite. "They can do that? Glamour cell phone conversations?"

"Cell phones, texts, emails, handwritten letters, telegraphs, photos, websites, on and on. Anything can be glamoured to seem like something else, especially when the targets don't realize they're being targeted."

"So coordinating a rescue from inside the city is out," Elena said. "We'll have to get in, but you say they're restricting travel. Is there a way to get close, sneak in below their radar? Maybe send in undercovers?"

"You won't get within fifty miles of the Bay," he said. "You'll drive your normal roads, of course, but then you'll suddenly forget to make the turn. Or you'll make the turn, only to end up right back where you began. Or you'll swear you left for the Bay hours ago, only to find yourself in the bathtub enjoying a good soak. Fae glamour has many facets."

Did we even stand a chance? Darkwinter seemed to have the advantage at every turn. And they had the Council's backing, besides.

What a mess.

"How did this even happen?" I asked, more to myself than anyone else, but Jael answered anyway.

"My sense is that Darkwinter and their allies have been planning this for some time, Talia's involvement notwithstanding. Recent conditions in the Bay have made the city ripe for such a takeover."

"How so?" Elena asked.

"The Bay was already in a state of chaos," Jael said. "After word spread of the rash of violence against witches, many of the others began to flee."

"It was safer for them to go," I said defensively, thinking of Gray and Haley. Of Reva. If they'd gotten out earlier, maybe they'd be safe now, too. Maybe Gray wouldn't be trapped in the Shadowrealm with a madman bent on killing her, and Reva and Haley wouldn't be locked in that awful prison. "What would you have them do instead? Wait around to be caught by a hunter? To be carved up and experimented on, slaughtered in their own beds?"

Jael finally set down his fork, deep pain flashing in his eyes.

Too late, I realized my mistake.

He'd lost someone he loved in exactly the way I'd so gracelessly described.

Nice move, asshole.

"Jael, I'm sorry. I didn't—"

"I wanted to take her away," Jael said softly. "But she wanted to stay. Sophie loved the Bay. It was her home. She loved Gray, too. I understand why you're so upset about this situation, detective." At this, he met my eyes again, his gaze fierce despite the calm, almost detached tone in his voice. "I'm asking you for the same understanding."

"I… Of course," I said. "I'm sorry, Jael. I should've been more… I'm sorry."

"Apology accepted."

In the awkward silence that followed, Elena cleared away some of the dishes and brought back a fresh pot of coffee, even stronger than the last one. She poured us each another cup—her fourth, my sixth, Jael's second. It seemed we'd all accepted that sleep wasn't an option tonight.

"I don't blame the witches for leaving," Jael finally said, stirring about half a cup of sugar into his brew. "I'm merely pointing out the facts. The power balance their absence created didn't cause this, but it *is* a factor. One we must consider if we're going to find a way to restore that balance."

"A factor, yes," I said. "Along with Darkwinter's aspirations, Talia's betrayal, and the hunters' endless quest for the magic they believe is rightfully theirs. Not to mention the Council's total fucking betrayal of their own oaths." I gulped down half my coffee, ignoring the burn in my throat. "Looks like we're about three kinds of fucked here, *amigos*."

Jael didn't disagree. "Another challenge we're facing is the existing unrest within each supernatural sub-community. The vampires in particular have become unstable. Several factions are vying for Darius Beaumont's territory. A group from the south has already taken control of his assets in town, including his apartment and the Black Ruby property."

"What?" This was news to me. Vampire hierarchy had a lot of very definitive rules. One group couldn't just move in on someone else's territory—not without a whole lot of bloodshed. "Darius hasn't formerly relinquished any of his holdings, and he isn't dead. Who are these upstart vamps?"

"They're unknown to me, but my understanding is that Darius lost respect in recent months after the slaughter of several of his own kind at Norah Hanson's home. His involvement with the Grinaldi family has not helped matters. None of the squabbling vampire underlings seem to know where his loyalties lie, other than with a witch who up until a couple of months ago was utterly unremarkable. And now the vampire seems to have vanished altogether."

"That's ridiculous, Jael. The vamps we eliminated at the

Hanson house were sent there to kidnap Gray and kill the rest of us. Hardly innocent victims."

"*Allegedly,*" Jael said. "Remember, detective. The official story is typically the one written by those in power, regardless of how they came into such power. At the moment, they've set up camp in our city, while you and your allies appear to have fled. Whom does that leave to tell the tale?"

I conceded the point, despite the fact that it made my blood boil to imagine some rag-tag bunch of bloodsuckers invading Darius's territory. He'd rip their throats out if he knew. Hell, I'd save him the trip and do it myself if I could get back there.

"So who's pulling the strings?" Elena asked. "Darkwinter and the hunters are doing the dirty work, but someone must be financing the operation. Coordinating the takeover. Do you think it's Talia?"

"I wondered about that, too, but..." Jael sipped his coffee, considering, then finally shook his head. "No. Talia has always thought very highly of herself, and her position on the Council does afford her some measure of power. But I'm fairly certain she's not the ultimate player here. Someone—or someones—is leading the charge at a much higher level."

"Probably sitting in a cushy office somewhere, keeping his hands clean."

"Or hers," Jael said.

"Or hers. Exactly." I pushed back from my chair and got up to help Elena clear the last of the dishes.

Jael had given us a lot to consider, and it all felt legit.

But something was still bugging me about it all.

Jael wasn't on the Council. As far as I knew, his family made an honest living in the Bay through Illuminae—at least, as honest as a fae could be. Back in the fae realm, he was Seelie court royalty, but here in our world, he was a club deejay. Venerated by the groupies who flocked to Illuminae to hear him spin, but not someone I'd typically think of as a covert operator.

How, then, had he come across so much intel about Darkwinter's actions?

I opened my mouth a dozen times to press him on it, but after putting my foot in my mouth about Sophie's death, I didn't want to risk offending him again. We needed him on our side.

Thankfully, Elena spared me the trouble.

Setting out a plate of homemade *alfajores* so thick with dulce de leche they were probably going to be the death of us all, she said, "Unfortunately, we can't make a move on this intel until we verify it. The last thing we need is to expose ourselves because of a misguided operation based on incomplete or unverified information."

"That's going to be difficult," he said, reaching for a cookie. "As I've said, communications into and out of the Bay are not reliable."

Diplomatic as ever, she waited for him to take a bite, then went in for the kill shot. "So, who's your source on this?"

Slowly, he finished chewing his cookie, clearly considering his next move. He held Elena in his gaze, but there was no malice there. If anything, he looked impressed.

Reaching for another cookie, he said, "My sister Kallayna has been working to infiltrate Darkwinter for quite some time. She'd heard whispers at Illuminae that the old lines were gathering strength, preparing to make a move in the Bay. Frightened by the possibilities, she encouraged these rumors, hoping to find out more information. Eventually, she became aware that a Knight of Darkwinter had been spending time at the bar. She took her time, slowly getting him to trust her. To enjoy her company. They became quite close."

"How close?" Elena asked.

"They'd started dating, and then Kallayna sensed things were getting more serious. He asked her to move in with him—he'd recently bought a home in the Bay. She was scared, of course, but she saw the opportunity for what it was and accepted his offer, pretending to be dissatisfied with our family."

"And this Knight… He believed her?" I asked, finally sitting down again.

"As far as we know, yes. Though communicating with her has been difficult. We staged a very public, very brutal fight over her decision to move in with him, all to lend credence to her claims.

She broke ties with me and turned her back on our legacy. Since then, she's been sending me encrypted messages through a secure, non-glamoured channel magically routed through our home realm, but the only way for her to access it is to leave the Bay, and she can't do that often without arousing suspicion."

"If you knew what Darkwinter was planning," I said, "why didn't you come to us sooner?"

"Just like you, I needed to be certain before acting on the intel. We didn't know exactly what they were planning—if anything. They could have just as easily been setting Kallayna up for a fall. I couldn't risk that."

"When was the last time you heard from her?" Elena asked.

"Two days ago—before the Knights secured the city." He pressed a napkin to his lips and closed his eyes, his shoulders stiffening. It was the closest he'd come to losing his composure in my presence. "The thought of losing someone else I love…"

He trailed off, but I knew the "someone else" he'd been thinking of in that moment. I realized just how much restraint he'd shown tonight in not asking me for details, for updates on the case, not even when the subject of Sophie had come up earlier.

He had a right to know where things stood.

"Jael, we know who took Sophie's life," I said gently.

"Oh?" he asked calmly. He didn't look up, didn't show any outward reaction at all, but I sensed the need in his voice, that one-word reply heavy with equal parts pain and hope.

"Sophie and the other witches in Blackmoon Bay were murdered by Jonathan Reese," I said. "He's the man currently imprisoning Gray and the others. We don't know whether he acted alone in the killings, but my gut says no. We already know he had accomplices in other attacks, including the one at Norah's house, so it's not a stretch to assume this is connected to the larger crime waves in the Bay as well as the Darkwinter takeover. I just wish I understood how all the pieces fit together."

"Jonathan Reese?" Jael met my eyes across the table. I could practically see the wheels of his mind turning. "Possibly a relative of Phillip Reese?"

"Yes," I said, recalling the name from what little I could find in

Jonathan's public records. "Phillip is his father—the hunter who killed Gray's mother when she was a teenager. Do you know the man?"

"Kallayna has reported that her Darkwinter Knight has accompanied a human named Phillip Reese to at least three or four meetings with other Darkwinter soldiers. I don't believe she knew he was a hunter. She hasn't been privy to the meetings themselves —only to his comings and goings."

"We already know from another source that Jonathan's motive isn't murder," I said. "He's developing the hybrid technologies, but his experiments often result in the death of his subjects. I just couldn't figure out how he was getting his research to Darkwinter, or if they were running their own operation. But that's it—it's his father. Phillip Reese is the connection."

"I thought Jonathan was estranged from his father," Elena said. "That everything he does is in direct opposition to his father's legacy."

"That's what we heard from one highly unreliable witness," I said. "Fiona Brentwood is a vampire with an ax to grind."

"Many people believe my sister and I are estranged," Jael said with a casual shrug. "Perhaps the rift between father and son was also an act."

We were all startled by my sister's phone. She hopped up from the table and fished it from her pocket, disappearing into the living room. "Alvarez. What have you got for me?"

I turned my attention back to Jael, who'd just snuck in a third *alfajor*. When all this was over, we'd have to send him a whole box of them.

"You could be onto something with that estrangement act idea," I said. "We hadn't considered it from that angle."

I popped an *alfajor* into my mouth, trying to process everything. It was entirely possible that there were multiple factions of hunter groups working together with Darkwinter, or that Jonathan and his father had set aside their differences to work against their common enemy. For all I knew, the prison was just one of *many* hybrid research sites.

The Bay needed our help, but right now, we needed to find out what was going on in that prison. That was the key to toppling the coup in the Bay—and anywhere else they'd set their sights on. I was sure of it.

"We need to get into that prison," I said. "We've got good intel that says it's here on the coast. Problem is, we can't actually locate it. It's fae spelled."

"I might be able to intercede," Jael said. "It's doubtful I can destroy the spell completely—Darkwinter have powers the rest of us can only dream about—but if I can weaken it long enough for you to get inside, that might be a start."

"It's worth a shot," I said. "But Jael, if Darkwinter figures out you were the one who brought down the spell..."

I let the silence speak for itself. Jael knew what Darkwinter would do to him if he got caught. He didn't need me to spell it out.

"They are, either directly or indirectly, responsible for the death of someone I love," he said, his catlike golden eyes suddenly blazing. "Possibly the torment of others. There is nothing I won't do, nothing I won't risk, to hasten their end. Are we absolutely clear on that, detective?"

I nodded once, accepting his offer. There was no point trying to talk him out of it. I knew what it meant to lay your life down for someone you loved—for vengeance, for a shot at saving them, for all of it. There would always be consequences, but not taking the risk at all? That was a shame I could never live with.

I sensed Jael felt the same way.

Elena returned from the living room, pulling on her jacket and gloves. "That was Lansky. We just got a hit on Norah Hanson's credit card."

"What does that mean?" Jael asked, reaching for another cookie.

"It means you'd better get a doggy bag, Prince." I grabbed the plate out from under his hand and rose from the table. "We've got a rogue witch to track down."

TEN

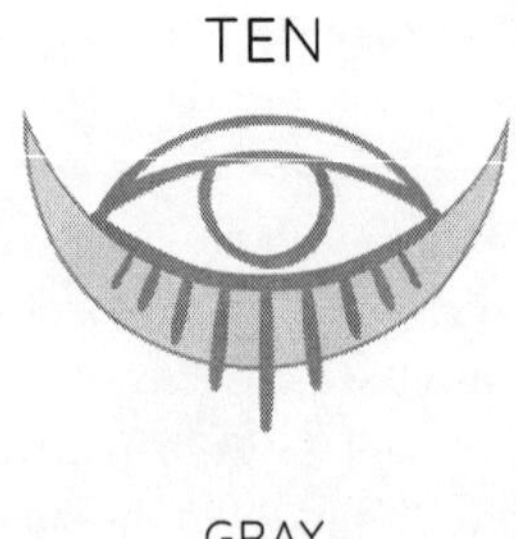

GRAY

It felt like someone had pulled the plug on my soul, and now I was being sucked down into oblivion, crushed by the weight of too much gravity as I spun and swirled and vanished down some ancient cosmic drain.

But just when I feared my bones would be pulverized, the spinning stopped, and I was breathing again, gulping down the precious air I'd been deprived of. I was alive.

And I was back on the material plane.

When I finally opened my eyes, I found myself resting on cloud-fluffy bedding, gazing up at a pristine white ceiling fitted with a stainless-steel fan that gently stirred the air. I'd been bathed and dressed in soft stretch pants and a loose gray hoodie that smelled like… like Ronan.

Like home.

God, how I wanted to close my eyes and sink back into that dream—the one where none of this was real. Where my rebels and I had never left the safe house, and instead spent our days cooking meals together and drinking good wine and playing Scrabble and making love. So much hot, passionate, incredible, amazing love in a bed big enough for the whole pack.

My core ached to think of it.

But despite the softness of his sweatshirt and the luxurious sheets beneath me, this was no dream. I'd just been betrayed by someone I trusted and evicted from hell, only to end up in a fancy hotel room I could never afford even if I *hadn't* lost my job at Waldrich's Imports.

Everything about Blackmoon Bay, about my old life, felt like it belonged to someone else.

And now, so did I.

I let out a tired sigh. The Prince of Hell would be expecting me soon, if he wasn't already. This hotel was probably his property.

Just like me.

Welcome to the first day of the end of your life, Gray Desario.

I waited another beat for the tingling in my arms and legs to subside, then sat up slowly, leaning back against a sleek ebony headboard. The room spun again, and when it finally righted, something else came into sharp focus.

The sight of him stole my breath all over again.

"Ronan," I gasped.

He stood at the foot of the bed in dark jeans and a black v-neck tee that clung to his muscles, a dark shadow of a beard lining his jaw, his hair practically begging for me to run my fingers through it. I wanted to touch him. To feel his hands and mouth on me.

But something was… different. His face had been bruised, with new, pink scars cutting across his jaw. His rigid, unmoving form was flanked by two terrifying canine beasts I recognized from our previous run-ins. There was no mistaking the matted, coal-black fur, the razor-sharp teeth, the glowing red eyes.

Hellhounds.

Despite the frightening and unexpected appearance of the hounds, a surge of gratitude swept over me. Ronan was here. Alive. He'd made it through the hell portal, and I'd made it back to him, and even if we only had one minute to say our goodbyes, I'd take it.

I couldn't help but smile.

"Ronan," I said, finding my full voice. "It's *damn* good to see you."

But Ronan wasn't smiling at me in return, or moving to capture me in a passionate kiss, or reaching for his phone to call Emilio and let him know I was okay. He was just standing there, still as a statue, his eyes blazing with fury while the hounds growled menacingly at his sides.

Ronan waited a beat. Two. Three. Made sure I'd finally seen the anger flashing in his eyes. Then, those beautiful hazel eyes that used to look at me as though I were the only person in the universe that mattered, turned demon black.

"Ronan?" Was this another trick? Maybe I hadn't made it out at all. Maybe I'd only found my way into another chamber in hell, full of fresh torments and hallucinations.

"Gray Desario," Ronan announced, his jaw clenched so tightly I thought he'd shatter his teeth, "your contract has been called."

His tone was stiff and formal, every one of those words pushed through lips that didn't want to yield.

But they did yield.

"I'm here in my official capacity as Guardian at the Crossroads to inform you of your eternal imprisonment and to escort you to your…" He paused, swallowing hard, stumbling. "To your master. Do not attempt to renegotiate. The terms of your contract are binding in accordance with the laws of the Crossroads and upheld by all the courts of the realms."

Ronan rattled off a bunch of rules and regulations, each one clearly regurgitated from memory. The ice in his voice reached into my heart, freezing me all the way down to the bone.

I wondered how many times he'd had to do this before. How many times he'd have to do it again once I was "escorted" into Sebastian's possession and no longer Ronan's responsibility. He was, after all, a crossroads demon, oathbound to serve at his master's pleasure.

From the sound of it, it was only a matter of seconds before that master was the very last thing Ronan and I would ever share.

"Stop!" I shouted, climbing out of the bed and rushing over to Ronan.

"Oh, but I can't," he said sardonically. "This is my job. You always wanted to know where I disappeared to all those times. What I did. Now you get an up-close-and-personal view."

"Don't do this," I whispered. "Just… wait. Five minutes."

He clamped his mouth shut, and I reached for his face,

running my fingers along his jaw. A shiver rolled through him, but before he fully leaned into my touch, he reached up and grabbed my wrist, yanking my hand away.

"Don't," he said. Cold. Dead.

Fear and confusion flooded my heart. *This* was how he wanted to say goodbye?

"What's *wrong* with you?" I asked.

Ronan took a breath, but before he could answer my question, the skin on my wrist—all the places where his fingers touched—began to smolder.

He released me as if I had the plague, his lip curling in disgust.

"Stay away from me, Gray." He held his hands up in front of him, slowly backing away. The hounds followed his every move, never leaving his side.

When I reached for his face again, they snapped at me in warning.

So that's how it's going to be.

"Let me guess," I said, pulling away and rubbing the heat from my wrist. "This new little trick of yours is courtesy of Sebastian, Prince of Hell, He Who Thinks He Owns Me?"

"It's not a trick, Gray. It's a price." Ronan sighed, finally dropping the stiff formalities. "He *does* own you. I've been fighting with him for a decade, looking for some technicality that could get you out of this mess, all for nothing. The only thing that kept you safe was the fact that you fucking stayed alive. But now?"

"Newsflash, Ronan. I'm still alive." I waved my hand in his face, displaying the red, angry welts quickly rising on my wrist. "Case in point."

"Colebrook was supposed to bring you back unharmed. Did he say anything about this?"

I took a steadying breath, trying to gather my thoughts. I didn't want to rehash the whole Death mantle thing right now, or give Ronan a reason to hate Liam. Despite my own anger toward him, I couldn't rule out the possibility of a future reconciliation. I already missed him so much—the flannel, the sun-kissed hair, the annoyingly philosophical conversations, the stupidly kissable lips.

The whole situation was impossible, but that didn't mean it wasn't worth fighting for.

And Liam owed me a fight. That was for sure.

As much as I wanted to deny it, Liam—Death—was a part of me, stitched into the fabric of my soul. I couldn't imagine my world without him.

"Liam and I came to an agreement with Sebastian," I said, glossing over the details. "The only way to get my soul out of hell and back into my body was to fake out the universe. We had to trick the natural order into believing I'm dead. Unfortunately, that means—"

"It means you're dead," he said with a defeated sigh. "At least as far as the contract goes. That son of a *bitch*!"

Ronan looked like he wanted to pulverize something. Or someone. I was grateful Liam wasn't here.

"It was the only way," I repeated. "I never would've agreed to it otherwise."

Ronan didn't argue the point. He bowed his head, shaking it slowly. "I never should've brought you through the hell portal. We wouldn't be in this mess if I'd found another way."

"We wouldn't be *anywhere*. We'd be dead, or zombies with no memories. We wouldn't even remember each other, Ronan." I took a chance and stepped close to him again, ignoring the protests of the hounds. Ronan's eyes locked on mine, his lips pressed tight together, the muscles of his jaw flexing.

I brushed my fingertips along his jawline. They came away singed, leaving a trail of charred hair in his beard.

I wasn't allowed to touch the man I loved. Sebastian's cruelty was truly limitless.

Swallowing the knot in my throat, I said, "What happened after we got through the portal? Where is Darius? Is he… Does he remember anything?"

Ronan met me with dead eyes. No longer black, but no longer warm and familiar, either. It was as if he was shutting down.

"He's in rough shape. He attacked a demon—the bloodlust is hitting him hard. And… No, Gray. He doesn't remember anything."

Tears blurred my vision. "Where is he?"

"Somewhere safe."

"I need to see him. You owe me that much."

"Gray, Sebastian—"

"Sebastian can wait."

"Try telling *him* that."

"He owns me for eternity. Another hour won't make a difference."

Ronan didn't respond.

"What about Emilio?" I asked. "Is he still with his sister? Have they found Asher?"

"Sebastian hasn't let me get in touch with Emilio yet." He shoved a hand through his hair, the sudden movement making the hounds jump. "All of this happened so fast... I barely had time to think from the moment those memory eaters attacked."

"I need to see Darius. Please, Ronan. He needs to know he's not alone in this."

"It doesn't matter, Gray. Don't you see?" He turned away from me, his body stiffening again. "I was *summoned* here. This is it. Game over. Don't even bother packing your shit, because everything you own belongs to him now. *You* belong to him now."

"I know."

When he turned to face me again, his eyes were rimmed in red, flooded with pain and regret.

My insides twisted into a pretzel. It was one thing to make the decision with Liam, floating on a hell boat with no other escape route in sight.

But this was really happening now. I was about to become Sebastian's eternal slave.

"It's time," he whispered. He held my gaze for another heartbeat, letting me see the real Ronan one last time.

"I love you," I whispered back.

A tear spilled down his cheek. Just one. In his eyes, I saw the immensity of his love for me, his devotion.

Then he turned away, the hounds close at his heels, all of them expecting me to do the one thing I thought I never would.

Follow them back into hell.

ELEVEN

GRAY

We walked briskly down a long, carpeted corridor decorated with garish orange-and-gold walls and a ridiculous number of chandeliers. Ronan stayed a few steps ahead of me no matter how hard I tried to match his pace, his angry footfalls audible even with the carpeting. The hellhounds trailed on my heels—Sebastian's insurance policy that I wouldn't bolt the first chance I got.

It was almost laughable. Where would I go? How could a demon sworn witch on a death march back to hell via some chintzy, overdone Vegas hotel possibly escape?

You must seek your own sword…

The voices from my vision on the hell boat floated through my mind, but at the moment, I had no idea what to do with that bit of advice. My own sword? From the sound of things, I'd be lucky if Sebastian even let me use a nail file again.

Better for him to keep me away from sharp objects. First chance I got, I'd be jamming something into his jugular, whether he was an immortal demon or not.

The corridor continued on forever, twisting and turning, taking us past doors that remained shut and walls that revealed nothing about my destination. After what felt like hours, we finally reached a large oak door that looked different from the rest, carved with strange symbols that glowed faintly at our approach.

Demon codes. Hell glyphs. Runes. I couldn't decipher any of them.

Ronan pressed his palm to the door, and the symbols pulsed brighter, rearranging into a different pattern. He turned to look at me over his shoulder and met my gaze, our noses nearly bumping, the warmth of his breath brushing my lips.

"Whatever you do," he whispered, "whatever you say, do *not* anger him. Sebastian is prone to melodrama and overreacting, and no matter what you might think, he *always* has the upper hand. Remember that."

"You don't know that. Maybe there's a bargaining chip we haven't—"

"There isn't, Gray. As long as you stand to lose something, he'll find it and exploit the hell out of it. There's nothing you can do here but listen and obey."

Obey. The word sent a shiver down my spine even as it filled me with indignation. I'd known what I was signing up for—at least, as far as committing myself to Sebastian before my time—but at the time I was more concerned with getting out of hell. Sometimes, you just had to deal with one shitstorm at a time.

But now the next storm was upon me, and I had to figure out my game plan—preferably before I was put in irons or sent into the fiery dungeons.

Because no matter what the contract said, no matter what the laws and order of the crossroads and hell and the Shadowrealm and everywhere else maintained, I was *no* one's prisoner.

* * *

The runes faded back to a faint glow, and the door swung open, the force of whatever was on the other side beckoning me to enter. The room was small, and as dark and cold as a refrigerator. I'd barely gotten a glimpse of it when the big door slammed shut behind me, the sound of it making my heart rattle.

There were no windows, and every corner was hidden in shadow. I could just make out a long table at the center of the room, with two figures seated in high-backed chairs at one end.

The only light came from a thick black candle flickering at the center of the table.

"Gray Desario," a slimy voice called forth from the shadows. I couldn't see the man's face, but I knew immediately who the voice belonged to. Ronan had always said Sebastian sounded like Colonel Sanders peddling used cars. "We've been waiting a long time for your arrival."

He leaned forward, his face illuminated by the candle. Instinctively I took a step back, reaching behind me for the familiar solidity of Ronan, but I was suddenly immobilized. I no longer had control of my body—it lurched forward, then marched itself forward to the table.

"Is that really necessary?" Ronan asked.

"Remember your place, boy," Sebastian barked.

Inside, my magic stirred, bringing my blood from a simmer to a boil. But outside, I was a prisoner in my own body, unable to move. Unable to blink. Unable to breathe. It was a wonder my heart was still beating. I was pretty sure Sebastian could've stopped that, too.

I'd never felt so utterly powerless. Not even when Travis had me pinned in the alley, or Jonathan had taken me prisoner. Not when Norah put a hold spell on me. Not even when I'd been trapped in the cellar watching my mother burn.

He'd wanted me to feel that way. To know the score here.

Just when I thought I'd explode from the fear, Sebastian's invisible bonds released me. I gasped, sucking in air, stumbling to the nearest chair and collapsing in it.

Ronan stood at my back, the hounds taking their places at my sides. Though he hadn't said another word since Sebastian's reprimand, I could feel the anger rolling off him, the ferocity of his love for me warming the air around me. I clung to it—the one good thing still standing in this place, no matter what curse Sebastian had put on us.

"Now that we all understand each other…" Sebastian drawled. "Gray. How are you feeling after your long journey?"

You are going to die a slow, painful, horrific death. I will carve you into pieces. Set the pieces on fire. And eat the ashes of your bones.

Out loud, I said nothing.

"It's natural to be a little nervous your first time, Miss Desario. But you have nothing to fear from me. As long as you behave yourself, I think you and I will get along like butter on grits."

The figure on his left shifted, and I caught a brief glimpse of a face. A woman's face, I was pretty sure. She had short white hair and light eyes. Blue, I thought. Like mine.

Did Sebastian have a wife? A *willing* wife?

"Do you know why I've worked so hard to bring you into the fold?" he asked, stealing my attention from the woman.

Again, I said nothing.

"Speak plainly, girl," he said. "No use standing on ceremony."

"It's okay, child," the woman said. She sounded old. Sweet, almost. I immediately relaxed, though I couldn't tell if it was because I actually felt better, or if she'd spelled me. "Answer his questions. You're safe in my presence."

Sure I am. But even as I had the thought, some part of me believed her.

"It is not enough to seek your own sword," she continued. "You must learn to use that sword as well."

I gasped. Had she read my thoughts? Was she actually encouraging me to kill Sebastian? What the hell was going on?

"Are you alright, girl?" Sebastian asked.

I blinked at him slowly. Numb. My eyes drifted back to the woman.

"He can't hear me," she said. "Only you."

Her mouth hadn't moved. It hadn't moved, I realized then, from the moment we'd stepped into this room.

Everything she'd said to me, she'd said in my mind.

I'd heard of witches who could telegraph their own thoughts into the mind of another. But how could she have known about my vision? I hadn't told anyone about that. Not even Liam.

I closed my eyes and took a deep breath, quickly trying to regroup. Despite the unconventional delivery method, the swords of the Tarot must've had a message for me, but what? Both the Three and the Four of Swords had come up in Sophie's book of shadows, in the reading she'd done just before she died. I'd seen the swords again in my nightmare in the Shadowrealm, and then again on the boat, when they'd pierced my heart.

But in the Tarot, swords weren't just about conflict. They were also about thoughts. Speech. Learning to harness your personal power and standing up for yourself and for those who needed protection.

Maybe that was the message I needed to hear today. It was time to stop cowering in the face of this devil and pick up my damn sword.

"Why have I brought you here, Shadowmancer?" Sebastian asked, and this time, I was ready for him. A surge of hot anger melted away the lingering fear.

"Let me guess," I said. "You want me to raise you an army full of corpses. Or better yet—magic up some poor lost souls and convince them to come work for you. Or maybe you want to run experiments on me, cut me open, see if you can figure out what makes a soul manipulator tick."

Behind me, Ronan shifted, a low growl rumbling in his chest.

"Simmer down, demon," Sebastian ordered. Then, to me, "Intriguing ideas, witch. But I'm afraid you've misunderstood. Soul manipulation is an extremely rare power, I'll give you that. But I'm not interested in your ability to raise the dead. Not today, anyway."

"You want to enslave my soul," I said. "That's obvious."

"Miss Desario! Wherever would you get such a preposterous idea?" He said preposterous like *pree*-posterous, and laughed as though I were the funniest girl in the world.

"You *are* the Prince of Hell, correct?" I asked. "Or is your whole dark, brooding, evil schtick just a smokescreen compensating for something else?"

Careful, the woman warned. *Don't push him too far.*

I kept my eyes fixed on Sebastian, not wanting to give her away. But why was she helping me? Was she a prisoner as well? She sat at his side as though they were on equal footing, and the way he angled his body toward her suggested a much more intimate relationship than master-servant.

So, whose side was she actually on?

Ignoring my dig, Sebastian cleared his throat, leaning forward so his face was once again in the light. The flickering candle made the pocks in his face deeper, his eyes more menacing. For all his southern-fried smoothness, Sebastian was downright frightening when he wanted to be.

"I don't need your soul today, witch," he said, his menacing tone sending shivers down my spine. "I need your blood."

"My… blood?" The same fear from before pulsed in my chest, but I let it pass, taking comfort in the familiar hum of my magic. I couldn't manifest it here, but I could still feel it simmering in my blood, tingling. Liam had been right about that, at least. My magic was still with me, even here.

"Why?" I asked.

"For a summoning." He said it as though it all made perfect sense, but I was lost. A summoning? Of what?

I glanced back up at the woman, who nodded slowly. Soothingly. I didn't know how, but we'd… connected somehow. Not just the telepathy, but some kind of link. I felt it tethering us, an invisible thread that allowed me to feel her emotions.

She was sending them to me. Infusing me with them.

Calmness. Reassurance. Support. And most oddly of all—love.

I lifted an eyebrow in question, but she remained stoic, her gaze fixated on the candle in front of her.

I was so thrown off by the whole thing that it took me a minute to realize Sebastian was talking again.

"…powerful line of witches that dates back millennia," he was saying. "Your bloodline was thought to have vanished centuries ago, relegated to the status of an urban legend. But some of us knew better, of course. When the opportunity arose to put you under my protection, well. Only a fool would have turned that down. And thanks to a series of unfortunate events perpetuated by some of your associates, here you are."

He spread his hands and beamed at me, waiting for me to speak. What did he expect? A thank you? A pat on the back for all his cleverness?

"I have no idea what you're talking about," I said, which was the truth. My bloodline? My biological mother had died when I was too young to even remember her. I knew nothing about my father. As far as I was concerned, Calla was my true mother. And if she'd been part of any ancient, urban-legend-inspiring legacy, she would've told me.

"You are Silversbane," the woman said reverently, her crystal-clear voice cutting through my thoughts. It was the first sentence she'd spoken out loud so far, and the sound of it reverberated through my very bones, igniting the magic within me and filling me with an odd sense of… belonging.

"But I've never even heard of Silversbane," I said. Ronan shifted behind me, his energy suddenly antsy. Did he recognize the name? "I'm not—"

My thoughts cut off abruptly as a memory arced through my mind, flashing behind my eyes like a bolt of lightning.

A woman enraged, her dark hair swirling around her head, whipped into a frenzy by the wind. A storm raging, inside and out. A creek, icy cold and rushing by my face so fast…

"I am Silversbane! This magic is my *legacy. Mine! Why should you have it when it was promised to me? My birthright! You have stolen it, Shadowborn filth!"*

Cold hands pressing on my shoulders, sharp nails digging into my flesh, and then… ice. Freezing. Gasping. A bolt of pain in my skull, pressure, my lungs on fire…

"Stay down! Stop squirming, little bitch!"

"Unfortunately, Silversbane was your mother's legacy, not your father's," the woman said, yanking me out of the memory. Or vision. What *was* that?

"Unfortunately?" I asked, blinking away the last of the images. I couldn't shake the cold, though. I rubbed my arms, pulling the sleeves of Ronan's sweatshirt down over my hands.

"Power is as much a gift as a curse," she said. "Though I suspect you already know as much."

At this, I arched an eyebrow. "Says the witch sharing the head of the table with the Prince of Hell? Not to be rude, but you seem a little old to be a princess."

"I'm not a princess, child. I'm Deirdre Olivante," she said matter-of-factly. "Your paternal grandmother."

"My… grandmother?" My mouth dropped open in disbelief. I had a grandmother? Alive? In league with the Prince of Hell?

We will speak of this in private later, she whispered in my mind. *I will tell you everything. Please just remain calm, no matter what he says.*

Before I could even process what she was saying, not to mention the fact that I suddenly had a grandmother I'd never heard of, Sebastian was rambling on about the bloodline again.

"Your ancestors are extremely powerful, even in death," he said. "I require access to that power. Unfortunately, as they have already passed on, I can not retrieve them through normal means. But you, Miss Desario, can."

Show interest, Deirdre said, her tone growing more insistent. *The sooner you let him get to the point, the sooner we can leave.*

I hoped she was right. I also hoped her apparent help wasn't a trap.

"How can I get the souls if they've already passed on?" I asked Sebastian.

"Through the blood summoning. You are their legacy. The souls will not be able to resist the call of their descendent—especially one as powerful as you."

"What do you want with their souls? Don't you have enough to choose from?"

"I do not owe you a reckoning of my affairs, Miss Desario. I'm simply informing you of your first assignment."

"I'm not—"

Let him speak, Deirdre snapped.

"You *will* summon their souls as required," he said, "then use your powers of manipulation to reintegrate them into new vessels, which will then be made available for my purposes."

I didn't bother telling him that Liam and I hadn't quite gotten to the Soul Reinsertion 101 portion of our lesson plan. Even if I wanted to help him summon my ancestors, there was no way I could do what he was asking.

"Let me get this straight," I said. "You want me to yank my ancestors out of their eternal rest by tricking them into thinking I'm summoning them, then imprison them in mortal bodies, and turn them over to you for some creepy purpose you refuse to divulge?"

"Well, you make it sound rather crass, but yes. That is your first duty to me, in a nutshell."

"*Oooh*-kay," I said.

I'd meant it as a pause, a breath before I told him exactly where he could stick his bloodlines and evil plans. But Sebastian clearly took the word as my acquiescence. His eyes lit up, the overeager smile making his lips twitch. He was doing his damnedest to hide it, but he'd just shown me his full hand.

This wasn't just some random errand he was sending me on. Something any one of his lackeys could do. Sebastian needed *me*. And only me.

And despite his bluster, a blood summoning wasn't something he could force me to do, either. It was magic. It required intention. Cooperation. You couldn't fake out a spell. If my heart wasn't in it, the magic would know, and it would backfire.

I pressed my lips together, hiding my own smile.

So, I *did* have a bargaining chip here. Maybe not the upper hand, but something close to an equal one, which was a hell of a lot more than I had when I'd walked into this dungeon.

"I'm so glad we've come to this agreement," Sebastian said. "Now, if you'll just—"

"Wait." I held up my hand, cutting him off cold. Now that I had his attention, and knew what he wanted, I decided to test the boundaries a bit. "If I do as you ask, I need something from you, too."

"Gray." Ronan grabbed the sides of my chair, his knuckles turning white. "Stop."

Sebastian let out a smarmy, patronizing chuckle. "Oh, let the girl speak her pretty little mind, son! There's no harm in hearing her request." Then, to me, "What would you like, Miss Desario? A shopping spree? A makeover? Some chocolates?"

"Actually, I'd like you to stop interfering in my relationship with Ronan. It has nothing to do with you, and I'd appreciate it if you'd undo whatever mojo you put on him to make us catch fire at every touch."

"This again?" He rolled his eyes. The Prince of freaking Hell rolled his eyes. "Sorry. No can do."

"That was never part of my deal," I said. "My relationship with Ronan didn't exist when my contract was executed."

"You're right," he said plainly. "It wasn't part of your deal. But it was part of his." He nodded toward Ronan, his smile stretching all the way to Texas.

"His?" Heart hammering a terrible new rhythm in my chest, I turned around and tipped my head up, trying to catch Ronan's eyes. It was a long time before he finally looked at me.

"I had to," he whispered. Regret filled his eyes. "It was the only way he'd agree to let us use the hell portal."

His earlier words came back to haunt me, their meaning clear only now.

It's not a trick, Gray. It's a price.

"What, exactly, did you pay?" I asked.

"You know," he said softly. His voice was breaking. So was my heart.

"Say it," I whispered.

"Oh, for the love of all that is unholy." Sebastian slammed his hand on the table, making the candle flame flicker. "You two are pathetic. It's your own damn fault for giving in to this temptation anyway. I'm doing you both a favor by putting an end to it."

I closed my eyes, willing myself to remain calm. Grief and misery were banging on the door of my heart, but I couldn't afford to let them in. Not with so much at stake.

I couldn't afford to lose it. I needed to hold on to that damn sword and figure a way out of this.

Opening my eyes, I looked across the table at my grandmother. "Could I speak to the Prince alone please?"

"No," Ronan said, at the time Deirdre said, "I don't think that's a good idea."

Ignoring the protests, Sebastian nodded, gesturing for Deirdre and Ronan to show themselves to the door.

Deirdre went first, and Sebastian's eyes never left her. For a brief instant, I saw the flicker of something almost human on his face. It was gone in a blink, but not before he'd given me another clue into his motives.

I had no idea what it meant. Only that what I'd seen was unmistakable.

Sebastian was in love with my grandmother.

"Gray," Ronan called, and when I looked at him, I saw the trepidation in his eyes. The worry. He didn't want to leave me alone with Sebastian, but I couldn't think straight with him in the room. Not after what I'd learned—what his deal meant for us. I needed to stay focused on Sebastian, on what I could use as leverage to buy myself some more time.

For so long, Ronan had been my rock. My protector. My best friend.

But at the moment, he was no more than a distraction. One I couldn't afford.

He lingered at the threshold with the two hellhounds, awaiting my response, refusing to join Deirdre in the hallway. But in the end, Sebastian showed him a single raised eyebrow, and Ronan caved.

I knew he would. That's how it was in this place. All of us were bound to Sebastian, forced to follow his orders or risk the life-altering consequences.

For now.

TWELVE

GRAY

Finally alone with the man who'd bought my soul, I squared my shoulders, sat up straight, and got right to the point.

"I'm sure you're aware that witches and the supernatural community at large are facing a massive new threat," I said. "Those who haven't been murdered outright have been taken prisoner, experimented on, tortured, and worse—used to create hybrid breeds and unstoppable supernatural weapons."

Sebastian stroked his goatee. "And you've come by this knowledge, how, exactly?"

I gave him the rundown on Jonathan and the prison—the horrors we saw there. "I don't know how or when, but the hunters are planning to unleash pure chaos. The entire supernatural community is in grave danger, as are humans."

Sebastian's oily laugh filled the room. "And this should concern me because…"

"You may not care about the fate of humanity, Sebastian. But if humans die off, you'll have fewer resources to exploit. Your demons will have fewer vessels to inhabit. Without the human capital that keeps this show running…" I spread my hands, indicating the tiny dungeon of the room, as well as the demon himself. "The whole seedy underbelly of your operation will come to a screeching halt."

He leaned back in his chair and folded his arms over his chest, not saying a word. His brows were stern and serious, but I saw the flicker of concern in his eyes. He'd heard me. Knew that the picture I was painting wasn't such a farfetched possibility.

"Get to the point, Silversbane."

"My name is Desario."

"I don't care what you call yourself. Just get to the point. Your obstinance is starting to grate."

I rose from the chair and crossed to the end of the table, standing before him. His lip twitched—the only indication that my presence affected him at all.

"My whole life, you've been making deals for my future—for my *soul*—with other people." Again, the magic inside me flared, giving me strength. Purpose. Power. "Now you're going to deal with me."

"You *are* a rebellious one, aren't you?" He laughed again, but it'd lost some of its earlier bravado. "You've spent too much time with demons."

"We could solve that right now." I jerked my head toward the door. "Let me walk, free and clear. Your absence from my life would mean one less demon to mess with my head."

"That's not how this works."

"Explain it again, then. I'm new here." I took a step closer, forcing him to look up to see me—to reveal the truth in his eyes. I unnerved him. He couldn't figure me out. He didn't like that one bit.

"If you refuse your assignments," he said, tapping the table for emphasis. "I return your soul to hell. There will be no brokering for its release after that. No deals, no trades, no begging, no rescue missions mounted by the bumbling, craven men who can't seem to think clearly where you are concerned. That, my dear, *will* be your eternity."

I watched him carefully. For a guy who owned a casino, his poker face left much to be desired.

He was totally bluffing.

"Do you think that scares me?" I asked, pressing my advantage. "That black, empty place Liam pulled me out of? That's not hell, Sebastian. Hell is turning your back on the people you care about and living the rest of your days knowing you could've helped them, but failed. Hell is watching someone you love burn before your eyes, powerless to save them. Hell is losing the people who matter to you most, no matter how hard you try to hold on. So let me tell you something, Prince." I leaned forward, making him flinch. "I'd rather spend a *lifetime* in your hell than one more minute in mine."

He lifted his hand, and a wave of power hit me, shoving me backward. I managed to stay on my feet, but barely.

I righted myself, and Sebastian smiled, thinking once again he'd gotten the upper hand.

"That's very poetic, girl, but this isn't open mic night at Luna's Café. Nor is this a negotiation. You're mine, and you're—"

"*Done.*" I drew myself up to my full height and stared him down, my voice unwavering. "Send me back to your so-called hell. Now."

"Don't play games with me. You won't like the outcome."

I glared at him, wondering how far I could push him. This was a dangerous game, with stakes higher than any I'd ever fought for.

But that was exactly why I couldn't back down. It was too important.

"You need to maintain the status quo in our communities, Sebastian. This isn't about games or me rebelling or anything like that. It's simple math."

"Okay. Let's say, for curiosity's sake, I consider your request." Sebastian glared at me for much longer than necessary, letting the echo of his forced Southern drawl creep over my skin like spiders. When I could no longer hold back my shiver, his eyes glinted at my response, and he offered me a twisted smile. "What exactly are you offering me, witch?"

I took a deep breath and closed my eyes, seeking reassurance from the magic inside.

This was it. My one chance at getting this right. So many had come to negotiate at this table, and so many had walked away in chains. I couldn't let that happen.

"I will do as you ask," I said calmly, opening my eyes. "I'll fulfill the contract and complete the assignments to the letter. I'll summon and bind my ancestors—no loopholes, no tricks."

Sebastian grunted. "And in return?"

I'd kept a respectable distance from him since he'd hit me with that invisible smackdown, but now I approached the table again. "In return, you'll allow me to return to Raven's Cape with Ronan and Darius, liberate Jonathan's prisoners, and deal with the immediate threats facing the witches and the supernatural community at large."

"I see. And how long will that take?"

"However long that takes," I said. "Unfortunately, there's not a manual for these things."

Sebastian shook his head. "And you think I can divert my resources for this little rescue mission of yours? Help you save the day and skip off into the sunset, everybody's favorite little heroine? A poster child for all the witches across the land?"

"No, Sebastian. I don't need you to help me." I leaned forward on the table, looking straight into his evil eyes. My magic surged, the electric hum of it making the hairs on my arms raise and the candle between us flicker. "I just need you to stay the hell out of my way."

THIRTEEN

EMILIO

From the outside, The Phoenix's Flame metaphysical shop was an unassuming little cottage tucked into the woods about fifteen minutes outside of the Cape, complete with a garden full of gnome statues and a curl of smoke rising from the chimney. There wasn't even a sign outside—this was strictly a word-of-mouth business.

Inside, the place was a witch's paradise. The main level had been opened up, filled with a mismatched collection of metal, wood, and glass shelving, display cases, and tabletops, each piece from a different era yet somehow working together seamlessly. Every surface displayed tools of the craft—crystals, wands, incense, books, DVDs, statues, beads, bells, cauldrons, jewelry. An entire wall of built-in bookcases was devoted to fairy, gnome, and gargoyle statues. A massive counter at the center of the store held a sprawling Tarot card collection that Gray would've loved.

"Merry meet, friends." A middle-aged woman with startling green eyes and a messy bun of curly red hair emerged from the back of the house, carrying a tray of pastries and tea. I got the distinct sense she'd been expecting us. "I'm Verona Braden. Please, make yourselves at home."

She gestured toward a small room off to the side, set up like a regular living room with two small couches and an armchair surrounding a coffee table made out of a massive tree stump.

It was seven in the morning, and Elena and I had just knocked on the door after staking the place out overnight. Jael was keeping an eye on things outside. At the moment, Darkwinter's focus seemed to be on the Bay, but there were still dark fae here in Raven's Cape, and we couldn't take any chances.

Elena and I thanked her and took a seat on one of the couches. When Verona set down the tea tray and sat across from us, I noticed she wasn't meeting my eyes, but staring at a spot just above my shoulder, her own eyes slightly unfocused.

She was blind, I realized.

"Have you met Roscoe yet?" she asked.

At the sound of his name, a russet-colored golden retriever padded out from the back of the house and joined us, sitting on the floor at my feet. I leaned forward and held out my hand, which he happily sniffed. Seconds later, he leaped up on the couch, curling up between me and Elena and promptly falling asleep.

"He likes you," Verona said with a kind laugh. "Okay. Now that I know you're good people, we can relax. Please, help yourselves to tea."

She remained amicably silent while Elena poured three cups from a teapot shaped like a cat.

Reaching for a pastry, Verona said, "So what brings you to my little corner of the woods? I don't get many drop-in visitors these days."

Elena introduced us and handed over our badges for the woman to inspect by touch.

"We're looking for information on a customer who came through here late last night," Elena said. "A witch by the name of Norah Hanson. Mid-fifties, highly knowledgeable. She's a coven leader from Blackmoon Bay."

The woman's eyebrow twitched—so slight a human wouldn't have noticed, but my shifter instincts picked up on it immediately. She'd recognized the name—if not from a personal acquaintanceship, then probably from the raised lettering on Norah's credit card.

"We don't believe she's a regular customer of yours," I said.

"Just passing through town. She paid with a credit card and made a fairly large purchase—just over five hundred dollars."

The woman nodded, concern tightening her warm features. "Yes, that name and purchase amount sounds about right. But the woman I helped felt much younger to me—in her early twenties at best."

"What makes you say that?" I asked.

"Obviously I can't see people the way sighted folk can, but I do have a different sort of sight. I get a sense for people, Detective. Everything from the way you speak, the words you choose, your scent, the feel of your skin when I shake your hand, the sound of your shoes against the floor, the swish of your clothing when you walk—all of those things reveal a lot about a person. If that customer was in her fifties, then Roscoe here is a toy poodle."

Roscoe let out a whimper of discontent.

"Do you think the credit card was stolen?" Elena asked me.

"Possibly," I said. "Or Norah has an accomplice."

"Would you like to see her?" The woman gestured toward the checkout counter in the center room. Next to the cash register sat a pale, milky-green orb about the size of a grapefruit.

"Is that a… crystal ball?" Elena asked.

"Indeed. But not just any crystal ball. Green aventurine is an excellent stone for attracting luck, money, and success." Verona winked at us, her smile sly. "Also, that one's got a hidden camera."

She headed out to the register and grabbed her tablet from beneath the counter, her steps quick and sure.

"Security footage," she said, then used voice commands to queue up the video. "I don't like to judge my customers, of course, but I have to tell you… There was something quite odd about her."

"How so?"

"For starters, Roscoe refused to go anywhere near her, which is very unusual for him."

"Do you think he sensed something sinister?" I asked.

"Not sinister, exactly," she said. "He would've warned me if he thought I was in danger. No, this was more like… confusion?

Like he didn't quite know what to make of her. And then there was… Well, see for yourself." She handed over the tablet.

Elena and I leaned in together over Roscoe, peering down at the screen. A young woman approached the register with a basket full of supplies. She was blonde, with chin-length wavy hair, brown eyes, and a heart-shaped mole above her left eyebrow. Her right brow was pierced with a tiny silver ring.

"Verona," I said, "would you mind giving us a moment?"

"Of course. Take all the time you need." She and Roscoe headed back into the main area of the shop, leaving me alone with Elena and the woman on the screen.

I felt like I'd just seen a ghost.

"Verona was right," I whispered, heart galloping. "This isn't Norah. It's Delilah Pannette."

Elena narrowed her eyes at the screen. "Who?"

"She's a witch from Norah's coven who went missing from the Bay not long after Sophie's murder. We feared she'd been killed, too, though we never found any evidence of foul play."

"Looks pretty alive to me," Elena said.

It was true, but there was something… off about her. When I'd spoken with her at Norah's house after Sophie's death, she was understandably upset, but I also sensed a fiery disposition inside her. She was talkative, alert, opinionated. The kind of witch who speaks her mind and doesn't back down from a fight.

The woman in this video was the exact opposite. She looked like a zombie, with glassy dead eyes, limp hair, and slow, jerky movements.

"Something is definitely wrong with her," Elena confirmed. The longer we watched the video, the more obvious it became. When Verona rung up the purchase, Delilah struggled to get her wallet from the purse, dropping the card several times. She never smiled, never asked questions, never said more than a few words, despite Verona's attempts at friendly small-talk.

"She looks like she's sleepwalking," Elena said.

"Or under a spell." My gut told me that was the answer.

Norah was staying out of sight. Whatever she was planning—whether an escape from the country, or something more sinister—

she'd coerced Delilah into doing her bidding. Using the credit card had been her first mistake.

Elena and I rejoined Verona at the register, tablet in hand.

"Would you mind if I forwarded myself a copy of this footage?" I asked.

"Of course not," she said.

"Do you remember what she purchased?" Elena asked. The camera angle hadn't really allowed for a clear view of her items. "Or if she said anything about what she needed the items for? Maybe when she first arrived at the shop?"

Verona shook her head. "She knew right where everything was, got it all gathered up so quickly I'd barely had time to ask if she needed help. I offered her tea, but she declined."

"But what did she buy?" I asked, at the same time Elena said, "Did she say anything about Norah Hanson, or where they might be heading?"

Verona hesitated, clearly uncomfortable at the sudden barrage of questions. "I'm sorry, detectives. I don't typically disclose information about client purchases. Some of the items we carry are rather sensitive in nature, as I'm sure you can imagine."

"Of course," Elena said, backing off. "We're just trying to do our jobs."

"Anything you can share would be a big help," I said.

Verona put the tablet back under the counter, then knelt down beside Roscoe, scratching his ears. The dog sighed happily, his tail swishing across the hardwood floor.

"What is this about?" she asked. "Has this Norah woman committed a crime?"

Elena and I exchanged a quick glance. After a beat, I nodded. Verona was a witch. She could be in danger. She had a right to know what was happening. Besides, maybe if she heard some of the gruesome details, she'd be more willing to share intel.

"Norah Hanson is wanted for questioning in connection with the disappearance of a teenaged witch from Blackmoon Bay and is a suspect in the kidnapping and murder of several others," I said, "including the woman seen here using Norah's credit card. The two may be working together, or there may be some sort of coercion going on, but it's clear that something is not right about the situation."

"But… you said Norah was a coven leader," Verona said. "You believe she's killing her own witches? That seems highly—"

"Ma'am," Elena said, the last of her patience finally snapping, "I appreciate your desire to protect your clients' privacy, but this is a police matter. If you're not comfortable volunteering information, I can go through more formal channels, but quite frankly that would be a waste of your time and our department resources."

Verona stood up, her mouth pressed into a grim line, her green eyes revealing nothing. They matched the aventurine stone, I realized now.

"We're talking about a child," I said gently, good cop to the rescue. "A runaway who was taken in by a very powerful witch, and possibly imprisoned and harmed as part of a larger crime we're only just beginning to uncover."

At this, she finally softened. "Perhaps we should have another round of tea."

We reassembled in the living room, though Roscoe had abandoned Elena and me, taking a seat at Verona's feet instead.

"There have been whispers of trouble," Verona said, stroking the dog's head. "Several practitioners have brought their concerns to me in recent months, seeking protective spells and amulets, advice, private places to meet. They say witches are being targeted again. That within the next few months, we'll experience another Great Hunt. At first, I didn't want to believe it. Rumors and old ghosts, I told them. Forty-five years I've been here, and though we've had our ups and downs, we've persevered. But this feels different now. Many have left Raven's Cape and the surrounding communities. Witches in other towns are getting worried, too." She shook her head, tears gathering in her eyes. "I keep assuring them that we'll get through this as we always have, but I'm not so sure."

"You *will* get through this," Elena said, surprising me by leaning forward and placing a comforting hand on top of Verona's. "We all need to work together, now more than ever."

Verona smiled. "Thank you. I know. I guess there's just a part of me that doesn't want to believe this sort of thing could happen again. Not in my lifetime."

She finished her tea, then said, "The woman pretending to be Norah did not tell me why she bought her supplies, but the combination of tools and ingredients she selected could only be used for one thing—a highly complex protection spell. One that, if done correctly, essentially erases a person's existence by changing her appearance and identity, altering her public records, and manipulating the memories of all who knew her."

"People actually do that?" Elena asked.

"Not often. If one thing goes wrong with that spell—the wrong word in the incantation, a single caraway seed more or less than called for, a mistranslated sigil, the wrong moon phase—the caster could die."

"Talk about erasing one's existence," I said.

"Precisely. There are other strong protection spells—those are the more common ones witches use, even in dark times. This one is not one to be trifled with."

"You didn't try to talk her out of it?" Elena asked.

"It is not my place to offer unsolicited advice to sisters of the craft, nor to pry too deeply into their affairs."

We finished our tea in silence, each of us contemplating what these revelations meant.

When we rose from the couch to say our goodbyes, Elena reached for Verona's hands. "Please be careful, Verona. It's not safe for solitary practitioners right now. Even covens are in danger. You must do everything you can to protect yourself."

"Don't you worry about that," she said, smiling at us both. "The witches of Raven's Cape will continue to do what we've always done. We will weather the storms upon us with a little bit of magic and a whole lot of common sense."

After promising to get in touch if Delilah or Norah returned, or if she thought of anything else that might help, Verona escorted us to the door.

"I'll be right out," I told Elena, lingering in the doorway. "There's, ah, there's something else I need to get from Verona."

FOURTEEN

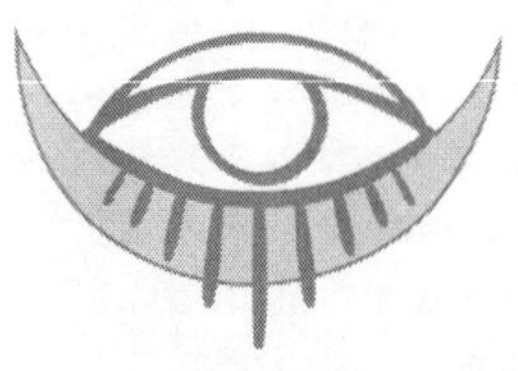

GRAY

"Rayanne! Are you hurt?"

Deirdre Olivante was waiting for me outside the chamber, concern deepening the lines between her eyebrows. In the sudden bright light of the hallway chandeliers, she looked even older than I'd originally thought, but her eyes were sharp and clear, the exact shape and shade as mine. It seemed I'd also inherited her cheekbones.

There was no denying our resemblance.

Wow. I have a grandmother.

"I… I'm fine," I said as the door shut behind me, blissfully separating me from the sleazy demon inside. Unfortunately, the moment the door sealed, the hellhounds reappeared at my sides, glaring at me with their mean red eyes as if they were daring me to try something.

I was too tired to be shocked, but their presence was as unsettling as ever.

"They do that sometimes." Deirdre waved her hand toward the hounds, careful not to get too close. "I'd say you get used to them, but I'm afraid you never quite do."

"Why don't you have a pair?"

"I'm not a flight risk." Deirdre sighed. "I've been with Sebastian a long time, Rayanne."

"Well, I don't plan on being here that long. Sebastian and I came to an understanding about a few things."

She arched an eyebrow, a smile playing on her lips. It warmed her face considerably. "It seems he's taken a liking to you. Sebastian doesn't usually give his demon sworn an opportunity to renegotiate."

"Lucky me." I was still wearing Ronan's sweatshirt, and now I pulled the hood up over my head, losing myself in a wave of his cloves-and-campfire scent. The back of my nose stung with unshed tears. "Where is Ronan? I really need to see him."

"He's taking care of some other business, but he'll meet up with you soon." Deirdre held out her arm. "Come. I'll show you around the casino while we wait."

I nodded, numb, grateful to let someone else make the decisions. The conversation with Sebastian had worn me out, and the unspent magic inside was making me feel fidgety, like I'd had too much caffeine. A walk would probably do me some good.

The hounds and I accompanied Deirdre back through the corridor maze to a sleek and silent elevator, which we took to the lobby level below, forty-two stories down. I had no idea what time it was; there were no windows anywhere in sight.

The casino, I learned, was called Inferno—a little on the nose for my taste, but the decor was a good fit, with deep reds and oranges on the carpeting and walls, accented with golden lights and a massive fountain in the center, lit up to look like real flickering flames.

If I didn't know so much about the owner, I might've been impressed.

The main gaming area looked exactly like the ones I'd seen on television—bright and glitzy, screaming with the sounds of music and cheers and beeping, blaring slot machines. The only difference was that this casino was packed with supernaturals, all of them blending right in alongside the clueless humans.

"I guess no one's immune to the siren call of the slots and the tables," I said, watching a fae woman blow seductively on the dice of her vampire companion.

"Sebastian's built quite an empire on our many vices," she said. "This is one of six properties he owns in Nevada." She told me a little bit more about the casinos, the demon security team, and the live shows, painting a glossy sheen over the less savory but even more lucrative parts of the business—prostitution. Drugs. Smuggling of all sorts. I pretended to be interested, and she pretended to be happy to give the tour, and a million unsaid things hung in the air between us.

I had so many questions for this woman, and under normal circumstances, I would've leaped at the chance to spend time with her. My grandmother. The mother of the father I couldn't even remember. A witch, like me, who'd somehow ended up in Sebastian's service.

But each time I opened my mouth, I lost track of my words. Every potential question felt loaded and dangerous, a Pandora's Box of possible pitfalls and fresh heartaches.

"Tell me about them," I said instead, indicating the hounds behind us, still glaring at me with those creepy red eyes. "I take it they're not invisible." People were definitely noticing them. The humans in the casino shot us curious glances, but the supernaturals gave us a wide birth.

"To humans, they look like service dogs," Deirdre explained, just as a man backpedaled out of our path. She let out a soft chuckle. "Big, scary service dogs, perhaps, but nothing so horrifying as their true form. Supernaturals can see them as they are."

"Are they always going to follow me around like this?"

Deirdre nodded. "They are charged with keeping you safe as well as preventing your escape."

"They've got their work cut out for them," I grumbled, but if Deirdre heard me, she ignored it. "Do they have names?"

"Sebastian has never bothered to name his beasts. As far as he's concerned, they're possessions like any other."

For some reason, that made me sad. Every being deserved a name. Even grotesque, cranky hellhounds. Especially hounds that were going to spend the rest of eternity getting up close and personal with me.

The last time I'd been this close to hellhounds, they'd damn near killed me protecting me in my magical realm. I hadn't forgotten the sharp pierce of their claws, the weight of those massive paws knocking me to the ground…

Toughen up, buttercup. You've stared down a lot worse than hellhounds in recent weeks.

Swallowing my fear and revulsion, I knelt down before them, meeting them at eye level. Their eyes glowed like hot coals, their breath carrying the stench of rotten meat and blood.

I really, really hoped I wouldn't be in charge of feeding them. Or cleaning up after them.

"Male or female?" I asked Deirdre, tentatively holding out my hand for them to sniff. They approached at the same time, their noses cold and wet as they pressed them to my palm.

When they didn't attack, I took a gamble and shifted my hands to their heads, rubbing just behind their ears. Their fur was coarse and matted, but not all that different from a dog's.

And, just like dogs, they melted into two happy, goofy puppies at my touch.

"Aww, you're not so tough after all, huh?" I laughed, moving in to scratch a little more. When I started showing one more attention, the other one nipped playfully at my hand.

Sophie had always wanted dogs. Two of them, actually. *Witches need familiars!* she'd said. *And we can't just get one. Two at a minimum. They need companionship, just like we do.*

I'd always shot down the idea—I didn't need a familiar, because I wasn't a witch. Not out loud, anyway. Besides, dogs seemed like a lot of work.

But now, as they snuffled and licked at my hands, wagging their tails as if we'd always belonged to each other, I was overcome with a sense of rightness so intense, it brought tears to my eyes.

It was crazy—this whole *thing* was crazy—but I suddenly knew without a doubt that these animals—these hellhounds—were supposed to be with me. Not because Sebastian had ordered it. Not because of any stupid contract or demonic spell. We just… belonged to each other.

"They are both females, actually," Deirdre said, surprise and amusement in her tone.

"Really? That's the best news I've heard all night." I laughed. "I could use a testosterone break."

"Couldn't we all."

"Sparkle and Sunshine," I said suddenly, the names Sophie had always imagined for our non-existent dogs now coming to mind. Her words replayed in my memory.

But don't let their sunny disposition and happy-go-lucky names fool you. Our dogs are some seriously *badass bitches…*

With a smile on my face and a little more lightness in my heart, I got to my feet and joined Deirdre once again.

"Sparkle, Sunshine. Come on, girls." The dogs padded closer, pressing against my calves. I wouldn't go so far as to call them doting pets just yet, but it seemed we'd made a little progress.

"Well!" Deirdre said, astonished. "I've never seen anything like it."

"What do you mean?"

"The hounds belong to Sebastian," she said. "All of them. They're assigned to demon sworn souls as needed, but their loyalty has always been to him. This is the first I've ever known them to bond with someone else."

A human couple loaded down with shopping bags bumbled past us, inadvertently nudging Deirdre closer to the hounds. Her hand brushed over one of their heads, and the beast let out a contented yelp, licking her wrist.

Deirdre laughed. "Well okay, then. Hello there, Sunshine."

"She's Sparkle," I said. "Sparkle has the underbite, see? And Sunshine has this notch in her left ear." It looked like something had taken a bite out of it, poor thing.

Deirdre stared at me for a beat, her eyes sparkling, her smile broad. In that moment, she really did look like a grandmother. Like someone who wanted to bake you cookies or teach you how to play bridge.

I was pretty sure I would've liked that.

"Would you like to get some coffee?" she asked. "I know the perfect place."

At the mention of coffee, my stomach did a full-on summersault, letting me know just how hungry I was. Shockingly, I couldn't even remember the last time I'd eaten real food. The safe house? It seemed like a thousand years ago, and suddenly all I wanted to do was wolf down a giant cheeseburger, six orders of fries, and a chocolate shake. And maybe some apple pie, too. And possibly some cheese sticks. And also, bacon. So, so much bacon.

I smiled at my grandmother, linking my arm in hers. "Throw in some dinner, Grams, and you've got yourself a deal."

"Careful mentioning the d-word around here," she said with a wink. "Deals are what got us all into this mess in the first place."

FIFTEEN

GRAY

Deirdre took me to a quaint little fifties-style diner a few blocks away from the casino, tucked down a side street just far enough off the main strip to give us a break from the crowds.

I wasted no time in ordering a full-on feast, and after I shoveled in enough greasy goodness to give me heartburn for a month, I finally felt human again.

Finally felt ready to face some of the questions swirling around my head.

Deirdre must've sensed the direction of my thoughts, because she ordered herself a double bourbon, then looked at me sternly and said, "Ask away. Now might be our last chance to talk freely in this city—Sebastian's goons don't come down this way. The place is spelled against demons."

The ominous tone in her voice made me shiver. I hoped she was wrong—that we *would* get another chance to talk. Despite the immediate chaos I had to deal with, including but not limited to the epic disaster formerly known as my love life, part of me hoped that my grandmother and I would get the chance to spend more time together. Maybe not right now, and maybe not even on the material plane. But she was beholden to Sebastian, too. I wanted to believe our paths would cross again, even if it was in this city.

It would've been nice to have an ally here.

It would've been nice to learn more about my family—my father—her son.

It would've been nice if we'd been reunited under any other circumstances but the ones that had actually brought us together.

I sighed, trying to mask my disappointment. The clock was always ticking, and right now, I needed answers. Answers that would help me understand what Sebastian really wanted with me and my ancestors. And more importantly, how the hell I could get out of this deal.

I waited until the server returned with her drink, then dove right in. "Back in that room, when I heard you talking in my head…"

"Projection," she said. "That's part of my particular brand of magic. I can transfer words and thoughts, images, emotions. But only to other witches—it doesn't cross any other barriers."

"So that's why Sebastian couldn't hear it? Or sense it?"

"Right. He knows I have that power, but he can't access it. It drives him crazy that he can't control it or even know for sure when I'm using it." A sly smile stretched across her face. "One of the few pleasures I take with him."

Again, I wondered if they were somehow… involved. But I wasn't ready to go down that path just yet. I needed to understand more about her powers, and my connection to this whole Silversbane legacy, whatever that meant.

"So can you read minds, too?" I asked. I reached for a French fry, then slipped it under the table. Sunshine happily lapped it up, but Sparkle didn't seem to like fried food. She'd had no problem dogging down half my burger patty, though.

"It doesn't work both ways," Deirdre said. "Not unless the other witch has the same power and can transfer thoughts to me."

"But you knew about the sword-seeking thing," I said. "From my vision."

She nodded somberly, then took a healthy swig of her drink. When she set her glass back on the table, her smile had turned grim. "I, too, am Shadowborn. But my shadow powers manifested in different ways. I can read a person's nightmares."

I stared, open-mouthed. That sounded absolutely horrifying.

"It's not like watching a movie," she continued, "so the details are often hazy. It's more like... I can pick up on the images and imprints left behind. The stronger, more visceral effect a nightmare has on a person, the more clearly I can connect with it. Sometimes it's a visual thing—I can see an object or a person that appeared in the dream. Other times, I can hear words. Sometimes I can only sense the lingering fear—and that feels very, very real to me." She took another sip of her bourbon. "Unfortunately, unlike with my projection power, I can't turn this one off or choose when to use it. Touching someone makes it stronger, sharper, but even without a touch, it's always there, tugging me into other peoples' darkness."

I blew out a breath, then reached for another fry for Sunshine. Reading nightmares? I'd never heard of anything like that. Psychic powers, mind reading, empathy, yes. But to connect with something so specific, so painful... That sounded a lot more like a curse than a power to me.

God. There was still so much about witchcraft I'd yet to learn, to explore. For so long, I'd denied that part of myself. Now, all I wanted to do was dive into it and research everything I possibly could.

I just didn't have the luxury of studying anymore. It was trial by fire, or not at all.

"Do you know what the swords mean?" I asked. "I've had similar nightmares a few times now, and the Four of Swords turned up a few times in Tarot readings with my best friend, Sophie." I told her about Sophie's book of shadows, and the readings I'd done since. "Sophie insisted the cards were about me. She'd said the four swords represented four witches—that the one in the ground was supposed to rise up, find the others, and give them purpose. She thought it had something to do with uniting the covens, but I wasn't so sure." I lowered my head. "She died before I could ask her anything more. She... she was murdered."

I wasn't sure how much if anything Deirdre knew about the story—about Sophie's death, the hunters, all of the things we'd faced in the Bay and in Raven's Cape—but I didn't want to rehash all of those details right now.

Then again, if she could read my nightmares, she'd probably seen every last bit of darkness in my soul.

I reached for my half-finished milkshake, taking a big, slurpy gulp. For an instant, I closed my eyes and allowed myself to pretend that I was a kid again, a normal one, out on the town for a day of fun with my grandmother.

But like all fantasies, this one came to an end much too quickly.

"Gray," she said gently. Tentatively. And when I looked into her eyes again, I saw the change come over her. Eyes that only moments ago shone with clarity and confidence now held a nervous, contagious urgency that made me squirm in my seat.

Beyond that, I saw only one thing.

Fear. Not the kind that came from bearing witness to someone else's nightmares, but the kind that came from knowing your entire world was about to go up in flames.

Deirdre reached across the table and grabbed my hand in a bone-crushing squeeze. "We need to talk about the Silversbane prophecy."

SIXTEEN

GRAY

"The Silversbane witches can trace their lineage all the way back to the first witches," Deirdre said. "It was the Silversbane bloodline that carried forth the honors bestowed upon all witches and mages by the Elemental Source."

"To become the guardians of Earth's magic," I said, recalling the history. The strongest human bloodlines were selected to receive and care for the magic, but the mages went mad for it, screwing everything up until the Source finally revoked their privileges, making witches the sole guardians. The mages didn't like that one bit. They blamed the witches for "stealing" the magic from them, and over time, their anger and desire for vengeance warped them into a vicious, bloodthirsty breed of humans we now called hunters.

"Precisely," Deirdre said.

"So how does the prophecy come into play?" I asked, picking up my pace to match hers. We were back on the strip now, losing ourselves in the anonymity of the crowd. As always, Sparkle and Sunshine kept watch—one up front, one behind, clearing the path from anyone who got too close.

"The original prophecy was said to be delivered directly from the Source, in a series of visions that appeared to a Silversbane oracle in a cave in the lands that later became Ireland. It was passed down orally for millennia, but never came to fruition.

Some centuries ago, the matriarch of the family—Dubheasa Silversbane—was concerned the oral traditions would be forgotten. She commissioned the greatest calligrapher known at the time to record the prophecy and other knowledge of the craft in a series of scrolls to be passed down from generation to generation through the maternal line."

"Let me guess," I said. "The scrolls were lost."

"Lost, destroyed, no one really knows. Witchcraft historians have found remnants of them—herblore, some spellcraft, details about certain rituals, references *to* the prophecy but nothing of the prophecy itself. Still, echoes of the original visions remained even after Dubheasa's time, and were once again passed down orally." Deirdre shook her head, disappointed. "So much of the original meaning has been lost in the translation since then, or embellished, or downplayed. Most consider it no more than a legend now, but there are many who still believe." The reverence in her eyes told me that she was one of those believers.

"What does the prophecy say?" I asked.

"Loosely, it states that four sisters will come to power, led by the third in their line—a Shadowborn, third daughter of a third daughter of a third daughter. She will be the strongest Shadowborn witch to live, and through her leadership and the bond of their sisterhood, the four will come to power with the strength to unite the fractured underground covens."

"Unite them to what end?" I asked, ignoring the goosebumps rising on my skin, the magic pulsing just beneath.

"Those who've studied the lore and the history believe that it's saying the unified covens will rise out of the ashes of oppression, reclaim their power, defeat the enemies who would stand against them, and bring the sisterhood back into the light. Remember, Rayanne, we were revered once. Beholden and respected as the true guardians and stewards of earth's magic. We kept all things in balance. Somehow, all of that got lost along the way."

"Thanks to the hunters." Bile rose in my throat. They'd been hunting us for millennia. Longer than that, even. Longer than they'd even called themselves hunters. And unless this prophecy was true—and the four witches could be found—they'd continue hunting us long after the current generation of witches was dead.

Deirdre stepped aside to let a group of jugglers pass. One of them dropped a tennis ball, and Sunshine bounded after it, but one growl from Sparkle had her running back.

I smiled, wondering if the hounds were sisters.

"Hunters, demons, supernatural factions who don't believe witches should've been entrusted with earth's magic," Deirdre continued. "Many have been seeking the witches of prophecy, in hopes of killing them and preventing the rise of power. But the hunters are less discriminating. They'll kill any witch, prophecy or not. They just want to eradicate us. Somehow, they think wiping us off the map would restore them to their former glory, complete with all the Elemental magic they once had."

"What about the Fae Council? Are they trying to get in on a piece of this prophecy action, too?" It wouldn't surprise me. Witches in power—in a big, united group—could really pose a threat to them. They'd be outnumbered for sure, and probably out-magicked.

"Officially, they've dismissed it as bunk—a rumor crafted by witches during the European witch trials as a way to legitimize themselves and avoid persecution. But there are many fae who believe magic is *their* sole domain, and they don't feel witches ever should have had access to it."

A small crowd had gathered on a corner, and we stopped alongside them to watch a group of street performers—a cellist and two guitarists. The blend of their music was as smooth and rich as dark chocolate, lulling us all into a state of peaceful contentment. They played with their eyes closed, their faces simultaneously serious and happy, and I couldn't help but envy them. I knew nothing about their lives, their struggles, but in that moment, they were free, carried away by the art of their music, their passion and talents bringing a group of random strangers together on a street corner. For five minutes, all of our problems were suspended. Nothing else existed but the music and the connection, a thread that held us all together in this strange city.

And then the moment passed. They finished their song to a

round of applause, and Deirdre slipped a few dollars into an open guitar case at their feet.

"This," she said, smiling as she watched the musicians pack up their instruments, "is one of the few things I truly love about this city."

We walked on in silence, each lost in our own thoughts. My head was already spinning, but I sensed there was so much more to this story. So much more we hadn't even begun to touch on.

"So if I'm a Silversbane," I finally said, "Sebastian must think I'm connected to this prophecy somehow. That I can find these four witches for him. Right?"

It made sense in my mind. He either thought they'd already died and could somehow be resurrected into new vessels, forced under his control, or he thought they were still alive and could be located with the help of their ancestors. *Our* ancestors. Either way, he wanted control of those witches. He wanted the power promised by the prophecy.

"*Connected* to it?" Deirdre gripped my arm, stopping me in my tracks and leaning in close. Her blue eyes were fierce, her voice low and serious. "Rayanne. You *are* the witch foretold to unite the covens. The Silversbane heir."

The Silversbane heir. The magic inside me roiled at her words, rising to the surface. Blue sparks lit up my hands, and I shoved them into my sweatshirt pockets to hide them. "That makes no sense, Deirdre. First of all, I'm an only child. And second—"

My words evaporated as the truth marched across her face, plain and obvious and... *No.* It couldn't be. It was completely impossible. Absurd.

"You're wrong," I insisted, shaking my head vehemently even as I felt the truth of it in my gut. In my bones. In my magic. Everything inside me was buzzing and warm, pieces clicking together in my mind, gaps filling in to form a complete story I hadn't even known I'd been missing.

As hard as I tried to fight it, I couldn't ignore the rightness of her confession. I was the Silversbane heir. That's why Sebastian had wanted me. Why the guys felt compelled to protect me. Why even Death himself couldn't predict my future. Why I kept defying expectations and breaking rules and doing things I never should've been able to do, even as a powerful Shadowborn.

The force of that realization nearly knocked me over.

"Breathe, Rayanne. Just breathe." Deirdre cupped my face, her smile kind once again. Her eyes twinkled, shining with something that looked a lot like pride. "It's true. You are one of the four Silversbane witches of prophecy. The Shadowborn. That is what the Tarot was trying to tell you."

"But… I have sisters?" My eyes misted, my heart hammering inside.

"Three of them. You were separated from each other when your parents died, adopted into different homes in an effort to protect you from those who sought to kill you."

Separated. Sisters. Parents died. Adopted. Kill you.

The words were coming at me so fast, I couldn't even grab onto any of them, let alone make sense of everything Deirdre was telling me. I closed my eyes, sucking in a deep breath of warm Vegas air.

Focus, Gray. Focus.

"I was practically still a baby when I was adopted," I said, opening my eyes. "Why would someone kill babies? We couldn't have had much power back then, even together."

"As the witches foretold to unite the covens under a single banner, you had immense power. Just by *existing,* you were a threat to anyone who benefited from keeping witches subjugated. We reasoned—"

"We?"

"My coven. You four were in my care after your parents died. We knew you would be hunted, especially as you came into your powers. Together, you'd be so impossibly strong, so clearly the witches of prophecy, we wouldn't be able to hide you. But we thought if you were raised in separate homes, there was a chance you might survive. As long as you didn't reunite, the prophecy could not be set in motion."

"But we were sisters! And we never had a chance to know each other!"

Sympathy and sorrow filled her eyes. "I regret that. Truly. But understand, Rayanne. If you'd been allowed to stay together, you never would've survived."

"And now? What happens next? Where are they? How can I find them?"

"Now it's out of my hands, and in the hands of fate. It seems the time of the prophecy is upon us. There is no way to stop the wheel of time, and no way to prevent you from reconnecting with your sisters. They will be called to you through the blood spell to contact the souls of your ancestors. Whether you want this or not, Rayanne, the four *will* reunite. And you will lead them."

An image flickered through my mind—the three women I'd seen in my dream, all dressed in white, carrying their silver swords. The muscular blonde. The dark-haired girl with a braid wrapped around her head. The one with a shaved head, dressed in a hospital gown—the only one who'd sparked any sense of familiarity.

Their images sharpened in my mind.

"Yes," Deirdre said softly, undoubtedly reading the imprints from my nightmares. "Those were your sisters. Their essences are reaching out to you. Consciously or not—they, too, sense that the time has come."

"Why does one of them feel so familiar to me?" I asked. "I don't think I recognize her, but there's something… I can't put my finger on it."

"Serena," Deirdre said. "She's the first born."

The first born. The oldest. My big sister. I have a big sister.

Hope flamed in my chest.

"She's familiar to you because you… You've already met her."

"Serena?" I scanned my memory, but couldn't recall a single person I'd ever met with that name.

"You know her under her adopted name." My grandmother met my eyes, her own cold and steely, unwavering in their brutal honesty even as my heart threatened to burst.

For so long, the closest thing I'd ever had to a sister was Sophie. As far as I was concerned, she *was* my sister, blood or not. When I lost her, I lost a piece of my heart I'd never get back. I lost Sophie as a person, as a friend. I lost her light, her magic, her laughter, her love. But I'd also lost the chance to be a sister. To have that bond with another woman. I'd grieved it, just as I'd grieved Sophie herself.

Now, Deirdre was about to change all of that. The next words out of her mouth were going to shake my foundations to the core. Change my world forever. Bring the impossible, amorphous idea of "you have three sisters" into a solid, firm, and very real person. A person I'd already crossed paths with at some point in my life.

A name had infinite power, and Deirdre Olivante was about to unleash that power on me.

"Who is she?" I asked, my voice shaking. "What's my sister's name?"

Deirdre closed her eyes and took a deep breath. "Haley Barnes."

SEVENTEEN

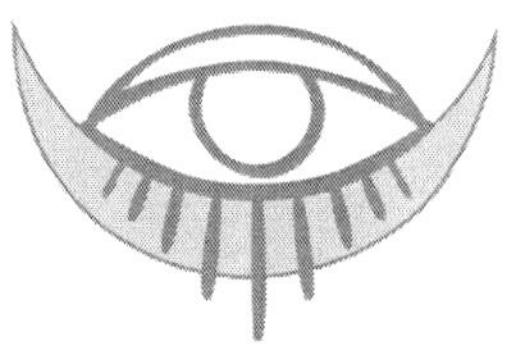

ASHER

"That stench is starting to become a situation." Haley wrinkled her nose at the dead heap of flesh and bones formerly known as Benson. "I can't believe they just left him here. Aren't they supposed to be brothers or something?"

"Brothers?" I thought of Ronan and Darius. Emilio. Hell, even Liam had a better chance of earning a place on my favorites list than these hunter pricks. I kicked Benson's boot through the bars. "These assholes don't know the first thing about brotherhood."

"Apparently they don't know the first thing about biohazard contamination, either." Haley resumed her pacing, trying to breathe through her mouth. "We need a plan. My hope-o-meter is starting to run dangerously low."

"*You* need to sit down, or it's not just your hope-o-meter you'll have to worry about, not that I ever want to say that word again. They're not feeding you enough to fuel all this fidgeting." I grabbed her shoulders, gently steering her to the center of the chamber to sit with the other witches. The rest of the group had gone eerily quiet—including my favorite trouble-maker, McKenna. Energy and hope were both in short supply.

Shit, Jonathan had really done a number on them. It was a wonder they were still alive.

I hope you're ripping that mother fucker a dozen new assholes, Cupcake. Preferably with a sharp knife.

"We'll figure this out together," I assured all of them. "But right now, we need to conserve energy."

"You seem to be doing okay," Haley teased. "And you haven't eaten anything either."

Of the twenty-seven witches imprisoned in this room, she seemed to be in the best spirits. I needed her to stay that way, to help keep the others relaxed and upbeat. The second doubt started creeping in, we'd all be doomed.

"I'm different," I told her. "I don't need food the way you do."

"So I've heard." She flashed a devilish smirk. "You know I'm going to make Gray spill all the details once we get out of this place, right?"

"You can try, Hay. But trust me. Gray is *not* a kiss-and-tell kind of girl."

Her eyes lit up, and she jabbed me with an accusatory finger. "So you *did* kiss her! I knew it!"

"You'll have to ask her," I said, not bothering to hide my own goofy-ass grin. Damn, just thinking about Gray again made my whole body buzz. I tried to imagine her telling Haley about our time together, her creamy cheeks blushing as she rehashed all the juicy details, acting out her soft moans of pleasure as we... *Fucking hell.* I was hard already. Talk about a situation.

Turning away from Haley, I adjusted my pants and said, "No more talking. I need time to think."

Haley laughed. "Whatever you say, incubus. But I'm telling you. As soon—"

Her words died at the sound of new footsteps in the corridor. A whole fucking lot of 'em.

"Everyone stay back," I whispered to the witches, slipping back into the shadows just before a group of fae soldiers marched into view.

Marched? Scratch that. It was more like a glide. I heard their footsteps like any other soldiers, but their feet never seemed to touch the ground. They were elite, that much was obvious. Every movement coordinated, not a step or breath out of place. Their uniforms were pristine—black, form-fitting fatigues that allowed for a full range of motion and plenty of places to stash weapons.

The black-and-gold insignia on their armbands marked them as Darkwinter.

Orendiel was at the head of the line. *Fuck.*

They lined up in perfect formation, and once they were all assembled, they fell so completely still and silent, I wasn't sure they were even breathing. Gone were the lackey, ragtag hunter pukes Jonathan had hired. These guys meant serious business.

My fucking hope-o-meter just dropped by about a thousand.

"Good afternoon, witches," a deep, commanding voice called.

From the back of the line came the shuffle and stomp of a pair of boots that most certainly didn't belong to the fae. They were clunky and intrusive, unleashing a grunt with every labored step.

A man appeared before the bars—human, about sixty-five, limping slightly, with broad shoulders that hunched beneath a loose-fitting flannel. His face was tired and weather-worn, the lower half covered with an unkempt white beard. His eyes, though. They were sharp. Deadly. Unfeeling.

Seeing him was like a straight punch in the gut. I solved the damn mystery before he introduced himself, and it took every last ounce of willpower I had not to rush the bars and tear out his fucking throat.

Dirty Beard. The fuckface, cowardly, piece-of-shit hunter who'd burned Gray's mother alive right in front of her.

"Most of you knew my son, Jonathan," the old man began, dragging his baton along the bars. The fae magic keeping us locked in here popped and buzzed at the contact. "I'm sure you're all great admirers of his work, as are we. Sadly, he's decided to move on to… other opportunities. I've brought in some new management."

Other opportunities? I wondered if this jackoff had any clue that his precious baby boy was probably being mutilated by the witch whose mother they killed ten years ago.

Probably not. Seemed unlikely he'd even care. From the looks of things, he and his little army had been waiting in the wings for the first opportunity to storm the castle. Now, with Jonathan missing and the rest of the hunters he'd commanded bumbling around in the chaos, it looked like daddy dearest was taking his shot.

"I'm here to assure you that Jonathan's work will continue," he said. "However, we'll be making a few changes to better suit our needs—starting with the location. Later this evening, you'll be transferred to another facility in the city—one with more equipment and better security. Any questions?"

"Where's our food and water?" one of the witches asked.

"Rations will resume upon arrival at our new location. Provided there are no *incidents* along the way. Next question?"

"Where are we going?" Someone else asked.

"That is classified. Anyone else?"

Man, I wanted to throttle this prick. He was really letting this fake-militia shit go to his head. Problem was, no matter how much of a toolbox he looked and sounded like—and it was a damn big one, don't get me wrong—deep down he was as badass as they came. One look into those dead eyes told me everything I needed to know. He was definitely the type of guy who spent his childhood mashing spiders, pulling wings off butterflies, and plotting revenge against every motherfucker who'd ever pissed in his Cheerios.

I'm guessing it was a long list.

Someone else was asking about the food again.

I nudged McKenna with my elbow. "Hey," I whispered. "Ask him about the escaped incubus." I needed to know how much they knew about me—where they thought I'd gone.

"What about the d-demon?" she asked, injecting a little fear into her voice. Nice touch.

"Demon?" Dirty Beard scoffed. "I presume you're talking about the incubus? He's been apprehended. Nothing to worry about."

I bit back a laugh. *You dumb fuck. I'm going to apprehend my boot so far up your ass, you'll be shitting footprints for a month.*

As Dirty Beard rattled off the rules and regulations he expected all the witches to follow during the transport, Haley, McKenna, and I huddled close, trying to come up with some semblance of a plan.

"What kind of fae are they?" Haley whispered. "I don't think I've ever seen any like that."

"Darkwinter," I said. "Take every terrible nightmare you've ever heard about the winter courts, and multiply it by a thousand. Oh, and that hunter yammering up front? That's the sonofabitch who murdered Gray's mother."

"Oh, shit." A chill rolled through her body, but Haley stood firm. "I'm not going to let them torture us for one more fucking day."

"Same page, Hay. But, ah, you got a plan?"

"I have one," a small voice said from the shadows behind me.

"You're the super-demon, Ash," Haley said. "What's *your* plan?"

I gestured toward the bars, where Dirty Beard was gearing up for another round of demands while Orendiel and the Douchebag Brigade stood around like stiff, well-dressed corpses. "In case you haven't noticed, I'm in a bit of a bind right now."

"I know a way out," the voice whispered again.

"What about Detective Alvarez?" Haley asked. "Surely he's found the cave entrance by now. They're probably working on a breakout plan as we speak."

"We don't even know if he got Reva's message," I said.

"Guys!" Reva shout-whispered, finally getting our attention. I looked down at her and sighed, hating that she had to spend even one night in this dank place. She was so small, so thin. No matter how long I lived, I'd never stop being surprised at just how monstrous men could be.

"What was that?" Dirty Beard asked, and I froze, clamping a hand over Reva's mouth.

"Someone in the back there. Another question?"

McKenna caught my eye, flashing me a cocky grin. Before I could stop her, she was on her feet, stalking toward the bars. "Hey, asshole," she said. "I got a question. You know what happens to guys who fuck witches?"

Dirty Bead laughed. "No, I don't. Do you know what happens to witches whose food rations are cut in half?"

McKenna imitated his laugh. Had to hand it to her—she didn't back down from a fight. "No, I don't. Do you know what happens to a hunter when a pissed-off, half-starved witch puts a curse on him?"

He slammed his baton into the bars, sending up a spray of sparks from the fae magic locking us in here. "No," he said. "I don't."

"Neither do I." She laughed again, high pitched, totally mental. "It's a new recipe I'm working on. Come back tomorrow and we'll all find out together."

"That's enough," Dirty Beard said. Unlike his son, he wasn't so easy to rile up. McKenna kept at him, though, giving us just the opportunity we needed.

"Alright, Reva," I whispered. "What've you got for me."

"I know a way out of here," she said.

I thumbed toward the retinal scanner at the front of the bars. "You got a spare eyeball?"

"Not out of the cell. Out of the whole prison." Her eyes lit up with renewed hope, brightening the dank, dark room. "There's another cave system past this one. None of them ever go back there."

"Reva," Haley said, "even if we could get back there without the guards catching us, the whole place is spelled. We'll never get out."

"Not the whole thing. I'm pretty sure they're only focusing on this cave system. I don't think they even know the other one exists." She told us about a small chamber she'd discovered when she'd been doing her shadowmancy business trying to get that message to Emilio. "It connects to the other system. The only way in is through a super narrow shaft halfway up the wall. It leads into the back chamber, then down another passageway. Eventually, it takes you back outside, way down on the other end of the beach."

"How far down?" I asked.

"Maybe a couple of miles from the pier. Three tops."

"You're sure?"

"I can go out at night," she said, nodding enthusiastically. "Once I get out, I'll find my way to town."

The idea had potential. But it also had a lot of pitfalls.

"Why don't you try to connect with Emilio again?" I asked. "Project, or whatever it is you do."

"There's no time, Ash. It was almost impossible last time. I'm pretty sure he has to be in wolf form to hear me, and even then, it was really hard. I don't know if I got through to him at all."

"I'm betting the Cape is crawling with hunters," Haley said. "Probably fae, too. It's not safe, Reva."

"I know how to avoid them. I'll go straight to the police and ask for the detective's sister."

"I don't like it," Haley said. "What if they catch you? They'll kill you. And they won't do it quickly."

Reva shrugged. "They think I'm a useless kid—not even worth experimenting on. They only reason I'm still alive in here is they've already forgotten about me."

"The so-called useless kid has a very useful point," I said.

"Trust me," she said. "They won't even notice I'm gone."

"You seem pretty sure about that," Haley said.

"I know how to disappear." She shrugged with all the cool confidence of a teenager who'd just gotten away with shoplifting. "I've been doing it my whole life."

Haley blew out a breath, her shoulders slumping. I knew how much she hated the idea—I wasn't too keen on sending Reva out alone, either. But Reva was right—she was small, the only one of us who could slip away undetected and fit through that shaft.

I put a hand on Haley's shoulder. "Hay, we—"

The crack of Dirty Beard's baton shut us up again. McKenna had finally gone silent.

"No more," the bastard snapped. "You all know what's expected of you. We'll be back at oh-six-hundred to start the transport. Any more outbursts, and you'll all be given electroshock treatment."

He shuffled out, the fae turning as one single unit to follow him down the corridor.

"Electroshock treatments?" Haley's eyes blazed. "Fuck this." She turned to Reva. "Okay, Reva. I'm in."

Reva gave me a high-five.

"So now we just need a way to get her out of this cell," Haley said. "We need some kind of—"

"Disturbance? Did somebody call for a disturbance?" I flashed them a big-ass grin.

"What's that look?" Haley asked, swirling her finger in front of my face. "I already don't like that look."

"You aren't supposed to like it."

"What are you thinking?"

"I'm thinking," I said, walking to the front of the chamber and peering out through the bars, "it's time to show these fae-fucking, limp-dick hunters where the big, bad incubus has been hiding."

EIGHTEEN

GRAY

Haley Barnes?

I wasn't even sure I'd heard Deirdre correctly, but the time for questions had passed. We were back in front of Inferno, too close to Sebastian's many spies to continue this conversation so candidly.

"So, that's Las Vegas," Deirdre said loudly, presumably for any of Sebastian's guards in the vicinity. "I'm so glad I got the chance to show you around. I'll take you back inside now."

She grabbed my elbow, steering me toward a service entrance near the back.

"But, what about—"

"There's no time, Gray," she muttered quickly. "Ronan's going to meet us any minute. He asked me to take you to see Darius first."

"Darius?" The idea of finally seeing my vampire and reuniting with Ronan was enough to settle my nerves and hit the pause button on my many questions. "Where is he? Is he okay?"

"He's... stable. The blood overdose is still working its way out of his system, and he—"

"Blood overdose?"

"He attacked and fully drained a demon after he got through the hell portal. I'm sure Ronan will fill you in on everything later. Come on—this way."

Knowing Ronan, he wouldn't fill me in on *anything* later, but what choice did I have but to shut up and follow her? I needed to see Darius, and I didn't know if and when I'd get another opportunity.

We took the service elevators down to the basement level, then followed another long series of hallways until we reached another wooden door. Unlike the last one, this didn't have any glowing runes or codes. Just a big-ass iron bar bolted across it.

Deirdre lifted the bar, then pushed open the door, revealing another dark chamber inside. This one was huge, though, and hot —nothing like Sebastian's little meeting room upstairs.

I stepped into the entry, waiting for my eyes to adjust. The floor was a dull, dirt-colored wood that looked like it hadn't been polished in decades, and the stone walls surrounding us were damp with moisture. Everything beyond the immediate entryway was cloaked in shadow.

Even my breath seemed to echo.

"Your vampire is inside," Deirdre said softly. "All the way in the back. But… a word to the wise? Keep your guard up. He's dangerous, Rayanne, despite the restraints and the hawthorn."

"Restraints?" My eyes welled as I pictured him tied up and sedated. What had they done to him? He'd lost his memories trying to save me, and this was the homecoming they'd given him? "Darius would *never* hurt me."

"But that's just it. This vampire is *not* Darius. You must remember, he's—"

I cut her off with a harsh glare, and she pressed her lips tightly together, as if she had to physically restrain herself from speaking her mind.

Darius had suffered memory loss. That didn't make him less deserving of respect and kindness. It didn't make him broken or some wild, untamed beast that needed to be restrained and beaten.

Deirdre hovered in the doorway a moment longer, as if she were still trying to decide whether to leave me alone with the man I loved. The man who'd saved me in the Shadowrealm. The man whose touch still smoldered on my skin.

"I love him," I informed her, ending the argument before it devolved into something worse. "I'm not leaving here until I know he's okay. Until I see it with my own eyes."

Her eyes softened, and she reached up to touch my cheek. Her palm was warm and soft, her touch kind.

"I understand." She smiled softly, then slipped outside with one final piece of advice trailing in her wake: "Just… don't get too close."

The door closed and bolted behind her, and I stepped deeper into the room, waiting for my eyes to adjust. It seemed the only light came from a sparse collection of electric wall sconces.

Everything about this room felt forgotten.

I turned to the hounds that'd followed me inside. "Sparkle," I whispered. "Sunshine. You two stay here and keep an eye out for me, okay?"

"Ah, there you are, lovely," Darius said. His voice came from the darkness, smooth as silk, sending a ripple of warmth across my skin. "Come closer so I can see your beautiful face."

"Darius," I breathed. Was that recognition I'd heard in his tone?

Or simply the charms of a smooth-talking vampire, just like the one I'd allowed to taste my blood that first time in Black Ruby?

That was the night we'd become blood bound, and it felt like a million years ago now. So much had happened since then. It was a wonder any of us was still alive.

But we are *alive,* I reminded myself. We'd already fought and survived so many battles. This was just one more.

Leaving the hounds at the door, I approached the back of the room cautiously, my heart thumping louder with every footstep.

Slowly, painfully, Darius came into view. He was seated on a long bench, his feet chained and bolted to the floor, his wrists chained and bolted to the wall. A hawthorn stake had been shoved through his left hand; the skin had partly healed around it, leaving a ring of dark blood.

My stomach twisted. I hated seeing him like this. Bound. Sedated.

I took another step closer, still assessing him.

His clothes were clean and looked new—dark sweatpants and a Vegas Golden Knights hockey jersey I was pretty sure he hadn't picked out from the souvenir shop himself. His face looked gaunt beneath a few days' worth of stubble, his eyes glassy, his brown hair wild and unkempt.

He flashed me a grin as I approached, as smooth and smokey as fine whiskey, but nothing like the real Darius. Nothing like the vampire I'd fallen in love with.

"You're afraid of me, beautiful," he said matter-of-factly. "I can sense it in your heartbeat."

I nodded, but not because it was true, or part of the long-standing joke we'd shared about how much he used to scare me before we'd finally come together.

"You're a very powerful vampire," I said, as if that explained the rapid-fire beat behind my ribcage. Playing the game was easier than admitting that my heart was shattering, sputtering out its last hurrah.

"I suppose I am," he said. His smile was composed, but the glint in his glassy eyes was feral. "I wish I could recall, but in the absence of memory, I'll have to rely on..." He sucked a breath of air through his lips, his tongue darting out to wet them. "...instinct."

I stepped closer, and those golden honey eyes darkened, his nostrils flaring as he scented the air around me.

"What do your instincts tell you about me?" I asked.

"Hmm. Something has changed. The last time we were together," he said, "you were quite a bit less lively. In fact, the demon said something about a missing soul?"

"My soul was trapped in hell, but that's old news. I'm back now." I forced a smile. "Better than ever."

He took another breath, then sighed. "More determined, perhaps. But I sense you've lost something along the way."

More than you could possibly imagine...

"Perhaps you could use a friend?" he asked.

I looked into those eyes, the dark lashes, the beautifully full lips, the face of the man I loved, and I wanted to open up to him, to confess everything that had happened, everything I'd learned. To tell him how scared I truly was.

But I'd be a fool to trust him now.

He was Darius, but… not. The man before me reminded me of an actor, changing his expressions and voice for a role. There was no warmth in his eyes. No recognition. And absolutely no love.

Darius's eyes suddenly darted to the side, and he scented the air again, his lip curling in disgust. Seconds later, I heard the scrape of the iron bar lifting from the door, followed by the click of the hounds' claws against the floor.

"*Demon,*" Darius practically spat. "If I never see or smell or taste another for a thousand years, it will be too soon."

I turned back toward the door as Ronan entered the room.

Anger smoldered in my gut like hot coals as I remembered his most recent devil's bargain, but I couldn't deny I was relieved to see him. Logically I knew he couldn't fix this any more than he could fix the mess he'd made between us, but his presence still comforted me. Ronan had been my best friend long before he'd become my lover. My life.

Nothing was going to change that.

"Why is he like this?" I asked as Ronan approached, hating myself for talking about Darius as if he wasn't in the room with us—wasn't glaring at me with raw, naked lust. But the change that had come over him went deeper than his memory loss. It was hunger, pure and simple. Bloodlust.

As far as I knew, Darius hadn't fed on living beings in decades, and he certainly hadn't overdosed. Yet Deirdre had mentioned something about him attacking and draining a demon?

"Is it just his instincts taking over?" I asked.

"Partly," Ronan said. "For a vampire, feeding on the living is primal. Feeding on donor blood or animals is the conscious choice in the equation."

"One he doesn't remember making." I sighed as the pieces clicked into place. Darius was centuries old. He hadn't come to his choices overnight. They'd been woven into the fabric of his life, shaped by his experiences, reinforced by decades of choices, every decision *not* to kill, *not* to drain the lifeblood of another being inexorably linked to his memory.

Memory that he no longer possessed.

"Well, this is rather enlightening," Darius said. "I don't recall ever being so thoroughly dissected before. Perhaps next time you might buy me dinner first."

"Gray," Ronan said, and the odd hesitation in his voice set a new flare of panic ablaze in my chest.

"Tell me," I breathed, my voice as fragile as an eggshell. "Just tell me."

"Before we came to the Shadowrealm, he was ambushed by hunters in a motel. They'd intended to kill him, but he… he destroyed them."

"Destroyed?"

"Drained," Ronan said, and the word punched me in the gut. Ronan gave me a moment to process this before continuing. "He fed on both of them, consumed by bloodlust. It was essentially an overdose—way too much, too fast, his system couldn't process it all. Somehow, he made it back to us, and we got him stabilized."

"Speaking of feeding," Darius said. "I don't suppose either of you knows where a vampire like me could get a… bite?"

"But then he attacked a demon?" I asked, ignoring Darius. "Deirdre said something about it."

"I came out of the hell portal with you, but Darius had already gotten through ahead of us. I found him feeding on one of Sebastian's guards."

"Now *that's* something I do remember," Darius said. "I'm not quite sure I'll ever get the taste of that filth out of my mouth." Darius laughed, a sound I'd never heard before. It wasn't *his* laugh. It belonged to some other vampire, some other time, some other place.

It occurred to me then just how fragile everything really was—for each of us. Every day was like walking on the edge of a knife. One misstep…

We had absolutely zero control.

Yet somehow, we kept walking along that blade anyway.

"Let's go." Ronan tugged on my sweatshirt, careful not to touch my skin.

I jerked away from him. Better that he not touch me at all. "We can't leave him here, Ronan. Not like this."

"There's nothing we can do right now," Ronan said, his tone suddenly gentle. This was hurting him just as it was hurting me. I had to remember that. "He doesn't know us anymore, Gray."

Darius scoffed. "The fact that you've detained me against my will, dressed me in these bargain basement atrocities, starved me, and poisoned me with hawthorn tells me *everything* I need to know about you, demon." He turned his gaze back on me, that same cold grin sliding across his face. "*You,* on the other hand…"

Darius closed his eyes and took a deep breath through his nose, inhaling my scent again. Naively, I waited for him to show me his real smile, to look at me with even the faintest glimmer of recognition.

But when he opened his eyes again, there was nothing. Only that icy smile that sent chills to my very core.

"You really are an absolutely lovely creature," he murmured, his deep voice sliding down my spine like a caress.

I felt my body inching toward him, seeking his touch as if by muscle memory. I leaned in close to the wall, right to where his un-staked hand was bound, just close enough for him to graze my face.

Ronan stiffened behind me, but didn't stop me.

Darius flexed his hand, reaching out to stroke my cheek with one elegant finger, his thumb pressing the dip in my bottom lip, and I shivered, my breath catching in my throat.

His touch was so familiar. If I closed my eyes, I could almost believe it was still him. That Darius was still with us. That he'd beaten the odds and regained his memories and—

"Gray." A firm grip on my shoulder, the too-warm touch that quickly led to smoke, and Ronan was easing me backward, out of Darius's reach once again.

Ronan released me.

I stood between them, Ronan at my back, Darius before me, and felt myself waver. Memories seized me, flashing images of our night together at the safe house, Ronan taking me from behind, Darius lying beneath me, touching me, bringing me endless pleasures…

I'd felt so loved, so cared for. So safe. In that moment, I'd known without a doubt that as long as we had each other, nothing bad could ever touch us.

If only I'd known that it was just that—a moment. Here, then gone.

That night, their touch felt like home.

This night, a touch from either of them could kill me.

Darius unleashed a faint moan, his eyes darkening with a look of pure, unadulterated lust.

"Whatever you're thinking about," Ronan told me, "whatever you're feeling, he's picking up on it."

I felt my cheeks flame and forced myself to look away.

"Deirdre said she'll brew something to ease his suffering," Ronan said. "It should help neutralize the effects of the overdose and diminish the bloodlust—Emilio's sister did the same thing before. But I'm afraid neither of them can do anything about his memories."

"Have they even tried?"

"What's to try? Those beasts that attacked us in the Shadowrealm weren't called memory borrowers or memory misplacers or temporary memory blockers. They're memory eaters, Gray. They destroyed his mind. I want to believe there's a way, but I just…" Ronan sighed. "Maybe there's no coming back from something like that."

Darius had no response to this. When I turned to look at him again, I saw his head hanging limply, his hair falling in front of his eyes. He'd gone still.

"He'll be okay, though, won't he?" I asked.

After all the secrets, the deceit, the misdirections, the cover-ups, all I wanted now was one more lie. I wanted Ronan to look me in the eye and tell me that Darius would pull through this. That we'd all pull through this.

But Ronan shook his head. "I don't know, Gray."

It was just as well. Lies never really fixed anything, anyway. They just prolonged the breaking.

"Did you know I was the Silversbane heir?" I asked Ronan. Emotionless. Cold. A throwaway question I didn't really expect him to answer.

"No," he said. "But I always suspected it."

I looked up into his eyes, searching them for some sign of hope. Something flickered there—a spark, maybe, and then it was gone.

"You were always destined for greatness," he said, leaning in close. "I never doubted that."

His smile reappeared, and for one brief instant, I thought he might actually try to kiss me again. But then he pulled back, shoving a hand through his hair.

"We… We need to find Asher," I blurted out. I wasn't sure why—it's not like finding Asher could do anything to bring back Darius's memories or break the chains Sebastian had put on my relationship with Ronan. But I had to stay focused on something—a mission with a definite end goal. Something we actually stood a chance at achieving.

"We will," Ronan said firmly. Definitively. Then, in a softer voice, "That's a promise, Gray."

I shook my head, biting back a snarky retort. There was a time when I believed Ronan's promises without question. When that firm, no-nonsense, no-bullshit tone had the power to pull me from the darkest depths of worry and fear. When one touch of his palm against my cheek could soothe the deepest ache in the darkest parts of my soul.

But he wasn't allowed to touch me now, and the ache bloomed unchecked, blackening me from the inside out.

I turned my back on both of them—my demon and my vampire, the men whose claims on my heart were burned into me like brands—and walked to collect my hounds.

Right now, our priority was Asher. He needed me to stay strong.

And I needed him to be… No, that was it. No more words necessary. I needed him to be. To just *be*.

NINETEEN

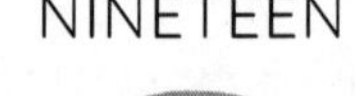

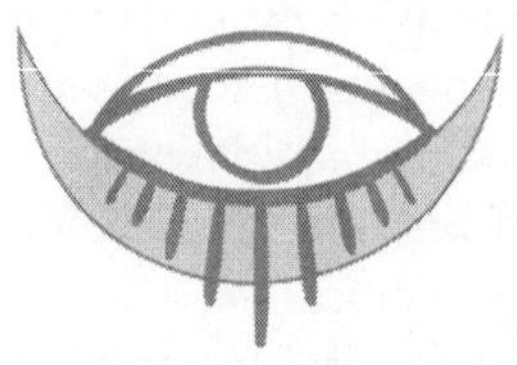

GRAY

"How soon can we get back to Raven's Cape?" I paced the hotel room, wishing I had a suitcase to pack or papers to shuffle or *anything* to distract me from the black hole eating away at my heart.

I was the fucking heir to the Silversbane legacy. The prophesied witch born with the power to unite the covens and bring order to the chaos and blah, blah, blah.

So why couldn't I save the men I loved?

Why did I grow up alone, isolated from my three sisters?

How did my parents actually die?

How did Deirdre end up in Sebastian's company?

Where were my sisters now? Did they know about me?

Who signed my original contract with Sebastian?

How much, if anything, had Calla known?

What did Sebastian want with my ancestors if he already knew I was the prophesied witch? Was it just my sisters he was after, so he could have the complete set?

I looked around at the hotel room, at Ronan, at the hounds pacing their own circles at the end of the bed. How had all of this come to be?

So many questions. So many impossible answers. And they just kept on coming, one leading to another to the next, each one more thorny than the last.

Destiny was cruel. That was the only answer. The only one I kept running up against, time and again.

Liam had once told me that destiny and choice were not mutually exclusive. *"But there are things about your path you must learn, must accept, no matter how difficult."* I wondered now if this was what he'd meant. The Silversbane legacy. Or my enslavement to Sebastian. Or something else entirely—something we'd yet to encounter.

How much of my current predicament had he already seen as one of his infinite possibilities? And if possibilities were, in fact, infinite, didn't it stand to reason that there were other paths we might still take? Other choices we just yet hadn't considered?

I pressed my fingertips to my temples, massaging my head. When this was all over, I'd eat and cry myself into a week-long coma with a few gallons of ice cream and a pan of Emilio's brownies, all of it topped off with a bottle of Darius's fancy wine. But for now, we had to keep moving.

"So Sebastian's letting you go?" Ronan asked. "Just like that?"

"For now."

"But how did that even happen? He doesn't—"

I held up my hand. "Ronan, it's a really long story, and I'll tell you all about it once we're on the plane. Okay? Right now, I just want to focus on getting the hell out of this city."

"We can't leave yet," Ronan said. "We need to find a safer situation for Darius. I'm not familiar with the vampire families in town, and we can't just leave him at Inferno. I don't trust Sebastian to—"

"Wait, *what*?" I spun on my heel to face him, my eyes wide. "Leave him at Inferno? Are you kidding me? We're not leaving him anywhere. We're *all* going back to the Cape. Together."

"Gray, he's not..." Ronan shoved a hand through his hair and blew out a frustrated breath. "He doesn't even know he's part of us. All he knows now is the taste of blood, and the fact that he's not getting it. It's driving him mad. Taking him back to the Cape in this state—likely against his will—is beyond dangerous. It's flat-out stupid."

"Then we'll take precautions. We're not splitting up again,

Ronan. The three of us need to get back to the Cape, back to Emilio. Then we need to help Asher."

Ronan crossed the room, reaching for my shoulders but stopping just short. I flinched away from him anyway.

He didn't even bother hiding the pain in his eyes.

"You think I *want* to leave him?" he snapped, making Sunshine yelp. "You think I wanted any of this to happen?"

I didn't need to answer that. Of course he didn't want this to happen. But it *did* happen.

I fell back onto the bed. My heart broke as much for Ronan as it did for me. Deep down I knew the truth, no matter what Sebastian wanted me to believe.

Ronan loved me. And it was killing him that he couldn't do anything about it. Ronan cared a great deal for Darius, too, and now he'd lost a friend. A brother.

"I'm sorry, Gray," Ronan said now, sitting next to me on the bed. "I'm so, so fucking sorry."

"Don't." I sat up next to him, careful not to get too close. "Look. I know that you're not allowed to love me, and Darius can't remember that he ever did. I know that Asher is still trapped inside that hellhole. And Emilio is probably going out of his mind trying to solve this case, and I have no idea how to help him once we get back." I turned to look into his eyes, and when I saw the love there, blazing as it always had, I took a risk, brushing my hand through the hair falling across his forehead. There was a second where it didn't hurt, didn't burn, but then the smoke came, and I pulled back.

In a much softer voice, I said, "But I *do* know that we all belong together. No matter what the circumstances. We're stronger together, Ronan. You know it. We need to get back there."

He watched me a moment longer, then finally nodded. "I know. You're right. I know."

"I don't want to split up again. Not if we can help it. The five of us are… We're a family, Ronan. No one can take that away from us. Not even Sebastian."

"And Liam?" he asked. "Where does he fit into all this?"

I forced a casual shrug, swallowing past the lump in my

throat. "I don't know yet. Liam and I… We have a few things to figure out."

"It seemed like you were figuring things out pretty well in the Shadowrealm. I saw the way you were looking at each other." He shrugged, all of this said without jealousy. Without disapproval.

Ronan had always made it clear that he wanted me to be happy—that he understood there was room in the human heart for the love of more than just one other being, and he'd never been jealous. Not of Darius, with whom he'd happily shared me. Not of Asher. Not of Emilio, who was just beginning to find his way into my heart. Ronan considered them all brothers. They all felt that way about each other.

But Liam was different. He'd always been just a little… outside of things. From the moment he'd arrived in Sophie's bedroom the night of her murder, he and Ronan had butted heads. They'd worked through some of their differences since then, but I wasn't sure Ronan was ready to hear the full story of me and Liam. And if he knew that Liam had made a bargain with Sebastian for my soul long before any of this had ever started…

My heart squeezed, tears springing to my eyes. I blinked them away, hoping Ronan hadn't noticed.

"Do you remember when I told you there was nothing I wouldn't do for you?" he asked. "I meant it, Gray. I want you to feel like you can be open with me about anything. Your feelings for Liam included. If you—"

"Why?" I whispered, fresh tears spilling, and in that one word —*why?*—he knew I wasn't talking about Liam or anyone else for that matter.

I was talking about Ronan. About what he'd done to get me out of the Shadowrealm.

It was a long time before he found the words to respond.

"This… this was one of those things, too," he said. "I said there's nothing I wouldn't do for you. That includes giving you up to keep you safe."

"There might've been another—"

"There wasn't. You were trapped in the Shadowrealm. Even Liam couldn't get you out. The thought of you there alone, facing those demons… I couldn't let it happen. Darius and I had to get to you, and the only way we could was through the hell portal. Sebastian never does anything without a price, and he knew I'd pay any price for you. So yeah, I gave you up. I did it because I wanted you to live. To love. To be that crazy, stubborn, beautiful witch you've always been." He offered me a sad smile. "As long as I know you're out there living your life, I… I have to be okay with that."

"But I'm *not* out there. I'm here. Trying to find a permanent way out of this bullshit deal with Sebastian. If I don't, there is no living my life, with you or without you."

"Don't say that," he whispered, his lips so close to mine I could already taste his kiss. "You're young, smart, passionate, powerful, beautiful… There's so much more you—"

I shook my head, cutting him off. All I could think about was his kiss. How long until I forgot the feel of his lips? The warmth of his breath? The soft velvet of his tongue? The intensity in his gaze as we…

I closed my eyes—the only thing I could do to break the connection.

"You have taken a piece of my heart, Ronan," I said. "Carved it right out and set it on fire. I'm so in love with you I can't even breathe to think of a life without you. Now you're asking me to accept this? To stand by and watch everything we are to each other burn to ashes?"

"Look at me, Gray. Please."

I opened my eyes. His own were red and glassy, heartbreak written on his face. The sight of his pain made my heart stop.

"There's nothing else we can do," he said. "It's over. It's just over."

My heart started up again with a painful sputter. And this time when it beat, it fell out of step, missing its twin. Missing my best friend.

"I will *never* stop loving you," I whispered, taking his face into my hands. It hurt to touch him, my skin burning with an ache I would never be able to ease. Not with words and promises. Not with dreams of a better future. Not with kisses.

"This isn't—"

"I love you, Ronan Vacarro. So, so much." I looked deep into his eyes and waited for him to say it. That he loved me, too. That nothing Sebastian said or did would ever change that, even if he couldn't act on it.

"Gray, I..."

Say it, Ronan. Just say it...

"You should... get some rest," he finally said, standing up unceremoniously from the bed. All traces of regret, of love, of friendship were gone in a flash. "I need to make arrangements to transport Darius. I'll come get you when it's time to go."

"That's *it*?" I stood from the bed and followed him to the door, shouting at his back. "That's all you're going to say?"

"What do you *want* me to say, Gray?"

I grabbed his shoulders and spun him around, ignoring the smoke. "I want you to look me in the eye and tell me you don't love me. Tell me this is really over between us."

I placed my hand on his chest, seeking the familiar drum-beat of his heart. It pounded behind his ribcage, harder and harder with every breath, even as my touch burned through his T-shirt.

He leaned in close, so close I could count his eyelashes. His breath came in short staccato bursts, each one kissing my lips.

"Say it again," I whispered. "Tell me again that it's over."

He clenched his teeth, grounding out every word. "This. Is. Over. We're done."

He pulled back and cleared his throat, shifting his gaze to a spot just above my eye. His face was neutral once again. Cold. "From now on, we are guardian and demon sworn. Nothing more."

"I'm never giving up on you," I said. "No matter what you say. No matter what Sebastian does. And I *know* you won't give up on me, either." I said it with all the confidence I could muster, needing to believe it for myself.

"It's too late, Gray." He turned away from me and wrenched open the door. "I already have."

TWENTY

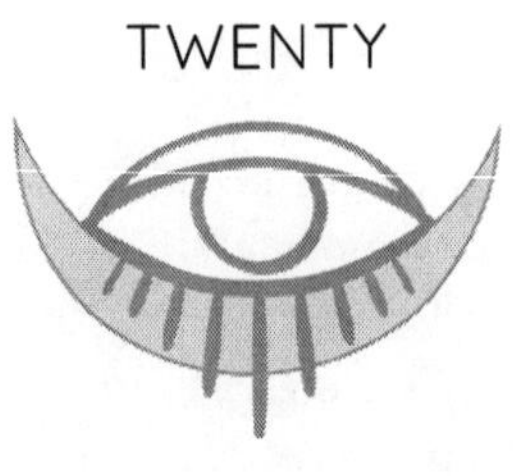

GRAY

After another long and brutal argument, Ronan finally agreed to ask Deirdre for help in transporting Darius. In a moment of sheer brilliance, she'd concocted an IV solution using essence of hawthorn, and with that, we were able to fully sedate him and get him on the plane without incident.

The plane wasn't Darius's private jet—one of the few things Ronan and I agreed on was that Darius's memory loss needed to be kept secret from the larger vampire community for as long as possible, including his pilots and other associates. So instead, we'd taken an aircraft on loan from Sebastian, no doubt a grand gesture designed to lull us into thinking he could be a friend. After all, Sebastian always had a price.

Ronan and I hadn't exchanged a single word since boarding the plane. By some miracle, I managed to hold it together for the entire flight, as well as the drive from the airport to Emilio's sister's house in Raven's Cape.

But the moment Emilio opened the front door and bounded down the front steps to greet us, I lost it.

"Gray?" He looked at me like he hadn't seen me in a hundred years and wasn't sure he could trust his own eyes.

I nodded, tears spilling freely, and collapsed into his arms, burying my face against his chest. His familiar scent enveloped me like a hug, all forest and sunshine and vanilla, and I slid my arms up inside the back of his jacket, soaking up his warmth. His strength.

Sparkle and Sunshine, my ever-present companions, ran circles around us both.

"I missed you so much," I breathed.

"You, too, *mi querida*. More than you can imagine." He wrapped his big arms around me tighter, holding me close, his hand cupping the back of my head. His thumb stroked behind my ear, the touch immediately soothing my jagged nerves.

"I see you brought… these guys," he said, not quite hiding his grimace as the hounds nipped at the hem of his jacket. He reached down to pat Sparkle on the head, and Sunshine nosed her way in for some loving, too.

"Sparkle and Sunshine." I pointed each one out. "Courtesy of Sebastian."

Ronan had given Emilio some of the details over the phone before we took off from Vegas, so news of my new arrangement didn't come as a complete surprise. But Emilio still winced when I told him about it—the meeting, the temporary stay Sebastian had finally agreed to. And of course, the hounds.

"You… named them?" he asked.

"I figured it was the only humane thing to do. Apparently, we're going to be spending a lot of time in each other's company. And by a lot, I mean an eternity." I smiled, trying to keep the mood light, but failed miserably. My face crumpled once again.

"Did Sebastian say how long you had?" Emilio asked gently.

"We left it kind of open ended. I'm hoping I can figure out another loophole in the interim."

"We will, Gray. That's not even a question." He put his arm around me and pulled me close again, big and protective and comforting, exactly what I needed. I let out a breath, some of my stress evaporating. Emilio had always had that effect on me.

Behind him, two men headed down the front steps from the house—shifters, I thought. Probably wolves. Jael came next—Emilio had told us he'd been staying with them, helping out. Then, bringing up the rear, a woman who could only be Emilio's sister, Elena.

I pulled out of Emilio's embrace and attempted to wipe away my tears and smooth out my hair, but I was probably making everything worse. I was still wearing Ronan's sweatshirt and the clothes I'd woken up with at the hotel, and I felt like my entire body was covered in a layer of grease from Sebastian's mere presence.

Clearly not my personal best, but Emilio's sister offered a warm, genuine smile anyway.

"Welcome to Raven's Cape," she said, introducing herself and leaning in to kiss my cheek. "I only wish you'd come here for a happier reason."

Her accent reminded me of Emilio's, and I wondered what else they had in common, what their childhood had been like, how long it had been since they'd seen each other before this. Emilio had never said much about her, but now I sensed a distance between them, a tension lingering just beneath the surface of their smiles. I wondered if she was the reason for the sadness I sometimes saw in his eyes. The regret.

I thought about his words back at the safe house the night I'd grilled Fiona Brentwood.

People do all sorts of misguided things when they're trying to protect the ones they love, querida. Let's just say I know something about that.

Maybe he'd been talking about his sister.

"Those are my guys," she said, bringing me back to the moment. She nodded to the shifters that were now speaking with Ronan and Jael at the car. "Detectives Aiden Hobb and Russel Lansky."

"They're helping with the case," Emilio said.

"Right now, they're helping with your vampire," Elena said. "But there's plenty of room in the house for everyone, so no worries. Even the… the dogs."

"They're not dogs, Elena." Emilio rolled his eyes playfully. "They're—"

"Shh!" She put her hands over her ears. "I have to tell myself they're dogs, or we're going to have a serious problem."

Emilio laughed. "Whatever you say."

"It *is* whatever I say. It's my house. Also, my jurisdiction." She turned back to me with a real smile. "You can set up in the spare room on the right, straight back from the front. There's a bathroom in there too if you want to shower. Once you're all settled in, I'll make us all a snack. Yes?"

"Thank you," I said. "That sounds great. Especially the shower and snack."

"By *snack*," Emilio said, "she means a seven-course meal, complete with appetizers and dessert."

I beamed. "Even better."

Elena went to help the others get Darius situated. Emilio told me they'd set up a room in the basement for him, trying to make sure he'd be as comfortable as possible.

"No stone benches," he promised me. "But we do need to keep him sedated and bound for now. Just until we can assess the situation and figure out how to best help him. Okay?"

"There has to be something else we can do," I said, my stomach knotting up again just thinking about Darius being… handled. That was the word for it. They were handling him, shuffling him from the car to the house, down into the basement, talking about him as if he were a stranger. A prisoner. "Emilio, it's *Darius*."

"Oh, *querida*," he said, his voice soft and reassuring. "This isn't right. I know it isn't. But it's the best we can do right now." He cupped my cheeks, his thumbs brushing away the last of my tears.

I wrapped my hands around his wrists and sighed, grateful for the contact. For a touch that didn't turn into smoke. When I looked up and met his gaze, Emilio was openly staring at me, his soulful eyes searching my face.

"What is it?" I whispered, suddenly shy. I didn't even want to *think* about how horrible I looked right now, but Emilio seemed completely captivated. "You're freaking me out, *El Lobo*."

"I'm sorry. It's just… it's really good to see you, *brujita bonita*. When they told me what you'd done in that prison, what it meant…" He closed his eyes and swallowed hard. When he spoke again, his voice was ragged. "I thought I'd never hold you again.

How did you even survive that place? And then you got stuck in *hell*?"

"That's... a really long story." I felt like I'd been saying that a lot lately, and I'm sure the other guys had their own tales to tell, too. We'd all been away from each other for so long, it seemed like it'd been years since we'd last shared a meal together, let alone talked. Really, really talked.

"I guess we have a lot to catch up on," he said.

"We will," I promised him. "After dinner, though. You got me all excited for Elena's seven-course meal."

Emilio nodded, lowering his hands from my face. I missed the contact immediately, but forgave him when he reached into his jacket pocket and pulled out a small box, gift-wrapped in pale turquoise paper and tied with a red ribbon.

"Is that for me?" I asked.

Emilio smiled. "Just a little something I saw and thought you might like."

A bubble of giddiness floated up inside, and I bounced on my toes, eagerly tearing open the paper. After so much darkness, so much insanity, it felt good to find the simple joy in something like a present.

The paper fell away, revealing a deck of Tarot cards.

And I gasped, tears blurring the colors and designs together.

I'd been mesmerized by this deck since I was a little girl.

"Are they... do you like them?" He asked. "I know you like to use Sophie's cards for your readings, but everything was so chaotic when we left the safe house, I didn't think to grab any of your things. When I saw this deck, I... I just got this image of you holding the cards. *These* cards. I felt like you belonged together. Does that sound nuts?"

"Emilio," I finally breathed. "It's not nuts. They're perfect."

"Are you sure? Because if you don't like them, I bet we can exchange them. There were at least a hundred different decks at the shop, and—"

"It's not that. It's...." I took a deep breath, the shock of it still washing over me. "This is the deck Calla used to use."

It was her favorite deck. The only card I had left from it was the High Priestess—I'd found it inexplicably tucked into my book of shadows the night we'd dug the book up out of my backyard. At the time, it'd felt like a message from Calla. An infusion of strength and wisdom and encouragement. Now, it felt like she was looking down on me again, wrapping me up in a gentle hug, reminding me that she was still with me.

"There was a time I'd be surprised to hear that," Emilio said, "but if I've learned anything from you, it's that there are no coincidences."

"No, there really aren't."

"You were meant to have those cards, Gray. I felt it from the moment I saw them in the case."

I nodded, unable to express how touched I really was.

When I finally looked up from the cards, Emilio offered me a shy smile. The sight of it filled me with so much warmth, it felt like the sun had finally found me again, thawing out my bones from a deep freeze.

There was so much going wrong. So much falling apart.

But here in Emilio's embrace, I'd found a moment of pure peace.

"You're trembling, *mi querida.*" He rubbed my back, as if I needed warming up. As if I could ever be any warmer than I was right here in his arms. "Are you okay?"

"More than okay." I pulled back and looked up into those soulful brown eyes again, my heart fuller and lighter than it'd been in weeks. "You make me believe we're strong enough to—"

He cut off my words with a kiss. A quick one, soft and pure, just this side of friendly, but a kiss nevertheless. There was a promise of more to come in a kiss like that—so much more—and for now I tucked it away for later, knowing that in the midst of all this chaos, there was at least one good, pure, beautiful thing waiting for me on the near horizon.

"Whatever you were going to say," he said, pressing his forehead to mine and closing his eyes, "it's true. We *are* strong enough. For whatever's coming our way. For whatever we need to do to fix this. For whatever we need to do to protect our pack."

* * *

Elena's dinner was amazing, and despite the challenges we were all facing, we still managed to laugh. To enjoy Elena's cooking, trading a few stories from their mutually trouble-making childhoods in Argentina. I learned that Emilio liked to chase away the chickens that his mother had meant to cook, and Elena had a knack for growing what she called a "very special medicinal herb of the smokable variety." Everyone got a good laugh at that.

Through all the laughs and the good food and the endless wine, there was only one thing missing. One thing that Ronan and Emilio both had deemed too dangerous to bring to the table.

My vampire.

TWENTY-ONE

GRAY

"Good evening, love."

Darius called to me before I'd even reached the bottom of the basement stairs, and I closed my eyes and stopped, hoping he couldn't sense the skip in my heartbeat at the sound of his voice.

Love. The sweetness of that word on his lips made my chest hurt. How many times had he called me that? Had he whispered it into my ear, his lips brushing my skin?

"I was hoping you might visit me," he said again. "It's dreadfully dull in this establishment. And the menu leaves *much* to be desired."

Thanks to Deirdre's potion, Darius had remained in a heavily sedated state for the entire trip home from Las Vegas. He'd been down here ever since, fed a steady IV drip of some kind of hawthorn-infused herbal tonic Elena had fixed up—just enough to keep him calm and slightly lethargic, but not totally immobilized.

In his current state, Ronan and Emilio said, he could still attack us. Even me. They said we had to be careful.

That didn't mean we had to be cruel.

The basement was finished, with warm yellow walls, and plush beige carpeting. Darius was seated on the couch, his legs free, but his upper body wrapped impossibly tight in what looked like a souped-up straitjacket. The IV was taped to his neck, the tonic in a clear IV bag hanging from a pole at the end of the couch.

I gasped, horrified. I didn't know what was worse—the chains at Inferno, or this?

"I'm sorry," I whispered.

He took in my appearance, his eyes drinking me in slowly, lazily. Elena kept her house warm, and after my shower, I'd pulled my hair into a messy bun and changed into the clothes she'd left out for me—a pair of soft cotton shorts and a black Dead Weather T-shirt, Ronan's sweatshirt tied around my waist. It wasn't especially glamorous, but Darius seemed to appreciate the outfit.

My cheeks heated under his gaze.

"Don't be," he said, a teasing smile tugging his lips. "I'm sure I've been in worse scrapes. Haven't I?"

I nodded, thinking of the time we were attacked at the morgue. The time we fought off those vamps at Norah's place. The time we battled memory eater demons in the Shadowrealm…

Darius had been through so much. This wasn't fair. It wasn't right.

I knelt on the carpet before him, resting my cheek on his knee and closing my eyes. The familiar scent of his skin emanated through the fabric of his borrowed sweats—whiskey and leather and something inexplicably his.

"Are you sure you want to do that?" he mused. "I'm quite dangerous, if popular opinion is to be believed."

I lifted my face, forcing myself to open my eyes and stare into his. He held my gaze, unblinking, studying me as I studied him.

"Whatever are you looking for, love?"

The tenderness in his voice was like a scalpel, so clear and sharp I could almost tell myself I didn't really feel it slicing through my heart.

But that would be a lie. Every moment Darius spent tied up here, his memories lost or locked away or entirely eradicated, hurt me in ways I couldn't pretend *not* to feel. I felt every bit of it. For him. For me. For all of us.

Tears escaped, despite my efforts to keep them prisoner.

"There, there." Darius ducked his head, offering a warm smile. "It can't be as bad as all that, can it?"

"It's *worse* than all that," I said.

"Tell me what's troubling you. Maybe I can help." He tried to shrug, but his movements were limited by the straitjacket. "Well, not *help*, exactly. But I can certainly listen. I'm an excellent listener."

That got a smile out of me. Darius had always been a good listener.

I untied the sweatshirt from my waist, setting it on the floor as I rose up on my knees, my hands sliding up his thighs. He opened his legs to allow me to get closer, and I did—as close as I dared. We were at eye level now, and I had no idea what would come next. There was no plan, no projection. Only instinct. And right now, my instincts were telling me that this was okay. That it was right.

"Darius, do you remember me at *all*?" I asked.

His face changed then, the teasing smile gone, his eyes smoldering as he stared deeply into mine, searching. I held my breath, waiting for the flicker of recognition to come. A smile. A word. A joke. A look that only Darius could give me.

But after another moment of searching, his face fell, his eyes filling not with recognition, but sorrow. Disappointment.

"For what it's worth," he said gently, "I truly wish I could. I'm so sorry, love."

He looked utterly pained by the admission.

I nodded, but I had to believe he was still in there. That his memories hadn't been erased, only misplaced, locked away behind a wall. We just had to figure out how to knock that wall down.

I took a deep breath and got to my feet, still standing between his knees.

Sliding my hands over his shoulders, I reached behind him for the straps of the jacket.

"Lean forward," I said.

"Gray, is this really the best course of action?" he asked.

"Don't you want to get out of this contraption?"

"More than you know. But the others… they think I'm a threat to you. Perhaps there's some truth to that."

"You would never hurt me," I said, needing him to believe it as much as I did. "You… you might not remember it now, but you care for me a great deal."

We're blood bound, I wanted to say, but held back. In his eyes, my words wouldn't make it so. Darius would need to remember that bond on his own, or it wouldn't matter to him.

"That very well may be, but I'm also not…" His eyes darted toward the IV bag. "I'm not in the best physical condition right now. I'm not sure that I could restrain myself. If I hurt you, even inadvertently…"

His eyes were pained. The thought of hurting me had upset him.

Hope surged inside me. Since I'd last spoken with him in the basement of Inferno, he'd clearly regained some of his awareness. His humanity. The fact that he was even thinking about my safety rather than trying to talk me into freeing him was a good sign.

"Lean forward," I said again, and he finally obeyed.

With new urgency, I worked at the locks and buckles and hinges at the back of the straitjacket until I'd gotten them all undone.

I pulled the jacket off, revealing his bare arms and chest, freeing him from the confines of this monstrous form of torture. It was as heavy as a bulletproof vest. I had no idea what it was made out of.

I tossed it to the floor. As long as I had a say in this, he'd never be forced into that thing again.

Darius kept his arms at his sides on the couch, slowly flexing his muscles. His pale skin began to regain some of its color. "That's… better," he sighed.

"We're not done yet." I reached up to unhook the IV, pressing my fingers against the skin of his neck. At my touch, he shivered, his thighs tightening around my legs.

Without the straitjacket, the IV was the last thing keeping him even remotely restrained. Once I disconnected it, the hawthorn would wear off quickly, and he'd regain his full strength.

If he decided to hurt me…

My hands trembled, but there was no going back now. He needed to know I believed in him. Trusted him. I *did* trust him.

Gently, slowly, I slid out the needle. A trickle of blood ran down to his collarbone.

And he was totally free.

"Brave move," he whispered through a smile. "Or maybe reckless. Either way… Thank you, little brawler."

"Darius!" I leaned forward and cupped his face, my heart ready to burst. "You remembered something!"

"I… did?"

"Little brawler! That's what you call me." I lowered my mouth to his, pressing a soft kiss to his lips. He hesitated only a moment before parting his lips, allowing me to deepen our kiss. Darius sighed into my mouth, a low moan rising from his chest.

I pulled back, searching his face. When our eyes met, something sparked in his. He was coming back to me. I could feel it.

"That's right," I urged, willing that spark to ignite into a flame. A fire. "You know me, Darius Beaumont. In every way that counts. Every way that means something, you *know* me."

"I…" Slowly, he lifted a hand to my face, tracing my brow bone with his fingertips. His touch was soft and gentle, a caress, a whisper.

His touch was all Darius.

I climbed into his lap, straddling him, sliding my hands into his silky dark hair. It'd gotten longer since we'd first met, almost to his shoulders now, and I tangled my fingers into it, drawing him closer.

His eyes darkened with a desire that bordered on pure, primal hunger, but he was no longer cold. No longer distant.

"I miss you," I said, emotion breaking my voice. It had only been days since we'd held each other in that cabin in the Shadowrealm, but even that had been too long, especially after nearly losing him.

"I'm right here, love." His gaze swept down my face, lowering to the pulse point on my neck. Beneath me, his cock stiffened under the thin sweatpants, already teasing me, making me wet.

I clenched my thighs to stave off the ache, and another low moan escaped his lips, his eyes fluttering closed.

"I'm yours," I whispered, rocking forward against his hard length. "Always."

Darius brought his mouth to my neck, his hands sliding up the back of my shirt. His touch set me on fire, every movement agonizingly slow, devastatingly perfect.

He kissed a line down my neck, across my collarbone, the points of his fangs grazing my flesh, but never breaking it. With each kiss, his tongue swirled over my skin, making me desperate for more.

In a move so fast I didn't even see it happen, he reached up and whipped off my T-shirt, tossing it to the floor. My bare breasts brushed against his chest, and he cupped them both, running his nose along the top curves, inhaling the scent of my skin.

I let out a whimper of pleasure, rolling my head back, arching closer.

Teasing my nipple between his thumb and forefinger, Darius captured the other in his mouth, flicking it with his tongue. The scrape of his fangs sent a jolt of white-hot pleasure to my core, and I gasped, losing myself in the warmth of his mouth.

He continued to tease me with his tongue, expertly swirling and sucking as I rocked against him, the friction building between my thighs.

"Mmm. Are you hungry, little brawler," he teased between kisses, sliding his hands inside the bottom of my shorts and underwear to cup my ass. His fingers dipped between my thighs, seeking my wet heat, teasing my entrance.

Warmth gathered, my core pulsing with a deep ache that could only be soothed by one thing.

"Starving," I whispered, reaching down the front of his sweatpants and fisting his cock. It was hot and velvet-smooth and as hard as steel, growing even harder at my touch.

"Fuck," he breathed, rolling his hips as I stroked him, teasing the head with my thumb. "That's…"

"*Mine.*" Something came over me then, a fierce possessiveness driving me wild with need. I needed him to kiss me. I needed him inside me. I *needed* to make him come.

I kissed him again, nipping at his lower lip.

Darius nipped me back, sucking my lip into his mouth, drawing blood.

He ran his tongue along the edge, growling at the taste of my blood, and in a blur of movement and strength, we were off the couch. He held me against his chest with one arm, my legs winding around his hips as he slammed my back against the wall.

Shoving a hand between us, he slid his fingers down the front of my shorts, pushing inside me, stroking me as I'd stroked him—fast and hard and faster still and oh my fucking *God* I'd never felt anything so hot.

My thighs trembled, my body tightening around his slick fingers…

"Is this what you want?" he growled, bringing me closer to the edge with every thrust. The question sounded like a threat. A promise. Danger and devastation wrapped in a silk scarf, and I nodded mutely, my eyes silently begging him for it.

And you will beg *me for it…*

His old words echoed in my memory.

"Say it," he demanded.

"This is what I want."

"Beg me, little brawler."

I was so turned on I could barely make words, but somehow, I forced them out.

"Please, Darius," I moaned against his lips. "I want you inside me. Fucking me." I grabbed the back of his head, fisting his hair and tugging hard. "Make me *feel* it."

A surge of wild, unrestrained need flooded his eyes, and without another word, he yanked the bottom edge of my shorts and underwear to the side and slid his cock inside me, thrusting deep. Hard. Banging me against the butter-yellow basement wall as I urged him to keep going, harder, faster, deeper, more, raking my nails along his back, biting down on his shoulder until we both came, hard and fast and shuddering, and I tasted the rich, coppery silk of his blood in my mouth.

* * *

He pulled away slowly, gently lowering me back to my feet. His eyes were wild, his hair knotted, his skin slick with sweat.

He pulled his sweatpants back up and tucked himself inside, and I did my best to clean up and straighten out my shorts. I was pretty sure the underwear was a lost cause—I'd heard them tear at one point, and now I felt the coolness of the air where the fabric should've been.

I was definitely going to wake up sore. I could already feel it starting—the ache in my thighs, the swollen mouth, the burns.

Darius flashed me a devious smile, and a fresh pulse of desire surged through my blood.

"Better be careful, little brawler," he teased. "Bite me one more time and you might turn into a vampire."

I rolled my eyes. "I'd have to bite you a lot more than once to turn into a vampire."

"That could be arranged." He held my gaze, his lush lips swollen, his smile light and content.

A flood of gratitude surged inside me. "I knew you'd come back," I whispered, pressing my palm to his cheek.

He watched me a moment longer, confusion drawing his brows together, and I waited for the gentleness to return to his eyes. The warmth.

The sex had been rough and wild and searingly hot—I was all for doing that again sometime. But suddenly I longed for a glimpse of the tenderness he'd shown me in the cabin in the Shadowrealm the first time we'd been together.

"Darius?" I asked.

"Hmm?" He cocked his head, still watching me with those honey-gold eyes, but where once there was friendship and familiarity and love, now there was only a mild amusement. The coldness had slid back into his gaze, a chill that went straight to the softest part of my heart and froze it.

"Vampire or not," he said with a low chuckle, "any man would come back for *that*, love."

I felt the blood leak instantly from my heart, pierced by the sharp arrow of that one word. *Love*. Where before it'd given me hope, somehow he'd managed to twist and mangle it into something cheap.

"Same time tomorrow, then?" he asked. "Perhaps I'll let you tie me back up. But not before I've had a chance to feed on something other than the shite they serve here."

I couldn't answer.

I felt dizzy. Lost. Darius and I were bound, yet even the taste of my blood hadn't been enough to bring him back to me. To heal him.

I grabbed my shirt from the floor and slowly dressed, the once-pleasurable burn of my muscles cooling into a stiff, bitter pain.

I wouldn't let him see it. Wouldn't let him know he'd broken me.

And I wouldn't let him out of this room.

I picked up Ronan's sweatshirt, holding it close as I approached Darius again.

"Whatever you want, bloodsucker." Pasting on a mischievous smile, I stretched up on my toes, capturing him in a deeply sensual kiss. He moaned softly, drinking me in.

It seemed Darius wasn't the only actor in the room.

Certain my devious mouth had captured his full attention, I pulled out the hawthorn stake I'd stashed in Ronan's sweatshirt and jammed it into the tender flesh beneath his ribcage, hating that Ronan and Emilio had been right.

Hating that I'd doubted Darius enough to bring the stake with me in the first place.

TWENTY-TWO

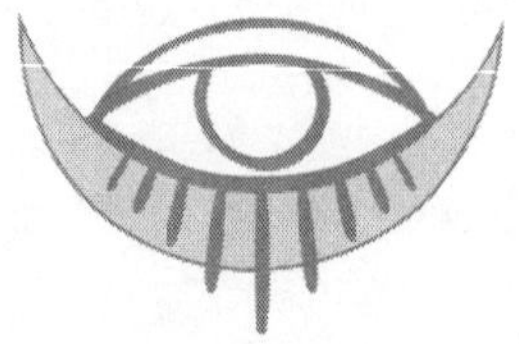

DARIUS

Intoxicating.

It was the closest word I could think of to capture her effect on me, yet it still felt woefully inadequate. The demon had told me she was a witch, and now I knew it must be true, for I was thoroughly bespelled.

I let her guide me back to the couch, where I promptly collapsed into my former position, my muscles turning numb from the effects of the hawthorn. Unlike the watered-down intravenous version, the stake was undiluted, its potency unmatched.

She'd chosen a big one, too.

"You wound me." I managed a weak smile, my words slurring. "And here I thought we had a real connection."

"We do," she whispered. "You just don't remember it."

"I could have killed you, love."

Her eyes shone with tears—tears I didn't deserve. After a deep, shuddering breath, she turned away from me, saying nothing more, disappearing up the stairs the way she'd come down.

Though she hadn't said the words, I felt them lingering in the wake of her exit.

You already have.

I realized then, with a sickening twist in my stomach, that she'd thought I'd remembered her. That she'd given herself so freely, so intensely, so… erotically, because she'd trusted me. Trusted the connection we were supposed to have had.

I wished things could've been different.

There was something so intensely familiar about her, but try as I might to find her in the dark recesses of memory, I couldn't recall ever having met her. I don't know how I'd managed to recall the nickname I'd supposedly given her. And though the brief taste of her blood had stirred something deep within me—something that spoke of a much more intimate history than she'd let on—it hadn't awakened any dormant memories.

Despite what she and the demon had told me about our relationship—that we'd even had one at all, that my memories of it had been stolen by some sort of shadow creatures in another realm—I looked into her eyes and saw nothing. Knew nothing.

Well, that wasn't entirely true. I knew she was going to stake me—perhaps even before she'd known it. Despite the pain and immobility it would bring, I'd let her do it anyway, almost welcoming the sharp pierce in my flesh.

It was better this way. She needed to understand I wasn't the man she'd fallen in love with before. I was a vampire. A hungry one. And being with her like that… I closed my eyes, still scenting her desire in the air. Remembering her now, the soft curve of her mouth, the heat of her breath as she moaned beneath my touch…

She'd nearly undone me.

And I'd wanted so, so badly to devour her. To sink my fangs into her throat and drain every last drop of that sweet, silky blood.

Shame burned inside me, but that was the truth of it.

Though I'd sworn we'd only just become acquainted, something about that final look in her eyes said I'd hurt her. Not physically, but in a way that was so much worse. A way that only someone who cared about you could manage.

An ache opened up in my chest, the bright pulse of it outrunning even the hawthorn working its way through my system.

Nothing the demon had said had affected me like this. Nothing the old witch had whispered as she'd plied me with her brew even came close.

But now, as I recalled the intense blue of Gray's eyes, the pain in them that *I'd* caused, I felt it.

For the first time since I'd arrived in this ocean-washed city, I felt the sting of something hot and fresh in my gut, the bitter taste of it coating my tongue like the very salt that coated the streets outside.

Regret.

TWENTY-THREE

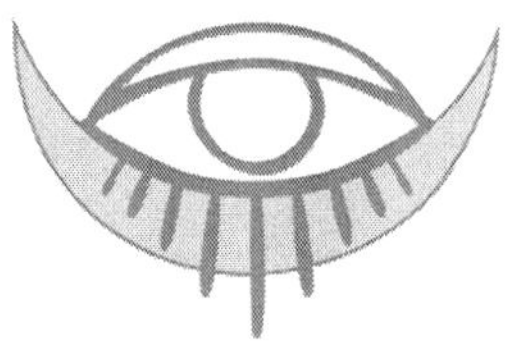

GRAY

The wind gusted, whipping the ocean into frothy white peaks and threatening to steal the breath from my lungs. Unperturbed by the cold, Sparkle and Sunshine bounded along the shore, chasing the receding tide and running from the surge like twin puppies.

Personally, I would've rather met Deirdre in a cozy little café in town, where we could sip hot mochas by a crackling fire. But it was better this way. Safer. We had a lot of ground to cover, and we couldn't risk being overheard.

I needed to know about the Silversbane legacy. My blood magic. If my blood was powerful enough to call my ancestors out of their eternal rest, surely it was powerful enough for other magic, too.

Like restoring Darius's memories.

It sounded crazy. Impossible. But after my disastrous reunion with Darius last night, I couldn't stop thinking about it. He'd remembered my nickname, and when he bit my lip, the taste of my blood had affected him deeply. Not in any way I could put into words. Just in a way I could feel, right down to my soul.

Darius and I were blood bound. Deeply connected. Mated, for all intents and purposes. And that connection hadn't broken. How could it? It wasn't linked to memory, but to blood—something he hadn't lost at all. I wanted him to remember our bond for my own emotional reasons, but physically, that bond still existed. I'd felt it drawing us close last night. I'd seen it in his eyes, even if it wasn't there in his mind.

When he'd healed me with his blood in the Shadowrealm, I'd connected to his past, sensing the memories of his former life, seeing them play out before me like a dream. It was as if he'd transferred them to me through the blood bond.

I didn't know what that meant, or how—if at all—that could help now. But there was something to it. I could feel it.

The memory eater demons had stolen the memories from Darius's mind. But maybe they weren't *gone*. Maybe there was a backup copy.

My blood was the key—I was sure of it. I just couldn't figure out how. The solution was there though, like a dream you try to chase into the waking hours, losing it at dawn only to get it back in flashes later on.

Right now, I was pinning my hopes on Deirdre. On my so-called super special Silversbane magic.

"Thank you for meeting me," I said when she finally crested the dune at the edge of the parking lot and joined me on the beach. "I didn't know who else to call."

Deirdre pulled her jacket close around her throat, the wind ruffling her short gray hair. Her eyes held the same grandmotherly warmth she'd showed me in Vegas. "I'm glad you called me, Rayanne. There's still so much I want to tell you. So much you need to know."

"How did you manage to slip away?" I asked her.

"Oh, I'm not really his prisoner." She lowered her eyes, her cheeks coloring. "Sebastian and I have an odd arrangement that dates back many years. I belong to him, and can never truly leave, but I'm not chained to him. I come and go, largely as I please."

"Do you *want* to leave him?"

She looked taken aback, as though no one had ever asked her the question before. Maybe they hadn't. I wasn't even sure what possessed me to ask, other than the fact that I was still trying to get a handle on how Sebastian operated. On whether I'd ever have a chance at truly leaving him after this momentary reprieve was over.

"No," she finally said, linking our arms and leading me further down the beach, Sparkle and Sunshine trailing behind us. "I made my choices. It's not always perfect, but this is my life now, and has been for a long time. *He* is my life."

"Are you… in love with him?" I did my best to keep the judgment from my tone, but I wasn't sure I succeeded.

To her credit, Deirdre didn't flinch.

"No," she said plainly. "Sebastian believes he's in love with me, but like many men before him, he confuses love with obsession, and that obsession has driven him to madness. His focus is single-minded, and when he fixates on something…"

She stopped along the shore, gazing out at the foamy sea. Far out on the horizon, the sun was struggling to peek through the clouds, but the clouds were winning that particular battle. Such was life on the Pacific coast.

When she turned to face me again, it looked like she'd aged a decade.

"So what is it you want to know about blood magic?" she asked, dropping the subject of Sebastian altogether. "I thought you didn't want to summon your ancestors until after you'd dealt with the conflicts facing your people here."

"I don't." I pulled my jacket sleeves down over my hands, blowing into them for warmth as we continued our walk. Elena had picked up a bunch of new clothes for me, but I forgot to ask for gloves. "I need to know how blood is linked to memory."

"To memory?" She narrowed her eyes, scrutinizing my face. "Is this related to the situation with Darius?"

Nodding, I took a deep breath of salty air, trying to put my jumbled thoughts into words.

Doing my best not to sound like a mad scientist, I told Deirdre about what'd happened in the Shadowrealm, and my tissue-paper-thin theory about a possible backup copy of Darius's memories.

It sounded crazy saying it all out loud. But if there was even a chance that my blood could heal him, could restore even a fraction of Darius's memories, I wanted to know how to try.

"Your relationship with Darius is unique," she said, stopping to pick up a piece of driftwood and throwing it down the shore for Sparkle. The hound bolted after it, chasing it into the surf, then promptly forgetting about it. "What you're trying to do… Well, to be perfectly honest, I've never heard of something like it before. But that doesn't mean it's not possible. A vampire blood bond is a deep, deep connection. You and Darius have that link. And yes, that link could store some residual memories."

Hope warmed my insides, and I let loose a smile—the first one of the day. "Do you think it's possible I could somehow transfer them back? Magically?"

"Possible, yes. Anything is possible. The fact that you're here instead of locked away in Sebastian's realm shows you that much. The problem is that it's too risky, Rayanne. If you attempt a blood spell, you may end up summoning your ancestors after all."

"But I wouldn't do a summoning spell. This would be something else."

"We don't know what this 'something else' would entail. It might be very much like a summoning spell." She shook her head, dashing my hopes. "I'm sorry. I have to advise against it."

"So what you're telling me is the only thing this Silversbane blood is good for is doing Sebastian's dirty work?"

"Don't say that," she said. "Blood as powerful as yours is a gift."

"My blood is a curse." I kicked at the rocky shoreline. If I couldn't use my blood or my magic to help the man I loved, what was the point? "And Sebastian wants to weaponize it against my ancestors."

Deirdre stiffened. "Rayanne—"

"Gray. I go by Gray now." Rayanne was a remnant of a past too painful to remember. The only other person who still called me by that name was Jonathan, and he wasn't even a person anymore.

"*Gray,*" she said, though I could tell she wasn't fond of the name. "He's not interested in your deceased ancestors. He's interested in your mother."

"Calla?" I asked, alarmed.

Deirdre shook her head. "Your biological mother. My daughter-in-law."

"Doesn't she count as a deceased ancestor?"

"Oh, child. There is so much..." Deirdre's face paled, her mouth pulling into a deep frown. The wind stilled. The hounds stopped chasing each other up ahead. Even the waves hushed, as if they, too, were waiting to hear her next confession.

"I'm afraid your mother isn't dead, Gray. A fugitive from hell, but very much alive."

TWENTY-FOUR

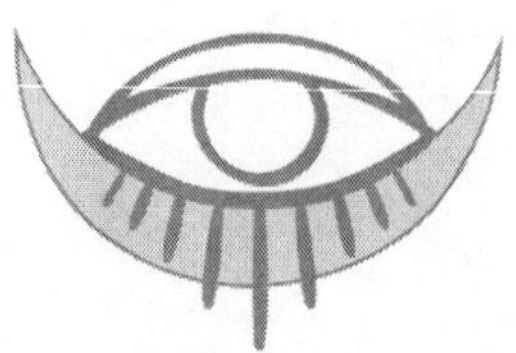

GRAY

Your mother isn't dead… A fugitive from hell… Very much alive…

Deirdre's words slammed into my chest, forcing all the air out of my lungs. She didn't even give me a chance to catch my breath before she continued, her sentences blurring together, each one another blow from which I didn't think I could recover.

"Trinity," she was saying now. "That was her name."

Trinity. I reached back in my mind, but found nothing. No connection. No recognition.

"When she became pregnant with you, she'd already had two of your three sisters—Serena, the oldest, and Adele, a year younger. But you, she insisted, were different. Special."

"Wait. Did I… Did I have another name? Before Rayanne?"

"Morgan Susanna," Deirdre said with a soft smile. "Your name was changed before your adoption to protect you."

"Morgan Susanna." I said it out loud, trying it on for size. It didn't fit. Not at all. Like Rayanne, it felt like someone else's name now. "I think I'll stick with Gray."

"If you must." Deirdre winked. "Anyway, around the twenty-fourth week of your pregnancy, Trinity began to have visions of a fourth daughter, and believed that you and your sisters would become great witches, one day uniting covens in war against supernaturals in a battle for magical dominion on earth."

"Like the prophecy," I said. But it wasn't. Not really. The

prophecy never said anything about a battle for magical dominion. Not specifically.

"Partially," Deirdre said. "But your mother was convinced. You four were the foretold witches, which must also mean she herself was an heir of Silversbane.

"The following year, your sister Georgie—the foreseen fourth daughter—came into being. One month later, your father…" She paused, pressing her hand to her heart. When she spoke again, her voice was thick with emotion. "My son, Thomas Derrick Olivante, disappeared."

Thomas Derrick Olivante.

The name echoed between us. My father.

"Disappeared?" I asked. "What do you mean?"

"The police suspected an affair, possibly a deadbeat dad situation. But I knew better. Your father adored you. He devoted his life to his wife and daughters, and no matter how unhappy or nasty your mother became, he never gave up hope. Never once complained about taking on the burdens of housework or meals or bedtime routines in addition to his regular work, all so your mother could have her endless 'free time.'"

"So what do you think happened to him?"

Her eyes grew cold. "Your mother murdered him, Gray. I was never able to prove that, but my son was not missing. He was dead. A mother knows. I felt the departure of his soul from this realm."

The wind whipped my hair into my face, stinging my eyes. I blinked back my own tears, snuggling deeper into my jacket. "What happened next?"

"Even without your father, you girls were thriving. It quickly became apparent that you were *extremely* powerful witches. Even as babies, you could heal each other's injuries, make flowers grow on barren dirt, find lost objects, predict the future."

Sunshine nipped at my hand, eager for another stick to throw, but I nudged her away, riveted by my grandmother's story.

"Everyone loved the four magical babies of Blackmoon Bay," she said, "but Trinity—"

"Wait. Blackmoon Bay?"

Deirdre nodded. "You four were born there, Gray."

"How is that even possible? I grew up on the east coast, and after Calla died, I just sort of… ended up everywhere else. Including the Bay."

"Yes, and you stopped ending up *anywhere* else once you reached the Bay."

"Because I met Ronan, and he helped me get set up."

"He did. But he would've done that anywhere. You stayed in Blackmoon Bay because the city is part of your soul. It called you home, Gray. Just like it called Haley home. And eventually, it will call your other sisters home, too."

"But Ronan already had a life in the Bay before I came along. Friends. A job."

"He did."

"Don't you think that's kind of a crazy coincidence?" I asked. But then I said, at the same time she did, "There are no coincidences."

We shared a laugh, breaking the tension just a bit.

As we walked a little further down the shore, I linked my arm into hers, suddenly wanting to feel connected to her. Grounded.

Deirdre tucked in closer, too.

"Trinity was a jealous woman," she continued. "Her own mother was quite powerful, too, yet she'd never inherited the gift. Trinity's witchcraft was mediocre at best, relying heavily on tricks and sleight of hand. The idea that her infant and toddler daughters possessed so much power, when she herself had virtually none, finally drove her mad.

"Desperate to claim your power for herself, she tried all kinds of magical experiments and spells on you and your sisters, but nothing worked—largely because she didn't have the skill, but also because it was against the natural order. Stealing another witch's power… It's an abomination. No force or entity or energy outside of her own greed would've aided in something so sinister. So, Trinity remained as weak as ever, while her daughters continued to grow in power. Finally, in a last act of desperation—"

"Oh, no." I closed my eyes, swallowing hard. "Don't tell me. This is the part where the evil villainess gathers up a bottle of blood and a box of chicken bones and heads down to the crossroads…"

"Yes, Gray," she said, her tone grim again. "Your mother made a crossroads deal—no bones or blood necessary. Sebastian, as you know, trades in souls."

A shiver ran through me, making my teeth chatter. Was my mother the one who'd sold me out to Sebastian in the first place? How could she have done such a thing?

I opened my mouth to ask, but Deirdre was already speaking again.

"The terms were simple: her daughters' magic in exchange for her own mortal soul, to be collected in ten years' time."

I sighed in relief. Something told me this story had a terrible ending, but at least my mother hadn't sold my soul. A dim light in a room full of darkness, but a light nevertheless.

"But like most people in their hour of utter desperation," she said, "Trinity neglected to read the fine print. She got her daughters' magic, sure, but not in the way she intended."

"What do you mean?"

"Well, from you, she got the ability to bring the dead back to life—so long as the deceased was a plant in need of some water and sunlight. From Serena, she got the power to summon spirits with a drop of her blood—but only the spirits of her long-dead childhood cats, Maise and Matilda. Adele's gift of foresight allowed her to see into the future—by fifteen seconds. And thanks to Georgie, who'd go on to become a talented herbalist by age three, your mother became adept at brewing tea."

"That's… it? That sounds like a practical joke."

"Oh, it was no joke. She'd asked for her daughters' magic, and that's what she got. She just wasn't specific."

"I'm assuming she didn't just let it go at that," I said. "Chalk it up to a lesson learned."

"No. She didn't." Deirdre shook her head, her eyes clouding with some ancient sadness I could only guess at. "Your mother wasn't well. Not by any definition."

An icy chill slid across my skin, my whole body erupting in goosebumps. Something dark and malicious slithered out of my memory, seeping into my mind, bringing with it flashes of something it'd long since tried to bury.

It was part of the same memory I'd recalled when Deirdre had first mentioned the name Silversbane in our meeting with Sebastian—the dark-haired woman at the creek, frantic, manic, forcing me into the water. Holding my head under, even as I fought for my last breath.

"I am Silversbane! This magic is my *legacy. Mine! Why should you have it when it was promised to me? My birthright! You have stolen it, Shadowborn filth!"*

New memories rushed in, filling in the gaps. My mother had promised to take us for a walk in the woods. She'd bundled us up in winter coats and hats, even Georgie, who still needed to be put in a carrier.

But she hadn't bothered with our socks or boots. She marched us into the winter woods, our feet freezing. All of us were crying.

"No, mama!" Serena cried. "Don't put Delly in there. She can't swim!"

Delly. Adele. My mother pushed her into the creek first, then me. Delly crawled out on her own. My mother held me under, waiting for the cold water to press the breath from my lungs.

"Stay down! Stop squirming, little bitch!"

"Mama, stop!"

The pain in my skull had been unbearable. The blackness closing in faster than I could fight…

"It was her," I gasped, the images finally receding. "At the creek in the woods behind our house."

Deirdre frowned. I waited for her to deny it. To provide some other explanation. But all she said was, "I'd always hoped you girls were too young to remember. But darkness like that makes an impression on your very soul. It never leaves you."

"My mother tried to drown us," I said, needing to hear the words spoken out loud, even if Deirdre herself couldn't say them. Even if they tore up my insides on the way out.

"Yes," she said. "All four of you."

"My mother tried to murder her babies," I said again, as if it would make any more sense the second time around. It didn't; this was a tale that only got more horrifying in the telling.

"I had long since suspected your mother in your father's disappearance, but without proof, there wasn't much I could do. She never prevented me from seeing you four girls, so I did what I could to protect you—charms, spells of protection, amulets sewn into the hems of your clothing. I visited as often as I could. It wasn't enough."

"So that's how we survived that day? Protective charms?"

"That may have been part of it. But there was also a neighbor walking his dog in the woods behind his property. He heard your sister screaming for help, and ran down to the creek to find out what was going on. He told us later that your mother had insisted she was trying to save you—that Serena and Adele had snuck you and Georgie out of the house while she was in the shower, knowing that you weren't permitted in the woods alone. She'd chased after you as soon as she'd noticed you missing. She said you and Adele had fallen in the water. He called me as soon as he got your mother and you girls back to the house. She was refusing to seek medical attention for you.

"That night," Deirdre continued, "I called on the help of my coven sisters. We cast a powerful spell to put your mother to sleep and to fully open her to the power of suggestion. While the sisters took the four of you out of the house, I worked to manipulate your mother's memory, making her believe she'd succeeded in killing you. The coven and I saw to your adoptions, ensuring your mother never knew what had truly happened."

Tears that had nothing to do with the bitter wind slid down my cheeks, as salty as the sea before us. My chest hurt, the pain of that day fresh in my lungs. In my skull. I didn't know what hurt worse—nearly drowning in icy water, or learning years later that your own mother had tried to murder you. Sunshine and Sparkle pressed against my legs, stopping me from walking. Absently I reached down to pet Sunshine's head, rubbing the notched edge of her ear. She nuzzled my hand, and the pain in my chest receded, just a little.

Wiping the tears from my eyes, I turned my attention back to

Deirdre, searching for the right question to ask next. This, I sensed, was only the beginning of a much longer, much more sinister story, and I needed to tread carefully.

I didn't know what other memories might be unlocked.

"How did she—" I began, but before I could finish the question, Deirdre's face paled, her eyes widening in fear.

The hounds yelped, taking off down the shore, and Deirdre raised her hands in front of her chest.

Magic, I thought.

"Down," she ordered. "Now!"

I didn't hesitate. Just dropped to the rocky shore and covered my head, barely ducking the blast of Deirdre's magic. Beams of bright, yellow-orange light shot out from her hands, and I twisted around to see the magic slam into a man charging toward us, gun drawn. The attack knocked him on his ass, unconscious, but more men followed in his wake, at least half a dozen goons not far behind. They rushed at us, even as the hounds bounded right for them.

"Hunters," she deadpanned.

"Where did they come from?" I got to my feet, bringing my hands to my chest, palms out. I hadn't used my magic since the battle with the memory eaters in the Shadowrealm, but it came to me easy now, blue flame sparking to life in my hands.

Still, it wasn't enough. I could feel it. I was out of practice, and the hunters were closing in fast.

"I don't know," she said, "but we're about to get up close and personal with a couple more."

Closing my eyes and calling on the magic of the earth, I drew more power into my core, pushing it out through my limbs, charging my entire body.

"Now!" Deirdre shouted, and I opened my eyes and sent a blast of energy outward right alongside hers just as two hunters drew their guns on us. Deirdre and I hit them at the same time. Her man went down, unconscious like the last. Mine only stumbled and gasped.

Ten feet away, Sunshine let out a primal growl that made the hairs on the back of my neck stand up. I saw her lunge at someone, knocking him into the water. Sparkle was still running down the beach—chasing after another hunter who'd turned tail.

Where had these assholes come from? Were they part of Jonathan's group? Part of the prison hunters?

"You're up again, Gray," Deirdre said, queuing up another blast as my guy righted himself and another one charged at Deirdre.

I took a deep breath and tried again, drawing in power as a spell took shape in my mind:

Goddess of the earth, Goddess of the sea
In this battle, I call upon thee
Lend me your strength, avail me of your power
Before this magic, make my enemies cower

Channeling my intentions into the words, I repeated the spell out loud, forcing the magic out through my palms.

The force of my attack was so strong, so unexpected, I had to fight to stay on my feet. It slammed into both hunters, simultaneously knocking them backward, dashing their heads against a sharp, rocky outcropping at the water's edge.

The tide surged forward, staining the beach with their blood.

"Oh, shit," Deirdre whispered. "That's… not good."

"We need to call Emilio," I said as the rest of the hunters took off, disappearing down the shore the way they'd come. "They might be part of the group he's looking for."

We jogged to catch up with the hounds. Sparkle had dragged her quarry back to Sunshine, and now the two feasted on his body.

His face was mangled beyond recognition.

"Sparkle," I called. "Sunshine. Come."

They stopped their gorging and stood at attention, wagging their massive tails, panting, tongues lolling, blood and flesh dripping from their razor-sharp fangs as they padded over to me.

They were a goddamn nightmare, and if I'd eaten lunch, I'd be spewing it all over the beach. Yet when I looked at them now, all I could feel was gratitude.

"So," Deirdre said, placing a tired hand on my back as she tried to catch her breath, "next time we plan a grandma-granddaughter outing, maybe we could try something a little more traditional? Knitting club, perhaps? Checkers?"

The leftover energy from the magic and the fight made me jittery, and I let out a nervous laugh, grateful for the small release. "Something tells me you're not the knitting and checkers type, Grams."

"No, child. I suppose I'm not." She let out a sigh, pulling her coat tight around her neck. There were so many words in that sigh, so many things still unsaid between us. But for now, she shook her head, looking at me with tired, knowing eyes. "And I'm sorry to tell you, neither are you."

I looked down at my palms, the center spot where my magic had emanated from. Two men had died by my hands, yet my hands were clean, the skin smooth and unmarred.

Inside, the magic stirred. Warming me. Comforting me. Reminding me that like Deirdre, I wasn't born to have a normal life. I could pretend otherwise, I could fight that fact as hard as I'd fought my mother when she'd held my head under that freezing water.

But in the end, the only choice I really had was acceptance.

I was a Silversbane witch. The witch of the prophecy. And my work was just beginning.

TWENTY-FIVE

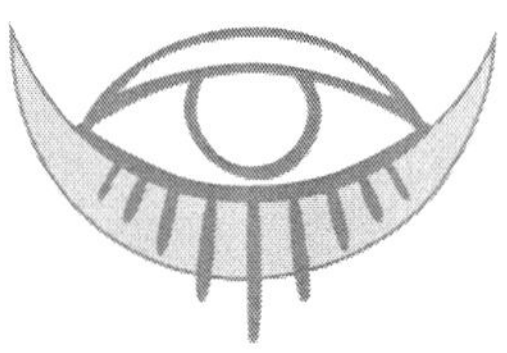

GRAY

Vita mutatur, non tollitur.

The words were printed on the Tarot card I'd drawn, and I repeated them out loud, tracing my finger over each one.

Life is changed, not taken away.

Emilio, Elena, and the RCPD shifter squad had arrived on the beach minutes after Deirdre's call. Emilio took our statements, then ordered Hobb to bring me and the hounds back to the house. Not wanting to leave town after the attack on my life, Deirdre checked herself into a hotel in the city. Ronan and Darius were gone when I got back. Now I was alone on Elena's couch, looking for guidance from the universe.

Be careful what you wish for.

It was the first time I'd used my new deck, and I'd drawn—of course—the Death card. Unlike the ominous Death card in Sophie's deck, this one was more peaceful, featuring a pale, nude woman lying on a moss-covered rock in a serene forest. The angel of Death stood behind her in his black cloak, come to claim her soul. Butterflies danced in the rays of light that illuminated her body, and lilies grew in the moss at the base of the rock. Carved in stone were those words, Death's ultimate message:

Vita mutatur, non tollitur.

Life is changed, not taken away.

It appeared to me now, the card and the message, reminding

me that I was in the midst of my own inevitable change. That even as one life died, another was just beginning.

I'd asked Sebastian for an extension on my contract—enough time to save my friends and deal with the threats facing us. Fighting, learning to grow and strengthen my magic, training, backing up my rebels—all of those things were important. But if I was truly the Silversbane heir—truly the witch of prophecy—then I needed to learn how to lead. How to inspire. How to save and protect the witches I loved as well as the witches I'd never even met.

I needed to find a way to bring us all together—witches and supernaturals alike—uniting us against the mounting threats facing our communities. Was I ready for all that?

For so long, I'd lived in the shadows, hiding my witchcraft, denying my magical heritage, pretending to be anything but who I really was. Eventually, destiny caught up with me. And now I was doing my best to keep up with *it*. Was I even worthy of the Silversbane legacy?

I closed my eyes, pressing the Death card to my chest. I wanted so, so badly to talk to Liam. This was exactly the kind of philosophical dilemma he loved to talk about, and his words of wisdom had never failed to open my eyes to new perspectives, new possibilities. I was still so angry with him. But I also needed him. Wanted him. Wanted his companionship, his hopelessly confusing explanations about the natural order, his jokes, his sweet kisses.

Yet he'd betrayed me. How could I reconcile the two? How could I hate a man I still cared so deeply for?

I couldn't. That was the answer. I couldn't hate Liam any more than I could deny I was Silversbane. Maybe that was part of what I needed to accept, too. That people made mistakes. That even Death made mistakes.

Oh, Liam. Where are you?

Ever since he'd confessed to me about his deal with Sebastian, I'd assumed that was the betrayal I'd dreamed about, the one the Three of Swords card had warned about in Sophie's book of shadows. But sitting here now, holding the Death card and reflecting on all the things Deirdre had shared today, I wasn't so sure anymore.

My heart felt like it'd been run through with so many swords. Liam's confessions, Ronan's deal that would forever keep us apart, my own mother trying to drown me. In light of the last one, how could I hold any anger toward Liam? He'd never meant for me to die. He'd never even meant to hurt me. And though it was the ultimate outcome, sending my soul to Sebastian had never been his intention—he'd honestly thought I'd be honored to become Death, just as he was. And at that time, he wasn't even human—not in the way I thought of him now.

My own mother had tried to drown me and my sisters. Her babies. And she likely killed my father, too.

"Things are not always what they seem," came a voice in my mind, warm and bubbly and belonging only to one person: my Sophie. She'd said those very words to me in my magic realm, right after I'd read about the Three of Swords in her book of shadows. I didn't dare open my eyes, didn't dare break the vision.

"Do you think I should forgive him?" I asked.

"Liam? I think you already have."

I shook my head, still resisting the idea. Could forgiveness really come that easily? *Should* it?

"Open your eyes, girl," she said, and even though I didn't want to lose her, I did as she asked. Sophie never led me astray.

The Death card came back into view, but when I looked up, I was no longer on the couch in Elena's living room, wrapped up in a blanket dotted with lighthouses. Instead, I found myself sitting on a carpet of velvety green grass in a meadow I'd missed for far too long. My realm. The source of my magic. A place I hadn't seen since Jonathan had taken me hostage.

"You shouldn't be here," a deep voice bellowed. "It isn't safe."

"Liam?" I looked up and met his gaze, startled at the force of what I saw there. Happiness. Longing. Sorrow. Regret. Love. All of it flickering through his ancient blue eyes, completely disarming me.

He was back in his shadow form, an uncanny reminder of the angel of Death in the Tarot card, but he was still Liam. I saw the humanity in his eyes—a depth and nuance that wasn't there when I'd first met him in this form. I wondered if he'd always carry Liam with him. Always carry our time together.

He sat down in the grass next to me, not too close. He was giving me space. Testing the waters.

"I haven't captured Jonathan yet," he said. "He's eluded me at every turn. If he attacked you here, I…" He trailed off, gazing out across the meadow, no longer looking at me.

"You're… still tracking him?" I wasn't sure why that surprised me, but it did.

"I've been hunting him since I returned from burning your scroll at the Great Hall of Records, Gray. This is your realm, and Sebastian has granted you temporary freedom. You shouldn't be kept away by the threats of a madman, or by anyone—or anything—else."

"I agree, but you didn't have to—"

"I wanted to. I *want* to."

We sat in companionable silence, the breeze caressing my skin. After my day at the beach, this felt warm and pleasurable, like the very end of summer when it's no longer hot and humid, but before the air turns chilly. The scents of lavender and lilacs filled the air, as sweet and clean as I remembered.

"I miss it," I said. "Being here. Back before I knew about… well, anything, really."

"That's the thing about knowledge," he said. "Once you know a thing, you can't unknow it. Unless, of course…"

He trailed off, and I knew he was thinking of Darius. The memory eaters.

I ran my hand over the grass beside me, the soft blades tickling my palm. "Well, here's something I now know. I have three sisters. Also, I'm the witch of prophecy. And my mother tried to murder us when we were babies."

Liam didn't say anything.

"I suppose you already knew all that," I said.

He nodded. I wasn't surprised, but it still stung. He'd kept so much from me. Not just as Death, but as Liam. As my friend. As a man I was starting to love. He was *still* keeping things from me.

Things about my future. About all the possibilities. Things about my past.

But maybe that was part of what it meant to love someone, too —shielding them from the painful truths. It wasn't always the best policy, but sometimes, you carried their pain so they wouldn't have to.

My heart hurt. Being this close to him… I wanted him back in my life. Back in my world. But that could never happen now. He'd failed to pass on the Death mantle to me. Now, that was his eternal calling. His prison.

"Will you seek them?" he asked.

"I already know about Haley," I said. "But as for the others… How could I not? We're supposed to band together and unify the covens." I drew my knees up to my chest. "I don't know what that means. I don't know what that would look like. I don't even know where to start."

"You've already begun, little witch." Liam smiled, his eyes shining with pride. "You've managed to get the upper hand with the Prince of Hell. I'd say that's a very good start."

I wasn't so sure about that. Sebastian had given me an extension, but he could call it back whenever he felt like it. For all intents and purposes, I was living on borrowed time, and a loan from the Prince of Hell came with the highest interest rates around.

"I need to ask you something," I said. "The woman whose soul you were supposed to bring Sebastian—the one who'd bailed on her contract. It was my mother, wasn't it?"

Liam met my eyes again, his smile fading. If he was uncomfortable with this line of questioning, though, he didn't show it, and I knew that whatever he said next would be the truth. I couldn't explain why, but in that moment, it felt like we'd come to a new understanding. Liam wouldn't lie to me about this. I knew it in my bones.

"It was," he finally said. "She made a deal with him many years ago, but when it came time to collect, she vanished."

"My grandmother says she's still alive. A fugitive from hell."

"Oh, Trinity is very much alive. Undetectable, though I'm

fairly certain she's still on the material plane. It's likely she has powerful allies protecting her."

"Powerful allies, like who? Who could be that powerful—or that stupid—to harbor a fugitive of hell?"

"If we knew, I'm certain Sebastian would've found her by now. There are many factions, Gray. Many groups and subgroups and beings who believe things should be different, and any one of those groups may have been sympathetic to your mother's cause, especially if they believed she could eventually connect them with the Silversbane heirs."

"She supposedly thinks we're dead."

"Yes. Let's hope it stays that way." On that ominous note, Liam rose from the grass, offering a hand to help me up. I took it, standing up and tilting my face up to meet his gaze once more.

"Where will you go after this?" I asked.

"I have been ordered to resume my duties, as I knew I must." The finality in his words pressed down on me like a physical weight, tightening my chest, making it difficult to breathe.

"Will I see you again?" I asked, fighting to keep the tremor from my voice.

"This is not goodbye for us, Gray. I assure you. But it may be some time before we see each other again."

"But… I don't understand. Can't you visit as Liam? Like you used to?"

"Not as Liam, I'm afraid. If I return to you on the material plane at all, it shall be in my raven form." He cupped my cheeks, his black gloves like spider webs against my skin. "Pray that I do not return, for if you see my raven by your side, know that I am there only to escort the departed soul of someone you love."

"I don't want to go back without you," I breathed, my eyes falling closed over tears. I was losing him all over again. "I'm not done being mad at you yet. And I'm not done forgiving you."

"Your words have given me more hope than you can imagine."

"Then why do I feel like this *is* goodbye? Why does it feel like… like you're dying?"

"*Vita mutatur, non tollitur.*" He lowered his mouth to mine, pressing a soft kiss to my lips that unleashed a shower of sparks between us.

"Please don't go," I whispered when he pulled away.

"I must." He stroked my cheeks, a few remaining sparks still lingering. "Though I didn't understand it at the time, this was always the only possible outcome for me, Gray. But your story has many, many volumes before you reach your final outcome, and most of them have not yet been written."

I nodded, and he released my face, the bright blue of his eyes fading as I slowly drifted back to consciousness. When I opened my eyes again, I was back on Elena's couch, still clutching the Tarot card to my chest.

This one wasn't the Death card, though. It was the Star. A card of healing and renewal. A card of hope.

TWENTY-SIX

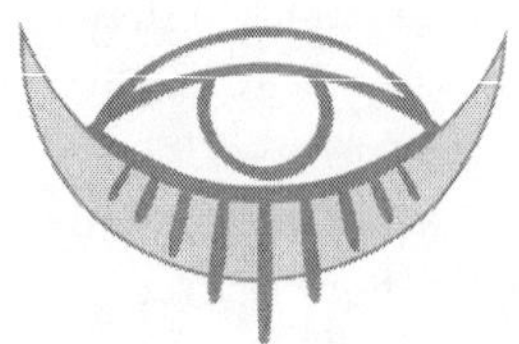

EMILIO

If ever there was a sight for sore eyes, it was her.

The moment I walked in the door and spotted her on Elena's couch, curled up with her new Tarot cards and a mug of tea, her legs wrapped in a blanket, my heart nearly stopped.

She was beautiful. She was here. She was whole.

Ever since she'd been taken from us at the safe house, I'd dreamed of this moment. Having her back. Safe. She'd been in Raven's Cape for days, back in my care, but I still couldn't get used to it.

And after today, when I saw the carnage on the beach and thought she'd been hurt…

I clenched my fists, wishing I could have torn those hunters apart myself. It was a wonder I let the ones we'd captured live.

If we hadn't needed their intel, I don't think I would have.

Gray sipped her tea, thumbing to a new card in her deck. She hadn't heard me yet, and I took a minute to watch her, to soak it all in, memorizing the image.

I could come home to this every night for a thousand years and never get tired of it…

When she finally sensed my presence and turned her face toward me, a smile stretched across her lips, lighting me up from the inside.

"Emilio," she breathed. She set down her cards and mug,

fighting her way out of the lighthouse blanket that'd tangled around her legs.

"Don't get up. I'll come to you." I took off my coat and my holster, then joined her on the couch, pulling her legs into my lap. She snuggled in closer, tucking her head beneath my chin. Her hair tickled my neck, and I breathed in her sweet scent, wrapping my arms around her, holding her close.

If I had my way, I'd never let her go.

"Tell me the update," she said.

"Do I have to? I'd much rather pretend we're here on vacation, taking a break from a long day of… well, whatever it is people do on vacation."

"That sounds nice," she said dreamily, letting us both live in the fantasy a little longer. I pressed my lips to the top of her head, kissing her hair.

She sighed contentedly, but despite her outward calmness, I felt the anxiety spike in her energy. She needed to know where we were at with the hunters.

Blowing out a breath, I said, "The guys Deirdre knocked out? We brought them in for questioning once they regained consciousness."

Gray swallowed hard. "And the… others?"

"After our investigation, we concluded they killed each other during an argument," I said firmly. If Gray thought I'd let her take the fall for killing the men whose sole mission had been to kill *her*, she was crazy. "Case closed."

"Any sign of the prison?" she asked.

"Jael picked up the signature of fae spellwork near the sight, but he said it was an inactive spell, already fading. There were no signs of any cave entrances or activity in the area. No footprints, no litter, no disturbed plant life. None of the things we usually see when we've got activity in an area near the beach. Ronan and Darius are still combing the shoreline, looking to see if we missed anything."

She arched an eyebrow. "So Ronan let Darius out on good behavior?"

"He seems to have mellowed out a bit since your… encounter."

She lowered her eyes, her cheeks darkening. The scent of her desire drifted on the air, threatening to send me into a frenzy. God, she was beautiful.

"Did the hunters give you anything to go on?" she asked, shifting so she could look up at me. The movement of her legs made my cock stand up and take notice.

Not a good time, bud.

"Not… especially." I shifted, trying to steer my wayward thoughts back to the topic at hand. The case, not the gorgeous witch sitting in my lap. "Lansky and I did the good cop, bad cop routine for hours, but all we managed to learn was that Jonathan has gone missing, and no one knows what the hell they're supposed to do now."

"I'm pretty sure he's still trapped in my realm," she said. "I… connected with Liam earlier, and he said he's been tracking him there, trying to make sure he doesn't get out. Even if he does, though, I doubt his men would even recognize him anymore." She shuddered against me, undoubtedly remembering her encounters with the deformed creature formerly known as Jonathan in the Shadowrealm.

I ran my hand down her back, calming her.

"It's hard to differentiate fact from fiction with these assholes," I said, "but from what we've gathered so far, it sounds like there's a separate faction of hunters that splintered off from Jonathan's group, and they're working more closely with the Darkwinter fae."

"So, Jonathan *wasn't* working with fae?"

"He may have been, but for whatever reason, others have moved in on his territory. Like I said, these guys are pretty tight-lipped, and half of what they're feeding us is probably bullshit, but it's starting to sound more like a coup."

"The ones you picked up from the beach—those were definitely Jonathan's guys?"

"Yes. They had brands on their arms that matched the ones

Darius saw on the hunters who attacked him in the hotel room, as well as the markings we found on—"

"Sophie and the other witches." She shuddered again.

"We still don't know what the markings mean, if anything."

"Probably some kind of sigil magic. Jonathan was so desperate, trying any combination of magic he could get his hands on, cherry-picking his way across all kinds of traditions and lore."

"What worries me is that this other group may have better resources. More capabilities." I pulled the blanket up around her shoulder, holding her close again. "It happens in the business world all the time. The little fish invents something useful, but doesn't quite know how to manage or market it. Big fish comes in and gobbles up the company, expanding on it, branching out. Taking it global."

We'd talked a little bit after dinner the other night about the situation in the Bay, and our theories about the wider implications of Darkwinter's involvement and the Council's treachery. We still hadn't put together the whole story, but we were getting closer, piece by painstaking piece. And the picture all these clues were starting to paint did *not* look good.

"So what happens now?" she asked.

"My sister and Hobb are taking a crack at the interrogation, trying to get more info out of these guys. But we can't hold them much longer without charging them. And without physical evidence of a crime—"

"They attacked me and my grandmother," she said, pulling out of my embrace to shoot me an incredulous look.

I shrugged. "And they're witnesses to the fact that you and your hounds killed four of their friends—something we *definitely* don't want getting out, especially to the human cops on the force. On the record, those assholes killed each other. And right now, the hunters left standing aren't going to push the issue because they believe we're getting too close to the truth as it is, and they're still loyal to Jonathan. They don't want to draw any more police attention than they already have. But if we start charging them with a crime, digging in deeper, they're gonna fight back like caged animals."

"This is… I'm so… God, I feel like tearing my hair out. Literally." She rose from the couch, fisting her hair and pulling tight, her eyes squeezing shut. "Maybe I should go down to the station, see if your sister can use me for anything."

"Elena and her team are handling things at the station," I said. "There's nothing you can do for her right now."

"But I need to do… *something*." She opened her eyes, piercing me with her fiery gaze. "I'm going crazy here, Emilio!"

"You need to take a hot bath and relax. You should take advantage now—no one else is here."

"But—"

"The case will still be waiting for us in the morning," I said. "I promise we'll all regroup and go over everything with fresh eyes and a big breakfast. Okay?"

She opened her mouth to protest, but then closed it, letting out a soft sigh.

"A hot bath does sound kind of heavenly right now." She smiled again, her eyes lighting up, the tension already lifting from her shoulders. "Okay, *El Lobo.* You win."

"Good. I'm glad you're going willingly. Now I don't have to strip you down and throw you into that tub myself."

She raised an eyebrow. "Was that an option? You didn't mention that in your initial pitch."

"I… uh…" *Oh, Gray. What are you* doing *to me?* I rose from the couch, turning away from her sexy, mischievous smile. "I'll… go find you a towel. And some bubbles. And candles."

And a cold shower for myself, thank you.

"You've thought of everything," she teased.

"Trust me, *mi brujita bonita.* You have *no* idea what I'm thinking."

TWENTY-SEVEN

GRAY

If thoughtful gestures and all-around sweetness were Olympic sports, Emilio would take the gold every time. He'd drawn the bath for me, filling it with lavender bubbles and lining the window ledge with candles, giving me a little spa retreat in the midst of the chaos. There was also a generous glass of white wine on the edge of the tub and a fluffy white bathrobe hanging on the hook behind the door.

He truly had thought of everything.

Stepping into the tub was pure decadence, my muscles instantly relaxing in the heat. I could've stayed there all night, waiting for my skin to prune. But despite the pleasure of the bath, all I really wanted to do was get back to Emilio.

Hoping he wouldn't mind too much, I cut my spa night a little shorter than I'd planned, wrapping myself in the fluffy robe and heading out into the living room. The warm, healing scent of fresh-baked brownies drifted on the air, making my mouth water.

I found Emilio on the couch, sitting before an untouched pan of brownies and two big glasses of cold, frothy milk on the coffee table.

I didn't even try to hide my goofy grin.

You crazy wolf. What would I do without you?

"Feeling better?" he asked.

"How could I not be? I just had a hot bubble bath and a glass of wine, and now I come out here to discover that a really cute guy made me brownies."

Emilio made a show of looking around. "What guy? I'll kill him."

Laughing, I took a seat next to him on the couch.

"And how do you know these brownies are for you?" he teased.

"Because torture isn't your style. You're too good to me to withhold such vital goodness." Not waiting for permission, I grabbed a spoon, then dug into the pan. It was, I'd learned, the best way to eat Emilio's sweet-and-spicy triple-chocolate brownies.

The warm, gooey, chocolatey goodness exploded on my tongue, chased with just the right kick of chili pepper. Orgasmic, as usual.

Emilio laughed as I shoved in a few more spoonfuls.

"Hey. Would you mind sharing?" he teased, nudging me in the ribs. "I did after all make them for both of us."

I scooped up a spoonful for him, cupping a hand under his chin as I spoon-fed him. His mouth engulfed the entire end of the spoon, soft lips brushing against my fingers.

We took turns feeding each other, demolishing half the pan before we even took a break for milk. Then, we dove back in.

Finally, when I couldn't take another bite of the rich, chocolatey perfection, I set down the spoon and leaned back on the couch.

"That's it?" he asked incredulously. "There's still at least a third left."

"I can't eat another bite," I said.

"Lightweight." Emilio leaned back, putting his arm around me. I snuggled in close, inhaling his sweet, outdoorsy scent. Everything about him was so good, so warm, so… pure. It was a strange way to describe a lone wolf shifter, perhaps, but it fit. At a time where everything was going dark, Emilio was goodness and light.

"What are you thinking about, *querida*?" He asked softly, brushing his knuckles along my upper arm.

I turned to look up at his face, his deep brown eyes shining, his glossy black hair catching the soft lamplight, chocolate staining the edges of his lips. In that moment, he was the most beautiful creature I'd ever seen. He made me feel lucky to be alive, to be here, to be sharing this moment in time with someone so incredible.

And he was looking at me in the exact same way.

"Thank you," I whispered, my throat tightening.

He smoothed his thumb over the corner of my lips, undoubtedly smeared with chocolate, just like his. "For the brownies?"

"Yes, for the brownies. But also for being in my life. For taking such good care of me. For keeping me calm and sane when everything around me is falling apart. For… for looking at me the way you do."

He cocked his head, a teasing smile playing on his lips. "How am I looking at you?"

"Like…" I swallowed the tightness in my throat, my heart thumping, everything in me hoping I was right. Hoping I hadn't misread his feelings. In a faint whisper full of that bright, gossamer hope, I said, "Like you want to kiss me."

He watched me a long moment, his eyes intense, his smile receding. For one mortifying, terrifying instant, I thought I'd made the wrong call.

Then he traced his thumb along the bottom of my lip, sliding his fingers along my jaw.

"I will always be in your life, *mi brujita*. That is a promise. As for wanting to kiss you…"

He held my gaze another agonizing moment, then dipped his head, capturing my mouth in a chocolate-infused kiss that was as hot as it was sweet, the spark of it traveling straight down to my toes.

I reached up and threaded my fingers into his hair, pulling him closer. Without breaking our kiss, he scooped me into his strong arms, lifting me up and carrying me back to his bedroom.

He laid me on the bed, kissing my lips, my neck, slowly working his way down my body as he unwrapped the bathrobe, revealing my naked flesh. He took his time, exploring every inch of bare skin with gentle kisses and soft caresses, his tongue swirling over my nipple, then sucking, his fingers trailing down between my thighs.

I parted for him, welcoming the touch of his strong hands, his warmth. He slid two fingers inside me, his thumb tracing slow circles over my clit.

Everything about his touch was slow and deliberate, gradually electrifying my nerves, winding me tighter and tighter until I was certain I'd burst if I didn't feel him inside me.

He seemed to sense this, and gently made his way back to my mouth, capturing me in a deep, sensual kiss.

He pulled away just a moment, just long enough to strip off his own clothes. He stood before me then, naked in the moonlight, his beautiful, muscular form standing over me like the sculpture of a Greek god. I drank in the sight of him, my eyes tracing the broad lines of his shoulders, the defined muscles of his chest and abs, the trail of dark hair that led down to his cock, hard and massive.

I nodded, giving him a soft smile, and he climbed on top of me, graceful despite his hulking form. Slowly, he lowered his full weight over me, his warmth sliding over my skin like water, like the hot bubble bath I'd just taken, and we lay like that for several long, blissful moments, our hearts beating as one.

Wordlessly, we both sensed when it was time. Emilio shifted, and I parted my thighs, arching my hips.

There was no awkward fumbling or second-guessing, no nervous giggles, no questions, no fear. From the very first brownies he'd ever baked for me, everything between us had been building to this, an ending of one chapter and the beginning of something brand new.

As Emilio slid inside me, stretching me, filling me, I let out a gasp of pleasure, sliding my hands into his hair and pulling his mouth to mine.

"Are you okay, *querida*?" he asked.

"I'm… perfect."

He nipped at my lower lip and smiled. "Agreed."

His eyes turned serious again, sensual, and he rolled his hips, taking his time with every thrust, allowing me to get used to him. We found our rhythm easily, though, our bodies arching, our mouths seeking the warmth of a thousand kisses as we brought each other closer and closer to the edge of bliss.

After an eternity of delicious, deliberate kisses and touches and slow, languid thrusts, I felt my core tighten around him, my nerves tingling.

The orgasm took its time, teasing me, waiting just out of reach as my thighs grew slick with sweat, my breath ragged, my heartbeat pounding a fierce drumbeat behind my ribs.

Emilio pulled out slowly, cupping my face, then slid all the way back inside, his eyes rolling back into his head in a look of pure pleasure, a low, sexy moan rumbling through his chest.

And that was it.

The wave crashed over me, explosive, powerful, rocking me to my core. My thighs trembled with the force of it, the pleasure impossible to contain, and I let go, calling out his name in ecstasy, losing myself in the tumultuous spin as shockwave after shockwave rippled through my body.

Emilio came with the same electrifying force, his body shuddering against me as he gripped my hips, holding me close, breathing my name into the moonlit night as if he were casting his own spell.

I closed my eyes beneath him and felt the hot pulse of our connection, throbbing like a heartbeat that spread throughout my entire body. It bound me to him, and him to me, and us to Ronan and Asher and Darius. Darius might not remember it, Ronan wasn't allowed to act on it, Asher was still a prisoner, but that didn't change what we were.

A family. A *real* family—not the kind who jealously fought to control each other's power, or harmed each other out of spite and anger. But the kind that had each other's backs, no matter how ugly things got. The kind that took turns lifting each other up, stepping up when someone else couldn't, picking up the pieces when someone else's world was falling apart.

Spent and blissed out, Emilio collapsed on top of me, then rolled us so I was on top of him. I laid my head on his chest, listening to the strong, powerful beat of his heart as he traced figure eights on my back.

We stayed that way for a while, sinking into the peaceful moment, the beauty of it.

I lifted my head, resting my chin in my hands against his chest, staring into his eyes.

Emilio smiled, melting me. "What are you thinking, *mi brujita bonita*?"

"I'm thinking…" I arched an eyebrow, unable to hold back my own smile. "Those were some of the best brownies I've ever had."

"*Some* of the best?" Emilio laughed, grabbing me and rolling on top of me once again, tickling me.

"Top five at least," I teased, and the tickling intensified, making me squeal. "Okay, okay! The best! The absolute best! I swear it!"

"Good." He stopped tickling me, once again capturing my gaze with his soulful brown eyes. One look had the power to convey so much, and right now, I felt the force of his love for me. His friendship. His fierce desire to protect our pack.

And there, between my thighs, I felt the force of his love in an entirely different way.

"I'm making another batch tomorrow," he teased, kissing my jaw, his cock hardening further. "And the day after that." Kissing my neck. "And probably every day for the foreseeable future." My collarbone. "I hope you're okay with that."

He slid inside me once again, and I sighed happily, welcoming him in deeper, losing myself in his warmth.

"Emilio Alvarez," I breathed, closing my eyes, a smile stretching across my lips. "I am *more* than okay with that. *So* much more."

TWENTY-EIGHT

GRAY

Even in the arms of my powerful, protective wolf, I still couldn't resist the siren call of those brownies, and an hour after he'd fallen asleep, I slipped out of Emilio's embrace and padded down the hall in search of a midnight snack.

"Gray? Everything okay?"

I jumped at the voice, shocked to find Elena sitting at the dining room table in the dark, sipping tea. She stood up to turn on the overhead light, wincing at the sudden brightness.

"I'm… good," I said, tucking my hair behind my ears. I was wearing the bathrobe, my hair still damp from the shower Emilio and I had taken after our third round of… brownies. "Just looking for a midnight snack."

Elena frowned. "Oooh, I hope it wasn't brownies. I might've finished those."

"No!" I teased, letting out a playful gasp.

"In my defense, *someone* left them out on the coffee table. Abandoned. Clearly, they needed to find a good home."

"Clearly."

"Have a seat," she said, rising from her own. "I'll fix you something."

"You don't have to—"

"It'll be quick, don't worry. I was about to make some more tea, anyway. Do you like *yerba mate?*

"I'm… sure it's amazing," I said, no idea what I was getting into.

Elena buzzed around the kitchen, insisting I stay put and relax. No less than ten minutes later, she was back, with two steaming mugs of the *mate* tea and a plate of toasted, crustless sandwiches, pressed thin with three layers of bread.

"*Sandwiches de miga,*" she said. "This one is ham and cheese, the other are roasted red pepper and asparagus. Try one."

She handed me a plate. I reached for a ham and cheese, taking a bite. Gooey cheese melted into my mouth.

"You just made these?" I asked, marveling at the culinary skills of the Alvarez siblings. I could only imagine what their parents were like in the kitchen. "Wow. Thank you."

"*De nada,*" she said, helping herself to a red pepper sandwich.

We finished our sandwiches and sipped our *mate* through a round of small talk, then her eyes turned more inquisitive, and I knew what was coming next.

"Can I ask you something, Gray? It's kind of personal."

I nodded, smiling into my mug.

"You and the guys…"

My cheeks heated, my smile growing broader.

"You're connected to all of them?" she asked. "Like, romantically?"

"I know it seems… unconventional," I said.

"No, it seems like a lot to manage!"

"As long as they're okay with doing their own laundry, I don't foresee any problems." I laughed. "Honestly? Having a relationship like this… It's not something I ever thought about before they all came crashing into my life. For so long, there was only Ronan. I had such intense feelings for him. I couldn't imagine caring for anyone else on that level."

"Did things between you and Ronan cool off when you met the others?"

"No, just the opposite, actually. This might sound crazy, but being with Ronan, loving someone so deeply like that… I don't know exactly how to explain it. But it made my heart expand. The other guys came together to protect me after I started coming into my powers as a witch. A lot of crazy stuff went down, and we all bonded really quickly after that."

"I can understand that. Intense circumstances can definitely have that effect."

"The more time we all started spending together," I continued, "the more it just felt… right. Like we belonged together. It's not that we don't have our challenges, just like any relationship. And all of this is still so new—I mean, your brother and I are still… getting to know each other." I lowered my eyes into my mug, feeling myself blush again. When had Elena even gotten home? I really hoped she hadn't heard us. Then again, she was a wolf shifter, with wolf senses. Not to mention a cop. And it didn't take a detective to put the clues together.

I sipped my *mate,* then looked up at her again. "I trust them with my life. We have each other's backs, no matter what goes down. I never doubt that, even in the middle of the worst kind of craziness."

"Like this thing with Ronan and Sebastian?" she asked softly, her smile open and compassionate. "Emilio told me a little bit about the situation."

I nodded. I didn't expect we could keep many secrets in this house. Not with all of us living in such close proximity.

"I'm so sorry, Gray," she said.

At her kindness, a blade pressed against my heart, carving a fresh mark for all that Ronan and I had lost.

I nodded again, blowing out a slow, even breath. "Ronan and I will get through this. Don't ask me how, since I still don't fully understand Sebastian's head games. But a bond like we have—it doesn't end just because someone else says it has to. I have faith that we'll figure it out together. Darius, too. I have to believe he's still in there somewhere, even if he doesn't remember me yet. I'm not giving up on any of them, and I'm not giving up on hope."

Elena's eyes twinkled, and she winked at me over the rim of her mug. "Sounds like a pack to me."

"In a lot of ways, it is." Then, eager to shift the focus away from my own romantic entanglements, I flashed a teasing smirk and said, "Maybe you should try it. Get yourself a few boyfriends, do a little test run."

"That easy, right?" Elena smiled, but the laughter quickly dimmed from her eyes. "I can't, Gray. I'm the Alpha. We mate with one, and we mate for life."

"Well, that doesn't sound like such a bad deal if you find the right guy though. Right?"

She shrugged, noncommittal.

"What about Detective Hobb? I've seen the way you two look at each other."

She reached for another sandwich, breaking it in half. Melty cheese dripped from the center, still warm. "I care for Aiden," she said, taking a bite. "A lot. But he's not my mate. Not in the true sense of the word."

Her eyes glazed with a deep, dark sadness, the cause of which I could only begin to guess at. She set down the rest of her sandwich, and for a moment I thought that would be the end of the conversation.

But then she looked at me and said, "I already found my mate. A long time ago."

My eyes widened in surprise. I was almost afraid to ask the next question, but she seemed to be expecting it.

"What happened?"

"Well, we married young. He was human—totally forbidden." The mischievous sparkle in her eye told me *exactly* what Elena thought about that particular rule. But despite the momentary smile, it was clear she didn't enjoy talking about this.

"I… didn't mean to push," I said.

"It's not that. It's… I haven't talked about this in so long. I just…" She swiped a tear that had escaped down her cheek, taking a shuddering breath. "To make a long and tragic story as short as possible… Back in Argentina, our pack was betrayed. Our people were slaughtered. Emilio got me out—just barely—but our parents…" She shook her head, fresh tears gathering in her eyes. "And my… my husband and my daughter… She was only three at the time." A bitter laugh escaped her lips. "At the time. I say it as if she'll ever be any older."

"Daughter," I whispered. Her words punched a hole in my chest, reaching right in and grabbing my heart. "I don't… I can't even find the words for this."

"That's because there aren't any."

My heart was breaking for her, my mind racing with so many questions, colliding into one another and making my tongue feel fat. How had their pack been betrayed? How had she and Emilio escaped? And what had happened since that horrible tragedy to drive them so far apart? It sounded like they were the last two of their family—of their pack. And somehow, they'd become estranged. For nearly two decades, if I remembered it right.

I took a breath, trying to corral my thoughts into the right words, into a single sentence that could offer even the tiniest bit of comfort.

But when I opened my mouth to speak, Elena held up her hand.

"It's not necessary," she said. "I've read every book on grief and loss and recovering from trauma. I even went to a few support group meetings in Seattle a couple of years ago, hoping I could find a connection, another person who understood and could help me feel less alone in it."

"It didn't help?" I asked.

"Yes and no. It helped soothe the sting in the moment. But there's just no balm for a wound like this. You carry the burden, and you learn to live with the pain, making room for it like another person in the house. It follows you everywhere—to the grocery store, to work, into your bed at night. You make peace with it. You make friends with it. And you survive, despite the hole in your heart."

She held my gaze, her eyes suddenly fierce, and I nodded. I hadn't suffered the loss of a child—I couldn't even imagine what that would do to a person. But loss was universal, and in my own way, I understood what she was saying.

Finally breaking our gaze, Elena brushed the last of her tears away and forced out a laugh. "Goodness, what's in this *mate*? Truth serum?"

I returned her laugh, glad to lighten the mood, just a little bit.

Her laughter faded, and now she looked at me with kind, honest eyes. The eyes of someone who might become a friend.

Maybe she already had.

"As long as we're being honest, Gray..." She took a breath, searching for her words, then said, "My brother cares for you a great deal. It's... it's good to see him like that. Happy."

The words seemed to stick in her throat, each one pushed out with great effort.

God, there were so many layers to her relationship with Emilio. So many sharp edges and dark corners I could only guess at. But I truly didn't want to push, and I sensed she'd reached the absolute farthest end of her comfort zone.

Exhaustion was settling into my bones, anyway. Stretching into a yawn, I rose from the chair and cleared away the dishes, ready to give her some privacy and head back into the warm embrace of my wolf.

But when I exited the kitchen and headed toward the hallway, Emilio was already standing there, unbuttoned jeans hanging off his hips, a wrinkled T-shirt tossed over his shoulder. The sight of his massive bare chest sent a fresh pulse of desire to my core, and I ogled him openly, hoping I wasn't actually drooling.

But the severe look in his eyes told me this was not the time for ogling.

"Get dressed," he said to us both, just as Elena's phone started buzzing on the table. "That'll be Lansky. I just got off the phone with him. Gray and I have a visitor at the precinct."

TWENTY-NINE

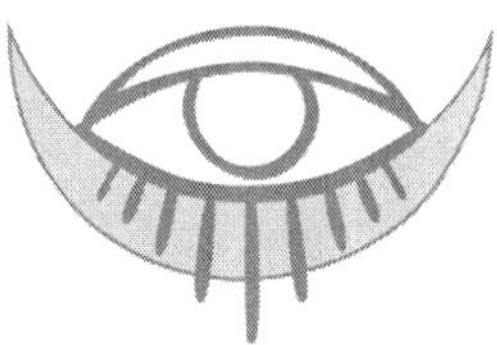

EMILIO

Nine minutes and one harrowing drive later, we stood outside the RCPD interrogation room, staring through the one-way mirror at a witch I hadn't seen—in the flesh, anyway—since Sophie's murder.

Reva Monroe was so pale and thin, she was practically see-through. Dark circles lined her eyes, making them stand out starkly against her china-doll complexion. Her head had been shaved, covered now with the fuzz of new growth.

One of the female officers had helped her clean up, and now she wore a set of RCPD sweats. They were two sizes too big, but she looked grateful for the warmth, sitting at the table and sipping hot chocolate from a styrofoam cup.

I could only imagine what her living conditions had been like.

"She showed up here a little while ago, asking for you and Gray," Lansky said to me. "She won't talk to anyone else."

"You get one of the EMTs to check her out?" I asked.

"Yes. She's refusing to go to the hospital," he said, "but they said she was stable. Dehydrated and hungry, a few scrapes, but no major injuries. She did tell us she hadn't been physically assaulted, but said that others had been… experimented on."

"Oh my God," Gray whispered, shaking her head. She clenched her teeth, her eyes sparking with rage. Her magic spiked —I scented it in the air between us. "Can I go talk to her?"

I put my hand on her shoulder, giving her a squeeze. "I'll go in with you."

Reva looked up from her hot chocolate as we entered, a smile stretching across her face when she saw us.

"I knew you'd come," she said.

Gray knelt before her, reaching for her hands. "Are you hurt? Did he hurt you?"

Reva shook her head. "Not like that."

"How did you even end up there?"

"Norah took me," she said. "Delilah too. She put Delilah under some kind of spell, but not me. She said there was only one way for me to help my friends."

"What way was that?" I asked gently, taking a seat across from her. I didn't want her to be intimidated. The kid had been through enough already—the last thing she needed was a bunch of hulking cops standing around, staring down at her, demanding answers.

"She sold me to Jonathan. I don't know how much she got, but probably not a lot."

Madre María, the sadness in those eyes.

I scrubbed a hand over my mouth, trying to keep my emotions in check. I glanced at the mirror, knowing Elena was there on the other side, thinking the same thoughts that I was.

Our theories about Norah were correct. She *had* betrayed her coven. Kidnapped Reva and Delilah, maybe others we didn't even know about. Likely she'd known about the vampire ambush at her house after Asher and Haley had been taken. Hell, she may have even sanctioned it.

"He has everyone in the cave prison," she said, glancing up at me. "Did you get my message before?"

"I did, kiddo. You did great. We searched the beach, right where you told us to, but the prison is fae spelled. Camouflaged." I glanced at Gray, then back to Reva. "But you're here now, physically. How did you manage to slip out of sight?"

"I knew there was another cave system behind that one, and it wasn't spelled. There was a shaft that led back out to the beach."

"How did you get out of the cell?" Gray asked.

"They said they were going to move us," she said. "Something about relocating into the city? When they came back to get us out of the cell, Asher and Haley started a fight with the fae guards, and I did my thing."

"Fae guards?" I asked. "Can you describe them?"

"Black uniforms, gold patches on their arms with a weird swirly kind of design. It kind of looked like tree branches, maybe?"

I shot another glance at Gray. "Darkwinter," I mouthed.

"Did the guards say anything about where in the city they were going?" Gray asked.

"No, the fae guards didn't say *anything*. The guy in charge was human—a hunter. Asher said he's the guy who…" She swallowed hard, her eyes filling with tears as she looked at Gray. "Who killed your mother in New York."

"Dirty Beard," Gray whispered. She was positively ashen. "Jonathan's father."

Reva nodded.

"Reva," I said, "I'm going to need you to remember as much detail as possible about the prison and everyone in it. Anything the guards or the old man said, things Jonathan might've mentioned before, things about what happened with Norah, anything you can think of at all. Nothing is too silly or insignificant to mention. Do you think you can do that for me?"

She nodded emphatically. "I told those guys my plan would work. I knew I could find you."

"And I'm so glad you did." I couldn't help but smile. "You hungry, kiddo? How do you feel about cheeseburgers?"

She grinned, her smile lighting up the room. "I feel like I love them."

I waved for Elena to come in.

"Did I hear something about cheeseburgers?" she asked.

"Make mine a double," I told Elena.

"Mine too," Reva said.

My sister rolled her eyes, but she was nodding. I even caught a smile on that grim face of hers.

Turning back to Reva with a smile of my own, I pulled out my phone and hit the voice recorder, setting it on the table between us. "Okay, Reva Monroe, stealth spelunker and master escape artist. Tell us a story, and make it a good one."

* * *

"Story checks out," Elena said a couple of hours later. "We've got them."

"That fast?" I asked.

"All thanks to this one." She smiled at Reva, who beamed right back at her. "I might have to make you an honorary detective, kiddo."

Elena gave us the lowdown, pointing out the site on a map on her phone.

After hearing Reva's account, she said, she was able to narrow down the possibilities to the most likely locations in the city—abandoned commercial buildings that had plenty of space to imprison captors and set up labs for their ongoing experimentation, all without attracting too much attention. From there, she had her guys combing through security camera footage, and apparently, Hobb had hit the jackpot with a condemned three-story building down at the intersection of Granite Top Road and Spring Street, right on the seedy outskirts of the Cape's warehouse district. The place had been on the auction block for a year, dead to all but the rodents who'd made it home. Yet earlier that night, cameras picked up on six nondescript black vans rolling into the alley adjacent to the property, right where the service entrances would be. The footage was grainy, she said, but they were able to zoom in on a partial view of one of the divers.

"Jael identified the armband insignia as Darkwinter."

"Sounds like we've got our target," I said. "So what's our play here, Chief?"

"Surveillance. We need to gather more intel. Then?" She blew out a breath, meeting my eyes. "We'll make our move. Together."

THIRTY

GRAY

"Can you do it?" I asked.

Jael nodded, peering through the binoculars, scanning the scene below.

It was well after midnight, and Jael, Darius, and I were in position on the second floor of an empty office building adjacent to the prison site. We sat in darkness, hiding in shadow from our enemies across the alley. The operation would begin in earnest in twenty-five minutes.

Sunshine and Sparkle were here with me, as always, ready to pounce at the first sign of trouble. In our short time together, they'd become more like companions than guardians, and we'd finally begun to trust each other. They knew I wouldn't bolt—wouldn't leave them—and I knew they wouldn't hurt me. In fact, they'd do anything to keep me safe.

Now, they were as much an integral part of the plan as the rest of us.

"Luck is on our side. Their security spell isn't fully operational yet," Jael said. "They believe they've still got time. Right now, it's strong enough to keep the prisoners in and curious humans out of the area altogether. But there are still a lot of loose threads for me to exploit."

"Threads?" I asked.

"Think of fae magic like a weaving," he said. "Complex spells like this—spells that need to cover a lot of physical ground, for example—require millions of different threads, each of them precisely woven together. This spell is still in progress. I can feel its threads, so it's essentially a matter of finding the right one and giving it a good tug."

"Will it destroy the whole spell?" Darius asked.

"No. But it will temporarily weaken the magic—long enough to give us a window," Jael said. "Once I give the signal, you'll have less than two minutes to breach the physical security. The moment they see you, they'll know the spell was compromised and they'll go on the offensive. Killing you brutally, of course."

"Of course." I rolled my eyes playfully, desperate for a little levity to break up the heaviness. "No one ever accused you of seeing the silver lining, did they, Jael?"

"Fae don't see silver linings. We make them." Jael surprised me with a conspiratorial wink. Seemed he needed a little levity, too.

We fell into silence, taking turns scoping out the warehouse through the binoculars. I couldn't see much—an occasional fae guard patrolling the entrances, a hunter stationed at the corner of the building, playing with his phone. It was quiet outside.

Inside? I could only imagine what was happening. We were assuming the prisoners were being held on the third floor—Darius and the shifters had all sensed the concentration of fear there. But we had no other clues. Reva hadn't been able to shadow travel—not since she'd escaped the caves. I suspected she was just weakened from her ordeal, but she was understandably distraught about the loss of her powers, no matter how temporary it might've been.

Poor kid. Deirdre had concocted a mild sedative for her, and we'd left her home tonight, with one of Elena's officers posted outside. When we said our goodbyes earlier, she was already camped out on the living room couch with Elena's Netflix password and enough pizza, potato chips, and ice cream to tide her over. Emilio had expected her to protest, but I was pretty sure she was relieved to be left behind. Reva was tough, but she was also exhausted, scared, and hadn't even begun to process the trauma she'd endured at Norah's hands, let alone Jonathan's.

All of us had already lost so much. And there was still so much more darkness to come. I was certain of it. Freeing the witches tonight? Getting back to Asher? That was just the beginning of a long, bloody fight.

One I was supposed to lead.

"It's time," Jael said, his hand on my back. His yellow eyes glinted in the moonlight that streamed in through the windows. "We need to get down to ground level."

"Jael…" I looked into those catlike eyes, wondering what he was thinking. He and I were connected by our love for Sophie, by the pain of her loss, but we had never spoken about her. Not really.

I hoped we'd get that chance someday.

"Doing this…" I continued, "There's no going back. If we fail and Darkwinter takes power, you'll be branded a traitor to your kind. They'll banish you from the fae realms, and probably worse."

"I am aware of the risks, and I fully accept any consequences, foreseen and unforeseen." He stood up straight, proud. But then his face softened, his eyes sparkling with new warmth. In a gentler tone, he said, "If Sophie were here, what do you think she'd have me do?"

The sound of her name on his lips brought tears to my eyes. But for once, they weren't tears of sadness. I felt his love for her. Felt the joy in her love for him. I was grateful she'd found that happiness, however briefly.

I smiled, blinking away the tears, and grabbed the lapels of his dark gray coat. "First of all, she'd probably add a little glitter to this jacket. It doesn't take much to go from drab to fab," I said, recalling one of her favorite lines.

Jael laughed, a sound that filled the room with warmth. When he met my gaze again, I saw my tears of joy reflected in his eyes. "Ahh, Gray. Sophie… She cared a great deal for you."

"She loved you, Jael."

He wrapped his hands over mine, giving me a reassuring

squeeze. "How could I honor her memory if I turned my back on you? On our home?"

"You're taking a huge risk."

"Yes." He leaned in close, whispering in my ear. "But I'm fighting alongside the heir of Silversbane. I like my odds."

And then he was gone, disappearing down the stairs that would lead him out into the alley. In less than ten minutes, Darius and I would follow.

I turned to Darius, taking a deep breath. We hadn't spoken much since the staking, but he had mellowed out, just like Emilio had said. He seemed to have gotten past the bloodlust. He no longer needed the hawthorn sedative.

He was practically back to his old self.

Except for the part where he didn't remember any of us.

Shoving down the pain inside, I said, "We clear on the plan?"

He gave me a stiff nod, as uncomfortable around me as I was around him. "Crystal, Miss Desario."

I took out the comms device Elena had given me and pressed the button to check in.

"Jael's moving into position," I said. "Darius and I are ready to rock. Sunshine and Sparkle will bring up the rear."

"Message received," Emilio said. "All good here, too. Elena?"

"Ready and awaiting the signal," she shot back.

I took another deep breath, trying to calm the nervous energy buzzing through my body. This plan *had* to work. Our friends' lives depended on it. *Our* lives depended on it.

Once Jael had temporarily neutralized the spell weave, Ronan, Emilio, Detective Hobb, and Deirdre would hit the front of the warehouse, taking out the hunters and fae guards stationed there, working their way up to the second and third floors. Elena, Detective Lansky, and a few other shifters from her local pack would cover the back entrances.

Darius and I would enter last, with an assist from Jael to disable any additional fae security inside. Our mission was singular: locate and liberate the prisoners.

The witches.

Asher.

My sister, Haley.

Fiona Brentwood, the vampire who I still believed wanted to help us, despite her earlier loyalty to Jonathan.

And every last one of the beings imprisoned and experimented on. Tortured.

I looked out the windows, watching the fae guard pacing across the alley, and my heart rate kicked up. This was really happening. Jonathan's twisted, bloody legacy was about to come to an end.

I just hoped the rest of us survived the fight.

THIRTY-ONE

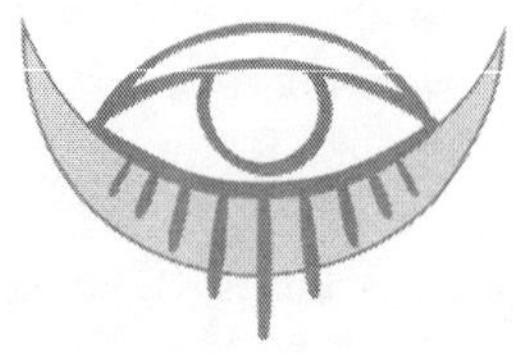

GRAY

The warm, gentle caress of a hand on my shoulder made my heart jump. Not because I didn't know who it was, but because I was surprised that he'd touched me at all.

"Darius," I whispered, my insides already heating, despite the protests of my brain. I couldn't deny our connection, even now, and being in his presence was unnerving enough without physical contact.

"Before we go into this," he said softly, "there's something I'd like to say to you. If you'll hear me."

I closed my eyes, unable to turn around. Unable to look into the eyes of the vampire I loved and not see that same love reflected back at me. I couldn't do it—not tonight.

I nodded, bracing myself for whatever twist in this tale was coming next.

"I didn't mean to be so cold to you, Gray," he said, the regret in his voice shocking in its pure nakedness. "So cruel. I am truly sorry."

At this, I finally turned around. I tilted my head back to meet his eyes, finding a tenderness I hadn't expected.

It wasn't love or recognition, but it was closer.

My heart dipped into my stomach, my breath hitching in my throat, stealing my words.

"Sometimes I look at you," he said, his voice silky and low in the darkness, "and I'm overcome with a... a strange feeling. Like we've known each other far longer than you've let on."

"Yes and no," I said, finding my voice, however frail it felt. "With us, it's kind of... complicated."

"I'd like to hear more about it, if you're comfortable sharing."

I closed my eyes and sighed. There was a time when "comfortable sharing" meant something entirely different between us. Briefly, I wondered how he'd feel if he could remember that night with Ronan, the love and passion and connection the three of us had shared with each other. It hadn't happened that long ago; I'd been so certain the three of us were forever. That our night together was only the beginning of something much bigger, much deeper.

Yet somehow, they'd both slipped through my fingers.

"You've known Ronan and the others much longer," I said. "You and I met several years ago, when I first came to the Bay. You... you helped take care of me when I was in no position to take care of myself."

Darius blew out a slow breath—an odd gesture for the vampire—and I felt the heat of it whispering over my lips. When he looked at me again, his gaze was heavy with sadness. "Several years of friendship, gone in a blink. How is that possible?"

"I wish I knew. Better yet, I wish I knew how to reverse it."

So much had happened since I'd talked to Deirdre on the beach, I hadn't had time to do any more research about blood magic. Part of me wanted to share my theory with Darius, but I wasn't ready. I needed more information. More... everything. And right now, we had other priorities.

"When I look at you now," he said, "I'm overwhelmed with..." He closed his eyes, took a deep breath. A scent. He reached out a tentative hand and cupped my chin, our skin barely making contact. Still, it was enough to set my heart on fire.

"I touch you," he continued, "and it's like I can *feel* everything we've lost. But I can't see the details of it. I taste your scent in the air around me, and it stirs something deep inside me, but brings back no memories." He opened his eyes, his honey-colored gaze intense and possessive and full of the same deep, desperate longing coursing through my veins. "I'm *certain* you've left footprints on my heart, Gray Desario, yet I can't recall the sound of a single step, and it's… it's breaking me."

His words mingled with the intensity in his eyes, the heat in his touch, the proximity of his body, the heartache in his voice, all of it wrapping me up in a spell I knew would soon shatter. But for the moment, I let myself take pleasure in it, indulging in the memories of *us*, the movie reel of our first kiss, the way we'd touched each other in the car outside Luna's, our shower at the safe house, the promises he'd made to take me to New York, the snow globe he'd brought back for me, our first time together in the Shadowrealm. Even the raw, lust-fueled night we'd shared in Elena's basement played in my mind, making my heart race, my core ache, everything inside me desperate for his touch, even now.

Each memory cut deep, but the pain was necessary, and I welcomed it. It reminded me that it was real. That everything Darius and I shared had really happened.

I'd lost him. I'd lost Ronan. I'd lost Liam. Each in very different ways, but each resulting in the same broken heart. Still, I wouldn't trade those moments and memories for anything, even if it meant a lifetime of suffering over this loss.

"Do you think it's possible that we might… become friends?" he asked suddenly, pulling me back to the present. "Maybe not overnight, of course. But in time, we might get to know each other again. Perhaps even enjoy each other's company."

"You mean starting over?" I asked, looking up at him. "From scratch?"

"I no longer have the memories that made me the man you knew and cared for. But in many ways, I'm still that man. It stands to reason that if you and I were destined to become friends once, it could certainly happen again."

"I think… I think I'd like that." I smiled. No matter how much I'd lost, no matter how hard life kept trying to hammer home the lessons of a broken heart, that glimmer of hope inside me refused to die. And now, at Darius's words, it surged brightly once again.

It was only for an instant, but it was enough to buoy me for the battle ahead.

Because if Darius and I could become friends again, maybe we could fall in love again, too.

The comms device buzzed at my hip. It was time.

THIRTY-TWO

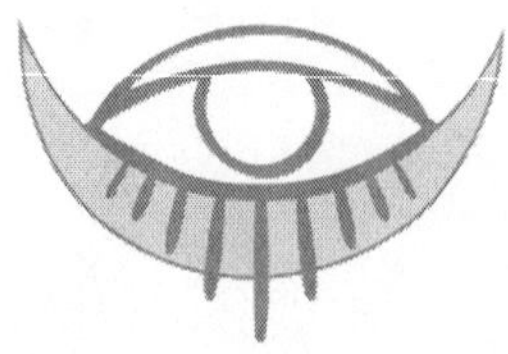

GRAY

From the moment Jael gave the signal, we were in motion. Darius and I ducked behind a Dumpster in the alley, watching as Emilio's team moved in on the front entrance, easily dispatching the lone fae and the hunter glued to his phone.

They were inside in under thirty seconds.

My heart was pounding in my ears, the dull thud threatening to drown out all else. I was relying on Darius's superior vampire hearing to let us know what was going on inside, because from the outside, everything was still and silent.

"They've been spotted," he said. "Ground floor. Fae guards are moving in."

That was our cue to release the hounds.

"Sparkle. Sunshine." I pulled out one of Ronan's T-shirts, letting them pick up his scent. "Go." I swatted Sparkle on the butt, sending them bounding off toward the entrance in search of Ronan.

"Elena's group is attacking the hunters," Darius said, cocking his head to listen.

The echo of gunfire reverberated across the alley, and a flash of Deirdre's yellow-orange magic lit up the second floor of the warehouse.

They'd made it upstairs. Now it was on us.

"Here we go," Darius said, his arm strong and solid around my waist. "Hold on."

Holding me tight, he took off, the alley around me a blur as he sped to the entrance. I closed my eyes against a wave of nausea, but there was no time to be sick. In a blink, we were already inside, the discordant sounds of battle assaulting my ears. The clash of metal, the howl of the hounds, gunfire, the agonizing wail of a hunter who'd fallen to Sunshine's brutal attack… I caught sight of her just in time to see her rip out his intestines.

Elena was the only one holding a gun. The rest of her pack, including Emilio, had shifted into their wolf forms, the beautiful beasts attacking the fae guards armed with sleek, lightweight swords undoubtedly infused with magic.

The unmistakable song of a blade cutting through the air sent chills down my spine, and I spun around to see it slice through the shoulder of a magnificent black wolf.

"Emilio!" I shouted, but he was already retaliating, lunging for the guard who'd hit him. He sunk his fangs into the guy's arm before I'd even taken a single step toward him.

"Keep moving," Darius ordered. "Their blades aren't silver. He's fine." He grabbed my hand and hauled me toward the back of a huge, open space littered with old metal shelving and discarded office furniture. We wove through the melee, dodging Elena's shifters as they held off the hunters and fae, our focus on the metal staircases crawling up the back wall.

We slammed into the wall with a grunt, but my feet didn't even touch the first step. Darius hauled me against his chest, dragging me up the staircase in another nauseating blink.

The second floor was a maze of cubicles and office equipment, all of it being decimated in the unfolding chaos. Fae guards darted around every cubical wall, leaping over office chairs and desks, desperately trying to get a piece of the witch at the center of the room. Deirdre wasn't letting anyone get close. The hum of her magic filled the air with a mix of smoke and an electric buzz that singed the back of my throat, and each time the fae charged, she shot out a burst of magic, forcing them back en masse. Sparkle fought by her side, mauling a particularly brazen hunter before he got within five feet of my grandmother.

Deirdre was a damn good fighter, but her magic wouldn't last forever. She was already losing steam, her shoulders trembling as she tried to focus her energy.

"We have to help her," I said, more to myself than to Darius. I knew we couldn't. There were too many obstacles between here and there, and we had to stay focused on reaching the third floor. On freeing the prisoners.

"Over there," Darius said, pointing to the next set of stairs. They were clear on the other side of the room.

I peered into the smokey haze, looking for a route. I'd just found a clear path when I felt two strong hands shove me from behind.

I stumbled to the floor and flipped around just in time to see Darius catch a hunter's blade in the chest—a blade meant for me. The hunter still had his fingers wrapped around the grip when Darius tore the man's arm clear out of its socket.

The arm and the body hit the floor. Darius pulled the blade free, wincing. The wound was already knitting back together.

I gasped in awe, but there was no time to wonder about the healing power of vampires.

"Move!" he shouted suddenly, and I rolled left, narrowly escaping the jab of a fae blade. The guard lifted his sword for another go, but Darius was already on him, tearing out half his throat with a vicious bite.

The sword clattered to the floor beside me. I wasted no time in picking it up and clambering to my feet.

I felt the ripple of its power immediately. It wasn't an electric buzz or even a hum, but a slow, silky current, clean and crisp as a mountain stream. An icy but not uncomfortable chill ran through my blood, and my own magic stirred in response, reaching to connect with this new power. I felt it the moment it happened—like a bolt sliding home inside me, locking itself into place.

The cold, new power raced through my body, twining with my magic, energizing me.

I knew nothing about how to handle a sword, but I swung it

anyway, slicing through the air with an ease I didn't expect. The blade was light but solid, the edges glowing faintly.

"Looks like you've found a new toy." Darius grinned, wiping the blood from his mouth. "Take it to go."

Grabbing my free hand, he led us through the cubical maze, both of us ducking low to keep out of sight. There was a crash behind us, and I heard Ronan's gruff voice cursing up a storm. I turned, catching a brief glimpse as he jabbed a dagger into someone's neck. Hunter or fae, I couldn't tell, but the guy dropped like a sack of rocks. Ronan wiped his forehead with the back of his hand, blood pouring from a gash above his eye.

Please, please let him be okay at the end of all this. Let all *of them be okay.*

I sent the little prayer up to the universe, hoping someone, somewhere, heard it.

Turning back toward Darius, I caught sight of a pair of fae soldiers heading right for us.

"Darius!"

"I see them. You take righty, I'll take lefty."

He let go of my hand and lunged for the guy on the left, barely dodging the guy's sword before sinking his fangs into his neck. On nothing but instinct, I swung my newfound sword in front of me in a smooth arc. I had no proper form, no real idea what to aim for, but I connected anyway, slicing a diagonal gash down his torso. Magic surged through the blade, burning a clean line through the fabric of his uniform, right down to his skin. I watched in fascinated horror as his skin appeared to eat itself away, revealing muscle and bone and blood, unleashing the frantic howls of a soldier being devoured by his own magic. His and mine.

The combination was deadly.

And impressive as hell.

"This way," Darius shouted. "Now."

I ran to catch up, taking his hand once again. Darting past the last row of cubicles, we finally made it to the staircase and up to the third floor.

Only to find a locked gate at the top of the stairs, barring us from entry.

"Get back," he shouted, and I backed down a few steps. He crashed through the metal gate, sending it clattering to the floor.

We rushed in, my sword raised, but there wasn't a single guard or hunter in sight.

"Trap?" I whispered.

"No," a voice said from behind us. It was Jael, looking a little worse for wear, but unhurt as far as I could tell. His yellow eyes were alert.

He slipped between us and moved into the room, hitting a switch on the wall.

Harsh, white light illuminated an even harsher, whiter room.

"Self-contained security," Jael said. "The gate was just a holdover from the building's previous occupants."

The room was windowless and surgically spotless, with white walls that shone so bright, it was impossible to tell where the light was coming from. The space was full of gleaming steel tables and shelves—a sight that reminded me of a much more high-tech version of the morgue in Blackmoon Bay, where Darius and I had once fought off a trio of vampires.

"Where is everyone?" I asked, fear gripping my chest. "There aren't any other floors in this building. They *have* to be here."

"Gray," Darius said. "Look."

I followed his line of sight. It took me a beat to realize that the walls he was staring at weren't walls at all—they were glass cells. Seven in all.

"Oh my god," I breathed. There, huddled on the floor in each cell, were three or four witches. Dressed in dingy white hospital gowns, their heads shaved, their bodies brutalized, they clung to each other, looking up through their glass prisons with wide, frightened eyes.

"Break the glass," I said.

"It doesn't work that way," Jael said. "It's secured with magic. Much stronger than the outer walls. I need time."

"We don't have it!" I approached the glass, scanning the faces for my sister. They didn't move as Darius and I approached. I pounded a fist on the glass.

No reaction.

"They can't see or hear us," Darius said. "They know only that the lights were turned on."

"Another psychological torment," I said. If they couldn't see or hear outside their cells, then any time the lights came on, they'd have no idea what awaited them. Food and water? Or the hunter's carving knife? "Jael, what do we do?"

"We wait," he said simply. He sat on the floor in the center of the room and closed his eyes, his hands outstretched. "Quietly. I need to concentrate on unraveling the spell weave. This one is much tighter."

Darius and I exchanged a glance. The chaos below was fading—I hoped it was because Deirdre and Ronan had managed to win the fight, and not the other way around.

I paced in front of the cells, searching in vain for Haley, but it was impossible to know if she was here. All the women had shaved heads, and some of them weren't facing us.

"I don't see Asher," I whispered.

"Nor do I," Darius said.

"Can you sense him?"

"Not specifically, no."

The fear inside me surged again, tightening my throat.

"We'll find him, Gray." Darius's voice, even at a whisper, was confident and sure. I took a breath, trying to borrow some of that confidence. Darius was right. We'd come this far. We wouldn't leave here without him.

"Oh, shite," Darius breathed, all his calm confidence evaporating.

He pointed at the ceiling inside one of the cells. Some kind of sickly yellow-green smoke crept out from the vents. I didn't need to smell it to know it was poison gas.

One of the witches started coughing. Then another. And another. Then, all at once, the screams began. I spun around on my heel. Tendrils of poison curled into every single cell.

"Jael!" Darius shouted. "We've got a problem!"

"I'm working on it."

I pounded frantically on the glass, watching helplessly as four young witches choked on poison air. Their mouths were foaming, their eyes bulging, their skin turning purple.

"Jael! They're choking to death!"

"Almost there…"

"Jael!"

"Got it!"

A tremble rolled through the room, rattling the metal tables around us. The lights flickered, then popped. A dim set of emergency lights illuminated the floor.

When the room finally stopped shaking, I glanced into the closest cell. The witches were lying in a heap on the floor, unmoving. The poison had dissipated, the air clear once again.

Seconds later, the glass windows slid open in a single, unified hiss. I set down my sword, and Darius and I rushed into the nearest cell, slowly rousing the witches to consciousness. One of them coughed, then sat up on her own, sucking in deep breaths of clean air.

Slowly, agonizingly, the others came to.

"Gray? Is that you?"

At the sound of a familiar voice, I darted over to the adjacent cell, my heart hammering in my chest.

Haley Barnes stood before me, her hand over her mouth, her eyes wet with tears of relief.

Her head was shaved, her skin gaunt, her bones jutting out where before she'd had curves for days. But it was still her, those light green eyes sparkling.

I beamed at her, pulling her into a hug so tight I was probably cutting off her air supply again, but I didn't care. She was my sister. I wasn't ready to tell her about all I'd learned just yet—there would be time for that later. But now that I'd found her again, I didn't want to let her go.

"I'm happy to see you, too!" She laughed, finally wriggling free of my embrace. Her smile didn't last, though. How could it, after what she'd been through?

"Tell me you've seen Reva," she said.

"She's safe," I assured her. "She made it to the precinct and told us everything. That's how we were able to track you guys down. Is this everyone?" I asked gently, gesturing toward the witches stumbling out of the cells. They were all pale and thin and severely exhausted, but it looked like everyone could walk. That was a good sign.

"If you've got Reva, then there are twenty-three of us here." She scanned the room, doing a quick count. "That's all of us. The only one missing is Asher."

My heart leaped at the sound of his name.

"They put him in solitary. Down here," she said, leading me to a white door I hadn't noticed. She opened it up, revealing a dark corridor. "There's another cell back there."

"Go with Darius. I'll be right back." Not wasting another minute, I darted into the cell and down the corridor.

I found the cell at the very end of the hall. It was smaller and dingier than the others, with bars rather than glass, and bare concrete walls and flooring that looked like they hadn't been cleaned since Nixon was in office.

And there, slumped in the center of the floor, sat a man in camouflage pants and a black T-shirt that had been torn to shreds. At the sound of my approach, he lifted his head, revealing a face covered in bruises, his nose clearly broken, a fresh gash carved from his ear to the corner of his mouth.

But then he smiled, and I let out a cry of happiness, drinking in the *very* welcome sight of one long-lost, sexy-as-sin, bad-boy smirk and a pair of piercingly beautiful eyes the exact color of the deepest part of the sea.

"Hello, Cupcake," Asher croaked. "You miss me?"

THIRTY-THREE

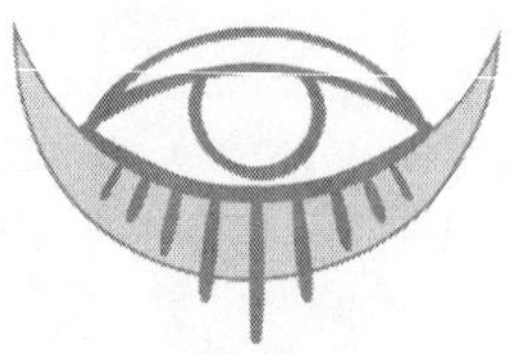

ASHER

Gray really was magic. One look at her, and all the fucked-up shit around me disappeared in a blink.

No longer electrified with fae mojo, the bars of my cell pushed open easily, and I stepped out from behind them and took a breath. I knew we weren't out of the woods yet, but I still felt free. It'd been a long time since I'd seen anything from this side of a cell.

And an even longer time since I'd seen anything as beautiful as her.

"You're hurt," she said softly, the spot between her eyebrows wrinkling. Tentatively, she reached up and touched my face. "They really did a number on you."

I pressed her palm to my cheek, soaking up the feel of her touch. "Nothing I can't handle."

"Tough guy."

"*Me*?" I laughed. "You're the one who made it through the Shadowrealm."

"Hell, too."

"Hell… what?" I closed my eyes, shaking my head. "To quote our friendly neighborhood vampire, I seem to have lost the plot."

At the mention of the vampire, sadness filled her eyes.

"What is it?" I asked, my heart thumping. "Is he—"

"He's okay. Just… there's a lot of plot to cover."

I sensed the weight of her words, the depth of everything that must've happened while I'd been locked up in these bullshit prisons.

"And Jonathan?" I asked. "Tell me you blasted that motherfucker into oblivion."

She shook her head. "I blasted him, all right. Multiple times. And he fell right into my magical realm. Liam is still hunting him. But that's—"

"More plot," I said.

Gray nodded. "We should probably stock up on bourbon and tequila on the way home. We have a *lot* of catching up to do."

Silence came between us, and I took her hands, stroking her soft skin with my thumbs. Just having her near me again, feeling the heat of her skin, my body was already responding, my wounds knitting back together, the force of her healing energy pulsing through my veins.

"When I didn't see you in that other room," she said, her voice breaking. "I thought…"

"You thought I'd checked out?" I smiled, pressing my forehead against hers, taking another deep breath of her sweet scent. "Not a chance. You kept me alive in there, Cupcake. You know that, right?"

"I'm glad my magic gave you strength. It—"

"No, not the magic. A thought. One simple thought." I pulled back and took her face in my hands, trying my damnedest not to tremble. I could seriously drown in those blue eyes. "I couldn't die in that fucking hole knowing I'd never kiss you again."

At this, her eyes sparkled, a smile playing on her lips.

"Is that right?" she teased, that smirk of hers driving me wild. She stood on her tiptoes and put her arms around my neck, pressing up against me. My body responded to her instantly, in all the obvious ways. I didn't even bother hiding how turned on I was. "Who says I *want* you to kiss me again?"

"Oh, let's not play games." I nudged her nose with mine. "I'm pretty damn sure you want me to kiss you again."

"Kiss a guy in camo?" She wrinkled her nose. "I don't know about that."

"Maybe you want to find out."

"Yeah. Maybe I do," she whispered, all the teasing gone. The look in her eyes turned ferocious, a passion that would never be tamed, and I crashed against her lips, stealing a bruising, breath-taking kiss. She moaned my name into my mouth, and I slid my fingers into her silky blonde hair, pulling her closer, closer, closer…

Fuck, I couldn't get enough.

I wanted to devour her, kiss by devastating kiss.

But that, too, was a plot we'd have to catch up on later.

Without another word, we broke apart, linking hands and heading out into the main room to join the others.

"If it isn't my favorite witch and my favorite pain-in-the-ass incubus." Haley beamed as Gray and I entered the room, her hope-o-meter off the charts.

"At your service, Hay," I said, giving her a wink.

"So, the witches are accounted for, but where are the rest?" Gray asked, looking around the room. "Fiona Brentwood? The other shifters and—"

"Not here," I said. "As far as we know, they only transferred witches to this facility. I'm only here because Dirty Beard can't get enough of beating me with his big stick."

I couldn't be sure, but I swore I heard Gray growling.

"Do you think they're still back in the caves?" she asked.

"No," Haley said. "It sounded like they were clearing out from that area altogether. My guess is they didn't want Jonathan coming back and screwing up the new world order."

"Alright, everyone," a commanding voice called from the other side of the room. "We still need to get ourselves out of the building, and that's going to take a group effort."

Darius.

"Good to see you again, bloodsucker." I crossed the room, pulling him into a hug that seemed to surprise him.

"Oh. Right, well, it's… lovely to see you, as well." He patted me on the back, then turned away, focusing his attention on the witches.

I looked at Gray, confused. Why had he been so stiff and awkward with me? We weren't exactly besties, but I thought we'd made some inroads.

"Later," she mouthed, picking up a badass looking sword from one of the metal tables. It glowed faintly at her touch.

Shit, a lot of *plot* to catch up on? Looked like I'd missed the whole fucking movie.

Shifting gears, I said, "I take it the rest of the boys are downstairs, beating those fae fuckholes into a glittery pulp?"

"Ronan and Emilio are," Gray confirmed. "With the help of the local pack. Emilio's sister is the chief of police. That's… another long story."

"What about Liam? I never thought I'd say this, but I actually miss his spooky ass."

Gray shook her head, her eyes glazing with pain. Before I could even ask about that, Darius was calling for us again, urging us to follow him down the stairs.

"With any luck," he said, "our people have cleared the way for our exit. But if there's any trouble, stay together, and stay down. We'll handle the fighting for now. Clear?"

The witches mumbled their assent, too exhausted to argue.

With Darius and Jael taking point and Gray and I bringing up the rear, we led the witches down the stairs.

Most of them could barely walk, let alone use their magic. Even Haley, the strongest of the group, was fading on me.

"You good, Hay?" I asked, putting a hand on her shoulder.

She turned to me and smiled, flashing a double thumbs-up. "Hungry as hell, but I'm hanging in."

"How's that hope-o-meter?"

"At least half," she said. "Let's see what happens when we got out of this shithole."

I had no idea what had been on the second floor before, but now it was a wasteland, littered with burning paper and overturned desks, dozens of gray cubicle walls smashed to bits.

We had to watch our footing, stepping over fae corpses. I hoped none of our guys were in this mess.

"Second floor cleared," Darius said, leading us to the stairs at the other side of the room, then slowly descending.

I could tell from the explosive chaos emanating from below that the first floor would be another fucking story.

And from the looks of things, this one wasn't going to have a happy ending.

THIRTY-FOUR

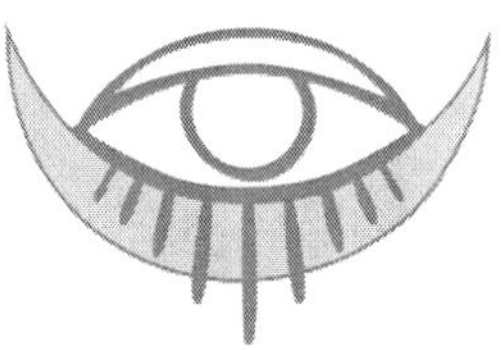

RONAN

In all our preparations, all our planning, and in every fucking scenario we'd run through, it wasn't supposed to go down like this.

I saw the scene unfolding in my mind before the wolf even made his move. It would end in blood—Emilio's—and there wasn't a damn thing I could do about it. No one else had seen it coming, and I was simply too far away to stop it. I charged ahead anyway, shoving aside bloodthirsty hunters and dodging fae attacks, shielding my eyes against the bright bursts of Deirdre's magic. Gray's hounds were at my heels, taking down would-be assailants. I was fifty feet away from the wolf, and closing in fast. *Forty. Thirty.*

Time slowed. Still in human form, Elena whipped around, taking out a hunter with the butt of her gun. *Twenty feet.*

From behind, another hunter attacked her, grabbing a fistful of her hair and wrenching her to the ground. *Fifteen feet.*

"Emilio, no!" I shouted over the melee, reaching out for him as I ran. But it was too late, as I knew it would be. Fighting on instinct, the wolf lunged for the hunter that had nabbed Elena, knocking him to the floor. He rose up on his hind legs, his sharp claws glinting, ready to shred the bastard who'd attacked his sister.

But Emilio was oblivious to the fae soldier hiding behind the wall. *Ten feet.*

Orendiel stepped into view, a silver dagger positioned perfectly, flashing like fire in the yellow-orange light of Dierdre's spells. *Five feet.*

Orendiel was quick. Efficient. The blade cut through Emilio's soft underbelly like a hot knife through butter. The wolf yelped, then dropped, hitting the floor with a thud that rattled my bones.

Elena screamed.

And shattered my fucking heart.

"Ronan! Incoming!" Deirdre shouted, and I jumped on top of Elena, shielding her from the blast of magic that exploded behind us. Something burst into flames, but it wasn't Orendiel. He was already running away from the destruction, fleeing our brutal assault like the coward he was.

I crawled over to Emilio, gently turning him onto his back. I gasped, unable to swallow the raw horror of it.

Elena said nothing, her face a mask of pure shock.

Her brother was covered in blood, more of it pumping out with every beat of his heart. Muscle and torn flesh glistened, the jagged edges of broken ribs protruding. The silver was pure poison, amplifying the effects of a regular dagger by a thousand. I couldn't even decipher where the blood was coming from—where the worst of the damage was. Confused by the silver poisoning, Emilio's body was stuck in limbo, parts of him shifting back into human form, while other parts remained wolf.

"*No*!" A gut-wrenching scream rang out across the room, and I looked up to catch Gray and Asher pushing through a group of witches, running toward us from across the room.

I caught her eyes and knew in an instant that she'd seen everything. That she'd watched the man she loved get gutted by the Darkwinter captain while I couldn't do a damn thing to stop him.

"Emilio," she breathed, falling to her knees before him. She took his human hand, tears spilling into her mouth as she reached up to touch his wolf snout.

He was stuck, half wolf, half man, his face twisted in excruciating pain. The sounds coming from his mouth were indescribable, each one tearing a chunk out of my heart.

Behind us, the fire crackled, superheating the air around us.

"Put pressure on the chest wound," I ordered, snapping my fingers in front of Elena's face to yank her out of her shock. "Now, Elena. Now!"

The sharp command woke her up, and she did as I asked, pressing her palms to the wound near his heart. Blood leaked out through her fingers.

"He needs to shift back into wolf," she said. "His body is using too much energy trying to shift back and forth between the two. We can't heal him like this."

"We damn well need to try," I said. "Unless you can force him to shift."

She shook her head.

I whipped the T-shirt over my head and tore the fabric into strips, tying them tight around his limbs, anywhere I thought might help slow the bleeding.

But nothing I could do was helping. Emilio's breath was shallow, fading. Blood pooled on the concrete floor beneath him, a glossy black slick that reflected the flickering firelight surrounding us.

"You fucking listen to me," I shouted at him. "You're not going anywhere. Don't even *think* about it. You hear me, asshole?"

A gentle touch on my arm made me flinch. I didn't need to feel the burn to know it was Gray.

"Ronan," she said, her voice broken and soft. I didn't even want to look at her. Didn't want to see the hopelessness in her eyes. The resignation.

Behind us, the flames surged, licking up the walls, consuming everything they touched. We had five minutes, maybe ten before they crawled across the ceiling, and then we'd all be fucked.

"Ronan," she whispered again, that soft voice trembling. I'd never seen her so scared. Not in the Shadowrealm. Not with Sebastian. Never. "Do something."

I finally met her eyes, the fierce need to protect her rising up inside me.

"Go with Ash and Darius," I said, blinking the sweat from my eyes. This place was quickly becoming an oven. "You need to get the others to safety. I'll take care of him."

Gray's eyes were wide in a pale face as she looked him over. Then, she turned to me again and nodded, locking her gaze on mine. Instead of the hopelessness I'd feared, I saw the exact opposite. Hope, so much of it, it made me dizzy. She was pinning it all on me, and I felt the weight of it on my heart. The importance of it.

"I won't let him die," I said. "I swear to you, Gray. I *will* get us out of here. *All* of us." My promises weren't worth much in her eyes these days, but it was all I had to give, and I gave it honestly. Emilio would survive this. He was the best of us, and he needed to be there on the other side when we got out.

Gray got to her knees and leaned forward, still holding Emilio's hand. She pressed her mouth to mine, her kiss fiery and all-consuming, hotter than the flames behind us. She tasted like smoke and ash and everything—*everything*—I'd ever loved. Everything I'd ever lived for.

When she pulled back, her mouth was red and swollen, her lips blistered.

"Don't you let go, Ronan Vacarro."

Asher hauled her up to her feet, and they followed Darius and Jael and the hellhounds, leading the witches out the front entrance, leaving a trail of bloody footprints in their wake.

Emilio's blood.

Elena gasped, and I turned back to feel a strange wind on my face that had nothing to do with the fire.

A majestic black raven flapped its giant wings before us, alighting on Emilio's chest as softly as a curl of smoke.

Emilio stopped breathing.

And there, from the space between his lips, the thin silver mist of his soul floated out.

"Colebrook!" I shouted at the raven, terrifying in its darkness. "Liam! Don't you dare take him from me. Don't you *dare*."

I screamed at him until my throat was raw, until I was coughing up ash, until I could no longer make a sound.

And still, the soul floated out, perfect and beautiful, made of pure silver-white light.

I lunged for the raven, but he opened his massive black beak, releasing a howling wind that blasted me and Elena onto our backs.

The flames behind us receded, the air immediately cooling.

When I got back on my feet and the dust finally cleared, Elena was still on the floor, unconscious. The few remaining hunters had scattered. The flames were out, leaving black, roiling smoke in their place.

In the space where Emilio had fallen, where the great black raven had sat upon his chest and ignored my desperate pleas, there was nothing more than a single black feather, floating in a glossy pool of blood.

How will Gray and her rebels endure this devastating loss? When it comes to fighting for the ones they love, will they ever catch a break? Read on to find out in ***Death Untold,*** book five in the Witch's Rebels series.

DEATH UNTOLD

BOOK FIVE

ONE

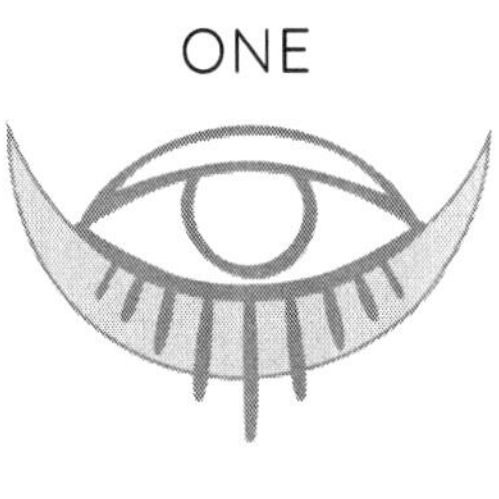

LIAM

Nothing was certain, they said on the material plane, but Death and taxes.

Yet the longer I lingered among them, the more deeply I came to understand that despite the frequency with which such platitudes were offered, Death and taxes were merely constructs in their eyes, words to encapsulate complex systems and ideas too vast for the human mind to grasp.

The only *true* certainty in their world—a world to which I so desperately ached to belong—was love.

It broke all the rules. It decimated once-immutable truths. It kicked down walls and spilled blood and burned so fiercely its heat possessed the power to bond that which, by all the laws of the cosmos, should have been severed.

Indeed, even as the fae's silver blade had severed Emilio Alvarez's spine, Gray's fierce love for him kept him tethered to her essence, against all odds.

His soul vibrated inside my raven form, guiding me on fierce winds high above the burning warehouse, far beyond the small town of Raven's Cape, through time and space and back again. When I finally felt called to stop, I found myself soaring through the deep indigo skies of Gray's magical realm.

It was as if she'd guided us both here, though she couldn't have known I'd already claimed him. I saw her now in my limitless vision, leading the witches from the warehouse, her incubus and vampire steadfast at her side.

All of her companions were fighters, just like Gray.

Just like Emilio.

Sighting the glow of her stone altar in the meadow below, I swooped down and dropped soundlessly to the earth, shifting into my human form just as Emilio Alvarez's broken body materialized on the ground before me—part man, part wolf, ruined and very near an end he didn't want to accept.

I suppose I hadn't wanted to accept it, either. If I had, I would have retrieved his soul, leaving the body for his loved ones to mourn and bury, as was their custom.

Instead, I'd brought him with me.

His blood soaked through the dark green meadow grass, and once again, his soul writhed and spun inside me, a frenzied dance that quickened beneath the shadow of the rune gate and the Shadowrealm beyond. Further down the path, its stone archway loomed, beckoning me to carry him through.

It was, after all, my sacred duty. My purpose.

Yet I was immobilized.

Whether it was his unfathomable strength in resisting Death's call, or my weakness in performing my task in the face of the pain I'd already caused, I could not bear the thought of escorting the soul of Gray's wolf to his eternal resting place.

Not until she had the chance to say her farewell.

One more day, one more hour, one more moment to hold a loved one close and whisper all the right words… Every human who'd ever suffered the loss of someone dear to them had wished for the same thing. Begged for it. They believed that the gift of time, however brief, would be a balm for their shattered hearts.

It was the least I could give the woman who'd captured mine.

As if he understood my intentions, Emilio's soul heated from within, making my skin glow silver. Human or raven or some other creature altogether, none of my vessels were strong enough to contain him long term. His energy was too bright, too strong, even in death.

The pentacle carved into Gray's altar pulsed a violet-blue, and ahead of us on the path, two of my strongest and most loyal ferriers appeared—a great horned owl and a white raven. They perched in the lower branches of a barren, oil-black tree, awaiting my orders.

But those orders would not come. Not yet.

"Tonight," I said, "in the realm where all things are still possible, we shall endeavor to stop time for them." I had no idea how long it would take Gray to arrive—only that she *would* arrive. Ronan would tell her of Emilio's passing, and she would find us. Find him.

I knelt in the grass beside his broken body and reached for his hand, his human fingers curled in agonizing pain against the forepaw of his wolf form, his entire body caught mid-shift. His death had been agonizing, but he felt no pain now. The blade had done its work carving through flesh and bone; the silver poison had done the rest.

I brought his hand to my chest, held it close. The blood of the wolf soaked my human clothing through to the skin, and an inexplicable wetness leaked from my eyes.

He deserved better.

Such was the way of all brave men.

"She is coming," I promised him in a voice so despondent, I hardly recognized it. "Gray will be here."

TWO

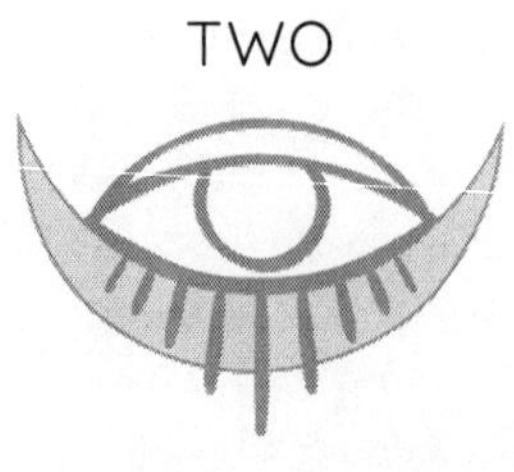

ASHER

Busting out of the smoke-filled warehouse and into the chilly night, I sucked in a deep breath. I almost didn't recognize the smell.

Air. Fresh, free, glorious air and a cloudless sky full of stars that not even the fire behind us could dim.

But as much as I wanted to drop to the ground and roll around in the grass like a puppy, there was no time. We had to get everyone to shelter, and pronto. The witches needed food and medical attention, all of us needed showers, and someone—hopefully not me—would need to come up with a plan.

Orendiel was still out there. Fucking coward. And I was pretty sure none of us would sleep until Emilio was well again, and we'd given that sick fae fuck the brutal farewell he so deserved.

"This way," one of the shifter cops shouted, and in a blur, our group raced down a side street, fueled on nothing but adrenaline and freedom, and fear that it could be snatched away again. We reached a row of unmarked vans and hurried inside—me, Darius, Gray, the witches, the cops, and the fae princeling who was now in the mix. Oh, and the hellhounds that had somehow, in my absence, attached themselves to Gray, and were now jumping on her lap in the back seat, yelping and licking her face like she was a piece of steak smothered in peanut butter.

Not much to look at, those two, but they were fiercely protective of her. Never thought I'd say it, but I was damn grateful they were on our side.

"Alright, we're rolling," one of the cops said into his comm device. Lansky, I thought Gray said his name was. After a quick head count and confirmation from the other two vans, we were off, Lansky phoning ahead for EMTs and food delivery, ordering his people to meet us at the rendezvous point.

The house belonged to Emilio's sister, I was told—another part of the story I was still trying to catch up on.

"It'll be tight," Gray said as we poured out of the vans and headed inside, the hounds halfway up her ass with excitement. Seemed they thought of this place as home, and they were glad to be back. "But it's warm and safe, and there aren't any electrified bars on the doors."

"Always a bonus," I said with a wink.

She was right—the house wasn't exactly set up for an influx of two-dozen witches. But for now, cramped as it was, we'd find a way to make it work. Whether they were from the Cape or the Bay or someplace else entirely, the witches couldn't go home yet. Not with the power balance so out of whack in all the surrounding communities. As far as we knew, Lansky had told me on the drive over, Blackmoon Bay had been the hardest hit, with supernatural crimes and violence mucking things up over there in a major way. But other cities would soon fall, and we needed time to regroup.

"It'll be awesome," I assured Gray as I took a look around the living room. It was open, with hardwood floors and bright orange walls. Seemed like a nice place. "Hot water, freedom of movement, food, drinks, safety? Hell, this place is a fucking palace." I gave her a smile, best one I had for the moment, and she blew out a relieved breath. I was about to pull her in for another hug when my eyes landed on a small lump at the center of the couch, snoring softly beneath a pile of blankets.

"Reva," she said, following my line of sight. "Safe and sound. Judging from that empty pizza box, probably suffering from food coma."

"Last time I saw this kid, she was slipping into the shadows of the caves like a pro spelunker." I knelt in front of the couch and ran my hand over her shorn head, careful not to wake her up. Even more careful not to let Gray see the tears of relief flooding my eyes.

Damn, is someone cutting onions in here?

"Brave girl," I whispered.

"Hey, help me get her out of here," Gray said. "I don't want her in the middle of all this tonight."

With a light touch, I scooped the kid up in my arms and followed Gray to the master bedroom down the hall, depositing her into Elena's bed. Reva yawned and turned over on her side, falling into a deep sleep once again.

"She'll be good in here for the night," Gray said softly, kneeling down at the side of the bed and pulling the blankets up over Reva's shoulder. "We'll figure out more permanent sleeping arrangements when Emilio and Elena get back later. He'll probably need his own room for a while."

"Oh, *hell* yeah," I said, forcing a smile I absolutely didn't feel. "Big motherfucker like that? He definitely snores."

She let out a quiet snicker. "Oh my God, you have no idea."

"I… Wait. How do *you* know how Alvarez sounds when he sleeps?" I teased. Clearly, they'd gotten closer—another part of the plot I'd missed. "Hmm. Something tells me we're gonna need to invest in a bigger bed for you, Cupcake."

Gray opened her mouth to shoot something back, but then shut it, emotion suddenly overtaking her face. Her brows drew together, and she shook her head, fisting the blanket at Reva's shoulder. "If Ronan can't heal him, Asher, I—"

"Hey. Don't do that. Ain't *nobody* got time for doubt tonight. *El Lobo* is a tough sonofabitch. He'll be back before you know it, along with Ronan and everyone else. And guess what? Tomorrow morning, we're gonna have the best fucking reunion breakfast you can dream up."

"With bacon?" she asked, that smile finally coming back to her lips.

"*So* much bacon. And scrambles and pancakes and OJ mixed

with whatever booze the she-wolf keeps in here, because after tonight, I think we *all* need a stiff one."

"You're telling me." She laughed again, and I took her hand and tugged her to her feet, drawing her close and nuzzling her neck and pretending I couldn't smell Emilio's blood congealing in her hair.

THREE

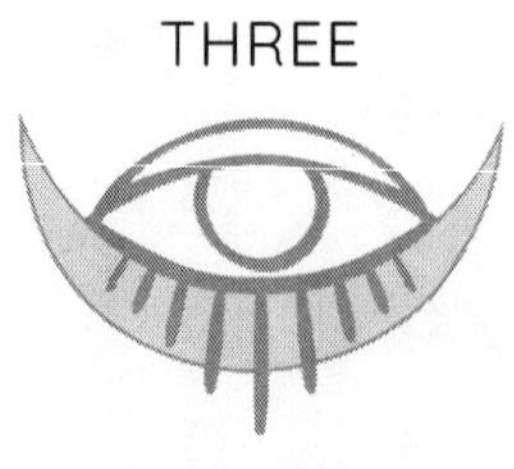

ASHER

The main living area was a hotbed of activity, and Gray and I dove right in, helping Darius, Lansky, and anyone else who had the strength to move furniture and set up the living room for triage. The two EMTs—panther shifters—had beaten us here, and those guys were already hard at work, checking vitals and administering IVs, patching up wounds, wrapping sprains, passing around clean T-shirts and sweatpants and blankets. No one wanted to risk exposure at the hospital—there was too much at stake now, too many questions with answers that humans wouldn't understand.

And here, at least, we could keep an eye on everyone, pool our resources, and figure out some kind of plan.

While Gray and I helped out the medics, Jael and a few of the more experienced witches who'd already been treated headed outside to set up more wards around the perimeter. Lansky called in a few men from a neighboring pack to help patrol the woods that backed up to the property. In the dining room, someone had set up a buffet of sandwiches and pizzas and Chinese takeout, and the witches who'd already been cleared by the medics were seated around the table picking at the food, the shock from their ordeal slowly receding. Not one to stand on ceremony, I helped myself to a slice of pepperoni-and-mushroom pizza and grabbed a chair between Haley and the smoky-voiced witch with the yellow eyes.

"Your friends came through for us," Yellow Eyes said approvingly. Then, reaching for an apple from a bowl of fruit hidden among the pizza boxes, "I damn near forgot what real food looked like."

"You came through, too, Ash," Haley said, rubbing the chill from her arms. "In a big way. Who knows what would've happened to us if you hadn't shown up."

"Come on, Hay. You guys would've figured things out." I licked the pizza grease from my fingers and shot her a cocky grin. "It just would've been a little less interesting."

"A little less bloody," she said, "that's for sure."

"Hey. He had it coming to him."

"Which one?" she asked, but then she just shook her head and laughed. "Dude. I still can't believe you took out Benson's eyeball."

I shrugged, swallowing a bite of pizza. "It was all part of my bigger… *vision*."

"Did you… did you really just say that right now?" Haley asked, cracking a smile.

"Look, Hay, I'm sorry we don't *see eye to eye* on this," I said, "but Benson was a little *short-sighted*."

"*Really*, Ash? *Really*?"

I grinned at her. "Girl, I could do this all night."

"Please don't," Yellow Eyes said, but she was laughing so hard she had to blot her eyes with a napkin.

When we all finally stopped busting a gut over poor Benson, I blew out a breath, the seriousness of the situation sending a chill down my spine. "The truth is… As far as I'm concerned? When it comes to men who think they can take away a woman's power, every damn one of them deserves to bleed. Matter of fact, soon as we find the rest of those hunters, I'm gonna take out more than just eyeballs, and that's a promise."

I wolfed down the rest of my pizza and grabbed another slice, along with a carton of something Chinese that smelled like spicy chicken and peanuts. I offered it to Haley first, but she shook her head, her brow creased like she was trying to figure something out. The chopsticks were halfway to my mouth when I felt her eyes boring into me again.

"Darius told us that Gray sacrificed herself to trap Jonathan's soul in the Shadow Realm," she said. Her tone held a mix of confusion and awe, even a shade of disbelief. "For *us*."

I nodded, and even though I hated remembering the moment Gray had ripped out Jonathan's soul and vanished before my eyes, I couldn't help but be proud of her for doing it. "She thought it was the best way to take him out and give the rest of us a chance to escape," I said. "Hell, maybe it was. Wished she didn't have to go there, though. We damn near lost her, from what I understand."

"How is she even alive?" Haley asked.

"No idea, but I'm looking forward to the story." I still wasn't sure what had gone down in the Shadowrealm—Gray and I hadn't gotten a chance to talk about any of it yet—but she'd beaten the odds and come back. That was the main thing.

"Fucking badass," Yellow Eyes said, taking a bite of her apple.

"That she is." I finished off the chicken and rose from my chair, overwhelmed with the sudden need to be close to Gray. To hold her, to take in her scent, to taste the sweetness of her kiss. "Speaking of which, I should probably go check on her. And *you* badasses need to eat. No more nibbling like mice, unless you want the EMTs to put you on an IV drip."

"Hard pass," Haley said, reaching for a plate and a slice of veggie pizza. Her skin was a couple of shades warmer than it had been a few minutes ago, and it looked like the fiery spark had finally returned to her eyes. Progress. The best kind.

FOUR

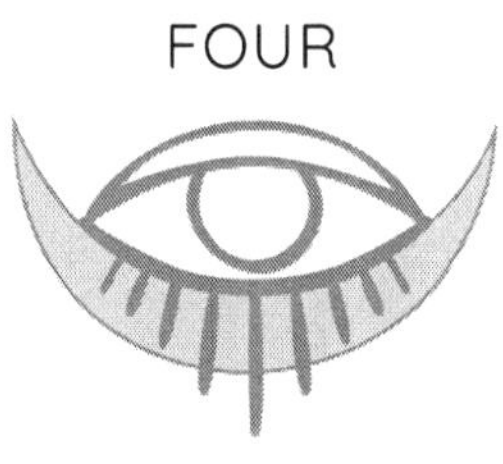

ASHER

At an agonizingly slow pace, I made my way through the press of bodies crammed into the house, everyone talking at once—cops asking the witches questions about our captors, EMTs admonishing them to back off, the witches trying to reach their loved ones on the few phones being passed around. It took some maneuvering and far more patience than I typically had, but I finally found my way to the back of the house. To Gray.

She was sitting in the bathtub in her pants and a bra, knees drawn to her chest, arms curled protectively around herself as the shower water beat down incessantly. She hadn't even bothered to close the door all the way.

The hellhounds—Sparkle and Sunshine, I'd been told—stood guard outside, but lucky for me, they gave me a quick sniff and let me pass.

Promising them I'd take good care of her, I stepped inside the bathroom and shut the door tight behind me. Through clouds of steam, Gray sat motionless, bra hanging half off her shoulder like she'd started to take it off but gave up halfway through. The hot, pounding water was turning the skin on her arms and chest bright red.

"Gray?" I asked softly.

She glanced up briefly and nodded, barely acknowledging my

presence. When I didn't say anything else, she looked down again, staring blankly at her knees.

Pain emanated from every inch of her skin. Her limp, blood-caked hair hung in matted locks around her face.

"Are the witches okay?" she finally mumbled.

"Damn straight. They're a strong fucking bunch, those witches."

Half of her mouth curved into a smile, but it fell just as quickly. "Any word from—"

"They'll be here, Gray," I said, knowing she meant Ronan and Emilio. "Give them time."

She pressed her forehead to her knee, her shoulders trembling. I could tell she was working overtime to keep her voice steady. "It feels like Emilio and I just found each other, and now…" She trailed off, her words like an anchor around my heart.

Not because I was jealous. Because I didn't know how to make it better for her.

There were a million things I *wanted* to say, and a million more I probably *should've,* but all of them felt big and dumb in my mouth. So instead of forcing it, I went for the diversion, kneeling down beside the tub and tugging on one of her matted curls.

"I realize I'm way out of practice at the moment," I said, "as I'm sure you can tell by my just-sprung-from-prison, don't-remember-what-soap-looks-like scent. But I'm *pretty* sure you're doing this whole shower thing wrong."

My attempt at humor fell flat. Gray lifted a shoulder in a gesture that barely qualified as a shrug, her bra strap sliding the rest of the way down. "I couldn't figure out the shower head. I wanted to change the pressure, but it wouldn't turn, and I just… I just kind of climbed in here and sat down. I don't even know how long I've been in here."

I got to my feet. "Okay if I join you?"

"Be my guest. I'm betting we smell the same right now anyway."

"Ahh, you'd lose that bet, Cupcake." Her scent had always driven me wild. Not even the stench of dirt and sweat and smoke and blood could change that. "I hope you don't mind if I disrobe for this one. I know how much you love a man in camo."

This—finally—got a smile.

Returning it, I stepped into the tub, trying not to wince. Mother*fucker*, that water was hotter than Sebastian's balls—at least, what I imagined the Prince of Hell's ball temperature to be, which I'd admittedly never done before that moment and would hopefully never do again.

Shielding Gray from the lava-water, I helped her to her feet, then fucked around with the ancient shower head until I got things to a more tolerable pressure and temperature.

"Better?" I asked, maneuvering her beneath the spray.

"Mmm." She tilted her head back to rinse her hair, exposing the pale expanse of her neck and throat. I reached up and stroked her, my thumb tracing her jaw, her neck, her collarbone, slowly working over to her shoulder. Her bra finally gave up and dropped away, and holy *fuck*, I wanted to kiss her. To bite her. To suck on every inch of her until she melted with pleasure and forgot every last one of her worries, just for a little while.

It wasn't long before she finally ditched her remaining clothes. She tossed them unceremoniously into the corner of the tub, then stood on her toes and looped her arms around my neck.

Her full body pressed against mine, skin on skin, warm and slick, making me instantly hard. I felt the pulse of her magic, calling to me, strengthening me, just like it had in the prison. The incubus part of me wanted nothing more than to bury myself between her thighs, but the man in me just wanted to feel her. To hold her close.

For now, the man was winning out.

Barely.

Ignoring the ache in my balls, I wrapped my arms around her and held tight, my chin resting on the top of her head as the water ran down our bare bodies and washed away the evidence of tonight's battle. The water swirled black and red down the drain, tinged with blood.

Wolf's blood, I reminded myself, and my gut clenched, my

mind flooding with nightmarish images of Emilio lying on that concrete floor, torn up and broken and writhing in pain, one faint heartbeat away from death's door…

No. I couldn't go down that road. Going down that road meant falling apart, and right now, I had to keep it together. For Gray. For Ronan and Darius. For Haley and Reva. For the other witches out there—strong, amazing women who'd just jumped out of the frying pan only to find out they'd still have to walk through fire, still have to face the Darkwinter and the hunters and whatever other crazy shit was waiting for all of us around the next corner.

"My hair feels like yarn." Too soon, Gray pulled out of my embrace and reached up to wring out her hair. "And not the soft kind."

Honestly, I was grateful for the distraction. Clearing the tightness from my throat, I pushed away the lingering thoughts of Emilio and grabbed the shampoo.

"Ever had your hair washed by a demon?" I teased, forcing myself to keep it light. Simple. Un-fucking-complicated in the face of the epically tangled, supremely fucked-up maze we were all stuck inside.

"No," she said. Despite the exhaustion in her eyes, her mouth curved into a playful smile. "Only by a vampire."

"Wait. What? You let *Beaumont* wash your hair? Seriously?"

She nodded, new mischief glinting in her eyes.

Keep talking. Keep distracting her from the blood still swirling at our feet…

"You're fucking kidding me," I said. "Well, screw that bloodsucker. I'm *way* better at this. Turn around."

With a small laugh, she did as I asked, and I eased her head back, squeezing shampoo into my palms and gently massaging it into her scalp.

She sighed, the sound of it more like pleasure than relief. I was taking that as a good sign.

"Told you," I said. "*Way* better than Beaumont."

"Not better. Just different."

"Oh, I beg to differ, Cupcake." I pressed my thumbs into the base of her skull and massaged upward, working my fingers across her scalp, unleashing the scent of mint and lavender—some expensive-ass spa shit that probably belonged to Emilio's sister. A soft moan escaped Gray's lips, and she shivered, despite the heat of the shower.

"Um, okay," she breathed. "Where did you learn how to do this, exactly?"

"First admit I'm better at washing hair than the bloodsucker, then I'll tell you."

"You each have different... strengths and... and skills," she said, the pleasure taking hold of her, making her gasp. "Okay. You... you're better at this. You're fucking amazing at this."

"Cosmetology school," I blurted out.

At this, she let loose a full-on laugh, turning around to meet my eyes. "Seriously, Ash? Cosmetology school?"

I nodded.

"You're kidding me."

"Hey. I wouldn't joke about something like good hair, Gray. Close your eyes and rinse." I guided her head back under the water, careful to block the soap from her eyes. "Natural talent can only get you so far. Crafting beautiful hair artistry takes training, practice, and experience, and you can't just—"

"You are the *most* full-of-shit demon I've ever met." She laughed and tipped her head up, blinking the water from her eyes and looping her arms around my neck again. *Fucking bliss.* "Asher, the friendly neighborhood demonic hairstylist? Please. You were just trying to pick up girls."

"Demonic hair *designer*." I lifted a shoulder. "Besides, maybe *they* were trying to pick *me* up. Ever think of that? Not that I could blame them."

"Of course not," she said, dragging a finger down my chest, tracing a spiral pattern on my abs that had my cock stirring again. "Who could resist this? Big, bad incubus on the outside. Sensitive, artistic hairstylist—sorry, hair *designer*—on the inside..."

"That does sound like a winning combo, doesn't it?" I grabbed her hand and brought it to my mouth, pressing a kiss to her fingers. It's not that I minded her touch—the opposite, actually. I just didn't know how much longer I could resist the siren call of her body, her smooth skin, her luscious lips, the tug of her magic… The last thing I wanted to do was scare her off with my insatiable appetite.

No matter what I felt about her, we'd only been together the one time, and that was just to save my ass from the devil's trap Jonathan had injected into my bloodstream. Now, despite the fact that we were both standing here naked, I still wasn't a hundred percent clear on her feelings for me. This thing between us—whatever it was now, whatever it was destined to become—it was all her call. It had to be.

Because the last woman I'd claimed as my own, the last one I'd claimed on my terms… she ended up dead.

So I held Gray's hand and smiled and waited for her to make another joke, some crack about me picking up girls or becoming a beauty school dropout, but the jokes didn't come. Her eyes had turned serious once again. She pulled her hand from my grip and slid her palm against my cheek, her thumb brushing my lips.

"I love you," she whispered.

My throat tightened with a lump the size of Texas. Damn near felt like it, anyway. Had she really just said that?

"I don't know what I would've done if you weren't there tonight," she went on. "If anything had happened to you, I… I don't…"

"Shhh." I took her face in my hands, my gaze drifting down to her mouth, then back up to her eyes, cataloging the curves and lines of her face, the blue of her eyes, the arch of her brows. Her words echoed in my mind, filling me up with something that felt a lot like magic.

I love you…

"Gray, I—"

"Asher," she whispered, her eyes fluttering closed, and suddenly I forgot how to fucking talk and just lowered my mouth to hers, brushing a soft kiss over her lips.

Threading her hands into my hair, she returned the kiss, deepening it before pulling back with a sharp gasp.

"Sorry," she said, pressing her lips together, then offering an apologetic smile. "Still stings a little."

I traced the edge of her mouth with my fingertip, finally noticing the redness. "What happened?"

"Ronan… I kissed him at the warehouse, and…" She shook her head and lowered her eyes, clearly flustered. "We can't… Whenever we touch now, it burns. Sometimes worse than this."

"It *burns*? What the fuck kind of fairytale curse bullshit is that?"

"Not a curse. A deal. When I was stuck in the Shadowrealm, he and Darius staged a rescue. They came through the hell portal."

"So this is Sebastian's doing." *Of course.* My blood began to boil, my hands clenching into fists. Why was that motherfucker so wrapped up in our lives? He had no claim on Gray. Not until her death.

Gray nodded. "It was the only way he'd let them use the portal."

I took a deep breath, trying to calm down. Fucking hell, so much had happened while I'd been stuck in that rotting hole of a prison cell. Where did I even *start* to put this story together?

Ronan… Shit. He must be gutted.

"Half of me wants to beat his ass for making another deal with that greasy soul-pimp," I said.

"Well, a full three-quarters of *me* wants to beat his ass, and that's when I'm feeling generous."

"I get it. But the thing is, Gray… I'd do the same damn thing a hundred times over if it meant getting you back safely. I can't blame him, and neither should you. You're here. Alive."

She nodded mutely, but she didn't look convinced. She just looked devastated.

"He loves you more than anything else in the world," I said. "He's been in love with you for basically ever, but he gave that up for you. He'd fucking *die* for you. You know that, right? From the moment you came into his life, that was never a question, and it never will be."

It was a long time before she moved again, and when she did, she looked up at me with the saddest eyes I'd ever seen.

"Newsflash, Asher." She blew out a breath, her shoulder lifting in a weak shrug. "I don't want him to die for me. I just want him to kiss me again without bursting into flames."

"Okay. Let me tell you something about our boy, Ronan." I grabbed her hands, squeezed tight. "He plays his cards close to the vest, and half the time you've got no idea what that motherfucker's up to, right? But we both know he's *always* up to something. He *will* find a way out of that deal—hell, he's probably already started renegotiating with Sebastian behind the scenes. And when this is over—when all this shit is back to normal and the witches have gone home and the fae fucks are in the ground with the hunters and our crew is back together, strong and fucking solid, we're gonna have a big party. A feast. Fucking massive. Cage dancers, live band, those guys who paint butterflies on faces. And the main course? Barbecued Sebastian nuts. What do you think of *that*?"

She tried to hold onto her sadness, her anger, but she couldn't —not completely. The laugh broke through, lighting up her face once again.

"I think I'll pass on the nuts," she said. "But I do appreciate your enthusiasm. Not to mention your brutally on-point sense of vengeance."

"Hey. Anything for you, Cupcake." I stroked my hand down the side of her ribcage and squeezed her hip, the moment turning serious again. "Absolutely anything."

"I know."

She closed my eyes, and beneath my touch, her body trembled. It was slight at first, a tremor that began in her shoulders and rolled straight on down.

I reached up over her head and adjusted the water so she'd get more of the warmth.

"You were right earlier," she said, her eyes still closed, the skin between them creased as if she were trying her damnedest to keep the images at bay. "When I found you in that cell, you asked me if I'd missed you. I missed you so much... so fucking much. I thought about you every day we were apart, and the picture of this moment right here…" She put her hand flat against my chest and shook her head. "It got me through some of the scariest shit I've ever faced."

"Hey. You got your*self* through that shit, because you're strong as hell, Gray. You fought some epic shit, and you still came out swinging. Every time. That's all you."

"All I wanted was for all of us to be together again," she went on. "Now you're here. We got you out of that prison. We saved the witches. But we can't exactly celebrate, because Ronan is bound by Sebastian's deal. I'm bound by my own deal with him. I found out my birthmother tried to kill me. Darius doesn't remember anything, and—"

"Wait. What? Gray, slow down. Breathe. I don't understand what you're saying."

She shook her head, but I couldn't tell if she'd even heard me.

"Emilio's hurt," she continued. "Really hurt. And Ronan and Elena were just… They looked like they'd already lost hope. How can he come back from that?"

She opened her eyes and looked to me as if I had the answers, but nothing I could say would make this right. Make it hurt less. I shook my head and reached for her face again, wishing I could kiss away the pain.

"I'm sorry. I'm so, so sorry."

"I know." She lowered her eyes, water droplets collecting along her dark lashes. "I'm sorry, too."

"You have nothing to be sorry for," I said. But before I could take another breath, she was stretching up on her toes again, pulling me close.

Her mouth covered mine in another kiss, this one so intense, it rivaled the heat of the water.

"Your lips," I mumbled. "I don't want to hurt your—"

"I don't care," she breathed. "I just… I want you. Us. Right now, Ash. I need to feel you inside me. *Please*."

Fucking hell, this woman was going to wring me right out.

"Gray, you're freaked out and upset and I get it. But…"

I trailed off, not sure where to take it. She felt so volatile right now—and who could blame her? But what the hell was I supposed to say? *No, Gray. I don't want you to use me as a painkiller. No, Gray. I want you to need me, not just because my touch feels good, but because it brings you happiness. Because you really do love me, just like you said…*

"Asher," she said, curling her hands into my hair, desperation seeping into her voice, "I can't… I can't think about this shit anymore tonight. I feel like my head is going to explode. Right now, I just need you. That's all."

That's all…

Despite her earlier declarations, the doubts crept in again. And there, in the darkest part of my tattered soul, pain flickered.

I forced a smile and pulled her close. "Whatever you need, Cupcake. You know that."

Didn't matter what I felt in that moment. I'd meant what I said —I'd give her anything she asked for, without question. I knew what it felt like standing on the edge of the cliff, staring down over the yawning chasm of grief, the fear of death nipping at your heels. Times like that, all you wanted was to feel alive. I fucking got it.

But it still stung.

I held her gaze, and her eyes softened, a sad smile just barely touching her lips.

"It's not like that, Ash," she whispered, as if she could read my thoughts. Hell, maybe she could. I could sarcasm my way out of just about anything, but I'd never been great at hiding my feelings —especially from her.

"I don't need sex," she said. "I don't need a distraction. I need *you*. I… there's so much more to say, so much I want to tell you about. But right now, everything feels so… so fragile. A lot of bad shit happened, and even though I made it out, I feel… off. Like, there's this thing inside me, this magic, and it keeps getting stronger, but I'm not sure what to do with that. There's this whole legacy thing we found out about, and I'm supposed to lead the witches… I don't even know what it all means. All I know is that sometimes, when I close my eyes, all I see is a big, black pit. And all I want to do is jump." She shivered again, her voice dropping to a whisper. "I don't even know what's real."

"You don't have to figure it out tonight." I cupped her face, tilting her up to meet my gaze again. "And you don't have to figure it out by yourself."

"I know. But for a little while, I thought I lost you." A tear slid down her cheek.

Brushing it away with my thumb, I said, "You haven't."

"I need to feel you inside me," she said again. "Not just to feel good and forget everything else, but to know that you're really here. That you're whole. That you're not going to disappear on me the minute I close my eyes again."

"That's not gonna happen," I said. "I'm never leaving your side again. *That* is a damn promise." I leaned in close, kissing her swollen lips, her chin, her collarbone, sweeping lower with each pass. Her skin was hot and slippery, and when I got to her breasts, she arched her back, pressing herself against my mouth as I sucked one of her nipples between my teeth, my fingers finding the other one and tugging, rolling, teasing her just right.

"Yes," she breathed, threading her hands into my hair.

Back in the cave prison, there'd been no time for teasing or slow, lingering kisses. I hadn't even laid eyes on her bare breasts before tonight—only her thighs, a quick blur of pale skin as she'd wriggled out of her pants and climbed into my lap, desperate to give me the strength to fight off the devil's trap poison coursing through my blood.

Well, it'd worked. She'd strengthened me in more ways than she'd even realized, and ever since that moment, I'd dreamed of *this* one—the chance to truly taste her, to inhale her scent, to make her gasp with pleasure at the hot slide of my tongue between her thighs.

I almost came just thinking about it, but I forced myself to hold out. Right now, it was all about her. All about bringing her to the edge of bliss and back again. I licked and sucked, kissing every inch of her silky skin as I worked my way across the lower curves of her breasts and down her ribcage, dragging my tongue over her hipbone, across her belly, and across the tops of her legs.

When I was finally down on my knees, I gripped the backs of her thighs and looked up at her through a spray of hot water. "You'd better find something to hold on to, Cupcake. Because I'm about to go all in on this gorgeous pussy of yours, and I'm not coming up for air until you damn well forget how to stand."

FIVE

GRAY

Without warning, Asher slid his tongue between my thighs, his mouth hot and demanding and insatiable and oh my *God* I was already trembling. I braced one hand against the tile wall and fisted his hair with the other, but there was no way I'd be able to hold out much longer.

With a surge of hot water sluicing down my back and clouds of steam smudging Asher from my view, I melted beneath invisible kisses, my body going wild for the teasing, fluttering strokes of his tongue and his soft moans of pleasure, each one vibrating through my core and making my knees weak.

"You're… amazing," I managed, wanting him to know how much I was enjoying this. How much he was unraveling me, one delicious kiss at a time. "Don't… stop."

Holy hell.

It was no surprise that an incubus knew how to please a woman. But before tonight, we'd only been intimate together once —for about ten minutes in the cave prison, if that—yet somehow Asher was reading the unique needs of my body as if he'd studied it for years, sensing my shifting desires before I'd even consciously registered them myself. Everything he did—every kiss, every hot breath, every nibble—felt like it'd been custom designed just for me.

I would've come five times over by now, but it turned out Asher wasn't just a master of my body's desires.

He was also a master of the epic tease.

I ached for release, but each time I felt those initial tingles building in my core, he'd pull back, easing the perfect pressure of his tongue, blowing a hot breath across my clit until the elusive orgasm slipped away once again.

And then he'd come back, his mouth whipping my body into a new frenzy.

I was going insane.

After everything I'd come through, every demon and battle I'd fought, *this* was going to be my end. Tonight, I would die in the shower by this man's mouth.

And I was pretty sure I'd be smiling when I did.

Asher shifted before me again, dragging his tongue along my clit, then dropping lower to leave a trail of light, fluttery kisses on my inner thigh, all the way down to my knee.

"This is torture," I groaned. I tightened my grip in his hair, tugging him back up toward my center, but that only seemed to encourage his incessant teasing.

"Torture?" He glanced up at me, his eyes fiery, his mouth wet with the evidence of my desire. "I can *taste* how much you love it, Gray."

He was right, of course, and he left me no choice but to give up the last bit of my control, putting my pleasure in the hands—and mouth—of the incubus who'd been driving me crazy since our very first meeting.

The incubus I'd somehow fallen in love with.

"You're beautiful," he murmured, then leaned forward again, his tongue flicking and teasing, his hands sliding up to cup my ass and pull me close. My hips arched to give him more access, and he slid his tongue inside me, stroking and sucking as his lips buzzed my clit.

"Ash," I breathed, tugging his hair, my body rocking against his face, desperately chasing the release he was holding just out of my reach. I felt the pressure building inside again, more intense this time, my core throbbing, and I bit my lip to stifle a groan of pure frustration.

He was going to stop again, and I was going to ache. To burn. If I didn't come soon, I'd explode.

"Please," I begged, my head lolling back as he plunged in deep, then pulled back, grazing my clit with his teeth before sucking it between his lips. His hair was silky on my palm, and I fisted it tight once more, desperate to hold him close.

"Don't stop," I whispered now, near tears from the slow build, the sheer intensity pushing me to the absolute edge of my limits. "Please don't tease me."

A sound that might've been laughter escaped his lips, and he slid a hand between my thighs, his fingertips grazing my entrance. Then, without warning, he thrust two fingers inside me, curling to hit the perfect spot with each thrust as he licked and sucked, faster now, deeper, more intense, almost there, and I…

"Asher! Don't stop! Don't… oh my God… That's…" I was out of my mind, babbling and gasping for breath as the heat rushed up my thighs and finally, blissfully, thank-the-fucking-universe-I-thought-I-was-going-to-die-fully exploded in a white-hot starburst of pure, unadulterated pleasure.

A tremor rolled through my body, starting in my thighs and working up my core, my chest, my spine, across my scalp, and down my arms. Whatever Asher was doing to me, I could feel it in my fingertips, my toes, everything warm and tingling, pleasure breaking over my body like waves against the shore.

And still, he didn't relent.

He kissed and sucked until I thought I'd burn up from the intensity, pushing past the sensitivity, the too-much, too-hot, too-good, too-*everything* rush of sensations until I suddenly felt the pressure building again, my muscles convulsing into another wave of bliss as a second orgasm burst inside, chasing the aftershocks that still lingered from the first, combining to ignite my heart, to steal the very breath from my lungs.

My knees finally buckled, and Asher laughed, catching me in his arms as he rose to his feet.

"Told you I wasn't stopping till you couldn't stand up anymore," he teased, holding me against his chest.

I nodded, leaning into his embrace. It was all I had left. Couldn't stand up? I couldn't even speak anymore. If it wasn't for the embarrassingly loud panting coming from my mouth, I would've thought I'd forgotten how to breathe, too.

Without another word, Asher lifted me up, guiding my legs around his hips. I had just enough strength left to wrap my arms around his neck and hold on for dear life as he spun us around and pressed my back against the tiles. Water streamed down his face from his hair, and with a fiery gleam in his eyes, he shifted his hips, giving me a taste of just how turned on he was.

"Yes," I whispered, answering the unspoken question with a bubbly laugh. "God, yes."

The press of his steel-hard cock against my entrance stirred me back to life, and I welcomed his touch once again, feeling every perfect inch as he slid inside me, filling me up.

The moment we connected, I felt the tug of his incubus hunger, an invisible force that unleashed an answering call in my own magic. I realized then how much he'd been holding back.

"Take it," I urged him, knowing he wouldn't unless I offered, despite everything we'd already shared. Everything he'd already given me.

He nuzzled my neck, kissing his way up to my ear. "You sure?"

I shivered in his arms, his voice and the proximity of his hot, wet mouth threatening to unravel me once again. Everything he did with his lips drove me wild.

"It's yours, Ash. *I'm* yours. Don't you know that by now?"

"Mmm. I'm starting to get the idea." Asher claimed my mouth in a bruising kiss I gladly returned, my burned, swollen lips all but forgotten. Beneath the saltiness of my desire still lingering on his tongue, I tasted his unique fire, like cinnamon and hot peppers. It made my mouth water for more.

Unlike our time in the prison, tonight there was no resistance on his part, no worries about what consequences awaited us on the other side. We were in love—the real deal. Only Sebastian meted out punishment for something so pure, so beautiful. The universe worked in mysterious, mind-bending ways I'd probably never figure out, but one thing was absolutely sure: when it came to real love, there were no consequences.

Pinning me against the wall again, Asher rolled his hips, sliding deep inside me. I felt my magic flowing into him, connecting with his own power, melding, strengthening. He grew harder with each thrust, his eyes full of love and lust and beauty as he held my gaze, our breath mingling, water running in rivulets over our curves and dips, both of us sliding closer and closer to the edge.

I clung to him, my heart beating strong and steady despite the terrors this night had brought. In Asher's arms, I was safe. Tonight, in this raging storm of grief and pain and confusion and fear, he was my anchor.

And for all his toughness, I suspected that I was his, too.

"Harder," I breathed, biting down on his shoulder to keep from crying out as he obeyed my wishes, plunging deep inside me, my back sliding against the tiles. I kissed his neck, his jaw, his beautiful mouth. I gave him everything I had. And I took everything he offered.

There was power in telling a man what you wanted. Power in claiming your desires. Power in recognizing his, and giving in to those as well.

Like me, he wanted it hard tonight, too. Hard and deep and soul-shattering.

"Harder," I said again, and I kissed him fiercely, feeling my body clench around him, and that was all it took. The now-familiar rush of pleasure snuck up on me fast, shattering me as Asher moaned into my mouth, coming hot and hard inside me, shuddering against me as tears spilled from my eyes.

He didn't ask me what was wrong. Didn't offer pity or sympathy or platitudes. In that instant, I knew he was feeling what I'd felt, and he just continued to hold me, to remain deep inside me, his gaze locked on mine as he waited for me to finally catch my breath.

Something strange and thrilling had just passed between us—

something that went beyond the magic and his incubus energy and the raw desire. Time seemed to stop. And there, in the ocean-blue depths of his gaze, I'd seen the ferocity of his love for me, his passion. I saw his loyalty to Ronan and the brotherhood he felt for the others. I sensed their presence, too—all of them. It was as if my connection with Asher was calling out to Ronan, Darius, and Liam as well.

And of course, Emilio. My wolf. *Our* wolf. His essence was fainter than the others', but he was still there, still with us.

Still alive.

Tears continued to spill, and Asher kissed them away, one by one.

"He's okay," I whispered, knowing Ash would understand. "He's still with us. I can feel him."

"Yeah. Me too," he said. "When we… finished… Something about it brought them all in. I even thought of Liam's spooky ass." Asher laughed. "Does that sound fucking crazy or what?"

"It's our bond," I said. "Being together like this brings us all closer. I think it's only going to get stronger now. Not just with you and me, but with all of us. Did you really feel Emilio, too?"

"Not as clear as the other guys, but yeah." He finally set me down, still holding me as I regained my footing on the slippery tub. The jeans I'd cast off earlier were balled up in a wet heap in the corner, still bloody. I'd be throwing those out the first chance I got.

"I know it was bad," I continued, toeing the filthy jeans. A stream of red water ran out beneath them. "But if Emilio…" I swallowed hard, unable to say the d-word out loud. *Died.* "I would feel it, if he did."

I *would* feel it. I knew that for a fact. Believed it with such unshakeable faith that even when Darius knocked on the door fifteen minutes later to tell us a car had just pulled in, even when I opened the front door and saw Elena's shocked, vacant eyes, even when Ronan met my gaze and shook his head, wordless, his whole body covered in wolf's blood, I still believed Emilio was okay. That any minute he'd walk in behind Ronan and Elena, naked, grinning his wolf's grin, cracking some joke about how he'd lost all his clothes during the shift that'd miraculously healed his body.

As we stood in the entryway, the door wide open, Asher's arm came around my waist, holding me up. Our bodies were still warm from the shower, hair dripping into our eyes, and even when I felt his own gasp of shock at Ronan and Elena's obvious despair, I kept looking past them, looking out into the darkness, searching for my wolf.

When was he coming back? Had he driven separately? Had he decided to stop for supplies? Did he have to file a report at the station?

My mind served up all kinds of logistical questions, because despite the painfully obvious evidence laid out before me, some part of me *still* believed that my thoughts, my intentions, my imagination, my heart, my bond with him, my hope, my faith, my magic… that all of those things were stronger than Death.

Stupid girl.

"We couldn't save him," Ronan finally said, his voice cracking, his face as pale as the moon. "Emilio is dead."

SIX

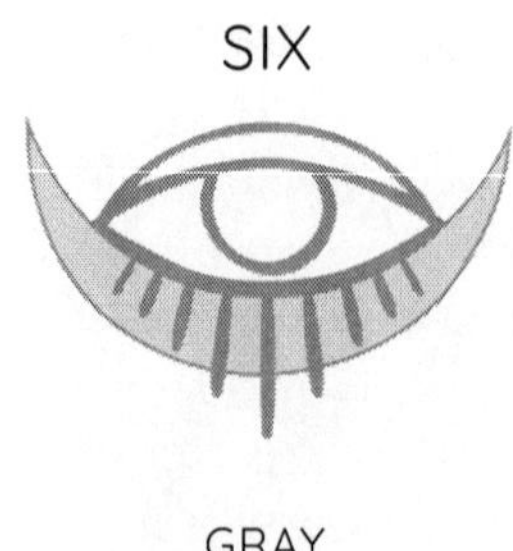

GRAY

"He isn't," I insisted. It was that simple. Emilio wasn't dead.

Which meant that Ronan and Elena had left him in that warehouse somewhere, bleeding and probably unconscious.

I was wearing only a thin robe I'd found hanging on the back of the bathroom door, but I didn't care. Ignoring Ronan's desolate stare, I pulled open the hall closet and grabbed the first jacket I saw, already shoving my bare feet into a pair of old boots.

"Let's go. We need to find him and bring him back here. He needs medical attention."

No one made a move.

"Why are you guys standing around? Let's go!" Now it was my voice that was breaking, a tiny crack on the first word that'd turned into a fissure by the last, huge enough for all the doubts and fears to seep in.

My knees buckled, and I felt a pair of strong arms come around my waist from behind, catching me before I hit the floor.

"He's gone, baby. He's gone." Asher's voice, which only moments ago had been a source of pure pleasure, was like rusty nails on a china plate now. I wrenched free of his hold, still refusing to accept that Emilio—strong, powerful, beautiful Emilio—was dead.

I could still feel his presence. His essence. Why were they all looking at me like I'd lost my mind?

I stepped toward Ronan, leaning in as close as I dared. My skin and hair were still damp from the shower, and here in Ronan's forbidden presence, steam rose from my body in iridescent swirls.

I searched his eyes, seeking the lie. The loophole that would let our wolf be okay.

But Ronan was a shell. His eyes were empty. It felt like his whole body was about to turn into dust and blow away.

I looked to Elena instead. She hadn't uttered a word since they'd walked in—just stood beside Ronan, her mouth opening and closing as if she couldn't suck in enough air, her hands coated in dark, dried blood.

"You'd *never* leave his body behind," I said to both of them. "So, if he's really dead, where's his body?"

No response.

"*Where?*" I demanded, feeling the eyes of the witches and the rest of our houseguests burning through my back. They'd all gathered in the living room behind me, keeping a respectful distance, but still. They were watching.

I wouldn't let myself fall apart in front of them. Not like this.

Stepping back from Ronan and taking a deep breath, I tried again, keeping my voice neutral. Even. Pushing out all the doubts and sealing up all those cracks and fissures behind them.

"Where is the body?" I asked again, calm. Collected. Logical. Behind me, I felt the presence of my hellhounds. They stood guard beside Asher and Darius, all of them apparently waiting for me to break.

I wouldn't, though. Not now.

"We searched the entire warehouse," Ronan said, his voice weakening with every word. "What was left of it, anyway. Inside and out. The raven came, and he's… he's gone, Gray. Just gone."

The words cut to the bone, but their bite quickly faded as my brain processed their meaning.

"Raven? Wait, you mean Liam?"

Ronan nodded. "He took him."

"His soul?"

"Everything."

"So he's not dead, then." I let out a shaky breath. Then, more firmly, I repeated it. "He's not dead. Not without a body. If Liam took everything, there has to be another reason. Something we haven't thought of."

"Gray, there's nowhere… We searched the entire area." Elena's voice was no more than a whisper, her eyes blank, her face gray. "There's nowhere he could be. I'm sorry. I didn't want to have to tell you this. He's just… *mi hermano*…" She blinked back tears, struggling to reign in her emotions in front of a house full of witches and shifters and strangers. "He's passed on. We have to accept it and mourn him and move on."

Move on?

I wanted to scream at her. To grab her by the shoulders and shake some sense into her. But the pain in her eyes snapped me from my anger, and instead, I drew her in and held her close. She was shaking.

Through the knotted tangle of her blood-drenched hair, I stared over her shoulder at Ronan, waiting for him to realize his obvious mistake. To finally connect the dots. To tell Elena they'd missed something and spring into action.

But he didn't. He just stood there, silently holding my gaze with a look I could read like an old book.

Pity.

It sparked a rage inside me that I couldn't contain. Without a moment to spare, I pushed Elena away and spun toward the now-empty dining room, a burst of magic erupting from my palms and slamming into the china cabinet, full force, totally out of my control.

The wood splintered. The glass panes on the front and the dishes inside shattered, exploding outward in a million razor-sharp projectiles before turning—instantly and inexplicably—to water.

Deirdre.

I hadn't seen her come in, but somehow she stood behind me with her hands raised, neutralizing my magic with a spell of her own. The shards fell like a harmless rain, soaking the leftover food spread across the dining table.

Her hands landed softly on my shoulders, gently squeezing. Heat emanated from her palms and warmed my damp skin.

"Breathe, Gray," she said softly, and I felt the gentlest push of unfamiliar magic against my own—probably a calming spell. The scents of lavender and honey and baby powder filled the air, and her soothing words felt like grandmotherly hugs. "Breathe in, exhale out. Release the anger. Call back the magic. Fill yourself with pure, white light."

I took a deep breath, exhaled it like she instructed, but… no. I didn't want this. Didn't want some magical numbing agent. I had important work to do. I was going to… do… something. Wasn't I?

"That's it, Gray," the soothing voice murmured. "Nice and easy. Come back to yourself."

Mmm. That sounds nice. Maybe I should *come back…*

Haze clouded my thoughts, smudging everything around the edges. *Wait… What was I just doing? Aren't I supposed to be somewhere? Meeting someone? But I thought…*

I glanced around the room, dozens of eyes on me. Why were they all so sad? Ronan, Darius, Asher… I looked over each one in turn.

"That's it, Gray," the soft voice said. "Follow my voice and come back."

Ronan, Darius, Asher…

Ronan, Darius… Emilio. Wait, where is Emilio?

I blinked rapidly, scanning the sea of faces—most of them unfamiliar—for the wolf.

"Where is…" I began, then shook my head, clearing away the haze. He wasn't here. He was… they were saying he was gone. Everything came rushing back, breaking through the spell and hitting me again like a bucket of ice water to the face.

"What are you *doing* to me?" I shouted, whirling around toward the source of the placating words. Deirdre was still whispering her soothing mantras, still bathing me in her magic, but I was done with that. I broke her magical hold, welcoming the rush of fury that boiled up inside, once again set loose. I *needed* this madness, this dark energy, this wild magic, no matter how ugly it got. No matter how uncomfortable it made everyone else feel. My skin was crackling with magical energy, the hairs on my neck and arms standing on end. It reminded me of that day on the beach in the Shadowrealm when Liam and I had kissed—those intense sparks, the moment just before lightning struck the sand.

"Emilio is still with us," I said, my voice trembling with anger. "Maybe not in this realm, but he's not gone."

At this, Ronan reached out, his palm facing up. There in the center was a black feather sticky with blood. "This was the only thing left behind."

"That's... good," I said, the barest blush of a plan formulating in my mind. "No, that's actually *really* good."

I turned around and searched the wide-eyed faces of the witches gathered in the living room for my sister. "Haley?" I said, and she got to her feet, smoothing a hand over her near-bald head. "You're with me."

Haley nodded without hesitation, crossing the room to join me. If I'd scared her with my outburst, she didn't show it, her eyes flashing with renewed determination that made me glad to have her on my side.

"Darius," I continued, "I need you to go into the kitchen and find me a clear glass bowl, some bottled water, matches, candles, salt, and the sharpest knife you can find. Ash? Your job is to keep an eye on the hounds and keep everyone away from us. *No* one disturbs us—and I mean *no* one—unless we come under attack or the house is literally burning down around us." Then, to Deirdre and the rest of the witches, "Are you guys up for a little protection magic? We need to keep this place on lockdown as long as we can."

They nodded in unison—even Deirdre, who was watching me with a mix of frustration and pride that almost made me smile.

"Where are you *going*, Gray?" Ronan asked, his voice barely recognizable now. He still hadn't moved from his position in front of the door. It was as if the weight of Emilio's near-death had fallen on his shoulders, cementing him in place. All he had to do was believe me. To have faith. But I knew from the look in his eyes that he didn't.

"Where am I *going*?" I snapped. "Where am I going?! Let me

tell you something, Ronan Vacarro." I shoved a finger into his chest, welcoming the brief burn. "This crew… Since all this shit started, we have fought demons together, hunters, rogue vamps, hell's curses, fae traitors, illusions, and every single sharp, pointy, flaming, cursed obstacle the universe has thrown at us. And you know what? I'm tired. I'm tired and I'm pissed off and I am *done* playing games. We deserve a break."

"Gray. You can't just—"

"Watch me." I snatched the bloody feather from his hand and turned around to find Darius with his arms full of the supplies I'd asked him to get from the kitchen. Haley and I took everything, and then I met Ronan's eyes one last time. "I'm going to find Emilio and Liam, and then I'm going to bring them *both* back here. Because I don't care what hell beasts are waiting for us tomorrow or which contracts and rules I have to break now. This crew—no, screw that. This *family*—we've just been fucked with for the *last* god damn time."

SEVEN

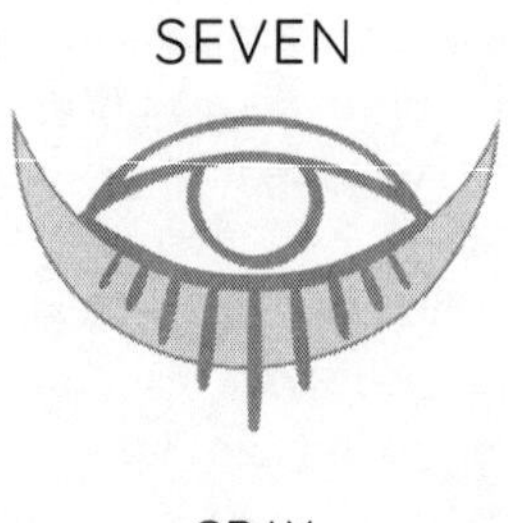

GRAY

"Nice speech, Aragorn." Haley closed the guest room door behind us, then turned to face me, her arms full of supplies. "I assume you have an actual plan?"

The shaved head made the fire in her eyes burn even more brightly, and despite the dark circles beneath them, she looked energized and ready to rock.

"It's percolating," I said, shedding the robe and grabbing a T-shirt and an old pair of leggings from the closet. "But here's the short version: you're going to help me do some blood magic to track them down."

"Gray, are you sure you—"

"Look, Hay. I don't have a lot of time for a debate." I quickly pulled on the clothes, then wrapped my hair in a bun. "Either you're in on this, or you're in my way."

I held her gaze, my heart hammering behind my ribcage. I needed her help—wanted her by my side through this—but if she wanted to bail, I'd find another way. There would be no talking me out of this—not even from the woman who shared my blood.

Haley rolled her eyes. "Of course I'm *in* on this, you crazy bitch. God." She set the supplies on the bed and plucked the feather from my hand. "I just wish we had more to go on. And better supplies. And maybe some of Nona's lasagna."

"Help me figure this out and I'll bake you a month's worth of lasagna."

"Do you even know how?"

I leaned in and kissed her cheek. "For you? I'll learn."

After that, I was a whirlwind, scouring the room for anything else we could use while Haley sorted through the stuff Darius had scavenged. The Tarot cards Emilio had given me were on the dresser, so I gathered them up into a neat stack and placed them with the other supplies, hoping we could harness the power of the cards as well as their connection to Emilio.

Stuffed in draws or shoved out of sight on the closet shelves, I found a lighter, which I slid into my T-shirt pocket, and a couple more half-melted candles. Then I unearthed a terra-cotta bowl, a half-spent tube of bright red lipstick, and—a more recent addition to the space—one of Emilio's T-shirts. I brought it to my face and inhaled, his woodsy-vanilla scent bringing tears to my eyes.

This was the room we'd shared together. The room where we'd spent one amazing night in each other's arms. The room where we'd shared our first time… and our last…

I closed my eyes, barely stifling the tears.

Focus, Gray. Get him back.

Shaking off the melancholy, I opened my eyes and tossed the shirt to Haley. She found a pair of scissors and got to work cutting it into seven strips.

"We need a circle," she said, toeing the dark green throw rug that covered the floor beside the bed. "Help me with this."

We rolled it up and shoved it out of the way, revealing the bare wood planks beneath. Dropping to my knees, I drew a pentacle on the floor with the old lipstick, then set the candles at each of the points.

As Haley lit each one, I poured a line of salt over the threshold before the door and along each of the windowsills. Haley poured the bottled water into the glass bowl and blessed it, and then we sprinkled that around the circle, too.

Between our actions in here, the witches' collective protection magic, and the perimeter Jael had set up, we'd be safe for a little while—hopefully long enough for me to track down my guys and bring them back. There were dark fae to hunt, threats to eliminate, people to save, order to restore… and I needed them by my side. We all did.

Certain we'd prepared the makeshift space as best we could, Haley and I knelt down at the center of the circle, the terra cotta bowl resting on the floor between us, the blade in her lap. Following her lead, I helped tie each of the T-shirt strips into seven knots, then placed all of them into the bowl.

From the deck of cards, I selected the two that most reminded me of the guys. For Emilio, I chose the King of Cups, honorable and compassionate, sensitive, full of love and strength and wisdom. For Liam, the Death card.

My eyes lingered on the words carved in stone before the black-robed angel of Death.

Vita mutatur, non tollitur. Life is changed, not taken away.

The last time I'd drawn this card, it'd brought me to Liam. I hoped now it would do the same. That the message would hold true.

I placed the cards on each side of the bowl.

Haley set the blood-drenched feather on top of the knotted fabric strips, then nodded at me.

It was time.

"Okay, blood priestess," I said. "Let's conjure up something good."

"Blood priestess. I like that." With a wicked gleam in her eye, Haley reached for my hands, clasping them tight over the bowl. At her touch, my magic sparked, and she let out a little gasp of surprise, then laughed. "Okay, we need to work on your grounding skills after this."

"We will," I told her. "We'll work on everything." *Including the part about us being sisters,* I thought. I still wasn't quite sure how to tell her—there were so many implications, so many unanswered questions. But that was a conversation for later. Right now, we had a job to do.

My magic settled, allowing me to feel the pulse of hers, our bond growing stronger the longer we held tight. Her touch was warm and solid, a reassuring connection in a night that had threatened to blow us all away.

My eyes misted again, but not because of Emilio or the struggles that still lay ahead. In that instant, I thought of Sophie, and a smile touched my lips. She'd brought Haley into my life, despite my resistance. She'd brought my sister and me together. I felt her presence now, her friendship. Her support.

I sensed Haley did, too. I saw my own emotion reflected in her eyes, and a silent understanding passed between us. She might not yet know about the nature of our relationship, but even if we *weren't* biological sisters, Haley and I were sisters in all the ways that counted.

And it'd all started with our connection to Sophie.

"She's here," I whispered, and Haley nodded, knowing exactly who I was talking about.

"She's always with us, Gray. She always will be." Haley returned my smile, a tear glittering on her cheek. Then, taking a deep breath and squaring her shoulders, she said, "It's time. Close your eyes, center yourself, and try to call up the ones you seek—images, feelings, emotions, sensations, words, anything that will bring them closer to you."

I obeyed, letting my thoughts drift to Emilio and Liam. It wasn't hard; they were always on my mind, always in my heart.

I saw Emilio's deep, soulful eyes. His warm smile. I tasted the rich, chocolatey brownies we'd shared. I felt the warmth of his kisses, his touch, his love for me. My palms tingled as I remembered stroking his coarse fur the first time I'd seen him shift into wolf form. My shoulders dipped as I recalled the time the wolf had pinned me to the ground at the safe house during our training, and the time he'd pinned me to the bed as a man. I heard the music of his laugh in my ears, and I held him close until his image was as firm and real as if he were standing right beside me.

Liam came to me just as easily, though not as comfortably. With Liam, there was no escaping the bitter taste of betrayal, the pang of something precious lost. But I wouldn't push it away. Acknowledging and confronting that pain was the only way I'd ever be able to forgive him fully, and I wanted to. More than anything. So I welcomed even that, the hollow ache in my heart, the twist in my gut that accompanied the rush of butterflies and the electric sparks of our first kiss. Goosebumps rose along my arms when I remembered our first meeting the night Sophie had died and he'd come to take her soul. My fingers tingled at the spider-webby touch of his robes, and a shy heat crept to my cheeks as I pictured the first time he'd taken his human form, just to make me more comfortable.

He was with me now, too. Both of them were, side by side in my mind's eye. Side by side in my heart.

I let out a deep, slow breath, and I felt Haley's energy shifting before me. In a soft, meditative tone, she reminded me to hold on to whatever images I'd called forth.

She was still holding my hands, and now she gently turned them so that my palms were facing up. I knew what was coming next, but I barely felt the bite of the blade as she sliced it across my hand. Instinctively I curled my fingers into a fist, squeezing my blood into the bowl.

Haley released me, and seconds later I heard the sound of a match being struck. The scent of sulfur filled my nose, and the contents of the blow flared to life in a blaze of light and heat that radiated across my face.

Haley began to chant, and I joined in, speaking the words like a mantra until I'd slipped into a deeply meditative state.

"Earth, air, water, fire. Earth, air, water, fire. Earth, air, water fire…" The words became automatic, and though Haley hadn't instructed me to do so, I continued the repetition dozens of times, not stopping even as she altered her own chanting to speak the spell:

Your connection runs deep
As blood in the vein
Let it guide you this night
Through distance, through pain
May your souls become one
Across time and space
And bring you together

In his resting place

The blaze of the bowl dimmed, and silence descended. My lips still uttered the chant, but I could no longer hear the sound of my own voice.

A gentle breeze stirred my hair, and I breathed in the scent of lavender and lilac. When the moment felt right, I opened my eyes.

Haley was gone. I was no longer sitting on the floor of Elena's guest room.

I was, unsurprisingly, back in my own magical realm, the now-familiar black trees glittering with silver threads. Slowly, I got to my feet, trying to get my bearings. The spell had brought me here, which meant that Liam and Emilio were somewhere in my realm, probably near the gate to the Shadowrealm.

The crunch of leaves and branches sounded at my back, and I spun around expecting Liam, my lips already curving into a smile.

But the gaze that greeted me was not the peaceful, ancient blue of Liam Colebrook's gaze.

The half-human, half-beast creature before me didn't even have eyes. Just two black pits oozing with foul blood, carved into a bashed-in skull that was covered in a patchwork of tattered flesh and bloody, matted fur. A long, crooked muzzle extended out beneath the pits like a door loose on its hinges.

He snapped his jaw, revealing a series of rotten, infected holes where his pseudo-vampire fangs should've been. And though he couldn't speak, the haunting words of the past slithered into my memory, filling my mouth with the taste of bile.

Leaving the shadows already, Sunshine?

It seemed the twisted monster who'd been hunting me for a decade had caught up with me once again.

EIGHT

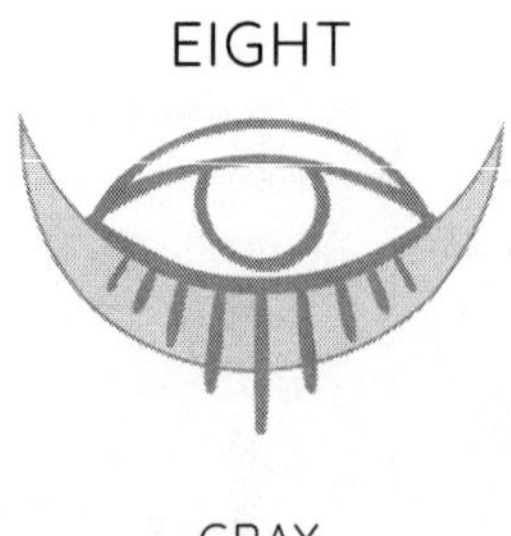

GRAY

My brain checked out, leaving my instincts in charge. I lunged, slamming Jonathan's deformed hybrid body to the ground and straddling him. My hands wrapped around his neck, fingers breaking through the loose skin and sinking into the flesh, right down to the brittle bones beneath. I swallowed back a gag as his putrid blood spilled over my hands, but still, he writhed and bucked beneath me, some unnatural force giving him superior strength.

In a blur, he shoved me off and rolled on top of me, pinning my arms at my sides with hands that were part human, part monstrous paw, tipped with razor-sharp claws that pierced my skin. Blood from his neck wounds dripped onto my face, and I closed my mouth and turned my head, trying to look for something in the grass—anything—to hit him with.

No rocks, no sticks. I had no weapons but the dinky lighter in my pocket, which I couldn't get to… and my magic.

Jonathan lowered his head and nosed my cheek, my jaw, my neck, inhaling my scent. The smell seemed to make him tremble, and something in his lower body—I didn't even want to imagine *that* deformed thing—hardened against my thigh.

I bit back another gag.

Oh, hell *no. This is* definitely *not happening.*

He shoved his cracked, bleeding muzzle into the curve where my shoulder met my neck and licked me, his tongue like sandpaper, his hot, sick breath coming more frantically. His jaw opened, and he bit down hard.

I braced for the pain that never came.

He had no teeth. No bite. Nothing but festering, stinking gums that smelled as rotten as the rest of him.

I took a deep breath through my mouth and closed my eyes, willing my heart rate to slow. I was in my own realm, surrounded by my own magic. Everything here was connected to me, including the Shadowrealm on the other side of the forest. This beastly *thing* might've had strength left in his body—hell, he might've been immortal, for all I knew—but he couldn't hurt me here. Not really.

In that moment, the truth blazed inside me like its own sun.

Jonathan was evil and repulsive. His appearance alone was enough to give me nightmares for the rest of my life, never mind the stench.

But I was no longer afraid of him.

He had no power over me.

A sense of utter calm descended on me like a heavy blanket, and I stopped struggling against his hold. Instead, I redirected my energy and sent a gentle call to my sacred place, pulsing my magic into the earth, sending it deep beneath the surface. I felt it trickle down through the grass like water after a rainstorm, slowly seeping into the dirt, through tangled roots and loose rocks, past earthworms and beetles and the decaying bodies of creatures long since buried. There were layers of bedrock, each colored band marking the passage of an eon, and the skeletons of creatures that no longer existed. It was a mirror of the earthly plane, one of many dimensions that touched and overlapped and called us home.

I wasn't sure how much time passed, but I felt it the moment my magic reached the source. The energies connected instantly, warming me, and the deep, ancient magic of this place twined with mine, inviting me to draw it upward, inward.

We are part of you, blood of Silversbane, came the whisper in my mind. *As you are part of us.*

My skin began to glow. The magic simmered inside me, heating my blood.

It was time.

There was no force, no explosion of sparks and violence, no out-of-control burst that shattered glass and splintered wood. Only a gentle nudge, and Jonathan was flat on his back, the air rushing back into my lungs in the absence of his crushing weight on my chest.

Unhurried, I slowly got to my feet, wiped my face on the bottom edge of my T-shirt, and searched the area for a piece of wood or a stick. I finally settled on a thick, foot-long chunk of tree bark near the forest's edge, wrapped in dried moss that seemed perfect for kindling. Certain it hadn't been there a few minutes earlier, I glanced up into the shimmering tree branches and smiled, sending the woods a silent thank-you.

A muffled grunt behind me alerted me to Jonathan's presence again, and I turned to face him, scrutinizing the sockets where his eyes used to be. "Why won't you just die?"

He shook his head in response, but I couldn't translate his answer. Maybe he didn't want to die, and haunting my realm would be his final stand. Maybe he *did* want to die, and just didn't know how. I couldn't imagine anyone—even a piece-of-shit hunter like Jonathan—would *want* to remain trapped in that form.

It wasn't a life.

It was a mistake.

Well, I certainly didn't owe him any favors, but if death was what he wanted, I'd be more than happy to put him out of his misery.

I fished the lighter out of my shirt pocket and lit the mossy end of the bark, blowing the red-hot embers to a flame.

"I'd cut off your head, half-vamp, but I didn't bring a blade. So, fire it is." I held up my makeshift torch, my own magic surging inside, warming me as much as the fire. "Fair warning… This might sting a little."

I lunged for him again, but he spun away out of my reach and dashed into the forest.

Using the torch to light my path, I chased him. He'd haunted me for far too long. This needed to end. With light, sure steps, I charged into the forest, hopping over tangled roots and fallen limbs, dodging sharp branches, ignoring the pounding of my heart as I hunted the hunter.

When I finally broke free of the thick, tangled trees, I found myself in a peaceful meadow. Jonathan was gone. I'd lost him.

But what I found instead more than made up for it.

Tears sprung to my eyes, and I extinguished and dropped my torch, blinking rapidly in the darkness until my vision adjusted, bringing them back into view.

"Emilio," I whispered. "Liam."

In the meadow before my white stone altar, Liam was on his knees beside my wolf. He looked as if he'd been there for hours, and now he stretched out a hand toward me, beckoning me forward.

"Hurry, Gray," he said, the urgency in his voice turning my blood cold. "There isn't much time."

"Time?" I crept closer, my muscles suddenly stiff with fear. Why wasn't Emilio moving? Was that… was that fresh blood on the ground? He still appeared to be trapped between his human and wolf forms, just like he had been at the warehouse. Why hadn't he shifted fully?

Why hadn't he healed?

Wordlessly I knelt down beside Liam and reached for Emilio's hand. He looked just like he had earlier tonight—gravely injured, caught between forms, carved up and poisoned by Orendiel's silver blade. But the face that had writhed in pain before had long since gone slack, and his skin was cold and clammy. His eyes were open, but they were glassy and vacant, holding no sign of the man I loved. No spark of life.

"Time for what?" I pressed, though I was pretty sure I knew the answer. My stomach was already twisting at the possibility, heart thudding in my throat.

Liam turned to me, human but for the glowing blue eyes and a faint pulse of silver-blue light emanating from his skin.

A soul, I realized. He was holding Emilio's soul.

Tears filled Liam's otherworldly eyes, and he reached for my face, touching it so sweetly and gently, it almost shattered my heart. He shook his head and closed his eyes, and the words came out slow and strangled. "It's… time to say goodbye, little witch. I'm so sorry."

NINE

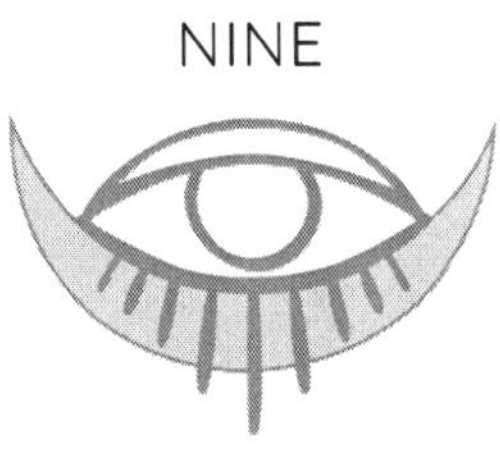

DARIUS

Ronan had nearly worn a groove in the living room floor with his incessant pacing, and if there weren't so many warm bodies in the way, I might've joined him. It'd been hours since Gray and Haley had sequestered themselves in the guest room, and other than a muffled conversation early on, we'd heard nothing. Saw nothing. No news. No updates. No sign of success or trouble but the iridescent glow of magic leaking out beneath the gap at the bottom of the door.

A trickle of worry crept down my spine, but I refused to let it take hold. Refused to show even a fraction of outward concern. The others wouldn't understand; in the wake of my memory loss, their claim on her heart felt much more legitimate than mine. But while my mind was unable to remember her presence in my life, some deeper part of me *did* remember. I felt it more and more the longer I spent in her presence.

And right now, that part of me wanted nothing more than to break down the bedroom door.

I glanced at the closed door down the hall, but the sentinel posted outside of it shook his head. Asher had taken Gray's demands seriously; he and the hounds would maim anyone who attempted to disturb her.

"Perhaps she's traveled to her realm," I reasoned aloud. "It's the most logical explanation, is it not?"

Ronan grunted something that might have been an agreement, though I couldn't be certain. "That thought doesn't bring me any peace," he said. "The freakshow hunter who's tried to kill her at least a dozen times already is supposedly running wild out there. She may as well have a target painted on her back."

"Liam will protect her."

Another grunt. "I don't like it. We should be there with her."

"Hmm." I rubbed my fingers over the stubble on my jaw. "My recollection is a bit hazy, but it's my understanding that the last time we tracked her to another realm, things went a bit sideways on us."

He stopped pacing long enough to glare at me, clearly not appreciating my attempt at humor.

"Regardless," I said. "We all know that when Gray sets her mind to something—"

Ronan's grunt turned into a growl, his eyes blackening as he stormed past me on his hundredth trek across the hardwood floor. "Don't tell me what I know, vampire. You can't even tell me what *you* know."

"I'm not sure I appreciate your tone, demon."

"No? Then why don't you take your smug face and your perfect little accent and go… I don't know. Go shove a scone up your arse."

"Ronan. Darius." Deirdre emerged from the kitchen, her presence stopping me from putting Ronan into a wall. "Why don't you redirect some of that toxic male aggression and help me with the coffee." She made her way around the room with a tray of steaming mugs, handing out coffee to the witches, some of whom had curled up together on the couch and chairs, others in smaller huddles on the floor. As exhausted as they must've been, no one had dared nod off. Not while Gray was unaccounted for and Emilio's fate still unknown.

"And if you can't make yourselves useful," the old woman continued, "at least make yourselves quiet. The last thing Gray needs is to come back and referee a pissing contest between—"

"You're something else, you know that?" Ronan shook his head, a look of utter disgust twisting his features.

"Ronan," she said, her eyes imploring him, "we will discuss our personal differences another time."

"Differences?" he snarled. "*Differences*?"

I felt the spike in his aggression mere seconds before his eyes turned demon black.

"So," he continued, "do you want to tell them about these *differences*, or should I?"

Deirdre visibly stiffened, but her eyes blazed with a new warning. "Now is *not* the time."

"You're right, witch. Twenty years ago was the time, but you failed. You made a bad call then, and every day you keep your secrets, you're making it a hell of a lot worse. For Gray, for yourself, and for everyone else."

"I had my reasons," she said. "As did you."

"Yeah? Why don't you come over here and remind me of them."

"Careful, demon. I'm not as old and docile as I look."

"Oh, for fuck's sake," I said, moving to stand between them. As much as I would've loved to see a brawl between a powerful old witch and a crossroads demon with an ax to grind, Deirdre was right. Now was *not* the time.

Fortunately, I was spared from having to intercede further by the opening of the front door and the sudden and rather grim entrance of the fae prince. His face was red with cold, his eyes full of something that looked a lot like fear. Real fear.

"I've finally made contact with my sister," he announced.

"Kallayna?" One of the witches on the couch asked. "Is everything okay?"

"It's... a long story," Jael said. "But the short version is that she's infiltrated the Darkwinter contingent in Blackmoon Bay under guise of a romantic relationship with one of their knights, and has been transmitting intelligence through a secured fae channel ever since. I hadn't heard from her in some time, but she finally managed to get a message out tonight, and the news isn't good."

Deirdre handed him a mug of coffee, which he accepted with a small bow. After taking a few sips, he pulled one of the dining chairs into the living room and took a seat.

"After the surprise attack and ensuing defeat in Raven's Cape tonight," he said, "Orendiel and the remaining Darkwinter Knights, along with the hunters still loyal to the cause, retreated to Blackmoon Bay to regroup."

"We figured that might happen," Ronan said, the argument with Deirdre seemingly forgotten in the presence of a far greater foe. "As far as we know, the Bay is still under their control."

"Yes," Jael confirmed. "But I fear the situation back home has taken a turn for the worse."

"How can that be?" I asked. "They've just suffered massive casualties and the loss of their most valuable prisoners. They retreated, presumably to lick their wounds."

Jael shook his head. "Apparently they've called in reinforcements. According to what Kallayna was able to uncover, two hundred additional knights have been dispatched to the Bay, and that's not counting the hundred or so already in place."

"Another two hundred?" Ronan let loose a heavy sigh. "We saw what they could do with less than half that number at the warehouse. It took all of us working together, with powerful magic and the element of complete surprise, just to survive the night. And not all—"

He cut off abruptly, but I knew what he'd been thinking.

And not all of us had *survived.*

I glanced down the hallway, hoping for a sign from Gray, but there was only Asher and the hounds, as still as marble statues. Asher's eyes were alert as he listened to our conversation out here, but he wasn't moving from his post for anything.

"There's more," Jael said, his face going a shade paler. "The Bay has been locked in a brutal winter storm for several days. White-out conditions, heavy accumulation, frigid temperatures."

"What?" Ronan asked. "But we never get weather like that. I can't even remember the last time it snowed there."

"Precisely," Jael said. "Kallayna believes the weather was conjured by Darkwinter. She hasn't found proof, but the timing and nature of the storm is too suspicious to be anything natural."

"To what end?" I asked.

Jael closed his eyes and sipped his coffee, lingering over every drop. He seemed to be avoiding the question, but just before I could press him again, he finally lowered his mug and met my gaze. "According to the official news reports, which are of course controlled by Darkwinter now, the storm has resulted in the closure of the two main bridges into and out of the Bay and all ferry service to and from Seattle and the surrounding areas. Without access to the city, vendors cannot deliver necessities like food, bottled water, medical supplies, and gasoline. Prior to announcing the road and waterway closures, Darkwinter Knights —with the backing of the law enforcement community that's also under their influence—seized control of the city's grocery stores and gas stations and began rationing out food and supplies."

"Holy shit," one of the witches—McKenna, I'd heard someone call her—said. "It's like martial law."

"Yes," Jael said. "Under guise of protection from the dangerous conditions of the storm, they've instituted a mandatory travel ban and curfew."

"And no one in the Bay has questioned this? Not even the humans?"

"Everything has been designed to look like a genuine emergency, including the extreme response," Jael said. "For the first few days, people were calm and orderly, trusting that the storm would pass, that the city officials would deal with any issues. But my sister tells me that panic has started to set in. Because of the curfew and restricted travel, many people—humans and supernatural alike—have not been able to go to work or open their businesses, and there have been reports of widespread looting and property damage. The Knights could easily quell this, but we believe it's all part of their plan to destabilize the city. Children are being kept from school. People can't get medical care. Sanitation services have been suspended, so garbage is piling up, and the water supply is now at risk. Boats have been frozen in the marinas, bringing the local fishing industry to a grinding halt. There are intermittent power outages, many of the older Victorian homes and original buildings do not have modern heating systems, and now the people are almost out of food. Rations or not, that is a terrifying proposition."

"It's a powder keg," I said, the implications hitting me full on. "All the pieces are in place."

"All that's left to do now is light the match." This from Elena, who'd just emerged from her bedroom. She'd excused herself to check on Reva soon after Gray and Haley had locked themselves in the guest room, and we'd all given her some space.

Her face was gaunt, with deep lines around her mouth and eyes. She'd showered, but she still smelled of wolf's blood.

My stomach twisted. The worse part? If I could detect it, she could, too.

I met her gaze, but then realized I had nothing to offer her. No compassionate smile, no words of encouragement, nothing that would truly help. For all intents and purposes, I was as much a stranger to her brother as most of the other guests in this house.

She nodded at me anyway, a gentle smile touching her lips.

Then, crossing to the center of the living room and addressing the group, she said, "The problem, of course, is that we don't know what that match looks like or when they plan to strike it."

"Sounds like we've got some things to sort out," I said, moving to stand at Ronan's side. I put a hand on his shoulder to let him know that for my part, all was forgiven. I had no interest in fighting with my brothers, even if I didn't remember them as such, and I wanted him to know that.

"Darius is right," he finally said, making no move to shake off my hand. "We need to make a solid plan."

"I'll put on more coffee," Deirdre said. "Something tells me this endless night is about to get a lot longer."

TEN

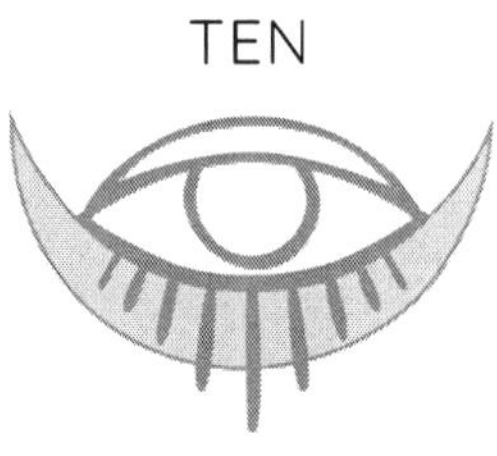

RONAN

It was damn near impossible to concentrate, but I was grateful for the challenge. It kept my mind off Gray and Emilio and Deirdre and all the other fucked-up shit swirling around inside, and right now, that was the best I could hope for. Distraction.

"So Darkwinter is amassing an army in the Bay," I said, still pacing, "where they've subdued most of the population and seized control of the city's resources. Meanwhile, we've liberated the witches, but not the hybrids the hunters created, or the other supernaturals they were experimenting on in the cave prisons."

"We're assuming they're being held elsewhere," Lansky said. "Possibly another warehouse in town, or—depending on how fast they bailed out last night—possibly in the Bay."

"You're assuming they're even *alive*," McKenna said. "From what we saw in there, none of them looked healthy. The hunters treated those guys even worse than they treated us."

"How do you mean?" I asked, though I suspected I already knew.

"Beat the shit out of them," McKenna said. "Tortured them. Basically, they were trying to trigger their predator response."

She wasn't telling me anything I didn't know, but fucking hell, those hunters were some sick bastards.

"If we're going to be prepared for all possible scenarios," Elena said, "we need to consider the *worst*-case scenario here. So yes, we're assuming they're alive, strong, and ready to attack on Darkwinter orders."

"You think the experiments worked?" I asked her.

"I think it's possible, and therefore I want to be prepared for that possibility." Despite the dark circles under her eyes, she glanced at her notes with extreme focus, tapping the notebook with her pen, totally absorbed in the task at hand.

Seemed I wasn't the only one who thrived on distraction.

"Before the warehouse mission," she continued, "Gray and Liam confirmed that Jonathan was still alive, albeit trapped in her magical realm. As Gray described it, he'd essentially transformed himself into some sort of human-shifter-vampire hybrid. If that's true, then there's a chance similar experiments were conducted on other beings, and possibly worked in the same way."

"But she also said Jonathan was falling apart," McKenna said. "Like, literally rotting away."

"True," Elena said, "but that doesn't mean he or the others like him can't do a lot of damage before they hit their expiration date."

Detective Hobb—a shifter cop I was pretty sure was banging Elena—spoke up next.

"So if we follow the logic here," he said, shouldering his way to the center of the packed room, "let's assume they've relocated these hybrids to the Bay—or they've created new ones at that location—and that they're at least somewhat operational as an attack force. Now we've got a city that's been isolated from the rest of the country, militarized by an invading fae army, stripped of most of its necessities, banned from traveling freely, and unable to communicate with the outside world—the only exception being Kallayna."

"Exactly," Jael said. "And we don't know how often she can reliably transmit information. She's already put herself at great personal risk."

"Fair point." Elena blew out a breath. "Okay, so if you're Orendiel, and you've got an entire city on lockdown and an army to back you up, and you want to cause the most damage in the shortest amount of time, what's your play?"

"Tell you what I'd do," I said. "Assuming I was a grade-A psychopath, which I'm not."

"Debatable," Beaumont said.

I shot him a death glare, but I let him get away with that one, mostly because I still felt guilty about the scone-up-the-arse comment. *Shit.* The sooner he got his memories back, the sooner he'd remember that insults and veiled threats were how we showed affection around here, and the better off we'd all be.

"I'd strategically unleash the hybrids," I went on. "Let them cause some ruckus at the local businesses, break into houses in the different supernatural neighborhoods, tear shit up, take a few people down in the process. Make the others believe they're being attacked from within—shifters burning down law-abiding vamp houses, vamps draining fae kids, fae manipulating shifter women, demons preying on witches, that sort of fucked-up shit. Then I'd sit back and watch the whole place turn on each other. Once that happens, they'll tear each other apart—we've never been totally at peace over there, anyway. Not even among our *own* kinds, let alone across species. And they'll have nowhere to go, no one coming in to help, because the 'benevolent' Knights of Darkwinter aren't going to break up that fight for anything. It's exactly what they want."

"Madre María," Elena said. "You're absolutely right—Emilio and I talked about this very thing after he'd found out about Talia's betrayal. Orendiel's going to light that fire, throw some gasoline on it, and watch the whole city burn to ashes."

"No," Beaumont said. "He won't let it burn to ashes. He'll be sure the humans get involved first. Think of it—it's the perfect scapegoat with a perfect message: Monsters have been living among you, and look what they've done to each other. They'll be coming for you next." He shoved a hand through his hair, losing some of the cool elegance he was known for. "He'll use that as leverage to get them to turn over even more of their freedoms. It starts in the Bay, and it spreads outward, especially when Darkwinter are controlling the messaging and communications."

"And that, my friends," Lansky said, "is how you stage a coup."

"We're talking about mass exposure of the supernatural community," Elena said, and a collective chill went around the room. "The Bay falls, then the neighboring cities, the state, the whole west coast…"

"This may already be happening in other places," McKenna said. "Haley and Reva were telling us that Norah had heard from some of the other covens in America and even a few overseas that weird shit was going down. Witch murders, disappearances, things like that. Norah didn't want to get involved—not even when they asked for her help directly."

"Gray told us about that, too," I said. "Haley and Sophie had apparently dug up some emails or something, and tried to confront Norah. She wanted nothing to do with it."

"Because she's in league with the hunters," the older witch with the yellow eyes said. "She sold out her own kind, and as far as we know, she's still on the loose."

"That's right," Elena confirmed. "We've got an APB out on her, but other than one credit card charge, we haven't heard a peep."

"She's the least of our problems," I said. "My gut tells me her part in this is over, and now she's on the run, trying to get ahead of the very nightmare she helped unleash. Right now I'm more concerned about Orendiel's plans in the Bay and the bigger implications for the country."

The room fell silent once again, hopelessness settling in like a death shroud.

"Let's not," Beaumont said, stepping out of the shadows to stand at the center of the room. "This is all very doom-and-gloom, and it's serious—no doubt about that. But we've faced down greater odds before, haven't we?" Then, he flashed a grin. "Well, *allegedly*. I don't remember the specifics, on account of my—"

"The point, vampire," I said, rolling my eyes. "Get to it."

"The point, dear demon," he continued, "is that we need a plan of attack, and we can't afford to get sidetracked with fear and speculation. While we know that witches have been kidnapped or murdered in other locations, we also know that the Bay, in particular, is under total siege. We have no such confirmation from any other cities or countries, so I humbly propose that we focus on the

Bay first. We can assess each new situation as we receive more information, but that one has to be paramount. It's my belief that Blackmoon Bay is ground zero for this entire operation."

"Agreed," Elena said.

"Thank you," Beaumont said. "Now, as I was saying. Yes, the situation is a powder keg over there. But the match has yet to be struck. And just like the warehouse siege, we have the element of surprise. They don't know that Kallayna is a spy, nor that she is still in contact with her brother."

"That is our hope, yes," Jael said. "But even so, we cannot physically reach them. They've isolated the city completely—not just with the storm and route closures, but with magic. Anyone who attempts to enter without Darkwinter knowledge and express permission will be turned around before they even get close. There is literally no way to breach city limits—not on foot, not with cars, not with planes, not even with tanks. Such is the deceptive nature of their magic."

"Fair point," Beaumont said, "But..." His lips curved into another grin, his eyes glinting with a look I'd come to know well. Hunger. "I believe I speak for all of the predators in the room when I say this: If we can't get to them, we'll just have to lure them out to us."

ELEVEN

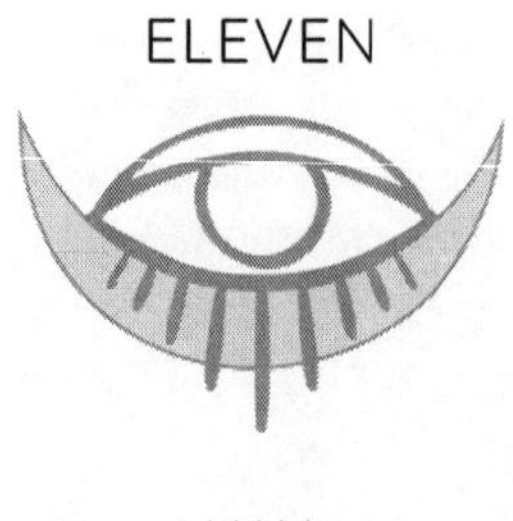

LIAM

Gray's twilight blue eyes clouded with ice, her whole body going rigid. From her energy, I felt nothing but cool detachment, even as Emilio's soul stirred into a hot frenzy inside me, recognizing her presence.

"I'm not here to say goodbye, Liam."

All the fear and concern and horror at Emilio's outward appearance vanished. She'd said the words simply, with a calm certainty I hadn't expected, as if there could be no other outcome.

I should've expected as much. Gray had always been determined, and she was fiercely protective of those she loved.

"You must," I said, though even I remained unconvinced. Still, it was my sacred duty to say these words, to inform her of his passing and offer her the option of escorting his soul to the Shadowrealm—or accompanying me, if she so chose. "It is your last chance before we—"

"There are *no* last chances here," she said, as resolute as I'd ever seen her. "I'm a necromancer, Liam. In the truest sense of the word. I have the capacity to give life, to save it, or to destroy it."

At that, I couldn't help but allow the faintest ghost of a smile to touch my lips. She was reciting my old words back to me, from the first time I'd told her about her nature. That was the night she'd lost Sophie, and she'd come so much farther since then.

"Clever girl," I said. "But did I not also tell you that all such beings are bound to me?"

She cocked her head, glaring at me with a power that would've frightened the strongest mortal. "It's a little late for that, Liam."

"Yes, I was afraid you might see it that way."

I had failed as her mentor. I had failed as her friend. And most of all, I had failed as a man who'd claimed to love her. There was nothing I could say now, no warning or long, metaphysical explanation, no truths or lies or anything in between that would alter her present course.

Gray placed a hand on Emilio's chest, her eyes softening for him and him alone. Then, turning back to me, she drew in a deep breath and said, "I am Shadowborn. I am the heir of Silversbane. And this man has my heart. If you think for one *second* I'm going to stand by and watch him vanish into eternity while I have the power to do something about it, you haven't learned a thing about me."

I offered a solemn nod, conceding her point. In truth, however, I'd learned more than she realized. For this moment, too, was a possibility I had seen. One I had hoped for, if I were being honest.

And here, at perhaps the most important meeting she and I would ever hold, honesty was my only choice.

"I know he hasn't yet passed on to the Shadowrealm," she said. "I can *feel* him. You have his soul."

"Indeed." I held up my hands, my skin glowing silver-bright in response. "Though I'm afraid I cannot hold him much longer. If I don't release him from my vessel, he will release himself, cursed to endlessly wander the realms without a guide."

She touched his face, her eyes softening once again. "So we'll put him back where he belongs."

"It's not that simple, I'm afraid. Even for a necromancer. His body is broken, Gray. His blood poisoned. His soul sensed the death of his physical form and departed of its own volition. To return it to his body now would simply trap him in pain and torment for all eternity."

"Not if we heal him first." She got to her feet and walked a circle around his body, her brow furrowed in concentration, her hands hovering before her as if she were trying to sense the last bit of his essence. "There must be something we can do. A spell."

"Perhaps," I said, standing to meet her eyes once again. "But there is no time. Not if we want to prevent his soul from wandering."

"Think, Liam. Think." Gray pressed her fingers to her temples and closed her eyes. "There's something we're not seeing here. Some way to heal him quickly or… something."

I watched her, in awe at her courage. Her calm. She'd come through so much in such a short time, and yet she still wasn't ready to concede defeat. With Gray, there was always another way.

"Well?" She opened her eyes, the moonlight reflecting on her hair, turning it silver in its pale light, and—

"Moonlight," I said, the answer coming to me now, sharp and clear.

And, like so many things I'd experienced since Gray had come into my life, completely forbidden.

But if it meant helping her restore the life of someone she loved, I wouldn't have it any other way.

"Moonlight what?" she asked, her hands on her hips. "Liam, we don't have time for your poetic riddles tonight. What are you—"

"Quiet, Gray. I must concentrate." Lifting my hands to the sky, I called upon the magic of the ancient fae, using it to channel light from the moon. I gathered it into my hands, so pure and beautiful it nearly hurt to look at. Then, with a spell as old as time, outlawed since the first Elemental Wars, I whispered the incantations and carefully spun in into a gossamer sphere no larger than a grapefruit.

Gray gasped beside me, but she remained still and silent, allowing me to do my precious work.

With a slow exhale, I released Emilio's soul, guiding the silver-white light into the moonglass. After a final incantation, the sphere sealed itself, encasing his essence in an unbroken bubble of protective moonlight.

"Moonglass," I said, holding the feather-light globe between us. "It will contain his soul until we are ready to release it."

My owl and raven ferriers, who'd been perched silently on the black branches overhead during our entire exchange, finally took flight. Despite the mesmerizing beauty of the sphere, they knew what its making had just called forth.

Gray and I had perhaps an hour by earthly reckoning to complete our task. Perhaps an hour before I'd be called to atone for my actions, sentenced to some punishment I could only imagine.

But that was a concern for another moment. Right now, Gray and I had more important matters to consider.

"What… what is it?" she breathed, still in awe. "How does it work?"

"It's a fae spell," I explained. "Almost as old as I am. It is the only known magic that can hold a soul indefinitely without damaging it."

"I've never heard of this before."

"Moonglass has been banished for more than four thousand years. While our purpose is to return life, the original intention was not so benevolent."

Her eyes widened as she peered into the glass. Its pearly sheen changed colors, shifting from silver to white to an iridescent pink, reacting to the soul inside.

"How do you mean?" she asked.

"The first fae tricked the moon into lending them her light, and they used it to create a device that would imprison the souls of their enemies. During times of war, they would call the light onto the battlefield, performing the spell and luring the souls of recently deceased enemy soldiers inside. Once captured, the souls could later be released into the most hostile fae realms, condemning them to an eternity of torment so much worse than anything they'd ever faced as soldiers."

She was silent for several moments, mesmerized by the beautiful, undulating sphere, and undoubtedly horrified by the tale of its origins. "Magic like this… It doesn't come without a cost," she finally said. "I know that better than anyone."

"No, it doesn't."

She swallowed hard, then met my gaze, the opalescent swirls of the moonglass reflected in her eyes. "What will this cost?"

"It matters not. The price will be paid."

Her eyelids fluttered closed, and she sighed deeply. "Liam, despite everything that happened between us, I don't want you to… I don't want something bad to—"

"I will not lie to you again, Gray," I interrupted. "I do not know what is to come of this—only that I will be called to atone for it. That is the truth. The moment I created the moonglass, I sealed my fate. I will take whatever punishment is meted out."

"But—"

"It is done. I've no regrets about that decision now, nor will I have them later. For there is no price I wouldn't pay to bring you even a moment's peace." I gazed into her eyes, needing her to understand the depths of my feelings for her, the boundlessness of my sadness that I'd caused her any harm at all. "You must know that, Gray."

My voice had softened to a whisper, and Gray nodded, a single tear slipping from her eye. She held my gaze a moment longer, but her thoughts were veiled to me. If she thought to say something more, she decided against it, quickly swiping away the renegade tear and nodding, once again resolute.

"What *you* must decide," I explained, "is whether you're willing to accept the risks and consequences for this decision and any that may come after as we endeavor to bring him back. If you're not, you may say your goodbyes now and leave this realm, as you should have already done, and I will face those consequences alone."

At this, she let out a hollow laugh and rolled her pretty eyes. "Come on, Liam. I thought you knew me at least a little better than that. I would never bail on you."

Nor I you, little witch. Not ever again.

"We're in this together," she went on. "Even if it wasn't Emilio's soul, and you'd asked for *my* help instead of the other way around, I'd still be here for you."

"That… that means more to me than you can imagine."

"I need you to know something. Everything that happened in the past—all the things you kept from me… It changes nothing. This means more to me than all of it. *You* mean more to me."

Emotion tightened my throat, but there were no adequate words to express my gratitude, my feelings for her. So instead, I lowered my eyes to the sphere and said, "This is the last important thing we will ever do together, Gray. Fitting that it will be the *most* important."

Without further ado, I handed her the moonglass. She took the sphere into her hands, delicately and reverently, fully aware of the importance of its contents.

"Guard it with your last breath," I warned anyway. "For if it breaks before the ritual is complete, his soul will have no vessel."

"And he'll wander forever. I understand, Liam. I won't let that happen."

"Emilio is lucky to have you as a friend. As am I." It was all I'd dare to confess. I held her unwavering gaze for the span of one more breath, and then I turned back toward her wolf. "And now we begin."

TWELVE

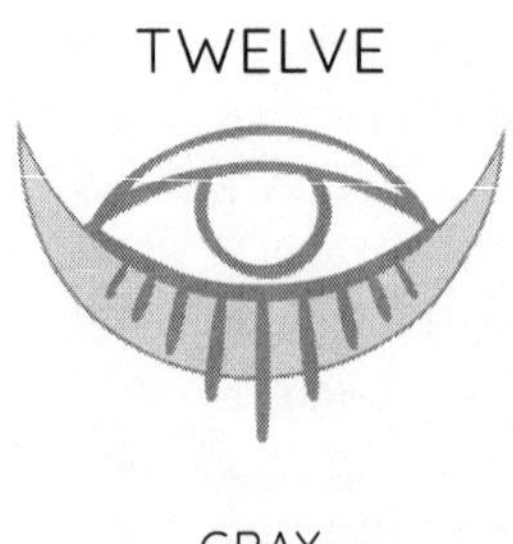

GRAY

The moonglass felt as delicate as a soap bubble, and I held it close to my chest, my skin warming at the contact.

Liam had said this was the most important thing we would ever do together, and I couldn't deny that. But the last thing? No. Neither of us knew what the future held, what the price of our actions tonight would be. But I had to believe this wasn't the end. Not for any of us.

Because I had to believe this would work—that we'd succeed in saving Emilio. And if we could do that, what *couldn't* we do? What challenges couldn't we overcome? What price couldn't we pay? What rules couldn't we break and re-write?

Love made all of that possible. And I *did* love Liam, I realized now. We had a lot to work through together, a lot of trust to rebuild, a lot of pain to heal. But that didn't change how I felt.

"Are you ready?" he asked, kneeling down beside Emilio's body.

I nodded, kneeling on the other side, careful to keep the moonglass safe.

"I will drain the poison from his body and attempt to heal his physical wounds," Liam said. "But you must do the rest. You have a bond with him—one that goes far beyond the physical. Your souls are connected as flames lit from a single candle."

"We are," I whispered, feeling a tug low in my belly, a warmth that stretched outward toward the sphere, longing to feel Emilio's touch.

"Gaze into the moonglass," Liam continued, his hands already moving over Emilio's wounds, assessing the damage. "Call on your love for him, your connection, and reach out to his soul. You must be as a beacon for him, Gray, for even with our guidance, if he loses his way back to his physical form, we won't be able to revive him. Do you understand?"

"Yes," I said firmly.

"Once he's found you, you must guide the soul precisely back into his body. That is done with intense focus, precise visualization, and your magic. You must imagine his soul as a river of light, and your magic as the gentle but immutable force of gravity that guides it along its path. It will require more magic than you have ever expended, more concentration than you have ever commanded, and above all, unshakable faith that you can complete this task. There is *no* room for error on this, Gray. Not unless you want to turn him into something… else."

"Bean," I breathed, and a memory flickered behind my eyes—a young girl in a unicorn hoodie, blood pooling on the pavement, her life force leaving as I held her in my arms. It was before I'd learned about my powers, about being Shadowborn, about any of it, and I'd brought her back from the dead with no clue what that would mean for her.

I'd turned her into something terrible, an undead monster, cursed.

Swallowing the lump in my throat, I nodded again. That would *not* happen. Not again. Never again.

"I can do this, Liam. I know I can." I cleared my throat, then tried again. "I will do this. I'll guide his soul, bring him home. There are no other options."

Liam stopped his ministrations and smiled, catching my gaze. "I have complete faith in you, little witch, or we would not even attempt it."

His smile was brief, but his confidence bolstered me further.

"I have complete faith in you, too," I said plainly, because that was the truth. Just as I wouldn't create another cursed soul, Liam would never disappoint me again. I knew that like I knew the taste of Emilio's brownies, the scent of his skin, the feel of his wolf's fur on my hands.

"His body is almost mended," Liam said. "There will likely be scarring, but that is better than the alternative."

"Agreed."

"Call upon your magic, Gray. It is almost time."

Letting my eyes drift closed, I sought the magic within me, urging the gentle warmth to a flame, pushing it outward through my limbs. In my mind's eye, I saw the black streaks cover my hands, slowly igniting into the blue flames I'd come to associate with my Death magic. It was hard to remember a time that I'd feared this power, that I'd recoiled from it in shame. It came so easy now, as natural a part of my being as any other.

"Good," Liam said. "You're doing great. Continue to follow my voice. I will guide you through the next steps." His voice was soothing and calm, easy to follow, like drifting down a warm and lazy river in the summer. "Use your power to tap into the source. Draw more magic into you."

I did as he asked, just like I'd done earlier when I'd been struggling with Jonathan. It took even less time now; the source seemed to be expecting my return, and eagerly connected with my magic, filling me to the absolute limits. My physical body began to vibrate, my heart racing, my teeth chattering, but I held steady.

"You're incredible, Gray," Liam said. "Now, you'll soon reach a point where you feel as if you'll absolutely burst if you take in even one more modicum of magic. Are you close?"

"I'm there," I said, my voice quavering. "I can't... hold... much longer..."

"You can, Gray. And you must," he said firmly, leaving no room for argument. "Actually, you must take even more. Push past your perceived limitations, Gray. Emilio's life depends on it."

I obeyed without question, drawing more magic toward my center, pulling it up through my chest, pushing it into my heart and lungs, my veins, filling myself beyond capacity. Brightness surged before my eyes, and I didn't have to open them to know that the light was coming from my own skin, barely able to contain this much power. My heart was now beating so rapidly it sounded like a snare drum in my ears, but I kept my breathing steady. Calm. Balanced. Even as every inch of me wanted to explode—to scream, to tear, to burst apart at the seams and unleash this magic.

But still, I held on.

Still, I drew more. I drank it in deep, fraying my nerves, grating my bones, squeezing my cells.

"You are almost there, Gray. Hold on."

I nodded, too afraid that opening my mouth now would let loose some of the magic.

"Okay," he continued. "When I give you the signal, I want you to open your eyes, smash the moonglass, and channel all of that magic into sending Emilio's soul back to his earthly vessel—just like we talked about. Can you do that?"

I nodded again, despite the dizziness making my head swim. My entire body was simply humming with magic, buzzy like a live wire after a rainstorm.

"Now, Gray!" Liam shouted. "Now!"

My eyes flew open, and I smashed the moonglass on the ground beside me. Emilio's soul spiraled outward, the purest silver-white I'd ever seen, so beautiful and breathtaking it brought tears to my eyes.

"Reach out for him, Gray. You must let him know you're here."

I blinked rapidly, refocusing, corralling the wild magic inside me. Lifting my hands, I sent out a concentrated pulse, guiding it around the silvery mist of his soul, urging the two energetic forces to connect. At first, I felt nothing—saw nothing—and a flare of panic rose in my chest.

But I ushered it out, quickly re-centering myself. This magic was mine. I could bend it to my will, direct it to my ends, guide it to bring back the man I loved. I had faith in myself, just as Liam had in me.

I relaxed, slowly increasing the pulse of my magic. It was a struggle to control it, but I held on. Familiar blue flames engulfed my hands again, surging bright, and I extended those flames, guiding them around his soul. At first, the mist recoiled, but then it finally stilled.

"Emilio," I said, pushing past the tremor in my voice. "It's me. Gray. Your *brujita*. I love you so, so much. Please come back to me. Follow the sound of my voice, and come back to yourself."

"Good," Liam said. "Keep talking."

"You have nothing to fear," I told Emilio. "I will guide you every step of the way. But you need to want this, *El Lobo*. You need to want to come to your family. Me, Ronan, Asher, Darius, and Liam, too. Elena and her partners. The witches we saved from the prison. All of us are waiting for you at home. Your sister is already preparing a big feast. Empanadas, I'm told." I kept talking, reminding him of all the guys, of the things we'd done together, the things we'd yet to do, the jokes we'd shared. Only good things. The sweetest moments, the happiest times, the love and camaraderie we'd all been building together. The moments, both big and small, that had bonded us together and made us a found family in the truest sense.

"You and the others found *me*," I reminded him. "Twice—when I'd first arrived in Blackmoon Bay, scared and alone. And more recently, after I'd lost Sophie. You helped me put the pieces back together, Emilio. You've healed my heart in ways you can't even imagine. Well, now it's my turn to come out and find *you*. To bring you home to us where you belong. So please don't make my job harder, *El Lobo*. Or you're going to owe me twice as many brownies later."

I didn't stop, not even to take a breath. For what felt like hours, I spoke to my beloved wolf, weaving a story of love and hope and friendship, of family and laughter, of joy, each shared memory a breadcrumb for him to pick up and follow home.

I spoke until my body was numb from lack of movement. And then, finally, when my voice was cracking and my tongue thick, I felt the change.

The magic inside me heated, and the air stirred, lifting the loose curls from my face and enveloping me in the familiar scents of trees and fresh-baked sweetness that could only belong to one man.

Tears spilled down my cheeks, and the words of my stories turned into a spell, coming to me unbidden, but absolutely welcome.

I am your guide
And you are my love
In body and spirit
Below and above
Blood follows heart
And heart follows soul
What was once torn apart
Shall now be made whole

I repeated the spell a dozen times, visualizing Emilio's soul returning to his body, just like Liam had instructed. Even when my voice had finally given out and my throat was throbbing and raw, still I said the words, no more than whispers of breath now, finally fading out as the last of the magic and strength left my body.

On my final word, I collapsed, falling backward onto the ground, my eyes glazed, the glittery night sky a swirl of blue and white overhead.

I took deep, cool breaths of night air, waiting for my body to come back to itself. To stop its vicious trembling. To still.

I did not even have the strength to turn my head or ask Liam whether we'd succeeded.

But then, I felt the warmth of Liam's touch on my cheek. Slowly, his face came into focus, his all-knowing eyes looking down at me, shining with something that looked a lot like pride.

"Gray, you did it. You did it."

Before I could even return his smile, darkness descended, and thick, black smoke settled over us like a cloak. The ground beneath me rumbled, making my stomach pitch, my head spin. I tried to sit up, but couldn't—some force far greater than my own weakness was holding me down, sitting on my chest like an invisible monster, crushing the breath from my lungs.

I couldn't see. Couldn't hear. For the longest seconds of my life, there was only fear, rising inside me like a new fire, ready to consume everything in its path.

And then, in the wake of seemingly utter chaos, a spark of hope.

The darkness pulled back, revealing the stars once again, and all at once, the sounds came rushing back.

Another breeze, stirring me back to life.

A sharp intake of breath from the body beside me.

A rattling cough.

Another deep breath, this one more steady than the last.

And the faint sound of a familiar name, the most beautiful music I'd ever heard.

"*Querida?* Is that you?"

THIRTEEN

LIAM

The earthquake in Gray's realm was merely a warning. I had just enough time to send Gray and Emilio back to the material plane before the ground before me split wide open, trees toppling into the gash, the stone altar cracking in two. The pentacle-carved slab on top slid to the ground and shattered. The stars winked out, and darkness veiled the moon, turning the realm a murky gray.

And then *they* arrived.

From the newly formed chasm in the forest floor, a smoky essence emerged, dark and dense, its presence turning the air acrid, burning my eyes and my flesh, sending me to my knees.

It was nothing I hadn't expected. I just hadn't realized it would be so excruciating.

Known only as the Old One, the essence was nothing and many things all at once. Eternity. Power. Emptiness. Completion. The void. The end, the beginning, and everything in between.

And, for all intents and purposes, my maker.

The Old One surrounded me, filled me, claimed my breath. Its formless voice was both singular and infinite, slicing through my mind and echoing in my skull, the raw, uncut power of it nearly shattering my vessel's bones.

"Lord of Shadows," the voices boomed. "It is long since we have last spoken. Longer still since we have been called to investigate the breaking of one of our most sacred laws."

It was an accusation, not a greeting, and though my instincts forced me to bow my head in deference to my superior, I wasted no time with return pleasantries.

"I could not let him pass into the Shadowrealm as such," I stated plainly, eyes downcast. "He is tied to her destiny in ways we cannot yet fathom, even with the gift of foresight."

"It matters not," came the emotionless reply. "He was to pass on. That was *his* destiny. The destiny of your witch is irrelevant."

"My witch, if you must call her so, is the Silversbane heir. She loves this man, and he loves her. I could not in good conscience allow that bond to be broken in such a way. Both of them deserve better."

"You are Death and Shadow, Lord of these lands and ferrier of souls between realms. Conscience does not concern you. Nor do the specifics of prophecies, Silversbane or otherwise, nor the emotional frailties of a witch who, for all the power inherent in her blood, is still scarcely more than a child."

At this, I got to my feet. The Old One had the power and right to scold me, to banish me, to torture me, as was their way in the face of abject disobedience. But I would *not* let them speak of Gray so dismissively. Not while I still had strength left in my vessel to defend her.

"The woman you call a child," I said, struggling to keep my tone respectful, "is destined to prevent the slaughter of thousands. *Millions*. Humans, vampires, shifters, fae, witches, countless others—your children. All of us would be wise to support her."

The smoke thickened around me, inside me, forcing a cough from my chest before it finally retreated, giving me a modicum of breathing room. Hovering over the ground before me, it roiled and twisted into the rough shape of a man, large and looming, with cavernous pits for eyes that glowed like lava. There was no mouth.

"Do not presume to speak to us of wisdom," the voice warned, and I stumbled a step backward from the splitting pain in my skull. "The witch is by all rights an abomination. She should have died long ago, many times over. Her life scroll has already been burned, has it not?"

It wasn't a question, merely another accusation. One I wouldn't deny.

"Yet she persists," I said. "Her strength, her fortitude, her compassion, her love for—"

"She survives by breaking our natural laws and mocking the semblance of order we've abided by since the dawn of consciousness. She simply should not be."

"That doesn't change the fact that she *is*." I regained my footing and approached the smoky essence again, my feelings for Gray propelling me forward. She was with me always; by my nature I transcended the bounds of time, experiencing her every wondrous touch as if it were the first again, as if it were merely moments ago, as if she were standing right beside me.

The memory of our last kiss arched like fire across my lips.

"There is a spark in her," I said, "the likes of which I've not seen in others of her kind. I have learned a great deal during the time and space I've shared with her, and—"

"Learned a great deal?" The voice was mocking now. Cruel. "It seems you have *forgotten* a great deal, as well. Including your sacred oath."

I closed my eyes and lowered my head, the collective weight of the Old One's accusations piling high on my shoulders. I would carry the weight of my discretions for the rest of my existence, for it was true—I'd broken sacred oaths for her. I'd strayed from my path. I'd… I'd changed.

I was Death, the Great Change, the Ultimate Transformation. How many times had I told Gray just that, trotting out the appellations like badges granting me supreme authority?

A smile touched my lips. In the end, it wasn't the Shadowborn witch who'd been changed so drastically by our relationship.

It was me.

"Indeed, I have forgotten things," I conceded, my eyes meeting those glowing pits once again. "But I cannot regret the things I've received in exchange. Despite all that I've forgotten or discarded, there is one thing I know beyond the shadow of all doubts." I recalled the sight of the moonglass, Emilio's soul swirling inside as Gray held him close. In that moment, I'd felt his thoughts, the ache of past regrets he'd feared he'd never have the opportunity to make right.

And I felt his love for Gray, burning brighter with every passing second.

"In the face of his sudden departure," I continued, "her spark would've been utterly extinguished. And the darkness of that loss would echo across the realms for eternity."

"For her, you have disobeyed your sacred duties at all turns. You say that her loss would've echoed across the realms, yet do you not believe that your own actions would have similar consequences?"

"It matters not," I admitted, "for I would do it all again, through time immemorial, if it meant sparing her even the briefest touch of heartbreak." Shame flared inside my chest for all the pain I'd already caused her, but I spoke the truth. "I will not bring the witch to harm again. *That* is my solemn oath now, and in obeying it, I must also serve those to whom her heart belongs. I must love and protect them as my kin."

"You've no obligation to her guardians."

"Obligation, no. But respect. Gratitude." And, dare I hoped, should we survive what was to come, brotherhood. Family, just like Gray had said when she'd brought Emilio back to his body.

For that is what we'd become, Gray's men and I. Regardless of their feelings toward me, regardless of my form on this realm or another, regardless of my many mistakes and missteps, our love for her bound us as family.

I knelt down in the grass again, placing my hands on the impression Emilio's body had left behind, making my final decision. "I will not carry him through the gates to the Shadowrealm on this night or any that follow. Nor will I defend my decision further. This matter is closed."

"Very well. In creating moonglass and sharing it with the Silversbane witch, you have brought it forth from the mists of legend and into the realm of thought, idea, and possibility once again. Your primal oath has been broken, and even now, you remain defiant. As such, you shall inherit the consequences of this decision, to be determined by cosmic tribunal at such a time as we deem appropriate."

I bowed as low as I dared, respectful once again.

But not remorseful.

Not regretful.

And not ashamed.

"So it shall be," I said, expecting—and hoping for—its immediate retreat.

But the Old One lingered.

The glowing eyes dimmed, the smoke thinning, but still, it did not vanish.

Suddenly I felt it inside me again, filling my chest, surrounding Liam Colebrook's heart. *My* heart. It beat frantically as a mouse caught by a predator, desperate for escape. My body flooded with fear. Adrenaline.

And beneath all of that, something else.

Hope.

"Your human heart shall be your downfall, Lord of Shadows," the voice echoed ominously. "And the downfall of those you've come to love as well."

Your human heart…

Hope surged, drowning out the fear. The Old One had touched upon something deeply personal within me; I'd never felt more human than I did in that moment, knowing I'd broken my sacred vows beyond all repair, knowing that I'd made my choices willingly, knowing that I'd sacrificed something precious so that others might have a chance at something even better.

"Perhaps," I countered, the beat of that almost-human heart as loud and steady as a drum in my ears, "it shall be our savior instead."

FOURTEEN

EMILIO

Snatches of memory flickered behind my eyes. The flash of magic… My wolf form lunging at a fae soldier… The metallic taste of his blood filling my mouth. The fierce clanging of swords reverberated off the walls. Ronan was shouting, running toward me. Elena in the line of fire. Ronan's face, stricken and panicked.

And then came the burning. Poison. My body feeling like it was consuming itself just to escape.

Pain. So much pain, and everyone around me screaming, all at once. Shouting orders. Ronan bent over me. Elena, tears leaking from her eyes. And Gray, holding my hand…

Fire. Smoke. So hot, and still so much pain.

And then…. Nothing. I was floating, soaring like a bird through the night sky until the inferno at the warehouse was nothing more than a tiny point of light on an infinite black canvas.

There was a tug, a presence, something telling me to let go. I wanted to. Anything to make the pain end. But then her voice broke through the mindless haze, clear as a song on a silent night.

Mi brujita bonita, calling me home…

Gray, I mouthed, but no sound came out. I felt the beating of my heart in my chest, the blood running through my veins, strong and clear once again. I smelled the antiseptic scents of floor cleaner and medicine and gauze. My skin crawled with an itch so deep, I was sure it would never fade.

But I was alive. I knew it with every fiber of my being. I was alive.

My head was heavy, my body trying to drag me back into a deep sleep, but I fought it. Where had I ended up? I had to see. Had to know. Slowly, I forced my eyes to open, recoiling at the sudden flood of white light.

I tried again. A peek. A little wider. Shapes and shadows emerged before me, filling in the light. Molecule by molecule, it seemed, my surroundings finally solidified.

I was in a bed, taped up with bandages, wearing nothing but gauze and a flannel sheet covering my lower half. It smelled like me. It smelled like Gray. The room was familiar, as was the woman keeping vigil at my bedside.

Gray, I mouthed again, but no, it wasn't her scent.

The woman beside me was my sister, seated in a chair next to the bed, her back ramrod straight, her hand resting on my forearm. Her face was turned in profile, her gaze focused on something outside the window.

She hadn't seen me yet, and I took the stolen moment to watch her. To re-memorize the shape of her face, the color of her hair. She had a few years on me, but when we were children, people used to think we were twins.

Same golden skin. Same wavy black hair. Same smiles.

It was a long time ago.

I finally shifted in my bed to let her know I was awake, and her head snapped toward me immediately.

I grinned, the last of the lingering fuzziness clearing from my mind.

Elena gasped at the sight of me, slapping a hand over her mouth. A smile peeked through around the edges of her fingers, making the skin around her brown eyes crinkle.

A flood of silent tears leaked down her cheeks.

"*¿Que pasa?*" I teased, testing out my voice. It was cracked and raw, but the words came out anyway. "*Jesús, María, y José.* You look like somebody *died,* Elena."

At this, my sister burst out laughing.

Dios mio, that was a good sound to come home to.

"You *asshole,*" she said, smacking my shoulder, but she was still laughing. "You had us all scared out of our minds, thinking we'd be planning a funeral this weekend, and now you're cracking jokes?"

"What better time for a laugh then when you're standing on Death's door?"

"Speaking of Death's door," she said, "where is your friend Liam? I've got a few choice words for him, too."

Liam… At the sound of his name, a new memory surfaced, but I couldn't hold onto it. He'd been there that night, I was sure of it now. Helped me somehow. But that was all I had.

"I haven't heard from him," I said, still chasing that memory. But it was gone, like so many others from that night. Perhaps that was for the best. "As far as I know, he's still tracking Jonathan in Gray's realm."

Elena narrowed her eyes, but if she knew more, she wasn't saying a word.

I sat up a bit, and Elena propped an extra pillow behind my head. That, too, smelled like Gray, and I glanced around the room, searching for her, though I knew she wasn't here. The scent of her on my sheets was fading.

"She's resting," Elena said, answering the question before my lips had even formed the words. "For the first time in days. It took all of us multiple attempts and a few threats to convince her to finally leave your side for more than just a quick bite to eat and a trip to the bathroom."

"So she's… okay?"

Elena smiled. "Tired from the ordeal, but yes, Emilio. Now that you're here, we're all okay."

"And the witches? Reva? Haley and the others?"

"All present and accounted for. Getting stronger every day. I should know—I'm feeding and housing them. All this time, Emilio, I had no idea how much these women could eat!"

"You love it, and you know it."

"Guilty as charged. It's been a long time since I've had a full house. As chaotic as it is, it's also kind of nice. Big meals. Late-night talks. Fighting over the bathrooms." She took my hands in hers, her smile slowly slipping away. She held my gaze a moment longer, then looked out the window again, her attention drifting back to whatever she'd been watching before I'd woken up.

Wind howled against the side of the house, lashing the windows with heavy, wet snow I'd only just begun to notice—fiercer than any storm I'd ever seen in the Pacific Northwest.

"Wow," I said. "How long have I been out?" I was sure it'd been months. I'd probably missed Christmas, missed New Year's. It might be past Valentine's Day for all I knew.

"Three days," Elena said. "In and out of consciousness as your body healed."

I blew out a breath. Three days? That was a relief. "What's with the snow?"

"They're saying on the news it's a once-in-a-lifetime storm," Elena said, though something in her voice had changed. Was that *fear* I detected? "It started in the Bay and has been working its way westward ever since. Most of the state is feeling the impacts." She rattled off snowfall amounts and temperatures, wind chill factors, all the facts and figures as if she were a weather reporter. But she was holding back the deeper truth. I could practically smell the lies of omission in her blood.

"Elena. What aren't you telling me?"

She shook her head, turning her gaze on me once again and forcing a smile. "There's plenty of time for catching up and making plans of attack now that you're awake. Right now, I want you to focus on healing. Can you do that for me?"

She swept the hair from my forehead, a gesture so unexpectedly sweet and motherly it made my throat tighten. She must've seen the emotion in my eyes, but this time she didn't look away or change the subject or feign some excuse about getting dinner started. Instead, she held my gaze, her own deepening with a mix of shadows and regrets and memories and even, most shocking of all, love.

"What are you thinking, Lainey?" I whispered.

The sound of her childhood nickname was foreign to us both, and the shock of it showed in her face. But still, she didn't break our connection. Not this time.

"I was thinking about that old saying about anger and forgiveness," she said. "How holding a grudge is like drinking poison and waiting for the other person to die."

I hadn't been expecting such a dark turn, but I shouldn't have been surprised. All evidence pointed to the fact that I'd nearly died in the warehouse that night. It made sense that my sister would be thinking about all the unsaid, unsettled things left between us—things we'd ignored for two decades. Hell, I couldn't be certain, but as I lay on that concrete floor, blood leaking out of my organs, I was pretty sure my own stockpile of regrets had flashed through my mind.

"For so many years," she continued, "I pretended you didn't exist. Did you know that?"

I shook my head. How could I know? The last thing she'd ever said to me was "Leave me, and don't ever come back," a broken whisper from a broken woman whom I would've done anything to make whole again. Until I'd called her about the Landes murder and Jonathan's connections in Raven's Cape, we hadn't spoken a word to each other in two decades.

"It's true," she said. "It was the only way I could let go of even a *fraction* of the rage I felt toward you." She closed her eyes and shook her head, pressing her lips together so tightly, they turned white. "Whenever anyone asked about my family, my home, I told them I'd been an only child, adopted by a couple in America when I was very young."

I sighed, my heart breaking. My for-public-consumption backstory had been similarly constructed, similarly terrible.

The only person I'd ever told about Elena was Ronan, and even he didn't know the whole story.

"That night at the warehouse," she continued, her face going a few shades paler, "seeing you on the floor like that, the blood… I thought I'd lost you, Emilio Alejandro Alvarez. I thought I'd have to see that name carved into a tombstone. And for the first time in twenty years, I realized you *hadn't* stopped existing for me. You never will."

Tears glazed her eyes, her pain so raw and real I had to look away. "We share the same blood, Elena. That alone connects us, even if we'd never spoken again."

"No, it's more than that." She wiped her eyes. "I spent so long wishing you'd never existed, and then I almost got my wish the other night. I was a monster, I realized. A fool. All that hatred, all that wasted time and energy, none of it ever brought my baby back. And now I was going to lose my brother on top of it all. When I got home that night, I went to my room and prayed. I prayed to *Jesús* and *Madre María*. I prayed to the saints. I prayed to the ghosts of Mamá and Papá and my husband and daughter. I prayed to every goddess I could name, and when I ran out of goddesses, I moved onto the gods, and then the universe, and then the stars, and anyone or anything else that would listen. Because in that moment, when I looked down and saw your blood covering my hands, I knew in the depths of my soul that I didn't want to lose you. Not again. No matter what happened in the past."

The force of her emotions hit me like a wave, and I closed my eyes, nearly drowning in the guilt I'd kept at bay for so many years. It was a constant force, and now it surged, as dense and heavy and dangerous as a black hole, threatening to drag me under for the last time.

"Emilio," she said softly, her hand against my cheek, and I opened my eyes to find her face streaked with fresh tears. "I don't want to waste any more time pretending I don't have a brother. We've lost so many years already."

"So many I've almost lost count." I swallowed the thickness in my throat. "I'm sorry, Elena. I'm so sorry. I was sorry then, and I've never stopped wishing for a time machine to go back and do it all differently. I never meant…"

I trailed off. She'd heard variations of this apology many times, and it hadn't changed anything.

I almost expected her to turn her back again. To order me out of her life, out of Raven's Cape, never to return. I wouldn't have blamed her.

If it weren't for me, her family might still be alive.

But instead, she looked at me, the look in her eyes more

vulnerable and hopeful than I'd ever seen, and said, "I want to let you back in. I just… I just don't know how. All that time, all that anger, still so many questions that I know you don't have answers for… There's a wall around my heart when it comes to you, and I can't find a way to crack it. Not yet."

I took her hand in both of mine and held it close, grateful beyond words that she'd shared that with me. For so long, I thought she was lost to me, and I'd tried to make my peace with that, though I'd never succeeded.

And now, she'd given me new hope, no matter how fragile. No matter how distant.

"So what do I do, Meelo?" she asked, her voice cracking on my old nickname. "Let you in, even after everything?"

"I can't answer that for you, Lainey." I pressed a kiss to her hand. "But I'm glad you want to try."

"But where do we go from here?"

"Nowhere. We just stay here. Right here. Take it day by day. Maybe one of those days, we'll find the first crack in the wall." I smiled, reaching up to smooth away the last of her tears. "Or maybe you'll get tired of me and decide to add some more bricks, make it even stronger, add some turrets and battlements on the top, a couple of armed guards, a canon, a cauldron of boiling oil…"

"Okay, okay, I get it." She rolled her big brown eyes, a faint smile touching her lips. "You watched too much American TV as a child. I tried to warn Mamá, but she never listened."

"Day by day," I repeated, my tone serious again. "Fair enough?"

She tucked her hair behind her ears and nodded, her smile growing a fraction wider. "Day by day. Yes, I think I can manage that," she said, and the heaviness that had descended between us dissipated in an instant, burned away like fog in the morning sun.

"He's awake?" A familiar voice called out from the doorway, and I turned to find my *brujita,* tears filling her eyes as she clasped her hand over her mouth, just like my sister had done. It made me smile.

"And doing much better now that you're here," Elena teased.

"Hmm. Look at that color in his cheeks! It's like someone just flipped him over and gave him a shot of adrenaline right in the—"

"Arm," I finished for her.

"Sure, Meelo. If you say so." She gave me a wink, smoothing her hand over my cheek once more.

"I'm... I'm sorry," Gray said. "I didn't mean to interrupt. I can come back later."

"Don't be silly." Elena rose from her chair and stretched. "We were just finishing up."

"For now," I reminded her.

"*Sí, mi hermano*. For now." She smiled one more time, her eyes bright, her shoulders squared. It was like a weight had been lifted, one we'd both been carrying for far too long.

I didn't dare admit it out loud, but that smile of hers did more to heal my wounds than all the medicine and bandages in the world. For the first time in twenty years, Elena had given me hope that she might one day forgive me. And in that forgiveness was the seed of something even more powerful: if my sister could find a way to forgive me after everything I'd done, maybe I could find a way to forgive myself, too.

"Elena," I called out, just as she reached the door.

She squeezed Gray's hand, then turned to look at me over her shoulder. "*Sí*?"

"Empanadas for dinner tonight. Lots of 'em. Piles and piles. With extra chimichurri."

"So demanding, this wolf! As if I'm his personal chef!" She let out a put-upon huff, but I saw the covert little wink she'd flashed at Gray, and I knew without a doubt there'd be a feast waiting for me tonight.

FIFTEEN

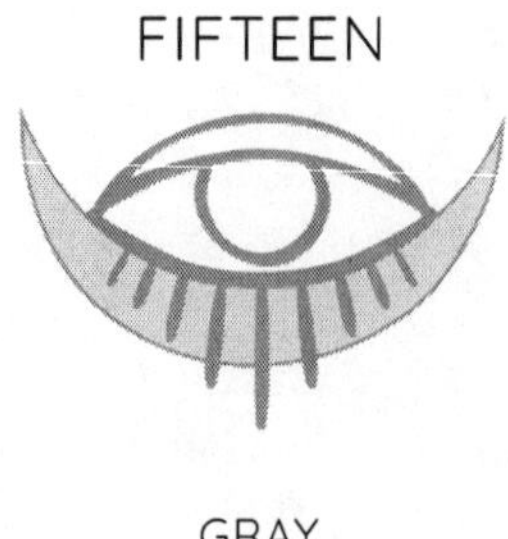

GRAY

It'd been so long since I'd heard Emilio's voice, I was afraid this was just another dream. Tentatively I reached out to stroke his cheek, rough with several days' worth of stubble. His black hair was getting long, curling over the tops of his ears in a way I suspected he'd hate if he could actually see it, but to me he was beautiful. Warm and alive and really, truly here.

"No need to wait for an invitation, *querida*." He opened his arms, waving me in for a hug despite the bandages wrapped around his chest. "I know you want a piece of this."

"But your injuries..."

"Paper cuts compared to how it feels not being able to hold you. Especially when you're standing right next to me, smelling like strawberries and sunshine and everything I want to be close to for the rest of my life."

His voice had faded to a whisper, his eyes serious and intense, and in that moment every last protest died on my lips. I leaned in close and buried my face against his chest, not bothering to keep the tears in check. They soaked right down through his bandages —tears of relief, tears of joy, tears of love, tears for every emotion I'd been struggling to keep in check since the moment I'd seen him fall beneath Orendiel's silver blade.

"Don't you ever scare me like that again," I whispered.

He cupped the back of my head. His hand was big and warm

and strong, and right now, it felt like the only thing keeping me from falling off the edge of the earth.

He was here. He was really, truly here.

"I'll do my best, *mi brujita*."

"That's not good enough." I lifted my head so I could look into his eyes. "I'm serious, Emilio. What we're building here… It doesn't work without you. *I* don't work without you."

He said nothing at that, only nodded, the depths of his brown eyes so beautiful it almost hurt to look at them. I leaned in close, brushing my lips across his mouth, my kiss as gentle as a breeze.

But before I could pull back, his hands were in my hair again, holding me close as he deepened our kiss. I parted my lips, and his tongue swept across mine, unleashing a soft moan from deep inside me as his sweetness flooded my senses.

It was so precious, so special. And I'd come so close to losing it.

Never again.

Without breaking the kiss, I slid into the bed beside him, leaning against his body, threading my hands into his hair. Heat emanated from his skin, and I breathed in his vanilla-and-pine scent, welcomed the scratch of his stubble against my chin, memorizing every sensation. This kiss was the first of the rest of our lives, the second-chance welcome-back embrace I'd been dreaming about, and I intended to carry it with me always. Forever.

He shifted beside me, pulling my leg across his hips, his hand sliding up the back of my thigh. *God,* I'd missed his touch, missed the feeling of being small and safe and well-protected in the arms of my big, muscular wolf, and under his powerful grip, it wasn't long before I'd forgotten all about his injuries.

We kissed long and hard, slow and sensual, teasing and gentle, every kind in every way until I could no longer feel my lips. When we finally broke for air, I turned over on my back, my head bent against his, staring at the ceiling and thanking all the forces of the universe for making this possible.

"Now look what you've done, *brujita*," Emilio teased.

I followed the line of his gaze down to the sheet draped over his hips, now tenting upward.

"Hmm." I nuzzled his neck. "That looks… uncomfortable."

"I'm not so sure about that. Would you like to try it on and find out?"

"Please." I laughed. "Spare me the crass jokes. Now you sound like Asher."

"Hey, I faced down Death and got another chance. If you think I'm going to waste any more time holding back my thoughts—even the dirty ones…" He turned toward me and kissed me again, a soft moan rumbling in his chest.

Desire flooded my core, but I didn't dare act on it. I'd just gotten him back, and from the dark circles under his eyes, I could tell he still needed a lot of rest.

The patient himself, however, had other plans.

"What do you think, doc?" he asked, turning on his hip. His hard length pressed against my outer thigh, and it took every ounce of willpower I had not to slide my hand beneath the sheet and touch him. "Is this wolf cleared for physical activity?"

"I'm not a doctor, Emilio," I said.

"Maybe not. But you can *definitely* make things better for me."

I gave him a playful eye-roll. "Who *is* this wise-cracking, innuendo-dropping beast in my bed, and what have you done with sweet, kind Emilio Alvarez?"

"You really want to know? Fine. I've fallen in love with a *bruja*, that's what I've done." His voice dropped to a sultry whisper as he traced my lips with his fingertip. "And nothing will ever be the same again."

I gave in to the magnetic pull of his words, his eyes, leaning into his embrace once again. Each kiss was deliberate now, intense, as if he were kissing me for the very last time and wanted to memorize the taste of me.

"I thought I'd never see you again, Gray," he whispered. "That night in the warehouse… It's a blur. But you were there. With me every step. I thought—"

"Shhh." I kissed him again, too scared to go down this path, to rehash the moment Orendiel's blade cut through the air, to revisit everything that had come after. But it was too much to hold back, and seconds later, I was breaking our kiss, my heart twisting, my eyes filling with tears at what tonight would feel like if he *hadn't* made it back. "I know," I said. "I know, because that night, when I saw the blood… I thought I'd never hold you like this again, or kiss you or watch the moonrise or eat a whole pan of brownies with you. It all happened so fast, and then Ronan was shouting at me to get the others to safety, and I just…"

I trailed off and closed my eyes, the memories still so fresh, so present.

"I'm so sorry, *querida.* To put you through that… I never… It was stupid."

"You have nothing to be sorry for, Emilio. You were there to help our friends. To liberate innocent witches. To help us restore the balance of power to our communities. You're a hero. You know that, right?"

"Hero? I could've ruined the entire mission." He shook his head, his earlier humor receding. "I was a fool. I left myself wide open for the attack—rookie mistake. But I saw Elena in the line of fire, and in that moment, all I could think about was saving her. I couldn't let her fall, Gray." His jaw flexed, his eyes going to some faraway place I couldn't see. "Not there. Not again."

"Not… again?" I placed my hand over his heart, my brow creased with confusion. "What do you mean?"

"Hmm?" He shifted his gaze back to mine, his eyes cloudy. Perhaps he hadn't meant to say all of that out loud, but now that he had, there was no taking it back.

"You said you couldn't let her fall again," I said.

"I… I did." He sat up higher in the bed, sliding an arm beneath my head, but not meeting my eyes. Instead, he watched the window, the snowflakes piling high along the bottom edge. It was a Darkwinter-induced storm, they'd told me. Fae magic meant to isolate the residents of Blackmoon Bay. Eventually, it would do the same thing here.

But right now, safe in the arms of my wolf, I thought it was beautiful.

After what felt like hours, Emilio leaned over and kissed the top of my head. Then, speaking softly into my hair, "Do you know why I became a cop, *querida*?"

I shifted onto my hip, trying to look into his eyes, but he was back to watching the snow fall.

"We never really talked about it," I said. "I guess I just figured you wanted to help people. Supernaturals, especially."

"I did. I do," he said. "And I'm good at it, Gray. I feel like I'm really, truly meant for this work."

"I *know* you are."

"But that's not why I do it."

I waited, slipping my hand beneath the sheet to find his. He laced our fingers together, and I squeezed him tight, sensing that he needed the reassurance.

"I… I'm atoning," he said. "I never put it into words before, but I see that now. I wanted to help our kind in Blackmoon Bay because I couldn't help them in Mendoza."

"Atoning? That's a strong word, Emilio."

"Not strong enough."

"But… atoning for what?"

He finally tore his gaze away from the window, turning to look at me once again. What I saw was shocking; there was so much pain and regret in his eyes, it scared the hell out of me. This man had faced death, come back from it. Yet whatever he was thinking about now had been more traumatic than even that. I had never seen him so wounded. So ashamed.

"Emilio," I whispered, squeezing his hand even tighter. "What is it? What's wrong?"

"Do you remember that night," he said, "when we got the call about Reva? When you and Elena were having a midnight snack?"

"Of course." I was still carrying the weight of my conversation with Elena—the things she'd revealed to me. Even after everything we'd endured since that night, her story still haunted me.

Her husband—her true mate—had been slaughtered, along with her three-year-old child.

"She told me that her husband and daughter had been killed," I told him, though I suspected he'd heard as much. He'd interrupted us to tell us about a call from the RCPD—that Reva was waiting for us at the station. Still, it seemed like he needed me to say it again. To make absolutely sure I knew where the rest of this conversation was headed. "She said the two of you barely escaped Argentina with your lives. That even your parents… Everyone… I'm so sorry, Emilio."

My words were useless, but I had to say them. I *was* sorry. They'd lost their parents, their family, their pack. Sometimes I wondered how they even found the strength to get out bed in the morning.

"We lost everyone we loved except each other," Emilio confirmed. "But Elena… Did she tell you why?"

"Not specifically. Just that your pack had been betrayed."

"It's true," he said, and by the sadness in his voice, I suddenly knew what was coming next, even before he said the words. I wanted to press my fingers to his lips and stop him, to kiss away his confessions before they escaped, to preserve his and Elena's private grief and the trauma of what was obviously a very personal, very terrible situation.

But when he met my eyes again, I saw the truth: Emilio *needed* to say these words. To confess.

Perhaps, I realized, it was the very first time he'd ever felt able to do so.

"Our pack *was* betrayed, *querida,*" he said. "By me."

SIXTEEN

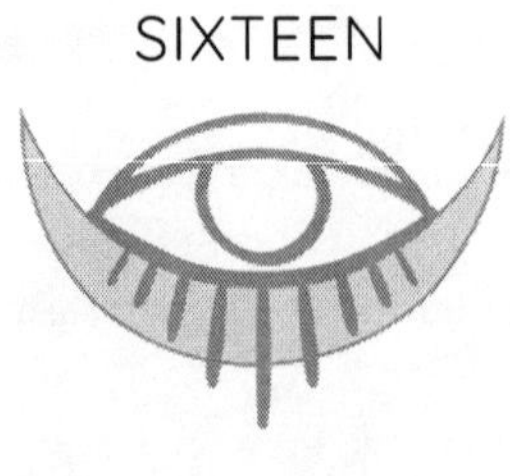

RONAN

"These roads are absolute shite," Beaumont grumbled.

"Be glad you're not the one driving." I took my foot off the gas again and peered out the windshield, trying to keep a little distance between our vehicle and the taillights in front of us—the van Lansky and Jael were in. But the task was proving futile. They were sliding around as much as we were, and even though the plows had been through recently, the snow was accumulating faster than they could keep up.

"This is insane," Haley said from the backseat. "I've never seen so much snow."

"That's because it's totally un-fucking-natural." I clicked on the wipers, trying in vain to keep my view clear, but it was useless. The snow was falling in big gobs, reflecting the light from our headlights until it looked like we were doing warp speed through outer space. The woods didn't help—the pines were several stories tall, their branches thick with heavy, wet snow, blocking out any ambient light we might've picked up from neighboring towns.

Our plans to lure the Darkwinter Knights out of the Bay had been temporarily put on hold in light of the crazy storm, and for the last couple of days our focus had been shoring up the house and making sure we had the supplies we needed to wait out the weather.

The five of us had just finished up a major supply run in Baldersville, a few towns down the highway from the Cape, middle of fucking nowhere. We'd tried all the stores in town closer to Elena's place, but they'd already been cleaned out. Same story everywhere we stopped along the highway until we'd gone about two hours out of our way and spotted a well-lit plaza with a couple of big chain stores—it'd felt like a fucking oasis in the desert, and we dove right in. The weather hadn't been as bad down there, either. But now that we were getting closer to the Cape again, forced onto the backroads due to highway closures, it was a frozen shitshow nightmare.

"I'm starting to think we might need a contingency plan," Beaumont said as I slowed down again. We were only doing about fifteen miles an hour now, crawling like sloths along the road, our little caravan the only fuckers crazy enough to venture out on a night like this. But we had no choice—with so many people staying at Elena's, we couldn't risk running low on anything, especially with this insane fae-mojo weather. "Maybe we should find a place to stop for the night."

"And day," I reminded him. "If we stop now, we won't be able to leave again until the sun goes down tomorrow."

"Better delayed and safe than frozen solid," he said.

"Look around. There's no guarantee this is going to lighten up. For all we know, conditions will be a hundred times worse tomorrow night."

"It pains me to say this," he grumbled, "but you make a fair point."

"Hey. We'll make it," I assured him. "Elena will beat our assess if we don't. She's got a whole feast planned, and I'm already working on my toast."

We'd just finished loading up the vans with everything on our list—bottled water, flashlights and batteries, matches, candles, every kind of food imaginable, blankets, sheets, pillows, air mattresses, extra clothing, coats, boots, winter gear, toiletries, paper products, herbs and crystals for some more warding magic, and of course, the all-important cases of booze everyone had begged for—when I'd gotten Elena's call. All five of us whooped and cheered in the parking lot at the welcome news that our wolf pup was awake and finally out of the woods.

Haley had insisted on running back into the plaza for a get-well gift, despite the fact that Emilio had already *gotten* well. Still, she'd gone ahead anyway, coming back out fifteen minutes later looking like a walking hospital gift shop. The woman had picked out at least four dozen roses in just about every color of the rainbow, all arranged in a giant vase she could barely get her arms around, three big-ass "Get Well" helium balloons trailing behind her. Looped over her elbows were two more shopping bags—one full of stuffed animals, the other crammed with boxes of chocolate-covered, well, everything.

"Seriously, Hay? Seriously?"

"What?" she'd asked, taking her time arranging all that shit in the back seat. "He was practically in a coma. He needs to be surrounded by bright, cheery things. Plus, he loves chocolate. Everyone knows that."

I peered into the other bag. "And the stuffed… cats?"

"Oh, those are for the witches. Kind of an inside joke."

"You've just thought of everything, haven't you?" I teased, but even I was smiling at that point. Girl really knew how to bring the silver lining.

The balloons bobbed beside her now, the massive rose bouquet strategically balanced on her lap. The whole van smelled like old lady perfume, but I wasn't about to tell *her* that.

Besides, she was right—it was a good idea. Emilio would love everything about it, the big fucking softy.

My gut twisted as my mind tried to serve up a replay on the night he'd been attacked, but I shut that shit down fast. Our wolf was okay. He'd fucking made it through the jaws of death, the crazy bastard. All because Gray had never lost faith that he would.

"I don't like this," Beaumont said suddenly, scanning the road ahead. "Something feels off."

"You think?" I reached for the console, trying to crank up the window defogger. "We're driving through a blizzard in a tin can with half-bald tires, on a sheet of solid ice, through the pitch-black woods, and I'm not even sure we're going the right way anymore."

"Thanks, as always," Beaumont said, "for the optimism. However, that's not what I'm talking about. Something doesn't feel right. Out there."

I tried to follow the line of his gaze out the side passenger window, but I didn't want to take my eyes off the road for more than two seconds at a time.

"Just a storm, Beaumont. You never seen snow before in your fancy-ass London house?"

"No, I haven't. But that's not—"

"You see anything weird out there, Hay?" I asked her.

"Yep. I spy something… white." She tapped her window, then said, "Well, look at it this way, guys. If we crash into a ditch and have to sleep out in the woods overnight, at least we're well-supplied."

"Awesome!" I flashed her a thumbs up in the rearview. Her sunny disposition was practically a foreign language to me—I swore the girl had a physical aversion to bitching and moaning. "You can be in charge of setting up camp, okay, Bright Side?"

"You got it! Your tent will be the one next to the bear den. I'll be sure to stock it with plenty of chocolate first." She gave the back of my head a playful smack.

I laughed. Since Gray couldn't touch me without starting a fire, I was pretty sure she'd given Haley carte blanche to knock me around on her behalf whenever the opportunity presented itself.

"No fucking with the driver," I teased. "Unless you wanna end up in a ditch."

"Pass," she said.

Silence drifted in, and for a while, the only sounds in the van were the squeak of the wipers on the windshield, the slow grind of the tires on the snowpack, and the occasional clank of bottles in the back.

"We seem to have lost Lansky," Beaumont finally said.

I narrowed my eyes and peered out the windshield again, as if I could see anything through the wall of white in front of us. Son of a bitch, he was right.

"Yeah, I don't even see the taillights anymore," I said. "How'd they get so far ahead of us?"

"Maybe they didn't," he said. "I doubt they'd speed up in these conditions. Perhaps they found a place to pull off."

"Let me try Jael." Haley dug out her phone, but that idea turned out to be a bust. "Shoot. No service. Sooo… anyone got a flare gun?"

"It's the trees," I said. "This stretch of road is pretty spotty for cell phones."

"You think they're okay?" she asked. "What if—"

"Fuck! Hold on!"

There was no warning. No time to course-correct. By the time I crested the hill and saw Lansky's taillights swerving off the road, we were already on a collision course with the jackknifed semi he'd clearly tried to avoid. We hit a fresh patch of ice on the downslope and the steering wheel jerked from my hands, and then we were spinning like a kid's toy, picking up speed as we careened downhill toward the wreckage, rose petals of every color falling around us like snow.

SEVENTEEN

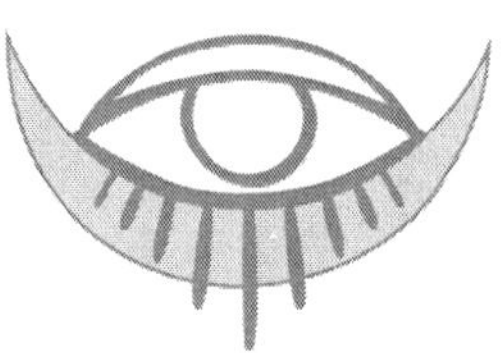

GRAY

It was one of those moments where you're lying totally still, holding your breath, willing your heart not to beat, and suddenly you feel the ground shifting beneath you, dropping away.

I was so certain I'd known what Emilio was going to say, so sure I could name the ghosts that had haunted his eyes every time I stared into them for more than a moment.

I tried to save them, I thought he'd say. *But I couldn't.* Or, *I should've been able to warn them. I should've seen the signs.* Or maybe, *I was just a scared kid. I ran and hid instead of being brave, and I've carried that shame ever since…*

But to say that it was his fault? That *he'd* been the one to betray them?

I swallowed hard, willing my muscles to remain still, hoping he couldn't scent the rush of pure shock flooding my body.

"Before we came together on this case," Emilio continued, tightening his arms around me as if he were scared I'd bolt, "Elena and I hadn't spoken for nearly twenty years. Did you know that?"

"Not… Not really," I said, willing my heart rate to return to normal. My skin felt hot and prickly, but not because I was afraid of Emilio or anything he might've done in the past, no matter how terrible.

No. I was afraid—terrified—that when he finally confessed his greatest regrets, I wouldn't have the words to make it better for him. To give him the absolution he'd been seeking most of his life.

"I knew that you'd emigrated here together after separating from your pack, but that was basically all," I said. "Ronan never said much about it."

"No, he wouldn't have. He doesn't know the whole story anyway—just the end." A warm sigh escaped Emilio's lips, stirring my hair, and he pressed a lingering kiss to the top of my head. "Actually, I guess I can say now that Ronan's part *wasn't* the end. For a long time, I feared it was, but my sister… Things are in flux right now. There's so much… I don't…"

I felt the sudden vibration in his chest, slowly turning into a tremor that shook the bed, and I realized he was trying—and failing—to hold back a storm of sobs.

All my words, all the right things to say, all the comforting thoughts, everything failed me. I didn't know what to say, what to do, how to help him, so I did the only thing that felt right in that moment—I snuggled closer to him and wrapped my arms around him, drawing his head to my chest, stroking his hair. I channeled all my love for him into this moment, sending it to him, strengthening him, trying to let him know without words that it was okay to let go. To let every horrible, ugly, scary, fucked-up thing go.

He seemed to sense it, and he clung to me as he wept, burying his face in my shirt, his tears damp on my skin as they leaked out in an endless river. Soon, my own tears followed, my heart breaking for the lost wolf he'd been, the family he'd left behind.

Of all the guys, Emilio had always been the most sensitive, the most compassionate, the most in touch with the emotional side of things. But I'd never seen him so vulnerable, so exposed. Whatever had happened in Argentina, whatever guilt and shame and grief he'd endured, he'd stuffed it into a bottle and shoved it into the darkest part of his soul, keeping it locked away… Until tonight.

When he finally ran out of tears, my wolf stilled in my embrace, but he didn't pull away. Didn't roll over or try to mask his pain or pretend it was something else, or worse—apologize for the show of emotion, like so many men would do. Instead, he held me closer, inhaling my scent, his breathing finally smoothing out again.

Our bedroom overlooked the backyard, and outside our window, the wind howled like a banshee, ushering in another moonless night. A fresh blanket of snow had descended on Raven's Cape, the windowpanes murky with frost. Throughout the rest of the house, we could hear the chatter of the witches, their laughter, their bickering, the occasional clink of dishes and silverware being set out on the table, Elena calling for wine and rum and a little more garlic in the sauce. It didn't take a detective to figure out that she'd be preparing a feast tonight; Emilio had come through the worst of things, and everyone whose lives he'd touched wanted to celebrate.

But right now, tucked into our bed, there was only me and my wolf, safe and warm and well-hidden from the happy chaos unfolding in the rest of the house, and for a long time we clung to each other without words, twin flames flickering in the window on a dark night, illuminating the way home.

I had no warning for just how dark that night was about to get.

EIGHTEEN

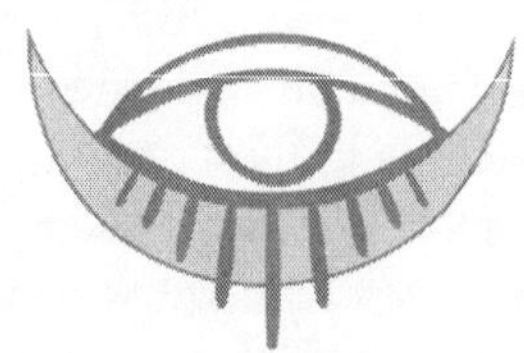

DARIUS

I blinked the fog from my mind, focusing on the skull-shaped indentation in the passenger window next to me. *My* skull shape, I realized, rubbing the side of my head. Blood trickled from a gash above my ear, but it was already healing.

Fortunately, I had a hard head, and though I was a bit dizzy, it seemed I was no worse for the wear.

"Ronan? Haley?" I sat up slowly, still trying to get my bearings. Both of the front airbags had deployed, and everything around me was coated in dust and rose petals. "Everyone okay?"

"Motherfucking piece of shit bullshit asshole snow! Fuck this shit! I fucking hate winter!" This, from Ronan.

"So the eloquent demon is still with us," I said. "Excellent. Haley?"

"Still with you," Haley piped up from the backseat, her breathing a bit erratic, but otherwise sounding like herself. "Which is more than I can say for Emilio's presents. What the hell happened?"

"We hit… something." I unhooked my seatbelt and tried to open the passenger door, but it refused to budge.

"A fucking semi, that's what we hit." Ronan wrenched open the driver's side door and stumbled out. "A semi that had no business being out on this back road, especially in a storm."

Haley and I joined him outside, the three of us standing in the middle of the road, trying to piece together the puzzle. The snow was falling so heavily, we had to constantly brush it from our eyes.

"The van is toast," Ronan said. From the looks of things, we'd slid down the hill, slamming sideways into the back of the rig. The passenger side took the brunt of it, the back end of the van securely wedged underneath the truck. Half of our supplies were scattered around the wreckage.

"So glad I picked the left side to ride on," Haley said, shivering. Whether it was the frigid night air or the realization that she'd just narrowly escaped death, I couldn't tell.

I took her by the shoulders and looked her over, checking her head, her neck, her arms, but she waved off my ministrations.

"You'd be the first to know if I were bleeding," she said.

I let out a brittle laugh. "Indeed."

"Hey!" Someone shouted from the other side of the semi. "Ronan, Darius! That you guys?"

"Lansky," I said.

"It's us," Ronan replied. "You guys okay?"

"A little banged up, but we'll live. You?"

"Same. Anyone check the guy in the truck?"

"Not yet," Lansky called back. "We're a little stuck at the moment."

"You got phone service?" Ronan asked.

"Negative."

"Alright, we're coming to you. Hang tight." Gingerly, the three of us stepped around the wreckage and made our way around the back end of the semi, following the sound of Lansky's voice. It was slow going on the icy road, with visibility at a minimum, and the danger of more vehicles sliding down that hill.

Fortunately, it seemed we were the only ones risking a drive tonight. Well, us and the semi, which seemed extremely out of place. Something about it didn't feel right. Not just the fact that it was out on a backroad in this storm, but something else I couldn't quite put my finger on.

The feeling of unease that'd crept up on me after we'd left the plaza had never really left, and now it intensified, putting all of my senses on high alert.

We found Lansky and Jael trying unsuccessfully to climb out of a ditch, their van tilted nose-first at such an extreme angle that its back wheels had lifted off the ground. Ronan and I helped them up the slope, everyone slipping and sliding on the rapidly accumulating snow.

"I swear that truck appeared out of nowhere," Lansky said. His eyes were still wide with shock, and I could smell the adrenaline surging through his blood. "One minute the roads were empty, nothing but this crazy snow. I'd just downshifted to tackle that hill, then all of a sudden, I'm hitting the brakes and swerving to avoid something that just… It just *appeared*."

"He's right," Jael said. Other than the falling snow flattening his hair, the fae prince looked as dignified and unruffled as ever, his yellow eyes glowing faintly. "I, too, saw nothing until the very moment of near-impact."

"Sounds like more of Orendiel's magical bullshit to me," Ronan said. "Let's check it out."

"I'm going to do a damage assessment on our supplies," Haley said. "Hopefully I can salvage a few things from our van."

"Good idea," Ronan said. "If we can get Lansky's out of the ditch, we might be able to drive it back. Ours is definitely a lost cause."

As I scanned our perimeter, keeping my heightened senses attuned to any vehicles that might've approached the top of the hill or any other threats coming our way, Ronan, Jael, and Lansky checked out the cab of the truck.

Ronan stepped up and peered inside the driver's side window, shaking his head. "Driver's definitely dead."

"Let's get him out," Lansky said, and Ronan hauled open the door.

The man inside—human, by the scent of him—toppled lifelessly into Ronan's arms, his limbs as stiff as those of a weeks-old corpse.

"What the fuck?" Ronan dragged the guy to the ground, propping him up against the truck's massive front wheel. "There's not a scratch on him, but he's a human popsicle."

Jael crouched down and checked for a pulse, then shook his head. After a beat, he closed his eyes and said, "This man did not die from exposure or natural causes. This is fae magic at work."

"Darkwinter?" I asked, approaching the body.

"Worse. The spell that took this man's life force has a dual signature belonging to two extremely powerful fae." Jael got to his feet, his typically smooth face creased with deep lines of concern. "Fenlos and Talia."

"The bloody *council,*" I said. Emilio had known Talia would turn up in all of this again, he just hadn't known how.

"The bloody council," Jael echoed.

"Looks like they're not hiding behind their bullshit pretenses anymore," Ronan said.

"No," Jael confirmed. "This spell could've easily been camouflaged, even from me. They wanted us to know of their involvement, and to draw the next logical conclusion."

"Which is?" I asked.

"That if the two highest-ranking members of the fae council are blatantly using their magic to sabotage us in a battle against the Darkwinter and the hunters, then the *entire* council has already chosen sides. It's just as Emilio feared."

Lansky crouched down to check the body. "Yeah, this guy's been dead at least two weeks. Which begs the question…" He stepped around the front of the cab to the other side of the road, then returned. "How did he get here? He's got no visible injuries and a fae magical signature. His truck literally appeared out of nowhere—there are no tire tracks on the other side of the road, and the only tracks on this side are from two vehicles—mine and Ronan's. Highway patrol has closed just about all the roads. No one else is out in this shit right now."

That was it, I realized. The thing that'd been bothering me about this. There were no tracks through the snow. The truck hadn't been driven here. It was put here magically.

Lansky blew heat into his hands, spinning around to take in the rest of the scene, putting the pieces together. "Jael, you said these fae wanted you to detect their signature—you're the only one of us who could."

"Yes, they know by now I'm working with you. Orendiel would've told them about my involvement in freeing the witches from the warehouse. The public fight Kallayna and I staged would also lend credence to the fact that I'd betrayed them all, including my sister."

"Okay," Lansky said. "So they know you're on our side. And they also knew, somehow, that we'd gone for a supply run today, and that we'd be taking *this* exact route back, even though we didn't take it on the way out, and there are three other routes we could've taken to avoid the highway closures. This is a setup."

"No, not a setup," I said, catching a new scent on the frigid air. Lansky's eyes suddenly widened—it seemed he'd caught it, too. "An ambush."

It was a sharp animal odor, but not completely natural. Shifters, I figured, though not a type I'd ever encountered before. "There," I said, nodding at a faint movement I'd just caught in the woods bordering the road. I was likely the only one who could see it through the snow. "In the trees."

"Haley, get in the van!" Lansky barked, and drew his weapon as the big cats shot out into view.

There were six of them, snow-white but for their reflective blue-green eyes. Their body shape gave the impression of mountain lions, but these creatures were about four times larger, with thick, corded muscles and powerful jaws that looked like they could crush bones very little effort.

"Why aren't they attacking?" Ronan asked as the beasts came to a stop at the edge of the road, about fifteen feet from us.

"Because you've got a witch in your pocket, dumbass," Haley said, and immediately the scent of human blood filled my nostrils. I turned to see that said witch was not in the van as Lansky had ordered, but kneeling down in the middle of the road, squeezing blood from her fist into a small pentagram she'd traced in the snow, her other palm facing out toward the shifters, as though she'd stopped them by her will alone.

When she'd squeezed the last drop of blood from her fist, she pressed the wounded palm against the symbol. The snow around it glowed briefly, then melted.

Before I could even *ask* what that was all about, she got to her feet, turned her palms face up, and began to chant, slowly pacing out a circle around us.

Spirits and guides, ancestors all
I call on you now, each one and all
I offer my blood in exchange for protection
Delay this attack from every direction
Let all who dare breach this circle I cast
Fall back to the moment of three minutes past.

She repeated the mantra several times, not stopping until she'd completed a full circle around us, magically cutting us off from the shifters.

"It's a confusion spell," she explained when she rejoined the group. "It's not much, but it's all the blood I can spare on short notice."

"What's with the three minutes thing?" Ronan asked.

"Each time they hit the boundary, their minds will revert by three minutes, so they'll feel like they haven't initiated their attack yet. It's essentially a time loop—it should make them retreat and start over. But seriously, guys. This is like, blood magic 101 stuff—totally makeshift. We've probably got about ten, fifteen minutes tops before it wears off."

Lansky took another look at his van. "We need to get that thing on the road. It's our best shot."

"On it," Ronan said, and Lansky and I followed him down into the ditch. Physically, we were the strongest and best able to push it out. But that meant leaving Haley and Jael unprotected—a prospect I didn't like one bit.

"Hold the circle, you two," I said. "The moment you sense the magic weakening, give us the signal."

"You think those things can understand us?" Lansky asked, jerking his head toward the beasts across the road.

"I want to say no," I said, "but I'm inclined to err on the side of caution these days."

"Alright. On three," Ronan said.

We crouched down and grabbed the bumper.

"One, two—"

All three of us jumped the gun, but after a few more attempts, we finally got the job done, shoving the two-ton van out of the ditch and back onto the icy road. It skidded to a stop, looking as tired as the rest of us undoubtedly felt.

Jael helped us out of the ditch, and we headed over to inspect the vehicle that would hopefully get us home.

"Can't believe the airbags didn't blow on this one," Ronan said, knocking on the hood. "You guys slid in face first."

"Yeah, remind me to bust Hobb's balls about that later," Lansky said. "He was supposed to take it in for a re-install after the dealer sent out a recall notice, but he blew it off." He crouched down to take a look underneath, inspecting the damage. "Okay. Aside from the obvious cosmetic shit, the front axle's bent, and the bumper looks like it's folded in against the front right tire. But if we go real slow and don't take any sharp turns, she'll get us home."

"Assuming she starts," Ronan said, wiping the icy slush from his eyes. All of us were wearing caps of snow three inches high. Poor Haley's teeth were chattering, but bloody hell, the woman was still smiling.

I left Ronan and Lansky to deal with the van while I checked on Haley and Jael.

"Five minutes," Haley told me. "Spell's fading."

"It's some spell, though." I put my hand on her shoulder and leaned forward, peering into the snowy woods. None of the shifters had moved from their posts, not even to attempt a breach. "They're completely immobilized."

"They're not the most predictable creatures, that's for sure." Haley shook her head. "I'm not sure if it's my spellwork, or something else keeping them at bay."

"Let's not look a gift horse in the mouth, shall we?" I winked at Haley, then turned to Jael. "Anything you can do?"

"I'm afraid not," he said. "Though not for lack of trying. Their minds have been secured against manipulation—likely they're only susceptible to Darkwinter influence."

"Darkwinter?" I asked. "So these aren't Jonathan's hybrids?"

"No way," Haley said. "Jonathan was too much of a loose cannon to make something this dangerous and, I don't know. Coordinated? They haven't attacked yet, but look how they're standing in formation like that. It isn't accidental. They're watching our every move. I wouldn't be surprised if there are more of them further down the road."

She was right. They'd positioned themselves at even intervals, and when I looked closely, I saw the slightest movements of their eyes, following Lansky's footsteps as he approached.

Jael and Haley were right. These weren't Jonathan's rotting, broken creatures. They were powerful, genetically altered, fae-made beasts bred for a purpose we could only begin to guess at.

We needed to get out of there.

"Bad news," Lansky said. "Engine won't turn over."

"Two minutes," Haley warned, and immediately I felt the shift in the energy around us, like an electrical current surging, then fading. At the edge of the road, one of the big cats took a step.

"Fuck," Ronan said. "This is about to get ugly. Anyone got weapons?"

"Nothing that would help against these creatures," I said.

"Can't you shoot them?" Ronan asked Lansky.

"Doubt it." Lansky drew his weapon again anyway. "These aren't silver bullets. They won't work on shifters."

"Might not kill them," Ronan said, "but maybe you can make them bleed."

Haley took a step backward toward the van. "Now or never, boys. Thirty seconds and we're totally exposed."

"Stay alert." Lansky took aim, firing off three shots into the chest of the closest beast.

The creature didn't even flinch, and if it'd bled at all, it'd been such a minuscule amount that not one drop had stained the snow.

"Great. Apparently, they heal faster than regular shifters, too," Lansky said, holstering the useless gun. "Guess we're doing this the old-fashioned way."

"Haley," I said, catching his meaning. "Now might be a good time for you to get in the van. You too, prince. See if you two can get it started."

The moment we heard the van door slam shut, we struck.

From the corner of my eye, I caught the dark gray blur of Lansky's wolf form, Ronan right on his heels. The shifters were just coming out of the spell-haze when we took down the first two —Ronan and Lansky on one, me on the other. I barged into him, biting, slashing, disemboweling. His blood tasted ashy and bitter, laced with some kind of chemical, but I drank deeply anyway, needing the fuel and—yes—needing to put on a show of dominance.

The wolf and the raging, black-eyed demon made quick work of their foe, Lansky mauling him with his massive claws while Ronan tore off hunks of white fur and flesh with his bare hands. The bullets hadn't made a dent, but the damned things were finally bleeding now. The three of us had no intention of letting them heal.

I scanned ahead for my next shifter meal, but was shocked to see the rest of the pack backing off.

Were they… retreating?

"Why aren't they attacking?" I growled, wiping the blood from my mouth.

Lansky pawed at the beast he and Ronan had shredded, drawing my attention to a black metallic object that appeared to be fused to its collarbone. It was circular and flat, about the size and shape of a watch face.

I tore the bone clean out of its carcass so Ronan and I could take a closer look.

"I'm guessing it's some kind of behavioral control device," he said. "Or tracker. I bet they all have them."

"Maybe that's why they're holding back," I said.

"If that's the case, then someone is watching. Someone's controlling them."

"Let's take them out," I said, already anticipating the bitter tang of blood on my lips.

But the big cats were already disappearing, loping away into the snow-packed forest on silent paws.

* * *

"I don't believe they weren't trying to kill us," Lansky said later, stepping into what was left of his clothing. While Haley and Jael had finished loading up the salvageable supplies into Lansky's van, Ronan, Lansky, and I had done a full sweep of the area, tracking the shifter prints a good mile out in all directions before the trees became too dense to continue. "Not for a second. Six cats that size against three of us? They could've done a hell of a lot more damage."

"We hit the first two pretty quickly, though," I said. "My sense was they weren't expecting our initial attack."

"No way. They knew *exactly* what we were up to. Exactly how we'd react. I'm telling you, guys. These aren't normal shifters, operating on instinct. They're following orders in real time."

"Detective Lansky is right," Jael said, securing one last box of food in the back of the van. "My belief is that Darkwinter is trying to unhinge us a bit. Consider it—Orendiel suffered a massive defeat that night at the warehouse, and he knows we're gathering strength here. What better way to keep us off guard and second-guessing our strategies?"

"Psychological warfare," I said. "Dark fae expertise."

"It is," Jael agreed, "and this is just a *taste* of what he might unleash. What he's already begun unleashing in the Bay. By his actions tonight, he's virtually guaranteed that whatever his actual capabilities, we're going to imagine much, much worse. Hybrid shifters? No. Try electronically-controlled hybrid super-shifters. A violent attack on our home? Yes, but let's add in a minor attack that cuts off the food supply during a storm. The point is, we don't know what he's fully capable of or what he's planning, and it could be virtually anything. That's how dark fae operate. He's counting on our fear of the unknown. Humans especially are conditioned to operate on worst-case-scenario fears, and that fear makes it much easier for the fae to manipulate their targets."

"Well, obviously that glitter-dicked asshole has never dealt with *me*." Haley leaned out the driver's side window of the van, now idling in the center of the road, ready to go. "I'm all about the *best*-case scenario, which at the moment is the prospect of ushering dozens of beautiful empanadas into their final resting place in my belly. Now, if you all don't mind... Can we *please* get the fuck out of here?"

NINETEEN

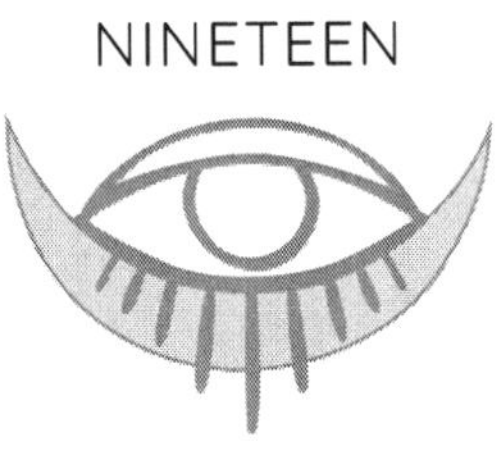

EMILIO

The ghosts that had laid siege to my heart had lingered there long enough. If Elena and I had any hope of reconciling, if I had any hope of being a brother and friend to the guys, if I had any hope of being the man Gray truly saw when she looked at me with those pretty blue eyes, I needed to evict them.

And I needed to do it now, before they slipped out of the light and into the dark corners once again.

"My sister and I were very close growing up," I began. "But at some point, she got involved with a new crowd, and she started spending all her time with them. Camping trips, road trips, last-minute parties I was never invited to. I hardly ever saw her that summer, and when I did, she was merely coming and going, picking up a change of clothes, bribing me not to tell my parents that her new friends weren't… our kind."

"They only wanted you guys to hang out with other wolf shifters?" she asked.

"They weren't like that with me, but my sister was the alpha of our generation, poised to take over leading the pack for our father. By the time she was thirteen, she'd already been promised to the alpha of a neighboring pack—a guy named Franco, who also happened to be my best friend—and it was just accepted that they'd eventually marry and mate as adults. But that promise was made years earlier—nothing she'd ever taken seriously. And these new friends of hers… They were human. They had no idea what she was. But I figured out pretty quickly that one of them was becoming more than a friend."

"As in…?"

"As in, she fell in love with him, Gray. A man named Jonah Shiley. He was the only one she'd told about her true nature."

Gray sucked in a breath. "She married Jonah. He was the forbidden love she told me about."

"Eloped, actually. None of us knew about it for a whole year. We'd thought she was living with a roommate, but it turned out that was just a girlfriend covering for her and Jonah whenever we planned to visit. She was nineteen years old, and he was twenty, and there was no telling them about the ways of the world or pack hierarchy or anything that even remotely implied their love was wrong."

"Because it wasn't," she said defensively, and I realized the subtext of my words.

Gray was a human witch. I was a wolf shifter. And nothing about us—about her touch, the way she looked at me, the way my heart seemed to grow big whenever she walked into the room—felt wrong.

"No, that's not what I meant, *querida*. You're right. Their love wasn't *wrong*. It was just… against the rules. My parents loved us, but they were also extremely practical, and extremely loyal to the pack. When they found out about the marriage, they basically disowned her. I saw her even less than before, as if that were possible. I missed her, you know? Missed getting into trouble together, missed her teasing me, missed just… Just hanging out and being goofy with my big sister."

"I'm sorry," she said, and I felt her own sadness wash through her. I wondered if she were thinking about Haley, or the other sisters she'd been separated from as a baby. Unlike me, Gray hadn't really known or remembered them. She didn't have anyone to miss.

I wrapped my arms more tightly around her, holding her close. When I finally felt her sadness retreat a bit, I continued.

"Anyway, the family she was promised to—Franco's kin—they

didn't take the news too kindly. My buddy dropped me, and our family became pariahs. People started disrespecting my father, then outright challenging his authority. Kids at school were fucking with me. It sucked. So there I was, basically still a kid, no sister, no friends, total outcast.

"Then the inevitable happened—I got jumped after school one day, five wolves, tore my ass to shreds—Franco and his brothers. They would've killed me, too, if this other pack hadn't shown up and saved me. They fought off Franco's crew and helped me patch myself back up."

I remembered them now, new in town, mysterious, all muscle and swagger. Chasing off Franco and his guys as if they were little field mice. I'd worried they'd beat me up themselves for being so weak, but they didn't say a word. Just took me home to one of the guys' apartments, patched me up, fed me. And from then on, they were always around.

"They saved me that day," I continued. "And they protected me every day after. Pushed me to get stronger, smarter, to develop my instincts. Basically, all the things my father should've been doing, but he was too busy defending our territory to worry about me.

"My sister got pregnant later that year, and once again, we didn't know a thing about it until Maya—" I stopped suddenly, my throat closing up over her name. My niece's name. I hadn't said it out loud since we'd left Argentina—Elena had forbidden it, even before she and I split. Hearing it now, feeling it, it brought everything rushing back in crystal clear, high-definition images. The good, as well as the bad.

Maya's first tooth. The sound of her sweet little laugh. How she couldn't say my name, so called me "Em-ee-o" instead.

My eyes blurred with tears, my throat stinging with the scream that wanted to claw its way out.

But Gray nestled in closer, her breath soft against my bare chest, and from her I took just enough strength to continue.

This, too, was part of the deal. No one said exorcizing these ghosts would be easy or painless.

With a cracked voice, I said, "Maya, my niece. My sister

showed up on our front porch three days after the baby was born, this little pink bundle in her arms. My parents melted. And just like that, she was part of our lives again. Maya and Jonah, too."

I stilled again, taking a moment to gather the rest of my thoughts. This was the inevitable turn in the road, the part of the story where the darkness began to seep in, and I felt it mirrored inside me now like a wisp of black smoke curling up from my gut, thickening around my heart.

"People heard about the happy little family," I said. "That's when the threats started."

"Against Elena?"

"Well, at first they were more generic. There were rumors of a rival pack moving in to the area from the north, looking for a challenge, and Franco's family were more than happy to fan the flames. They started spreading lies about my father, about his ability to manage and provide for the pack. Someone threw bricks through my parents' windows painted with curses and crude, violent images. They cut the brake lines of my father's car—fortunately, he'd only made it down the driveway before he figured it out. They slaughtered the chickens and cows on my parents' land. My father started getting anonymous calls and emails demanding that my sister be tossed out of the pack, stripped of our protection. When he refused, the threats escalated. This went on for a couple years, but my parents always managed to stay on top of things, to not lose hope.

"Then one day, someone physically assaulted my sister in the grocery store parking lot, trying to get at the baby. She fought the guy off and Maya was unharmed, but that was the last straw. My father decided my sister and her family needed to go into protective custody."

"Holy shit," she whispered. "How did he even set that up?"

"Well, he was a cop—no surprise there, right?" I laughed, grateful for the chance to relieve some tension. "In our family, you were two things: a wolf first, an officer of the law second. He'd always known it was only a matter of time before Elena and I followed in his footsteps."

I swallowed through another painful lump of emotion. My

father hadn't lived long enough to see either of his children follow in his footsteps.

"Anyway," I said, "he had some help from a high-ranking shifter friend a few jurisdictions over, and they made all the arrangements. He and my sister staged a big public blow-up, and he officially disowned her, basically banishing her from the town. A few days later, we got them set up with new IDs in a small mountain town about an hour-and-a-half from where we lived. Other than my father and his friend, I was the only other person who knew the location. Even my mother couldn't know—that'd been her choice. She was too worried she'd break down and go visit them, blowing their cover."

Gray shook her head, her silky hair brushing against my skin. "That must've been the hardest thing for her to do. Especially after all the ups and downs she'd had with Elena, and finally getting close again, only to have to let her go…"

"Oh, she was miserable," I said. "My father, too. Our family was torn apart, and there was nothing we could do about it—not if we wanted to keep them safe from the threats and attacks. My sister didn't even dare send us letters or pictures—we were all so worried they'd be traced back. My mother started drinking. My father buried himself in his work, taking overnight shifts and walking beats he'd long since graduated from, just to avoid the emptiness at home."

"What about you?" she asked.

What about me.

It was a loaded question, the answer weighted with so much guilt and pain I felt it now, eating away at my insides, flaring up all over again. For this was the root of it. The domino that fell and knocked down all the others.

My hand began to sting, and I realized Gray was gripping it so tightly, her fingernails were making half-moon indentations in my skin. Gently, I extracted myself from her grip, wrapping her hands in mine instead. It seemed we were both waiting for the other shoe in this painful story to drop. The difference was, I knew what was coming.

And I needed to anchor myself to her. To hold on for all I was worth as the memories came at me full force, the fiercest, most brutal waves that hit me full-on and pummeled me against the shore.

I could still feel the old resentments, the shamefully hot burning in my gut when I thought about what Elena's choices had meant for our family. I loved her, I loved Maya, and even Jonah was starting to grow on me. But because she'd broken the rules, she'd broken our family, too. I lost my sister, but I also lost my parents. She'd cost me my sense of home and place and belonging. She'd cost me my friendships and dignity and standing in our pack. She'd cost me everything. That's how it'd felt.

So when my friends—the guys who'd looked after me when Franco went crazy on me—started showing up again, I welcomed it. We were all a little older at that point, a bunch of wild-eyed wolves looking for trouble. I'd started drinking with them, staying out all night, looking for girls, generally disturbing the peace. There was always some party to go to, always some ruckus to cause.

Stupid boys.

Telling Gray about it now, I could see all the signs. All the fucking clues. But back then, I wasn't much different from my sister with her friends—no one could've convinced me that any of it had been a bad idea.

"One night," I went on, "the guys took me out to this expensive new club in downtown Buenos Aires, insisting they pay for everything, that they wanted to show me a good time since I'd been so down about my father disowning my sister. I drank a lot that night—more than I ever had—and we were all just letting off steam. I started opening up a little more about my fucked-up situation at home, and next thing I know, I'm telling them about the threats and how my sister wasn't really disowned, just relocated for her protection."

I felt the shift in Gray's body immediately, her muscles tensing, her heartbeat kicking up. Even she could read the writing on the wall—the message it cost me absolutely everything to finally translate.

And by the time I had, it'd been far too late.

She pressed a kiss to my shoulder, warm and comforting. It was like she could sense me slipping under the waves and wanted to pull me back up again before I drown.

"It's okay," she whispered. "I'm right here."

I gripped her hands tighter, and squeezed my eyes shut, forcing myself to watch the scene unfolding like a movie. It would be—I promised myself right there, right in her arms as the storm raged on outside our window and inside my heart—the very last time I watched that movie. The very last time I forced myself to relive it.

"They listened attentively," I said, "asking for more details, their eyes full of fake concern. They said how sorry they were—that they'd had no idea I was dealing with all this shit at home. They reminded me how they'd had my back with Franco's crew, and how I was like family to them. How that automatically made my parents and sister their family, too. How they wanted to help me protect her. A few more drinks, and I believed them. I'd felt like I'd been carrying that burden on my own for so long, it was a relief to get help. A relief to know that this big, strong, ragtag pack could fight for us. That they could put an end to the threats and bring my sister and her family home where they belonged."

Silent tears leaked from my eyes again, but I didn't bother to wipe them away. Like the ghosts, like the movies, they needed an outlet, too. And through it all, Gray just held me, kissed me, touched me, let me know without words that she wasn't going anywhere. Wasn't judging.

"By the time we left the club," I said, "the boozy feelings had faded, but the sense of relief had only intensified. I felt damn near euphoric. I couldn't wait to go home and talk to my parents—see what we could do to bring these guys into the fold, strengthen my father's position as alpha, and put our family back together.

"They drove me back to the house, but as soon as we turned down my road, I knew something was wrong. Then we saw the firetrucks at the top of the driveway, and a blaze of orange that lit up the sky." I reached for the bottled water on the bedside table, taking a long swig. The long-remembered taste of acrid smoke and the scent of burning animal flesh curdled in my mouth.

"The guys stayed by my side that whole night," I continued, "waiting for the fire chief to come out of the ashes and tell me the answer to the only question I cared about—whether my parents were inside. But I knew before he'd even spoken the words. The house and outbuildings had been torched. The remaining animals had all burned alive. And my parents… my parents died in their bedroom closet, huddled together until the very end."

By now, Gray's tears were flowing, too, running like a tiny river down the side of my chest. My need to comfort her overwhelmed my own pain, and I stroked her cheek with my thumb, pressing a kiss into the top of her head. I would never be able to express how much this meant to me—that she'd been willing to listen, to feel this pain, to help me carry it.

"I knew I had to get to my sister. That she and her family would be next, if they hadn't already been found and targeted. The guys drove me there as fast as they could, breaking just about every traffic law on the way. I never once hesitated to tell them the address."

I took another slug of water and a deep breath, forcing myself to unclench the muscles that'd tightened like piano strings. This was it. The worst part. The last and most treacherous and most deeply buried memories, the ghosts with the sharpest teeth and claws, the ones who'd fight me every step of the way as I tried to finally release them.

"It was my fault, *querida,*" I said, my words like broken glass in my throat. Each one cut deep, cost me something, but I couldn't stop. Not until every last one was out. "All those years with the rumors about the rival pack, it was them. My so-called friends. They were in league with Franco's family the whole time, and they'd been working me for years, slowly laying the trap. I took the bait, because they made me believe—no, scratch that. I *let* them make me believe—that they could help me. But when we finally got to Elena's home, the second we got out of the car, I knew. I just knew, and there wasn't a damn thing I could do about it.

"Two other cars pulled in immediately behind us, full of shifters I'd never seen before—bigger, angrier, their eyes wild with bloodlust. To them, it'd been a hunt years in the making, and they'd finally cornered their prey. I knew it that instant that these monsters were responsible for the fire at my parents' home, and now they'd come for my sister's family, too.

"I ran inside and woke up Elena and Jonah, trying to get them out, but we were the little field mice now. The monsters loped into the house like they hadn't a care in the world, a dozen guys against the three of us. Elena and I didn't even have time to shift —it all happened so fast. It was… It was a slaughter, Gray. The pleasure they took…"

The scene flashed behind my eyes once again. The sound of Elena's desperate screams as they'd ripped Maya from her arms. The way Jonah had dropped to his knees and begged, tears streaming down his face. The blood splatter arcing across the bedroom wall as they'd cut his throat. The soft, muted cries as the biggest of the pack had smothered Maya against his chest, pressing all the air from her tiny lungs and discarding her on the bed like a rag doll. They beat the shit out of me and Elena both, leaving us for dead. Lying on the bedroom floor, barely conscious, we watched their filthy boots stomp out of the house, the sounds of their laughter and whoops of victory like another round of blows to the head.

"Then I smelled the gasoline. Saw their silhouettes outside the window, flickering behind the orange flames that rose up suddenly from the base of the house. Their laughter went on and on… I swear it was still ricocheting around my skull even after I heard all their cars peel out."

The only reason we'd survived that night was thanks to the kindness of an elderly neighbor, who'd risked his own life to drag us out of the fire mere moments before the house crumbled.

"Elena and I woke up two days later, side-by-side in the local hospital, both of us in utter shock. Part of me feared the pack would be back to finish the job, but then I realized they'd left us alive on purpose. They let us go, because they knew we'd never pose a threat again. They'd defeated our family, killed our alpha. Elena and I were broken wolves without a pack—like some pathetic cautionary tale that would go down in the history books as a lesson to anyone that might try to challenge their dominance in the future.

"The moment we were released from the hospital, we went into survival mode, fueled entirely on shock and adrenaline. We had some money—some accounts my parents had set up when we were kids—and we used it all to pay off the right people, get passports and all the papers and tickets we needed to get to the states and disappear. From Los Angeles, we made our way north, seeing the forests and mountain ranges that reminded us of home. We found work and a cheap house to rent in a small seaside town called Raven's Cape, and for a little while, we lived in relative peace, haunted only by our own demons and the nightmares we never spoke of out loud."

"Raven's Cape," Gray whispered, lifting her head and glancing around the room. "This was your house?"

"No," I said with a faint smile, smoothing the hair from her forehead. The side of her face where she'd been resting against my chest was pink, her eyes still glassy with tears. "Elena has significantly upgraded since we lived together. The house we'd rented before isn't even there anymore—it was probably condemned and put out of its misery."

Gray settled back against my chest again, and for a while we just lay together in silence, the snow still swirling outside, the sounds of the household drifting in along with the mouthwatering scents of Elena's cooking: ground beef and onions frying, parsley and garlic being chopped up for the chimichurri. My stomach rumbled, and Gray let out a soft laugh, trailing her fingertips back and forth across my abdomen.

"It was a mistake, Emilio," she said softly. "A terrible mistake. You didn't intend for anyone to get killed. You thought they'd help keep your family safe."

I appreciated the sentiment, even though I suspected she knew her words would offer little comfort. When you'd carried a matched set of luggage stuffed to the gills with guilt, self-blame, and regret for two decades, it wasn't a simple matter of dropping the bags on the curb and moving on just because someone said you could.

"Of course I didn't intend for anyone to die, *querida,* but that doesn't change the outcome. What does intention matter in a situation like that? If a drunk driver kills someone you love, and later says they didn't mean it, does that change how you feel? Does it ease your pain or change the fact that you've lost someone forever? Does it bring them back?"

"But a drunk driver... You could argue that's negligence."

"You could argue that what I did was negligence, too. A drunk driver is blinded by alcohol and overconfidence, and they make a shit decision in a moment. I was blinded by a lot of things back then, too. Anger. Resentment. A fierce need to prove myself to a pack where I'd never be alpha. And a deep, endless ache for the family that I'd once had. If I'd been thinking clearly, if I'd kept my promises to protect my sister's secrets, perhaps..." I trailed off. Those thoughts, too, were part of the haunted house of horrors in my mind. And as such, they needed to be brought out into the light, and released, along with all the rest.

"Elena and I stuck together in America out of necessity, and Elena was still so fragile. Shock, mostly. I knew I couldn't leave her, even though I was terrified of the day she started asking questions.

"It took six months, but then it happened. The grief... It was like walking through mud. When it finally started to recede, just a little bit, her mind cleared up. The story wasn't adding up. She began asking more questions—hard ones. Ones with complicated answers I didn't want to give her. I dodged, redirected, distracted her, tried to convince her it was unhealthy and we had to let it go, had to board up that part of our lives and keep focused on the future. What a load of bullshit that was."

"How did she finally find out?" Gray asked.

"I'd gone out to pick up a pizza, and when I came back inside, she was sitting at the kitchen table with a half-spent bottle of pineapple vodka and that faraway look in her eyes she'd often get, her hands in her lap. I held up the pizza box and made a joke about how we could've just gotten pineapples on the pizza instead of having to drink them. She laughed, but there was something wrong with it. It was totally foreign, like it belonged to another person. A chill went down my spine. Then her smile died, and she lifted her hands and pointed a gun at my chest."

Gray gasped.

"'It was you,' Elena whispered. All the blood drained out of me, and I knew she'd finally figured out the truth. Enough of it, anyway. Enough to know who'd led the wolves to her door. And my God, *querida*, I'd never seen such despondence. It was like the last thread holding her together just snapped.

"'I've got two silver bullets in here,' she said. 'One for you, one for me. That's how it has to be, Meelo.' I didn't even try to argue with her. She was going to kill us both. I was certain of it. And the worst part of it was, I wanted her to. I saw the emptiness in her eyes, and in that moment, I really believed death would be the better option for both of us."

A shiver raced through Gray's body, and she reached for the sheet and pulled it up to our shoulders. "What changed her mind?"

"You know how you say there's no coincidence?" I said.

"Yeah, that's a lesson I've been forced to learn over and over."

"Okay. So here's where shit gets *really* insane."

"You mean it gets worse?"

"Not at all. It gets better." At this, a smile slid over my face. She was going to like this part of the story—a little levity, a slightly-happier-than expected ending. "That was the night I met our boy, Ronan."

TWENTY

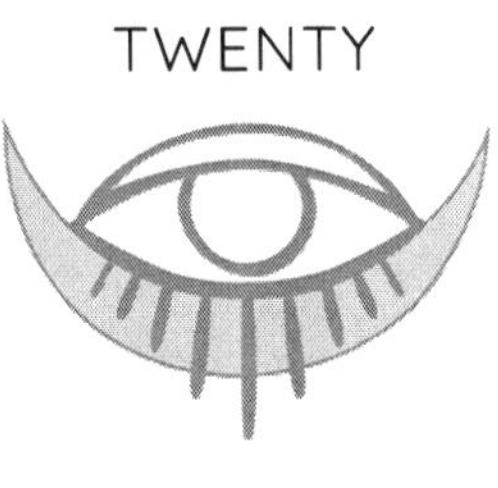

GRAY

"What?" I bolted upright in the bed, sure I'd misunderstood him. "Ronan just happened to show up on your doorstep at the exact moment you and your sister were about to die?"

"As crossroads demons are known to do, I guess," he said. "See, Elena had told me she was going to kill me, and then she was going to kill herself. It was *going* to happen, the forces already set in motion. I saw it play out like a movie, and I knew there'd be no talking her out of it—not even if I'd wanted to. My sister has always been stubborn—you might have picked up on that."

I let out a soft laugh. I *had* picked up on it. It was one of the things I really, really liked about her.

"Anyway," he said, "she flipped off the safety, steadied her aim. And I nodded and told her I was sorry, and that I loved her, and I understood why she had to do this. Then I closed my eyes, waiting for the bite of that bullet. Praying it would be quick, but knowing it wouldn't. Silver poisoning is… unpleasant."

I shuddered again, remembering his tortured body in the warehouse, the way the silver had eaten through his flesh and bones, slowly killing him. A hundred years could pass, and I'd never forget that sight. The fear. I only hoped that *he* hadn't remembered it. That he'd passed out long before the full gruesomeness of his predicament had set in.

"But instead of the pop of a gun," he continued, "I heard Elena gasp. I opened my eyes to see her staring at a point just past my shoulder, her mouth hanging open in shock. So I turn around, and there's this brooding, black-eyed demon leaning back against our kitchen counter, cracking a beer and tossing the bottle cap into the sink. 'Oh, don't mind me,' he said, taking a swig. 'Just here for the show. Continue, please.'"

Emilio's soft smile turned into a full-on laugh, and the sound of it unleashed the floodgates. It was like a needle popping a balloon that just kept expanding and expanding, and now I laughed, too. The things he'd shared with me had been so dark, so tragic, I marveled at the fact that we still remembered how to laugh—that we could do it so soon after talking about everything else. But I cherished that laughter, too. It felt like my wolf and I had been lost in a dark, dangerous forest together, so certain we'd never find our way back to the light. And now here we were. Laughing.

I closed my eyes and took a moment to send a prayer of thanks to the universe.

What bodies, these. What magic. What love.

Then I laughed even harder as the picture of Ronan sharpened in my mind. "Oh my God, he's *such* a drama queen!"

"Well, he knows how to make an entrance, I'll give him that."

"But how did he get there? How did he know what was going on?" I had so many questions, all of them rushing out at once. "What was he even *doing*?"

"To put it bluntly, Elena was about to commit murder *and* suicide, and apparently this is one of Sebastian's favorite combos. Not to mention the fact that I had the most guilty conscience of anyone alive. I guess he thought we were good candidates to go darkside, so Ronan was dispatched to negotiate a deal for our tarnished souls and carry us back to hell."

"But you *weren't* good candidates, obviously."

"Oh, you should've seen Elena's face! The mere idea of working for the Prince of hell got her all riled up again…" Emilio shook his head, almost like he still couldn't believe the turn of events. "You might say Sebastian gave her back the will to live. Ranting and raving at Ronan the entire time about how presumptuous he and his boss were, she emptied out the bullets and chucked them out the window right then. And when she turned back to meet my eyes, there was so much rage and disgust and fire—fire I hadn't seen in years. In that moment, I knew she'd survive. Not because she'd get over it or forgive me or forget what'd happened in Argentina, and not because she'd find a healthy way to deal with it. No. I knew that the anger in her now would fuel her for as long as it took."

Emilio blew out a breath, the earlier levity slipping away again, just as I knew it would. Humor existed even in the darkest corners of a tragedy, but wounds like this didn't just disappear after a good laugh. This was the first time Emilio had ever talked about all of this—I felt that, deep in my bones. He still had a long way to go to releasing his shame and all the pain that came along with it, and to putting the pieces of his relationship with Elena back together, if that was even a possibility. But he'd done the hardest part tonight—starting the process. Speaking the words. Freeing himself of having to carry it alone.

"After giving Ronan a piece of her mind, and telling him he owed her three bucks for the beer, she looked me dead in the eye and told me to pack my bags and leave the Cape. She said she never wanted to see me again.

"Just the fact that she'd survived the night, that I'd survived the night, that all felt like a gift, and I didn't want to take that for granted. I knew I'd caused her so much pain already, I just... Honoring her wishes—leaving, for good—it felt like the only decent thing left to do."

"So you ended up in the Bay," I said, connecting the dots. "Ronan helped you."

"You know he has a thing for strays." Emilio laughed again—not quite as exuberant as the last one, but a laugh nevertheless. "He offered to help me get set up in the Bay, and the rest, as they say, is history. I got a job on the force, met Darius soon after that, did some consulting with him. He was still practicing law back then, before he traded all that in for Black Ruby. Ronan and I didn't see each other all that much—he had his work, and I had mine, and our paths crossed only on occasion, but we always had that unspoken bond. And he knew, without my ever having to say as much, that when the time came when he needed me, I'd be there. No question."

I let the magnitude of his words settle over me. "So before I came into the picture, you guys weren't really all that close?"

"Well, yes and no. Like I said, we had that unspoken bond. But when you did come, it brought us closer once again. And then when Sophie passed away and you started coming into your powers and everything else happened, well…" Emilio sighed. "Now I can't imagine Ronan *not* being a part of my life."

I poked him in the ribs and smiled. "So you're saying that my craziness is the glue that bonds you guys?"

"No, Gray," he said seriously. "You coming into our lives and bringing us all together like this… It's the best thing that's ever happened to me. And I'm pretty sure the rest of the guys feel the same way."

"Me, too," I said, holding his gaze, still marveling at all he'd been through, at everything he'd survived in order to end up here. In my arms. In the home of a sister he'd once thought he'd have to turn his back on forever.

During one of our infamous brownie sessions, back before anything romantic had happened between us, Emilio had told me, *People do all sorts of misguided things when they're trying to protect the ones they love, querida. Let's just say I know something about that.*

At the time, I'd sensed that he'd endured some terrible losses in his life, that he'd carried a truckload of regrets. But I'd had no idea the depths of his pain.

I'd seen real glimpses of it in his eyes tonight, felt his broken heart in the tears that'd soaked my shirt.

But when he looked at me now, his eyes were clear, flickering with something new and shiny. Something that brought a warmth to my chest I couldn't even describe.

Hope.

"Tonight," he said through new tears, "just before you came in here, was the first time since Elena had pointed that gun at me that she gave me any indication that we might have a relationship again." He smiled faintly, lowering his eyes and focusing on a loose thread in the sheet. When he looked up at me again, he said softly, "*Querida*, I died that night, didn't I?"

It took me a beat to realize he was no longer talking about what had happened between him and Elena, but the warehouse battle. The sudden shift nearly gave me whiplash; it felt as if I'd been yanked back in time, back to those ugly moments of seeing him lying in a pool of his own blood.

"You... you'd been badly wounded in the fight," I began, my throat thick with emotion. "Cut with a silver blade. Bleeding..."

"Badly wounded enough to die, then." He shook his head, as if trying to clear away new cobwebs. "I remember trying to shift out of my wolf, and I couldn't. Not all the way. I remember having all the heightened senses and instincts of the wolf, but the pain felt like a man's pain. The fear was... indescribable."

"There was a while there where you got kind of... stuck," I explained. "You couldn't quite shift one way or the other. Ronan and Elena didn't know how to heal you."

"So how *did* they heal me?"

I pressed my fingertips to his lips and shook my head. I wanted to shush him, to tell him there was no point in revisiting that awful night. That the important thing was that he did survive, never mind the hows of it all.

But secrets and lies were the twin snakes that kept looping back to bite us, time and time again. Whether it was Emilio lying to his sister about how her family died, or Liam lying to me about our relationship, or Ronan keeping my deal a secret, or me lying to him initially about what I'd done to Bean... Secrets like ours were heavy burdens, and eventually, they came crashing down on us, and the truth slithered out, all the more venomous for the time it'd had to fester.

I made a vow right then and there that I'd never lie to the men I loved. Not even to protect them.

"The warehouse was burning," I said, "and I was on one side with Ash and Darius and Jael, along with the witches we'd just liberated. We were running for the exit, and I just... I saw you go down. I got to you as quickly as I could, but you were... you were in bad shape."

I told him the details, as best as I could remember.

"Ronan promised he'd save you, and so I left. We had to get the witches to safety. So I came back here with Ash and Darius and everyone else, and we just waited for word from Ronan and Elena. When they finally showed up, you weren't with them. Ronan said that Liam arrived in the form of the great raven to claim your soul. He saw it leave your body. You were… mutilated." I shivered as the images flooded my mind again, unbidden. Emilio lying in all that blood, his chest cleaved open, his body shifting between man and wolf, stuck in limbo. "Liam took you, but Ronan and Elena didn't know where. You were just… gone."

Snuggling in close, I told him the rest of the story—how I knew he wasn't totally gone from us. How Haley and I did the blood spell, and I'd tracked them to my realm. How I'd fought Jonathan, how when I finally found Emilio and Liam, it looked as if they'd been waiting for me. I explained the ritual Liam had guided me through, trying to remember all the details—the moonglass, the magic, the feel of his soul as I gently guided it back home.

"And together," I finished up, "Liam and I brought you back. I'm not sure what happened in the realm after that—there was a strange earthquake sort of event, but then it stopped. And you called for me. That's when we knew you were okay. I took your hands in mine, and then… Well, the next thing I knew, I was waking up in this bed next to you, and Haley was shouting for Ronan and Elena, and someone told Lansky to call the medics back to the house. I was fine the next day—just needed a little rest after the energy expenditure from calling up and using so much magic. You needed a little more time." I kissed his shoulder again, dropping my voice to a whisper. "And here you are. Back with me where you belong."

Emilio was silent for a long time, and though I was dying for his thoughts, I let him be. It was a lot to process, coming back from the brink of death.

"I heard your voice," he finally said, a little awestricken. "Felt your presence all around me. I felt this… this energy pulling me toward the gates. I guess some part of me *knew* I had died—that I was supposed to go through them. But suddenly you were there, your spirit. It was pulling me, too. And no matter how strong the call coming from the other side of that gate, I knew I didn't want to go through it. Not as long as you were standing on the outside, calling me home."

"As if I'd *let* you leave without me." I tried to laugh, but Emilio seemed to be stuck in that moment, uncertain of how to feel about the whole thing.

"Gray, that kind of magic… There's always a cost."

I offered a faint smile. I'd said something similar to Liam when he'd made the moonglass. "Doesn't mean it isn't worth it."

He nodded, but I could tell he wasn't convinced. He brought my hands to his mouth, pressed a kiss against each palm. When he looked at me again, he said, "What was the price, *querida*?"

"I don't know. Honestly. I connected with Liam briefly last night—He's still in my realm, still hunting Jonathan. He told me he's been called to appear before… Well, I think he called it a cosmic tribunal? We don't know exactly what that means for us yet."

"Maybe nothing," he said.

"Maybe nothing," I echoed, but the words felt as thin as the frost on the edges of the window.

"Gray, you shouldn't have—"

"Don't even think it."

"But—"

"I have the power to raise the dead, Emilio. To manipulate souls. I don't know why that power was entrusted to me. Or how it even works, exactly. Or what my bigger purpose is in all of this. I don't even know if the Silversbane prophecy is legit, or just some wishful thinking by generations of witches desperate for answers and hunters even more desperate to get their hands on that kind of mojo. But I *do* know that I can't lose you. That in that moment, I was facing that very real possibility of having to say goodbye to you forever. So yes, maybe there *is* a bigger consequence, an astronomical price tag we can't even imagine, and it'll drop on us all like an atomic bomb when we least expect it. But I would do it again in a god damn heartbeat. You know why?"

He didn't say anything. Just turned his head away, his eyes focusing on the ceiling.

"Because I love you," I said softly. Taking his face between my palms, I turned his head toward me again, stroking my thumbs over his cheeks. "You snuck up on me, Emilio Alvarez. From the very first, you showed me so much kindness and compassion during Sophie's murder investigation. You supported me even when I violated police procedure. You bought me shower poofs and baked me brownies and watched the moonrise with me. You protected me. You let me into your heart. And somewhere in all of that, through all the insane stuff that's happened between the first time you showed up at my house with your messy bed-hair and San Francisco T-shirt, and right this very moment, I fell in love with you. *That's* why."

Another tear escaped down his cheek, but still he hadn't spoken. His brown eyes seemed to darken.

Emilio was healing remarkably well, especially considering the extent of the original damage. Elena was right—his color was looking good, and the wounds crisscrossing his body were no more than battle scars now, his skin red and raised, but completely healed.

Still, the experience had clearly changed him. He'd died that night, and I'd brought him back. Despite the fact that he'd just unburdened himself of one of his greatest secret shames by telling me about his past, there were new shadows swimming in the depths of his eyes. It seemed to me that he'd aged, somehow. Not physically, but… cosmically.

"I don't know how to ask this," I began. "So I'm just going to blurt it out. Are you pissed that we brought you back? Or freaked out or… I don't know. Confused? I need you to be totally honest with me."

At this, he immediately shook his head, surprising me. "You brought me back to my sister. To a chance to set things right between us—a chance that she is finally willing to consider after twenty years of stone-cold silence. You brought me back to my brothers. To my life's work. To the new friends and partners we're making here in Raven's Cape. And most importantly, you brought me back to *you, mi brujita.* To the woman I fell *madly* in love with. So sure, I could sit here on this bed and tell you that what you did was wrong, unnatural, that it never should've happened, that I was supposed to die that night and you should've let me go." He closed his eyes and let out a deep breath, and when he looked up at me again, his gaze was full of fire. "But that would make me a damn liar, because there is *nowhere* else I'd rather be than right here in your arms."

He slid his hands into my hair and pulled me against his mouth, stealing my breath with a wild, feverish kiss that had me wishing we had the house all to ourselves. I wanted him to claim me in every room, in every way, both of us running around naked and howling up at the moon and celebrating the fact that we'd survived another crazy night. But for now, that kind of celebration would have to wait. I was grateful for the kissing anyway.

I finally pulled back to catch my breath, my lips stinging with the intensity of his welcomed attack.

"You're blushing, *querida,*" he teased. "Something on your mind?"

"Maybe." More heat rushed to my cheeks. I felt like a kid with a crush, and I loved every minute of it. "It's just… You… you fell in love with me, too?"

"You think I buy shower poofs and twelve bottles of fruity conditioners for *every* woman I meet?" He grabbed me by the arms and flipped us so that he was on top of me, the sheet between us barely hiding his desire. "What kind of—"

He cut off abruptly, taking a deep whiff of the air, his face twisting with concern. I felt the change in his body immediately—his muscles stiffened, then bunched, and I recognized the movements for what they were. He was about to shift.

"Emilio, don't!" I gripped his arms, his muscles hot beneath my touch. "You're not totally healed yet."

Without a word, he jumped up from the bed and headed for the door, naked and stumbling as he went.

"Wait!" I shouted, chasing him down the hall, nearly tripping over Sunshine and Sparkle on the way. "You're still healing! You can't just—"

"The guys are in trouble!" he shouted, barely avoiding a collision with Elena, who seemed to be on the same trajectory toward the front of the house. Someone managed to haul open the front door just in time, and the pair launched themselves out, transforming into wolves before their feet even touched the snow-covered ground.

TWENTY-ONE

GRAY

The question about whether Emilio could fully shift in his current condition was swiftly answered.

They were magnificent together, two sleek, black wolves streaking across the bright white snow like arcs of dark lightning. I was so mesmerized by their power, their grace, that it took my mind a minute to process the sight unfolding before me.

The team that had gone out for supplies in two relatively newish vans was now stumbling out of a single, completely jacked-up van that had somehow gotten wedged into a snowbank at the end of the driveway.

Haley, Jael, Ronan, Darius, and Lansky—I counted them twice just to be sure. They were all there. All standing on their own two feet.

But three of them were covered in blood.

"Ronan!" I ran outside, following the path of the wolves to the end of the driveway, where Emilio and Elena were frantically sniffing around the van and the perimeter of the yard. Sparkle and Sunshine joined them, tracking some unknown threat.

"It's not our blood," Ronan said, and I stopped just before him, reaching out to touch his jacket for a quick second. He lowered his head to catch my eyes. "Hey. I'm okay, Gray. We all are. I promise. Which is more than I can say for half the shit we bought and one of the vans, but hey. Priorities, right?"

I nodded, the adrenaline spike slowly fading. "What happened?"

"We—" Ronan began, but his attention suddenly shifted to the super-hyper wolf circling us, wagging his tail and yelping like a puppy.

"What? Look at *you*!" Ronan let out a full-on laugh, dropping to his knees to grab Emilio's huge wolf head. He scratched him behind the ears and brought his face close, inhaling Emilio's scent, his eyes full of emotion. The whole thing was so adorable and touching, it basically turned my insides into a puddle of goo.

"Who's back in action, huh?" Ronan wrestled Emilio to the ground, teasing him like he really *was* a puppy. "Who's the biggest, baddest wolf that ever was? Who's a good boy?"

The two of them went at it, rolling around in the snow until Emilio finally pinned Ronan by the shoulders. He licked his face from chin to forehead, and then, shocking us all, shifted back into his human form.

Asher and a crowd of witches had gathered on the lawn now, and all of us busted up laughing at the sight of a very hot, very naked man straddling a very stunned demon.

"Dude, are you fucking *kidding* me?" Ronan shoved Emilio off and got back to his feet, dusting himself off. "I didn't miss you *that* much! For fuck's sake, put some clothes on."

"No!" McKenna shouted. "Don't cover up on our account, hot stuff."

"Seconded," Kasey, another witch from the prison, called out. Elena had bought everyone new phones, and she had hers out now, probably filming a livestream of the whole thing. Not that I blamed her.

"Even *I* got a little buzz from that display," Asher said, kicking snow at Ronan.

Emilio smacked Ronan on the shoulder. "You love it and you know it, hellspawn."

"I feel totally violated," Ronan said, but he was grinning like an idiot. Rubbing the snow from his hair, he said, "Shit, it's good to see you walking, brother."

"Good to *be* walking."

"All sorted?" Darius asked. Then, without waiting for a reply, "Excellent. Perhaps you might consider dressing, preferably before that summer sausage of yours turns into a cocktail wiener? It *is* ten below out here, you daft bastard."

Emilio wasted no time in hauling Darius in for a hug. Unlike Ronan, Darius took the "violation" in stride.

"You look much better than the last time I saw you," Darius said, his voice heavy with relief. He might not remember everything about Emilio, but he'd come to care for him all over again. That much was obvious.

"Unlike you guys." Emilio wrinkled his nose. "What *is* that stench? I thought I smelled shifters. Elena and I bolted out here, thinking you'd been attacked."

"We were waylaid by a pack of hybrid shifters," Darius said. "Mountain lions. The whole thing was a mind-fuck cleverly disguised as an ambush."

"Orendiel?" I asked, snapping my fingers for my hounds to come back. Though the wolves had decided we weren't under immediate attack, my hounds were already patrolling the street in front of the house. I couldn't blame them—they'd been cooped up most of the day on account of the snow. Seemed it was lightening up a bit now, though.

"Yes," Jael said, coming out from behind the van with an armload of grocery bags. "Along with his associates on the fae council. They left us a message."

"I don't care what it takes," Lansky was barking into his cell phone, pacing in the snow alongside the van. "Get a team up there. I need barricades between the seven-mile marker and the twelve. That whole section is officially closed until they can clear out the vehicles and the body. No, no ID. Let the M.E. figure it out."

"Body?" I asked.

"Girl, you have no idea." Haley handed me a package of toilet paper about the size of a small condo, then returned to the van to retrieve some kind of crate. With a bright, trademark-Haley smile, she said, "The good news? The alcohol survived the crash. I repeat, the alcohol survived the crash."

TWENTY-TWO

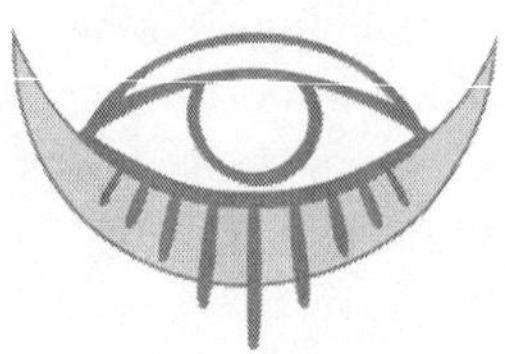

RONAN

In celebration of our wolf pup's triumphant return from the land of the near-dead, Elena had outdone herself in the culinary department, setting up a massive buffet in the dining room featuring all of Emilio's favorites from the homeland. It was so good to be home, to be surrounded by everyone I cared about... All the Orendiel bullshit began to fade into the background.

Liam was still in the Shadowrealm, and part of me actually missed the guy, despite my feelings about what he'd done to get Gray's soul back from hell. The longer I'd sat with it, the faster my rage had started morphing into something pretty damn unfamiliar to me.

Gratitude.

We'd all done things to keep her safe. To keep each *other* safe. I couldn't fault him for that. Not when I caught her blue-eyed gaze across the table, the soft smile on her lips just for me. The woman still loved me, even after everything.

I gave her a wink, then reached for my glass. We may have been temporarily without everybody's favorite surfing philosopher, but we still had a lot to celebrate tonight. It was the first time the rest of us had all been together in a long-ass time, and that alone deserved a toast.

So all around the dining table and spilling into the living

room, we raised our glasses of whiskey and wine—and chocolate milk for Reva—and for the span of one incredible meal, we allowed ourselves to relax. To drink. To laugh. To just be.

But by the time the dinner dishes were cleared and the coffee and *tres leches* cake appeared, the mood had shifted. It was like we all sensed it at the same time—an invisible threat, still hanging over our heads, still lurking just outside the door.

"I feel like we're still missing a lot of pieces to this puzzle," Gray began, sneaking something under the table to one of her hounds. "But we can't sit around waiting for answers that may never come. Especially not after what happened to you guys on the road tonight. We need to make a plan of attack."

"Attack?" Reva set down the bite of cake she'd been about to take, the color draining from her face. She looked up at Gray, who was seated next to her. "I thought you guys were done fighting. Everyone's here. Everyone got out. Even Emilio is better."

Gray ran a hand over Reva's fuzzy head. "We didn't get *everyone* out, sweets. Jonathan had been keeping and tormenting other supernaturals besides witches. We can't just turn our backs on them."

"I know, but… What about their own people? Why does it have to be you guys?" The poor kid looked terrified, and I couldn't blame her. These witches had become her family. We all had, in a very short time at that. She didn't want to lose a single one of us.

"Because we know about the situation," Gray said, "and together, we have the power to do something about it." She took Reva's hand in hers and smiled, her whole face lighting up with pride. "It's kind of like when you guys were stuck in the caves. You were the only one who knew another way out, and even though it was a huge personal risk, you took it. You slipped away from the guards and snuck out right under their noses. Right?"

"I guess."

"Look around, Reva. All these amazing witches sitting here tonight? That smart-ass demon over there snarfing down his fourth piece of cake, even though everyone else hasn't even had one yet?" Gray grinned at Asher, who laughed with his damn mouth full, then shrugged and shoved in another bite. "They're all here because of you. Because they were in trouble, and you had the power to do something about it, and you did it. No questions or second-guessing."

"I'll drink to that." McKenna raised her glass again, nodding at Reva, and the rest of the witches and Ash followed suit.

Reva's cheeks glowed pink once again, and she nodded and took another big gulp of her chocolate milk, looking about six years old instead of sixteen. Damn, sometimes it was easy to forget she *was* just a kid—one whose sense of security and normalcy had been stolen from her, time and again. By Norah. By whoever shit-ass adults abused or just plain lost track of her in the first place.

We're not gonna let that happen again, kiddo…

"One thing's for sure," Ash said now. "The whole lure-them-out plan is shot to shit. From what you said about those mountain lion shifters, they've definitely got eyes on us. No way they're taking the bait."

"Agreed," Beaumont said. "So that's where our plan of attack comes in. It seems we'll have to take the fight to them after all."

"You talking about the Bay?" Emilio asked. He gestured for Elena to pass him the cake, and cut himself a hefty slice. I still couldn't believe how good he looked—even better than before the fight at the warehouse. The fact that he was even sitting here with us was a damn miracle. But smiling? Happy?

"You still thinking about our roll in the snow?" he asked, and it took me a half-second to realize he was talking about me. The whole table erupted in laughter. "You're looking at me like you want to make out or something."

"There's not enough whiskey in this whole town to make that happen." I lifted my coffee mug, which was half full of the stuff anyway, and grinned, taking a big gulp. "I was just thinking that the whole coming-back-from-the-brink-of-death thing is a good look on you."

"And I'll drink to *that*." He lifted his mug and stretched across the table to clink it against mine.

"We're all drinking to that." Elena laughed and reached for the bottle of whiskey at the center of the table, topping off her own coffee, then passing the bottle to Gray. Around the table it went.

When we'd all settled down again, McKenna said, "Okay, so how can we bring the fight to the Bay? Jael said there's no way in, not even by a sneak attack. We can't even get close."

"Anyone got any ideas?" I asked. "Any magic we haven't thought of, spells we could use, weapons, something…"

Reva raised her hand. "Oh! I have an idea."

I bit back a laugh, totally picturing her in school, squirming out of her chair to answer the teacher's question. *Pick me! Pick me!*

"If it's your idea, it's bound to be good," Gray said, and Reva grinned. "Let's hear it."

"What if I did something with my shadow traveling? I don't know anything about disabling fae magic, but I might be able to get into the city astrally and snoop around. Maybe I could, like, spy? Find out what kind of spell they're using or what else is happening over there? Anything could help."

"It's… possible." Jael tapped an elegant finger against his coffee mug as he considered it. "Since she wouldn't be physically trying to get into the Bay, the magic wouldn't necessarily register her presence. She may be able to slip through."

"Wouldn't they have accounted for something like that though?" Haley asked. "Seems like a pretty big flaw in their security."

"But they don't even know about her," Ash said. "You saw this little badass in the caves, Hay. She snuck out right under their noses, and they never gave it a second thought."

"Shadow traveling *is* quite rare," Jael said. "I don't believe we've come across a witch with that power in decades. It's unlikely that Orendiel and the hunters would've concerned themselves with something like that—they can't possibly account for all variables. They're more focused on Gray and the other supernaturals sitting around this table. Honestly, they may not even realize how strong the rest of the witches are. They may believe they're still in a weakened state after the prison ordeal."

"Yeah, underestimating us is kind of a hunter specialty," McKenna said. "Dicks."

Elena reached for the coffee carafe, topping off a few of our mugs. "Okay, in theory, I like Reva's idea. We can protect her physically, and she can sneak into the city with her shadow mojo. But she still has to get close to the Bay, and I'm not sure how to do that. Between the storm, the road closures, and the risk of exposure to Darkwinter spies, it'd be a pretty big gamble."

"Well, it's not so much the distance that's a problem," Reva said. "I was able to get to Gray in that fireplace, right? And that was while I was here in the cave prison, and she was staying at the safe house near the Bay. So, it's the same distance, basically."

"So you think you can do it from here?" Elena asked her.

"Not at the moment. I mean, I could *get* there, sure. But I don't think I could hold a clear connection for very long. Like that time with Gray, I was only able to get a few words out. Same with Emilio the first time I traveled to see him in the woods."

"Right," Emilio said. "It'd felt like a bad connection. It was easier for me to pick up on it in my wolf form, but even then, it was spotty and didn't last very long."

"And for this to work," Elena said, "you'd need more time in there. Not just to spy, but to be sure you weren't seen in the process. If they spotted you, even astrally, they'd know about our secret weapon, and you'd be on their radar in a big way. I won't take that risk."

"I can do it," Reva said. "I know I can. I just need to practice. I need to work on sustaining the connection and keeping it clear."

"We can all help her with that," McKenna said, and the other witches nodded. "It's not like we're going anywhere with this storm, anyway."

Elena finally agreed. "Let's see how the practices go. We'll check in a couple of days and figure out next steps."

"Okay, so that's a good start," Gray said, passing Asher yet another piece of cake. I didn't know how that bastard wasn't four hundred pounds by now. "Hopefully Reva's insights can help us track down Orendiel and pinpoint his base of operations. That way, if we can figure out how to break the magical security, we'll know the primary target in the city."

"I still feel like there's someone higher up pulling the strings," Emilio said. "Not just the council, but someone else. Someone with much bigger aspirations."

"Bigger than wiping out supernaturals from the inside out, and stealing witches' power?" Gray asked.

"I mean, those are major things," Emilio said. "But hunters have always wanted that. And no offense, Jael, but you can't tell me the fae are totally cool with witches and other supers having magic. That's always been a sore point with the Council."

"Snobs," Asher fake-coughed into his hand.

"No, you're right," Jael said. "I'm afraid my kind has always held a bit of an elitist attitude toward magic. But most of us have made peace with the fact that we have to share it. Most of us have no interest in subjugating witches or anyone else for that matter."

"Still," Emilio said, "*some* of you do. Darkwinter, specifically. So this is really nothing new for them, it's just happening on a much bigger scale. But at the end of the day, Orendiel is still just a soldier. And so are Talia and Fenlos. I'm telling you guys, my gut says there's more to this than just a coup."

The house fell silent, all of us sipping our spiked coffee, nibbling on the last crumbs of cake. I sensed the mood shift again, the hope we'd built up slipping dangerously close to despair once again.

Not tonight. No fucking way.

"Look, guys," I said. "The other night, Beaumont said we can't let fear and speculation sidetrack us, and he's right. We need to stick with the known quantities, and right now, that's Orendiel and the Bay."

The vampire nodded at me across the table. "Thank you, hellspawn. I didn't know you'd been listening."

I grinned at him. "What can I say, bloodsucker? I'm full of surprises." Then, to the rest of the group, "So we're in agreement? Gather intel on Orendiel and the Bay, figure out a way to get in there and neutralize the Darkwinter Knights, and take it from there. With enough witches on our side, I'm pretty sure we can show those hunters *and* the dark fae straight to the fucking door."

"With enough witches?" At this, Gray's eyes suddenly lit up. "Wait. I might have an idea on how we can get in."

"Don't keep us in suspense, Cupcake," Asher said.

"We all know that witches help keep the power balance in check," she said. "That's why it was so easy for Orendiel's Knights to destabilize the Bay and lock it up with fae mojo. Most of the witches had been imprisoned, murdered, or chased out, leaving the city wide open for a new power to slip in."

"Yes," Emilio said. "By the time we left the Bay to come here, the power structure was already crumbling. That's when we started seeing a rise in supernatural-related crimes. The Bay was essentially falling apart before our eyes, and there wasn't a damn thing we could do about it."

"So… What if we could counteract Darkwinter by restoring some of the power balance in the city?" she asked.

"What do you mean?" McKenna asked. "How?"

"We've got about two dozen witches in this house alone." Gray rose from her chair, her excitement building. "I'm sure we could bring even more into the fold if we put the word out in the Cape and some of the neighboring towns."

"You know, that's not a bad idea," Elena said. "We can check in with Verona Braden—she owns the metaphysical shop where Delilah was last seen. If anyone would know how to get in touch with the witches of Raven's Cape, it'd be her."

"Here's what I'm thinking," Gray continued. "We start putting the word out. Get everyone together. Bide our time a bit, train, figure out when it's right for Reva to slip in there and poke around. Using her intel, we'll narrow down our main targets and anything else we need to know. Then, assuming we get a large enough contingent of witches, we ride out to the Bay, see if we can break that spell with our own collective magic."

"And once we're in," Haley said, "we take back our city. Fuck yeah, Desario."

"Storm the castle, so to speak," Darius said. "Excellent. I'm told I own a club in Blackmoon Bay. And a rather nice car."

"I can attest to that," Gray said, her cheeks darkening in a way that set a flare of jealousy straight into my chest.

Really? In Beaumont's car?

I grabbed my drink, drowning the flood of images that thought unleashed. It's not that I was jealous she'd been with him.

It was that she still *could* be with him. He may not remember everything about their relationship, but he could still touch her.

My heart burned with a now-familiar ache, but I shoved it way down. Regret had no place at this table. We were so close to figuring this shit out. Close to taking back what was ours.

"I think," Emilio said, reaching for the bottle of whiskey once again, "we've got ourselves a plan. A damn good one. And that calls for another round."

Everyone cheered and banged on the table, laughter exploding like fireworks once again. And for a minute I closed my eyes and soaked up all the warmth and let myself believe this was home. That we were all part of a big, crazy, obnoxious family celebrating a holiday dinner that we'd make last all week.

It's almost enough to ease the pain of our reality.

"Personally, I think it calls for a group hug," Haley said, rising from her chair and waving everyone close. "Come on, guys. You too, grumpy demon over there. Bring it in."

She was talking about me. I got up and joined the knot of people that'd formed at the head of the table, never losing sight of Gray.

I stood as close as I dared. I caught a hint of her scent, a touch of her sweater brushing along my forearm as I reached in to hug Ash. But all I could think about was touching her. Holding her in my arms. Pressing my lips to her forehead and promising her that everything would work out. That we'd be okay, just like always.

I couldn't do that, though. Couldn't even graze her skin without burning her. It was the ultimate fucking punishment.

And after everything we'd been through together, all the shit we'd somehow come out on top of, this would be the thing that would finally break me.

The others let out another collective cheer, the celebration kicking back into high gear as more hugs and more booze got passed around, and I grabbed a jacket and one of the hounds and slipped out the back door unnoticed, out into the snow-globe night where I could temporarily lose myself in the backwoods, breathe in the icy-fresh air, and—for a little while, anyway—pretend I wasn't dying inside.

TWENTY-THREE

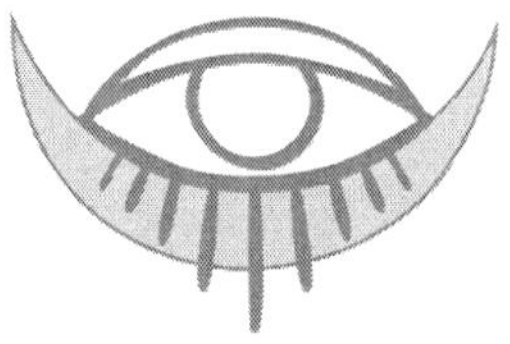

GRAY

The morning after our insane feast, the hounds and I found Elena in the kitchen at dawn, cracking dozens of eggs into a huge bowl. The sun was giving us a rare show, the snow finally letting up a bit, and the light streamed in through the kitchen windows, illuminating her like an angel.

After everything Emilio had told me about what they'd gone through—about what Elena had lost—it was hard to look at her without getting choked up.

"I know I look good from the back," she called over her shoulder. "But damn, girl. Take a picture or something."

I laughed, the knot of emotion loosening. She'd probably scented me long before I'd even approached. It was hard enough to sneak up on a regular shifter, never mind a cop shifter.

"Girl, did you even go to bed last night?" I asked.

"I did. But I was wide awake an hour ago, so I put on the coffee and got to cooking."

"Again?"

"Honestly?" Elena laughed. "I love cooking. Besides, it's easier than doing dishes."

I glanced around the kitchen, taking in the mountains of dishes piled up on the countertops, plates and mugs practically spilling out of the dishwasher. Other than Reva, we'd all gotten a little tipsy last night, caught up in celebrating Emilio's recovery and enjoying a little fun before tackling the challenges ahead.

"You want some help?" I asked her.

She looked at Sunshine and Sparkle, panting and excited, and then at me, taking in my puffy coat, snow boots, and the huge, fur-lined hat I'd found that made me look like a Russian soldier. "Looks like you three already have plans."

"I promised them a walk in the woods this morning." I scratched behind Sparkle's ears, and she let out a little yelp of pleasure. "But I can be back in fifteen minutes to chop or wash or whatever."

"No, Gray. It's a beautiful day, and who knows how long it'll last. You need some fresh air and alone time." She offered me a warm smile, then nodded toward a basket covered with a towel. "Take two blueberry muffins to go."

I reached for the basket. "Two? These things are huge."

In response, she leaned her head out the kitchen doorway, calling across the dining room to a pile of witches in the living room, most of them crashed out on the air beds and sleeping bags they'd brought back from the supply run. Elena had set some of the beds up in the basement downstairs, but most of them had wandered back up here sometime in the middle of the night. It seemed they'd gotten used to close quarters in prison and didn't want to be separated.

I couldn't blame them. Now that I had my rebels back under the same roof, I didn't want to be separated from them, either. The five of us had crashed in the room Emilio and I had shared, Ronan taking a sleeping bag on the floor, lest we accidentally bump toes and start a fire.

"Haley!" Elena shout-whispered, as if that wouldn't wake up the entire room. "Haley! Get dressed."

"Hmm?" came the groggy reply, and like a litter of kittens piled up in a box, the rest of them stirred, too.

"Get up, girl," Elena said, and Haley's head finally popped up from the pile.

"I'm up, I'm up." She stifled a yawn, slowly getting to her feet and picking her way across the floor. "What's going on?"

"Gray needs your help outside with the hounds," Elena blurted out, and I almost smacked her. "I don't want any of you wandering out there alone. Even during the daylight hours."

"No worries. Give me five minutes." Haley stretched, then disappeared into the bathroom.

"What is *wrong* with you?" I asked the minute Haley was out of earshot. "I thought you said I needed alone time!"

"You do—alone time with your sister. You have to tell her, *loca*," Elena said. "You keep putting it off, and you're going to miss the chance and regret it forever."

I opened my mouth to argue, but Elena was right. If anyone knew about regret, and potentially rocky sibling reunions, it was her.

Still, I wasn't ready. Telling Haley she had not just one but three sisters, that I was one of them, that we were all part of some ancient witchcraft legacy, that our mother had tried to kill us... The conversation was a lot more involved than dropping one simple truth-bomb about a long-lost sister.

"Aren't you happy that she's your sister?" Elena asked, cutting right to it, as usual. "Don't you want her to share that joy?"

"I'm thrilled," I said, because I truly was. "It's just that... I don't know. I guess I keep waiting for a sign from her. Like some kind of guarantee that she'll feel the same way."

"Oh, Gray." Elena wiped her hands on the towel tossed over her shoulder, then cupped my face. "How could she not?"

I shrugged. I know it seemed obvious to her, but I'd been alone for so long, I felt totally clueless about how female friendships worked, let alone sisterhoods. Sophie was the first and only female friend I'd ever really had, and I'd kept her at a distance, too. It was kind of ironic that she was the one to bring Haley into my life. And though Haley and I had gotten pretty close since Sophie died, I had no way of knowing how she truly felt about me.

What if it totally freaked her out? Or worse—what if she already knew we were sisters, and didn't want to tell me because she didn't want the burden that came along with that? The obligation?

What if *she* didn't want to claim *me*?

"No, no, no. Don't do that." Elena whipped me on the butt with her towel, recapturing my attention. "You're overthinking it, Gray. You need to just tell her, get it all out, and let things unfold naturally from there. Haley will listen. She'll—"

"Listen to what?" Haley appeared in the doorway looking as fresh and perky as if she'd already downed half a pot of coffee. She was all bundled up, just like me, her cheeks pink, her eyes bright. We looked like a pair of snow-beasts about to embark on an Arctic adventure.

"I'll… tell you outside," I mumbled. My heart fluttered with fresh nerves, but they weren't necessarily bad ones. Just… nervous ones.

Brilliant, Desario. Really.

Haley shrugged, then spotted the basket on the counter. "Ooh, muffins!"

"I already got one for you." I laughed, catching Elena's eye. Yeah, it was time.

Thank you, I mouthed.

Elena winked, then shooed us all toward the back door, Sunshine and Sparkle practically peeing themselves with excitement.

"Brunch will be ready in an hour," she said, "so don't go too far. I'm counting on you two to referee the bacon plate. You know how guys are about their meat."

Haley cracked up. "Gray *is* the expert on guys and their meat."

Holding back a laugh of my own, I shoved her out the door before she could make any more jokes about my arrangement with the guys.

"Don't knock the meat-lover's sampler platter until you've tried it," I said.

"*Knock* it? Seriously? Girl, I'm over here trying to figure out where to order my *own* sampler platter." Haley giggled and linked her arm in mine, and together we followed the hounds into the woods, Elena's laughter trailing us all the way there.

TWENTY-FOUR

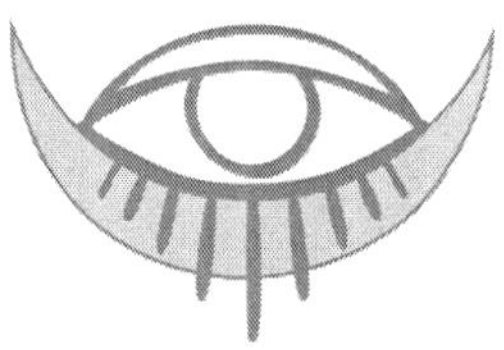

GRAY

The snow out back was hip-deep in parts, and though Haley and I had to push ourselves to plod through it, it was no match for the hounds. They bounded around like a couple of pups, carving figure eights in the thick layers of white as Haley and I fought for every breath. When we finally reached the shelter of the backwoods, the snow leveled off, and we scouted around for a good place to take a muffin break.

"There," she said, pointing out a huge nurse log lying in a copse of trees, mostly untouched by the snow.

We sat on the log side by side, unwrapping the muffins while the hounds waited at our feet, their hypnotic eyes fixated on our every move.

"Haley," I began, at the same time she said, "Can we talk about the hounds?"

We both laughed, then she said, "I'm sorry. You go first."

"No, it's fine. They're kind of new to the family. Courtesy of Sebastian."

She hadn't spent much time with them yet—other than for a few brief hours with Emilio last night before dinner, they'd hardly left my side since we'd all escaped the warehouse.

"So basically, they're your jailers?" she asked.

"More like my protectors," I told her. "And my friends. I don't think that's how Sebastian intended it, but that's how it worked out. Right, girls?"

They wagged their tails and licked their chops, probably thinking I was about to hand over the muffin. Not happening.

"Their cuteness is definitely in the eye of the beholder," Haley said, narrowing her gaze on them. "But I have to admit… they're kind of growing on me."

"They have that effect."

"Can I…?" She held out her hand, tentatively, and Sunshine nudged it with her nose.

"Be my guest. Looks like they like you."

She stroked Sunshine's muzzle, and of course, Sparkle wanted in on the action too. Soon they were competing for her affection, plodding around the woods in search of sticks and rocks and other gifts for their new friend.

Sparkle came back with a huge, snow-packed pine bough about the size of Haley herself, and we both cracked up.

"I'm so honored, Sparkle," Haley said. "What a beautiful gift. I shall treasure it always. From a great distance."

The sun peeked through the clouds overhead, rimming the snow-covered pines around us in a golden glow, and a calmness came over me. The sound of my sister's laugh filled me with pure happiness, and suddenly I felt lighter, knowing that the moment was right.

It was time.

"I need to tell you something, Haley," I said softly. "It's important."

She stopped petting Sparkle and glanced up at me, expectant. "Everything okay?"

"More than okay. You're… you're my sister."

"Oh my God, I'm *so* glad you said that." Her eyes filled with emotion, and she leaned over to pull me into a hug. "I feel the same way, Gray. I know we got off to a rough start at Norah's place, but that was just growing pains, you know? We make a kickass team. Remember that time at the morgue, with that security guard? I wonder what he's—"

"Haley." I pulled out of her crushing hug and grabbed her

arms, blinking the happy tears from my eyes. She was such a crazy witch, in the best possible way, and she was mine. All mine. How did I get so lucky? "Listen to me. You're my sister. My *real* sister. As in, we have the same biological parents. The same blood. The same grandmother—Deirdre."

Haley's eyes widened. For a moment, she went totally still. She didn't breathe, didn't make a sound. I held my breath, too, worried she was about to bolt on me, or laugh, or just… not react at all.

But then she just started laughing again, happy tears like mine streaking her cheeks, and I let out a big, fat sigh of relief.

"Sisters?" she asked, bewildered. "But… how?"

How? I wanted to make a sex joke. Like, *Well, Haley, when a mommy and a daddy love each other very much…*

But I couldn't. Our mother *hadn't* loved our father. She'd murdered him. She'd made four babies with him, and then snuffed out his life, nearly snuffing out ours, too.

"There's… more," I said.

Haley was still beaming. "I'm all ears. Tell me everything."

"No, I mean more of *us*. Our parents had four daughters. Somewhere out there in the world, we've got two other sisters. We were all separated as children and raised separately to keep us safe, because there's this whole prophecy thing and our mother wanted our magic and… God, this is a long story."

My heart was in my throat, my magic buzzing beneath my skin as I thought of our mother again. Even the hounds picked up on it—they bounded back over to me, pressing against my legs, sniffing all around.

"It's okay, girls. Mama just needs to chill." I blew out a frosty breath, then steadied myself, waiting for my magic to settle. When it did, I turned to Haley and told her the whole story—as much as Deirdre had told me, anyway: The Silversbane Prophecy, and our mother's visions about it during her pregnancy. The four of us. How she'd desperately wanted our magic. How Deirdre believed she'd killed our father. Our near-drowning at her hands, and all the ways our lives had irrevocably changed as a result.

"Drowning…" Haley closed her eyes, her voice soft in the

winter air. "When I was younger, I used to have this recurring dream. There were four little girls—sometimes I was one of them, and other times I'd be watching them like a movie—you know how dreams are weird like that. Anyway, the girls were always dressed in white, and we were always walking through the woods. Sometimes we'd pick berries, or build a tree fort, or look for cool rocks. That part was slightly different each time, but the dream always ended the same way. Whether I was one of the girls or just an observer, we'd reach the river, and then one by one, we'd vanish. I was always the last one left standing—or I'd watch the last one standing, and she'd become a spitting image of me. And in that moment, I'd be overcome with this feeling of such loneliness…" Haley shook her head. "Sometimes the feeling would stay with me for hours after waking up. Like, some part of me knew that something was missing."

"Something *was*. All of us—we were missing from each other." I put my arm around her shoulder, and we bent our heads together, our breathing synchronized.

"I grew up with good parents," she said. "But they died in a car crash fairly young. My mom's mom—Nona—she raised me after that, but she passed away when I was a freshman in college. I couldn't afford the tuition. I ended up in the Bay—like a lot of witches without a family."

"You had a family, though. We both did. We just didn't know about each other."

Haley nodded, snuggling in closer. "I guess that's why I ended up joining Bay Coven. I wanted that family. That sisterhood. It didn't turn out exactly as I'd hoped, though."

"But it did," I said. "Never mind Norah. You got Sophie out of the deal. And Delilah and Reva and all the others. And after that, you got all the sisters you kept safe in the prison."

"No, you're right."

"You also have me, Hay. And guess what? Now that I've found you, I'm not planning on letting you out of my sight again."

"And I can't escape you, even if I wanted to." She reached

down to pat Sunshine's head. "You'd send these two to hunt me down."

"Don't tempt me."

We sat in silence for a moment, both processing things in our own ways. I sensed Haley had a million more questions, as did I. Deirdre might be able to fill in some of the gaps, but the last time I'd seen her was when I'd come back from the realm with Emilio. Once we knew Emilio was out of the woods, she'd said her goodbyes, telling me she had to check in with Sebastian and would be back when she could.

I hadn't heard a peep from her since.

"There's a lot more that Deirdre hasn't told me yet," I said, "but we'll figure it out. We'll find the others."

"We're sisters," she said, her smile widening. "I still can't believe it. And we've got two more."

"Do you think they're in a coven?" I asked. "Or practicing magic at all? I wonder if they're in Washington, close to the Bay. Deirdre said we'd all be drawn there eventually, but right now it's like looking for a needle in—"

Two low, dangerous growls stopped my stream of consciousness babble, raising the hairs on the back of my neck.

"Sunshine? Sparkle? What's going on?"

"Do you feel that?" Haley held out her hands, then hopped off the log, looking around the woods as she rubbed the chill from her arms. "It's like it just dropped by about twenty degrees."

"Now that you mention it, yeah." My breath, which had been a thin white mist all morning, was now a dense cloud. I stood up and peered through the trees, looking for a patch of sunlight I was sure had been there seconds earlier.

When had it gotten so dark?

"What time is it?" I asked. "How long have we been out here?"

Haley glanced at her watch. "It's only half past eight. Less than an hour."

"We'd better head back."

Overhead, the treetops swayed and creaked, dumping another load of snow on the forest floor. And then… silence. Stillness.

Not the good kind.

A chill crawled across my skin. The dogs closed ranks, flanking me and Haley. Then, they began to bark, but there was no one around—not that I could see.

"Something's not right." I closed my eyes and reached out for a connection with the earth. But for the first time since I'd gotten back in touch with my witchcraft, I felt nothing. It wasn't just that I couldn't sense the earth's magic or draw up the energy. It was like there was no energy there at all. Something was actively blocking it.

"We need to go," I said urgently. "Now."

But it was too late. We'd been spotted. Not by a person or shifter or fae magician.

By something else entirely.

TWENTY-FIVE

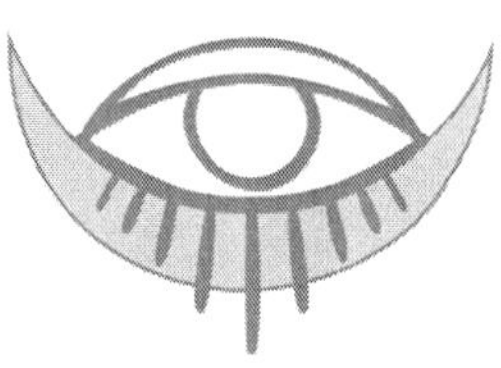

GRAY

"What's happening?" Haley's eyes widened. "It feels—"

A gust of arctic wind stole the rest of her words, and she gasped for breath, her lips turning snow white right before my eyes.

Holy. Shit.

"Haley! Move your ass!" I grabbed her hand and bolted, dragging her behind me. I had no idea what was happening, but I felt the frigid air close on our heels as if it were an actual monster chasing us through the woods. Without breaking my stride, I glanced over my shoulder to make sure the hounds were following, and the sight behind me threatened to steal my breath, too.

It was as if the woods had been hit with a tsunami, but instead of sweeping over the landscape with water, this one was invisible, and it turned everything it touched to ice. Glittery, silver-white crystals solidified behind us, freezing the air in a narrow path that wound through the trees, heading right for us.

It was no more than fifty feet away.

"Move!" I shouted, tugging her forward. "Faster!"

This was no ordinary storm. Not even the freakiest weather event could explain it. All I knew was that if we didn't beat this thing to the house, we were going to be encased in ice.

We were going to die.

"Haley, faster!"

With a burst of new energy, she pushed forward, linking her arm in mine as we hauled ass toward the backyard. My lungs burned, my lips cracking and bleeding from the cold, my fingers and toes already going numb, but the harder we pushed, the further away the yard was starting to feel.

"We won't make it!" Haley shouted. "There's too much—" The wind howled between us, carrying away the rest of her words.

She was right. That thing was coming too fast, we were already bordering on exhaustion, and the backyard would be another trudge through hip-high snow. We had one last recourse, a realization we both seemed to reach at the same moment.

Magic.

"We need to connect blood!" She shouted. "Bite your hand!"

Still running, we each bit into the soft webbing between our thumb and index finger, drawing blood. Without speaking, we clasped hands again, pressing our wounds together. I felt the touch of her blood immediately; my magic sparked to life in response.

"Channel my power!" she shouted. "Now!"

Holding onto her hand for dear life, I stopped and turned toward the invisible enemy, raising my other palm and calling on the last of my reserves, drawing on whatever power I could from my sister. I felt her own magic move through me, much liked Darius's power had when we'd fought the memory eaters in the Shadowrealm.

An electric bolt of bright blue magic shot from my outstretched palm and slammed into the icy torpedo heading our way. It exploded in a shower of sparks, and for a moment, everything stilled. It stopped, mid-air, and I bent over at the waist, trying to catch my breath.

"Calm before the shit-storm," I panted. "We need to keep going."

Haley nodded, still clasping my hand. The magic had bought us a precious few seconds, but it'd weakened us both severely, and now we stumbled awkwardly through the trees and out into the yard, pushing ourselves beyond all physical possibilities.

Everything below my waist was numb.

Sparkle and Sunshine were barking like mad, clearing a path ahead of us.

Slowly, the back deck came into view, and the sliding glass door opened, Emilio and Asher bolting out, their eyes wide with shock.

"Get back!" I shouted at them, knowing the ice-missile was already back in motion. "Move!"

They ignored me, both of them leaping off the deck and charging toward us at lightning speed. They reached us at the same time, grabbing us by our jackets and yanking us backward, half-carrying us back to the house. They practically threw us onto the deck, where Ronan and Elena were already reaching for us, hauling us in through the doorway. All four of us plus the hounds tumbled inside, and someone slammed the door shut behind us.

We all watched in horror as the white path that had been targeting us spread out, then crested, peaking as a giant wave that towered over the house.

"Everybody, duck and cover!" Elena shouted. "Away from the windows!"

Then the wave crashed. It broke upon the house, shaking it down to the foundation. Windows shattered. Shelves rattled, dishes crashed to the floor, door frames cracked under the pressure of trying to stabilize the walls.

And then, just as quickly as it had burst on the scene, the mysterious vortex was gone.

Gingerly, we all got to our feet, rounding up everyone inside and making sure no one got hurt. Miraculously, everyone was okay—just completely freaked.

Outside, as far as we could see, the entire property and the forest beyond—was encased in ice, a child's fairytale wonderland that would've been beautiful if it wasn't so absolutely deadly.

"What the hell is happening?" I asked, still panting. My heart was in my throat, hammering so hard I wasn't sure I could even speak around it. "Is this all Darkwinter's doing?"

"No," Jael said. "The magic that made this is much more ancient. Much more deadly."

"What the fuck is it?" Ronan asked.

A familiar voice echoed across the house, his ominous words sending a chill down my spine that had nothing to do with the ice palace outside.

"It seems the price of our actions in the realm has just gone up," Liam said. "And our debtors are ever eager to collect."

TWENTY-SIX

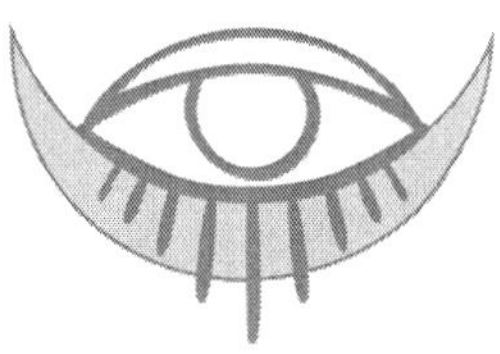

GRAY

"I've been banished to the material plane," Liam said. "Delivered, in essence and body, to your doorstep. I fear my arrival is what brought about your current predicament."

I picked a path across a sea of broken glass in the kitchen, slowly making my way over to Liam. He was in his human form, dressed in dark jeans and an olive green V-neck sweater that made his blue eyes look even more ethereal than usual. To say I was happy to see him was an understatement, despite the bad news he'd brought. Despite all the things that still lingered between us.

He'd brought Emilio back to us. And now he was here.

I pulled him in for a tight hug, my heart still pounding from the ordeal we'd all just been through. He seemed surprised by the contact, stiff in my arms, but I didn't carc. I'd missed him. Having him here… Well, it felt like the band was back together again. There was no other way to put it.

"How can the ice bomb be your fault?" I asked, pulling back to look him in the eye. "And what do you mean, you've been banished here? You can't travel to the Shadowrealm?"

"In this form, I am unable to travel *anywhere* now, unless it's on foot or by other normal means of transportation." Liam lowered his eyes. "My powers have been temporarily suspended. I can still take on my raven or owl forms, but that is the extent of my magic.

Even as an avian being, I must remain tethered to the material plane. I can no longer manipulate soul energies, travel to or between realms, or perform any of my sacred duties as Death. For all intents and purposes, I'm human."

"Human?" I gasped. Liam had wanted a chance to live out the rest of his life as one of us, but something told me this wasn't what he'd had in mind. "But if you're here, without your powers, who is serving as Death?"

"There is none," he replied somberly.

"But how can that be? For how long?"

"I know not. For as long as it takes the Old One to reach a decision, I suppose."

"So you're on probation, huh?" Asher chuckled. "Never thought I'd see the day *you'd* break the cosmic rules, Spooky."

If Liam was surprised by *my* hug, he was downright shocked by Asher's uncharacteristic display of affection. Ash tackle-hugged the poor guy, nearly knocking him onto his very human—and very nicely packaged in those jeans, I noticed—ass.

"I am… pleased to see you liberated," Liam said, awkwardly patting Asher on the back. "I am pleased to see all of you, though I wish it were under better circumstances."

He broke free, then looked at Ronan, who nodded in greeting. Liam's gaze finally came to rest on Emilio, and the two locked eyes for a long moment, a silent understanding passing between them.

"Where's the vampire?" Liam asked.

"Basement," I said. "Sleeping. Someone should probably go check on him."

"I'll go," Elena said. "I need to check in with the department, too. I want to know if anyone else was affected by this—"

"Arctic missile," Haley said. Then, to Liam, "Yeah, so getting back to that… I thought Darkwinter created the storm? But Jael said it was some kind of ancient magic. Now you're saying it's *your* fault?"

"The dark fae did indeed create the storm, but due to my predicament, it is now growing even larger and more brutal than they'd envisioned. My arrival here seems to correspond with the polar weapon that targeted this precise location. It was as if the stripping of my powers had an immediate and equal reaction on the material plane."

"I thought it was targeting us," I said. "Haley and I were in the woods, and everything just turned into this insane winter wonderland."

"Only not so wonderful," Haley said. "More like a winter wasteland."

"I believe it was drawn toward my energy," Liam said. "Understand… The suspension of my powers is not just about human souls. I am Death, the Great Change, the Ultimate Transformation. Without me, life energy such as that which balances nature cannot—well—transform. We will now experience a state of perpetual winter, compounded infinitely by unchecked fae magic and spellcraft, and a complete power imbalance resulting from the disruption of the witch communities here. All of those forces have conspired in this moment to bring about the destructive forces you've just witnessed."

I leaned back against the kitchen counter, trying to stabilize myself. "This is insane. You all know that, right?"

"I'm afraid there's more," Liam said. "The longer I'm stuck here, powerless, the worse those inhabitants of the material plane will suffer. Living souls will not be able to pass on in death."

"What, like no one can die?" Asher asked.

"People will still die. And their souls will vacate their bodily vessels. But I won't be available to guide them, to call upon my ferriers, to move them through the transition. The souls will wander on the material plane as ghosts, trapped, and growing increasingly confused and frantic at their inability to move on. The more restless a spirit becomes, the more dark energy it draws to itself. That's when you begin to see poltergeists and hauntings, non-demonic soul possessions, things of that sort. That happens now with restless spirits, but consider it on a mass scale, where *all* spirits are restless."

"Humans will go insane," Emilio said. "They will absolutely break with reality."

"Yes, that is my prediction as well," Liam said.

"So we've got a winter weather lockdown," I said, "with the possibility of random, deadly, unpredictable events like what we saw today. We've got ghosts, possibly angry ones. We've got hauntings and possessions. And that's on top of the militarization of cities by the dark fae and the hunters."

"It's a lot to face," Haley said. "But remember what Ronan and Darius said. One thing at a time, deal with the known, figure out the rest as we go."

Footsteps echoed up the basement stairs, and I turned to see Elena emerging from the doorway, cell phone in hand. "No reported injuries from the arctic blast," Elena said. "Not in Raven's Cape, anyway. And Darius is fine, too. Sleeping like a vampire. I decided to let him be. He'll have a busy night ahead of him—as will the rest of us."

"So you got through to the department?" Emilio asked.

"Mayor's office, actually," Elena said. "It seems that what happened here was localized to my property—a rare weather anomaly, they're calling it. But another band of heavy snow is moving in fast, and the rest of the region is still dealing with the accumulation and frigid temperatures we've already experienced. The governor has declared a state of emergency. They're requesting federal aid, with military intervention a strong possibility, should things continue on this trajectory."

"But that means more humans flooding into the Cape," I said. "Right into the path of danger."

"That's exactly what that means." Elena's lips pressed into a grim line.

I looked around the kitchen, cataloging the damage. Broken glass. Broken windows. Cracked walls. Outside, I thought of all the living creatures that must've been buried under that ice fall, and my heart broke.

The full implications of what Liam and I had done in the magic realm were slowly sinking in.

"This is my fault," Liam said.

"No," I said. "It's mine. I'm the one who tracked Emilio to the Shadowrealm. It was my decision to bring him back. You were simply honoring my wishes." I turned to look out the back door, beyond the edge of the property where the trees now sparkled like diamonds in their icy prisons. "I risked all of you… All of this… I put everything on the line to bring Emilio back." I turned back to face them, their outlines blurred by my tears. When I found Emilio's warm gaze, a smile touched my lips. "But I won't apologize for it. I'd do it again in a heartbeat, for any one of you."

"As would I," Ronan said.

"Ditto," Asher said.

"Same," Haley said. "Come on, Gray. Really."

"That isn't up for debate, love." Darius peered out from the other side of the basement door. It seemed he didn't want to sleep through the excitement, after all, but he still couldn't risk sunlight exposure. "All we've left to do is deal with the outcome. How we arrived at that outcome is now irrelevant."

Emilio laced his fingers through mine, giving my hand a squeeze.

"Alright, we need to divide and conquer on this one," he said. "Let the governor coordinate with emergency services and deal with the human population. As for the rest of us, our job description hasn't changed. We need to stay on track with our plans."

"The mayor wants all hands on deck at the precinct," Elena said. "I don't see how I can refuse."

"No, don't refuse," Emilio said. "You, Lansky, and Hobb should do whatever you have to do to maintain status quo. We don't want to arouse any suspicion from the humans, so if coordinating from the precinct is what you'd normally do in extreme weather, then that's what you need to do now. But Elena, you need to be very, very careful out there. Don't travel alone, and don't take any unnecessary risks. Your job is not worth your life. Are we clear?

Elena nodded. "We're clear."

"In the meantime, I'll reach out to Verona and start coordinating with the witches in the area," Emilio said. "It's more important than ever that we stick together on this."

"We've *always* been stronger together than scattered," Haley said. "It's time we start remembering that."

"It's happening." In a swirl of cold air, Deirdre stepped in through the front door, her coat and boots thick with snow, her eyes wide with excitement.

Either she knew something the rest of us didn't, or she'd finally gone off the deep end.

"I sensed a sudden shift in the universal energy," she said, breathless. "Can't you feel it? I came as soon as I could. We have so much to prepare for, and very little time to do it."

"Deirdre, slow down," I said. "What's happening? What are you talking about?"

She beamed at me, locking me in her bright blue gaze.

I knew in a flash what she was going to say next.

"The Silversbane Prophecy, child. This is how it begins."

"With the blizzard from hell?" I forced out a laugh, but a bolt of nervous energy shot down my spine, and inside, everything was trembling.

"You've already begun gathering witches," she said, gesturing toward the sea of faces around us. "And now you will gather more."

"Okay, and then what?" I laughed again, but anyone in that room who knew me could've seen right through it. "I just stand on a chair, bang on a glass, and roll right into it? Like, Hi! I'm Gray, third daughter of a third daughter of a third daughter, Silversbane heir, destined to unite everyone. By the way, how do you all feel about uniting? Hope no one's got any plans tonight! Let's do some icebreakers!" It sounded ridiculous, even without my added snark. These women were strangers. Many of them had their own covens or had been practicing solitary for years. Who was I to come in and claim such a powerful legacy?

Who was I to unite them? To lead?

All the old doubts rushed in. But then Emilio squeezed my hand again, and Haley came to stand at my side, and Ronan gave me a crooked grin, and Asher winked, and Darius offered a single nod of unwavering support.

And Liam's eyes blazed bright, just for a moment.

"Yes, Gray," Deirdre said, her own eyes softening. "You do just that. Perhaps with a little more finesse, but the principle is there. You tell them about yourself. Your magic. What you've learned.

What's to come. Remember, child. Most witches are already aware of the prophecy. And while some have dismissed it as legend, many still believe. Many still hope."

Hope. That little word again, four letters and one syllable, strong enough to carry the most powerful essence we had.

But was *I* strong enough to carry *it*?

Maybe not on my own. But I wasn't on my own anymore. I had my rebels. My grandmother and my sister. Two more sisters still to meet. New friends like Elena, Lansky, and Hobb. And the kind, supportive smiles of all the witches surrounding me now. I hadn't even made time to learn all of their names, yet here they were, ready to cheer me on. Ready to trust me. Ready to help me carry that hope for our entire sisterhood.

My blood warmed, the magic settling into a comfortable hum. Suddenly, a sense of purpose rose inside me like a helium balloon, and I finally felt it. The energetic shift Deirdre had mentioned, like a warm wave of energy that radiated across my skin.

I smiled—a real one this time. "I think I'm… I'm actually ready for this."

"Sounds like shit's about to get real, Silversbane," Asher said with a big grin of his own.

"First order of business better be figuring out a new HQ," Ronan said. "Or shit's about to get *really* real. As in, fifty people sharing a bathroom real."

"Not to mention sharing a bed," Ash said.

Haley laughed. "As if you guys have a problem with that."

"We're very selective about it, though," he said, winking at me.

"Ronan's right," Emilio said. "We're already stuffed to the brim here. And now with all the damage, it's not safe for any of us. We need to relocate. Tonight, if possible, before that next band of snow hits."

"Leave that to me." Elena hit a button on her phone and pressed it to her ear. "Start packing up, people. I know just the place."

TWENTY-SEVEN

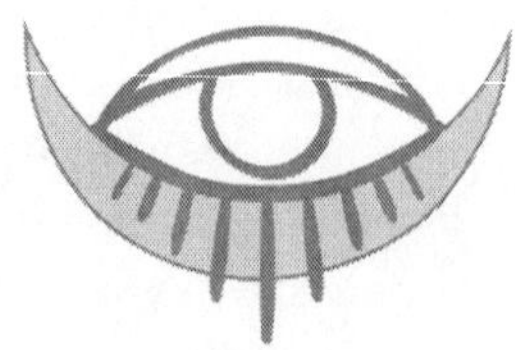

EMILIO

"I hope no one is allergic to dogs." Verona Braden laughed as she reached for my arm, allowing me to guide her up the front steps and into the place we'd all be calling home for the foreseeable future. Roscoe, her golden retriever, followed behind us. I was honored he'd let me take over for him, temporarily standing in as Verona's eyes.

"I think it's pretty safe to say we're all dog people here," I said. "Elena and I are wolf shifters, for starters. In case you haven't figured that out."

Verona let out another hearty laugh. "Detective Alvarez, I can smell you a mile away. Same goes for your sister, and her partners as well."

"Hmm. I'll try not to take that as an insult," I teased. "Elena's not here, though. She'll be in later tonight."

"You carry her with you, Detective. Always." Then, holding out her hands as we entered the front foyer, "This place is lovely. Absolutely lovely."

Verona had her own ways of seeing a place, and her assessment was absolutely right. I still couldn't believe we'd scored it.

Apparently, one of Hobb's cousins owned a large stretch of oceanfront property about ten miles south of Raven's Cape, and was in the process of building a bed and breakfast. The lodge had been completed earlier this month, but because of the freak weather, the family decided to postpone the public opening until springtime. So, after a decent amount of begging completely unbefitting to my alpha wolf sister, and the promise of a few more dates, Elena finally convinced Hobb to call in an old family favor.

Three hours later, we found ourselves moving in.

Nestled against the forest and facing the sea, the property had a rustic quality to it that I loved, with rough-hewn timber framing and dark pine walls, and huge bay windows overlooking the beach. Behind us, the landscape was thick with massive, old-growth pines and a canopy of lush foliage that protected us somewhat from the heavy snowfall and provided a sense of privacy and security.

The ocean was relentless, the frothy waves churning nonstop, creating a stunning soundtrack for all of us.

It felt good here. Clean. Alive. And perhaps most importantly, spacious. The main lodge was two stories high, with ten bedrooms upstairs and a professional kitchen, huge dining room, and three other large living spaces on the main floor that we could further divide for sleeping and training areas.

"You're doing a good thing here, Detective." Verona turned back toward me with a smile. "Bringing us all together like this."

"That means a lot coming from you," I said. When we'd first met Verona, she'd told us she'd been aware of the change in the air, the fear and rumors about another witch hunt already churning through her community. But she'd insisted that no matter what evil befell the Cape, she and the other witches could weather the storm as they always had.

Between the *literal* storm that'd hit, along with everything I'd shared with her about Darkwinter and the other information we'd been able to gather so far, she soon realized how deep this went. How much we *needed* to stick together—all of us.

I didn't mention anything about Gray or the prophecy. That was for my brujita to share, whenever she was ready.

Verona had traveled with a small caravan of local witches she'd been able to persuade to the cause, and now they mingled with the witches we'd brought up from Elena's house, making quick, friendly introductions as everyone tried to make themselves useful and settle in for the long haul. Hobb had managed to sneak away from the precinct for a little while to help us get set up, but Elena and Lansky had their hands full at the RCPD, coordinating emergency response with the mayor and other local officials. She'd promised to drive up with Darius after sunset, but we didn't know how long she and the other detectives would be able to stay.

All of us had some long nights ahead.

The next couple of hours were a blur. Between assigning bedrooms and organizing our essentials inside the lodge, setting up and warding our perimeter outside, and figuring out dinner plans for our quickly-expanding army, I'd only seen Gray in passing. She'd helped the witches find beds, cleanse and ward their spaces, and consolidate and inventory the food and magical supplies everyone had brought with them.

But I could tell from the tense, anticipatory mood that Gray had yet to fully introduce herself, or make mention of the prophecy. Of her heritage. Of how crucial it was that the witches join forces—not just to stay safe from the immediate threats of the storm and the hunters, but to unite. To fortify. To start looking ahead to a time when—hopefully on the near horizon—witches didn't have to hide or practice in the shadows anymore.

When they didn't have to fear for their lives, but could embrace them fully.

The first chance I had for a break, I tracked her down in the kitchen, where she'd been filling ice cube trays as if it were the most important task in the world.

She'd put her hair into a loose bun, and now I slipped my arms around her from behind and pressed a kiss to her nape, breathing in the strawberry-sweet scent of her skin.

"Hiding out?" I murmured.

"No. I mean, sort of." She leaned back into my embrace and blew out a breath, and I felt her heartbeat level out, her tense muscles relaxing just a fraction. "Okay, fine. I'm totally hiding out."

"Consider yourself busted."

"Busted, huh?" she asked playfully. "Does this mean you'll have to cuff me, Detective Alvarez?"

Dios mio the thought of Gray in handcuffs… I bit her earlobe and groaned, an ache blooming below the belt that was only going to get worse. It'd felt like a thousand lifetimes since I'd had her to myself. Since I'd felt the press of her warm body, heard the soft sounds she made as we…

Cold shower, Alvarez. It's gonna be a long night.

She turned around in my arms and slid her hands over my shoulders. Her eyes were full of a new ferocity, a purpose. But beneath that, I sensed the current of her trepidations.

And I marveled.

The woman who'd chased me to the very edge of death and snatched me out of its jaws, breaking every last rule in the universe to bring me home… That same woman was still reluctant to claim her birthright. To stand up and claim herself.

How could she not know that the witches would follow her anywhere? That *I* would follow her anywhere.

"What if I don't know what I'm doing?" she whispered, answering my unspoken questions. "What if I say all the wrong things, or make the wrong choices, or lead them astray, or cause even more infighting? What if they hate me?"

"What if they do?"

The question took her aback, and she blinked up at me, surprised. "Then… then… I don't know."

"No, you don't, and neither do I. But here's something I *do* know. If you don't try, if you don't tell everyone what's coming and convince them that when the shit hits the fan, we all need to be standing on the same side, then we *will* fail. Wrong choices and infighting and their opinions of you will be the least of our problems." I grabbed her hands in mine and pressed a kiss to each palm, trying to send her all the love I could. To make her feel it. "This is life or death, *querida*. For all of us. You know better than most what we're up against."

She shuddered, and I saw the fears play out across her eyes. Hunters, dark fae, hybrids, perpetual winter, imprisonment, all the other things Liam had warned us about—most of them invisible and probably impossible to defeat.

"I don't say this to frighten you," I said. "I say it to remind you that you've already faced down a lot of those things, and you've come out swinging every time. Every day, your magic gets stronger, and so does this." I pressed my hand flat against her chest, feeling the steady beat of her heart.

Gray closed her eyes, blowing out another breath. After a beat, she turned away from me again, refocusing on her ice cube trays. "I guess I just need some time to figure out what to say."

"You *will* figure it out, though. I know you will. Gray, you're—"

"Alvarez, you got a second?" Hobb's voice cut in from the doorway. "Colebrook spotted something we need to check out on foot."

Liam had set off in his raven form a couple of hours ago to check out the area from above, keeping a particular eye out for anything that suggested we'd been followed or tracked. Fortunately for us, any attackers would have to come in through the forest, which was dense and slippery and difficult to traverse, or along the beach, which meant they'd be spotted quickly.

Assuming we could see them.

Still, Liam's bird's eye view would come in handy. The shoreline up here was similar to the one near the original prison, with lots of rocky outcroppings and cave systems perfect for hiding.

"Be right with you, Hobb." I turned my attention back to Gray, hoping to give her one more kiss, one more vote of confidence.

But *mi brujita* was already gone, the ice cube trays abandoned on the counter half full.

TWENTY-EIGHT

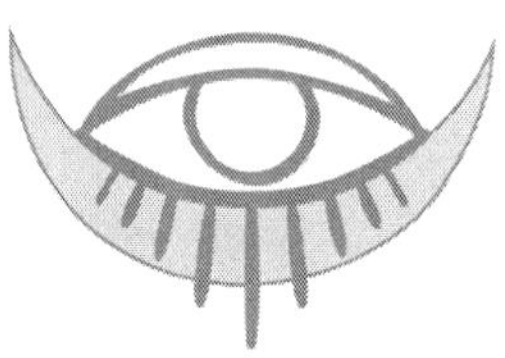

GRAY

Even hidden away in the last bedroom in the farthest corner of the second floor, the ocean roaring all around me, Sunshine and Sparkle panting at the foot of the bed, I still couldn't drown out the sounds of the voices. Still couldn't breathe under the unspoken weight of the expectations. Under my *own* expectations.

Sitting on the bed I'd claimed, I stared at the Six of Wands card in my hand. In the deck that Emilio had given me, the card featured a man standing on top of a mountain behind a massive lion. In one hand he held a crystal ball, in the other, a flame-tipped wand. Five wands surrounded him, and overhead, two ravens circled in a blood-red sky.

The man in the card looked much more confident—not to mention qualified—than I felt, but the message was clear: I needed to be fearless. Bold.

I felt it inside me. I truly did. Deirdre was right—the time had come. All of us could feel it.

But I'd barely gotten used to the twenty-some witches in Elena's house, and now our makeshift coven was rapidly expanding, with more witches set to arrive in the coming days. Verona had done her job in putting the word out, and her network of witches had picked up and run with it, organizing volunteers with vehicles to drive out and pick up any witches within an hour's drive.

I wanted so badly to help them. To lead them. I felt it burning inside me, brighter than the fiery torches in the Six of Wands card. When I thought about what the Silversbane legacy actually meant to me, it wasn't about power or magic at all. It was about bringing people together. Mending old, generational rifts between women who probably couldn't even remember why their mothers or grandmothers had been fighting in the first place. It was about breaking down old structure and building something stronger. It was about eliminating any force or being that sought to keep us from doing just that.

And most importantly, it was about sisterhood.

For so long, I'd been a solitary witch, so deep in the broom closet I could barely *say* words like "witch" or "magic" without breaking out in hives.

Now I was part of something big. Something important. Something with life-or-death stakes not just for everyone here, but for witches and supernaturals everywhere.

The fire inside me surged, mixing with the magic and burning so hot, I feared I might just combust.

I swept the cards into a pile and tucked them back into the box. There was no advice to be found in the Tarot tonight—nothing I couldn't divine myself.

Outside my door, I heard someone clomping up the stairs. The rhythm of the footfalls was a dead giveaway.

"Here's how it's gonna be," Asher announced to the entire lodge. Subtly had never been his strong suit. "I'm going in there. Anyone comes through that door who's not bleeding from a major artery is gonna get flatlined. Got it?"

His protectiveness brought a smile to my lips, and I opened the door, shooting him a glare I didn't really mean. "I'm fine, Ash. I just needed some space."

"I know. That's why I'm here."

"You know I need space, so you invited yourself up here to invade it?"

"I… Um…" He scratched the back of his head, clearly at a loss for words.

His slightly embarrassed smile was so endearing, I couldn't

help but return it. "Damn you and your sexy incubus charms, Asher O'Keefe."

"You're not the first woman to say that, Cupcake."

"No." I arched an eyebrow. "But I'd better be the last."

"No question."

Laughing, I stepped aside to let him in. Rather than taking the invitation graciously, he marched to the end of the bed, clapped his hands once, then pointed at the door.

"Sunshine," he said, "Sparkle-butt, you know I love you. But you need to vamoose."

"Oh, good luck with that," I teased. "They only listen to me."

But my loyal hounds, traitors to their name, hopped up and marched out the door, which Asher promptly shut behind them.

"You're something else," I told him.

"What? You think you're the only one who can't resist me? I've got those girls wrapped around my finger like you wouldn't believe."

"So you've been bribing them."

"What?" He pressed his hand to his heart, mortally offended. "Sunshine and Sparkle and I have a deep relationship based on mutual respect and—"

"Bacon?"

Asher cracked up. "You know it."

"So what was the deal with Liam?" I asked, sitting back on the bed.

"He spotted a cave system not too far from here that looked like it could be trouble, but the shifters checked it out, and it's clear. Hobb's posting two guards there, anyway, just to be safe. Reva volunteered to go with them and do some of her shadow spelunking, but they squashed that idea pretty quick." Asher shook his head, smiling. "Crazy girl."

"Aww. She just wants to help."

"Yeah, I get it. But if she thinks we're letting her anywhere *near* a place like that, forget about it. Kid already spent enough time locked away in a cave."

"Where is she now?"

"I gave her my phone and my app store password, so, I'm

guessing she's hiding in her bedroom, running up my credit card."

I laughed. "You're kind of a softy, aren't you?"

"Don't let *that* get out." Asher sat next to me, and I leaned my head on his shoulder, taking in his fire-and-cinnamon scent. It stirred something inside me, doing nothing to cool the flames I'd been contending with before his arrival.

Despite the desire smoldering between my thighs, the mood turned serious; the weight of the moment felt impossibly heavy on my shoulders.

"Gray, I know what it's like when everyone is turning to you for answers you don't have," he said, his tone so suddenly gentle it made my heart squeeze. "When you're carrying the weight of the world on your shoulders because you know one wrong move can send the whole thing tumbling to the ground. I know what it feels like when you want more than anything to do the right thing, only you don't know what the fuck that thing might be. And most of all, I know you. Not as well as Ronan does. But I know you."

I lifted my head to meet his eyes, and he pressed his hand to my heart, fingertips grazing my collarbone.

"I see you, Gray Desario. I feel the dark magic pulsing through you. The doubts. What they're doing to you. I feel everything you feel, and if I could, I'd take it all away from you. Carry it so you wouldn't have to. Even the most painful parts."

"I know." My voice threatened to break, but I wouldn't fall apart. Not now. Not when everyone was counting on me. "I have to learn to live with it, though. To control it, channel it. It's my fate, right? Powerful Silversbane magic, and all the responsibility that comes along with it."

"Maybe so. But let me tell you a secret: Every once in a while?" He leaned in close, his breath no more than a faint whisper against my lips. "It's okay to fall apart."

Asher's words undid me, tender and unexpected and exactly what I needed to hear. I fell into his embrace, letting him wrap me up in his warmth. His strength.

He pressed his lips to the top of my head and said, "Let it go, baby. I've got you."

The emotion that I'd strangled back for weeks broke through the surface, finally erupting.

I wept shamelessly in his arms, releasing my heartbroken frustrations about Ronan's deal with Sebastian, my pain at all we'd lost when the memory eaters stole Darius's history, the betrayal I'd felt toward Liam, all of the fears I'd buried when we'd come so close to losing Emilio. I wept for the women downstairs, for all they'd endured at the hands of the hunters and the dark fae, for all they'd lost before then, for all they'd grown up afraid to say and do and be. And I wept for the little witch I once was, the little girl full of magic and possibility, one of four magical sisters whose mother attempted to drown them out of petty jealousy.

When I'd cried enough tears to compete with the ocean outside, I looked up into his eyes once again, trying to find the words to apologize for the outburst. But there, reflected back at me, I saw so much love and support that in that moment, I truly felt like I could do anything. My crying turned into laughter, bubbling up from some deep, magical place inside me.

Wordlessly, Asher took my face in his big hands and kissed the tears from my cheeks. From my chin. From my neck.

It wasn't enough, though. With Asher, I was always hungry, always desperate for more.

He was kissing my cheek again, and I turned toward him, capturing his sensuous cupid's bow mouth, my core melting as his tongue slid between my lips.

We tumbled backward onto the bed, tearing off clothing as we fell, mouths and hands seeking warm flesh, seeking unmet desires, seeking love.

And then he was inside me, anticipating my every need once again, bringing my body to the very edge of my limits, making me cry for an entirely different reason.

TWENTY-NINE

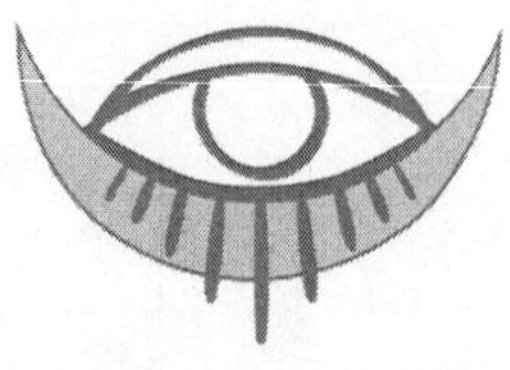

GRAY

"Not that I'm complaining, Cupcake, but what are you smiling about now?"

I traced a path along the black symbols tattooed across Asher's chest, every muscle in my body relaxed and happy. We'd been locked away for an hour; eventually, someone would come looking for us, and I'd have to go back downstairs and face the music—more specifically, the magic. But for now, I was perfectly happy to hide away in a bubble of bliss with one of the men I loved, basking in the glow of all the ways he'd just made my body sing.

"I was just thinking about the day we met," I confessed. "Officially, I mean."

"At Bloodstone Park, across from Norah's place," he said.

"I'm surprised you remember."

"How could I forget? You were *so* into me. I thought I was going to have to restrain you."

"What?" I laughed, smacking him on the stomach. "I was so *not* into you! You were the biggest jerk I'd ever met. And that's saying something, because I've met a lot of jerks in my life."

"And *you* were wearing a tight pink-and-white hoodie that made you look like a giant cupcake. All I wanted to do was pin you down and lick off all the frosting."

I sat up, the sheet falling down to my waist. "Wait… *that's* why you call me Cupcake?"

Asher grazed his palm over my exposed breast, threatening to stir my body into a new frenzy.

"It suits you." He leaned forward and captured my nipple between his lips, his tongue sliding out to tease me. "Mmm. Very lickable."

"You are such a beast. You know that right?" I laughed. "For your information, that sweatshirt was Sophie's. I don't own anything pink."

"As someone who just spent half the day hanging out between your thighs, I beg to differ. You've got plenty of pink—"

"Asher!" I smacked him again. Did this man ever stop?

He pointed at me, his grin stretching even further. "And now your cheeks are pink, too. Perfect."

"Now you're just trying to embarrass me."

"It's a skill. Seriously. Don't play a game of wits with me, Gray. You will lose."

"Say whatever you want, Mr. Big Bad Incubus. I know your secret."

"You think so, huh?" He kissed my jaw, my earlobe, his soft lips buzzing over my skin and making me shiver. Somehow he'd gotten me horizontal again, the sheet around my waist mysteriously vanishing. He rolled onto his hip, propping his head up on his hand, watching me intently. "Which one?"

I trailed my fingers down his chest, down over the ridges of his abs, lower still until I reached his velvet-smooth cock. He was already hard again, but stiffened further at my touch, the beat of his heart pulsing just beneath his hot skin. "The one where your heart is almost as big as your—"

"*Almost,*" he said between kisses, groaning softly into my ear as I began to stroke him. "But not quite."

"Hmm. Lucky me."

"Lucky?" Asher rolled on top of me and grabbed my wrists, pinning them over my head as his solid weight settled over me. His cock teased my entrance, unleashing another moan from my lips despite my best efforts not to let him win.

"You don't even know the meaning of the word," he said. "But before the sun comes up? You damn well will."

I lost the ability to speak, my retort melting into a puddle of sighs as he rocked his hips and plunged inside me again. I felt his incubus hunger tugging lightly at my magic, and a rightness pulsed through my veins, warm and delightful and perfect. I loved the way we filled each other up, loved knowing that my magic could make him strong, could take care of him, just like he'd taken care of me.

I opened myself up to him fully, slowly sending out a warm pulse of magic, and Asher deepened our kiss, his body seeming to hum with it. He was close to the edge, thrusting in deep and perfect, faster and faster until I was certain he'd explode. But then, without warning, he stilled inside of me, pulling back to see my face.

In one big, impossibly strong hand, he cupped my chin, searching my gaze with an intensity that made me gasp. For a brief moment, I fell right into his ocean-blue eyes.

I saw his soul there. All the pain and regret and love and hope.

And he saw mine. I felt it, knew it. And for the first time in our relationship, I dropped every last wall, leaving myself completely open. I let him see it all—the brave, the scared, the shameful, the beautiful, all of the parts of me that made up the whole.

"I've never wanted anyone like I want you," Asher whispered. He dipped his head and stole another kiss, stole my breath, stole my heartbeat. And I let him take it all, because in that moment, as he slid back inside me and finally brought us both over the edge of that cliff, as I fisted his hair and shuddered beneath him and sighed his name into the darkness, I knew without a doubt that I was his.

To protect.

To love.

Just as he was mine.

After a quick shower, we crept back into bed, sliding between the sheets and wrapping up in each other's arms once again. I felt him growing hard again, and I was certain we'd spend the rest of the night just as we'd begun it. But instead of slipping inside me, he turned me onto my side, snuggling against me from behind and wrapping me up in his embrace. With a fluttering of kisses on the back of my neck, he whispered, "You need to rest, Gray. It might be your last chance for a while."

I opened my mouth to argue, but a yawn escaped instead, and before I could even find the strength to rally for another round, I was fast asleep.

I didn't know how much time passed, but eventually, the soft, pleasant rumble of low voices woke me. I opened my eyes to find Ronan and Asher by the window on the other side of the bedroom, their heads close together, deep in conversation. Darkness had fallen, the moonlight illuminating their silhouettes. Ash was bare-chested, a pair of sweats hanging low on his hips. He had one hand on Ronan's shoulder, his other hand gesturing emphatically. Ronan's head was bent low, nodding at whatever Asher was saying.

My heart swelled. I loved them both so much. I opened my mouth to tell them just that, but before I could get a word out, Ronan's smile glinted in the darkness.

"Looks like Sleeping Beauty's finally awake," he said.

Both of my demons left the window and joined me in bed, Ash curling up behind me, snuggling in close, Ronan sitting on the very edge before me, careful not to touch me.

Though mere inches separated Ronan and me, it felt as if another person had wedged himself between us. That invisible, formless monster was a constant companion we'd always carry, reminding us of everything we used to have. Everything Sebastian had stolen.

It was a sharp contrast to the closeness Asher and I had shared tonight, and it lit me up with rage.

There *had* to be another way. But until we could find it, we'd take what we could, stealing glances, breathing in each other's scents, memorizing the sounds of laughter and voices and whispers, which had their own sweet cadence.

Keeping our voices low in the moonlit room, the three of us talked about the plans for the days ahead, which would be full of magical and combat training, Reva's shadowmancy practice, intelligence gathering, big speeches, and above all, constant vigilance.

After what felt like minutes but had probably been an hour, Ronan rose from the bed and stretched, wishing us both good night.

"There's room in here," I said, patting the space in front of me. "If we slept in our clothes, and didn't get too close..."

I trailed off. It was ridiculous that it'd come to this, and we both knew it.

"Emilio and Darius are on beach patrol tonight," Ronan said. "I should probably go check on them. Good excuse to take the hounds for a stroll, anyway."

"Aww, leaving so soon, demon?" Asher asked. Despite the teasing tone in his words, I knew he could sense how badly I wanted Ronan to stay.

I could sense the same feeling from him.

Ronan turned his back on us and opened the door. When he spoke again, his voice was rough. "You know I have to."

"Ronan," I said firmly, and he shook his head, refusing to look at me. I could almost feel the demons inside him, threatening to tear him apart.

Threatening to tear us *both* apart.

"He owns our souls, not our hearts," I whispered, and he finally turned around, locking his fierce hazel eyes on mine. "Stay with us tonight," I said. "Please."

Ronan closed his eyes and let out a sigh, but he finally pushed the door closed, sealing the three of us away in this perfect bubble once again.

With Asher still behind me, Ronan resumed his place in front of me, but this time he stretched out on his side, closer than he'd been before. His breath stirred the hair around my face, and he stared deeply into my eyes, reading me even as his own thoughts remained veiled.

"I wish I knew what you were thinking," I said softly.

"You know *exactly* what I'm thinking, Gray. I'm *always* thinking it. Same thing, every minute of every hour of every day." He lifted a hand to my face, keeping it just shy of actual contact.

Heat radiated from his palm as he traced an invisible caress down my cheek. "Every time I see your face. Hear your voice. Feel your presence. All I can think about is how much I need to touch you. How it's eating away at me inside, knowing that I can't do it without hurting you."

Asher's body went rigid behind me, anger pulsing from his skin. "One day, I'm going to kill that Kentucky Fried fuck."

"You and me both, brother," Ronan said.

"There has to be a way," I said.

"To kill the prince of hell?" Asher said. "You bet your sweet little ass there's a way. And as soon as we figure it out, we're all getting a plane to Vegas, and we're going on a motherfucking crime spree. Because we're not just killing Sebastian. Hell no. We're taking out every one of his minions and burning his casinos to the ground, too. And after that, we're gonna piss on all the ashes."

Ronan laughed, shattering the dark, dense weight that had settled over us. "You've got it all planned out, huh?"

"I've got *sketchbooks* full of ideas. Just you wait."

"Okay, boys," I said, rolling my eyes. "I appreciate your vivid imaginations when it comes to tormenting Sebastian, and believe me, I'm all in. But when I said there has to be a way, I meant a way for us to be together tonight."

Asher's hand slid over my hip, his lips tickling my shoulder blade. "Now *there's* a sketch I'd like to see."

"Will you guys try something with me?" I asked.

Asher cracked up, and Ronan gave me a crooked smirk.

"Let's see," Ronan said, tapping his lips. "You're lying in bed next to a beautiful woman, who also happens to be naked, and she asks you if you'd like to try something with her. Your answer is… Ash, would you like to field this one?"

"Hmm, it's a tough one. I might need to phone a friend," Ash said. "But… No. Let's go out on a limb here and say…"

"Fuck yes," they both said, laughing so hard the bed shook. Then, from Ronan, "What are you thinking, Desario?"

"I can't *wait* to hear this," Ash said.

"Sebastian is all about the fine print," I said. The idea was gathering momentum inside me, making my heart flutter. I gazed into Ronan's eyes, hoping this didn't freak him out. Hoping it would bring us closer, not push us further apart.

But some part of me knew it would bring us closer. That we needed this tonight, maybe more than we ever had before.

Be bold, girl. Fearless, just like the Six of Wands.

Okay, maybe Tarot *hadn't* been referring to the demons in my bed, but still. The fire inside me surged anew, reminding me that living a fearless life wasn't always about big, courageous acts of bravery in the face of life-threatening adversity.

Sometimes it was just about making a small, bold leap in the quiet space of your own heart.

"The deal specifically says you can't touch me," I said, and Ronan nodded. I tugged the sheet down and grabbed Asher's hand, pressing it to my bare breast, a slow smile stretching across my lips. "But it doesn't say you can't watch."

THIRTY

GRAY

Ronan's eyes darkened with lust.

"No," he said, his voice suddenly hoarse. He swallowed hard. "It doesn't say that."

Emboldened by the new intensity in his gaze, I kicked the sheet off completely and slid closer to him, bringing my lips within a hair's breadth of his. Everything about this moment felt dangerous and delicious, a heady mix that was already making me dizzy. Ronan's cloves-and-campfire scent called to something deep inside me, a familiar longing I'd associated with him ever since I'd started to have feelings for him—a longing that had only intensified since we'd finally crossed that boundary together.

"I want to do this for you," I whispered. "But only if you're okay with it."

He nodded, the tip of his tongue darting out to wet his bottom lip. My thighs clenched; that one little gesture flooded my core with so much heat, I thought we'd start a fire even *without* touching. I wanted nothing more than to slide my tongue into his mouth, to taste him, to unleash everything we'd been forced to hold back since we'd escaped the Shadowrealm.

"Take off your clothes," I said, arching back against Asher. "Both of you."

Ash slid out of his sweatpants, and Ronan followed suit, yanking the shirt over his head and kicking off his jeans and boxer briefs. My two fierce, beautiful demons stretched out on either side of me again, and Asher kissed my neck, swirling his tongue behind my ear, his fingers trailing slow circles down my ribcage, my hip, my upper thigh, then back up to my breast.

Both of them were hard as steel, Asher's cock pressing urgently against my backside, Ronan's so close to the apex of my thighs, if I closed my eyes and thought back to our last time together in the woods of the Shadowrealm, I could almost feel him inside me again.

"Touch yourself," I said to Ronan, soft but fierce, my breath hitching as a flood of raw desire coursed through my veins.

He did as I commanded, fisting his cock and stroking himself slowly, a soft moan escaping his lips.

Asher rolled my nipple between his thumb and forefinger, the sensation sending ripples of pleasure straight down to my core.

"Ronan," I breathed, as Asher increased the pressure on my nipple, tugging and teasing, making me writhe. "Tell us what you want to see."

"I want to see your face," he said. "Your eyes. I want him to fuck you from behind and drive you absolutely wild… But your eyes are *mine*."

At those words, Asher growled in my ear, more than ready to comply. I arched backward again, and he slid inside me from behind, his hand on my hip as he slowly rocked against my backside.

My body was still buzzing from our earlier time together, my skin hypersensitive, but holy *fuck* he felt good. I bit my lip to keep from crying out.

Ronan's eyes blazed with new heat.

Asher grew harder inside me, his fingers digging into the flesh at my hip as he plunged in deeper, his teeth nipping at my neck, my shoulder.

Ronan leaned forward, dragging his nose through my hair and inhaling my scent, careful not to let our skin touch. His chestnut hair tickled my cheek, and I skimmed my fingers in front of his chest, feeling the heat rise from his body, our energies connecting even as our bodies couldn't.

"Touch yourself," he whispered, and I obeyed, slipping a hand between my thighs. I was hot and wet, two fingers gliding over my clit as Ronan stroked himself harder and faster, Asher's chest slick with sweat against my back.

Finally, I *did* cry out, the intensity almost too much to bear.

All three of us were getting close, the heat and energy and magic rising between us, invisible tendrils pulling us close, wrapping us in a cocoon of love and desire.

Then Ronan sucked in a sharp breath, the space between his eyebrows creasing, his eyes glazing suddenly with emotion.

"You okay?" I whispered. "What's wrong?"

"It's torture, Gray. Watching you… My hands are on fire to touch you… I just… *Fuck.*" His voice was raw, his chest rising and falling rapidly, his body trembling from the effort of holding back. "I'd fucking *die* tomorrow for a chance to kiss you tonight. To taste you just one more time."

I blinked back tears, the passion in his words threatening to unravel my heart.

Asher stilled behind me, resting his forehead against my shoulder blade. I knew without asking that he'd end this in a heartbeat if he thought we were causing Ronan pain. Both of us would.

"Do you want us to stop?" I whispered to the demon in front of me. My best friend. The man I loved. The one who'd agreed to this torment just for a long-shot, one-in-a-million chance at bringing me back from the Shadowrealm in one piece.

Ronan's eyes went demon-black, his voice a low growl in his throat. "Don't you fucking *dare* stop."

Ronan couldn't touch me, couldn't physically participate beyond the closeness and the watching and the dark, desperate wanting. But I knew by the look in his eyes that he needed this. *We* needed this—this unexpected, unconventional way to be together, to break the chains Sebastian had tried to tighten around our hearts.

Asher shifted behind me, sliding in slow and deep.

My eyes fluttered closed, and I felt Ronan inch forward, the heat of his body reaching out to me once again.

Still stroking his rock-hard cock, he leaned in closer. "Don't close your eyes, Gray," he whispered. "Stay with us tonight. Please."

I smiled at the echo of my earlier words and did as he asked, my gaze locking onto his as the three of us continued to chase that pure, unadulterated bliss lingering just out of reach.

"Gray," Asher moaned, and I knew he was *right* there. In that instant, all of us were mere seconds from beautiful oblivion.

I increased the pressure on my clit, and my body tightened around Asher, my stomach muscles clenching, the now-familiar tingles gathering in my core.

"Gray… *fuck…*" Ronan's body tensed, and then he let go, setting off a chain reaction. Asher came hard inside me, his body shuddering against my backside, and with his gravelly voice in my ear and Ronan's gaze locked on mine, I finally let go, too.

The orgasm washed over me in a hot rush, stealing my breath as my body trembled beneath its power. I came for Asher. I came for Ronan. I came for all of us, my heart beating like a wild animal, my whole being alight with pleasure.

At the final gasp, I was finally permitted to close my eyes, and the three of us lay in silence, floating on a cloud in some other sky, on some other realm.

It was one of the most intense experiences I'd ever had, and somehow, despite the fact that Ronan still couldn't touch me, I felt like it had brought us closer.

All three of us.

"I love you," I whispered. "Both of you. So much."

Asher tightened his hold on me, and I opened my eyes to see Ronan watching me close. Neither of them said a word. They didn't have to. I saw Ronan's love for me burning in his eyes, the fire of it more intense than the fire that sparked whenever we touched. I felt Asher's love surrounding me now, holding me close, keeping me safe.

Asher reached across my shoulder and wrapped his hand around the back of Ronan's neck. "You good, brother?"

Ronan gave him a silent nod and closed his eyes.

The intense moment between us had crested and receded, and

the three of us finally broke apart, getting out of bed to stretch and change the sheets.

After another quick round of showers and a raid on the fridge downstairs, we crept back upstairs, stripped down once again, and climbed back into bed together. Ash took the middle this time, making sure Ronan and I couldn't get too close and accidentally set the mattress on fire. I curled up against Asher's left side, and Ronan did the same opposite me, meeting my eyes across the tattooed expanse of our incubus's chest.

There was nothing awkward about it; we were family. The love we shared transcended all boundaries, and as we drifted off to sleep, I found a moment's peace in the knowledge that somehow, we'd find a way to transcend Sebastian's imposed boundaries, too.

We fell asleep quickly, and didn't stir again for hours.

Not until we heard the screams.

THIRTY-ONE

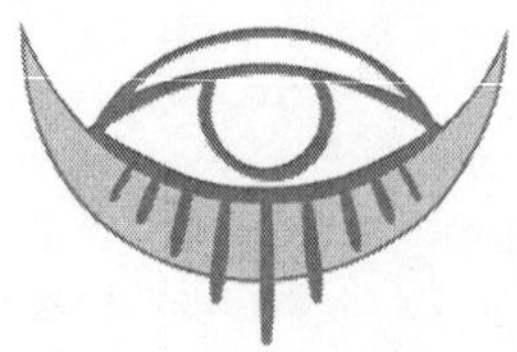

DARIUS

For hours I paced the rocky shoreline south of the lodge, my fingers wrapped around the handle of a fae blade we'd procured from the warehouse, all of my senses attuned to my surroundings. I tasted the ancient salt of the coastal air on my lips, felt the pounding of the surf beating in my chest, braced myself against the sharp bite of the wind on my face.

Despite the circumstances, I couldn't help but feel invigorated. Hopeful, even. Emilio had survived insurmountable odds to return to us, whole and unbroken. The witches we'd liberated from the hunter's prisons were growing stronger through practice and new, shared knowledge, combining their magics in unique and powerful ways that made victory feel a little more possible with each passing day, despite Liam's dire warnings. Gray was finally beginning to embrace her legacy, and though I suspected she'd need a little more time to fully claim her birthright, I felt the greatness in her, so close to the surface she practically hummed with it.

For the first time since I'd returned from the Shadowrealm without my memories, things were beginning to look up.

Other than the brutal cold and the frenzied state of the great Pacific, the night had been calm. Emilio and Elena were patrolling the southern end of the property, with Detective Lansky and another wolf shifter from the department keeping watch at the forest's edge. Two more shifters were posted at the mouth of the cave system Liam had discovered, and all was quiet there, as well.

But for an occasional wandering witch raiding the kitchen for a midnight snack, the occupants of our lodge had finally settled in for a good night's rest. After the energy and excitement of relocating to the lodge and settling in with the new witches and animal companions that'd arrived with Verona, it'd been a surprisingly peaceful evening.

So peaceful, in fact, that when a desperate scream broke through the rhythmic roar of the waves behind me, it took me a moment to comprehend what I'd heard.

Reva.

And she was in grave danger.

I spun around and caught sight of her cowering in the sand at the base of a massive sea stack. Her eyes were wide with fear, her whole body trembling in the wintry mist.

"Reva!" I knelt down before her, reaching out a hand to help her up. "How did—"

My words cut off abruptly as my hand passed through the mist. It wasn't Reva after all—only a shadow projection. Which meant her body was somewhere else, and I had no idea how to find her.

"Reva, where are you?"

"They're all around me!" she shouted. It didn't seem like she'd seen or heard me at all. "Leave me alone! I can't… Help! Somebody help me!"

I took off at a run toward the lodge, the ocean blurring in my peripheral vision, the icy wind tearing at my hair. I arrived on the scene at the same time as Emilio and Elena, the three of us tearing across the front of the property, straight for the forest behind the lodge.

"In the woods. There!" I shouted, catching sight of the melee just inside the tree line. Witches and wolves alike had teamed up against an enemy whose scent turned my stomach.

Vampires.

Gripping the fae sword, I charged into the trees, swinging at the first bloodsucker I saw, taking his head clean off.

I didn't even spare him a glance as I spun around, catching another one in the chest as Gray staked him from behind. He stumbled backward, and I beheaded him post haste.

"How many?" I shouted.

"A dozen at least," she said, yanking the stake from his back. The hounds were by her side, their fangs already dripping with blood. "Maybe more. We all bolted out here when we heard Reva screaming. The wolves had already taken some of them down—it all happened so fast, we—."

"Duck!" I hauled Gray to the ground and covered her with my body just as a vamp lunged at her from behind. Overcorrecting for his miss, he slipped on the snow, and the moment he righted himself, a huge raven swooped in and clawed out his eyes. One of the hounds lunged at him, knocking him flat on his back. The other dove in to finish the job, gnawing his throat, snapping the bones of his neck.

It was the most gruesome vamp-killing I'd ever witnessed, but I wasn't complaining.

Leaving the hounds to sniff out a new victim, Gray and I ran deeper into the woods, chasing the sounds of snapping wolf jaws and tearing flesh. Intermittent flashes of blue and violet light lit up the forest like a nightclub, magic sizzling in the blood-soaked snow.

"Reva!" Gray shouted, her stake at the ready. "Where are you? Reva!"

"Over here," I said, scenting the demons close by. "This way."

We caught up with Asher and Ronan, who'd just tackled a hulking bloodsucker with a ridiculous bright red mohawk. I did the whole world a favor and chopped his head clean off.

Gray and the incubus headed deeper into the pines in search of our youngest witch while I teamed up with Ronan on a pair of vamp females.

We made quick, bloody work of them, then circled back around the edge of the forest, searching behind every tree for any other vamps lying in wait.

"Coast looks clear on this side," Ronan said, wiping the spray of blood from his face. He cocked his ear toward the woods again, the sounds of the skirmish finally beginning to fade. "Sounds like the worst of it is over. Fuck, that was intense. I was sound asleep."

"The wards held," I said, eyeing the lodge. Other than a single, one-way track through the snow from the back door leading into the woods, the rest of the area between the back of the lodge and the woods was still blanketed in unbroken snow. There were no footprints on the side or front areas, either.

"Our witches know their shit," Ronan said. "So. Local gang, you think?"

"Judging from their attire, no. None of them wore jackets or winter gear of any kind. I suspect that's what allowed us to get the upper hand so quickly—they came here looking for an easy score, but they weren't expecting the weather."

"Great. Vamp tourists." Ronan spit out a mouthful of blood, then dragged his sleeve across his mouth. "I'm guessing it means word is out that the council is no longer enforcing the rules. How long until this shit turns into a total free-for-all? Hell, maybe it's already happening in other places."

"Let's hope this was a one-off," I said. "It's possible these vamps are connected to the rogues we slaughtered at Norah's house. Hollis aside, some of those pricks were definitely out-of-towners. Not to mention the southern visitors Gray and I had the pleasure of entertaining at the morgue."

I shuddered at the memories. The female had been Gray's first kill.

"We're just making friends wherever we go, aren't we?" Ronan gave me a smirk that probably worked significantly better on Gray, but I appreciated it anyway. "Well," he continued, "at least we—wait. Wait, wait, wait."

"Did you hear something?" I asked, the sudden urgency in his tone putting me on high alert once again.

But Ronan hadn't moved. He just stood before me, his smirk turning into the brightest smile I'd ever seen on the demon.

And then, he launched himself at me.

"Fucking hell, Beaumont. Fucking hell!" He hugged me so tight, if I'd actually needed to breathe, I was quite certain I would've passed out. "You just remembered something, you scone-eating son-of-bitch! The vampires we iced at Norah's, Hollis, the morgue… You remembered!"

"I… huh. I supposed you're right."

"This is major. Major!"

He finally set me free, and I ran a hand over my head, trying to chase down those memories again, desperate to crack open a few more. But the moments from the fight at Norah's were already fading, Hollis's face slipping back into the shadows.

"It's okay," Ronan said. "Don't push it. You remembered something. That means it's all still in there. The rest will come."

"Let's hope you're right. I don't—"

"Here! I've got her!" The voice was Hobb's, and now he emerged from the trees, tattered clothing covering his body, a passed-out young witch cradled in his arms. "She's okay. Just a little spooked."

"Oh my God, Reva!" McKenna rushed over to inspect the girl herself. "What happened? How did you end up outside?"

"I just thought… I want to practice traveling," she said, stifling a sob. Tears streaked her dirt-smudged face, and she sniffled, her body still trembling in Hobb's arms. "The forest is so quiet, and it has so many shadows… I thought I could get a stronger connection."

"You thought wrong," Hobb snapped. "You could've been mutilated. You put all of us at risk, and—

"Detective," I interjected, giving him a stern glare. "Perhaps we should let McKenna take Reva inside and get warmed up."

"Come here, sweet pea." McKenna took the girl into her arms, swiftly shuttling her back inside the lodge.

"I found her hiding in a hollowed-out tree," Hobb told us, "half frozen, surrounded by four bloodsuckers. If the kid hadn't started screaming, we never would've gotten to her."

The rest of the group began trickling out of the forest, two and three at a time. The crew was a little scraped up and a whole lot exhausted, but for now, it appeared we'd all survived the latest attack.

"What the fuck was she doing outside by herself?" Hobb

asked. "Fucking kid. How many times did we tell her? No one goes outside alone. Especially not a fucking—."

"She's a sixteen-year-old child, Detective," I said. "One who is still learning to control a powerful magic none of us fully understands, and one who desperately wants to help the witches she considers family."

"Well she damn near got herself killed, along with half my men. When that kid wakes up tomorrow, she's gonna have some serious explaining to do."

"Perhaps," I said, "you should seek explanations from your men instead. Despite their years of experience, not to mention their wolf shifter instincts, this child managed to slip beneath their careful net of surveillance, as did a nest of vampires—"

"We don't have the manpower to patrol the whole forest," he barked. "The vamps weren't anywhere near the lodge. I found the kid all the way on the other side of the creek."

"Again, I have to ask, how was she able to slip past—"

"Darius?" The whisper was faint, but panicked, the sound of it sending a bolt of fear down my spine. "I think… I fucked… up…"

I spun around just in time to see Gray collapse to her knees, her arm wrapped tightly around her midsection. Blood spilled out between her fingers, staining the snow a sickening shade of crimson.

"Gray!" I dropped to my knees before her, catching her just before she face-planted. "What happened?"

"Last vamp." She nodded toward the direction she'd come from. "Still alive. Staked him. But… not before he…"

"He's a dead bloodsucker now." Ronan's eyes turned black. With one of Gray's hounds on his heels, he grabbed my sword and took off running.

"Did he bite you, love?" I asked Gray.

She shook her head. "Knife. I was… stupid. Left my… inside unguarded…"

"Shh, it's okay. Let me take a look." Gently, I pulled her arm away from the wound, inspecting the damage. It was a nasty gouge about five inches long, slicing straight down beneath her breast. The blade had carved through clothing, flesh, and muscle.

Milky-white slivers of rib shone through the gash, the wound pulsing with blood.

"Gray! Holy shit!" Haley emerged from the forest with Asher, both of them crouching down beside us. "Oh my God, what happened?"

"Stay calm," I told them. "She's going to be fine. Just give her some room."

"Beaumont…" Ash's tone was a warning, but I glared right back at him.

"Take off your sweatshirt, hellspawn. Put it behind her, then kindly back off."

He finally obeyed, and I turned my attention back to Gray, easing her backward onto the sweatshirt.

"I've got you, love. Try and relax." I leaned forward and brushed a kiss across her temple, a trickle of her blood coating my lips. It melted in my mouth, stirring my own blood to life. Something in my chest flickered, but I ignored it, focusing instead on the woman before me.

Using my fangs, I pierced the vein at my wrist, then held it over her mouth, allowing her a few drops before moving my wrist to her wounds.

It was an inelegant solution, but the best we had in the moment. Unlike when I'd healed her in the Shadowrealm, she was conscious now; my blood would burn inside her wounds like living fire. But once the pain subsided, it would bond with her blood, along with her magic, and start the healing process.

Too bad we don't have our own private cabin…

My eyes drifted closed, and in that quiet darkness I watched the memories of our time together in the realm like a movie I'd never tire of. There, in the cabin nestled in a snowy wood, was the first time I'd made love to her. It was the time and place where I'd fully, unapologetically fallen in—

My eyes opened with a start.

Memories. Real memories. More of them, coming in faster and more clear now. Like the attack at Norah's house, saving Gray from the avalanche and all the time we'd spent in the cabin after had occurred *before* our final moments in the Shadowrealm.

Before the memory eaters had stolen my history.

"Thank… thank you." Gray was sitting up on her own again, wiping my blood from her mouth, when two things hit me at once.

I'd just saved Gray's life.

And I'd just remembered the absolute most precious piece of my own.

I took her face between my palms and tilted it toward me, capturing her beautiful blue gaze.

Then, as if I'd just figured out the answer to a complex question that had been plaguing me for years, I said, "Don't take this the wrong way, but I'm fairly certain I'm in love with you."

THIRTY-TWO

GRAY

"He remembered something, Hay." I measured out two more cups of dried lavender and another cup of amaranth flower into a glass bowl for Verona, who was busy in the common room sewing protective mojo bags. "Not just something, but a *major* thing."

Haley held up a finger to silence me, then continued counting the crystals spread out on the counter before her, piles of smoky quartz and black tourmaline that would also be sewn into the bags. Since the vamp attack three days ago, Verona and some of the other witches blessed with protective magical skills had been working nonstop, shoring up our defenses around the house as well as around our bodies. No one had been seriously injured that night but me, and Darius had healed me on the spot. After Ronan had killed the vamp who'd knifed me, he, Darius, Emilio, and Detective Lansky scoured the forest, identifying and then burning all the vamp bodies and ensuring none had escaped alive.

Darius had been right—they were out-of-towners, a group from the Carolinas that he suspected had connections to the three that attacked us in the morgue the night we'd gone looking for intel on Sophie's murder. We couldn't be certain, but the detectives thought there might be some kind of supernatural bounty on my rebels and me. Lower-level vamps were fickle with their loyalties, and after the slaughter at Norah's house, it wouldn't have taken much for them to get the word out that Darius Beaumont was "a traitor" to his own kind.

With so many enemies breathing down our necks—known and unknown—Verona didn't want us taking any chances. "An unprotected witch is a sad story just begging to be written," she'd said.

Other than a freak hailstorm the following morning, our last couple of days had been fairly low-key, and we'd spent them working on magic and spellcraft with Verona, inventorying our weapons and magical ingredients, and helping Reva practice her shadowmancy. After the attack, none of us wanted to let her out of our sights. Liam had been especially helpful in that department, spending long hours instructing her on the nature of physics, space-time, and astral travel. I didn't understand most of what they talked about, but he made her laugh and kept her out of trouble, and with his patient tutoring, she seemed to be gaining both confidence and skill.

"That's good, though, isn't it?" Haley finally looked up from her task, her crystals all counted out into neat rows. "That means he's getting his memories back."

"What else *could* it mean?"

Darius hadn't remembered much—just snatches of the time we'd spent together in that cabin, the way he'd felt about me in those moments, and a little bit about the vamp attacks at the morgue and at Norah's place. Nothing more, and nothing since, but it was the first real glimmer of hope any of us had gotten that he might actually regain his memories.

"I don't know much about how memory works," Haley said. "I'm the blood girl, remember?"

I gave her my best, your-my-favorite-sister smile. "Speaking of being the blood girl…"

"*Gray.*" She lanced me with an admonishing gaze. "I thought Deirdre was totally against the blood spell idea."

"Deirdre isn't here."

Haley and I still had so many questions for our grandmother, but since her first visit to Raven's Cape, she'd flitted in and out of our lives so often, she might as well be an apparition. Since the ice bomb and our subsequent relocation, she'd gotten slightly better at checking in by phone. But even then, whenever I tried to question her about the legacy or our mother or anything else having to do with the past, she suddenly had a hundred reasons to get off the phone.

Since I'd told Haley about our sisterhood and our bloodline, she hadn't even gotten time alone with Deirdre yet. But our family dynamics, crazy as they were, would have to wait.

"She's just worried it will summon our ancestors," I said.

"Which will set in motion your end of the deal with Sebastian, imprison the ghosts of our relatives, and probably get you shipped off to hell where you'll spend the rest of eternity worshipping a glorified pimp who calls himself a prince."

"I appreciate your thorough and vivid imagination, Hay." I sealed up the jars of lavender and amaranth and set them back on the shelf with the other non-lethal herbs. "But I don't think it will work that way. Magic is all about intention. As long as we're clear on our desired outcome, we should be fine."

"Should be fine? You know that's just a stand-in phrase for 'I might blow everything to shit but I don't care because… *reasons*?'"

"Honestly? I don't even think the ancestor thing is Deirdre's main issue. She's just… I don't know. She thinks it's a distraction." I lowered my voice, crushing a bud of lavender between my thumb and forefinger. "She's worried that I haven't spent enough time with the other witches yet. She says if I'm going to lead them, I need to roll up my sleeves, get over my trust issues, and start participating as one of them."

"She has a point."

"I know, but she's also missing one. A big one."

"Which is?"

"We can do all the physical workouts Emilio and Elena come up with. We can learn sword fighting and martial arts. We can crush herbs and meditate and do group spells and swap secrets from everyone's books of shadows every single day, and yes, all of those things are important—I'm not saying otherwise. But they pale in comparison to the most powerful tools we have: Ourselves. Our bonds. Our own unique magic. Our instincts."

"Yes!" Haley pointed at me, a grin lighting up her face. "That's the kind of poster-worthy shit you should be saying to the group, Silversbane."

"Get me a bullhorn and some glitter cannons, and we'll think about it." I flicked the lavender bud at her, and she laughed again. "Anyway, I'm serious. Without his memories, Darius isn't whole. He still has instincts, but he doesn't remember his experience. All the things he's learned and honed along the way. All the people he's learned to trust—"

"And learned to love," she sing-songed, batting her lashes at me.

"And love, yes. Love and friendship are bonds that strengthen magic, Haley. Witches, vampires, shifters, demons, fae, humans… We're all stronger for it."

Haley ran her hand over the neat rows of her crystals, a soft sigh escaping her lips.

"You're already saying yes," I said. "I can feel it."

She rolled her eyes, but then smiled, and I knew we were in business.

"Thank you, thank you, thank you!" I stepped around the counter and hugged her close, planting a big kiss on her cheek. "You really are my favorite sister. You know that, right?"

"I'm going to remember you said that when we meet the other two." She squirmed out of my embrace and made a big show of wiping my kiss off her face. "If this goes sideways, *you're* telling Grams."

I nodded, keeping my thoughts to myself. Because if this thing went sideways, Grams would be the least of our worries. Sebastian, on the other hand…

"Okay," Haley said. "Let me get this stuff to Verona. In the meantime, you put on the kettle and crush up some dried rosemary, forget-me-not, and vanilla bean."

"For the spell?"

"Those herbs are associated with memories, so I'm going to have you and Darius drink an infusion before we start. Can't hurt, right?"

"Good idea."

"We're also going to need black sea salt, water, six red candles, a sage bundle, and some matches. I'll ask Verona for some crystals to help keep out negative spirit energy. That should create a magical barrier against any of our dead relatives, *just* in case any of them get curious."

I was already rummaging through the pantry for the ingredients. "Is that everything?"

"Actually, we could use an assistant," she said. "This spell is pretty intense. Once we get into the ritual, it might be helpful to have someone on the sidelines keeping an eye on things."

"I would like to help, if you'll have me." Liam leaned against the doorway, hands in his pockets, his casual stance completely at odds with the hope and excitement in his eyes.

Since we'd moved into the lodge, I hadn't spent much time with him, but his presence had been comforting. He'd been there when I'd brought Emilio back from the brink. He'd been there when I'd saved Asher's soul from the devil's trap in Norah's attic. It seemed fitting that he'd be there when we brought Darius back. Looking at him now, at the flannel shirt buttoned crookedly, the messy blond hair, those bright blue eyes that never seemed to dim, I felt a flicker of hope and excitement, too.

"Liam Colebrook," I said with a grin, "you're hired."

THIRTY-THREE

GRAY

"How are you guys feeling?" Haley asked, checking her supplies one last time before finally shutting the door to the outside world. "Still good to go?"

Upstairs in the back corner bedroom I'd claimed as mine, Darius and I sat on the floor across from each other in the lotus position, gazing into each other's eyes. A thick red candle burned between us, carved with runes, its golden light reflecting in his eyes. Beside us, sage smoke rose from a stone bowl, purifying our space.

It was just after sunset and the room was dim at the day's end, yet for us, it felt like a beginning. A brand new day full of promise, potential, and possibility.

I was nearly giddy with it.

"Excellent," I said, and Darius nodded. He hadn't said much since we'd started, but I saw the hope in his eyes. He wanted this to work. Believed that it could.

"Liam," Haley said, "go ahead and serve the infusion."

Liam poured out two cups of liquid from a ceramic teapot on the dresser, passing one to each of us. The scents of rosemary and vanilla filled the room, wrapping me in a comforting embrace.

"As you're sipping your tea," Haley instructed, "I want you both to close your eyes, relax, and call up a particularly strong shared memory—one that comes to you easily, Darius."

His full lips parted into a grin, and my insides fizzed. "The cabin," he said. "Where—"

"TMI, vampire," Haley teased. "We don't need details. You guys just need to call it up for yourselves. In silence. Try to bring in as many sensory details as you can—sights, smells, sounds, tastes, feelings, intuitions, all of it. Once you've got that firmly in place, and your tea is finished, you can open your eyes again."

We closed our eyes, and I let my mind wander back to the Shadowrealm, back to the snowy wood where we'd found our perfect hideaway. I heard the crackle of the fire he'd build, felt the warmth of the flames against my bare legs and the soft T-shirt Darius had dressed me in. The scent of the cabin's bare wood interior mingled with the intoxicating whiskey-and-leather scent of my vampire, and my heart rate kicked up—both in the memory, and in the present moment. I drew in other details, too: the soft touch of his fingers on my skin as he'd traced circles across my forehead, calming me. The taste of his kiss, and the desperate need I felt for his touch. The warmth of his mouth between my thighs. The desire in his eyes when he'd finally claimed me, his words echoing in my memory… *You absolutely intoxicate me…*

My body was wound tightly, my breath coming in short bursts. I'd just finished the last of my tea, and I was certain I'd had a firm hold on the memory.

For me, those moments weren't going anywhere.

I opened my eyes, and found my vampire with a hard-on.

He offered a devilish smile, but no apologies, and I couldn't help but laugh.

"I see we *were* thinking about the same thing," I said.

"I've been thinking about it every day since it came back to me, love. Dreaming about it, reliving it, replaying it. In fact, I'm considering commissioning Asher to make some sketches for me."

"Great," Haley said, and I flinched. I'd almost forgotten there were other people in the room. "Judging from the state of Darius's pants and the crimson flush on Gray's cheeks, I'm giving you both an A for that part of the assignment. Moving on."

Verona had given us several large crystals to help keep our magic contained and protect us from any potential visitors from beyond, and now Haley placed them in the corners of the room and on the windowsill—black tourmaline, labradorite, black obsidian. Next, she set the six red candles in a circle around us, standing a Tarot card against each one. They were all cards I'd consciously selected earlier from the deck Emilio had given me, hoping to draw on their particular energies for the ritual:

Six of Cups, for nostalgia and good memories, and a childlike faith that our blood spell would work as intended.

Judgment, symbolizing the rebirth of Darius as a whole being, memories restored and intact.

Three of Cups, a card of friendship and sisterhood, for the deep bond and gratitude I felt toward Haley.

Queen of Swords, to aid Darius with mental clarity.

The Lovers, representing our eternal bond, blood and heart and—though it was an odd choice of words considering Darius was a vampire—soul.

And finally, The Star. I'd drawn it on the day Emilio and I had first been intimate together. The day Reva had turned up at the RCPD. It'd brought me a sense of calm and peace and hope, and I was channeling all those feelings again now, bringing them into the ritual that would bring my vampire back to me.

As Liam lit the surrounding candles, Haley knelt inside the circle next to me and Darius and unsheathed her athame, a slim silver dagger with a handle fashioned from raw quartz. She passed it through the sage smoke and whispered a few incantations in Latin, then used it to slice Darius's fingertip.

"Place a single drop of blood on Gray's tongue," she said. "No more, no less."

Darius did as she instructed, and I closed my eyes, letting the blood soak in like it had in the Shadowrealm. Again, I tasted the richness of it, smooth and slightly bitter, like dark chocolate without a grain of sugar.

A flood of images cascaded through my mind's eye, I gasped.

"Tell me what you see," Haley said.

"I can see Darius!" I said. "You... you're in London, meeting with clients in an old-fashioned looking office, with ornately carved furniture and shelves full of books and scrolls."

"Yes," he said softly, "I suppose that was where I practiced law."

"Now I see you at Black Ruby... You're filling out a liquor order. Wait, now you're unpacking blood from the deliveries. And now you're... Oh." My cheeks flamed again as I watched an image of myself through Darius's eyes. He'd just taken my blood, sealing our bond, and though he'd teased me with more sultry innuendo than I could handle, I sensed from the memory that he was practically on fire inside. I felt the strength of our connection surge through me, both in his memory of that moment and in my own mind, right now.

The movie reel spun onward from there, forward and back, showing me glimpses of his past I could only guess at. Centuries, cities, faces, feelings, all of it spinning into a blur.

I opened my eyes, my heart threatening to burst from my chest. I couldn't process it all.

"His memories are still there, locked away in his blood," I said. "Or connected to it or... something. I don't know. There was so much... I'm sorry." My eyes filled with tears, my body suddenly overwhelmed with emotion.

Darius reached for my face, silently wiping a tear with his thumb. His own eyes were intense, his gaze heavy. I sensed a hundred thoughts forming in his mind, in his heart, yet he seemed unable to find the words to voice a single one.

Instead, he smiled, and I let out a breath, steadying myself again. Reminding myself that we were in this together. That this was absolutely going to work.

"No, that's a good thing, Gray," Haley said. "That means your theory actually holds water, and with a little luck and a whole lot of magic, we might be able to kickstart Darius's own recall abilities."

She held up her athame again, instructing us to hold out our hands, palms up.

"Essentially," she continued, "we need to recreate the blood bond, connecting you both in an unbroken circle. The idea is that your blood, your magic, and the magic of your existing bond will flow from one heart into the other, into the other, into the other, continuously, until there is no longer a separation between the two. Magically speaking, of course."

"If we need to recreate the bond," I said, "shouldn't Darius drink from me? That's how we did it initially." Memories of that moment in Black Ruby rushed back, stirring me up inside.

Across from me, Darius arched an eyebrow, his lips twitching with the effort of holding back a smile. He knew exactly what I was thinking about, exactly what that memory was doing to me. He could scent the desire in my blood.

"To create the unbroken circle effect," Haley said, "you'd both have to drink from each other, and that's a no-go. We can't risk turning you. No witch can survive the change."

I nodded. It was an old refrain, one all witches had learned from a young age. Though we were human, the magic in our blood didn't mix well with vampire blood. Other than the witch Jonathan had claimed to turn, for which we'd seen no evidence, none of us had ever survived an attempted change. I needed no further proof than Sophie and the other Bay witches Jonathan had murdered by injecting them with vampire blood.

I shook off the cobwebs of those old thoughts. Right now, I had to stay focused on Darius. On our ritual. On what it would feel like later tonight, holding my vampire in my arms, kissing him, talking about all of the things he'd remembered.

We kept our hands steady, and using the tip of her athame, Haley carved runes into our skin, cutting just deep enough for blood to rise but not drip. It stung, but I welcomed the pain. It kept me focused on the moment, on its importance.

When she finished, Darius and I clasped hands over the candle between us, pressing our palms together and lacing our fingers tight. The moment we connected, my palms began to warm, then tingle, the sensation slowly spreading up my arms and into my chest.

"Do you feel it, Gray?" Haley asked, and I nodded, stifling a giggle. It made me feel light and happy inside, like getting laughing gas at the dentist.

"Now," she continued, "I want you both to gaze into each other's eyes and focus on your connection. See it reflected in your gazes. Note the different colors and facets in the eyes of your beloved. The exact shade and shape of the lips you've kissed so many times. The sound of breath, the scent. Feel the way your skin tingles when you touch, the way your fingers are so tightly entwined, the sting of the rune carvings. Imagine your blood flowing from your heart, Gray, down your left hand and into Darius's right. Darius, feel yourself receiving that gift of blood and magic from her, bringing it deep into your own heart, then sending it back out to Gray through your left hand and into her right. Imagine it's a circle of fire, spinning slowly at first, then heating, quickening, binding you together as it grows brighter."

Everything around us was silent but for the soft popping of the candles and the strong, wild beat of my heart. As I felt the magic working through us, my body warm and tingling, the circle of flames growing stronger, I gave in to the deep pull of Darius's gaze. The emotion reflected in his golden honey eyes was indescribable; the moment felt shockingly intimate, despite our company.

As the circle of flames continued to spin, Haley rose to her feet, then paced her own circle around us, chanting a spell as she moved.

Blood is the bond, blood is the key
To unlock the cage of these memories
What flows from one heart shall flow to the other
As mysteries past will soon be uncovered
Trust in this magic, trust in this love
Restore what was lost, below and above.

She repeated the verse three times, once for each circle she walked. As she chanted, the flames inside me heated, my magic spinning, twining, connecting. My heart was beating hard enough to burst, but each time I feared it would, I felt the magical rush of Darius's blood into my body, steadying me. With each circle Haley completed, more of Darius's memories surfaced, flickering through my mind only to rush away again before I could fully grasp them.

I hoped they were rushing back to him.

"Rise," Haley said, "keeping your hands clasped."

When we'd gotten to our feet, she said, "I want you to close your eyes and imagine the circle of flames slowing down, dimming, slowly fading like embers in a fire. Reclaim your magic, your blood. Feel it filling you up again, spreading throughout your body, renewing you. Once the flames have completely subsided and you feel whole again, you may release each other, and the ritual will be complete.

This part took a bit longer than the chanting, but Darius and I seemed to get there at the same time, slowly releasing each other. It was hard to let him go; after the deeply intimate moment we'd just shared, it felt like I was breaking the connection all over again.

Like I was risking losing it all.

When I looked into his eyes, I saw a flicker of sadness, and knew he'd felt the same way.

"Darius," I whispered, reaching for his face. If this was supposed to restore him, why did I suddenly feel so empty? So lost?

"I'm afraid I was right," he said softly, a smile tilting at the edge of his lips. "I *am* in love with you."

And then his eyelids fluttered closed, and Darius swayed on his feet.

THIRTY-FOUR

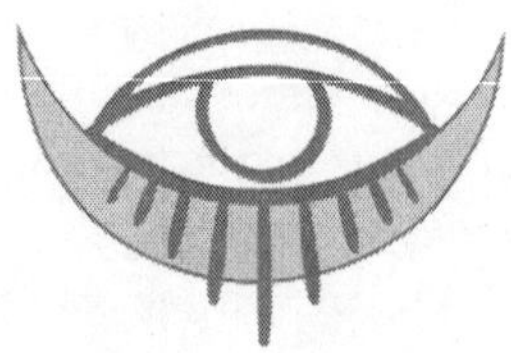

GRAY

"Liam," Haley ordered, and in an instant, Liam was at my vampire's side, catching him before he collapsed. Slowly and gently, he guided Darius onto the bed, pulling the blankets up to his shoulders, tucking him in.

My heart melted, and I blew out a breath.

"All part of the process," Haley assured me. "He just needs to rest now. How about you? Feeling okay?"

"I… I'm fine. Just a little dizzy. Nothing some OJ and chocolate won't fix."

"Here, hold this." She pressed a piece of smoky quartz into my left palm, folding my fingers around it. "It will help ground you. Take—"

I gasped as a new image jolted my mind, accompanied by a sharp burst of pain that had me dropping to my knees and clutching my head.

"Breathe, Gray." Haley knelt by my side, rubbing circles on my back. "Deep breaths. Count backward from ten if you need to."

"There's another image," I said, trying to focus on it. On *her*, I realized. "A woman. I don't think she's from Darius's memories."

"A woman? What does she look like?" Haley asked. Her voice held a note of concern.

"She's sitting at a desk in the middle of a huge office, flipping through old books. She's wearing modern clothes—a black pantsuit, blue silk blouse. Her jacket has some kind of silvery-looking pin in the shape of a crown, with two swords crossing underneath."

Haley sighed. "Dark braid over her left shoulder, a little too much eye makeup?"

"You see her too?" I opened my eyes, slowing getting to my feet. Just as quickly as she'd arrived, the woman was gone, taking the head-splitting pain with her.

"Not at the moment," Haley said, "But I had a similar vision while I was chanting. When I saw her, though, there was with a younger woman with her—same color hair, glasses. It looked like they were packing up boxes together. Papers, files, office stuff."

"Why did we both see her?"

Haley shook her head, blowing out the candles in our circle.

"It's possible," Liam said, "she's one of your ancestors. Despite the protective crystals, her essence may have felt drawn here. Both of you possess very strong, very special magic, amplified by your bloodline. Working spells together is bound to have unforeseen effects."

"That would make sense," Haley said, "but I'm pretty sure the women I saw weren't dead."

"I'm with Haley on this one, Liam. It didn't feel like a spirit or even a memory, like when I'd seen people from Darius's past. It felt like we were spying on someone."

"Yeah," Haley said, "I didn't get the sense she knew we were there. She definitely wasn't watching us. The minute she appeared in my mind, I let her drift past, bringing myself back to my breathing and chanting."

A shiver rolled through my body, and I rubbed my arms.

"Not to worry," Liam assured me, resting his hands on my shoulders. "Shared visions are perfectly within the realm of possibility in a situation like this."

His warmth brought me back to the moment, a few tiny sparks zapping my skin where he touched me. That was one thing that *hadn't* changed—his effect on me. No matter what we'd gone through or what the Old Ones had done to his powers, Liam still had the ability to electrify me with the simplest touch.

"Sorry," he continued, releasing me, and immediately I missed the contact. Missed him.

Why did everything have to be so complicated?

"Anyway," he said, "sometimes witches inadvertently connect with the energy fields of others, especially during intense spell-craft. It's possible you picked up on a remnant of something that happened in this lodge in the very recent past, or something that's happening nearby as we speak. There are other properties in the area."

Liam's explanation made sense, and Haley and I shook off the lingering creepiness and set to work picking up the candles and other materials from our ritual. We decided to leave the protective crystals in place, and to leave the main candle burning—the one that had sat between me and Darius, casting his face in a warm glow.

I moved it to the bedside table, smiling at my sister and Liam. "I couldn't have done this without you. Both of you."

"Maybe not," Liam said with a wink, "but knowing you, you would have found another way."

"Are you calling me stubborn?"

"I am. And I believe it's one of the best qualities a witch can possess."

I laughed, then took my place in the chair next to the bed, where I'd remain until my vampire woke up. I wanted to be the first person he saw when he did.

I brushed my knuckles over his stubbled jaw, marveling at his grace, his beauty, the power of our bond. "So what happens now?"

"Now, we wait," Haley said. "He should remain in stasis for about six hours, and when he comes to, he will likely be confused. The memories could rush back in a flood, competing with new memories or ideas about his identity he's formed since the attack in the Shadowrealm. Or it could happen more gradually, with bits and pieces coming back to him out of order, or melding together. Or it might not…" She trailed off, not bothering to voice her doubts, which I appreciated. Tonight, I had no room for those kinds of thoughts. His memories would return, even if it took months. There was no doubt in my mind.

"I'm just a few doors down the hall if you need anything." Haley leaned in to kiss my cheek, then saw herself out, shutting the door softly behind her. Liam stood at the end of the bed, hands in his pockets, rocking forward on his toes.

"You once told me that memories don't exist," I said to Liam, a smile touching my lips as I remembered the conversation. We were still at the safe house where Ash used to live, and my incubus and I had just survived an attack by zombie animals I'd inadvertently brought back from the dead. "That they're only stories we tell ourselves, and the way we let them change and shape us is our fatal flaw."

Liam let out a quiet laugh. "Yes, well. I believe we both had a lot to learn back then, didn't we? You about magic. And I about humanity. Heart. What it means to be a true friend." He came to stand beside the bed, placing a hand on Darius's arm. "What you're doing for him, Gray… He's quite blessed to have someone like you in his life."

"You say that as if you *don't*. Liam, you've got me, too. I know we're not perfect, but that doesn't make it any less real."

After a beat, Liam finally nodded, still struggling to accept that I cared for him. Still struggling, I sensed, under the very heavy, very human weight of his guilt.

"There's… something else I wanted to discuss with you," he said softly. The sparkle in his eyes dimmed, and I felt the energy in the room shift. "I have been called to hear the final sentencing. Tonight, at exactly midnight, I'm to travel out over the ocean in my raven form. One of the servants of the Old One will collect me, and I'll be brought before the tribunal one last time to hear their decision."

"Tonight? Already?" My eyes widened, my heart thumping with a mix of anticipation and fear. "Maybe that's a good thing, though. Right? If they've made a decision that quickly, maybe there's a chance they'll overturn everything and restore your powers! What if I went with you? I could testify for you, tell them about Emilio and what's coming and the prophecy and—"

"It doesn't work that way, Gray." Liam smiled, but it didn't match the new sadness in his eyes. "Though I do appreciate the show of support."

I rose from the chair and met his gaze. "Don't give up, Liam. You never know what might happen."

"In the long and spiraled history of time, a cosmic tribunal has never overturned its decision, nor have they issued a lesser sentence for such a crime. But if there's one lesson I've learned from you," he said with a wink, "it's that impossible odds are no reason not to try."

"Liam." I lowered my eyes, my lashes wet with tears. There was so much to say, and once again, no time to say it. I slid my arms around his waist and pressed my cheek to his chest, breathing him in. His heart beat strong and steady, human, the press of his chin on the top of my head simultaneously comforting and heartbreaking. "Why does it feel like we're always saying goodbye?"

"No, not goodbye. I promised myself I would stop saying goodbye to you, Gray Desario. So let me say this instead." He took a step back, then tilted my chin up toward his, forcing me to meet his infinite blue gaze once again. Stars collapsed and were born again in those eyes as I awaited his words. Galaxies. Universes. "Be well, little witch. I shall keep you in my heart, and ask—though I don't deserve the kindness—for you to do the same." He bent down and kissed me, soft and gentle, pressing something cool and smooth into my palm.

There was a final spark across my lips, and then our kiss was broken.

Once again, Liam Colebrook was gone from my life.

I opened my fingers to find a heart-shaped piece of granite, worn smooth by the constant tumble of the ocean. Carved onto its face was a tiny raven's feather.

THIRTY-FIVE

GRAY

I was starting to become an expert at bedside vigils—a skill I hoped I wouldn't have to call on too often. Finally alone with him, I sat by my vampire's side, holding his hand, reliving every one of our shared memories. I didn't want to risk interfering with Haley's spellwork, so I didn't add any additional magic to the mix, but it felt like the right thing to do, letting those moments replay in my mind. Letting them fill me with happiness and hope, with the love I'd felt for him, the connection we'd shared from the first moment he'd tasted my blood that night in Black Ruby.

Exquisite, he'd said then, and I smiled now, seeing the moment with new eyes. We'd already had a connection by then; our blood promise had only solidified it. But neither of us could've predicted where that promise would lead, or how much deeper that bond would become.

"You'll remember," I whispered, pressing a kiss to his palm. A tear slipped down my cheek, but it wasn't from sadness or worry. It was hope. Faith. It might not happen overnight, but Darius would regain his memories. I knew it in the way that I'd known Emilio was still alive. In the way I knew Asher would survive the prison. In the way I knew Ronan and I would find a way to break Sebastian's curse.

"You just take your time, D. All the time you need. And when you're ready, you find your way back to me, and I'll be here waiting for you. I promise."

Darius didn't stir. He didn't toss and turn, seeking the coolest part of the pillow. Didn't twitch or fidget. He didn't even breathe. Just lay perfectly still, one hand over his heart, the other in mine. He was utterly at peace.

I shifted in my chair, trying to get comfortable. I'd just started to get feeling back in my butt when I heard a soft knock at the door.

Emilio. I sensed him before he announced himself, and wasn't the least bit surprised when I opened the door to see him standing there with a triumphant look on his face, his now-shaggy hair sticking up all over the place, hands hiding behind his back, a chocolate smudge on the side of his mouth.

"I've got something for you," he said with a grin.

"Hmm. I bet." I leaned up against the doorframe, my arms crossed over my chest. "Does this something start with a 'b' and rhyme with 'rownies?'"

"Is it that obvious?"

"You're wearing the evidence, Detective." I stretched up on my toes and kissed the edge of his mouth, licking the smudge of chocolate.

"Damn," he whispered when I pulled back, his eyes darkening with desire. "I should've been more strategic in my chocolate smudging. Wait—be right back."

"Oh no you don't." I was about to smack him on the shoulder —I still wasn't quite used to his flirty innuendos—but he saved himself by pulling his arms out from behind his back and revealing a plate of still-steaming brownies.

I nodded for him to come inside, then shut the door behind him. "Only *you* would think to bake brownies in the middle of a multi-pronged crisis."

"Trust me, *querida*. There's no better time. Baking calms me, and the scents of chocolate, cinnamon, and vanilla make others feel at home. But hey, if you've got some kind of moral opposition to them, I'm sure I can find another taker."

"And another girlfriend, while you're at it." I grabbed the

plate from his hands and took the brownie from the top of the stack, shoving in a bite. "Defaulting on the gift of chocolate?" I mumbled, not even caring that I was talking with my mouth full. God, his brownies were incredible. Sweet and decadent, with that deliciously spicy kick at the end. "Definitely grounds for a breakup."

"Girlfriend?" He arched a teasing eyebrow and grabbed a brownie for himself. "Is that what you are?"

"Pretty sure we've established that." I set the plate on the bedside table next to the candle still burning for Darius, then pulled Emilio in for another kiss.

He tasted like the richest, darkest, most velvety chocolate ever, and as he deepened the kiss, a flame of red-hot desire flickered inside my core. My libido went from zero-to-sixty in a single heartbeat.

Emilio must've scented the change in me. He let out a quiet moan against my lips, his kiss becoming more insistent, his hands sliding inside my shirt, huge and warm on my back.

I leaned into his touch. I'd missed it *way* more than I'd missed his brownies, and it'd been entirely too long since I'd felt him against my bare skin.

We weren't alone, exactly. But here in my bedroom with only a passed-out vampire for company, it was the closest we'd gotten to actual privacy since the night before the warehouse liberation, and I wasn't about to let the opportunity pass.

"Come here." I dragged him across the room to the closet on the other side. It wasn't a walk-in, but it was large enough for two people to get into just the kind of trouble we were looking for. I pulled him inside and closed the door partway behind us, leaving it open just a crack so we could keep an eye on Darius.

"But Darius—"

I pressed a finger to his lips. "Haley said he'll sleep for at least six hours."

"Are you sure?" he asked, but he was already slipping out of his shoulder holster, setting the weapon on the top closet shelf. His shirt and jeans were next, along with everything else, until he was standing naked before me, fully erect.

I slid my hands over his shoulders, taking in the feel of his smooth, golden skin, marred only by the faint residual scarring from the silver blade. "I haven't even unzipped my jeans yet, Detective Alvarez, and you're already naked. So much for your noble protests."

"If there's one thing my trip to the other side taught me, it's not to take anything for granted, and not to wait around for a better moment when the present one is perfectly damn good."

His mouth was on mine in a heartbeat, claiming me, marking me, making up for all the time we'd lost. Without breaking the kiss, he unbuttoned my cardigan, sliding it off my shoulders, his hands roaming every inch of exposed skin. I kicked off my jeans and underwear, and Emilio lifted my arms up, guiding my hands to the bar that ran the length of the closet.

I curled my fingers around it, holding tight as he kissed me senseless, devouring my mouth, my neck, my breasts, his massive hands and lush lips everywhere at once, heating my blood from a simmer to a boil.

"I can't get enough of you," he breathed, kissing my stomach, licking a path from one hipbone to the other. His fingers fluttered between my thighs, teasing me open, his hot breath swirling over my clit. Emilio inhaled my scent, burying his face against my flesh, moaning as he tasted me.

He felt incredible, and part of me wanted to close my eyes and sink into his kiss, let him claim me with his mouth, again and again, teasing and sucking and licking me until my legs trembled.

But I needed him inside me. All of him. And I couldn't wait another second.

"Emilio," I begged, sliding a hand into his hair and fisting it. "Kiss me."

He grabbed my ass and pulled me closer, his tongue sliding inside me, deeper, pure ecstasy, but it wasn't enough.

"Not there," I panted. I tugged on his hair, guiding him upward, losing myself again in the pleasure of his mouth as he kissed a path up my stomach, through the valley between my breasts, alongside my neck, my jaw, finally claiming my mouth in another breathless kiss.

As always, Emilio seemed to know exactly what I needed in that moment, what I craved, and as I wrapped my fingers around the bar again, he lifted me up, his hands cradling my ass, guiding me onto the tip of his massive cock. I sank onto him, feeling every inch as he plunged inside me.

"I missed you," I breathed, my thighs clamping tight around his hips. I held him there, and he buried his face in my neck and breathed me in, slowly rolling his hips as I braced myself on the bar. Despite his earlier hunger, my wolf's frenetic energy shifted, and once again, he was the slow, tender lover he'd been the first time we'd shared a bed together. With one arm holding me up, he cupped my face with his free hand, kissing me softly, sensuously, tasting me as if every time was the first. His hand trailed down my throat, grazing my collarbone, my nipple, my ribs, slowly sliding between us. With a soft, gentle pressure, he traced slow circles over my clit, drawing me closer to the edge as he shifted inside me, slow and steady, deliberate.

It snuck up on me, that heat. That deep, dark pulse of pure pleasure, bursting inside me like a dam. As my thighs trembled around him, I held on tightly to the bar and turned my head, biting my upper arm, muffling my cries of ecstasy. Emilio gripped my ass, pushing in deeper and holding me steady, his breath coming out in a sudden rush as he bit my shoulder and finally let go, shuddering against me until he was finally spent.

I let go of the bar and looped my arms around his neck, slowly sliding down his body, kissing him as I went.

My feet had just hit the floor when the closet door swung open, and we both turned with a start to see a smirking, bed-headed vampire looming in the doorway.

"You've dragged the wolf into the closet." Darius glanced around the dark space, his eyes glinting. "Is this some kind of metaphor? Perhaps your subconscious is telling you he's not the man for you."

Emilio let out a hearty laugh, his hands still firmly gripping my ass. "Judging from the sounds she was making, bloodsucker, I'm guessing that's not the case."

"Yes, I did wonder about that." Darius stepped fully into the closet, looking around again as if he were considering moving in. "Does she always do that?"

"You tell me."

"You guys." I rolled my eyes. "I'm right here."

"Mmm." Darius's gaze drank us in, head to toe and back up again. "Indeed, you are."

"How are you feeling?" I asked, reaching forward to sweep the hair from his eyes. I didn't care that I was naked. In fact, standing there in that closet with a still-erect wolf shifter by my side and a mischievous looking vampire in front of me, I was pretty damned turned on.

"Haley said there might be some initial confusion," I said. It was hard to keep the hope from my voice. She'd also said he'd sleep a few more hours, yet here he was, wide awake and already teasing me. Was that a good sign?

Do you remember? Did it work?

"I seem to recall something about that," Darius said, offering no further explanation.

"So…?" I gave him an encouraging smile, but my insides were tying themselves into knots. His thoughts were hidden from me, his face a mask. Only his eyes held a glint of their former mischief, the only hint that a bit of the old vampire might have resurfaced

"I'm feeling," he said, stroking an elegant finger along my cheek, "in the mood for a story. The one where a devilishly handsome vampire spends an evening with an entrancing young witch in his Astin Martin Spitfire in the parking lot of Luna's café. Are you familiar with that one, love? Because I'd *really* like to know how it ends."

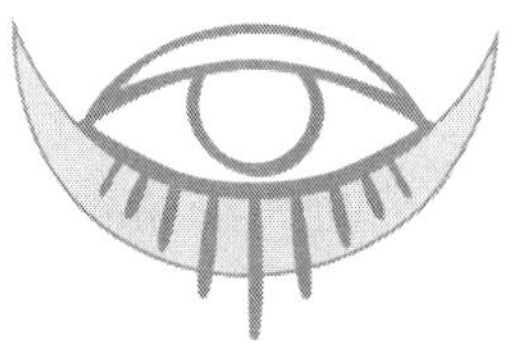

DARIUS

"Cookies!" she shouted, unexpectedly throwing herself into my arms. I couldn't help but embrace her, despite the fact that her luscious scent was currently being overpowered by the wolf's. Her skin was warm and soft, her body curving against mine as if it'd been created to do just that.

"Cookies, huh?" Emilio laughed. "And here I thought she only had eyes for my brownies."

"No, the story." Gray pulled back from my embrace and beamed at me with tears in her eyes, her gorgeous smile nearly as bright as the sun. "After the… the car stuff… We ended up inside the café, and you bought me a latte and chocolate macadamia cookies and told me how you loved cheeseburgers and sweet potato fries."

I nodded, the once-familiar flavors rolling over my tongue again, unleashing flashes of other memories. Black Ruby—the club I owned. Late nights balancing the books, eating the leftover fries.

"Now that you mention it," I said, "I do love those things. I remember… pieces. It's just… I'm not sure the spell has taken hold. I'm afraid there are still so many gaps."

"I know, but don't you see? It's just the beginning!" Gray's enthusiasm refused to be tempered, and I couldn't help but return her smile. It was absolutely infectious. Regardless of what I'd remembered, I'd spent many hours since our return from the Shadowrealm gazing into the haunted depths of her eyes, wishing I could erase every last worry, every last fear.

This was the closest I'd come to bringing her pure happiness in a long, long time.

"Tonight was just our first attempt," she continued, her skin glowing. "Haley and I are daughters of Silversbane. With our combined power, her blood magic expertise, and a little more practice, we'll figure this out, D. I promise you that."

D. The nickname floated into my consciousness, settling into my chest. That, too, I was remembering.

"Wait, can we go back to that part about the parking lot sex?" Emilio asked, sliding a hand over the curve of her hip. The man was rock hard, and had made no effort to control or cover himself on my account. "As an officer of the law, I feel it's imperative to gather all the evidence for detailed analysis."

Gray laughed, then turned to me again, her eyes shining with fresh hope. "What else do you remember about that night at Luna's? Any other details, conversations, anything?"

I closed my eyes, traveling back in time to that night, back to the butter-soft leather seats of the car. I was in the driver's seat, Gray sitting beside me, whispering my name as I kissed the pale skin of her inner arm.

"I've tasted you," I said now, opening my eyes, and I could tell from the surprise in hers that she knew the *exact* moment I'd just recalled. I'd whispered the words in response to her own breathless utterance: *I don't know how you do that… It's like you know exactly how to touch me…*

"I can smell the blood running through your veins," I continued now, the words echoing strong and clear in my memory. "Hear the tempo of your heartbeat."

Then, just like I had that night, I leaned in close, inhaling her sweet scent, my body burning with desire. "I can feel where you *ache.*"

Gray gasped, and without hesitation, I claimed her mouth. Emilio steadied her hips, kissing the back of her neck, her ear, his soft black hair brushing against my cheek as we both tasted her.

Gray's hands dipped inside the waistband of my jeans, fumbling with the button and zipper. I was already in a state of intense arousal, one brush of her fingertips had me gasping with pleasure.

"Are you absolutely sure, love?" I asked her. "Both of you?"

All teasing aside, I didn't want to make any assumptions—not about either of them. I was fairly certain I'd never shared her with the wolf, and though he and the others had assured me time and again that we were brothers, bonded by our deep love for and loyalty to this woman, that didn't mean I could invite myself into their most intimate moments like this. Especially when my memory was still so spotty, with no guarantees it would ever return.

"There's nothing I want more," Gray whispered, her hands coming up to cup my face. "I love you, Darius. And I know you love me, even if you're still trying to remember how we got here."

"There's no need to stand on ceremony with me, Beaumont," Emilio said, still nuzzling her neck. "You could come back from all this convinced you're a damned toy poodle, for all I care. You're still one of us. Still my brother."

Not wanting to waste another precious second, I kissed her again, giving myself over to her touch. She slid inside my jeans again and gripped me, stroking me with absolutely perfect pressure.

Without warning, she and Emilio knelt down before me, Gray sucking me between her lips, slowly guiding me into her hot, velvet-smooth mouth as Emilio took her from behind, her soft moans of pleasure vibrating across my skin.

Everything inside me came undone. Gray had me at an absolute disadvantage, her mouth on my flesh, licking and teasing with such perfect, knowing strokes I could only assume she'd done this before.

I slid my hands into her hair, fisting her silky curls, my gaze trailing down the graceful arch of her back to the place where Emilio plunged inside her, the muscles of his abdomen rippling with the movement. Everything about the moment was perfect, beautiful, and as he brought her to her second epic orgasm of the night, I lost the very last shred of my own control, exploding in a white-hot burst of intensity, my body shuddering as she brought me back from the dead.

She leaned back against Emilio, breathless and breathtaking, her cheeks dark, her eyes glassy. I sat down on the floor beside them and leaned back against the wall, waiting for my heartbeat to steady.

None of us spoke.

Moments later, the closet door swung open, and a swath of light fell on Gray's face.

"What the hell?" she gasped, her cheeks darkening further as she scrambled for her clothing. It took her a moment to recognize the figure looming in the doorway, grinning at her like a dammed idiot.

"Who has an orgy and forgets to invite the fucking incubus?" Asher demanded.

"Did it occur to you, hellspawn," I began, "that the oversight was intentional?"

"Then you should've gotten a hotel across state lines, because the energy you three are giving off is like a nuclear sex bomb calling out across the miles."

"And you felt you had to answer that call because..."

"Because I'm *super* into sex bombs, bloodsucker." He stepped into the closet, crowding us. There'd been very little room to begin with. Now, I couldn't move without feeling the warm brush of someone's breath on my neck. "Besides, I couldn't sleep."

"There are lots of ways to pass the time, demon," I said. "Perhaps you could play a game of hide-and-seek on the other side of the city. Or better yet, the country."

"Don't be rude," Gray teased, nudging me with her foot. "There's plenty of room in here for everyone."

"In *where,* precisely?" I slid my hand across her thigh, spreading her legs and slipping two fingers across her clit. She gasped, no doubt still sensitive, but her hips rocked into my touch.

That was apparently all the invitation he needed.

With a speed and grace that would impress any vampire, the

incubus was out of his clothes and kneeling before Gray, claiming her mouth in a savage kiss.

I took the gentlemanly route and removed my hand from between her thighs, allowing him a turn. He pulled her into his lap, wrapping her legs around his midsection, burying his length inside her. Gray whispered his name, then Emilio's, then mine, and though we'd only just finished devouring her, she reached for us both again, stroking, teasing, taking. I was instantly hard again at her touch, ready to give her anything she wanted, to take anything she had to offer.

As before, she touched me like she truly knew me.

And for the first time since those damned memory eaters stole my history, I allowed myself the faintest flicker of hope that maybe I'd remember how she liked to be touched, too. That I'd remember not just flashes of stolen moments in the car or in the Shadowrealm cabin, but every precious moment we'd shared together.

On my knees at her side, I leaned in close, kissing my way up the curve of her neck, sucking her earlobe between my teeth, grazing her flesh with my fangs. She arched her back like a feline, rising up on her knees until Asher was nearly completely exposed, then sliding down on him once again, driving the incubus wild. The scent of her desire pulsed from her body, in her blood, in the air, mingling with ours into a divine perfume that had my head spinning, my cock throbbing, my entire body aching for more.

Asher was the first to lose control, setting off a chain reaction that, in a matter of mere minutes, had us all trembling and weak.

Again, we sat in silence, heartbeats and breath and heat cresting, then receding, slowly bringing us back down.

The wave of shared pleasure had only just begun to fade when a hard and most unwelcome rap on the bedroom door had us all scrambling for our clothes.

"Shite," I mumbled under my breath, at the same time Asher shouted, "Fuck off!"

"Emilio?" Elena called. "Sorry for the interruption, but we've got something."

"Better be something good," the wolf snapped, but he was already on his feet, awkwardly stuffing his considerable bulk into his jeans and reaching for his weapon on the top shelf.

The rest of us followed suit, spilling forth from the closet and stumbling into our various undergarments and bits of clothing. It was a terrible end to an otherwise magnificent evening, but it was an end none of us would fight.

We all knew the deal. Elena wasn't banging on the door like a woman offering a round of coffee or even one telling us to keep it down in here.

She was banging on the door like a cop.

"Just got a call from Seattle PD," she said from the other side, all business. "Two women were just detained after an altercation at Sea-Tac, boarding a flight bound for Toronto. They're being transferred to Raven's Cape PD as we speak."

"We got IDs?" Emilio asked, opening the door.

Elena handed him a folder, her face severe. "Norah Hanson and Delilah Pannette."

THIRTY-SEVEN

GRAY

"Multiple counts of kidnapping. Human trafficking. Assault. Abuse of a minor by a person in a position of trust. Aiding and abetting a fugitive. Murder one. Forgery. Fraud. And this is just off the top of my head." Emilio dropped a thick folder onto the table, and the woman cuffed to the chair behind it flinched.

The woman. Staring through the one-way glass into the RCPD interrogation room, I couldn't bring myself to call the prisoner Norah Hanson. She looked nothing like the leader of Bay Coven. Where Norah had been tall and elegant, with steely-gray hair and intelligent eyes, this woman was easily fifteen years younger, with cropped, jet-black hair, violet eyes, and a scowl that would make most people cross the street just to avoid her.

"My name is Donna Calabrese," the woman insisted, her voice flat and exhausted. Rehearsed. "I'm traveling to Canada with my daughter. You've got the wrong—"

"Save it, Hanson. Your fingerprints don't lie. And once that protection spell wears off, your face will corroborate the evidence."

She tried to feign ignorance again, but I'd seen the twitch of her jaw at the mention of the word spell.

Verona had told us that Delilah had come into her shop a while back, using Norah's credit card to buy a combination of magical ingredients that would only ever be used for a particular spell. According to Verona, that kind of magic was intended to erase a person's existence by altering the way they looked, their identity, their public records, other people's memories of them, everything.

We'd gotten lucky that Norah had done the spell in haste. She'd missed a few crucial steps, and while it'd changed her appearance, everything else had remained the same—including her fingerprints and public records. The fake IDs she'd procured for herself and Delilah might've helped her slip beneath the radar, but apparently, she and Delilah had gotten into a heated argument on the jet bridge during boarding. An airline employee tried to calm things down, but Norah hit her, and everything escalated from there.

I turned to look over my shoulder. Delilah sat on a bench between Elena and Haley, wrapped in a blanket, sipping hot chocolate that Detective Hobb had brought her. Norah had been magically coercing her for months, manipulating her into doing her bidding. But like Norah's identity spell, the magic she'd been using on Delilah required precision and clear intent, and Norah, in her haste to escape, had gotten lax. Delilah had begun to remember her true self. And just before they'd stepped onto the plane that was supposed to ferry them out of the country, Delilah pushed back.

"Let me be *real* honest here, Hanson," Emilio said. "You're facing multiple life sentences. I'm not here to play good cop or offer you any favors in exchange for your cooperation. No matter what happens in this room, or in any lawyer's office or courtroom hereafter, you're going to die in a cell. You're going to die alone. And you're going to die with the knowledge that you were responsible for the slaughter of your own people, and possibly the downfall of humanity."

I didn't expect Emilio's dire speech to have any effect on the woman, but in the heavy silence that followed, her head slumped forward and her shoulders began to tremble. Tears slid down her cheeks and plopped onto the folder in front of her.

It was a long time before she spoke again, but Emilio waited her out, his hip cocked against the table, arms crossed over his chest, his breathing steady and even as if he had all the time in the world.

The strategy worked.

"You're right," she finally said, and I heard the break in her voice. The moment when she'd finally realized there was nothing left to do. No tricks, no spells, no lies. Just the truth. "The walls are closing in on me, and I've got nowhere left to turn. No hope for a future. No hope for freedom. So what, Detective, could you possibly do for me?"

"You tell me," he said.

"Shoot me. Right now. Tell them I became violent and belligerent. That I attacked you, left you with no choice."

"Not gonna happen. But I can offer you one thing, Norah."

It was the first time he'd used her given name, and she looked up at him, a flicker of hope flashing through her eyes despite the reality of the situation.

"You give me the information I need—information that leads to the capture or death of the dark fae and hunters behind this, the rescue of additional supernatural prisoners, and the liberation of the city of Blackmoon Bay—and I might be able to offer you a few nights' sleep, knowing that at the end of all your scheming and machinations and plotting, you were offered one last chance to do the right thing, and you took it."

He picked up the folder and tapped the papers into place, then left her alone with her thoughts, joining the rest of us behind the glass.

"She's not going to crack," Emilio said. "I've got nothing to offer her. No leniency, no community service, nothing. She's broken too many human laws for that, and she knows it." He crossed the room and crouched down in front of Delilah, offering her a compassionate smile. It reminded me of the first time I'd met him officially, the night of Sophie's murder, when he'd come to our house to investigate. His kindness was one of the few bright spots I remembered from that night, along with Ronan's rock-steady support.

"How are you holding up?" he asked her.

Delilah blew out a breath. "I'm… okay. I just wish I could

remember more. I was with her this whole time, and I've got nothing to show for it."

"Be gentle with yourself," he said, squeezing her knee, and Haley grabbed her hand, holding it tight. "You've been under her spell for months—no one blames you for anything that happened."

"I know. I just wish…"

Emilio nodded. "We all wish we had more to go on here. But we'll get there. Together, we'll figure it out, piece by piece, just like we've been doing. Okay?"

She smiled, faint but true, and Emilio rose, heading out with Hobb to get hot chocolate and coffee refills.

When they returned, I downed the coffee Emilio offered me, then said, "I need to see her. Face-to-face."

"Gray, that's not the best idea," Elena said. "She's unstable, and as we already know, a master manipulator. We've got her cuffed and warded, but that doesn't mean she couldn't call up some spell, something we haven't thought to protect against."

"She won't," I said.

"How can you be sure?"

I glanced through the glass again, taking in her dead eyes, the dejected bend of her head. She looked nothing like the Norah I remembered, but there in her eyes, I saw a piece of her broken soul, and I knew. Her guilt ran bone-deep, and it was eating away at her like a poison.

"Because she's already given up," I said. "She didn't lose control and slip up at Sea-Tac today. She wanted to get caught. She's ready to end this."

"Then why didn't she turn herself in to the authorities?" Emilio asked.

"And tell them what? That she's a rogue witch who betrayed her coven by aligning with witch hunters and dark fae in a magical plot to destroy supernatural and humankind?" I shook my head, biting back a sarcastic laugh. It all sounded so ridiculous, I couldn't believe this was my life. "She knew if she got booked, Seattle PD would get in touch with you and Elena right away. She's been a fugitive for months, and she's known since

Sophie's death that you've been investigating her. Then she risks Delilah using her credit card at The Phoenix's Flame? I'm not buying it. She's not dumb, Emilio. She's just... She's just done."

Emilio closed his eyes and sighed, and I knew I'd finally gotten through to him.

"Let me talk to her," I said, reaching for his hand. "The minute anything starts to feel wonky, I'll back off. You can be in there with me the whole time."

"You bet your witchy little ass I can be." He wrapped his hand around my fingers, his touch warm and protective, like always. Then, pressing a kiss to my palm, he said, "Alright, *mi brujita*. Let's see what kind of interrogation skills you've got."

THIRTY-EIGHT

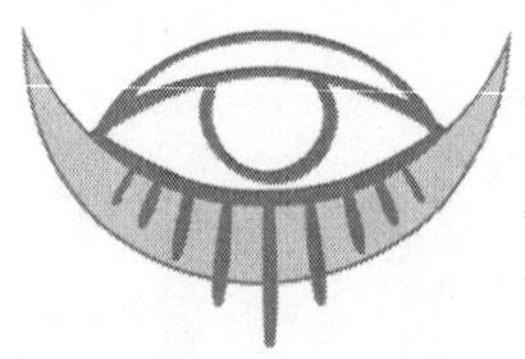

GRAY

"Why?" I asked, knowing I didn't need to elaborate.

It was the same question I'd asked Fiona the night Darius had brought her back from New York. The same I'd asked Jonathan. The same I'd asked anyone who'd ever gotten to such a dark place in their lives that they truly believed bringing harm and death to witches—to anyone who was different than them, for that matter—was the only way out.

But unlike Jonathan, who'd always treated his mission as if it were God's work entrusted to him by an army of holy messengers, or Fiona, who'd been temporarily blinded by love and devotion to a despot, Norah had no such convictions. And when she finally glanced up and met my gaze, I saw the echo of a thousand regrets in her eyes.

Her shoulders trembled again, her face crumpling like wet paper.

Like Emilio, I crossed my arms over my chest, prepared to wait her out. It didn't take long; it seemed she was almost out of tears.

"I had two… two… d-daughters once," she said, suddenly and softly, the words barely finding their way out of her mouth. I got the sense she hadn't said them in a long time.

"Did you know that?" she asked.

I shook my head, shocked. I'd always assumed Norah was a

self-contained, self-sufficient, superwitch. The idea of her raising children was almost impossible to reconcile, even knowing she'd taken Reva in. Of all the words I'd thought to describe Norah over the last few months, motherly hadn't even been a contender.

"No, I suppose you wouldn't," she said, a small, faraway smile touching her lips. "It was a long time ago. They were around Reva's age back then—fourteen and seventeen. Their father lost his battle with cancer when they were just out of diapers. I'd raised them up by myself."

"I… I'm sorry," I said, hating the flicker of sympathy in my chest. Hating that Norah was getting under my skin, but letting her do it anyway. "That must've been difficult."

Norah nodded. "Oh, but it was worth it. They were beautiful. My greatest challenge, yes, but also my greatest joys. There's nothing I wouldn't have done for them, nothing I wouldn't have given them." She took a deep, shuddering breath, and my skin erupted in goosebumps. Whether it was more manipulative bullshit or the purest truth Norah had ever spoken, there was no way this story had a happy ending.

"I will spare you the gruesome details," she said, "because they are irrelevant. Suffice it to say my daughters died at the hands of witches. Witches who sold them out to the highest bidder, leaving me to linger, to try to make some semblance of a life when all I wanted to do was evaporate clean out of existence."

I glanced at Emilio and shook my head. It wasn't that I didn't believe her; I knew what it was to crawl through the endless hellfire of grief searching for a loved one who would never return, no matter what bargains you whispered into the darkest hours of the night. The pain in Norah's voice rang true.

I just couldn't believe what I was hearing. Could anyone really be so blind? So willfully ignorant?

"You've done the same thing, Norah," I said. "Can't you see that?"

Norah shook her head, willful till the end. "I know you think I'm a coward. I can see it in your eyes—all of you. Delilah, too. Even after she'd been under my enchantment, I'd still catch her looking at me that way. Judging. Pitying." At this, her face twisted into a scowl, and she turned a fiery, wild gaze on me. "But *you're* the one who turned your back on who you really are, Gray. It was so easy for you, wasn't it? Walking away. Pretending that the witch inside you—that sick, flawed part of you—had never even existed, when all along it was festering, rotting you from the inside—"

"Alright, we're done here." Emilio reached for my hand again and nodded toward the door, but I held firm. I appreciated the backup, but I *wasn't* done here. Not by a long shot.

"What you call sick and flawed?" I leaned across the table, getting right in her face. "That has *nothing* to do with witchcraft, Norah. It's called being human, and it exists in all of us. Even you, and yes, even me. *Especially* me. I've made a lot of mistakes in my life—hell, I'm probably making a few right this minute. But I have *never* sold out my own kind. Never turned a sister over to the hunters. Never bought into their bullshit about witches being evil and wrong. That's on the witches who murdered your daughters. That's on *you*."

But Norah only laughed, bitter and manic, the sound of it making my skin crawl. "Do you know what it's like to hate yourself so completely, to look in the mirror every single day and force yourself to find another reason not to carve out your own eyes? Not to slice open your veins and spill your own blood down the drain?"

I exchanged another glance with Emilio, then shook my head, fighting off a shiver.

Even at my lowest points, even when I'd cocooned myself up in blame and guilt over the deaths of the people I loved and all the pain and suffering they'd endured, I still couldn't imagine such self-loathing. Such emptiness. Such a desperate need for the final escape.

"You are blessed, then," she said with a defeated sigh. "Truly blessed. Perhaps you should take that blessing, turn your back on all of this once again, and walk out that door. Because trust me, Gray. This is not a road you want to go down."

I turned toward the glass and closed my eyes, trying to gather my thoughts.

All the time I'd been thinking about Norah, going over every detail of our conversation at her house the day she'd banned me from the coven, poring over Sophie's book of shadows for more clues, looking for something that would tie her to Sophie's death or to the disappearance and murder of the other witches… In all that time, it'd never once occurred to me that she might be suffering so deeply. That something—someone—had broken her, just like someone had broken Jonathan. Just like someone had tried to break me.

Again, I was reminded of this lesson, this simple truism that we as people—as witches, as supernaturals, as gods and goddesses, as cosmic forces and elemental energies and unfathomable beings as old as time—just couldn't seem to grasp:

Hatred was made, not born.

And unless someone did something to stop the cycle, it continued. I could rally a hundred witches, a thousand, a million. Unite all the covens on the planet, kick that prophecy up into high gear, wipe out the hunters and dark fae, and establish a new world order where everyone wore yoga pants to work and spent our free time playing with puppies and having amazing sex and coloring mandalas in adult coloring books. But even with all of that, hatred would always be the biggest threat, the poison that could seep in undetected and rot us from the inside out.

If we didn't find a way to end it, it would surely end us.

THIRTY-NINE

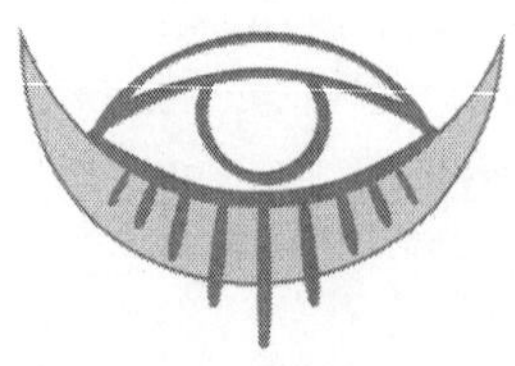

GRAY

"You can still honor your daughters, Norah," I said softly, compassion sneaking into my voice against my better judgment. I turned to face her once again. "It's not too late."

Another bitter laugh. "They're dead. It doesn't get any later than that."

"So honor their memory and do the right thing here. Help us." I leaned across the table again, close as I dared. The violet in her fake eyes was starting to fade, the natural slate gray peeking through underneath. "Who is Orendiel of Darkwinter working for?"

"I was not involved with the dark fae specifically," she said, breaking our gaze. Her whole body had gone rigid with fear. "My arrangement was with the hunters."

"Jonathan Reese?" I asked.

Norah shook her head. "Phillip Reese. Jonathan was just a pawn."

"Our understanding," Emilio broke in, "was that Phillip didn't become involved until shortly before Jonathan's disappearance."

"Your understanding—or, rather, your lack thereof—is the reason this was able to escalate so quickly."

"Explain," he demanded. And this time, whether she truly was ready to cooperate, or just wanted to make us suffer at the telling, she obeyed.

"This has been an operation years in the making, detective. Phillip has never lost track of his son's whereabouts, nor his aspirations. And while Jonathan has always been unstable, Phillip recognized the genius in many of his ideas, if not the execution."

She went on to tell us that Phillip allowed Jonathan to develop his weapons and run his experiments under the misguided belief that he'd rid himself of his father's influence. But Phillip had a hand in things all along, sending rogue supers to infiltrate Jonathan's operations under guise of joining the cause, tracking Jonathan's every move and discovery. He'd been aware of the experiments with vampire blood, of Fiona Brentwood's involvement. Even the hunters in Raven's Cape that we'd assumed were loyal to Jonathan had been moles planted by Phillip.

"What about the witches in other states?" I asked. "Countries? Washington wasn't the only state affected by this. Sophie told me that she and Haley had found communications from other covens, asking you for help."

Norah closed her eyes, her lips pressed into a thin line. When she looked up at me again, her eyes were fully back to their natural color.

And fully engulfed in regret.

"Jonathan had already begun experimenting in other locales long before they reached the Bay, making a lot of mistakes and risking exposure at every turn. But through those mistakes, he also revealed much about the inner workings of his mind, about his plans, about the hybrid technology he'd been working on. Phillip saw the seeds of true brilliance there, but knew Jonathan could never pull it off himself. That's when Phillip took a more active role, sending in his spies and surreptitiously nudging Jonathan toward the Bay. From that point forward, things began to coalesce quickly."

"So you knew all along," I said, unable to keep the venom from my voice. "The witches from the other covens that'd reached out to you for help—you turned them down. Not because you wanted to keep your head down and protect the Bay Coven witches, but because you wanted to protect Phillip. You wanted to protect yourself."

Norah didn't bother denying it. "Phillip and I have known each other a long time, crossing paths many, many times over the years. For most of that time, we kept an uneasy truce and stayed out of each other's business. It'd been a few years since we'd even communicated, when he suddenly reached out for a meeting. There, he shared with me a glimpse of his plans, and offered me a deal. Protection, survival. All I had to do was give him a little bit of information now and then, and turn a blind eye to his and Jonathan's activities."

"You are unbelievable," I said.

Norah merely shrugged. "At the time, I thought he was my best shot at survival. This war was coming whether I helped Phillip or not. The hunters had come out of the woodwork, developing an international underground network that, unlike the witches, was united in a single purpose. There would be no stopping the coming storm. Who are witches to stand up to this kind of power, Gray? Who am I? We can't even agree on the best way to cast a banishing spell."

Rage boiled in my gut at her words. How could she doubt us so much? How could she take such an easy way out?

I took a deep breath, reeling in my anger. Hadn't I doubted us, too? Wasn't I *still* doubting us? How many witches had gathered in the lodge, all of them willing to come together against a threat with a thousand faces, all because they knew fellow witches were in trouble? That our community was in grave danger? And I'd yet to trust them. To fully join them. I was there, sharing the space with them, helping with odds and ends, sitting in on some of the trainings. But I was still separate. Still holding myself apart. Still not claiming my magic or my blood.

"How does Orendiel fit into all this?" Emilio asked, and I turned my attention back to the interrogation. "You claim you don't know who's pulling his strings, but Phillip must've mentioned something about the fae involvement."

"Orendiel has his own agenda," she said. "But according to Phillip, when he heard about Phillip's work—presumably through a rogue fae that had been working with Jonathan to capture supernaturals for experimentation—he approached

Phillip with a deal: the dark fae and Phillip's hunters would join forces, working together to hybridize supernaturals for their armies, then eradicate both the witches and other problematic supernatural races. Phillip would have access to elite Darkwinter Knights as well as fae technology to meld with Jonathan's research, Darkwinter would have access to the hybrids they created, and once the war was over and the only groups left standing in power were the dark fae and the human hunters, they would divide the spoils. The fae would become the ruling class, and in return, the magic of the witches would be returned to its rightful keepers—the hunters."

"Back to this again," I said, throwing my hands up. It was always the same story. Power and magic. Magic and power. "Do the fae even have the capability to do such a thing? Magic can be manipulated, even channeled. But it can't be extracted and transferred. The hunters have been trying it for centuries, and it's never worked."

Norah frowned. "Greed blinds us all to logic and reason, Gray. I'm sure Orendiel knew exactly how to play on Phillip's base desire for the eradication of witches and the reclaiming of their magic—the hunters have never made their manifesto a secret. I imagine Orendiel spun quite a tail, and Phillip heard exactly what he wanted to hear, and here we are. Darkwinter doesn't *need* to have the capability to extract witch magic, because they have no intention of keeping up their end of the bargain. My guess? Darkwinter will turn on the hunters the moment their usefulness has run its course."

"So in the end, it's only Darkwinter that's left standing," I said with a shudder.

"And their hybrid army," Emilio said. "One way or another, we need to get to Blackmoon Bay and end this."

"You're too late, detective," Norah said. "Blackmoon Bay and the experimentation in Raven's Cape were just testing grounds. For years, they've been quietly installing magical infrastructure and soldiers in other cities across the globe. Those soldiers—dark fae and hunter alike—are simply awaiting orders. Once those orders are issued…" She trailed off, blowing out a breath and closing her eyes. Her face was even paler than before, with deep grooves lining her forehead.

"Is there anything else you can tell us?" Emilio asked. "Any other details, names, locations, anything you may have seen or overheard?"

"What's the point? There is nothing you can do to stop this, Detective. The wheels were set in motion long ago, and now they're spinning, full speed ahead. Your only chance is to gather up the ones you love and find a safe place to weather the storm."

"This isn't a storm," I said. "It's a war. One that you helped facilitate. And if we don't do something to end it, there won't *be* a safe place to weather the storm."

She nodded, resignation heavy on her shoulders.

"There's an outpost," she said. "About sixty miles southwest of Blackmoon Bay, hidden away inside the Olympic National Forest. I can show you on a map. I've been there twice, both times to deliver… to deliver prisoners."

"Witches," I clarified. "Women and girls that you kidnapped and sold."

"Witches," she confirmed. "It's fae-spelled to look like an abandoned cemetery, but there's a modern facility beneath it, with a high-tech lab, prison cells, and bunkers. That's where witches and other supernaturals are evaluated and processed for Phillip's higher-level experimentation. Phillip has since relocated to the Bay with Orendiel, but I'm sure the outpost is still operational. If any of the prisoners are still alive, that's where they'll be."

"How can we trust you're not sending us into a trap?" Emilio asked.

"Oh, but it *is* a trap, Detective. Just because Phillip isn't there doesn't mean he's left it unprotected. It's likely still under heavy guard, magical and physical. Enter at your own risk."

"You'd like that, wouldn't you?" I asked. "Send us right to the slaughterhouse, then collect your reward from your masters for being such a good little witch-slave. Right?"

Another bitter laugh escaped her lips. "There's nothing left they can offer me, Gray. I've got nothing more to give them, and nothing more to bargain with. Everyone I've ever cared about is dead. And I've sent dozens—maybe even hundreds—of innocent people to their deaths."

Her shoulders began to tremble again, and she squeezed her eyes shut tight, as if she were trying to force her tears back inside.

"That feeling?" I said. "That jackhammer in your head, the acid eating through your gut, the fire licking up your spine? That's guilt, Norah. And you deserve every ounce of pain it brings you. I hope you—"

"Gray." The touch of Emilio's hand on my shoulder silenced me, and I closed my eyes, breathing in his scent, letting his presence steady me once again. He was right. Ranting against Norah wouldn't do us any good. For all her lethal mistakes, she *had* given us good intel. At least we had the big-picture view of their plans now, whatever that was worth. And what she'd said about the outpost could prove useful, even if it *was* a trap. We'd find a way to get in there, just like we always did.

"Oh, Gray," Norah whispered. "You can't even begin to imagine the guilt I'm carrying."

"You made your own bed, Norah. You—"

She held up her hand cutting me off. "Sophie… I need to tell you about Sophie."

I gasped, the pain of hearing my best friend's name passing through this woman's lips almost unbearable. Not because I couldn't handle hearing the sound of Sophie's name, or because I felt like I had some claim on her memory.

But because in that moment I just *knew*. Right here, right now, handcuffed to a chair and facing down the very end of a life she'd squandered, Norah would only have one reason to bring up Sophie in that way.

Tell me about her? No. She wanted to confess.

A shiver rolled through me, starting between my shoulder blades and working its way down, making my knees weak, my stomach roil, my mouth go dry.

"What… what did you do?" My voice was no more than a whisper, no more than a breath. Again, I felt the calming touch of Emilio's hand on my shoulder, but he knew, too. I could feel it, the change in his body, the tension tightening his muscles.

"I visited her in your home in South Bay that night," she began. "Before our coven meeting. We had a pleasant enough conversation."

"Did you…?" I let the question hang there between us. *Kill her? Did you kill her? Did you fucking murder my best friend…*

"Did I inject her with vampire blood? No, I did not," she said firmly, and I blew out a breath. But then, "I merely unlocked her bedroom windows, setting the rest of the evening in motion."

The room spun, the walls closing in on me even as bits of conversation flashed through my memory of the night of Sophie's murder.

No sign of forced entry…

The front door was unlocked… her bedroom windows were wide open…

Maybe she knew him…

Maybe they came in through the windows…

The pieces clicked into place in a flash. Norah was already working with Phillip at that point. They'd known Jonathan was searching for me—that he'd been searching for me his whole life. Under Phillip's orders, Norah aided and abetted Jonathan in murdering her. She *knew* Sophie was going to die that night. She made it happen.

I couldn't breathe. I felt myself being dragged back into that hellfire of grief, the weight of Sophie's death pressing on my lungs, squeezing out my air. Sophie was never far from my thoughts, from my heart, but hearing Norah's confession now was like being set on fire all over again.

Something inside me snapped, and I lunged across the table, my hands wrapping around her throat. Magic sparked across my skin, electric currents that pulsed into Norah's pathetic body, calling forth her broken soul. I felt its pull, its resistance, and I shattered it, willing it out of her body. The first gray-black wisps of it emanated from her mouth as she watched in resignation.

"Do it," she choked out.

As if I needed her permission. Her pathetic encouragement.

You are going to die, bitch…

I tightened my grip. Her eyes bulged, her soul slithering out. All I had to do was reach out and grab it…

"Come back to me. Come back to me, *querida.* This isn't a road you want to go down." Emilio's hand was on my back, warm and steady, his words reaching across the void of pain and anger, filling me with his love. His patience. His support.

"This isn't going to bring her back, Gray," he said softly. "Nor will it bring you even a moment's peace."

My hands were still locked around Norah's neck, but my magic pulled back, releasing its thrall on her soul. The gray-black wisp sunk back into her mouth, then vanished completely.

"Come back to me," Emilio whispered, and that was it.

I let her go, allowing Emilio to guide me to my feet again. He led me out of the interrogation room, through the back room where the others had been watching through the glass. He took me down the hall, out the back door of the precinct, out into the freezer-burned Raven's Cape night, where the snow swirled before our eyes in feather-sized flakes and the cold air filled my lungs, washing away the fires once again.

Emilio held me close, his heart hammering against my ear, his hand on my back, the other caressing the back of my head, his breath warm in my hair.

"I'm… I'm okay," I finally whispered, pulling back to look up into his eyes. In their beautiful depths, I found my center, my heart. "I'm sorry I lost it in there."

"There's nothing to apologize for, *querida.* I'm just glad you're back. You were…" He blew out a misty-white breath. "You were in another realm."

I fought off a shiver, snuggling into his embrace once again.

Emilio had been right to stop me. Killing Norah, stealing her soul, it wouldn't have done a damn thing to bring Sophie back. There was *nothing* I could do to bring her back—her soul had already moved on.

I closed my eyes, reaching out for her now, remembering her passion, her drive, her love of life.

For Sophie, solving the mystery of the other rumored witch murders and visions she'd had about uniting the covens had never been an obligation or a burden. For her, it wasn't about some ancient prophecy or magical blood curse or an inexplicable power she spent half her time losing control of, and the other half recoiling from.

No. For her, it had been about something else entirely: love and friendship, sisterhood, the things that truly made life worth living.

More than anything, I wish she were still with me. Right here, right now. She would know what to do.

Oh, Sophie. What am I supposed to do now? Go to this cemetery outpost? What will we even find there?

Immediately, an image appeared in my mind—two Tarot cards from Sophie's favorite deck. I recognized the cards and their placements from the reading I'd found in her book of shadows.

She'd drawn the Six of Wands, featuring a winged creature with a face shaped like a moon, rising from the center of a flower bud. Five hands raised wooden staffs in her honor, ready to follow her leadership. Then, crossing the Six of Wands, she'd drawn the Four of Swords. In that card, the moon-faced creature was buried in the ground, surrounded by dirt and roses. One sword was buried next to her, with three others piercing the earth above.

There are four of you, Sophie had said. *The swords represent four witches. Three standing their ground, waiting for the fourth to rise, to find them and give them purpose.*

And then, when I'd pressed for more details, *You have to find the others, Gray. The four of you must unite the covens…*

Back then, I'd had no idea who the four witches could be. But it was clear to me now. They weren't just any witches. They were me and my sisters.

I blinked back tears, gulping in a fresh blast of cold air as the implications of those cards—of Sophie's message—hit.

Yes, we would go to that cemetery. And whatever else might've been waiting for us there, we'd find my sisters. We'd find the power to unite the covens and take down the hunters for good. I knew it with utter certainty—more than I'd ever felt about anything in my life, with the exception of the love I felt for my rebels.

My best friend died wanting to help her fellow sisters. She died wanting to help me and every other woman who'd ever called herself a witch, whether that witch was ready to claim her power or not.

So no, maybe I couldn't save her from Norah's treachery or the hunters' twisted plans. I couldn't even bring her back from the dead, despite my powers—her soul had already moved on.

But I could honor her memory. I could carry on *her* legacy… by finally accepting the responsibilities inherent in mine.

I could pick up my sword, find my sisters, and rise the fuck up.

"Let's get back to the lodge," I said suddenly, my voice steady and resolute as I blinked the snowflakes from my eyes. "We've got some troops to rally."

FORTY

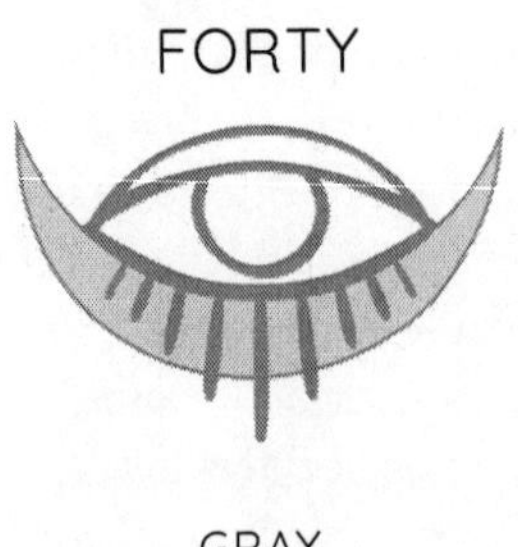

GRAY

The fireplace crackled to life at the back of the common room, around which every occupant of the lodge had gathered. Some were sharing couches, others had brought in chairs from the dining room. Some were sitting cross-legged on the floor, shawls wrapped around their shoulders, coffee mugs in hand.

All eyes were fixed on me.

Tucked into my shirt pocket, close to my heart, three small objects gave me an infusion of strength: the Page of Cups card, in honor of Sophie. The High Priestess, for Calla, the only mother I'd ever known. And the granite heart Liam had given me, carved with the feather I would forever associate with him, no matter how long we might be apart.

I pictured the three of them standing by the fireplace now, their eyes shining with love. With encouragement. And with unshakeable faith in me—faith that I was finally starting to find for myself.

I looked out over the sea of faces gathered before me. Some of them—Haley, Darius, Ronan, Emilio, Asher—I'd come to know, to love. Others were quickly becoming like family, too—Elena, Detective Lansky, Reva, Sunshine, Sparkle. And a few were virtual strangers I'd seen only in passing, women whose names I hadn't even fully learned.

But all of them were part of this. And all of them deserved my gratitude. My trust. My authentic self, flaws and fears and all.

"Thank you all for being here," I said, my voice steady despite the jumble of nerves inside. "For those of you who don't know me, my name is Gray Desario."

Haley let out a whoop, and everyone laughed. Leave it to my sister to turn this moment into a pep rally.

Grinning at her, I continued.

"I am a Shadowborn witch. My birth name is Morgan Susanna Sil—" I hesitated on the last word, knowing that this moment would change my life in so many ways. It felt big and important, all-encompassing, and I took another steadying breath, letting the feelings wash over me. Inside, my magic simmered, sending tendrils of heat and electricity crackling through my veins.

"Silversbane," I finally said. "I am the third daughter of a third daughter of a third daughter, all of us descended from the first witches—those chosen by the Elemental Source to be the guardians of earth's magic."

A murmur rippled through the group, and I felt the energy in the room rise and warm in response, but no one laughed at me. No one called me a heretic or rolled their eyes or pelted me with crystals. No one stormed out or tried to talk over me. No one called me insane.

Letting out a breath, I caught Ronan's eye, and he winked at me, flashing that crooked grin I'd always loved. Next to him, Asher gave me the thumbs up. Darius was next, offering a supportive and seductive smile—I was pretty sure he couldn't differentiate between the two. Then Emilio, his hand on his heart, his eyes locked on mine, sending me his love. Haley was at the end, smiling brightly, a beam of light I felt down to my very soul.

I touched the cards in my pocket and continued.

"My sister Haley and I, along with two other sisters we haven't yet found—Georgina and Adele—are part of a prophecy that dates back millennia. It states, among other things, that under my leadership, we're to unite the covens against all who seek to oppress us, and bring our global sisterhood—witchcraft, in all its many forms and practices—back into the light."

I told them everything I knew. Everything I'd learned from Deirdre, all the details she'd shared about the original prophecy and the scholarly interpretations that'd followed. I told them the little bit I knew about our birthmother, about what had happened to us as children. And I told them about my belief that we'd find the remaining Silversbane heirs—my sisters—at the cemetery outpost Norah had told us about.

"Whether you're a believer in all of this prophecy talk or not—and most days, I'm not even sure where *I* fall on that scale—one thing is certain," I continued. "We *are* under attack. A threat is upon us, not just here in Raven's Cape and Blackmoon Bay, but in cities and states throughout our country and beyond. Witches have been kidnapped, tortured, experimented on, murdered. And this threat, this looming black cloud of death and destruction… It's no longer just about witches. Every living being is at risk now, supernatural and human alike."

At this, Emilio and Elena joined me at the front of the room, sharing all the details they could about the ongoing investigations, about the information Norah had provided, and about the Fae Council's betrayal, putting every last one of our theories on full display.

No stone was left unturned, no puzzle piece unexamined. Some of the witches asked questions. Others shared their own observations from their time in the cave prisons or from rumors and whispers they'd picked up in their covens. Reva told us about things she'd witnessed as she'd traveled the shadows of Norah's house, back when she'd been living there, corroborating a lot of what I'd discovered in Sophie's book of shadows. And others remained quiet, simply taking it all in.

But again, no one laughed, or shouted, or turned their backs on us. They were with us. One hundred percent.

I took center stage again, knowing that the next part had to come from me. Knowing that every moment in my life had led me here, to this one.

Liam and I had spent countless hours debating destiny versus free will, fate versus choice. He'd always insisted I had some grand destiny, a special path that had been mapped out in the stars long before I was even born. I'd always believed I made my own choices—that no universal forces, no bloodlines, no supernatural conspiracies, no magic could conspire to bend my will, no matter what the prophecy or Death himself said.

But choice and destiny weren't mutually exclusive. They could both exist, they could both be honored. Perhaps destiny merely nudged us in certain directions, placing opportunities in our path at every step. The rest? That would *always* be up to us.

I smiled, knowing I wouldn't have wanted it any other way.

"We all took a different road to get here," I said, looking out again at the witches and loved ones that'd gathered. "Some of you were imprisoned, and you ended up here because by the time you were liberated, it was too dangerous for you to return home. Some of you had no homes to return to. Others came because there's safety in numbers. Some of you just wanted to be part of something bigger than yourselves. But one thing we have in common is our sisterhood. Our magic. And our desire to live and love and practice in peace."

"Give peace a chance, y'all," Haley said, again making everyone chuckle. She had a knack for shining a light on the dark places, that was for certain.

"Unfortunately," I continued, "that peace now comes at a price." I took a deep breath, again drawing on the love and support of my rebels, my sister, my friends. "In three days, we'll be leading a team to the cemetery outpost in the Olympic National Forest to liberate any remaining prisoners and gather additional intelligence about the siege in Blackmoon Bay and the enemy's larger plans. We'll need protective magic, offensive and defensive spellcasters, healers, fighters. What we're facing there… It's likely going to be brutal. We'll fight monsters that used to be men, and men that made monsters out of their brothers. We'll fight dark magic the likes of which we've never encountered before. And worse—we'll fight the ideologies that allowed that magic to manifest in the first place."

Fighting off a shiver, I pressed on. "Some of us may die. And those of us who do make it out alive will come back here, only to regroup for a bigger, deadlier mission: reclaiming the city of

Blackmoon Bay—the place that many of us in this room once called home. Make no mistake—this is just the beginning of a much longer, much more difficult battle, and none of you signed up for it. So, if any witch, shifter, demon, or other ally wants out, now is your chance. There are *no* judgments here. You will still be protected, still have a home here, still be welcomed. Understood?"

Everyone nodded. I had no idea which way this was going to go, who would be left standing at the end of it all. I was running on those two magic words again—hope and faith.

Taking a deep breath, I made my final declaration. "I ask that we all close our eyes now. Those who wish to remove themselves from consideration for the upcoming operation can quietly leave the room. For those who remain in this room after a count of one hundred, we'll break up into groups, assess everyone's skills and abilities, and make our plan of attack."

I watched as everyone closed their eyes, then closed mine and began the count out loud. Over the sound of my voice, I heard the soft rustling of people rising from their chairs, shoes scuffing against the hardwood, footsteps bearing witches to the perceived safety of some other place.

I tried not to let my disappointment show. I'd made my choices, after all. It was only fair to give them the same opportunity, and to stand by my promise not to judge.

"Ninety-nine… one hundred." I opened my eyes.

And my heart nearly stopped.

Every chair and couch was empty.

Because every person in the room was now on their feet, standing before me. Not a soul remained seated, and not a soul had left. They'd merely risen, closing the spaces between them, drawing together.

From the center of the group rose a sparkling mist of the palest pink light, pulsing warm and bright, and their faces turned toward it, smiling. It was their magic. Their hope. Their solidarity. Their promise.

Haley looked up at me with tears in her eyes, her own smile bold and beautiful as ever.

"We're with you, Gray," she said. "All the fucking way."

FORTY-ONE

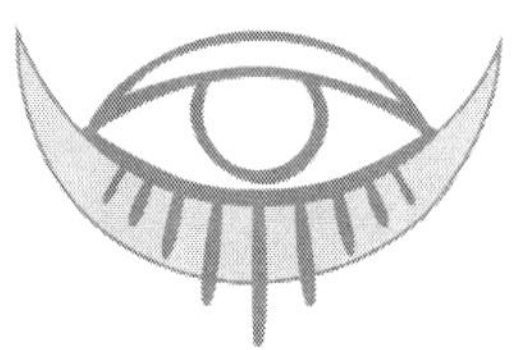

RONAN

Fucking hell, I hated the cold. Hated the waiting. Hated standing around in balls-deep snow with my thumb up my ass, counting down for the signal from the witches on the other side of the hill.

But once that signal came—the night sky lighting up with a fireball of bright orange attack magic— you bet your ass I wanted nothing more than to go back to that waiting. Back to the part before all hell broke loose.

But going back wasn't an option. Not tonight.

"Ronan!" Ash shouted. "On your left!"

Heeding the warning, I spun around fast, swinging my sword for all it was worth. The Darkwinter soldier bearing down on me caught it in the face, dropping like a bag of wet sand. I had no idea whether he was dead or just wounded, and no time to check. I was already on the move.

Seven days to the hour after Gray's meeting, after some of the most grueling magical, combat, and strategic training we'd ever endured, here we were, converging on a cemetery in the middle of the damn forest like a virus attacking its host.

Ten witches had comprised the first wave, slipping through the snow-covered forest from our makeshift basecamp on light feet, getting into position to launch the spell that would alert the whole forest to our presence. For the rest of us, there would be no sneak attacks, no quiet infiltration. Our best chance, we'd decided, was a full-on blitzkrieg.

Motion on my right, and Beaumont blurred into view, tearing out the throat of a hunter who'd had his sights set on Haley. She and Gray stood back to back a few feet ahead of me, channeling each other's magic to fight through a cluster of Darkwinter guards who looked like they'd just been caught with their dicks in their hands. Hell, for all I know, they *had* been standing out here, pulling off a big old circle-jerk, no idea what was coming for them. It wasn't every day your secret cemetery hideout got invaded by a bunch of pissed off, kickass, magic-toting broomstick riders.

One of them opened his mouth to shout something, but he didn't get the chance. Gray lit 'em all up like firecrackers.

That's my girl.

"Lansky!" I shouted, spotting three more hunters ahead, charging toward two more witches fighting on the east side of the cemetery. "Twelve o'clock! Take those motherfuckers out!"

Lansky, who'd remained in his human form for just this purpose, raised his weapon and took aim, squeezing off three rounds. The hunters dropped out of sight, off the fucking planet.

Elena and Emilio were in full-on wolf mode, and now they charged ahead, barreling into a group of hunters and taking them down like bowling pins.

The snowmelt ran red with their blood.

I crept up behind an unsuspecting hunter trying to get the drop on Lansky, carving a fresh path from his shoulder to his kidney. Ahead of me, Jael lit up one of the dark fae with his own brand of fae magic—a golden orb that surrounded his prey and squeezed the life right out of him. Apparently, that particular spell only worked on other fae, but it was a neat trick, and way more effective for him than swinging a sword.

On the other side of the cemetery, Sunshine and Sparkle had staked out their own live buffet, devouring any hunter or Darkwinter snack in their path.

I never thought I'd be so grateful to roll with a pair of hellhounds.

"Heads up, hellspawn!" Beaumont blurred past me again, and I followed his path, teaming up with him on two more dark fae. One of them got a good jab in, slicing my forearm down to the fucking bone, but I repaid him in kind.

"Nothing says thanks like a sword to the throat, dickhole." I watched him gurgle and choke on his last breath, then I spit on his corpse.

"Alright?" Beaumont asked, glancing at the blood soaking through my jacket sleeve. Looked like he was wearing the same amount, but the blood spilled down the front of his clothing wasn't his.

"I'll live." I took a deep breath, shaking off the pain. That was one good thing about the cold—shit went numb a whole lot faster.

Fae-glamoured or not, everything about the cemetery was absolutely real: headstones jutting out of the ground at odd angles, just waiting to catch someone in the shins. Short, wrought-iron gating buried in the snow like caltrops, eager to tear through the soles of our feet. Crypts looming up out of the frosty mist, providing the perfect cover for a hunter damn near pissing himself at the chance to jump out and knife one of us.

Despite the odds, we persisted.

Side-by-side, with a combination of magic, speed, bloodlust, and brute force, my crew and I—no, fuck that. My *family* and I—we fought our way through three dozen guards, a combination of Darkwinter Knights and hunter pricks just like the ones we'd taken down in the warehouse back at the Cape. The brutal cold, slippery conditions, and fake-cemetery obstacle course made tonight's assault a hell of a lot more challenging, and I was pretty sure we'd all be getting stitched, bandaged, and dosed up later.

But somehow, we survived it. We always fucking survived it. Gray, Darius, Emilio, Asher, and I—hell, even Liam, wherever his spooky ass was at the moment—we made sure of it. After everything we'd already been through, there was no way we were letting anyone on *this* frozen wasteland take us down.

"We clear?" I asked Ash, catching up with him after icing one last fae guard.

"Looks like." He waved to Beaumont across the cemetery, and

the vampire gave a thumbs-up. After doing a final sweep to ensure we'd obliterated every last guard spotted aboveground, we plundered the bodies for whatever useful weapons we could find, then regrouped in the middle of the cemetery to catch our breaths. So far, everything had gone according to plan. Norah's intel had proved solid.

At least the traitorous bitch had been good for something.

She'd told us about a crypt at the end of a flagstone pathway in the southwest corner of the cemetery that would lead us underground, down into the facility proper. The location itself was easy to find—a large stone mausoleum, an archway carved with pentacles and moon symbols, an iron gate marking the entrance. Problem was, we had no idea what to expect beyond the gate. Because of the weather and the remote location of the cemetery, we weren't able to do a full surveillance. We'd hiked a mile in from our makeshift basecamp, doing our best to stick to the paths with the most tree cover and the least amount of snow, but the first wave of witches had to move in fast. Once we'd gotten a visual on the place, we knew it was only a matter of time before they'd get a visual on us.

Now, we stood before the gate, wondering how many guards were down below. Did they have surveillance? Had they set a trap? Or had they all rushed out during our initial attack, leaving the rest of the place unguarded, free for the taking?

What, exactly, was worth taking down there?

"Alright, guys," Gray said, wrapping her hand around the gate. "Let's see what fresh hell awaits us next, shall we?"

She turned and caught my eyes for just a second, and I mouthed the only words I knew in that moment. The only ones I wanted her to know.

I fucking love you, Desario.

Without another word, Gray turned back toward the gate and wrenched it open.

But not before I'd caught that smile.

FORTY-TWO

GRAY

Blood. It was all around me, filling my nostrils, filling the air, coating my tongue with its acrid tang. It made *my* head spin, and I wasn't a vampire. I could only imagine how Darius was dealing with it.

But dealing with it he was, never leaving my side, not for an instant. His hand on my shoulder kept me steady as I waited for the initial shock to recede.

"Breathe through your mouth, love," he whispered, his lips brushing the shell of my ear. "It will be less unpleasant that way."

After descending the dark and twisted staircase to the lower level, we'd assumed the lack of guards meant a trap, some mind-fuck designed by the fae to lure us deeper into their maze of chaos.

But now, standing in the center of the large chamber that held the facility's prison cells, I realized the truth.

At the first sign of our attack, any guards that might've been stationed down here had probably abandoned their posts, grateful for any excuse to get out into the fresh air, even if they had to risk death to do it.

The room was nearly identical to the one we'd found on the top floor of the warehouse back at the Cape—brightly illuminated, with morgue-like steel tables and shelves surrounded on three sides by glass-fronted prison cells. But where the warehouse room had been surgically spotless, this one was filthy. Each cell was smeared with blood, inside and out. The tables were slick with it. Walking across the floor was like walking across a viscous shallow river, each step more treacherous than the last. There were drains at the center of the room, but they'd overflowed long ago.

The worst part, though, wasn't the blood.

It was the prisoners.

A dozen witches, two or three to a cell, all of them so weak and drained they hadn't even flinched when we'd hit the lights. Eight shifters—a mix of wolf, panther, mountain lion, fox, most of them in their animal form, all of them trembling with fear. There were two deceased human males—vessels, Ronan and Asher determined. Demons that had likely been injected with Jonathan's infamous devil's trap venom, left to die. Three female vampires lay near death in another cell, chained to the wall, surrounded by blood yet prevented from drinking any of it.

One of them was Fiona Brentwood, so far gone she didn't recognize any of us. Not even Darius.

I felt my mind trying to shut down inside, to block out the horrifying scene. But I forced myself to stay present, to take in every gruesome detail. I needed to see this. To feel it. All of us did.

If anyone had come here tonight with even a shred of doubt about the importance of our mission, the sight before us surely eradicated it.

"I'll get to work on the security," Jael said. The cells were locked by the same type of magical weave he'd found in the warehouse, and he needed a few minutes to untangle its complicated threads.

As he worked in silence, and the others spread out to guard the entrances, I grabbed Haley's hand, holding it tight. Her face was as pale as mine must've been, and with good reason.

Somewhere in these cells were our sisters. I'd felt the connection as soon as we'd entered the chamber—a tug on my magic, on my heart. It was the same feeling I'd gotten when Haley and I clasped hands during the ice storm behind Elena's house—when we'd transferred magic through our blood.

Like attracted like. Silversbane blood ran through my veins. It ran through Haley's. And it ran through Adele's and Georgie's.

And right now, that blood was singing a siren song.

I only hoped we weren't too late.

"Got it," Jael announced, and the glass doors slid open.

Still, the prisoners didn't move.

"They're all in really bad shape," McKenna said. She and Yvonne, another witch gifted with healing magic, tried to assess the situation. I didn't know much about healing, but it was obvious that these beings had been imprisoned for much longer than the ones we'd found in the warehouse.

I didn't even want to *think* about what kinds of torments they'd been subjected to.

"Gray," Haley whispered, tugging on my hand. "Over here."

I followed her to a cell in the far right corner, where three witches huddled close, their eyes glazed. They were no more than skeletons with a thin layer of skin, barely breathing, unblinking.

"Adele?" she whispered. "Georgina?"

"They might not go by those names," I reminded her.

"No, but hearing them might bring something back. A memory, a flash, anything."

"Adele?" she tried again. "Georgie?"

My heart hammered in my throat, my stomach twisting. It was all I could do not to vomit, not to scream, not to break.

Please say something. Anything. Please.

"Adele?" she said once more.

And then, it happened.

One of the witches twitched. Slowly, agonizingly, her head turned toward us.

And I knew. I just knew.

The realization crashed over me, hard and fast. I'd seen her before. Blonde hair like mine, expressive brown eyes. Long limbs that held the ghost of muscles. And though she'd been brutalized to within an inch of her life, nearly unrecognizable, I knew in that instant she was our sister.

"It's her," I said to Haley. "I saw her in a vision. You and Georgie were there too." It was the dream I'd had in the Shadowrealm, when they'd tried to warn me not to follow the man chasing the deer. They'd appeared again on the boat with Liam, floating on one of Hell's lakes. They'd told me it was time to seek my own sword.

The one with the shorn head had been Haley. This one was Adele.

"Do… do I know you?" the blonde croaked out, her lips barely moving.

Haley burst out laughing, and I cried silent tears, both of us falling to our knees in relief.

"We're your sisters, Adele," Haley said. "And we're here to liberate you from this one-star shithole."

FORTY-THREE

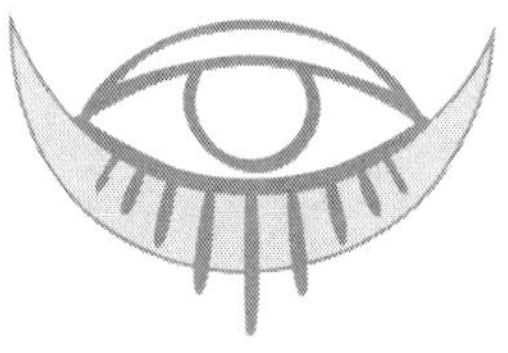

GRAY

It took all of us the better part of three hours to transport everyone from the underground cells. They had to be triaged and temporarily healed as best as McKenna and Yvonne could manage, bundled into warm gear, and slowly brought up to the mausoleum, where Lansky, two more RCPD wolf shifters, Sunshine, and four more of our witches would stand guard, waiting for the rest of us to do a full sweep of the underground facility.

After that, we would begin the long trudge back to basecamp, and then, to the lodge. We had about eight hours until sunrise to get all of the vampires to safety, and something told me we'd be using every last second to finish this job.

It had been a long and brutal night, and the end was nowhere on the horizon. But fatigue and soreness were no match for the joy that Haley and I felt at finding Adele, and as we watched Ronan carry her up to the top, my heart was instantly lighter. I wanted nothing more than to stay with her, to keep her in my sights, but I had to believe we'd have plenty of time for that later.

Right now, we had a lot of work ahead of us.

Including locating Georgie, who—much to our frustration and concern—had not been among the imprisoned witches.

"Okay, the prison is clear," Ronan said when the last vampire prisoner had been taken upstairs. "Time to move."

After securing everyone in the mausoleum, there were only a dozen of us left down here—Haley, me, and two other witches named Bex and Sasha from Verona's group; Ronan and Ash; Darius; Jael: Sparkle; Elena and Detective Hobb in their wolf forms; and Emilio, who'd shifted back into human form. We fanned out down a long corridor that branched off from the prison chamber, creeping past dozens of abandoned offices, unoccupied cells with barred entries, and bare-bones sleeping chambers without them. Asher managed to find a couple of dead tablets and a cell phone, and Darius tracked down a file box containing four thumb drives, a few maps of Washington, two hand-written notebooks, unused shipping labels to an address in Blackmoon Bay, and a bunch of receipts, all of which we'd sort through later.

Other than that, we'd come up pretty empty on the intel front.

"Seems like they started clearing out days ago," Emilio said. "The food wrappers in the trash cans are at least that old."

"You're right." Darius sniffed the air. "No human or fae has been down in this section in at *least* that long, maybe longer. They've probably moved on to Blackmoon Bay."

"And left their prisoners behind?" I shook my head. "No way. There has to be more to it than this."

"The prisoners we've just liberated couldn't possibly be of use to them anymore, Gray," Darius said. "To the hunters and fae, transporting them probably seemed like a liability—look how long it took us just to get them aboveground. Perhaps they decided to cut their losses."

"I might agree with that," Emilio said, "but something isn't adding up. Why leave so many guards behind just to deal with a couple dozen prisoners who don't even have the strength to stand, let alone mount an escape or attack?"

"We need to keep looking," I said, and Haley nodded. Our other sister was here somewhere, or, at the very least, she *had* been —recently, too. My instincts were screaming at me loud and clear. I wouldn't leave until we found her, or found some clue that would indicate her whereabouts.

We continued down the corridor, checking every single room, until we finally reached the T at the end. There was a large, locked door in the center of the T, made of heavy oak and carved with runes, bigger and stronger than any of the others. From there, the corridor branched out again in both directions.

We cleared the corridor first—just more of the same abandoned office spaces with a few rooms in between that looked like doctors' exam rooms.

I tried not to linger too long in those—the dried blood smeared on the floor and exam tables was enough to make the bile rise in my throat.

The only additional pieces of intel we'd come up with were a couple of folders containing some kind of medical records, presumably for the prisoners.

None of them bore my sister's name, or anything that sparked even a glimmer of recognition.

We finally converged again at the large door in the center of the T. Those of us who'd brought weapons drew them, Haley and I readying our magic as Emilio kicked in the door.

For such an imposing piece of wood, it splintered and swung open easily, the runes remaining as dead as everything else. Motion sensors triggered the lights, bathing the space before us in a warm, pleasant glow.

Leaving Elena, Sasha, and Detective Hobb to patrol the corridors, the rest of us headed into the office. Instead of the same basic setup we'd expected to find, this one was massive and ornate, with gleaming hardwood floors, floor-to-ceiling mahogany bookshelves stuffed with dusty old tomes and lore books, a wall of high-tech computer peripherals, a small conference table with six leather chairs, and a huge mahogany desk situated square in the middle—something you'd expect to find an in an executive suite in Manhattan rather than in an underground outpost.

"Whoever worked here was pretty high up the ladder," Bex said, running her hand along the conference table. Like Sophie, Bex was able to pick up on the psychic imprints people left behind on objects, and now she let out a deep sigh. "A lot of people got fired in this room. Some of them were killed."

Suppressing another shiver, I glanced at Haley, who had the same wide-eyed look on her face as I felt on my own.

"I've been here before," I whispered, images of the place flickering through my mind's eye.

"Me too," Haley said. "It was the place we saw in our vision during the blood spell for Darius."

She was right. I could almost see the woman again now, paging through the books spread out across her desk.

"She's a vampire," Darius said, his voice holding a note of surprise. He scented the air again, then slid open a recessed panel on the far wall, between two bookcases. The space he'd revealed lit up immediately.

"It's a refrigerator," he said, and I peered over his shoulder to peek inside.

Every shelf was lined with neat, unbroken rows of the same thing.

Blood. Bottles and bottles of blood.

"This is the expensive stuff," he said, opening one up and sniffing it. I waited for him to take a sip, but he didn't.

"From the blood bank?" I asked, though I had my doubts. In all my time delivering blood orders for Waldrich's Imports, I'd never seen anything like that.

"I'm afraid not." Darius capped it without drinking it, and set it back on the shelf. "This collection was bottled at the source, so to speak."

My stomach churned. Humans. She'd been draining humans, bottling their blood for her own personal collection. Who knew whether she'd kept them alive; perhaps they were the people whom Bex had thought died here.

After making my way back to the center of the room, I looked through the books on the desk, finding nothing of particular interest, then moved on to the drawers. There wasn't much—just a few random office supplies, a phone charger, a chocolate bar.

And then the pin. Shaped like a crown, with two swords

crossing beneath it, it shone like liquid silver, catching the light and reflecting it in tiny prisms that scattered rainbows across the ceiling.

"It's definitely her office," I said, passing the pin to Haley. "She was wearing this on her jacket lapel in the vision."

Emilio caught sight of it, his face ashen. "Are you sure, *querida?*"

"Positive. I saw a silvery crown with two swords underneath, exactly like this. Do you recognize it?"

"It's the council's insignia." He met my gaze, the space between his eyebrows pinched with new concern. "As far as I know, there is only one pin—*this* one. I'd heard the custom had fallen out of favor decades ago, but back then, they used to give it to the ultimate ranking member."

"So the woman we saw in the vision was Talia?" I asked.

Emilio shook his head. "Talia is powerful, but the title of ultimate ranking member is typically reserved for fae royalty. One who has the last word in all council matters, but who seldom visits our realm. He or she typically sends emissaries. I wasn't even aware the council had someone in the position right now."

"Emilio, why would Gray and I get a vision from some random royal fae?" Haley asked. "And if she's so important, why would she have an office at the bottom of this outpost? Wouldn't she have more important things to focus on?"

"Like plotting the downfall of the entire human race?" Ronan asked. He and Asher had been quietly searching the bookshelves up until that point, and now they joined us at the desk, a large leather attaché case in hand.

Inside, they'd found a half-charged tablet containing all kinds of unencrypted notes and plans. There were digital and paper maps, travel itineraries for an entire staff that appeared to have been regularly moving into and out of the Bay from other international destinations for at least a year. There was a leather calendar, also full of notes and details about meetings and missions.

"Darkwinter isn't interested in eradicating all supers and

humans," Jael said, scrolling through the tablet. "They're planning to enslave them. Once the witches are out of the picture and the hybrids have done their work ushering in the destruction of most of the world's communities, those left standing against the dark fae will be captured and enslaved."

"Bloody hell," Darius said.

"There are a bunch of passports, too," Ash said, fishing them out of one of the attaché pockets. They were all from different countries, issued in different names, but the photo inside every single one was identical.

"It's her," I said, and Haley confirmed with a nod. "The woman we saw."

"Employee ID badges," Ash said, pulling them out of the bag as well. "Same chick. Looks like her actual name is… Trinity O'Leary. Same name on three badges, plus some of the paperwork and notes we found."

"Trinity," I whispered, my heart pounding. "She's… she's not a random fae royal, Haley. She's not fae at all. She's a witch. And apparently a vampire. And I believe she's our birthmother."

"Holy shit," Haley whispered. Her face was sheet-white.

"Looks like there's an assistant, too," Ash said, flipping through more of the paperwork.

My chest constricted, all the air whooshing out of my lungs. I knew what he was going to say before he'd uttered another sound.

"Georgina Mertz."

The last name didn't matter. No witch in her right mind would use the name Silversbane.

Just like with Trinity, the first name was all the confirmation I needed.

Our mother had infiltrated the fae council, using them to spearhead a plan of mass destruction—to what end, I had no idea. And my sister, *our* sister, the one who—along with Adele—was prophesied to help us unite the covens…

She was our mother's right-hand woman.

Haley's mouth rounded into a pale pink O. But before she

could formulate a single question, Asher dropped the case, his eyes wide with panic.

"Uh, guys?" Asher said, and Sparkle issued a low, warning growl behind him. "We've got a serious fucking problem, and it ain't your family tree."

FORTY-FOUR

GRAY

Shadows came to life, peeling themselves from the walls, morphing into the brutal monsters of nightmares. In the span of three heartbeats, we were completely surrounded.

No, not shadows, I realized. Hybrids. Part shifter, part vampire, part wild creature I couldn't even identify, they'd emerged from a passageway that'd been spelled to look like a bookcase, baring sharp teeth and wielding razor-sharp claws that glinted in the light. By the time we realized what was happening, they'd already divided our group in half, six of us on the inside, six near the outer door we'd entered through.

They outnumbered us four to one.

All that was left to do now was fight.

Instinct took over as the office erupted in pure chaos, a blur of gore and flashing blades and gnashing teeth. Deep underground, my connection to the earth was strong, and I called on its magic to infuse my own, drawing it deep within, then sending it out through my palms in white-blue electric arcs.

All of this happened in an instant. My first attempt crashed into one of the bookshelves and fizzled out, but my next hit was true, igniting one of the hybrids in flames. I didn't have time to watch him burn; I was already charging up for another hit, shooting it at one of the beasts just before he swiped at Bex.

In the blur of my peripheral vision, Darius was in perpetual motion, grappling with one vamp-monster after another, fighting off their attacks. They seemed nearly evenly matched in speed and strength, and for every one he managed to take down, another took its place. Two wolves charged in through the door—Elena and Hobb—trailed by Sasha, wielding her own magic, yellow-green flames bursting from her palms.

"Asher, duck!" Ronan shouted, and Ash dropped to the floor just as Ronan threw a silver dagger into one of the beasts' chest. Part vampire, part shifter, the thing dropped to the ground instantly, the silver poison already wreaking havoc on its bloodstream.

I had no vampire superstrength or speed, no shifter instincts, no weapons but my own magic. It took every ounce of strength and focus to control it, but somehow, I managed to take out three more monsters, burning each one to a crisp.

Unfortunately, the office was now burning too. If we didn't get to the exit soon, we'd all be engulfed.

"Jael, behind you!" Darius shouted, then put up his arms to fend off another attack. Jael was near the doorway, but it wasn't an escape route. Hybrids had surrounded him on all sides, closing in fast. He swung his fae blade, decapitating one of them, but another took a chunk out of Jael's arm. The sword clattered to the floor.

"Ronan, help him!" I shouted, firing another bolt of magic at a monster charging Emilio, who was back in his wolf form, his powerful jaws descending over a hybrid's throat. Sparkle took down two more, all of us desperately trying to reach Jael.

I'd nearly broken through when I saw Ronan's eyes go wide with fear, clear on the other side of the room. He opened his mouth to shout at me, but it was too late. In an instant, I was slammed into a bookcase, the wind knocked out of me, my skull cracking against the wood. I hadn't even seen my assailant, but he was on me now, one impossibly-strong hand around my neck as he lifted me a foot off the ground.

I felt the insistent push of his vampire influence on my mind, paralyzing my body as he flooded me with images of all the things he wanted to do to me.

Fangs shone inside a wicked grin, his chin already stained with blood.

The room was darkening around me, acrid smoke and the monster's tight grip choking off the last of my air supply. I couldn't call on my magic, couldn't even swing a fist.

I was fading.

The beast hauled me close to his mouth, inhaling my scent. His tongue darted out to lick my cheek, the rotten funk of his breath and the low, desirous growl in his chest my final warning. My final goodbye.

I'd never felt so weak. So powerless.

I am going to die…

I closed my eyes, waiting for the bite of those teeth.

And then he dropped me.

My ass hit the floor hard, my shoulders crashing into the bookshelf behind me. I had just enough time to cover my head before an avalanche of books cascaded down on top of me.

When the room finally swam back into view and I could actually breathe again, I saw the monster at my feet, his head cleanly separated from his body, blood pooling beneath him. I looked up to see an outstretched hand reaching for mine. Grabbing it, I got to my feet and came face-to-face with the man who'd just saved my life.

The ancient blue light of his eyes called me home.

"Liam," I breathed.

"No time," he said, a fae sword held firmly in his other hand, dripping with blood. "We need to move, Gray. Now."

"Jael!" I shouted. "Go help Jael!" But Liam shook his head, his grip on my hand tightening. He wouldn't leave my side, not when we were still surrounded by deadly hybrids, with more emerging from the walls with every passing heartbeat. Smoke billowed around us, thickening, blotting out the light.

At a painfully slow pace, Liam and I fought our way to the doorway where I'd last seen Jael, but it was too late. In the intermittent flashes of my magic attacks and the fire eating up the walls behind us, we watched in horror as the beasts dragged our fae prince down the left corridor, descending on him like a pack of rabid dogs. Seconds later, a wall of flames cut him off from us for good.

"Jael!" I screamed, my throat raw, my legs propelling me forward, even as a strong arm looped around my waist and hauled me backward. Eventually, I stopped fighting it, and I collapsed against Liam's chest. Tears streaked my face, my insides burning with shame and grief. None of us could reach Jael. None of us were even close enough to hear his final cries.

"Move, Gray! Now!" Liam's panicked voice shook me out of my stupor, and I slipped out of his hold just in time to avoid a strike. I dropped to the ground as Liam swung his blade, taking our attacker's head clean off.

He hauled me to my feet again and we spun around, looking for another exit, some way to lead everyone to safety, but every corridor was rapidly filling with hybrids. With nowhere else to go, we ran back into Trinity's office, trying to discern friend from foe amidst the chaos.

With the notable exception of Jael, I spotted everyone in our group. They were all still on their feet, still fighting hard.

And then Haley went down.

I charged back into the melee, shooting an electric bolt at a hybrid who'd jumped into my path. When I got to my sister, she was on her knees, her head bent back at a severe angle, her eyes half-lidded. She seemed to be in a deep trance.

In one hand she gripped a bloody dagger. Her other hand was clenched in a fist, dripping with blood.

I knew at once she was doing a spell.

Calling up another surge of earth magic, I channeled everything I had into protecting her, drawing up an iridescent shield around her as Liam continued to swing his blade at any beast in our periphery.

Temporarily safe inside the shield, Haley used her blood to draw a pentacle on the floor, then pressed her palm against it. The symbol glowed at her touch.

All around us, the team continued to fight. And the beasts continued to emerge from the darkness.

And then, the chanting began.

It started soft—so soft I almost wasn't sure it was Haley. But then her voice grew stronger, louder, more powerful, the tenor of it reverberating inside my chest.

The words felt sinister, dark, so unlike anything I'd ever heard come out of my sister's mouth, I had to check again to make sure it was her.

Slowly she got to her feet, her eyes closed, her head bowed, her words rising above the sounds of our battle, raising the hairs on the back of my neck.

Blood of hell, blood of night
I call on the darkness to show us the light
May evil and malice and violence intended
Return to its hosts uprooted, upended
Dark Goddess I bend, Dark Goddess I bow
Hear my petition, and thusly I vow
My service is yours, by blood and by blade
Until my last breath shall deem it unmade.

Nine times she spoke the spell, her words growing more impassioned with each repetition. My shield was dimming, revealing Haley in her full, terrifying glory. Blood shone on her lips, her eyes wild, her face stark white. A deep and chilling darkness seemed to emanate from within her, but still, I held onto that shield for as long as I could, pouring all of my magic into it, all of my power, all of my love.

I had no idea who she'd petitioned or what, precisely, she'd promised, but I didn't dare disturb the spell.

Haley's magic was working.

Slowly at first, and then all at once, the tide changed. There was a single heartbeat of silence, as if someone had hit the reset button.

The smoke began to clear.

All of us looked on with awe and wonder.

And one by one, the hybrids turned their attention away from our group and onto each other.

I'd never seen such brutality, such gruesome violence. Such

single-minded determination. They tore into each other, shredding flesh and bone, destroying, devouring.

I was mesmerized.

Strong hands suddenly gripped my arm—Asher's? Emilio's? I had no way of knowing. Snapping out of my near-trance, I grabbed my sister's hand, and all of us charged for the door.

Just like the monsters in the office, the hybrids in the corridors seemed bent on self-destruction, their bone-chilling screams of agony providing the gory soundtrack to our escape. After a quick head count, we rushed down the main corridor, back through the prison chamber, up the winding staircase to the mausoleum.

I didn't dare let go of Haley. Didn't dare open my eyes. Not until the pounding of my heart subsided, and I finally felt the sweet relief of snowflakes melting on my cheeks.

FORTY-FIVE

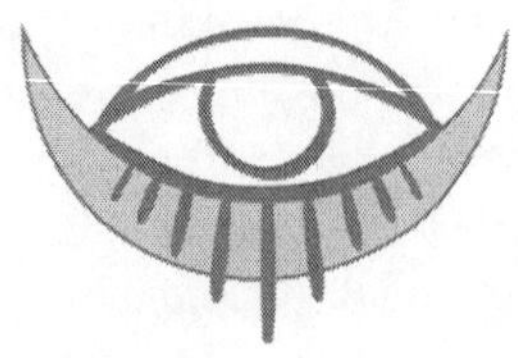

LIAM

Sitting on a bench on the outer perimeter of the cemetery, I cupped my palm, mesmerized by the snowflakes melting against my skin.

Snow felt different now. The warmth of Gray's presence beside me felt different. My heartbeat felt different.

Everything felt different.

"I'd all but forgotten what it meant to be human," I said softly. "I used to think humanity was destined to fail, and that my responsibility in escorting your souls out of these vessels and into the Shadowrealm was a kindness as much as a duty. What, after all, was the point of all this so-called living?" I shook my head, my very human breath condensing before me. "What a fool I've been."

Gray leaned her head on my shoulder, and I turned to press a kiss to her crown.

"And now?" she asked. "Do you still wonder what the point is?"

I left her question hanging in the cool air between us, where it lingered a moment longer before drifting away in the breeze.

The tribunal had ended. I'd been permanently banished here, all remaining powers stripped. I'd no longer be able to shift into my avian forms, no longer see a thousand upon a thousand upon a thousand possible outcomes. I was vulnerable now, just as any other man. Powerless but for that which I drew from within.

I'd been condemned to the fate of humanity, possibly condemning humanity in the process.

For with my banishment and the permanent dissolution of my duties, there would be no Death. No transformation, as I'd warned them before. Winter had already begun its deadly dance, but soon it would spread. Soon the restless souls would gather. Soon the hauntings would begin.

The Old One had offered only one alternative, only one service for which they'd grant a full reversal of this curse: I must sacrifice another Shadowborn witch, forcing upon her the mantle I'd once so proudly carried.

The refusal was on my lips before they'd even finished the proclamation.

Their only concession, their only grace, was in allowing me to serve out my remaining days as a mortal man in the company of the woman I loved, for as long as she would have me.

I'd explained all of this to her as we sat on our bench, watching the others make arrangements for the return to base-camp. They'd managed to salvage some of the intelligence they'd found inside, and were organizing that now, along with treating injuries.

Jael's body had not been recovered. When the wolves returned to the corridor to investigate, they found only ashes.

"I would do anything to fix this, Gray," I said now. "Anything."

She didn't say anything for a long moment. And then, just when I thought my human heart would arrest, she tilted her head to meet my gaze, and a soft smile touched her lips. "You and I are a lot alike, you know."

"Rule-breakers and seekers of trouble. Defiers of cosmic law." I laughed softly, but Gray's eyes had turned serious.

"People who'd do anything to protect the ones we love," she said. "People who've learned, deep down, the most important lesson." She slipped her hand into mine, melting the last of the snow between our palms. "No matter what the risk, love will *always* be worth it."

She leaned forward, brushing her lips across my mouth in a kiss I felt all the way to my toes. There were no magical sparks this time. Only the ones I felt inside.

I returned her kiss, slowly deepening it, tasting her with a new appreciation for all of life's richness. For all of its blessings.

I kissed her as I'd loved her—without hesitation, without regret, without fear.

When we finally broke apart, I cupped her face, gazing into the depths of her twilight blue eyes.

"I'm in love with you, little witch. So much it makes my heart feel like it's going to go supernova every time you're near me. Is that… Is that normal?"

Gray laughed, her eyes lighting up despite the heaviness of tonight's battles. She pressed a hand to my chest, and I covered it with my own, feeling the frantic pounding of my heart through both.

"It's normal," she said. "I'd say you get used to it, but you don't. And that's a good thing."

"I shall take your word for it."

Silence drifted between us once again, and in the calm, I spoke the words in my heart.

"I cannot say I've come to this banishment unwillingly," I said. "For I've longed to return to my human form, to live out the remainder of my days as a mortal. But I would not have wished this upon you. Upon any of you. My one regret, Gray, is that when I am gone from this realm, you and those who carry on your legacy will still be dealing with this fallout. Yes, I will die, and without another to carry on the sacred duties, my soul will be as cursed as all the rest. But in so many ways, I am getting the easy way out."

"No, Liam. You're not." She shook her head, staring at me as if I'd just spoken the most ridiculous words known to man. "You gave up your life for me. For Emilio. For us to have another chance at life and love. You gave up your eternal soul. And you did it all over again when they gave you a chance at redemption, and you turned them down."

"I will not sacrifice another."

"I know. And in that refusal, you gave up absolutely everything."

I took her face in my hands, pressing another kiss to her lips. "And I will do so again," I whispered. "For as long as I have something left to give, for as long as I am here to give it."

"Okay," she said firmly, rising from the bench and brushing the snow from her legs. "Here's the deal, Colebrook. I love you, too. Don't ask me how it happened, because there are too many little moments, too many conversations, too much anger, too much laughter, too many sparks. But it *did* happen. You're as much a part of this family as the rest of us. And that means you're bound to us, and we're bound to you, and mortal or not, you're not going *anywhere* without us. We won't give you up without a fight. We won't give *any* of this up without a fight."

She turned to head back down the path.

"Where are you going?" I asked.

"To make damn sure we win this fight, and the next one, and every single one we're facing after that. Because guess what? This little witch still has something left to give, too."

FORTY-SIX

GRAY

I trudged through the snow, back the way Liam and I had come, back to the mausoleum. The injuries had all been treated, and now the group huddled together, checking over the liberated prisoners one last time. Haley had her arm around Adele, their heads bent together, both of them sitting on the mausoleum steps. Adele's eyes were closed, but some of the color had returned to her cheeks.

Haley's eyes were haunted. She hadn't wanted to talk about the blood spell she'd done, about what dark energies she'd called upon, about what it would mean for her later.

About what it would mean for any of us.

But I knew she'd sacrificed something important.

Just like Liam had done. Just like Jael had done. Just like the prisoners had done. Just like everyone from our group had done—all the brave witches and allies and my strong, beautiful rebels standing before me. Every single one of them had put their lives on the line, making their own personal and private sacrifices, all because I'd asked them to follow me into the darkness, and they'd come without question.

I hadn't guaranteed them a victory. Hadn't even guaranteed their survival. Yet they'd put their trust and faith in me, and they'd come anyway.

Now it was my turn to step out over that endless void, to leap with no guarantee of a net below. To be bold and brave. To trust that I was making the right decision—not just for me, but for all the witches I'd led here. The ones I'd yet to meet. To unite. For the men who would give their lives for me. The men who'd already given me their hearts.

We'd lost a friend tonight. A man who died protecting us, honoring the memory of the woman he loved—my best friend.

We'd fought a ravenous army of vampire-shifter hybrids, terrifying and brutal, yet no more than a fraction of the size and skill of the armies that likely awaited us in the Bay. That may also be waiting in the shadows of other cities, in other countries, their masters counting down to Armageddon.

We'd discovered that my mother was the mastermind behind a worldwide supernatural conspiracy that left the fate of humankind hanging in the balance, and my sister—a sister whose existence I'd only just discovered—was doing her bidding.

We'd liberated another sister, who—along with other witches and supernaturals—was fighting her way back from the edge of death, and would heal from her physical wounds only to unleash the horror of all the emotional torments she'd endured at the hands and direction of our mother.

And Haley… I had no idea what was in store for her, but from the haunted look in her eyes, I knew it wasn't going to be pleasant or easy.

Despite all we'd lost, all we'd endured, there were still so many battles to face. Still so many nasty surprises on the horizon.

I closed my eyes, recalling the moment of utter powerlessness I'd felt at the hands of that hybrid. I'd felt his thoughts, seen the glint of blood on his fangs. His breath had misted on my cheeks, and in that moment, I'd known it was the breath of death.

If not for Liam, I wouldn't be standing here.

I didn't know what awaited us around the next corner. But I did know this: I would *not* be made to feel that way again.

It was in our blood, I realized. The key to everything.

Darius's blood had healed me in the Shadowrealm, and my blood had begun to restore his memories. With help from my magic, Asher's blood had built up an immunity to Jonathan's devil's trap nanotech. Haley's blood had saved us tonight, causing our enemies to turn on each other. Silversbane blood had brought us together, had led us to our other sisters, had carried the legacy of our magic from one generation to the next.

Silversbane blood had allowed my mother—a witch—to survive the change and become a vampire.

And it would do the same for me.

FORTY-SEVEN

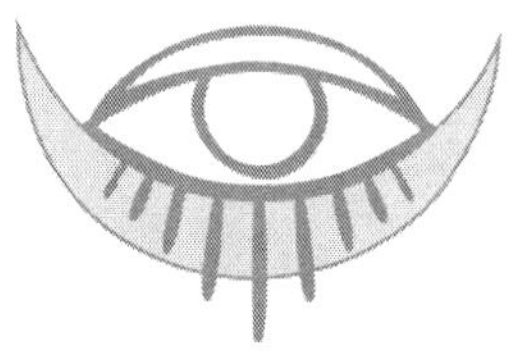

GRAY

"Out of the question." Darius folded his arms over his chest, his mouth pressed into a grim line.

Lined up inside the mausoleum, Asher, Ronan, and Emilio stood at his side, the fire in their eyes smoldering, the stiffness in their muscles telling me exactly where they stood on the matter.

Only Liam stood at my back. Only Liam understood.

"I'm asking you to give me the strength to protect myself," I said. "The power. The freedom of choice."

"You're asking me to condemn you to a life of blood and death," he snarled. "You will lose your soul, Gray. I cannot—I *will* not facilitate that."

"I won't lose my soul." I placed my hand over his heart, offering a tender smile. "My soul is here. With you. All of you. As long as we're together in this world, it—"

"No, Gray." He grabbed my wrist, his grip almost painful. Anger coursed through his blood, making his skin hot. "That's not enough. As far as I'm concerned, this world doesn't even exist without you. *You* are the beating heart of it, love. *Our* beating heart. If we lose you, none of it is worth it. There's no more fight. No more reason."

"My soul is promised to Sebastian!" I shouted.

How many more times would we have to go over this? Why couldn't they understand?

"There are two outcomes here, guys," I continued. "Only two. Either we lose this war, and I die fighting, because I'm not immortal like Darius and Ronan and Ash. Or by some miracle, we win, and after all the dust settles, Sebastian shows up to collect on my contract. I'll never see any of you again. Don't you get that?"

"You don't need immortality," Darius said. "You've got magic, and—"

"My magic isn't enough. You saw what happened in there tonight. If it wasn't for Liam, I'd already be gone. I need strength. Speed. Predatory instincts. There's a full-on war coming to our doorstep, Darius—"

"One you don't have to fight alone." He gestured beyond the flagstone path to the spot where the rest of the group had gathered, waiting for us to take them back to camp. "All those witches out there—"

"They're depending on me to lead them! To rise up and claim my legacy!"

"And you *will*. You'll rise up like the witch you are. That power is already inside you, Gray."

"It sounds nice, doesn't it?" I asked. "Like something you could print on a T-shirt or make into an internet meme, right? But the reality is... We don't stand a chance. Not a real one, not for the long haul. How many more nights like this can we take? Jael is dead. Everyone else is beat up and exhausted. And we haven't even scratched the surface of what's coming. We're lucky we survived the night. How do you think Blackmoon Bay is going to roll out? And that's assuming we can even get there in time."

I clutched my head in my hands, drawing a deep breath, trying to dial down the anger. I didn't want to fight them on this. I just wanted to make them understand. To feel the rightness of this. To grant me my choice.

"I know what I'm asking you to do," I said. "I know the risks. But for the first time since I was a little kid, I have real faith in my magic. In my intuition. And most importantly, in my blood. My mother survived the change because she's Silversbane, just like me."

"You don't know that's what allowed her to survive," Darius said. "There could be any number of reasons—"

"There *could* be, but there aren't." I pressed my hands to my chest, the magic rising to the surface, pulsing against my palms. "I can *feel* the rightness in this. *This* is my path. Please, Darius. I want this, but I won't do it without your support." I turned to look at each of them, imploring them. "That goes for all of you. I'm asking you to back me up on this. I'm asking you to trust that I know what's right for myself, for my body. I'm asking you to trust *me*."

"You *will* lose your soul," Darius said again, but his resolve was finally weakening, and I smiled, shining a light through the tiny crack he'd left behind.

"Actually, my soul might have another option." I looked at Liam as a new idea dawned and rose inside me like the sun, fresh hope filling my chest, bolstering my plan.

Liam understood my intention immediately, but his eyes dimmed, and he shook his head. "I would do anything for you, Gray. But I'm fully human now. I no longer possess the power to create moonglass or to guide your soul into its orb."

"Perhaps not," a voice echoed from beyond the shadows of the mausoleum, and we all turned toward the sound. Weak and bloodied, burned and weary, but alive, Jael stepped through the doorway at the top of the stairs, his yellow eyes glittering in the darkness. "But I do."

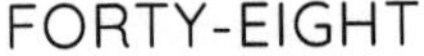

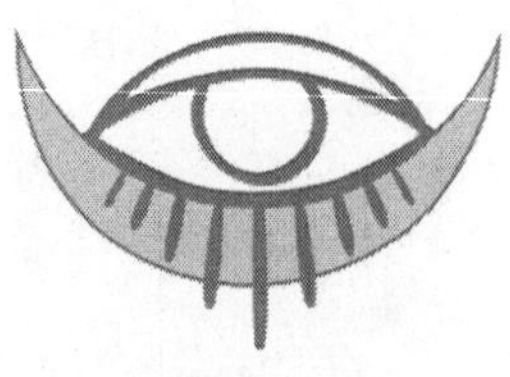

GRAY

We'd been blessed with a full moon, and now Jael stood in the center of the cemetery, snow falling on his shoulders, an opalescent orb glowing in his hands. "It is time, Gray."

Asher. Emilio. Liam. Ronan. Darius. Each one stood before me, their eyes filled with secrets and emotions and all the things they hadn't said. There hadn't been time.

But we didn't need words. The love and trust we shared transcended every last one.

What they'd given me tonight was a precious gift: their trust and support. Their unconditional love. I wouldn't squander it.

I stood before Asher, claiming his mouth in a kiss that burned all the way to my toes, giving in to the familiar call of his incubus hunger, offering him one more dose of my magic.

I moved on to Emilio, who blinked back tears, enveloping me in a bear hug that infused me with strength.

Liam was next, a shy smile that turned into a passionate kiss the moment our lips met.

When I got to Ronan, the demon held my gaze, unwavering, his eyes saying a million things. He didn't want this for me. None of them did. But he would stand by my decision no matter what. He was my first love, my best friend. And no curse or transformation or war would ever change that.

Swallowing the tightness in my throat, I took a chance and

pressed my lips to his, both of us ignoring the burn, just for a moment.

And then there was Darius. My vampire. We'd shared so much already, come through so much. And there was so much more to do, to see, to reclaim.

I smiled at him, and stood up on my toes, my lips brushing his ear.

"You're still taking me to New York after all this," I teased. And then I kissed him, deep and delicious, his whiskey-and-leather scent enveloping me once again.

We broke our kiss, and Darius pierced the skin on his wrist, pressing it to my mouth, gently holding my head against it. I closed my eyes and drank, letting the richness fill me, warm me.

Too soon, he pulled away.

And then he spun me around, my back against his chest, and swept the curls off my nape.

In front of us, Ronan gave a single nod.

The vampire's mouth descended on my flesh.

I cried out as his fangs pierced my skin, deep and deadly, their purpose singular. The pain was fierce, delicious, intense, my head spinning as he began to suck.

I don't know how much time passed, how long he drank from me, because for me, time stopped. There was no yesterday, no tomorrow. Nothing but the heat of his lips, the pure pleasure of the bite.

I tried to stay conscious, tried to hold on to everything about the moment, to follow the pleasure to its logical end. But a numbness spread throughout my body, and from my mouth, a cloud of gossamer smoke emerged, a deep and velvet gray, shot through with bright silver threads and indigo points of light.

My soul.

The iridescent pulse of the moonglass loomed large before my eyes, and I finally gave in to the numbness, letting it sweep me out of the snow-blanketed night, far and away to another world where pain no longer existed and everything was blissfully, unapologetically black.

* * *

When darkness descends, who will survive the Battle for Blackmoon Bay? ***Rebel Reborn,*** the sixth and final book in the Witch's Rebels series, is waiting for you! Read on to find out what happens!

* * *

REBEL REBORN

BOOK SIX

ONE

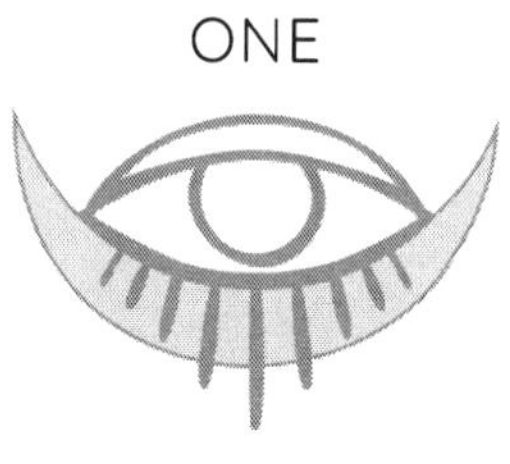

DARIUS

From the moment my fangs pierced her flesh, I knew only her blood on my lips, the warm and salty taste of it bursting across my tongue as it slowly filled my mouth. I swallowed once, twice, unable to stifle a groan of raw pleasure as I continued to suck.

A flame flickered to life inside my chest, then ignited.

I was burning. Raging.

All for her. My witch. My love. My eternal mate, in this lifetime and all that would follow.

I would die for you, Gray Desario…

The words escaped my lips unbidden as I finally broke our connection, forcing the orgasmic flames in my blood to smolder, ignoring the ache in my very being that so desperately wanted more. That would *always* want more when it came to Gray. But she hadn't yet turned; some part of me knew that if I took even a single swallow more, I would certainly kill her.

I lifted her off the ground and held her against my chest, burying my face in her hair, inhaling her scent. The gray mist of her soul had already slipped from between her lips, and now it floated freely, mesmerizing us all.

Jael whispered his fae magic, the very cadence of it so lovely it seemed to be weaving a spell around my heart as well. Slowly, peacefully, Gray's soul drifted toward the moonglass held reverently in the fae prince's hands.

"Holy shit," Asher whispered, and we continued to watch in awe as the essence of the woman we loved filled the glass sphere like smoke caught in a bottle, light pulsing from its misty depths.

Even the very winter's night seemed to be holding its breath until the last wisp of her soul was safely contained, and Jael sealed the glass and lifted his hands toward the moon, thanking her.

Tears streaked Liam's face, his wide, blue eyes like twin orbs in the dim. Gone was the omnipotent, ancient being we'd come to know as Death; he seemed in that moment quite young, and quite human.

His origins, his mysteries remained his and his alone. But there was one secret even the Great Transformation Himself could no longer hide:

He'd fallen in love with her.

I averted my gaze, feeling the need to give him privacy.

The woods surrounding our moonlit cemetery had gone silent during the spell. Before we'd begun, we'd sent the remainder of the group back to base camp under the protection of Elena, her shifter team, and one of Gray's hounds. The other paced a perimeter twenty feet out, keeping one ever-watchful eye on Gray, the other on the darkness beyond.

Snow continued to fall all around us, collecting in tiny drifts on the headstones, filling in our blood-soaked boot prints, erasing all evidence of our earlier battle. Gray's body began to tremble in my arms, but that was to be expected; the transition was never easy.

"It is done," Jael said softly, bringing the orb close against his chest. We locked eyes in that moment, mirror images, each one cradling a precious piece of the woman I loved.

I nodded, and he bowed his head in acknowledgment.

It was a moment of peace and understanding in an otherwise treacherous night, and everyone seemed to feel it at the same time, all of us releasing a collective sigh.

Then the others looked to me, to the woman lying limp in my arms.

"She *will* survive the change," I said, even as the tremor continued to snake through her body, even as the white mist of her breath ceased, her lungs no longer requiring air. "I can feel the life force inside of her. She's stronger than any of us ever realized."

"Stubborn as hell, too," Emilio said, and the rest of us let out a quick laugh. Stubborn as hell? Yes, that about summed it up. Who else could've talked us into undertaking such a risk but the fiercely beautiful, determined, impossibly stubborn witch we'd all fallen in love with?

Lowering my eyes to the moonglass in Jael's hands, I asked, "What of her soul?"

I was as desperate for the answer as I was afraid of it. Caught up in the intensity of Gray's plan, none of us had stopped to talk through the logistics of what would come after. By the time we'd agreed to support her plan, it had been enough to know that her soul would not be instantly damned.

But now?

"I must take her to my home realm," Jael said plainly. "It's the only safe place for her now. My family will protect the moonglass until it comes time for her to honor the contract with Sebastian."

"Your *family*?" Ronan's eyes turned demon black, his shoulders bunching with tension. "And what happens when the wind changes direction, and Queen Sheyah decides it's a fine day to stab us in the nuts?"

"My mother may be cold and calculating," Jael said, "but she's not cruel, nor is she a traitor to her blood. She will honor my wishes, Ronan. You have my word."

"Jael, there is *no* room for error on this," Emilio said firmly. "No room for petty squabbles, judgments, or old vendettas. This is Gray's *soul*. Should it fall into the wrong hands, even in your realm…"

The wolf trailed off, turning his face toward the moonlight, casting the new worry lines around his eyes into sharp relief.

I couldn't blame him. I didn't know which vendettas he referred to, but I didn't need specifics. The Seelie queen was a notoriously conniving woman; she never formed an alliance unless there was something in it for her, and like most bargains struck at an hour of desperation, her allegiance never came without cost.

I suspected she was one of the reasons—if not *the* reason—Jael and Kallayna had left their realm and made a new home in the Bay in the first place. Now Jael wanted to bring Gray's soul back there? Under the protection of the woman who—if the centuries-old rumors held even a whiff of truth—had once burned an entire village of humans and their livestock on the mere *suspicion* that they'd been harboring a runaway fae child?

"I have given you my *word*." Jael's yellow eyes glowed fiercely, his brow drawn tight. "Never mind that Gray has become important to me as a leader, a warrior, as well as a friend. Her soul will be well-protected. I shall give my life to that end, if it comes to it."

"You've been more than loyal, prince," Liam said.

"It's not his loyalty we're worried about," Asher said. "It's that whole 'if it comes to it' part."

"It *won't* come to it," Jael insisted, but I wasn't convinced. None of us were, and in the uncertain silence that followed, the fae prince finally exploded.

"Gentlemen," he began, his voice full of fire, "I have risked my sister's life and my own to bring you intelligence from the Bay. I have fought by your sides in battles I could just as well have left behind, narrowly escaping an army of hybrids intent on burning me alive and nearly succeeding. I have risked eternal banishment from all the realms by calling upon forbidden moon magic, all in service to the woman I've come to call a close friend. I did not take such actions only to betray her at the very last."

"Jael," I began, but he would not relent, his entire body tense but for his hands, in which he held the moonglass as gently as a soap bubble.

"I would not take her within a *galaxy* of my realm if I believed for one moment my family would bring her harm." Jael's voice shook with defiance. "I understand your concern for her, but I beseech you to take an accurate accounting of my proven fidelity before accusing me *or* my family of future treasons."

Emilio lifted his palms in a gesture of peace, but Ronan and Asher were still wound up.

That Jael believed he could protect her was obvious. But could we really trust Queen Sheyah, regardless of Jael's noble intentions? And what of her royal guard, her servants, her subjects? When had Jael last communicated with his family? How could he be certain he'd even find welcome in his realm, let alone protection for the soul of a human witch-turned-vampire he'd just risked his own eternal existence to save?

I closed my eyes and pulled Gray tight against my chest, my blood humming in recognition at the blood now flowing through her veins. We were beyond connected, beyond bound, beyond mated.

We were one.

Trust him…

The message was faint but clear, imprinted from one vampire mind to another. The realization nearly made me weep.

She truly was assimilating.

Unconscious as her body was, Gray's mind was right here with us—right here with me. She trusted Jael. And as much as I hated the idea of letting her soul out of our sight, I knew what Gray had known from the very moment she'd made the decision to turn:

There were no other options.

Opening my eyes, I looked from Ronan to Emilio to Asher to Liam, nodding at each before my gaze finally came to rest on Jael's still-smoldering yellow eyes.

"Gray entrusted you with the extraction and guidance of her soul," I said, granting him the same small bow he'd offered me earlier. "We entrust you now to protect it in whatever way you deem best."

Ronan blew out a tense breath, but no one said a word to contradict me. We'd all come together to support Gray in her decision to change, and that—like so many things we'd done and shared together on this journey, whether I could remember the particulars or not—bonded us once again as brothers.

Jael wasted no more time.

"We must move quickly," he said, "while night still holds. I need to draw upon the moon's power once more, if she'll allow it, and weave a portal spell to open a doorway back to my realm."

"How long will it take?" I asked, eyeing the expanse above the snowy treetops. The sky was still inky black, but soon enough the sun would begin her ascent. I'd very much prefer Gray and I were back at basecamp with time to spare before the first rays touched the earth.

"Can you guarantee me complete silence and zero interruptions?" He headed off to find a clear spot beyond the headstones. He knelt upon the snow, nestling the moonglass into a downy drift at his side. "If so, it shouldn't take more than—"

The rest of his words cut off abruptly as a blinding pain split my skull.

It unfolded like a car crash—time slowing for an eternity before zooming forward, leaving my mind in a frenzied blur, uncertain where one moment ended and another began.

The agony and confusion brought me to my knees.

It was all I could do to shield Gray from the impact as we hit the ground, my head spinning.

"Beaumont!" Ronan shouted, but I couldn't see him, barely registering the motion of his body lunging for me. Someone else scooped up Gray, and I bent forward and pressed my forehead against the snow, desperate for something—anything—to numb the pain.

Useless.

My body shook, head to toe, the tremble so violent I bit my tongue. Blood filled my mouth, and the walls inside my mind burst like ancient dams, ushering in a flood of disconnected images and sounds and scents, each one unlocking another and another and another, slicing through me like hot blades. Arms and legs wild with spasms, I roared into the night, unable to contain the torment, certain my ears were bleeding.

"Darius? What's happening?" Someone was at my side, a warm hand on the back of my neck, another flat on my back. Ronan's? Liam's? I had no idea. There was only the torture unfolding behind my eyes. Only the haunting howl of a thousand ghosts inside my skull. Only the taste of Gray's blood welling up from within.

Only… only memories.

I managed to get to my knees again, and clamped my hands around my head, desperately trying to keep my skull from exploding. A flurry of images and sights and sounds poured unbidden into my mind, imprinting themselves all at once, disconnected and fragmented, but… but *mine,* I realized suddenly. Every last one of them was mine—flashes of the life I'd lived and lost, the lifetimes I'd rebuilt in the decades and centuries that followed.

Memories.

Memories of my wife and children, the family I'd mourned on so many long, lonely nights.

Memories of my brother, my turning, the anger that had burned like hot coals inside my chest when he'd stolen my mortal life.

Memories of friends come and gone, of careers, of homes.

Memories of everything I'd once loved.

And then—impossibly sweet, impossibly precious—memories of a brand new love, unfolding as gently as a spring bud, then rapidly growing into a flowering vine that had somehow crept in behind my walls and blossomed, wrapping itself so thoroughly around my heart I could scarcely remember a time when it hadn't been part of me, nor I part of it.

Gray. My witch. My little brawler. My vampire. My queen.

I remembered the night we'd spent in the cabin in the Shadowrealm, making love until we'd nearly no strength left in our bones, chasing away the cold with kisses and caresses. I remembered the heartbreak in her eyes as I told her how I'd been turned. I remembered the taste of her kiss, the promises inherent in each and every one.

I remembered the words she'd uttered so breathlessly at the mouth of the hell portal.

I love you, Darius…

I remembered my own words sliding into my consciousness, balancing on the tip of my tongue, desperate to be heard.

It seems I've fallen in…

The last had remained locked inside, stowed away as we came under attack from the demons that would steal my memories—memories that had just been returned to me.

Gray had saved me in all the ways that counted—then and now.

Her blood, our connection… she'd been right to trust it.

I would never doubt it.

My love for her knew no limits, no bounds, and deep inside me, that feeling expanded endlessly, chasing away the worst of the pain, steadying my hands. I was falling, experiencing each moment with her for the very first time, again and again and again.

"I'm in love with her," I announced, my tears turning to laughter as I felt the force of that love hit me full on. With Ronan's help, I got to my feet, swaying against his side. I was unsteady, but suddenly I felt unstoppable.

"For fuck's sake, Beaumont." Ronan gave me a shove. "We thought you were dying, asshole."

"Ah, but I was. And now I've been reborn!" Again I laughed, bordering on maniacal, and grabbed his shoulders, hauling him in for a fierce hug. "You don't understand, demon. I fell in *love* with her. I know I did."

"Yeah, you and me and everyone here." He pulled back and narrowed his eyes at me. "What's going on in that head of yours?"

"More than you know, friend," I said. "I *remember* it. All of it. All of you!"

Ronan glared at me a moment longer, then his eyes widened as the realization finally dawned. He gripped my arms, a smile cracking his stoic face. "You're shitting me. You fucking remember?"

"It must've been the—"

"Hate to break up the lovefest, but, uh…" Asher crouched

down next to Sparkle and followed her line of sight to a dense copse of trees beyond the cemetery. The hound's haunches were raised, a menacing growl reverberating from her chest.

Asher got to his feet and rolled his neck, the bones cracking. "Fight or flight, assholes. We got company."

TWO

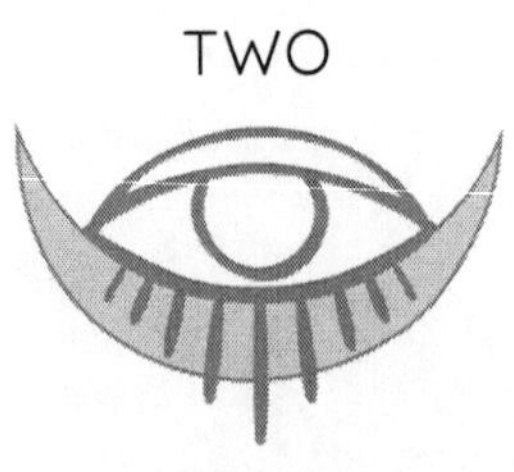

DARIUS

"Sellouts." Asher spat at the ground, leaving a smattering of blood in the snow. His jaw was red and swollen where he'd taken a hit, and his blue eyes blazed in the darkness, the adrenaline from the fight still zipping through his blood. "My guess? The inside team called for reinforcements, but these fucks wanted no part of it. They took their time getting here like a bunch of pussies, waiting until our numbers thinned out and the spellcasters left so they could get the drop on the rest of us."

"Agreed." I bent down to scoop up a handful of snow, using it to rinse the taste of hunter blood from my mouth. After the incident at the motel when I'd attacked two of them and overdosed—a brutal scene I now remembered with utmost clarity—I refused to swallow even a drop of their bitter poison.

There'd been about a dozen of them tonight, all human, hiding out in the dense trees and waiting to make their move. They'd underestimated us, though, as hunters with big egos and small pricks were wont to do. With Gray's loyal hound leading the charge and Emilio's wolf a close second, we'd left Liam to watch over Jael and Gray, bolted into the woods, and sliced through their ranks like a hot knife through butter.

Back on the other side of the cemetery, Jael continued to work on the portal spell, Liam doing his best to stand guard. He'd wrapped Gray in another cloak, and now he held her close, stroking her hair. The sight brought me comfort.

Liam was one of us now.

We're definitely *going to need a bigger bed…*

"You think we're in the clear?" Ronan asked, reclaiming my attention.

I turned to see him rubbing snow into his hands in an attempt to clean the blood. Moments earlier, when the last hunter standing had given us a rather detailed account of what he'd been planning to do to our witch, I'd watched with delight—and a good measure of awe—as Ronan tore out the bastard's throat with his bare hands.

I scanned the woods behind him, taking in as much sensory detail as I could. Save for our movements, the night had fallen silent once again. The air was tinged with the scent of human blood, but if any hunters had survived our attack, they'd scampered back the way they'd come.

"The last of the rats have either expired or fled back to their cages," I confirmed.

"For now," Asher said. "But we're still exposed out here. Gray's immobilized, Liam's got no defensive powers, we can't risk anything happening to the moonglass, and we have *no* idea what other surprises are waiting for us in the woods."

"You think there are more fae out there?" Ronan asked.

Hunters were one thing; relatively easy to contain, they didn't stand a chance against a vampire, a wolf, a hellhound, and a pair of demons. But the dark fae could present a serious challenge—especially if there were a lot of them.

"Unlikely," Asher said. "The fae aren't fucking cowards. If they were anywhere in the vicinity, they'd already be on top of us. Nah, I'm more concerned about hunters playing games. We're stronger and faster, but that doesn't mean they can't fuck with us. Sun's not too far off now, and like I said, Gray and Liam are basically sitting ducks. They need to get the fuck back to the lodge. You too, Beaumont."

I nodded, conceding the point. All the vampire strength and

speed in the world couldn't compete with a sunrise. "But we're not going anywhere until Jael—"

The force of the explosion knocked us to the ground, the light blinding.

"What the *fuck*?" Ronan shouted. We got to our feet and shook off the impact, trying to see through the thick blanket of smoke engulfing the entire cemetery.

Seconds later, Liam walked out of the smoke like an apparition, carrying the still-unconscious Gray.

A bolt of horror pierced my heart.

"Where is the moonglass?" I demanded.

But Liam seemed unfazed, his eyes cold and mysterious once again, just like his voice. "Jael has completed his mission."

"Successfully?" I asked.

"He and the moonglass have vanished, along with all signs of the portal."

"I'll count that as a win," Asher said.

"He could've been a bit more subtle about it," I snapped, brushing the snow from my backside. But with Gray's soul safely out of harm's way, and her body still whole, still assimilating, it was nearly impossible to hold onto my anger. By the time Liam placed her back in my arms, there wasn't even room inside me for mild annoyance. Her presence immediately calmed me, steadied me, and again I buried my face in her hair, taking in her scent.

She was still unconscious, which was a blessing. Yes, her mother had survived the turning. But Gray was the first witch I'd ever personally known to survive the change—to begin the assimilation process. I had no idea how her body would react once it completed the transition—I only knew that she'd be hungry. Ravenous.

We needed to get her secured and sedated before she became conscious of that.

Holding her tightly against my chest, I nodded toward a clearing in the distance—our way out. "We've still got a bit of a trek ahead of us, and it looks like the snow is picking up again." I stepped over the blood-soaked body of one of the hunters we'd dispatched. "Let's just hope this was the last and only ambush."

"Hope isn't a viable strategy, bloodsucker." Asher spit out another mouthful of blood, then rubbed his swollen jaw and sighed, exhausted but resolute. He looked to Ronan, as if asking permission.

"Do what you gotta do, brother." Ronan clapped him on the back, then whistled for the hound, who bounded out of the dense knot of trees, her fangs and muzzle dripping with hunter blood. Seemed Ronan had interrupted her midnight snack, but if she harbored any resentment, she wasn't showing it. She pressed her nose against Ronan's leg, and he reached down to scratch behind her ears.

"What is it you have to do?" I asked Asher.

"Tie up a few loose ends." Gesturing for the wolf, he said, "*El Lobo* and I will meet you guys back at the lodge in the morning. Don't wait up."

"Where in the bloody hell are you going?" I asked.

At this, Emilio cocked back his massive furry head and howled at the moon, his battle cry haunting and clear, a chilling warning to all who'd dare cross his path tonight.

Asher flashed a feral grin, teeth glinting in the moonlight. "We're going hunting, brother. Take care of our girl."

THREE

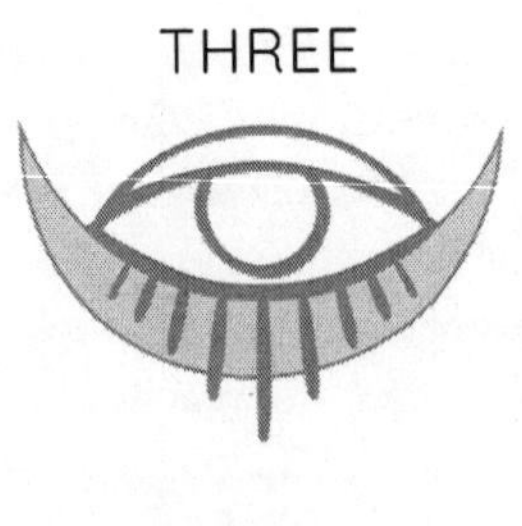

GRAY

So. Much. Blood.

The taste of it in my mouth, the smell of it in my nose, the viscous feel of it sliding deliciously across my tongue. My veins hummed with it, magic and power and strength, all of it crackling to life with a fierce intensity that made me feel like I could burn down the world with little more than a pointed glare.

I was born for this…

Flat on my back in nothing more than a T-shirt, underwear, and a thin sheet over my legs, I opened my eyes to complete darkness and tried to sit up. My body refused to obey. The blood inside me was buzzing and alive, my senses finely attuned, but my muscles felt slow and sluggish.

I sucked in a cool breath—the first I'd taken since I'd awoken—and realized at once we'd made it back to HQ. I could smell the familiar mix of salty ocean air and fresh-cut wood from the lodge's timber framing, and the scents of all the witches and men and shifters who'd occupied it, every one of them clear and distinct. Strongest of all was Darius's—that heady blend of leather and expensive whiskey that always made my blood sing.

Again, I tried to rise.

No luck.

My belly turned over with a terrible growl, empty. Craving. Demanding.

"You're hungry," announced a familiar voice, and slowly I turned my head to find my vampire standing near my bedside, still as the darkness itself. My eyes had already adjusted to the lack of light, and now I saw him as clearly as if he were bathed in afternoon sunlight. I blinked, not believing it, but the shape of him only sharpened—glossy dark hair, full lips that made my thighs clench with fresh, hot desire. His eyes narrowed as he took me in, his honey-brown gaze both tender and severe.

"Darius," I whispered, but there was no time to wonder about his breathtaking beauty or my enhanced vision. My stomach turned over again, bringing with it a wave of nausea so severe it made me gasp.

I needed to move, to feed, and again I tried to sit up, but the firm, comforting press of his palm against my chest steadied me. I hadn't seen the movement, but now he was standing right next to me, the scent of him nearly overpowering my senses.

I wanted him. Badly. My mouth watered for it, my core suddenly burning with the unquenched flames of desire. Everything inside me craved his touch.

My hunger for him was even more desperate than my hunger for blood.

I'm going to die without it...

"What's.... happening to me?" I sputtered. "I feel like... like I'm..." I tried to reach for him, but my arms were locked in place, immobilized despite the fact that my skin felt like it was on fire.

No, not immobilized. Restrained, I saw now. Same with my legs and torso. I tugged hard against the binds—thick leather straps fastened tightly around my wrists, ankles, and across my lower rib cage.

They'd tied me to the bed. Under any other circumstances, I might've been turned on by the idea. Now, it just made me rage inside.

Still. I knew it had to be done. After all, I was a deadly predator now, recovering in a lodge full of warm bodies, every single one of them pulsing with thick, sweet blood.

A whimper escaped my lips.

"It's temporary," Darius assured me, his voice measured and

tight. "Once we've regulated your blood intake and weened you off the hawthorn infusion, this arrangement won't be necessary."

"Infusion?"

He lifted the sheet covering my legs, revealing an IV taped to the top of my foot. I followed the tube to the bag dangling from the poster at the end of the bed, slowly meting out a clear liquid drip.

"It's on a time-release," he said.

Well, that explained the sluggishness I was feeling.

"After our return," he said, "I bathed you and helped you get settled in here. I've been with you ever since."

"Ever since when? How long was I out? Is everyone else okay? What about Jael? My sisters? Sparkle and Sunshine?"

"One question at a time, little brawler." Darius let out a low chuckle. "Let's see… Everyone is present and accounted for. Your sisters are well, chomping at the bit to see you, though we all agreed it would be best for the humans of the household to wait until you've fully stabilized before visiting. The hounds have scarcely left your side—I had to bribe them with raw steak just to get a few moments alone with you tonight. We've not heard from Jael, but he completed the portal spell and disappeared with your moonglass before we left the cemetery that night, and the queen has not declared war upon us, so we're assuming no news is good news on that front. All of the liberated prisoners are being treated for various medical issues and injuries, but everyone is expected to recover. As for you, you've been in and out of consciousness the better part of two days. This is the first time you've managed to stay with me for more than a few moments—speaking, besides."

My head was spinning. "Two *days*? I feel like I haven't eaten in months."

"Hours, actually." He rolled up his sleeve, revealing a muscled forearm and a wrist covered with punctures, dark bruises welling angrily beneath the skin.

The sight of it made me wince. For Darius to bruise and not immediately heal, I must've been pretty brutal, and I must've taken a lot from him.

"I'm sorry," I whispered.

"It's nothing, love. Few more hours, I'll be good as new. But my blood is a stopgap—not nearly enough to sustain you. You need non-vampire blood—preferably human. Quite a bit of it, at that."

My stomach growled again, and Darius replaced his palm on my chest, as if he'd sensed I needed his touch, needed him to keep me from slipping away. I closed my eyes and tried to ignore the parched feeling in my mouth, focusing instead on the rest of my body. My blood, singing and alive. My magic, crackling as always inside me, but more solid and sure than it'd ever felt before. I could hear laughter down on the first floor, the sounds of cooking in the kitchen, the splatter of wet snow against the windowpanes. The curtains were open to let in the moonlight, but the night was dark and cloudy. When I inhaled, the wisdom of the sea filled my senses, sharp and ancient and as powerful as I felt inside.

My heart now beat more slowly than I remembered, but it was stronger, responding to Darius's touch with a deep familiarity.

"I survived," I said, the word itself bringing forth a rush of laughter. "I survived the turning."

"Yes, it appears your body has fully assimilated the change," he confirmed, his voice thick with a mixture of relief, surprise, and there, lurking just below the rest, a hint of sorrow.

I understood. This hadn't been his choice, after all, and I wasn't out of the woods just yet. Not until I could exist in the presence of others without trying to murder them.

A shudder wracked my body, but instead of passing as I'd expected, it intensified, rolling from head to toe and back up again. My teeth chattered, my fangs cutting through my gums, then sliding back in. Again and again. The taste of my own blood filled my mouth.

"D-D-Darius? What's happening now?"

"Shh, it's alright, love." Darius lifted the sheet and climbed into the bed next to me, his hand sliding under my T-shirt to trace a soft pattern on my belly. "This will pass."

"What is it? Why am I sh-shaking like this?"

"You're a vampire, little brawler," he said plainly. "A hungry one at that. Your instincts are telling you it's time to hunt."

Vampire…

Instincts…

Hunt…

The bed shook with my renewed efforts to escape—instinctual more than logical at this point—but the hawthorn had done its job. I couldn't break the binds.

"We can't grant you your freedom yet, Gray. You're too strong. If that primal part of you takes over, you could—"

"I get it, D," I snapped, but then I closed my eyes, forcing myself to count backward from ten, focusing on the feel of his touch until the tremble finally subsided.

None of this was Darius's fault—he was just doing what he had to do to keep everyone safe, including me. This was my choice, and I had to live with it. Besides, for the power and immortality of a vampire, hunger pangs and a few bouts of the shakes were a small price to pay.

I just hoped the transition period wouldn't last too long. Every hour I wasted in bed was another hour we were leaving Blackmoon Bay in the hands of Orendiel and the hunters.

And in the hands of my mother, a vampire-witch we now knew was the deadly, vulgar head of the world's most poisonous snake.

"My mother killed to feed herself," I said absently, my thoughts drifting back to the darkness of the crypt, the evidence we uncovered there.

"You will not be reduced to such savagery. Elena has reached out to her connection at the local hospital to procure what we need, and at present, our demons and the wolf are braving the weather to retrieve it. You'll have a fresh, humanely-harvested supply very soon."

"What about after? What happens when that runs out?"

"Then we'll find more."

"Darius, you need to eat, too. As will the vampires we rescued, including Fiona. We can't just drain the city's donor supply."

"No, I suppose we can't."

"And until we can figure out how to deal with this winter apocalypse," I said, glancing out the window as a fresh bout of wet snow slapped against the pane, "I'm pretty sure imported goods are in short supply."

"All true," he said, though he seemed completely unconcerned about our predicament.

"At some point, we'll need to—"

"At some point, at one point, another day, tomorrow, next week, next year, next century… All pointless frames of reference for us now."

"How do you figure?"

"Gray, you're an immortal. If you start worrying about everything that can go wrong, everything that can throw a wrench into your day…. Well, there are a hell of a lot more days to worry about now."

I closed my eyes as the brutal wind whipped another wave of slush against the lodge. Darius was right. I had to take things day by day or I'd drive us all mad.

"All things considered," he said, forcing a note of cheer into his voice, "you're handling this extremely well. Much better than most."

I nodded, forcing the desperate gnawing inside me to settle. I knew from the stories I'd heard—not to mention the things Darius had shared about his own turning—that things could've been *so* much worse for me.

"I guess that means I didn't slaughter anyone in the night, right?" I asked, only half-kidding.

"Well, let's see…" He tapped his lips, his tone light and teasing. "As of our last accounting, the casualties stood at four shredded bath towels, one shattered windowpane, an upended china cabinet full of porcelain shards formerly known as priceless antiques, two splintered dining chairs, and a fruitcake Verona was particularly proud of, but the rest of us secretly cheered for *that* loss. Oh, you also punched Asher in the mouth."

"Holy shit, Darius! Are you serious?"

Darius shrugged as if this was all par for the course. "To be fair, he had it coming. Your incubus gets rather mouthy when—"

"But how did I manage to do so much damage? I don't even remember coming home. I don't remember anything after the bite. And I'm tied up, besides!"

"Initially, we thought we could forgo the restraints, relying only on the hawthorn. But you're too strong, Gray. The few times you surfaced into consciousness were brief, but wild. You needed to feed, but my blood left you… Well, it left you a bit mad, to be honest. Asher insisted on trying to reason with you, convinced he could sweet-talk his way past thousands of years of predatory evolution." Darius shook his head, holding back a laugh. "The moment he unfastened one of your restraints, you clocked him."

Now I was laughing, too. The whole scene sounded pretty ridiculous—and one hundred percent Asher. "What did he do then?"

"Complimented your right hook, cursed up a storm, then retreated to a dark corner of the lodge with a bottle of tequila and a bag of frozen peas while I secured your restraints and got you calmed down. He hasn't gotten close since."

"I suppose I'll have to make it up to him at some point."

"I suppose." Darius nuzzled the skin behind my ear with a string of kisses I felt all the way to my toes. "But it seems you're through the worst of it, anyway."

"I hope so."

Most newborn vampires went absolutely wild with bloodlust. Without a present sire to tame them, to guide them through the early part of the change, to feed them and help them see the difference between instinct and choice…

I forced away the thoughts, unwilling to follow them any further. That wasn't going to happen to me. I *did* have a sire. One I trusted with my life.

With my heart.

"So I guess I have to call you *sire* now," I said, another laugh bubbling up as I turned to meet his eyes.

Darius flashed me a sexy smile, tracing his thumb across my bottom lip. "I wouldn't refuse a nickname like that, if you insisted, of course."

"You mean you like it better than D?"

"Hmm. That one *has* grown on me since our halcyon days in the Bay, but only because it's from you." He leaned forward, pressing a chaste kiss to my lips that only left me wanting more. Apparently, it left him wanting more, too. The hot, hard press of his cock against my thigh told me everything I needed to know about that.

I shifted closer to him, as much as I could with the binds, the movement inspiring a low groan from my vampire.

"So what now, *sire*?" I teased.

Darius laughed again, his breath tickling my cheeks. His honey eyes sparkled with a thousand new facets, flecks of other-worldly colors and bottomless depths I was seeing with all new vision.

"Oh, little brawler," he breathed, the length of him growing harder. "First my delivery girl, then my witch, and now my vampire… You really *are* going to be the death of me, in this form or the next."

This form…

It hit me all over again—the magnitude of what we'd done. The magic of it. Sure, I was hungry, but I'd survived the change. I was a fucking *vampire*. A bloodsucker. An immortal supernatural. A fearsome, apex predator.

I must've said all of that out loud, because Darius suddenly laughed and said, "Yes, all of those things and more. So much more."

"Right," I said. "So, *how* is it that I'm not freaking out right now?"

At this, Darius could only shrug. "Because you're *you*, love." He kissed my eyebrow. "Completely baffling." The tip of my nose. "Wholly unusual." Then, just as softly as before, my lips. "An utter mystery, the likes of which none of us will ever fully solve."

I rolled my eyes. "In other words, a total weirdo."

"Yes," he teased, his lips still dangerously close to my mouth. "But you're *our* total weirdo, and that's the important bit."

I longed to touch his face, his hair, his lips. The tremor had returned, but this time it wasn't a side effect of the change. It was a side effect of the sexy, dangerous, seductive vampire in my bed, and the fact that my desire to feel him inside of me had sparked to life once again, smoldering between my thighs.

Why are you next to me instead of on top of me, vampire?

"What is it love?" he asked softly, his voice holding a note of playfulness. He knew damn well what it was, and he was enjoying every minute of tormenting me.

"I feel… hot," I said, my body already beginning to writhe under his intense gaze. "Under my skin. Inside me. Everywhere."

"Is that so?" He ran his finger down the front of my T-shirt to the top edge of my underwear, sliding it back and forth beneath the lace, his touch kindling the embers inside me into a blaze.

"Darius," I whispered, my eyes fluttering closed. "I'm dying."

"And I'm not unsympathetic to your plight." His fingers dipped lower, but not low enough. I arched closer, but he only pulled back, starting the whole torturous process again. He trailed those teasing fingers slowly down my T-shirt, back to the lace, sliding lazily down, down, down… then back out again.

Holy hell, bloodsucker.

"Could've fooled me," I snapped.

"Mmm. I remember the first thirst of a newborn vampire," he said, every word laced with seduction. "The need. Bone-deep, all-consuming, a blinding fire that rages unchecked. It's not just the blood you burn for now, is it?"

I shook my head, my mind and body both unraveling. Vampire influence had no power over another vampire, but Darius's words were having the same effect, winding me tighter, leaving me wet and aching for his mouth between my thighs.

"I cannot feed you," he said, his voice a liquid whisper against my mouth, "but perhaps we might sate a *different* sort of hunger tonight."

FOUR

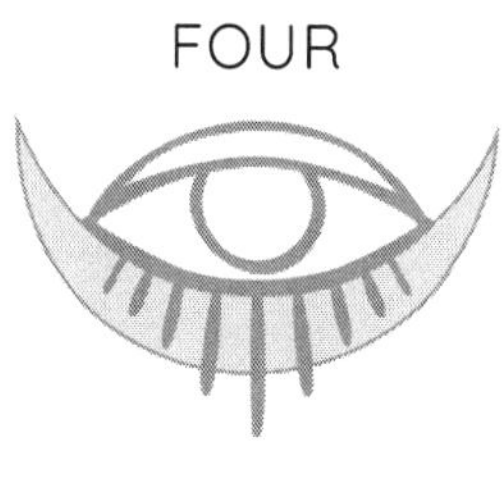

GRAY

"Tell me," Darius said, his nose grazing my jawline, making me shiver. "Tell me what you need, love."

I needed to touch him. To taste him. To feel him inside me, on top of me, all over me. Straining hard against the straps, I said, "Untie me and I'll *show* you what I need."

"Untie you? I think not." Darius arched an elegant brow, a smirk sliding across his mouth. His fingers ghosted across my wrist, caressing the thin swath of skin exposed along the edge of the leather strap, then feathered down the inside of my arm to the crook of my elbow. "Even if you *weren't* a dangerous newborn predator, I rather like this look."

Swallowing the thickness in my throat, I whispered, "Helpless and hungry?"

"Hmm." His eyes ignited and he leaned in close again, soft lips buzzing my own, his erection pressing urgently against my hip. "*Bound.*"

I strained against the straps, desperate to uncover both the promises and the demands inherent in that single word. The leather creaked at my effort, but the hawthorn had dulled my strength just enough to prevent me from breaking free.

"Don't struggle, love," he said. "No point in it, really."

"Touch me," I begged. "Please, Darius."

"Do you trust me?"

"You know I do."

"Then let me take care of you." Without waiting for a response, he glanced around the room, then opened a dresser drawer, fishing through it until he found what he was looking for.

"You want to… blindfold me?" I asked, dragging my gaze down from the wicked gleam in his eyes to the black bandana in his hand.

He folded it into a long strip of fabric, tugging it tight, the snap making me flinch.

"If I may?" he asked.

I nodded, struck mute by the sudden force of my arousal. I'd never been tied up or blindfolded before—rendered nearly powerless, putting a man in complete control of my body, my desires, my pleasure. The idea sent a thrill down my spine, and my slow-but-steady vampire heart kicked up into a quick staccato beat.

"Close your eyes, little vampire," he ordered, and I did as he asked, my body laced tight with anticipation as he fastened the blindfold around my head and tied it tight.

"Darius, are you—"

He cut me off with a violently passionate kiss, fangs scraping across my bottom lip, drawing blood.

"You will not speak again unless I command it," he said, licking the blood from my lip. "For the next hour, I will decide what you feel, when you feel, and most importantly…" He shifted away from my mouth, and seconds later, his hot breath misted at the apex of my thighs. "…*where* you feel. Is that perfectly clear?"

I opened my mouth to respond, but then shut it, nodding instead. The domineering alpha side of Darius's personality had always been there, simmering just beneath the surface, but he'd never unleashed it on me in the bedroom. Not like this.

And oh holy *hell*, was I on *fire* for him right now. My body had erupted in goosebumps, my nipples tight beneath the T-shirt, begging to be sucked.

Darius pressed a hot, wet kiss between my thighs, his tongue lingering, heat emanating through the silk of my underwear. The teasing pressure of his lips hinted at the devastating kisses to come.

Groaning softly, he bit the fabric and tugged it down, exposing my bare flesh to the cool air and the all-too-brief brush of his mouth. His silky hair tickled my inner thighs, and my hips arched closer, demanding more. But the restraints left little room for maneuvering, and the harder I fought for control, the quicker it eluded me.

Darius pulled back and released the fabric from his teeth.

"Naughty little vamp," he teased, clearly enjoying the game. "I believe you need a lesson in manners."

I groaned in delicious frustration, but didn't dare speak out, didn't dare break his rules. My senses had never been so sharp, so attuned to every little movement, every current of air, every stroke of his tongue, and he'd never teased me so relentlessly before. He was going to bring me to pure ecstasy, but first, he was going to torment me to within an inch of my life.

And I was going to love every impossible, crazy-making, panty-melting second of it.

"Would you like to watch me, love?" he asked. "Watch me taste you, touch you?"

I nodded emphatically, but this only made him laugh.

"Sorry, not a chance. Tonight is all about… Yes. Feeling." A soft kiss alighted on my hip bone like a butterfly, then vanished, only to reappear on my knee. "Tasting," Darius said, his tongue dragging seductively down my calf, swirling over my ankle bone. Then, fingers fluttering between my thighs, "Anticipating."

He let the word linger on the air as he increased the pressure, grazing my clit with teasing strokes that quickly turned hot and fiery—and then stopped.

I am going to die. And then I'm going to come back from the grave and kill him, too.

Pressing my lips together to hold back a desperate moan, I waited breathlessly for his next kiss, his next teasing touch.

It didn't come.

Minutes passed, then slowed, then stretched into an eternity. Scenting the air, I noticed his whiskey-and-leather scent had faded. Save for the storm raging against the window and the muted sounds filtering from the rest of the lodge, the room had fallen into complete silence.

Did he actually leave *me like this?*

Rules be damned. I opened my mouth to call out for him. No man *or* vampire got me all worked up, only to leave me helpless, unable to even take care of myself.

But before his cursed name reached my lips, my sexy, sneaky, commanding vampire was on his hands and knees on top of me.

Naked.

Hard.

And still not close enough. Never close enough.

"You seem flustered, little vampire," he teased, grazing my throat with his fangs, his tongue. The tip of his cock brushed my clit, still shielded by the underwear I was quickly growing to hate. "Are you not enjoying the game?"

"No, I'm not," I huffed.

"Liar. I could scent your desire clear across the room." Without warning, he tore my T-shirt down the middle, as far as it would go with the straps locked around my lower ribs.

My nipples pulled tight, and he took one into his hot, wet mouth, sliding his palm across the other. He sucked and licked, teasing me with his fangs, buzzing his lips over my flesh until I ached, my hips undulating beneath him.

I arched my back, ever so slightly, and Darius bit down, then soothed me with his tongue. The pleasure was so concentrated, so intense, so…

Oh, fuck… How is this happening already?

"Darius!" I cried out as the orgasm suddenly claimed me. I clenched the sheets at my sides, straining once again to break my binds. He hadn't even fully touched me yet—not where I needed it most—but somehow, he'd brought me all the way to the edge and pushed me right over.

Darius moaned softly, but he didn't relent. His hair spilled forward over my flesh as he tongued me, and I longed to run my fingers through it, to hold him against me and ride out these insane waves, but I'd surrendered my body to him completely, and it was clear my vampire wasn't going to relinquish even an inch of that control.

I'd just started to regain my balance from the retreating orgasm when his touch evaporated once again, only to be replaced by the weight of his full body pressing down on top of me. In no more than a heartbeat, he tore off my underwear and slid inside me, steely and hot, his own control quickly unraveling.

The rules of the game continued to blur as we lost ourselves in each other, Darius no longer pretending to have even a *modicum* of restraint. He wanted this as badly as I did, and as much as he'd enjoyed teasing me, raw desire had finally claimed us both.

He was wild, kissing and biting, lips and teeth and hands exploring every accessible inch of skin. He gripped my ass, and without warning, slid a finger between my cheeks, delicately teasing. At my soft groan, he slipped a finger inside, and I gasped, the shock immediately replaced with pure pleasure.

"You like being touched like this," he said. Not a question.

I nodded, mute. Lost to the new sensations he was unlocking inside of me.

"Have you ever…?"

I shook my head, knowing what he was asking. No one had ever touched me or done anything else to me there, not like that, and the feel of it as he stroked me in time with the thrusts of his cock had me bracing for the next wave. The pressure was already building, winding me tighter.

"Perhaps," he said, pushing in deeper, slowly, "we'll try something a bit larger next time."

Fresh heat flooded my core.

"With so many of us desperate to touch you," he said softly, seductively, "we may need to start getting more creative. One from behind, another in front…"

God, he was making me even wetter. How was that possible?

Darius claimed my mouth, his tongue sliding between my lips as his cock thickened inside me, and I couldn't help but imagine what it would feel like to have him take me like that, sliding into me from behind while Asher took me from the front, Emilio sucking my nipple, Liam running his tongue along the side of my neck, Ronan touching himself before me…

The image of all of my rebels together, naked, surrounding me and filling me up… I couldn't hold out another minute. My body began to tremble with the force of the explosion building inside me.

"Darius," I breathed. "I can't wait. I'm too close… I…"

"Come for me, love," he said. "Let yourself go."

His liquid voice undid me, and I shattered, heat surging through my core, racing down my limbs, lighting up every nerve ending with an intensity I'd never felt before. It was so wild, so impossibly intense, I thought my blood would literally boil. My body began thrashing, and Darius pressed his full weight against me, shuddering as he came, both of us making the bed shake so hard I worried it would splinter and send us both crashing to the ground.

It was several long moments before I regained the power of speech, and when I finally did, my voice came out hoarse. "Is it always going to feel like that now?"

"Mostly," Darius said. "Vampires are quite sensual, and we feel things *very* acutely, especially for the first few years." He laughed softly, nuzzling my ear. "As I recall, there were moments when even walking outside during a stiff breeze posed a distinct challenge. Emphasis on the word *stiff*."

"So you're saying being a vampire comes with a constant, insatiable horniness?"

Darius laughed again. "That's one way to put it, yes. But like all hunger, we learn to mediate it—when to indulge, when to refrain, when to spend several hours in an ice-cold bath."

"How many hours of your life have *you* spent in cold baths?"

"Since I met you? More than I care to count, love."

Goosebumps slid across my entire body at the thought. Being with him… Everything had felt sharper, deeper, more connected —the slide of his hot length inside me, the touch of his fingers, the mist of his breath on my nipples, the scent of him filling my senses, threatening to overwhelm me in the best possible way. I was already revving up again, a low throb pulsing between my thighs like a warning.

"I suppose you should consider yourself very lucky," he said, trailing kisses across my jaw and lightly brushing my lips. "You've got five men practically banging down the door, waiting for a chance to touch you. All you need to do is ask."

"Darius?" I breathed, the ache in my core deepening as he slid a hand across my belly. "You're not helping."

"Hmm. What would help?"

I strained against the straps again, the leather stretching, but not quite snapping. "Untie me. Please."

"I'm sorry. I can't do that just yet. But I think we can get rid of this for now…"

Darius finally removed my blindfold. I still couldn't run my fingers through his hair or pull him into an embrace, but as he leaned close, I stared into his golden eyes, once again mesmerized by the kaleidoscope of colors glittering before me. He was so beautiful it almost hurt to look at him now.

Darius flashed his sexiest grin. "To answer your next question? Yes. I have *always* been this devastatingly handsome."

I rolled my eyes. "That's not what I was going to say."

"You were thinking it, though."

"Maybe." I tried to laugh, but it quickly turned into a yawn. The hawthorn was kicking in again, and my body was tired, desperate for rest and the blood that hadn't yet arrived. As hard as I tried to stay conscious for this—for all of it—I was losing the battle.

I'd just about drifted under again when a sudden bolt of realization slammed into my skull, forcing my eyes open.

"Darius!" I gasped.

"Ahh, and there it is," he said, touching the tip of my nose. His grin stretched wider now, his eyes dancing with pure joy. "The realization has finally dawned."

"You said something about when you'd first turned! The whole stiff breeze thing?"

"Indeed, I did."

"And earlier, you told me you remembered the thirst of a newborn vampire." I reviewed our entire conversation in my mind, his words hitting me now as if he'd just spoken them. "And our time in the Bay, when I was still delivering imports to Black Ruby!"

"All of those moments, and so many more."

"Does this mean…?" I held my breath, my heart hammering wildly.

Dare I hope?

He'd had flashes of memory before, but never enough to call it restored. This was the first time he'd remembered something so far back in his past—so many different details. It *had* to mean something.

"It means exactly what you think it means," he said, still smiling.

Tears blurred my vision. "But… How? When?"

"Turning you, taking in so much of your blood… It unlocked something for me, Gray. You were right all along. The connection was there. Whether your blood held my memories and returned them to me, or simply unlocked them from some dormant place deep inside my own mind, it matters not."

"How did it happen?"

"All I know for certain is that within moments of drinking from you, I was struck by a pain inside my skull so blinding, it drove me to my knees. It was like something literally cracked open, and everything just… It all came flooding back."

"Just like that? In one big rush?"

"Everything was a bit topsy-turvy at first, but eventually the memories sorted themselves into the right order. I remembered everything I'd ever lived through, all the things I'd done, falling in love with you." He cupped my face, tracing my jawline with his thumb. His eyes were filled with love for me, blazing bright, but soon the smile began to diminish, and the look in his eyes turned to regret. "I remembered becoming a vampire, all the choices I made since that day. The people I hurt along the way. I—"

"Don't do that to yourself." I shook my head, my eyes pleading with him to stop before he went any further down that dark path. "We've all done things we're completely ashamed of. Things we'd die before even *thinking* about doing now, consciously, in our so-called right minds."

"Yes, but I've had much longer to do such things—and much longer to regret them. Lifetimes upon lifetimes of bad decisions and—"

"And lifetimes of good ones." I wriggled my fingers until he grasped my hand, and I squeezed it tight, needing him to understand. "Do you remember what you said to me that night in the Shadowrealm, after I told you how sorry I was for what you'd gone through?"

He lowered his head, his hair falling into his eyes. "That all of it had brought me to you."

"And you wouldn't wish for another outcome."

"That's still true, love. Don't ever think otherwise." He brushed his knuckles along my cheek, smiling faintly, then frowning again. "I suppose I'd simply gotten used to carrying my regrets—after so many decades, they'd simply become background noise. But losing those memories, only to have them return full force… It's as if I'd committed some of those most terrible mistakes only yesterday."

"But you didn't. You're a different man now, Darius. And a hundred years from now, you'll be a different man yet again." I squeezed his hand again. "The difference is, now you'll have an immortal witch-vamp by your side, keeping you out of trouble."

This, finally, got a small laugh. "Causing it, more likely. Especially if you let me tie you up again."

"Again? That implies you actually untied me, which you haven't." I squirmed again, but Darius only shook his head.

"Not a chance, little vampire. You're just lucky I haven't been able to figure out the camera on my phone."

"Guess you'll just have to hold on to this memory extra hard."

"Oh, you can count on it."

He leaned down and kissed me, tender and sweet.

"Thank you," I whispered when he pulled back. "For that night in the cemetery. It's the greatest gift you could ever give me."

"Turning you into a bloodsucker?"

I shook my head. "Honoring my choice, and helping me see it through."

Darius nodded, but suddenly, he seemed lost. Regret flooded his eyes. "Gray, I… I know how badly you wanted this. And logically, I understand your reasoning, just as I understood it the other night in the cemetery."

"Then why do you look so conflicted?"

"I feel like a bit of a fraud."

"How so?"

"You're thanking me for this so-called gift, but I have to confess… If I'd been myself when you'd asked, I wouldn't have changed you—not for all the pleading and logic in the world, no matter how badly I wanted to support you."

"Irrelevant. If you hadn't changed me, you wouldn't be yourself."

He flashed a smile, but it faded before it even reached his eyes. "Being a vampire… Yes, you're stronger. Faster. Immortal. But this fate isn't—"

"This has nothing to do with fate, Darius Beaumont." Now I was getting pissed. "This was a choice. *My* choice. And your choice was to support me, just like you've always done."

Darius nodded, but said nothing.

"How much have we lost?" I asked. "How much has been completely outside of our control? From the moment Sophie died, we've taken hit after hit. For every win, we've got more losses and setbacks than I can count."

"Like I said, Gray. I get your reasons. I just wish there'd been another way that didn't involve risking your soul."

"We're about to turn the tide. All of us. The odds we're facing? That doesn't happen without big risks."

"I know all of this, love. There's no need to rehash. You're a vampire now—there's no going back." He closed his eyes and shook his head, and I feared this would turn into a bigger argument. But when he opened his eyes and looked at me again, his gaze was warm and clear, full of love and appreciation. "But you're mine, love. And *that's* something I would never change, no matter which form you've taken."

He pressed a kiss to my forehead, and the last of my anger evaporated.

"Finally, something we agree on," I said.

"I'm so sorry. I don't want to argue with you. Not about this or anything else."

"Hmm," I teased. "So what *do* you want to do with me?"

"For starters…" He rolled on top of me, hard and ready, his eyes darkening with pure desire. "This feels about right."

"More than right," I whispered, and he sank inside of me, deeper and deeper as my body welcomed his touch. I wasn't as sensitive as I'd been earlier, but despite the hawthorn, I could still feel every inch of him.

But just before he whipped me into another white-hot frenzy, a herd of beasts crashed through the front door and up the stairs, carrying with them the scent of two demons, a wolf shifter, and—most importantly—my dinner.

"It's them," I announced, unable to keep the excitement from my voice. My stomach tumbled with fresh hunger, my mouth watering.

"Bloody hell," Darius grumbled. Then, loud enough so they'd hear him, "Brilliant timing, you gits."

"We've got maybe thirty seconds before they get all their boots off and come crashing through the bedroom door," I said.

Darius shot me a wicked grin, sliding inside me again, faster this time. "Then I guess we'd better hurry."

FIVE

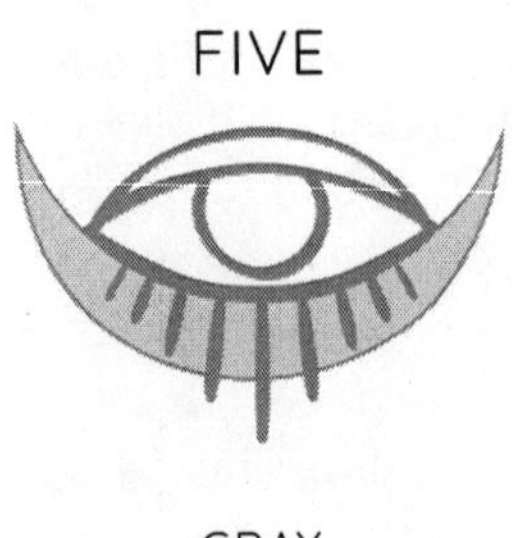

GRAY

I was still seeing stars from the insane rapid-fire orgasm Darius had just delivered when the guys barged in, spilling through the door in a wild tumble of arms and legs and takeout bags, Sparkle and Sunshine right on their heels.

Asher took one look at the vampire lying on top of me and laughed. "Did I call it, or did I call it?"

"*Dios mio*." Emilio shook his head, a grin lighting up his face. "We told you to *check* on her, not *climb* on her."

"Huh. I could've *sworn* you said climb." Darius, who still hadn't bothered to extricate himself from between my thighs, shook his head, feigning confusion. "Must be your accent."

Asher was still cracking up. "Must be you're an insatiable sandbagger who offered to keep watch tonight just so you could get our girl alone and steal her vampire virginity."

"I assure you, Mr. O'Keefe," Darius said, finally climbing off the bed and covering me with the sheet, giving me a covert wink as he did. My vampire was completely naked, totally unfazed as he turned to face the firing squad. "Nothing was stolen in this room tonight, save for our privacy."

"Privacy, huh?" Asher scanned him head to toe. "I can see you're pretty concerned about that."

"Victim-blaming will get you nowhere." Darius gave Asher a

playful smack on the cheek, then finally located his pants, taking his time picking them up off the floor while I enjoyed the view.

"So that's how it's gonna be, Cupcake?" Asher turned his playful blue gaze on me. "You haven't seen the rest of us in days, and suddenly you've only got eyes for the bloodsucker?"

"He's the only one who's naked," I said matter-of-factly.

Asher grabbed the hem of his T-shirt, lifting it to give me a mouthwatering peek. "We can fix that right now."

The briefest glimpse of his tattooed, rock-hard abs had me damn near drooling.

But Darius grabbed Asher's wrist, stopping the show just before it got good. "She needs to eat, and then I'm taking her for a shower. So whatever thoughts are tumbling through that lecherous mind of yours, incubus, put them on ice."

"A shower, huh?" Asher rubbed his jaw, slowly approaching my bedside as Darius ducked into the bathroom to wash up. "Better give her an extra shot of hawthorn this time. Girl's got quite an arm on her."

The teasing smile hadn't left his face since he'd first walked in, and now I returned it with one of my own.

"Consider it payback for the time you took me down at the safe house," I said.

"That was for your own good. And anyway, you're way stronger than me now." Asher swept the curls from my forehead and pressed a kiss between my brows, his eyes twinkling with a mixture of happiness and that seductive, bad-boy edge he'd never quite lost. "You feeling a little less psychotic now, bruiser?"

"Why don't you kiss me for real and find out," I teased.

"You fight dirty, Cupcake."

"I learned from the best."

Never one to turn down a dare, Asher planted one right on me.

"You're looking good, Desario," Ronan said when Ash finally pulled away, the relief in his eyes belying his lighthearted tone. "Color is back to normal."

"What do you mean?" I asked.

"For a while there, your skin was the shade of warm milk," he said.

I winced. That didn't sound like a good look.

"Three guesses as to what put *that* fresh shade of pink on her cheeks," Asher said.

"You're welcome, love," Darius said, returning from the bathroom, freshly showered and fully dressed.

"Yeah, you're welcome for my contribution, too," Asher said.

I laughed. "What contrib—"

He cut me off with another kiss, this one so deep and delicious I couldn't help the moan that escaped my mouth.

"Okay, kids," Ronan grumbled. "Knock it off before this shit turns into a health code violation. I've got dinner here, remember."

He set two large paper bags on the dresser and emptied out the contents, consisting of several take-out containers from Marcella's Diner and a twelve-pack of beer, along with what I could smell were a few large hunks of raw meat for the hounds, wrapped up in butcher's paper.

"So Marcella's is still up and running, even with the storm?" I asked, keeping my eyes peeled for the only meal I cared about in that moment, which would arrive neither in take-out containers nor butcher's paper.

Ronan nodded. "Pretty sure it's the only restaurant in town still open. Place was crowded as hell."

The smell of all that hot food drifted toward me—burgers, fries, fried chicken, pancakes, pie. Ronan crumpled up the empty bags, then said, "Okay, remind me who ordered what."

Panic gripped my limbs. Was that all they'd brought back? "What about the—"

"I've got you covered, *querida.*" Emilio held up a small cooler I hadn't noticed, then popped it open and pulled out two opaque bags of blood. "Still cold though. Should I warm it up?"

My body reacted on instinct, arms and legs straining hard against the straps, my stomach growling like a wild animal. I felt the slide of my fangs, the sharp points piercing my lips.

It seemed like I wasn't in control of any of it.

"Relax, Gray," Emilio said, his voice gentle. "You're okay. We'll take care of this right now." He passed one of the bags to Darius, then cut the corner off the other one with his pocketknife and tilted it toward my lips.

My body settled instantly, the moment I tasted the first drop.

Relief. It was the only word in my mind as the tangy liquid flooded my mouth. Drinking cold blood felt a bit like drinking warm beer, but at the moment, I didn't care. It was food—the only kind that would truly sate me—and for that reason alone, it was practically a gourmet feast.

Besides, I didn't want so much as a *smear* of warm blood touching my lips. Better to not know what I was missing than to ever develop a real taste for it.

The guys watched me closely, a mixture of wonder and curiosity on their faces as I downed the entire bag. Even Darius seemed mesmerized, despite the fact that we were sharing the same meal.

When I'd literally sucked it dry, I let out a small burp, then smiled, feeling much more like myself. "Okay, you guys are starting to freak me out. Why are you staring at me? It's like you've never seen a bloodsucker before."

"We've seen plenty," Emilio said. "Just... Just not you."

"Am I that revolting?" Suddenly self-conscious, I licked my lips, hoping I hadn't spilled anything.

"Revolting?" Asher laughed. "That's a negative, Cupcake."

"I think we're all still a bit awestruck, love," Darius said. "You're quite different now."

"Different how?" I asked.

"You're kind of radiating," Asher said. "Like, you've always been super-hot, right? That hasn't changed. But now you're... well, you're just more."

"More hot?" I rolled my eyes.

"More everything. Not just how you look, but your vibe. Your energy. We can just... feel it." He shifted uncomfortably from one foot to the other, and I glanced down, finally noticing the massive bulge in his jeans.

"Yeah," he confirmed, before I could even ask. "That's exactly what I'm talking about."

"Seriously?" I couldn't help but laugh. "Are *all* of you getting hard watching me eat, or is that just another special incubus thing? Because I realize some guys have food fetishes, but if you're sprouting boners every time I take a snack break, we're going to have a serious problem."

"One person's problem is another person's opportunity," Ash said.

"Your power affects us, Gray," Emilio said. "Each in different ways, maybe, but there's no denying it."

The more I thought about it, the more it made sense. Darius had always had an effect on me—even before we'd become blood bound.

I looked from Emilio to Asher, to Ronan, to Darius, and my chest tightened with a fresh wave of emotion. The last time we'd all been together, I was convincing them to let Darius turn me.

And they'd stood by my side through all of it.

"It's so good to see you guys," I said, tears flooding my eyes.

"You have *no* idea," Ronan said. The relief in his voice was plain.

Emilio squeezed my foot, and Ash ran his fingers through my hair, while Darius held my hand.

They were all here with me save for Liam, who now fell under the "no humans allowed" restriction. I really wanted to see him, as well as my sisters and the others, but it was better to wait. Tied up, bloody mouth, still a little wobbly inside from the hawthorn… Yeah, I wasn't exactly a welcome sight.

As everyone dug into their takeout, they updated me on everything that had happened since my turning, including Jael's decision to take my moonglass back to his home realm—a move the guys didn't seem too thrilled about.

"But Jael… he's okay, right?" I asked.

"All evidence suggests he made it back to his home realm with your soul intact," Emilio said, sharing a few more details about Jael's portal and the hunters they'd taken out in the woods, as well as the ones he and Asher had chased down after the ambush.

"Lucky for us, they weren't very careful about covering their tracks," Emilio continued. "We followed the path they'd made back to an abandoned park service lodge a little deeper into the woods. By our estimate, the whole group had been holing up there, roughing it for the past few weeks at least. Seems most of them were dispatched up to the cemetery during our attack, but two hunters hung back."

"What happened to them?" I asked, though I already knew the answer.

"Let's just say the glamoured cemetery is no longer the only burial ground up there," Asher said. "After we took out those two, we tracked in a little deeper, then circled back up to the spot where they'd tried to jump us. No one was left. *El Lobo* and I made damn sure of that."

I didn't doubt it.

"So it seems we made it out of the whole mess in pretty much one piece," I said, blowing out a breath. I was still getting used to the whole not-needing-air thing, and the gesture felt a little forced. Darius had always seemed so natural.

Years of practice, I supposed.

"The issue now," Darius said, "is that we've got no communication with Blackmoon Bay. Kallayna—via her brother—was our only link."

"We've still got Reva," I said. "I say we stick to our original plan—keep practicing with her until she's ready, and then let her do her thing. I know she can get in there remotely—she's a strong kid, and just as dedicated to this as the rest of us."

"Her dedication isn't an issue," Emilio said, raking a hand through his dark hair. "I hate putting her at risk like that, but I'm afraid it may be our best shot at getting any sort of intel. Otherwise, we're heading in blind—and that's if we can get in at all."

"She's just a kid," Ronan said. "If they find her snooping around like that... No. There has to be another way."

"There isn't," Emilio said. "We've been over it from every angle. Between the fae spells, the unpredictable weather, the Council's treachery, and the beating we've taken at nearly every turn... We're up against a wall here, Ronan."

Ronan shook his head. "Liam's been working with her for days, and she still hasn't made any progress. We can't just turn her loose like that. What if she get's caught? What if—"

"Guys. Seriously?" I looked around from one gloomy face to the next. The air was suddenly so thick with their collective hopelessness, if I actually *had* to breathe it, I'd probably choke. "We saved all those lives the other night—witches, shifters, and vampires alike. We destroyed an army of insane hybrids. Wiped out another pack of hunters. We got more intel from the inside—okay, maybe not as much as we'd hoped, but a hell of a lot more than we had when we started. Haley and I found our sister. And hey, guess what? I'm a scary immortal vampire now—bonus!"

I bared my fangs and hissed, hoping to make them laugh, but only Asher cracked a smile.

"Hey!" I said. "Where's the sense of accomplishment here? The hopeful optimism?"

"Now you're starting to sound like your sister," Ash said. "Always trying to find the bright side."

I smiled, taking it as a compliment. From the moment Haley and I had started getting closer back in the Bay, she'd been a bright spot in my life. Not that she never felt down or scared or pissed off, but even in her darkest moments, she still had a way of bringing out the best in everyone.

"Maybe my sister has a point," I said, channeling a little bit of Haley's eternal optimism. "If Haley were standing right here, she'd make each of us share one thing we're grateful for."

Ash groaned. "Thank fuck she's not standing right here, because that exercise sounds completely—"

"Okay, Ash, you go first." I grinned at him, big and bright, letting him know there was no way out of this.

"You want gratitude? Fine." He huffed and puffed, then finally found his answer. "After we took out those hunters, we looted the park service lodge. Brought home a few more fae blades, some tactical gear, shit like that."

"See, that wasn't so hard," I teased. "Emilio?"

He squeezed my foot again. "You survived the change. That's enough to get me through whatever shitstorm comes next."

I smiled. I was grateful for that, too.

"Darius, what about you?" I asked.

Without missing a beat, he said, "I just got laid by the hottest vampire-witch in existence. That's my final answer."

The crass declaration from the otherwise proper vampire shocked us all into a bout of laughter.

"I should probably smack you for that," I said, "but I'm tied up."

"As if I could forget," he said with a wink. Then, to Ronan, "Alright, hellspawn. You're not getting out of this, either. What's your answer?"

Ronan locked me in his fierce autumn gaze, his eyes burning with some new urgency.

"Everybody out," he demanded. "I need to talk to Gray alone. *That's* my answer."

SIX

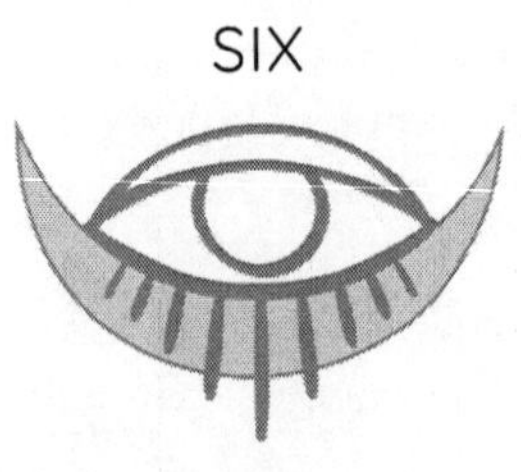

RONAN

The guys gave me a world of shit, but eventually, they took the hounds and cleared out, leaving me alone with Gray for the first time since she'd changed.

I couldn't stop staring at her.

"I must be a total mess." Gray lowered her eyes, her smile suddenly shy.

"A beautiful mess, though," I said. So beautiful it broke my fucking heart. She was immortal now. In a matter of one short night, the number of things that could kill her had been slashed from infinite to two. Only two.

Incineration and beheading.

But that built-in safety feature had come at a cost, and she'd given up a part of herself to get it. And no matter what she believed—no matter what Jael had promised about her soul—I wasn't convinced she'd ever get it back.

Still, she'd survived. That was the important part.

And her eyes glittered with new facets, the depths of which I'd only just begun to explore. Staring into her eyes, losing myself there, it was almost enough to make me forget about the fact that I still couldn't touch her.

"You've got a little…" I swiped my thumb across my lower lip, indicating the blood smeared across hers. I wasn't sure I'd ever get used to the sight of that, but as long as she was healthy, it didn't matter.

She licked the blood clean, then offered another faint smile. "Sorry. I'm still a little—"

"I love you," I said, my voice breaking on the words. I knelt at her bedside, leaning as close as I dared, wishing I could take her face into my hands. "I loved you as a witch, I love you as a vampire, and I'll never fucking stop. I need you to know that. To truly know it. My heart has and will always be yours, even when I'm acting like a fucking asshole."

She closed her eyes, a tear streaking down her cheek. "I do know it," she whispered. "I always have."

"All that shit I said to you back at Inferno, when you'd first returned from hell… I thought I was doing the right thing. I was so twisted up about Sebastian cashing in on your contract, so fucked up about not being allowed to touch you… I guess I just lost my shit. All I could picture was you locked up in one of his dungeons, and him sending me to retrieve you each time he had some bullshit job for you, and you just looking at me with this… this broken look in your eyes, wondering how the fuck the man you loved so much could ever do something so low." I pinched the bridge of my nose, trying to keep my own tears in check. It was a losing battle. "I thought it would be better if you just… If you forgot you'd ever loved me."

"Yeah?" She opened her eyes and glared at me with new fire. "That makes you a fucking asshole *and* a fucking idiot, Ronan. I could *never* forget how I feel about you. All that stuff about letting me go, about things being over between us… Did you honestly think I'd believe you?"

I shook my head. "Deep down, I guess I knew you wouldn't. Hell, I *hoped* you fucking wouldn't. I was out of my mind, Gray, and I didn't know how to handle it. So I fucked up, and I hurt you, and I've spent every night since then haunted by the look in your eyes and silently begging you for the forgiveness I know I don't deserve."

She lowered her eyes, and silence wrapped us up completely, save for the constant roar of the wind and the ocean. She didn't move or speak for so long, I wondered if she'd drifted off to sleep. I was about to stand up and head out when she finally met my gaze again, pinning me in place.

"I forgave you the moment those stupid words fell out of your stupid mouth. I forgave you because I knew you didn't mean them, and I knew you were only trying to protect me from some future heartbreak. I love you, Ronan, even if you never touch me again. Even if you're marching down to my dungeon every single night for the rest of eternity to do Sebastian's bidding. So the next time you get the bright idea to break up with me, go ahead and stick it right up your ass, because I'm not going anywhere."

Her eyes were full-on blazing now, swirling with a mix of anger and love and desire and yes, forgiveness too.

My heart damn near pounded out of my chest, and I had to shove my hands into my pockets to keep from reaching out to her. Touching her. Making up for all my shit with one devouring kiss at a time.

"You're my best friend, Desario," I whispered. "And the love of my life. I will never break your trust again. So you want to know what I'm grateful for? What's my one piece of good news in all of this?" I shrugged. "It's the simple fact that you haven't given up on me. On us."

"I never will."

I blew out a breath, the weight of my guilt lessoning a fraction. Her faith in me, however undeserved it may have been, was a precious gift. One I wouldn't risk losing again.

"Your soul is under the protection of the Seelie Queen," I said, shifting gears. This was a conversation we couldn't avoid, no matter how much I wished we could sweep it all under the rug. "It's likely your situation with Sebastian has changed."

"You think we finally found that loophole?" she asked.

"I don't know. He's got no jurisdiction in the fae realm, and I doubt the Queen would make a deal with the prince of hell. But depending on the exact language in your contract, he could see this as deception on your part."

"Who cares what he thinks? If he can't get his hands on my soul, he has no claim over me."

"I'm not sure he'll see it that way, Gray. Sebastian is nothing if not resourceful. Once he finds out that you're a bloodsucker, he's probably gonna come at you. I just think we need to be prepared for it."

She nodded, the space between her eyebrows creasing with new worries.

"I'm not telling you this to freak you out," I said. "More than anyone else in my existence, you seem to have some influence over him. You just need to figure out how you want to spin this."

Gray flashed her fangs—a look that terrified me as much as it turned me on. "Can't I just bite him and be done with it?"

"He's a demon—the most powerful one in existence. I'm afraid you'll have to get a little more creative than that." I leaned in close again, inhaling her sweet scent, now mixed with the faint tang of blood. "Hey. We've got this. Don't ask me how, but we've got this. You and me? We always figure shit out, and this is no different. Okay?"

She smiled up at me, her eyes sparkling. "Ronan Vacarro. Is that a note of optimism I detect?"

I grinned, my lips just a hair's breadth from hers, and whispered softly, "Don't tell a soul."

"I wish you could kiss me," she said, and I nodded.

"You and me both, Desario."

A wicked smile slid across her face.

"What kind of trouble are you brewing up now?" I asked.

"No trouble. I was just thinking... Apparently, I've got vampire influence now."

"Comes with the territory, I suppose."

"I thought you might want to help me test it out."

"You don't really need my permission," I said. "That's kind of the thing with influence, right?"

"Probably not, but I'm still going to ask. So?"

"Fine." I got back on my feet and stretched, stifling a yawn. "But don't make me see anything too crazy. It's been a long few nights already and I still need to take the pooches out for a—holy *fuck*, Gray."

I stumbled a step backward as the images invaded my mind.

Gray, breaking her straps and pulling me on top of her. Kissing me. Grinding up against me and begging me to take her, right there…

I blinked rapidly, and the scene evaporated.

Back here on planet reality, my dick hard as stone and my witch still strapped tight in her bed, I shook my head. "Well, that was… interesting."

She smiled up at me like a little imp. "See anything you like?"

"Not sure I quite got all the details," I said. "Maybe we should try another—oh, okay, that's… fucking… nice…" My eyes drifted closed as I let the hallucination wash over me, Gray on her knees before me, freeing me from my jeans, taking me into her mouth, one luscious lick at a time. It was all I could do not to grab myself right there and finish the job, but that would kill the vision. Right now, hallucination or not, I only wanted it to be her, not my own damn fist.

She moaned as she took me in deeper, and I had no fucking idea whether it was the real Gray or the hallucination making that noise, but I didn't care. Both of them had the same effect.

And both of them were about fifteen seconds away from making me come.

"Don't stop," I said. Whatever she was doing to me with her mind, it felt fucking amazing, her mouth hot and hungry, her soft little sighs sending jolts of white-hot electricity skittering across my skin…

I felt the sudden tingling in my balls, my heart hammering, my body about T-minus five seconds from exploding—

"Everything alright in there?" The fucking vampire asshole knocked on the door, shattering the vision, breaking my concentration, and earning himself a permanent spot on my shit list.

"Awesome, asshole," I grumbled. My dick went instantly limp, and I opened my eyes, blinking away the last remnants of that beautiful dream. "Give us a few more minutes."

"Very well," he said. "Tell Gray I've drawn her a bath and will be back to help her post-haste."

"Post-haste?" I whispered to Gray. "Who the fuck says that?"

"I heard you, hellspawn. You've now got one minute to say your goodbyes."

I flipped him off.

"I heard that, too," he said.

Gingerly I got to my feet, the ache in my balls throbbing. Yeah, that was gonna be a situation.

"Sorry about that," Gray said, biting her lower lip. "I was really hoping we could see that through."

"Another time," I said. "Definitely another time."

"At least we know my power works, right?" She beamed at me, and I couldn't help but laugh.

"That's an understatement."

"What are you doing the rest of the night?" she asked.

"Cold shower," I said, limping toward the door. Shit was brutal. Wouldn't trade it, though. Until I could finally touch her, this was the next best thing—something she'd chosen to share with me and me alone.

"Ronan," she said, and I turned back to catch her wicked smile.

Seconds later, another image flooded my mind, Gray in the shower with me, suds sliding down between her breasts…

I braced myself against the door, cursing under my breath. "Not helping, Desario. Not fucking helping."

"You know you love it."

Hell, she was right.

"Yeah, I do love it. And you. Now please put your new toy away and let me go put this little situation on ice." I opened the door, grabbed my stiff dick, and hobbled out into the hallway with a smile on my face. Sure, I felt like I'd just gotten kicked in the nuts by a four-hundred-pound gorilla, and Beaumont was out there smirking at me like a total prick, but my girl was alive. She was safe. She was immortal. She had a dirty-as-fuck mind, and she was more than happy to give me a peek.

And the best part? After everything, she still loved me.

For the first time in months, it seemed the universe was finally on our side.

"Wait, Ronan? Serious question this time. I promise."

I turned back to see her wriggling against her straps.

"When do you think I'll finally get sprung from here?" she asked.

"Soon. We just need a couple more days to make sure everything's cool once we stop the hawthorn."

"*Days*?" She pressed her lips together, and I knew she was biting back another argument. But ultimately, she relented. We all knew she'd never put the people she loved in danger—particularly her sisters and Liam, who wouldn't be able to fully defend against her vampire instincts if it came to that.

"Fine," she finally said. "What happens after I'm cleared for takeoff? We rally the troops and ship out for Blackmoon Bay? The longer we wait on making a move, the—"

"Slow down, Desario. There's one *very* important thing we need to do first, *post-haste*," I said for Beaumont's benefit.

"What thing?" she asked.

I grinned at her, raking my eyes over her body from head to toe and letting out an appreciative sigh. "First day you get your official hall pass? The boys and I are taking our hot new vampire-witch out for a test drive."

SEVEN

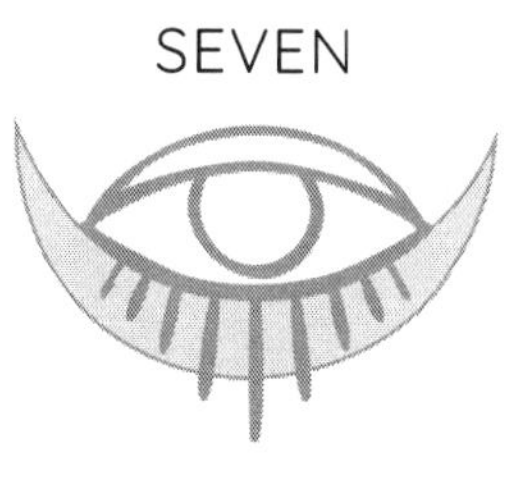

GRAY

Two nights later, I found myself standing next to Darius in a narrow ditch at the bottom of an icy hill, excitedly bouncing on my toes. He'd run me up and down the steep incline so many times, we'd melted a path through the thick layer of ice and snow clear down to the mud beneath.

And still, I wasn't even winded. I had energy to burn, and after being on house-arrest for the last few days, I was more than ready to light it all up.

"I think we've established that I'm faster than you, D," I teased. I'd beaten him nine out of the last ten runs, and the ones we'd done before that were all ties.

Doing his best to hide his frustration, Darius nodded toward the top of the rise, where Asher, Ronan, and Liam stood waiting for us. Liam was holding a stopwatch and clipboard, while the demons took turns cheering us on and keeping Sparkle entertained with an old tennis ball she'd dug up. Emilio was around somewhere, too—he'd shifted into wolf form, and he and Sunshine were keeping an eye on our perimeter, making sure we didn't have any unexpected drop-ins.

The guys still thought it best that I steer clear of the humans for another night or two, at least until they could run me around out here and assess my strength and control. But Liam, who was so used to disappearing and appearing at will, was having no part of it. While the guys had attempted to whisk me away under cover of darkness, he'd snuck into the back of the SUV and hid under a tarp without anyone even noticing, surprising us all by leaping out of the back when we finally arrived at the trailhead.

There was a lengthy argument about whether to drive him back, but in the end, Darius's logic proved no match to Liam's philosophical counterpoints, and he was finally given permission to stay and make himself useful—provided he and I didn't make any physical contact.

About half-a-mile down the dark forest trail, while the others had drifted ahead with the hounds, I grabbed Liam and dragged him behind a tree, stealing a long-overdue kiss.

He gladly returned it, wasting no time deepening the kiss, sliding his hands into my hair and backing me up against the tree, his every touch making my whole body shiver.

"I missed you," I whispered, breaking away just long enough to let him catch his breath before stealing another kiss. We didn't stop again until his cheeks were bright red, he was panting for air, and Darius was shouting from the trail ahead for us to keep up.

"According to Liam," Darius said now, "we've not yet achieved statistical significance. Until we do, the fact that you're so-called *faster* than me remains unproven, from a scientific perspective."

"It's okay," I teased, turning and stretching up on my toes to plant a kiss on his cheek. "I know you're just letting me win to boost my confidence. I'm sure it won't happen on the next run."

He grumbled something unintelligible, even for my vampire super-hearing, then pulled away. "Pay attention, Gray. This is important."

I nodded, biting back another retort. Despite his grumpiness, Darius was a great coach, and this was the best night I'd had in a long time. Together with my rebels, running around in the snow, stretching my new legs… For a little while, it was easy to pretend we were just out for a fun romp in the woods on a chilly winter's night. The winds had died down, and the snow that managed to reach us through the thick canopy of evergreens was light and fluffy, the kind made for catching on your tongue.

It was all kind of romantic, actually.

Or it would be, if they weren't assessing and training me for the attack sitting on the horizon.

Stealing myself for another run, I held up my hand to let the guys know we were ready, then Darius counted down from three.

We were off, racing up the steep hill at a clip so fast, the trees around us were no more than an inky smudge across the snow-white canvas. When I reached the top and spun around, I caught Darius just cresting the rise.

This time, I couldn't help myself. "Have I kicked your ass enough times for it to be statistically significant yet?"

"I concede, little vampire. You are faster than me. But your instincts could use some work." Without warning, he darted close and grabbed me, his body a blur. It happened so fast, I didn't even realize what he'd done until I felt the sudden, icy bite of snow between my boobs.

I squealed, desperately shaking the snow from inside my shirt as I chased him back down the hill, then up again, scooping up snow along the way. I slowed down and waited until he thought he'd bested me, then charged again, pelting him with a wet snowball right between the eyes.

"Nice shot!" Asher shouted as I blurred past them again. I was so puffed up about my snow-fighting skills that I didn't see my enemy lurking behind the trees. Too late, he leaped out from the shadows and tackled me, both of us rolling back down the hill, my lungs aching from laughing so hard.

When we finally reached the bottom, tangled up in each other's arms and legs, tears of laughter were already freezing on my cheeks.

"Concede my victory yet?" Darius nudged my nose with his, a grin stretched across his lush mouth. "Or do you need another lesson?"

He lifted a hand from behind his back, threatening me with a full-on snowball to the face.

Still cracking up, I squirmed in his arms, begging for mercy. "You win, you win! You're the best snowball fighter there is."

"And the most handsome."

"And the most handsome. As well as charming, intelligent, and sexy."

"That's more like it." Darius brushed a quick kiss across my lips, then stood up, hauling me to my feet and dusting the snow off my ass.

I turned and flashed him a mischievous grin. "But I'm still faster than you."

I raced back up the hill, leaving him to chase after me once again.

"And that's another win for Gray," Liam announced, marking the time on the sheet. "We can safely say that her superior speed has been scientifically proven."

"That one doesn't count!" Darius finally made it back to the top, his hair crusted with snow, his eyes bright and happy. To me he said, "Asher was right, love. You fight dirty."

"Not as dirty as we do," Ash said, and I turned just in time to duck before he and Ronan launched a volley of hard-packed snowballs right at Darius's head.

Darius charged, tackling both demons in one swoop, all three of them rolling around in the snow like puppies. Liam tried to take a step back to avoid the chaos, but he was too slow; someone's hand—not sure whose—reached up and snagged his boot, dragging him down and into the brawl.

I was laughing my ass off, no idea who to even cheer for as the four of them pummeled one another with snow, Sparkle yelping as she ran circles around them. Seconds later, Emilio and Sunshine appeared, tails wagging, both of them jumping right into the fray.

"Boys!" I shouted, still trying to get my laughter under control. "We're supposed to be working!"

"Oh, you're going down, Desario!" Ronan shouted, beaming me in the chest with a well-aimed snowball.

"That was wholly unwise, hellspawn." Keen to defend my questionable honor, Liam pounced on Ronan from behind, taking him down and shoving his face into the snow.

We spent the next hour chasing one another through the woods in an epic winter battle, making alliances and breaking them, pushing faces into the snow, shoving snow down shirts and pants and anywhere we could find an easy opening. By the end of it, all of us were laughing so hard I wasn't sure we'd ever be able to talk again.

Poor Liam was shivering his human ass off, but the smile hadn't left his face. Through chattering teeth, he finally said, "I'm fairly certain my vessel has never seen snow in his life, let alone gotten up close and personal with it."

"I'd say the perpetually wind-tossed surfer hair and the pineapple tattoo on your hip are pretty solid indicators," I teased.

"Dude… what?" Asher cracked up. "You have a *pineapple* tattoo? On your *hip*? Did you lose a bet or something?"

"I'm not sure what gambling has to do with my vessel's choice in body art," Liam said, pulling down the waistband of his pants and boxers to reveal the tattoo in question. "Are pineapple tattoos offensive on the material plane?"

I tried not to stare, but couldn't help it. It'd been a long time since I'd seen any part of Liam's unclothed skin, and seeing the flash of well-defined abs transported me right back to our time on the beach in the Shadowrealm. To the moment of our first kiss, so passionate and intense, all those sparks…

"Gray, you okay?" Asher's hand on my shoulder snapped me out of the memory, and I looked up to find Liam staring at me, his eyes twinkling with mischief. Something told me he and I had been thinking about the same thing.

"The snow has been an interesting experience," Liam said, refusing to break our gaze, "but I prefer the beach."

A smile twitched at his lips, and I returned it, feeling the heat rise inside me.

But the moment passed, and it wasn't long before the guys were back in coach-mode once again.

Ronan grinned at me now, shaking his head like he still couldn't believe any of this was actually happening.

I knew the feeling.

"She's fucking fast, Beaumont," Ronan said to Darius. "Faster than any vamp I've come across."

"Don't remind me," Darius said, but he was smiling, too. "Gray, you're a natural. Truly. And you've assimilated the change better than any newborn I've ever encountered—your magic seems to be neutralizing the worst of the side effects."

"I feel great," I told him. "Better than ever."

"Yes, and I can't tell you how relieved we are at that. But don't let it go to your head just yet. Speed, strength, and fortitude are just a few aspects of your new form. You've got a lot more to learn if you want to be able to fully leverage all of your strengths and skills."

I nodded, more eager than ever for the next lesson. "Hit me with your best shot, boys."

EIGHT

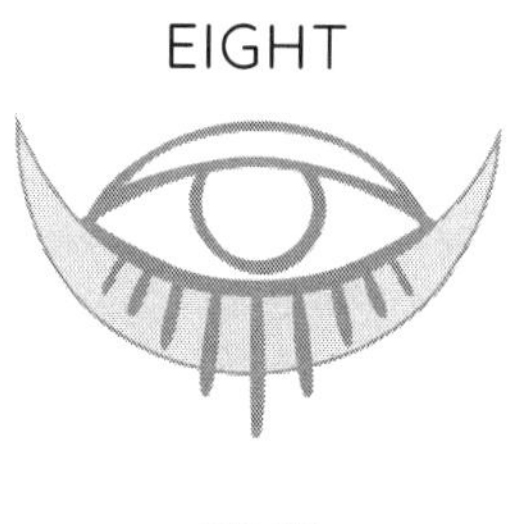

GRAY

"Use every advantage you've got," Darius shouted, his voice an echo from the dark woods behind me, one I couldn't pin down no matter how hard I tried.

After running through numerous exercises testing my strength and agility, all of which I'd passed with flying colors, the guys decided it was time to test my instincts. They'd blindfolded me and led me deeper into the forest, none of them speaking as we marched for what felt like an hour.

If it wasn't for the feel of Darius's firm grip on my arm and the sound of Liam's chattering teeth, I wouldn't have known they were still with me.

Eventually, the trees thinned out, the snow thickening at our feet an inch at a time until I was pushing hard through hip-deep snowpack. The wind was chillier out here, too—compete with wet, heavy snow that splattered against my cheeks.

They'd brought me to the middle of what I could only guess was a wide clearing, leaving me with no warning of what was to come. All I had to go on was Darius's final instruction: *Don't let anything touch you.*

"I'm fresh out of advantages!" I called out now. "I can't see, and everything smells like ice—my nose is useless." Hearing was also a challenge; the wind was picking up again, howling through the treetops behind me, making them shiver and creak. My instincts were screaming at me to take off the blindfold, but I promised Darius I'd leave it on. That I'd see this through, no matter how frustrating.

But frustrating didn't even begin to cover it. After doing so well with all the physical tests, I felt like a total failure out there.

I lost my sense of time, waiting for what felt like hours for something to happen, only to feel everything speed up again at the first sound of footsteps breaking through the icy snowpack. I had no way of knowing whether it was one of the guys or something else, but I wasn't taking any chances. I spun around, arms out, bracing for an attack that never came.

Seconds later, something brushed along my arm, and I yelped like a scared puppy. So much for instincts.

"Try harder, Gray," Darius called, his voice still far away. Clearly he wasn't the one touching me, but no matter how hard I tried to get a sense for *something*—the fiery scent of one of the demons, the feel of Emilio's thick wolf coat, the sound of Sparkle or Sunshine panting—I just kept coming up empty.

I took a deep, unnecessary breath, the familiar gesture calming me, helping me to refocus. I'd just gotten my bearings when something shoved me from behind, knocking me face-first into the snow.

"Fucker!" I shot to my feet, spun around, and lunged, but again, there was only air. Only snow. Spinning back around, I tried my best to scan my surroundings with my available senses, but all was silent and still.

It reminded me of the night we'd invaded Norah's house to rescue Asher—the cloaking spell inside that had rendered all scents and sounds invisible.

"Guys, this isn't working. Let's try something—"

Impact.

I was flat on my back, snow falling wet and heavy on my face as I tried my best to keep the tears locked down. Emilio could see right through it, though, even in his wolf form, which was currently pinning me down in the snow.

He let out a soft whine, then licked my face, refusing to stop until he finally got a laugh out of me.

"If that turns into frostbite, you're in big trouble." I reached up and sunk my fingers into the coarse fur at his neck, taking comfort in his warmth, in the familiar touch, in his presence.

I gave myself about two minutes to enjoy it.

And then I gave him a good shove, launching him clear off my body.

"Vampire strength for the win," I said, but when I got to my feet and turned around, he was already gone.

Footsteps approached in the snow behind me, and again I whirled around, only to feel a tug on my hair from behind.

They were totally screwing with me.

I wanted to scream. I was literally fighting blind.

"Alright. I'm done!" I called out, reaching for the blindfold. There was no point in continuing this particular test. Clearly, I'd already failed.

"You're *not* done," Darius said firmly. No longer an echo in the distance, he was standing right in front of me. His hands came to rest on my shoulders, and I relaxed as his familiar scent finally broke through the cold. "You've simply forgotten, little vampire, and you're letting it upset you."

"Forgotten what? How to fight invisible monsters in three feet of snow?"

"Your newly acquired senses are not your only assets, Gray. That's what you've forgotten."

"What do you mean?"

"You're a witch, are you not? A Silversbane at that. If your vampire senses are incapacitated for any reason, draw on your magic to guide you."

I wanted to argue back, to lash out from the place of wounded pride I'd found myself in. But Darius was absolutely right. The answer was so obvious, so ridiculous, I could only laugh. "Wow. I'm kind of an idiot."

"Don't even think it," he said, tilting my chin up, then stealing a quick kiss. "This is all brand new for you, love. You can't expect to master everything there is to know on your first night of training."

"But we don't have much time, D. We don't have the luxury of weeks or months to explore the finer points of being a vampire-witch. People are dying."

"No, we don't have weeks or months. But a few nights? We have to take that, at least. We can't risk going in unprepared. Doing so could make everything worse—not just for you, but for the very people we're trying to save."

"Alright," I said, deciding to leave the blindfold in place for now. "One more try. Let's see if I can connect with my realm out here. I need—"

"I would advise against it," Liam said. I had no idea whether he'd been by my side through all of this, or had just crept up, but he clearly didn't like my plan. "Your realm isn't safe, Gray. Not with Jonathan's whereabouts still unknown."

"It's the source of my magic," I said.

"No, Gray. *You* are the source." He placed his hand against my chest. "In here. Your realm helped you connect with it more deeply, but it has and will always be within you."

"But half my power comes from the Shadowrealm, and it's connected to my realm through the rune gate," I said. "Accessing that power is my best shot at defending myself."

"Your Shadowborn powers flow through *you*," Liam said. "Always. You do not need to access them from the realm any more than you need to breathe air. Gray, listen to me, please. I wasn't able to locate Jonathan in your realm. We have to assume he's still there, waiting for you to return."

"I took care of him last time. The only reason he got away from me was that I'd found you and Emilio, and that was the priority."

"You can't assume the situation will be the same. For all you know, Jonathan has gotten even stronger."

I shook my head, not wanting to accept this. I'd ignored my realm for so many years I'd almost forgotten what it even looked like. But since I'd started connecting with it again, reclaiming my magic, it'd become a part of me. Important.

Maybe I didn't *need* it, but I wasn't ready to say goodbye to it, either. And I damn well wasn't about to let a cockroach like Jonathan Reese lock me out.

If and when I let it go, I would do it on my own terms.

I told the guys just that, but Liam was adamant.

"There will likely come a time when you have to face Jonathan again," Liam said, the tone in his voice imploring. "That is the nature of such conflicts. But that time does not need to be tonight."

"Spooky's right," Asher said, squeezing my shoulder. Apparently, they were all there now. "No unnecessary risks, remember?"

I steamed for another minute, then finally relented.

"No unnecessary risks," I said. They were right. There was no need for me to go to the realm tonight, no need to waste energy fighting an enemy hiding in the shadows. There would be plenty of time for that later.

Besides, I was a leader now, not some rogue witch playing dress-up with her powers and hiding out in the shadows of Blackmoon Bay. Those days were long gone. The witches were depending on me to see this through. And the guys had stood by me when I'd made the decision to become a vampire, despite their own personal feelings on the matter. I owed it to them to do this thing right. To learn my new strengths and weaknesses, figure out how they meshed with my old ones, and leverage all of that to become the most powerful vampire-witch I could.

"I'm good," I said, finally shaking off the funk of all my failed attempts. A new burst of energy shot through my limbs—I was so ready to do this. "Let's see how much mojo I can access without tapping into my realm."

Still blindfolded, I waited a few minutes to give the guys time to scatter, then I stretched my arms wide, reaching for the energy around me, beneath me, inside me. It took a few minutes, but then I felt it again—the familiar tug, the warmth, the buzz of my magic as it connected with the earth and sky.

The sensations felt the same as they always had when I tapped into external magic, but tonight, with my vampire senses on high alert and my mind newly focused, everything was so much clearer.

I could sense the cold kiss of every snowflake alighting on my skin, feel the cool air whispering across the hairs on my neck, taste winter's breath. If I concentrated hard enough, I could hear the snow falling, feel the earth shifting beneath it to accommodate its weight.

I am part of this. All of it.

Power surged inside. I felt amazing, like there was literally nothing I couldn't do, no foe I couldn't best, no battle I couldn't survive.

"Come at me!" I shouted, a giggle bubbling up to the surface.

And come at me they did. Rather, come at me they *tried*.

For the next hour, they played the same game as before. But this time, no one even got close. I could feel the shift in the energy around me as they approached, sense the change in the air when they moved to grab me. I could scent each one of them, my mind seeing their moves a millisecond before they made them.

I danced and sidestepped every attempt easily, as smooth as water flowing over stones.

"You were right," I said, when Darius finally called an end to the exercise. "The key was my magic. I felt like it unlocked something inside me—all that vamp potential. I feel incredible."

I couldn't help the smile that stretched across my face, but I could tell from the tight feeling inside that Darius wasn't smiling back. I could sense him more clearly now, too—not just his presence, but his emotions. More than any of the other guys, I felt like I had a direct link to him now.

"What?" I asked him. "What's wrong?"

"You definitely have an advantage over the rest of us mere single-entity beings," Darius said. "Many advantages, actually. But you're not wholly indestructible, Gray, and neither are any of us. We all have to fight hard, and we have to fight smart. You've still got a long way to go. I'm not ready to give you a medal just yet."

"I think I'm doing pretty damn great for my first time out," I said, a little defensively. Hadn't I just proven that? Hadn't I spent the last few *hours* proving that?

"For your first time out, absolutely," he replied. "But that's exactly what this is—your first time out. Liam's right about statistical significance. We need more time to train, more time to know this isn't just a fluke."

"A fluke? Are you—"

"Sunrise isn't for a few hours yet," he said, leaving no room for argument. "I think we should run through that exercise one more time. After that, I've got some mental tests I'd like to…"

His words trailed off as I headed back the way we'd come, ditching my blindfold on the way.

"We're not done yet!" he shouted, his voice echoing across the meadow. "You can't possibly tell me you're tired."

I wasn't tired—the opposite, actually. My body was buzzing with energy, glad for the exercise and the fun night out, despite the few hiccups and Darius's apparent inability to dish out a compliment.

But I was also eager to get back to the lodge, to rest up before tomorrow night. I'd proven myself stable enough for public exposure—that much was certain. After a day's rest, I'd finally be able to spend some time with my sisters.

I hadn't even spoken to either of them since we'd gotten Adele out of that cell. The three of us had so much catching up to do.

"You guys can stay if you want," I called over my shoulder, "but I'm ready for some hot chocolate and a nice roaring fire with—"

The howl of the wolf pierced my eardrums, and I spun around just in time to see Emilio charge at Liam, knocking him to the ground.

Liam struggled in vain to fight back.

And then Emilio, the man I loved, the one I trusted with my life and the lives of everyone I'd ever cared for, tore out Liam's throat.

NINE

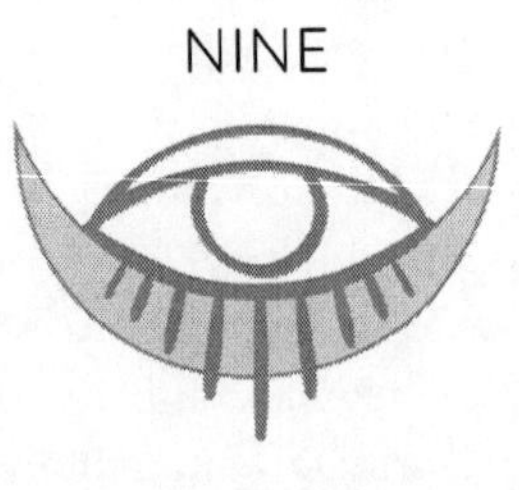

GRAY

"Liam!" I shot back across the meadow, launching myself at Emilio, desperate to put an end to the carnage…

I face-planted into the snow.

Emilio vanished. Liam vanished. The crimson pool of snow… All of it was gone.

What the fuck is going on?

I got to my knees, blinking away the lingering images, shocked as Liam came back into view.

He stood between Ash and Ronan, shivering in the cold but otherwise unharmed. All of them were watching me like I'd totally gone off the rails, which I basically had.

"Gray?" Liam's brow furrowed as he knelt before me, reaching up to touch my face with a gloved hand. "What's wrong?"

"I don't…" I closed my eyes, then opened them, certain I was losing my mind.

"You're trembling," he said.

"But… You're alive!" I blurted out, hauling him against my chest in a crushing hug. Seconds later, Emilio bounded toward me, still in his wolf form, and pressed his nose against my thigh.

There was no blood. No vicious snarl. Only my beautiful, gentle wolf. I reached out and stroked behind his ear.

I'd imagined the whole thing.

"I heard Emilio howling," I said, trying to piece it together.

"Then I saw him… He attacked Liam. He… he killed him."

Liam pulled out of my embrace and narrowed his eyes at me. "Gray, are you feeling alright?" Then, to Darius, "Perhaps we should get her home. The drop in external temperature seems to be adversely affecting her, or maybe the stress of all the activity after her lengthy bedrest."

Darius shook his head. "I can assure you, Liam. Neither of those things is affecting her."

"Then what the fuck was that?" I demanded, my limbs still vibrating, my heart heavy. Even with Liam in my arms, the grip of loss and grief had yet to fully retreat. "I saw him lying in a pool of his own blood."

"That," Darius said, hauling me to my feet, "was a lesson in the power of influence."

"That… That was *you*?" I glared at him, my mouth dropping open. He'd actually made me hallucinate—made me believe—that one of the men I loved had just brutally murdered another.

How could he have been so cruel?

"I'm sorry for springing that on you," Darius said, softer now. He took my face into his hands, swiping my tears with his thumbs. "It was the only way to make you truly see."

"See what?" I asked. "You made me think Emilio… That he…. I watched him tear out Liam's throat!"

"Dude, seriously?" Asher turned a fiery gaze on Darius. "That's a little fucked up, even for you."

"What you call 'a little fucked up', hellspawn, I call making a very important point." Turning his attention back to me, Darius said, "It was the first thing that came to mind—something I knew would blind you to all personal risk and send you charging in without a second thought. And you took the bait without question. You bolted straight for them, didn't you?"

"I thought he was *dead*, asshole!" I shoved him in the chest, expecting to meet a solid wall of muscle, but sending him sprawling on his ass instead.

Right. Vampire strength.

The realization offered little consolation.

Darius got to his feet and brushed the snow off his backside, unfazed.

"You are physically stronger now, Gray," he said. "Your speed and agility are almost limitless, your raw power like nothing I've ever encountered in a newborn, and your instincts—once you learned to start trusting them—are spot on. Your magic enhances all of those qualities, and we've only just begun to tap into that potential."

"So what's the problem?" I snapped, turning away from him. I wanted to keep my eyes on Liam and Emilio, to make sure they were still here. Really here.

"Despite all of that," Darius continued, "you're still not immune to the powers of a sadistic vampire bent on getting inside your head. If we run into rogues in the Bay—which we almost certainly will—they're going to exploit you the first chance they get."

"Then you're basically saying we don't stand a chance," I said. "If anyone can make me hallucinate images like that, I'm toast." I bent down and put my hands on my knees, still trying to catch my—well, breath wasn't the right word anymore. More like my equilibrium.

That little mind trip had left me absolutely reeling.

"They can *try* to make you," he said. "But they won't succeed. Not if you learn to shield your mind."

"That takes a lot of concentration, Darius. Not to mention energy. Not the most reliable tactic in a full-on combat situation, when I might have five other assailants coming at me, not to mention trying to keep track of the witches and you guys and everything else going on."

"For a witch, yes, it would be a lot of energy," he said. "But for a fellow vampire? It's just a matter of learning the right technique. Then it becomes second nature."

I let out a bitter laugh. "That simple, huh?"

"I never said anything about simple, love. Just possible." He folded his arms across his chest and glared at me, driving home the point. "You're the one ready to call it a night, so sure you've learned all you can. Perhaps next time you won't be so hasty to dismiss the idea of additional training time."

I stepped into his space, glaring at him right back. "Perhaps next time, *bloodsucker*, you won't break into my head with a vision guaranteed to scar me for the rest of my damn life."

Darius exploded, fisting the front of my jacket and hauling me close, nose to nose. Through gritted teeth, he said, "And how long do you expect that life to last if you refuse to learn even the most rudimentary—"

"Darius." Ronan stepped in, a firm grip around Darius's arm. "Can I have a word, please?"

His eyes had gone completely black.

Darius finally released me, and I turned my back on him, grateful as Ronan practically dragged him to the other side of the meadow. When I turned back to look at them, I saw Darius standing firm, arms crossed over his chest while Ronan paced in front of him, arms gesturing wildly.

Good. I hope he's tearing you a new one.

"You okay?" Asher asked, offering a warm smile. It felt like the first I'd seen in a year, and when he opened his arms for a hug, I gladly accepted the offer, waving for Liam to join in.

A few minutes later, Ronan and Darius returned, Ronan sparing me a sympathetic glance before marching ahead, back toward the woods. His eyes had returned to normal.

The others headed for the path, too, and I turned to follow them. But a soft touch on my shoulder stopped me in my tracks.

"I don't want to talk right now, D," I said.

"Then just listen. Please, Gray."

Folding my arms across my chest, I nodded and turned around.

"I'm so, so sorry for putting you through that," Darius said, his eyes glazing with unexpected emotion. "I wouldn't have gone to such extremes if I thought I could make the point any other way."

"So you're sorry, but you're standing by it?"

"I don't know what else to say. I'm trying to protect you."

"Darius. You have to know that if any one of you went down like that, not even a freight train could stop me from getting to you."

"I understand. Which is why I needed you to see just how easy it would be to get inside your mind. If that happens when we're fighting in the Bay, even for an instant, there's nothing you'll be able to do to regain the upper hand. You may not even realize you've lost it."

"So we just have to make sure that doesn't happen," I said. He'd been right about that part, anyway. I still had a lot more to learn, and not a lot of time to learn it. "I get it, Darius. You made your point. Mission accomplished."

"Hey." Darius hooked a finger beneath my chin and tilted my face up, but I refused to meet his gaze. "Look at me, love. Please."

I finally gave in.

"I meant what I said," he continued. "I'm deeply sorry. I never meant to hurt you, only to shock you. Understand, Gray… I'm your sire. Yes, becoming a vampire was your decision, but ultimately, you would not have undergone the transformation if I hadn't agreed, regardless of the state of my memories at the time."

"What does that have to do with anything?"

"I made you. It's my responsibility to guide you through this. To ensure, to the absolute best of my ability, that you can come into this new power fully, to explore every facet of it, to know your strengths as well as your weaknesses. If I overlooked something, and you got hurt as a result, or worse…" His voice broke on the word, and he closed his eyes, shaking his head. "It was a bad call on my part. I should've found another way."

"I… I accept your apology." I wrapped my hands around his wrists, and he opened his eyes, his hands still cupping my face. His gaze softened as he looked at me, sweeping down to linger on my lips.

I swallowed, my mouth already watering for the taste of his kiss, sweet and tender and full of the love I knew he felt for me, sealing the momentary gap that'd come between us. But I couldn't kiss him. Not right now.

Offering a small but brief smile, I pulled out of his touch. "I said I accept your apology, and I do. And I promise I'll do whatever it takes to learn the shielding techniques, and any additional training you want to put me through. But I just…" I closed my eyes, the image of Liam's bleeding corpse still flashing through my mind. "I need a little space, okay?"

When I opened my eyes again, Darius was still standing before me, his lips pressed together, his face tight with guilt. With pain.

He hadn't moved, hadn't granted me the space I'd requested. But I didn't need to wait for it anymore. I was faster than him now, and without another thought, I blurred out of sight. The guys were still clomping through the snow along the trail, the hounds keeping guard at the rear, and I sped past the whole lot of them, not stopping until I reached the car.

By the time they all got back, I was already tucked safely into the back seat, wrapped up in a blanket, pretending to be fast asleep. Only Liam dared to sit near me. Dared to take my hand. I squeezed it tight, holding it close for the drive home, taking comfort in the warm and solid reality of it.

The weight of Darius's guilt felt like another person in the front seat. I didn't want him to feel that way, but I couldn't find the words to make it better for him just then. He didn't understand—I wasn't even particularly angry with him anymore. Yes, his choice of imagery had been shocking and cruel, but I understood why he'd taken such an extreme measure.

It wasn't that I'd needed space from *him,* or from what he'd done. It was that I'd watched Liam's blood soak into the snow until he had none left to lose. In that brief moment, it had been real to me.

And for the first time since the Lord of Shadows visited my bedroom with talk of necromancy and the rare powers of the Shadowborn witch, for the first time since our journey through the Shadowrealm and hell, since he'd kissed me, since he'd confessed his betrayals, since he'd given me a rock carved with his signature raven feather, since he'd helped me bring Emilio back from the dead, since he'd sacrificed his eternal soul for us, since I'd fallen in love with him... For the first time in our long and winding relationship, I finally and truly understood that Liam—the Great Transformation, Older than the Seas, formerly known as Death Himself—could die.

TEN

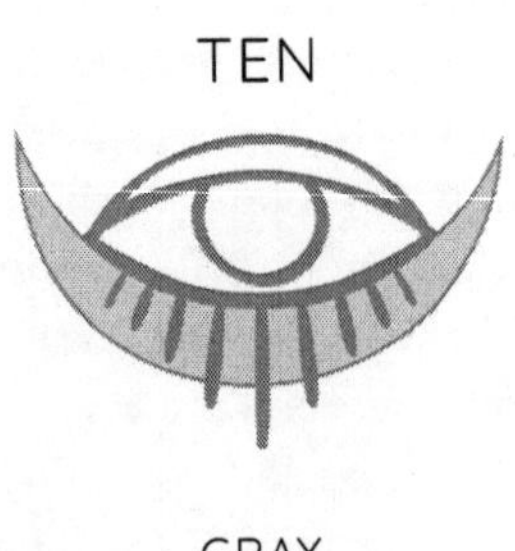

GRAY

I spent the early morning sleeping in my own bed, blissfully alone and free from the restraints, blinds drawn tight against the daylight, door locked and guarded by both hounds to keep any would-be visitors away.

By the time I woke up, the sun had just set, and the lodge was buzzing with activity. I crept downstairs on quiet feet, hoping to catch my sisters alone. I found them in the kitchen; Verona had them working hard, pulverizing dried herbs and portioning them into glass jars while several other witches fluttered around them, collecting and labeling the full jars, looking over ingredient lists, taking stock of the herbs in the pantry.

They didn't notice me at first, and I lingered in the doorway, taking a moment to soak it all in.

Haley was practically buzzing, talking a mile-a-minute, her smile bright and warm. If she was still dwelling on the blood oath she'd sworn in the crypt, she didn't show it one bit. Her curves were coming back, as was her hair—the fuzz I'd gotten used to was now a cute pixie cut that made her green eyes pop.

Adele looked a hundred times better than when I'd last seen her in the cemetery, which was a huge relief. Her face was still gaunt, tattooed with the bruises and scrapes her captors had given her, but those marks were already beginning to fade. Her color had completely returned, those beautiful brown eyes sparkling. They were kind eyes, open and trusting despite the fear lingering there.

Despite our different eye color, she looked a lot like me. Same cheekbones, same blonde hair, though hers was a bit longer. Apparently, her captors hadn't cut it, and now it curled over her shoulder in a low side ponytail.

I blinked back tears. I still couldn't believe I had sisters, that they were here, that three out of the four of us had finally been reunited after more than two decades apart.

And we'll find Georgie, too. Whatever it takes.

"Gray! You're up!"

Haley's squeal of delight snapped me out of my thoughts, and I stepped in through the doorway, beaming at her as she darted across the kitchen and launched herself into my arms.

"You look fucking amazing, girl." She laughed as she pulled back and took me in, head to toe. "I missed you so much! I've been trying to get in to see you for days, but your supreme protectors were having none of it."

"That was for *your* protection, not mine." I pulled her in for another quick hug. It was so good to see her, to feel her, whole and alive. Despite all the obstacles we'd yet to face, I felt stronger just knowing we'd be doing it together.

"How… how are you feeling? I mean, is it… Am I… Do you…?" Haley trailed off, but I read the questions in her eyes.

Giving her a reassuring smile, I said, "I'm feeling better than I've ever felt in my life. It's super weird. And no, you're not in any danger from me."

Haley laughed. "Good to know, because now that I've got you back, I'm not leaving your side. Well, other than when you need to pee, or you're having 'special' time with—"

"*Special* time?" I rolled my eyes, cracking up. "That's not… Hay, you *really* need to get some 'special time' of your own. Sooner rather than later."

"I keep asking if the guys have any hot brothers, but no luck." Haley linked her arm in mine. "Come on. Come meet Addie—officially, this time. She's dying to talk to you."

She led me to the counter at the center of the kitchen, where

Adele and McKenna, the boisterous witch who'd helped Asher and Haley take care of the witches in the cave prison, were pouring some kind of herbal powder into bottles through a paper cone. The cone tipped, and I grabbed it, catching it just before it spilled all over the counter.

"Thank—" Adele looked up, her eyes going wide when she saw it was me. McKenna winked at me, then slipped out of sight, leaving me alone with my sisters.

"Addie, meet Gray," Haley said softly. "Gray, meet our sister, Addie."

Adele—Addie—smiled, her eyes glazing as she took me in. "Gray, I… I just…"

She was suddenly overcome with emotion, unable to get the rest of the words out, and seeing her tears broke the dam on mine. Righting the cone, I walked around to the other side of the counter, then pulled her in for a hug. She stiffened at first, and I worried I'd done the wrong thing—maybe she didn't like touching, or wasn't ready for that kind of intimacy with me yet.

But just before I released her, she softened in my arms, her shoulders shaking as she finally let loose the sobs she'd been holding in.

My own tears falling freely, I held her close, rubbing her back, letting her get it all out. She'd just been through a torturous hell I could only imagine, and whether she'd known about us before or not, finding out you had a built-in family was beyond intense. The poor woman was on an emotional roller coaster—I had no idea how long she'd been on this ride, and no idea when she'd be able to get off.

When her breathing finally evened out, she pulled out of my embrace and met my eyes.

"Gray," she said again, this time with a steady smile. Then, in a clear, determined voice completely at odds with her red nose and glassy eyes, she said, "Thank you for saving my life. For everything you're doing here. For all the… I mean, Haley told me about the prophecy and the covens, and everything that's happened, and the stuff in Blackmoon Bay, and your friend Sophie, and… Shit. I'm sorry. I didn't mean… *God.*" She let out a nervous laugh, swiping away the tears from her bruised face. "How am I fucking this up so badly already? Five minutes into meeting you—that might be a new personal record."

"You're not fucking *anything* up," I assured her, then smiled. "The first time I met Haley, she practically decked me."

"Hey!" Haley said. "You're conveniently leaving out the part about you acting like a complete bitch."

"Okay, first of all, I wasn't acting. And second of all, my best friend had just died. I should've gotten a free bitch-pass." I winked at her to let her know I was teasing. I would never joke about losing Sophie, but somehow, making light of my own feelings felt okay—almost as if Sophie herself were watching, egging us on. As painful as that day at Norah's house had been for me, it was also the moment Haley had come crashing into my life, slipping a note into my pocket that would lead me to Jael and Sophie's book of shadows, and to everything that had come after.

Everything that had brought us closer. As close as sisters.

I wouldn't trade it for the world.

Haley tossed a dried rosebud at me, pegging me between the eyes. "If I'd known I was your big sister back then, I probably would've skipped the *practically* part and gone straight to kicking your ass, so consider that your free pass."

"Oh, you want some of this?" I teased, spreading my arms. "Take your best shot, girl."

"Hmm. Hard pass. You weren't a super-powered bloodsucker back then." She grabbed a clean cutting board and knife from the drying rack next to the sink, then handed them to me, her eyes twinkling with laughter. "Now wash up and get to work. Bloodsucker or not, there's no such thing as a free lunch around here, Desario, and you've been laying around for days."

"Yes ma'am." I knotted my hair in a loose bun and washed my hands, excited to roll up my sleeves and dig in. It felt good to be doing something tangible, something other than practicing violence, or worse—executing it. After everything that had happened with the guys last night, a few hours of peaceful herbcraft with my sisters sounded like just what the doctor ordered.

"So, what are we working on today?" I asked brightly, joining them at the counter. "Healing potions? Protective charms? Dinner?"

Addie held up a vial marked *hemlock*. "The fine art of poison-making."

I laughed. So much for a day of peaceful herbcraft.

"Sounds like a party." I rubbed my hands together and grinned. "Where do I start?"

ELEVEN

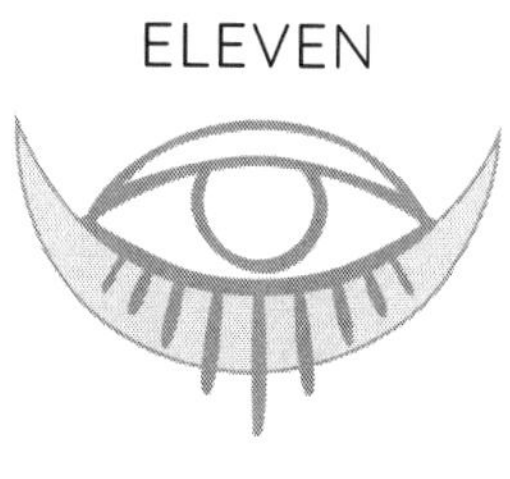

GRAY

"Crafting the perfect poison is both an art and a science." Verona, who'd been supervising all the activity in the kitchen, set an armload of clean vials and jars on the counter before us, then handed me a sheet of instructions.

I scanned it carefully, memorizing the ingredients, measurements, and specific incantations necessary for crafting the deadly poisons our witches would be carrying into battle, just in case.

Not everyone had built-in offensive powers. But we'd make damn sure they weren't left defenseless, either.

I closed my eyes, took a moment to set my intention for this deadly work, then grabbed the kitchen knife and a bottle of what looked like tiny twigs, ready to chop.

Everyone in the lodge was working on something—poisons, spells, protective charms, healing potions, combat training, weapons inspection and inventory, meal planning, cleaning, mending, weatherizing the windows and doors against the insane winter. Half the guys were on guard duty with Elena's men on the beach and in the woods, Liam was working with Reva on her shadow traveling practice, and the rest had gone out with Elena on another grocery run which, according to Haley, was starting to become a real challenge. A handful of local stores were doing their best to stay open and stocked through the storms, but they were having trouble getting supplies delivered. Most of the major roadways into the Cape and surrounding communities had been intermittently shut down, leaving the National Guard and emergency services to pick up the slack.

If things had gotten that bad here in the Cape, I could only imagine what they were experiencing in Blackmoon Bay—ground zero for the entire disaster.

It took me a few minutes to get into the groove, but once I did, the work became easy, almost meditative. My sisters and I got our own little assembly line going, with me chopping, Haley measuring and mixing, and Addie portioning everything into bottles.

Everywhere I looked, people were in motion. Bodies moved. Hearts beat. Blood flowed, warm and sweet and seductive.

I couldn't say the presence of so many people didn't faze me, but I meant what I'd told Haley: no one in this house was in any danger from me. The times I felt the hunger welling up, I just stepped outside for some air, or took the hounds for a romp in the snow, or grabbed some blood from the stash Emilio had brought back for me.

It got the job done, just enough to take the edge off. But it wasn't satisfying. Not in the least. Drinking donor blood was a choice I made *every* time, and I was only a few days in.

Darius had been doing this for centuries.

Darius…

I hadn't spoken with him since our argument last night. I'd gone straight to bed after we'd arrived at the lodge, and last I heard, he was out patrolling the beach tonight.

I missed him. I needed to see him, to let him know I was okay. That I understood what he'd done and why, even if the image of Liam still haunted me…

Desperate for a distraction, I turned to Addie and blurted out, "So what's your superpower, sis?"

Haley cracked up. "Nice, Gray. Way to ease into it."

"Well, we're all witches, right? Magic isn't exactly a four-letter word around here."

Haley shot me a smug glare, and even though my magic

didn't come with mind-reading powers, in that moment I could read her thoughts like a book.

I'd come a long way since that first day at Norah's, when I was willing to do just about anything to keep my magic on permanent lockdown. Back then, I really believed I could outrun my destiny.

Anyway, Addie was our sister. I wanted to know her, just like I wanted to know Haley. And I wanted them to know *me*, too. Maybe it wouldn't happen overnight. Maybe we'd fight and keep secrets and avoid any subjects that cut a little too close to the bone.

But magic? That was neutral territory. It was something we all had in common, and a good place to start.

"I guess you'd call it foresight," Addie replied, and I nodded. Deirdre had mentioned as much.

"But not in the usual ways you hear about," she went on. "I don't literally *see* the future so much as sense it. Like, they're not visions exactly, but I get these impressions—feelings and smells, mostly. Sometimes I'll hear things, like a song or a voice or some other noise that helps me home in on whatever it is I'm sensing."

"Sounds like Sophie's gift," I said. "She'd pick up on emotional impressions whenever she touched something. Like, a piece of furniture or jewelry or clothes. People too. I used to call her the human lie detector."

"Haley told me about that." Addie smiled. "But it's not so much about touching objects for me. It's more like… like there's something out there, right? A force, divine intervention, an invisible time-traveling multi-dimensional being, something. It taps into my intuition, and then stuff just sort of… appears. From there, it's up to me to put the puzzle together."

"What do you mean?" I ask. "How does that even work?"

"Let's say I pull a Tarot card, and the message I get from it has to do with children. Six of Cups, maybe." She tapped a small bottle against the counter, settling the powder inside before sticking a rubber stopper in it. "Once I accept that message or keyword or whatever, that's when I open up. Suddenly I'll smell crayons and paste, or hear kids playing outside, or taste school lunch. That tells me something is going to happen at an elementary school. So I might draw another card to try to pull in more clues—is this an emergency situation, or just something I need to know about? Does this affect someone I care about? These are really simplistic examples, though—usually I'll get a lot more intuitive hits, all at once. I just try to stay open to whatever messages are trying to come through, and from there, I can usually piece together a prediction."

"That's fucking cool," I said. "Just that you can do that. I feel like I'd get totally overwhelmed."

"Sometimes I do. I mean, it *is* cool. But it's also maddening, especially when I *know* there's something important trying to come through, and I can't quite figure it out." She reached for an empty bottle and set it up with a fresh paper cone. "Like you guys, for instance. Looking back now, I can see that I've been getting bits and pieces about this moment for years, but I had no context for it. I didn't know what the hell the universe was trying to tell me.

"I grew up in North Carolina—about as far as you can get from Washington, at least in the states. I'd always assumed I'd been there. I didn't learn about my adoption until two years ago—my mother finally told me, but she left out a lot of details. I thought my real parents had died."

"That's what we all thought," I said. "I take it you don't have any memories from before?"

"Just flashes, but nothing that ever made sense. Haley told me about our mother, about what she did to us…" Her hands stilled around the bottle, and her eyes went far away, narrowing as if she were trying to pull the memories out of the mists of time. But then she blinked and shook her head, blowing out a breath. "I don't know if I blocked it all out, or someone altered our memories, or what."

"Maybe a little of both." I scraped the latest batch of chopped twigs into the big bowl in front of Haley, then dumped another batch onto my cutting board.

Altered memories. That was the theory Haley and I had come up with. Ultimately, I'd remembered that day at the creek when our mother had tried to drown us, but Haley never did, and she was the oldest—she would've been about four when it happened. Deirdre had told me she'd altered our mother's memories to make her believe she'd succeeded in murdering us, so it wasn't much of a stretch to assume our grandmother had "adjusted" our memories as well.

After all, she was trying to keep us apart. To keep the prophecy from coming true.

"Anyway," Addie continued, "A couple of years ago, I started getting this massive influx of impressions—way more than at any other time in my life—and they all had to do with the west coast. Like, the wind would rustle the trees outside my house, but I'd hear the sound of the ocean instead. Or I'd be eating barbecued chicken at Mom's Sunday dinner, but it would taste and feel like fresh crab. In bed at night, I'd feel like I was on a boat—you know, that rocking sensation, the wind in my hair, the smell of the sea. Or I'd be watching the sunset over the hills, and suddenly I'd see it setting on whitecaps instead. One morning I just woke up with this urge—a need, really—to go west. Washington, specifically. Don't ask me why—I'd never even been here."

"You sensed us," I said. "Deirdre said that would happen. We were all born in the Bay—she said we'd all be drawn back to it."

"That's what Haley told me." Addie sighed. "I was always a little on the impulsive side, so when it got to the point where I couldn't sleep anymore because all I could think about was making my way west, I did it. I gave notice at work, broke my apartment lease, packed my belongings into my car and took off. My parents thought I was nuts, but they'd always encouraged me to have a sense of adventure. Mom was a witch, of course, so she knew all about intuition and feelings and signs. Well, and obviously she must've known that my origins were here, but she never said anything. It's only now that I realize it."

She got that faraway look in her eyes again, and lowered her head, her hands fidgeting with the bottle.

After a beat, I put my hand on her arm. "Addie, have you been back in touch with them since you got out of…?" I trailed off. I couldn't bring myself to say the word prison, or cell, or crypt or torture chamber of nightmare hell, but she knew what I was asking.

Addie shook her head as a tear slid down her cheek. "The hunters... It was one of the main ways they kept us all in line. They'd show us pictures or video of our families every few days —they said they had people watching them at all times. If we disobeyed, if we tried to escape, if we tried to get in touch with anyone on the outside, they'd...."

I glanced at Haley, wondering if anyone had tried to reach out to Addie's parents, but Haley only shook her head.

"Addie, listen to me," I said firmly. "We left *no* one alive in that compound—not hunter, not hybrid, not fae, not a soul. Even if they *did* have someone watching, the hunters have much bigger problems now."

"I know." She sniffed, dashing away the tears. "That's exactly what I've been telling myself. But I'm not going to risk calling them—not until we're out of the woods. At this point, it's almost better that they think I'm..." Addie shook her head, blowing out another breath.

"Addie," Haley asked, putting her hand on our sister's back, "how did you get mixed up with the hunters in the first place?"

"They nabbed me in Port Franklin about ten months ago. I was their prisoner, plaything, and medical experiment every day from that moment until you guys came busting into that crypt."

"Holy shit," I whispered. Haley coughed, doing her best to hide her own gasp of shock.

Swallowing the lump in my throat, I said gently, "How did they get to you?"

"I'd been living there just over a year by then—it was the first place I'd landed after leaving North Carolina, and I'd fallen in love with it immediately. It had the small-town, artsy vibe I'd always wanted, and the people were so friendly and open. I found work right away, waitressing in a place that catered mostly to witches. I'd recently started dating, and saving for my own place. I thought I wanted to set down roots, you know? I still wasn't sure why I'd felt called to move there, but at that point I was happy to roll with it, trusting that when the time was right, all would be revealed. But then things started getting weird."

"Weird how?" I asked

"A few of my regulars—they'd started acting kind of paranoid. At least, that's how I saw it at the time. Whispering about old hunter conspiracies, and witches being murdered in their beds… I… Sorry, Gray. I didn't mean…" Her cheeks darkened, and when she met my eyes again, her own were full of compassion. "I know they weren't rumors after all, but at the time, no one had heard from the hunters in decades. It all seemed a little far-fetched—like everyone had heard it from a friend of a cousin of an ex-husband, but no one had any firsthand info.

"The vamps and shifters," she continued, "who normally stayed pretty sequestered in their own territories, started getting into skirmishes. One night a family of lynx shifters was slaughtered in their home, little kids and everything, and their whole community blamed the vampires. After that, things started going downhill fast. My restaurant shut down, and I was laid off. I was in shock, literally wandering the streets with my head hung, wondering what my next move was going to be. I swear—the second the question was in my mind, I felt it."

"Felt what?" I asked. I'd long since given up on chopping. Haley and I, along with the other witches in the kitchen, were all riveted by the story.

Sadly, I was pretty sure a lot of them had similar tales to tell.

"That foreboding. Like when every hair on your body stands on end, and your heart just starts banging away for no reason. I reached in my bag for my mace, but by then, someone was already on top of me, jamming in the needle." She closed her eyes, a full-on shiver working its way through her body. I could sense the uptick of her heartbeat, the adrenaline spiking through her blood as remembered panic set in. "I woke up in a cell. You can pretty much figure out what happened next."

It was a good thing I'd already set down the bottle of herbs I'd been working with, because I was pretty sure anything in my hands would've shattered in that moment.

"Addie," I said softly, forcing myself to keep my voice calm.

Gentle. For my sister's sake. For the sake of every witch in the room who'd gone through the same impossible hell. "You're safe here. All of you are safe here. And I promise you, we're going to kill every last one of those motherfuckers if I have to tear their throats out myself."

I was shaking with rage, so consumed by it that I didn't even notice Haley standing in front of me until she reached out and grabbed my arm. "Gray? Take this. Please."

I blinked back to reality, taking the steaming mug from her outstretched hand. Closing my eyes, I took a second to dial it down, then managed a tight smile. "I appreciate the effort, but I don't think Merry Mint is going to do the trick this time."

"This brew is." She winked at me. "My own special blend. I call it Vampire's Delight."

I brought it to my nose, inhaling the scent. I smelled the mint first, then a subtle pinch of dried hawthorn—nothing that would knock me out, just strong enough to blunt my sharp edges—finished with a spoonful of O-positive. I sipped it slowly, forcing myself to relax.

"Thank you," I said. "That's actually… really good."

"Told you." She handed a mug to Addie. "This is straight-up honey lavender. No blood, unless you're into that sort of thing."

Addie laughed, happily wrapping her hands around the mug. "I think I'll stick with the honey-lavender, thanks."

We sipped our tea and got back to work, giving Addie a few moments to gather her thoughts. Whatever she'd gone through, it was clear this was the first time she was talking about it out loud, and I knew this was only the very first crack. Eventually, that crack would turn into a fissure, and all hell would break loose.

The difference now was that she wouldn't have to go through it alone. Not anymore.

After a few moments of companionable silence, Haley turned the conversation toward our other sister. "How do you guys think Georgie got tangled up with Trinity when the rest of us managed to stay under her radar?"

"I don't know," I said. "I'm guessing Trinity found her somehow. Maybe that's how this whole thing got started. Now that we know she's involved with the Fae Council, we can connect her to Orendiel and the hunters. So it's possible that Trinity found out that we were still alive, and set the wheels of her plan in motion."

"But why would she track down Georgie and not the rest of us?" Addie asked.

"Maybe she's still looking for us," Haley said.

That thought sent a shiver down my spine, but there was no room for fear. I grabbed Verona's instruction list, scanning for the next batch of poisons. If and when Trinity came for us, we'd be ready for her.

"You guys said that we were all called to the Bay," Addie said. "That we sensed each other somehow."

"That's what Deirdre thinks," I said.

Addie capped off another one of her bottles. "Do you think Georgie senses us, too? What if she's trying to get back to us, and Trinity's holding her hostage?"

"We can't assume Georgie is a hostage," I said. "For all we know, she and Trinity are working together." I hated myself for saying it, but someone had to. The girl we'd seen in our vision during the blood spell hadn't looked like a hostage to me.

Haley looked up from her bowl of herbs, glaring at me across the counter. "Do you actually think our sister is evil?"

"I'm not saying she's evil, Hay. But we can't know her motivations. She might not realize what's going on. Our mother may have twisted everything, manipulated her into doing her bidding."

"She's not a child, Gray," Haley said. "She's a grown woman."

"That doesn't mean she couldn't be misled or manipulated or threatened," I said. "All we know is that she's working with Trinity. We have no idea what her situation is, but at the end of the day—"

"God, I hate that phrase," Haley said. "At the end of the day? We're talking about right *now*, Gray. Our sister is in trouble, and you want to sentence her before we've even—"

"I think what Gray is trying to say," Addie said gently, reaching out to touch Haley's hand, "is that even if Georgie *isn't* evil, she's still fighting on the wrong side, whether she realizes it or not."

"Thank you," I said, blowing out a breath. "That's all I—"

"And," she went on, cutting me off with a kind smile, "I think Haley is trying to remind us that no matter whose team Georgie is on, she's still our sister, and we owe it to her to give her the benefit of the doubt. To try to help her, just like you guys helped me. Just like you're helping each other."

I looked into Addie's eyes, my momentary annoyance at Haley floating away.

Haley sighed. "Addie's right. Look, Gray, the last thing I want to do is fight with you."

"Same," I admitted. "I get what you're saying about Georgie."

"And I get what *you're* saying," Haley said. "I think we just... We can't make assumptions either way. But we also can't abandon her without trying to figure it out.

"Agreed," I said, and Addie smiled.

"Guys," she said, "I think I just broke up my first sister fight."

I nudged her in the ribs. "Don't let it go to your head just yet."

Magical or not, I was starting to think that her gifts went well beyond foresight. Addie was a natural peacemaker.

"So where do we go from here?" I asked.

Both of my sisters opened their mouths to respond, but the voice that reached my ears wasn't from either of them.

It was the dark, deadly, deep-fried twang of the only man I hated worse than the hunters.

"I'll tell you where you're *not* going, Miss Desario," Sebastian drawled. "How about we start there?"

With fire in his eyes, he snapped his fingers, and every witch in the kitchen disappeared.

TWELVE

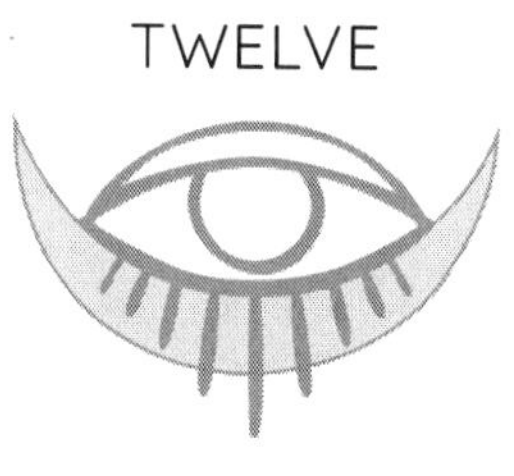

GRAY

Instinct took over.

In a blur of movement, I grabbed my knife and leaped over the counter, lunging for him, fangs and blade bared.

But even with my vamp speed, I was no match for the prince of hell. A single raised hand, and I slammed into an invisible wall, my knife clattering to the floor.

I scrambled to my feet. "What have you done with them?"

"Relax," he said. "I've safely relocated them to another part of the lodge, where they will remain, none the wiser, so long as you give me the right answers."

"I'm not answering anything until I know for sure they're safe."

His eyes turned completely red, the vein at his temple throbbing with barely-contained rage. "I'm sorry, bloodsucker. Have I given you the impression that you're in any position to negotiate?"

I backed off, but I didn't back down. I had no idea how he'd found out about my vampire transition, but now that he had, I had to play this very carefully.

"What can I do for you, prince?" I asked, folding my arms across my chest.

"See? Civility. That's much better." Patting his stomach, he glanced around the kitchen, his eyes returning to normal. "I suppose I can't expect hospitality, though. What have you got to drink in this dreadful establishment?"

I didn't respond.

"Never mind. I'll help myself." He rummaged through the cupboards, locating the liquor stash and pouring himself a generous glass of bourbon. Gesturing to the table at the other side of the kitchen, he said, "Sit."

It wasn't a request.

I did as he asked, and he took the chair across from me, eyeing me up as he sipped the bourbon. I couldn't read his thoughts, and didn't dare try to influence them, lest he sense my interference. But one thing was clear—Sebastian had a lot on his mind.

"Let's get one thing clear before we proceed." He set the glass on the table, locking me in his frightening glare. "The fact that you are at present a soulless monster does not negate our deal. Soul or not, you *will* find a way to do as I demand, per the rules of your contract."

I waited a beat. Two. Three. Then, "The contract is for my soul, Sebastian. Which, as you can see, is long gone. I'm not sure we have anything left to—"

He snapped his fingers again, and my throat constricted. It was as if I were being choked by an invisible hand. No, I didn't need oxygen, but I needed my windpipe intact.

"I think we're well past semantics, Miss Desario." He lifted the glass to his lips, watching with pure amusement as I clawed at my own throat, my eyes bulging. Saliva pooled in the corners of my mouth, my neck about five seconds from snapping in two, and still he drawled on. "I *own* you, just as I own Ronan. Body, mind, soul, blood, bones. I own those sharp and shiny new fangs of yours. I own those curls that probably drive the boys wild. I own your heart, your smile, your eyeballs. I own the soles of your feet. I own your fingerprints. I even own your thoughts."

He took another long sip, then set the glass down, finally releasing his choke-hold.

I coughed, rubbing my throat, glaring daggers at him.

He was full of shit. Sebastian was nothing if not a stickler for details—his entire organization was predicated on it. My contract was specific—my soul was promised to him. Nothing else.

"So you can see why attempting to avoid your fate is not only futile," he said, full of the kind of confidence that could only be achieved by the truly mediocre, "but extremely dangerous."

I nodded, deciding to play along for now.

"At any rate," he blathered on, "the task I've set for you doesn't require the presence of your soul, per se. Only your magic."

The lodge had fallen silent, save for the wheezing of his breath. I couldn't even hear the ocean outside. He'd truly sealed us in a bubble.

And he still hadn't told me what he wanted, or why he'd shown up at all. He liked keeping me off balance, that was for sure.

Maybe it was time to throw him off balance instead.

"I know it's not my ancestors you're really after," I said.

"You know nothing."

"You sure about that?"

He waved away my words with a swat of his fat hand, but I saw the flicker of surprise in his eyes. He was playing games, as usual.

"Tell me what you want with Trinity O'Leary," I said, point blank.

The name itself was like a spell, unleashing all his pent-up rage. He slammed his glass onto the table, shattering it and slicing his hand open in the process. My eyes widened at the sight of his crimson blood, but the scent that followed was rotten, a stench so foul it made my stomach turn.

"I've told you once before, and this is the *last* time I'll say it," he warned. "Ronan and the other strays you've picked up along the way may be lining up to lick your boots, but you do *not* dictate orders to me. I'll reveal information to you if and when it's pertinent. Is that clear, witch?"

I glared at him, saying nothing.

"Is that *clear*?" he shouted, this time flipping the table between us. His eyes had gone back to red, his voice shaking.

Whatever my birthmother had done, her betrayal had cut deep. That much was clear.

But Sebastian's outbursts wouldn't scare me off—not this time. Despite his show of force and the choke-hold he'd sprung on me earlier, Sebastian's power over me wasn't physical. Deep down I knew he wouldn't break me. Scare me, yes. Hurt me, sure. But break me? Not a chance.

He needed me in one piece. He needed me willing. My magic wouldn't work without my intent, and my intent could not be faked.

I'd gotten him riled up, off-kilter, and unfocused. I had to press my advantage with him, however small it might be.

I decided to call his bluff.

"I know she bailed on her deal," I said, "but so do lots of people. You can't honestly tell me you'd invest all this energy into tracking down one nearly-powerless witch, especially when you've got the Silversbane heir on the payroll now."

Sebastian closed his eyes and bowed his head, folding his hands in his lap as though he were the picture of self-control. But without the table between us, I could see his legs now, the anxious bounce of his knee.

Again, I wished I could read his thoughts.

"Who made the deal for my soul?" I asked, certain it was all connected. My mother, my legacy, Sebastian's obsession with me. How could it not be?

"How could someone make a deal for a soul that wasn't theirs?" I pressed. "And why were you so willing to accept it?" Then, in a voice that came out much softer than I'd planned, "Why am I so important to you?"

Sebastian sighed. After what felt like an hour, he finally met my eyes again. He seemed to be taking a measure of me, and I forced myself not to fidget.

For the first time in our strange, antagonistic relationship, I swore I saw a flicker of sympathy in his eyes.

"The answer to each of those questions," he finally said, all his earlier rage gone, "is a long, complicated story."

"You've got a captive audience and all the time in the world," I said.

Ignoring this, Sebastian rose from the chair and righted the table he'd knocked over, then headed back to the liquor stash to fix a new drink.

This time, he returned with two.

Handing one to me, he said plainly, "Be careful what you drag out into the light, Silversbane. Some things can't be shoved back into the darkness, no matter how hard you push."

Surprising myself, I took the offered drink, clinking my glass against his before taking a sip. The bourbon stung, but after a moment, my tongue seemed to remember that it'd once liked the taste, and I tossed back a bit more.

Sebastian sat down across from me again, eyeing me with the same assessing gaze. We seemed to be on another level with each other, both of us dropping some of the bluster and mind games, though I couldn't figure out how we'd gotten there.

After another impossibly long stretch of silence, I said, "I've agreed to your terms, Sebastian. I've made a vow to carry out your bidding. I think I have a right to know who sentenced me."

"If circumstances were different, I might agree with you." He tossed back the rest of the drink, but it wasn't enough to erase the humanity from his eyes. "I'm sorry, Gray. The story of your binding is not mine to tell."

The sincerity in his voice was utterly shocking. Now *I* was the one off-kilter and unbalanced, knowing I could never trust him, but seeing something else beneath the surface nevertheless.

In that moment, the Prince of Hell seemed ancient, as though he were carrying the secrets and regrets of every lost soul he'd ever enslaved.

"Then whose story is it?" I asked, clinging to a last desperate hope he might share some clue, some insight, as if knowing one more thing about my past could untangle every last mystery in my present.

"It's mine," came the sharp, clear reply, and I turned to see Deirdre storming into the kitchen, her eyes blazing. "This has gone on long enough, Sebastian."

Sebastian slammed his fist on the table, but the moment he met my grandmother's fiery eyes, his own softened considerably. In a voice entirely too tender for the moment, he said, "This doesn't concern you, Deirdre."

"You're damn straight it concerns me. You promised me you'd leave my granddaughter alone until it was time for her to fulfill her vow."

"That was before I knew she'd become a bloodsucker," he said. "I can only imagine why you didn't feel this change in circumstance warranted a discussion."

"I've only just learned about it myself," Deirdre said. She flashed her eyes at me, and I heard her warning in my mind.

Don't say another word, Gray. We will discuss this later.

I downed the rest of my drink and pressed my lips together, but that was more out of frustration than following her orders. Since I'd met my grandmother, she'd left me with more questions than answers, popping in and out my life as it suited her. At this point, I felt very little allegiance to her.

I just didn't know what the hell else to say.

"Be that as it may, Deirdre," Sebastian drawled, "my patience on this matter is just about gone. I think it's time the witch returns with me to Inferno."

All the sympathy, the humanity, the gentleness I'd seen in him evaporated, replaced once again by the oily, underhanded wheeler-dealer I'd always known.

"We've got a penthouse suite all set up for you," he told me with a smug smile, as if this was a selling point.

At this, I let out a hollow laugh. "Is that a euphemism for dungeon?"

"Hardly," he said. "As long as you do as I ask, you'll want for nothing, I assure you."

"Sorry if I don't take you at your word."

"I've given you no reason not to trust me," he said. "In fact, I've given you more leeway than any other in my possession."

In my possession…

The words crept uneasily down my spine. Technically, he *had* given me leeway. From the moment Liam had burned my life scroll, Sebastian could've called in my contract with a snap of his greasy fingers.

But I needed more than leeway now. I needed time.

Steeling myself, I said, "You and I have a deal. You agreed to grant me my freedom until I've figured out the situation here. As you can see, we're still dealing with that situation, and it's only gotten more complicated."

"I don't see you dealing with anything," he said, glancing around the kitchen. "I see a bunch of witches playing at spellcraft while the world outside falls apart."

"Sebastian," Deirdre said. "A word, please?"

"The world outside is exactly what we're trying to save," I reminded him, ignoring my grandmother's pleas. "And if we fail, your operation fails, too. No more human vessels, no one making deals… It's all just… Poof." I made a starburst with my fingers. "So I'm *real* sorry the apocalypse isn't sticking to your ideal timeline, but unless you're willing to let it all burn down—including hell and your place in it—you should probably back off and let me do what I need to do here."

"So let me get this straight," he said, rubbing his fingers over that ridiculous goatee. "You refuse to trust me, yet at every turn, you're expecting *my* trust. Demanding more and more of it. Attempting to break your contract."

Deirdre's voice echoed through my skull again. *Gray, that's enough. Tell him what he wants to hear and get him the hell out.*

But telling Sebastian what he wanted to hear was the fastest way into another devil's bargain you couldn't talk your way out of, and I was *not* signing up for that.

"I made a vow to you that night at Inferno, Sebastian," I said. "If that vow is broken, it will be because I've made you a better offer, not because I've reneged."

After a beat, he rose from the table and came to stand beside my chair, towering over me.

Screw that. I stood up, meeting him at eye level, refusing to submit.

"Two weeks, Miss Desario," he said, his breath sharp and boozy. "That is all the time I'm willing to grant, and that is more than generous. See to it that you handle your affairs before then, as there *won't* be another extension. And should you even attempt to negotiate for more time, I won't hesitate to smoke your beloved demons out of existence."

His eyes glittered as he watched that threat hit the mark, worming its way into my mind. No matter how tall and tough I stood, I knew I couldn't hide the fear in my eyes.

I was a fool to think for even a second there was anything humane about Sebastian.

"Show yourself out, prince," I said, keeping my voice solid. "I'm sure you know the way back to hell."

I turned my back on him, feeling both terrified and more powerful than I'd ever felt in my life.

I sensed his instant departure. Just like that, the air in the room cleared.

"Gray," Deirdre said. "You must find your sisters."

I turned to look at her, shocked by the sight. She was slumped in one of the kitchen chairs, her eyes watery, her whole body radiating exhaustion.

"What's wrong?" I asked. "Are you okay?"

Deirdre held my gaze a long moment, then shook her head, a tear sliding down her cheek. "I need to speak with the three of you. It's urgent."

THIRTEEN

GRAY

I found Addie and Haley with Verona and the other witches in the common room, all of them sitting around the fireplace, chatting and laughing over tea and cookies as if the last twenty minutes hadn't even happened.

"Deirdre's here," I said to my sisters, deciding to leave the Sebastian stuff for later. "She needs to talk to us. Says it's urgent."

Haley and Addie headed back to the kitchen with me, Addie smoothing her hair on the way. She'd yet to meet our grandmother, and I had no idea how she'd feel when she finally did, but I was pretty sure this wouldn't be a happy reunion. Not for any of us.

We found Deirdre sitting alone at the table, exactly where I'd left her. She spared a brief glance for Addie as we approached, her eyes misting at the sight, but then it was like a wall slammed down over her emotions, locking the rest of us out.

Immediately, she warded the kitchen, making sure no one would disturb us.

"There is no easy way to say this, girls, so I'm just going to come out with it," Deirdre said. "I'll fill in the details after. Okay?"

She didn't give any of us a chance to disagree, or even wait until my sisters and I had gotten settled in our chairs. She just plowed on with the words that seemed to be tearing her up from the inside.

The ones I'd been afraid to hear since she'd first appeared in the kitchen, announcing that the story of my contract was hers to tell.

"Gray." She took a steadying breath, then met my gaze, her face a mask of control.

It was inevitable, what she said next, and I couldn't say it came as a surprise. All the clues had been there, and now that I looked backward, I could see them all line up neatly, waiting for me to solve the mystery on my own.

But I hadn't, and hearing it said aloud rattled me to the core.

"I'm the one who sold your soul to Sebastian," she said.

Ignoring my sisters' gasps, I closed my eyes and let the confession wash over me. Word by word, it sank into my skin, winding its way around my heart and squeezing tight.

It was one more betrayal in a long line of broken promises and shattered trusts. So why the hell did it hurt so bad?

The table cracked before me.

I hadn't even realized I'd been gripping it.

"Gray?" Haley touched my arm, gentle and kind, and I focused my energy on it, coming back into myself. Slowly, the anger receded, settling into a cold stone at the pit of my gut.

I released my death grip on the table and rose to put on the kettle, grabbing a bag of blood and some crushed hawthorn for myself. Something told me this fucked-up fairy tale was just beginning, and I was going to need a lot more than Haley's touch on my arm to keep from tearing Deirdre's head clear from her body.

FOURTEEN

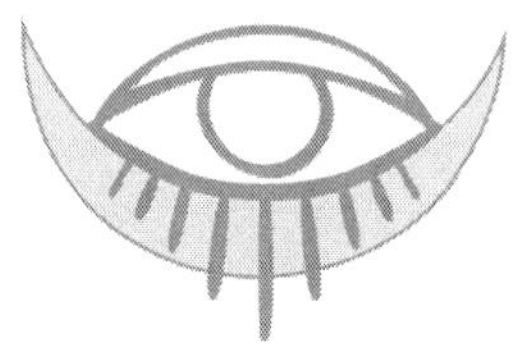

GRAY

When the tea was ready and I felt like I could rejoin everyone at the table without destroying anything, I wrapped my hands around the mug and settled back into my chair, barely meeting my grandmother's eyes.

"Talk," I said, staring at a point just above her left shoulder.

"Sebastian and I go back a long time," Deirdre began. "Before any of you were even born, when I was still young and beautiful."

Is that a twinkle *in her voice?*

"Save us the trip down memory lane," I snapped. "Get to the point."

"Oh, but this is the point, Gray. Every step, every decision led to the ultimate one. I could no more unravel this thread from the story than I could undo the outcome."

I brought the mug to my mouth, biting back another nasty retort. For so long, all I'd wanted to know was who signed my contract—who sold my soul into demonic slavery, condemning me before I was even old enough to know what hell even was. But now that I had my answer, I wasn't even sure I wanted to understand the hows and whys of it.

But Deirdre didn't give me a choice then, and she sure as hell wasn't giving me one now.

"I was fairly powerful in my own right," she continued, "but hungry. Hungry to prove myself to my parents, who were well-regarded in our community but cruel and cold to their children. Hungry for bigger, more expansive magic, which always seemed to elude me. And most of all, hungry to make a name for myself. One night, after a particularly brutal fight with my parents, I was just angry and volatile enough to do the one thing I'd always known was absolutely forbidden—call upon the demon at the crossroads."

A chill went through the room, and both my sisters shivered. I wrapped my hands around my mug, willing myself to sit still. To not leap across the table and throttle her.

"At the next full moon," she continued, "I gathered up my supplies and headed out into the woods just before midnight, looking for the fabled place where two paths crossed—a dark, ominous part of the forest where most witches in my circle had never dared to venture. Once I knew I was in the right spot, I performed the ritual, spilling blood to call forth the demon servant who'd carry my plea to his master.

"Imagine my surprise when the master himself showed up. Oh, he was quite charming back then—in a different vessel entirely, mind you—and he knew exactly what to say to wrap me around his finger. I made my first deal that very night."

"You sold your soul?" I asked.

"Not then, no. Sebastian doesn't always trade in souls. There are other favors, other promises, other bits of knowledge and sacred information a witch might offer, and there were many things Sebastian wanted to know about my family. As I said, they were influential in the community, and my mother was a prominent witch from an even more prominent family. So Sebastian and I continued on in this way for years, meeting at the crossroads in the woods, making deals. We used to joke that I'd signed my name in blood so many times I could've fed an entire vampire coven for a year." At this, she glanced at me briefly, but didn't have the courage to hold my gaze.

"Why are you telling us all of this?" I asked.

"I want you all to understand that Sebastian and I knew each other very well by the time you girls came into my life. Call me a fool for trusting the Prince of Hell, but he'd never betrayed me, which was more than I could say for my own family."

She paused to sip her tea, and I took a moment to process all of this. I didn't want to feel sorry for her—not at all. But I also knew what it was like to finally find the one person you could trust after all the people in your life—the people you were *supposed* to be able to trust—had shit on you.

But my empathy could only go so far. I knew the ending of this story, and the person who'd gotten shit on this time wasn't Deirdre. It was me.

"Fast forward to the night your mother tried to kill you," Deirdre said. "By then I had a solid coven, backed by the power of Sebastian, who we'd been working with as a group for some time. After we succeeded in removing you four from your mother's home, we did a binding ritual on you."

"Why the hell would you do that?" Addie blurted out. It was the first she'd spoken since Deirdre had begun this story, and though she was initially eager to meet our grandmother, her demeanor toward her had flipped like a switch, as had Haley's. The three of us now sat close together on one side of the table, shoulders practically touching, staring down our grandmother on the other side, like some kind of tribunal. We were in this together now—three out of the four witches of prophecy, united after more than two decades, never to be torn apart again.

"We thought binding your powers would allow you to blend into human society more seamlessly," Deirdre explained. "But it didn't work. Already you were all too strong—even Georgie, who was only a baby then. I knew it was only a matter of time before you were truly discovered—before people in the larger magical and supernatural communities learned the truth about your legacy. We knew the witches chosen to adopt you into their care would do their best to shield you, but it wasn't enough. It would never be enough. I didn't… I didn't know what else to do."

"Sounds exactly like the kind of desperation Sebastian thrives on," I said, draining the last of my tea. I'd added a little too much hawthorn, and now I felt it working its way into my bloodstream, quickly mellowing me out.

It was probably for the best. All that anger, all that bitterness was making it hard to think, and now that Deirdre had started weaving the full tapestry of this story, I realized I *did* want to know.

Every last detail.

"In exchange for your eternal protection, I offered him my own soul, my own blood. I'm no Silversbane, but as I said, my line is powerful in its own right, highly coveted by demon lords."

"What demon lords?" Haley asked. "I thought Sebastian was the boss."

"He has been in power a long time, Serena—"

"It's Haley now."

"Of course. Haley. But like all men in positions of power, he knows his is not guaranteed. There will always be challengers—someone hungrier, dirtier, more desperate, more willing to do whatever it takes to secure that ultimate power."

"So you thought having access to your magic and your blood could somehow help keep him in power?" I asked.

"That was part of it, yes. But more than my powerful blood, I knew I had another advantage: In all those deals, over all those clandestine meetings at the crossroads, Sebastian had fallen in love with me."

"Holy shit," Addie said. "Are you saying Sebastian is our—"

"No. Your grandfather was human, I assure you. With all the same weaknesses and frailties as the rest." Deirdre shook her head, the muscle in her jaw ticking. "He was long gone by the time you four came into the picture. In any case, I knew as well as Sebastian that my offer meant I'd become his—body, magic, and soul. There was no way he'd turn it down."

"Well, apparently prostituting yourself to the Prince of Hell wasn't enough after all, was it?" I asked. Under the table, I felt the touch of Addie's hand on my thigh, offering a gentle squeeze.

Deirdre shook her head, her eyes glistening with fresh tears. "Nothing is simple when it comes to Sebastian, and this deal was no different. He had conditions, the first being that I allow him to make me immortal."

Haley gasped. "You're immortal?"

Nodding, she said, "My soul would always be his regardless, but he wanted my body, too—and not just for however many years or even decades I had left. He wanted to be sure that I was well and truly his possession—for eternity. So yes, I'm immortal, but it's not the gift you might think. I was sixty-three when he turned me, so sixty-three I am cursed to remain."

"You agreed to this?" I asked, a flicker of warmth suddenly worming its way back into my heart for her. An immortal existence as Sebastian's lover sounded like a special kind of hell. "You traded your eternal freedom just so he'd protect us?"

She looked up at me again, a faint smile crossing her lips. In a soft voice full of pain and regret, she said, "Understand, child. There's nothing I wouldn't do, even today, if I thought it would help keep you four girls safe. I truly believed that by sacrificing my eternity to Sebastian, you and your sisters might have a chance at living your *own* lives, far away from the legacy and all who'd seek to use it against you."

"How exactly was he supposed to protect us?" Addie asked.

"Sebastian promised to assign each of you a demon protector, charged with guarding you against hunters and—should she discover my trickery and come searching for you again—your mother. For many years, your guardians did just that, and though I quickly grew to despise Sebastian, I took comfort and joy in knowing that you were all safe. For the first time since you were born, I was beginning to feel like I could breathe again. Your mother believed you were dead. And the guardians were keeping you from danger. To me, every moment spent with Sebastian felt like an investment in your future, and it was a small price to pay.

"Sadly and regrettably, like most desperate people standing at the crossroads, I failed to read the fine print." At this, she looked up to meet my gaze again, her own burning with shame. "What I didn't realize, Gray, was that in addition to protecting you for the rest of your life, Sebastian would lay claim to your soul upon your natural death."

"All of us?" I asked, alarmed.

Deirdre shook her head. "All of you are spoken of in the prophecy—the witches who would ultimately unite our kind. But

Gray, only you are the third daughter of a third daughter. The powerful Shadowborn witch foretold to lead the covens. That was the power Sebastian most craved."

"I still don't understand how you could make a crossroads deal with someone else's soul," I said. "*My* soul. It wasn't yours to bargain with."

Inside, I felt my dark magic swirl, pulsing into my blood, looking for an outlet. My mind was screaming at me to put that woman through the wall, but apparently the hawthorn was keeping me in check.

At least, that's what I was telling myself. If not, I'd have to admit that my heart was breaking for her. That if this were merely a story about someone else's life, I'd already be cheering for the old woman to come out on top, despite all her missteps.

That she'd wanted to protect us was clear. That she'd truly believed she was doing the right thing was clear.

But none of that changed the outcome, and that's the part I just couldn't get past.

"You were a baby, Gray," she said. "A minor child."

"This isn't family court," I snapped. "Why would my minor status make a difference?"

"No. I fear you would've had a better chance in family court." Deirdre offered a quick smile, but it didn't touch her eyes. "In the court of hell, only Sebastian's rules matter. As your sole guardian at the time, I was able to assume temporary power and dominion over your soul, which allowed me to make the deal for your protection and sign it with my own blood on your behalf."

"But it's not your blood he's after now," Haley said.

"No. That honor goes to the Silversbane witches. You four, and your mother, of course, though she's managed to evade him thus far—a fact that torments him endlessly."

"What is it that makes Silversbane blood so special?" Haley asked. "There has to be more to it than magic words in an ancient prophecy."

Deirdre sighed. Under the guise of making more tea, she got up from her chair and headed to the stove, but it was obvious she was merely steeling herself for the rest of the story.

The tension in the room felt thick and sticky, and my sisters and I exchanged dark glances, just as rattled as Deirdre seemed to be. Even without speaking the words, I knew we shared the same understanding: things were about to get even more complicated—for all of us.

"There *is* more to it than the prophecy," Deirdre confirmed, her back to us as she watched the flames flicker to life beneath the tea kettle. "A *lot* more."

FIFTEEN

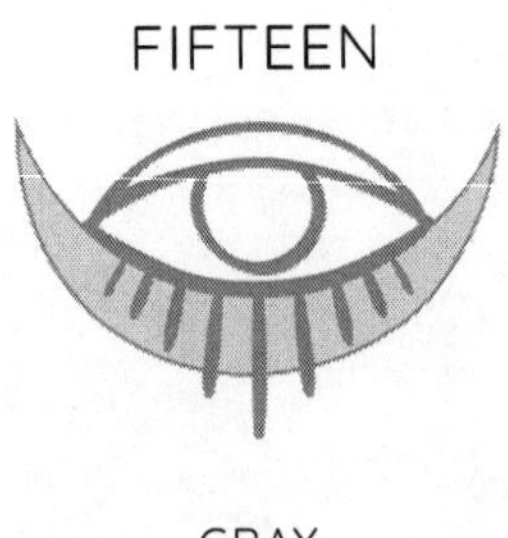

GRAY

Time slowed to an impossible crawl as we waited for Deirdre to prepare her tea, my sisters and I perched on the edges of our chairs, desperate to hear the rest of the story.

My mind was swirling with possibilities, none of them good.

By the time Deirdre rejoined us at the table, the only thing I knew for certain was that nothing she revealed, nothing she said, nothing she did would ever come between me and my sisters again.

"Your matrilineal ancestors lived in what we now know as Ireland," Deirdre began, and my sisters drew closer to me. I reached for each of their hands beneath the table, clasping them tightly, making physical the connection I'd already been feeling. Magic hummed in their veins, calling out to mine as we touched, wrapping us all in a blanket of support and rightness.

It felt like coming home after a day spent trekking through the snow, that first wave of welcoming warmth as you opened the door, the rich scent of hot chocolate beckoning you to step inside and take off your boots, slide into your slippers, and come sit by the fireplace.

"They were among the first witches chosen by the elemental source as guardians of the earth's magic," she continued, and I nodded—she'd told me that part of the story the day we'd met in Las Vegas, when I'd first learned about the Silversbane prophecy.

"At that time," she said, "the fae, who were among earth's first inhabitants, had already been living here for eons. They'd had their own magic, and had successfully connected with earth's innate magic to become quite powerful beings—perhaps even more so here than they'd been even in their home realms. So you can understand why they'd be reluctant to share. They were not pleased to learn that the source had gifted humans access to that magic, as well as naming them its sole guardians."

"They've always believed magic was their domain," I said. "They've never fully trusted us—that hasn't changed."

"No, it hasn't," Deirdre agreed, blowing across the top of her tea, making the steam swirl before her. "This is all legend, of course, but there is always some kernel of truth to be found there. As the tale was told to me, the fae decided that the best way to keep the magic within their sphere of influence was to mate with the first witches and mages, creating a new, even more powerful fae bloodline, melding the best of both magics."

"But witches can't become pregnant by supernaturals," I said.

"Not naturally, no," Deirdre said. "But with a bit of fae magic, all things were thought possible."

An image flitted through my mind—Sophie and Jael. I wondered if they would've had children together. Beautiful, magical babies with her gorgeous red hair and Jael's penetrating yellow eyes...

"Humans had always been enamored of the fae," Deirdre said, pulling me back to the present. "And a bit intimidated by these beautiful, otherworldly beings who'd kept themselves largely apart for so many years. When the fae rulers brought the proposal to the covens, the witches, who were quite open-minded and keen to further the protection and stewardship of all forms of magic, saw it as a great honor. And so the mating rituals began, but no children were born. Years passed, and still, not a single heir, though not for lack of trying."

At this, Deirdre smiled, lost in the story. I felt my own lips twitching into a smile; fae were rumored to be extremely passionate lovers.

"According to the old tales," Deirdre said, "a young fae prince had a prophetic dream about a witch who was recently born in the mortal realm to one of the first witches, with violet eyes and silver-white hair. In the dream, her mother allowed him to hold the child, and the moment he gazed upon her face, he fell in love with her. When he woke up that morning, he told his court of the dream and declared his intent to marry her, sending his emissaries to scour the mortal realm for the child who matched the description. She was found in Ireland, and her family was presented with the prince's proposal, along with the promise of more wealth than they could ever imagine.

"The family saw this as a high honor, and accepted the proposal, on the condition that they be allowed to raise their daughter Finnabair and keep her at home until she reached the age of twenty. The prince agreed, and the wedding date was set.

"But the prince, who dreamed of her nightly, grew impatient. When the child was only four years old, he sent his emissaries to her home to request that she be released into his care immediately, vowing to raise her himself until she came of age, at which time they would marry as planned. Horrified at the thought of losing their precious daughter sixteen years sooner than they'd agreed, her parents outright refused." Deirdre's eyes misted. "The emissaries slaughtered her parents and siblings, kidnapping the girl to the fae realm and presenting her to the prince anyway."

Deirdre paused to sip her tea. Next to me, I felt Addie curling inward, her shoulders hunching. After everything she'd just been through, I wasn't surprised the story was upsetting her.

"Addie, do you want to get some air?" I asked softly, squeezing her hand. "We could take a walk."

My sister shook her head. "I want to hear how this ends."

"I'm sorry to upset you," Deirdre said kindly, "but know that this particular story has a happy ending—at least for Finnabair. You see, she was a clever child, and though the prince had treated her kindly, and sworn his love and loyalty until the end of time, she still remembered her homeland, and what had been done to her family on his orders. Biding her time, she waited until midnight the night before her twentieth birthday—what was to be her wedding day—and made her escape, knowing it would cause the prince the most pain to lose her so close to the moment she was set to become his for eternity."

"Fucking badass," Addie said, and we all laughed, breaking up the tension a bit.

"Oh, but the story doesn't end there," Deirdre said. "The prince did not take her departure lightly. The moment news reached his ear that his bride-to-be had run away, he called in a favor to an allied court in the north, rumored to have the most powerful and destructive army in the realms. The ally sent him four elite fae warriors, and the prince sent them to hunt Finnabair down. He wanted her executed on site, and as proof that they'd completed their duty, they were to return with her long silver braids as both a trophy and a lesson to anyone who might think to betray the prince in the future."

"So much for his so-called love and loyalty," I said. "Asshole."

"Though the prince claimed issuing such an order broke his heart," Deirdre said, "he could no longer trust her, and could not allow such a betrayal to go unpunished, for to do so would be a sign of weakness, and his rule would most certainly be challenged."

I rolled my eyes. It always came down to the same thing with these guys—power. They spent their whole lives coveting it, and once they got a taste of it, they spent the rest of their lives trying to hold on to it before the next upstart got his claws in. It was a vicious cycle with no end and no winners.

Beyond that, something else about the story was making me uneasy, though I couldn't quite put my finger on it. A question struggled to form from the mist of my mind, but no matter how hard I tried to focus, it wouldn't coalesce.

"The soldiers tracked her down in a matter of days," Deirdre went on, "for though she was clever, and very much at home in the forests of fae she'd essentially grown up in, she did not know how to get back to the mortal realm. But despite their training and the prince's orders, none of them could bring himself to execute her. They continued to send dispatches back to the prince that they'd yet to locate her, hoping they could buy themselves enough time to figure out what to do, but they were running out of options. Eventually, Finnabair cut off her own hair, soaked it in animal blood, and had the men send it to the prince, declaring they'd done their duty—that she was well and truly dead and buried. But the prince knew this was another trick, and demanded the soldiers return to him immediately. If they refused, he would consider it an act of war from the allied court—the soldiers' homeland—which would leave him no choice but to retaliate."

"Please tell me they told him to fuck off," Addie said.

"Essentially, that's exactly what they did. The soldiers had fallen in love with Finnabair. They refused to turn her over to such a cruel fate."

"So wait—all four of them fell for her?" Haley asked.

"Yes."

"Hmm." Haley nudged me in the ribs, laughing. "Where have we heard this story before?"

"What happened next?" I asked, ignoring Haley's teasing.

"The prince followed through on his threats, and a long, bloody war ensued. There are differing accounts as to how it turned out, but one outcome was certain: the allied court was completely ostracized. They were branded as traitors, their reputation destroyed along with most of their lands and a good deal of their people. Despite the skill of their armies, they could not defend against the prince and the other allies he'd rallied against them."

"I thought you said this story had a happy ending?" Addie said.

"For Finnabair, yes." At this, Deirdre smiled. "Ironically, the union of the warrior fae and the silver-haired witch was the first of its kind to create a child. From their love, a new bloodline was born."

"Silversbane," Haley whispered, and a shiver rolled through my body. Silence floated between us, and I closed my eyes, walking backward through Deirdre's story, back to the start. I'd been so caught up in Finnabair's tale, I'd forgotten why we'd started talking about it in the first place.

And now that I was thinking about it more clearly, the nagging question I'd been chasing finally reared it's big, ugly head.

I opened my eyes, meeting Deirdre's across the table.

"Which court?" I asked, my voice low, my jaw tight. Deep inside, where magic and intuition lived, I feared I already knew the answer, but I had to ask anyway.

Deirdre nodded slowly, her smile fading. She'd known this question was coming. "You're asking about the northern allies. The warriors."

"Our ancestors, Deirdre," I clarified. "Aside from Finnabair, whose blood runs through our veins?"

"Your lineage can be traced back to Darkwinter," she confessed. "That is why you're so powerful. You—all of you—are descendent from the powerful union of a daughter of a first witch and the warriors who sacrificed everything they'd ever known and cared for to keep her safe."

Addie was out of her chair, pacing the kitchen before her. Haley got up to get her some water, but I was pretty sure nothing would ever wash away the memories of what she'd suffered. The memories of the torture and torment Orendiel and his knights had doled out.

"Understand, girls," Deirdre said, "Darkwinter were not always as they are today. Their hallmark hatred and violence—that was made, not born. Your line was not created from such darkness, but its opposite. The Knights of Darkwinter called upon by the prince were brave and true. That they loved Finnabair, that they protected her, that they sacrificed so much to keep her safe —*that* is where the true source of the magic of Silversbane lies. The friendship, love, and union of the fierce witch and her brave, honorable fae… All of it came together to create the most powerful bloodline in history."

"That may be so," I said, "yet somehow along the way, that line became corrupted."

"I will not excuse Darkwinter's actions now, but as I said, that hatred was born of war, evolving over centuries of being ostracized and attacked on the orders of a cruel, vicious prince bent on power."

"Do they know who we are?" I asked, my head spinning from the direction this crazy story had spun. "Orendiel and his army of glitter-dicks? Do they know they're hunting their own…" I trailed off, unsure what to call it. Blood? What the hell did that even mean anymore?

The word itself felt strange to me now, its meaning so diluted it may as well have been a foreign language. Did it mean family? A bond? A promise? Or was it no more than the red stuff oozing through us all—the stuff that made my heart beat? The stuff Darius and I and others of our kind needed to swallow in order to survive?

"They know of the stories, I'm sure," she said. "It's part of their ancestral lore as much as it's a part of yours. But you have to remember, Gray. It's not as if you're *fae*. We're talking about thousands of years, hundreds of generations of blending bloodlines. They don't necessarily know that you girls are the four Silversbane descendants—the witches of prophecy."

My sisters joined me back at the table. Seeing Addie's red, puffy eyes made me want to stab something.

"I think it's time for you to go," I said to Deirdre. I'd been caught up in the story about Finnabair, but that didn't change the fact that my grandmother was the one who'd sold my soul to Sebastian. I understood her reasoning—why she thought she had no other options—but no matter how hard I searched my heart, I just couldn't find forgiveness there. Not for her. Not yet.

"Gray, I understand you're upset with me," she said, "and you have every right to—"

"I'm not upset," I snapped, but that was just a reaction. The moment the words were out, I knew they were true. All the anger I'd felt when Deirdre had first begun this confession had somehow evaporated.

I wasn't upset. Wasn't mad. Wasn't even marginally annoyed.

The only emotion swirling in my gut now was disappointment.

Again, I thought of Finnabair. Not the woman who'd fallen in love with the fae warriors sent to execute her, but the violet-eyed, silver-haired newborn the prince had first dreamed of.

Deirdre had glossed over that part of the story, but in my

mind, it was the most important part. The origin, without which the tale could not have unfolded as it did.

Emissaries of the fae prince had arrived with promises of prestige and money, and without a second thought, Finnabair's parents made a deal. She was days old, and they'd agreed to trade her away, completely trampling her sovereignty, cashing in her future for their own personal gain.

And right here in America, thousands of miles and thousands of years away from Finnabair's Ireland, the same cycle played out again when a sixty-three-year-old witch made a bet on the devil and lost.

I looked at my sisters, wondered again at the abuses they'd suffered, both at the hands of the same men. Hunters who'd been trying to kill us for millennia. Fae who had no idea they'd been chasing down their own descendants.

I thought of Norah, a witch so many others had trusted and venerated. A witch who later turned over her own kind to the enemy, trading their lives, their blood, their souls for a shot at saving her own ass.

I thought of my rebels. I thought of all the battles we'd faced so far, all the power games we'd been forced to play and play again, all the fights still banging on our door, looking for a way in.

We had so many enemies, yet in the end, the people with the greatest power to destroy us weren't our enemies at all.

They were our own flesh-and-blood families. The ones we hadn't chosen ourselves. The ones who hid under the twin banners of blood and loyalty while they sharpened their swords, waiting for the day when they'd shove them straight through your heart.

"Girls, what can I do to make this right?" Deirdre asked. "What do you need from me? Please tell me."

In her eyes, I saw the same desperation she must've felt when she'd realized her granddaughters would never be safe—the same desperation that had driven her to Sebastian—and I knew she'd meant what she said earlier. That she would do absolutely anything, even now, to help keep us safe.

All I had to do was ask.

I reached for my sisters' hands, holding them tight, the three of us a unified front. The tight, unbreakable bond of our magic flowed between us, connecting us, strengthening us.

I had a single thought, and in that moment, I knew my sisters shared it.

"We need you to leave, Deirdre," I said. "Permanently."

SIXTEEN

ASHER

"Ace of Cups. Drink."

Tossing the Tarot card on the discard pile, I pushed a glass of whiskey toward Gray, amber liquid sloshing up over the sides.

Clear-eyed and resolute, she held my gaze and downed it, never blinking.

"That's not how Tarot works." Haley rolled her eyes. "You can't just say *drink* every time you draw one of the cups cards, Ash."

"And *you* can't ask me to give you guys a reading and then tell me how to interpret the cards." I picked up another one from the pile on the table between us. "The Fool. Oh, this one's got your name all over it, Barnes. Drink up."

"No way," Haley said. "I'm tapping out. Two is my max, and I've already had three."

"I'll take one for the team," Gray said, downing the glass I'd set up for her sister.

I shook my head, flashing her a grin. "You're a lot harder to drink under the table as a bloodsucker."

"Bloodsucker *fae*," she corrected.

"That too." I'd been sticking to beer, but now I poured a round of whiskey for myself and picked up the glass, lifting it in salute before downing it. When I finished, I caught her gaze again, seeing right through the jokes to the soft parts inside her—the parts that still felt like the lost, confused kid who'd first washed up in Blackmoon Bay all those years ago. Couldn't blame her, though. Seemed like every time she finally solved another piece of her mysterious origins, she uncovered another betrayal. Another painful tale she wished she could close the book on for good.

But shit didn't work that way. We didn't get to flip through the fairytales of our lives, picking out only the best ones, the happy ones to keep. They were all part of us, the good as well as the terrible.

I just wished she'd gotten a few more good ones lately.

"Pick another card," Addie said. "It's my turn."

"You got it." I did as she asked, revealing the next card in the deck—Three of Cups. This one had three women sitting side-by-side on the rocks before a lotus pond, the full moon shining down upon them. They each held a chalice, and their eyes were closed, heads bent as if they were casting a spell.

"It's you three for sure," I said.

"Does this mean we all have to drink? I think it does." Without waiting for an answer, Addie reached for the bottle and poured three shots, then downed hers like a champ. "Cheers, fae bitches."

"I should've quit while I was ahead," I said. "I'm no match for three drunk-ass sister-witches, especially if you keep ganging up on me."

"The big bad incubus is afraid of three little girls?" Haley teased. "That's rich."

"We should totally start a band," Addie said randomly. "Drunk-Ass Sister Witches. It has a nice ring to it, don't you think?"

"I'd definitely pay to see that show," I said.

"Your turn, Ash," Gray said, flashing a smile I know she didn't totally feel, despite my best efforts to cheer her up. To cheer them all up. "Pick a card for yourself."

I picked up the deck, giving it a good shuffle before turning over my card.

"Seven of Swords?" I picked up the card for a closer look. There was a dude on the front, with black angel wings, kneeling in the snow to pick up two swords, one of which he'd grabbed by the blade—total fucking amateur. Five ravens circled him, each one holding its own sword. The storm clouds behind him felt pretty damn ominous to me. "This guy looks shady as hell. What's his deal?"

"Oh, you know," Gray said. "Deception, trickery, the usual." She folded her arms across her chest, eyeing me up and down as a sexy-ass grin stretched across her mouth. "Maybe the cards are warning me to watch my step around you, incubus."

I reached for my beer again, tipping it back to take a swig. "You needed the cards to tell you that?"

Still grinning, she slid out of her chair and joined me on the other side of the table, straddling me, seemingly oblivious to the fact that we weren't alone. "I'm not so great with learning lessons. Maybe you should teach me the hard way."

I wrapped an arm around her back, ensuring she wouldn't wriggle away. "Why the fuck are you so sexy?"

"And on that note… *Barf.*" Haley stood up, making a show of yawning and looking at her phone. "Wow, would you look at the time?"

Addie laughed. "Subtle, girl. Real subtle."

"Stay for the show if you want," Haley said, "but the two of them have enough chemistry to set the whole lodge on fire, and trust me, you don't want to be at ground zero when it happens."

"Alright, alright." Addie stood up and grabbed her glass, along with the unfinished bottle of whiskey. "You two kids have fun. Try not to incinerate anything."

"No promises," Gray said.

And then two of the three drunk-ass sister witches were gone, leaving me alone with a woman insisting on being taught the hard way.

Emphasis on hard.

Gray leaned forward, licking a path across my lips.

Three, two, one, and… yep. Hard as fuck.

"You taste like beer," she said, her voice low and sultry.

I kissed her again. "You taste like trouble."

"Mmm. We make a good combo, don't we?" She looped her arms around my neck and sighed, her breath warm on my lips. "A vampire-fae-witch with the worst gene pool in history, and an incubus with… well, let's just call it your garden variety mysterious origins."

I laughed. "My origins aren't all that mysterious, Cupcake. You take one incubus, find him a succubus mate, throw 'em together, shake well, and garnish with a cherry."

"That's it?" she asked.

I shrugged and ran my hand up her spine, cupping the back of her neck and pulling her mouth to mine. Kissing was better than talking. Always had been.

But eventually she broke our kiss, pulling back and staring into my eyes in a way that completely undid me. She wanted to know more. She wanted to know *me*—all the things I'd never told her, the things I'd been trying not to tell myself.

"Last I heard they were somewhere in Italy," I said. "I haven't had any contact with them for at least a hundred years, give or take."

Her mouth fell open, and she stared at me for a good full minute before finally finding her voice. "Ash, your parents are still *alive*?"

"No idea, but I haven't heard otherwise, so that's my assumption."

"You don't talk to them at all?"

I reached for my beer again, tossed back another slug. Normally the booze kept the memories at bay, but every once in a while they snuck back in.

Like whenever I had to watch Gray live through some fucking trauma her own family had caused. That shit always stirred up old ghosts.

Hundreds of years wandering this forsaken rock, and I'd never understand why so many of the world's worst people in existence insisted on procreating. Most of the population—human and supernatural alike—had no business bringing kids into this world.

"Alright, Cupcake," I finally said. "You want the whole sob story? You got it."

I sighed and closed my eyes, breaking off her intense gaze.

Saying the words was one thing. Seeing her eyes change from sexy and flirty and curious to sad and pitying was another—one I wanted no part of.

"My parents never bothered to tell me what I was. I grew up thinking I was a regular kid with serious fucking problems."

"How did you finally figure it—oh. Oh, fuck, Asher." She leaned forward, resting her forehead on my shoulder, and in that moment I knew she'd answered her own question. "The girl," she said softly. "The one from your drawings."

"The one and only." The same girl I'd drawn night after night for decades, though the drawings had stopped not too long after things heated up between me and Gray. Somehow, whenever I tried to draw her after that, I'd end up drawing Gray instead, which was just fine by me.

"I saw her," she said. Confessed. "The night I… When I had your soul. I saw the whole thing."

"I figured as much." The night she'd taken my soul to save me from the devil's trap in Norah's attic, our souls connected. She relived my worst memory as though it were her own, and I was pretty sure it'd haunted her ever since. "If I could erase that from your memory, I would."

"I'd erase it from yours, too."

"My parents thought they'd have more time, but they waited too damn long. If they'd just been honest with me from the start, I could've learned to control it. And I *damn* sure wouldn't have gotten involved with a human girl. Fuck, Gray. Carina was innocent, and I just…"

I held Gray close and clenched my jaw, willing the wave of memories to recede, but of course they wouldn't. *Carina…* It was the first time in centuries I'd said her name out loud, and in doing so, I'd called forth her ghost.

Every single memory I'd ever shared with her came crashing back, from the first day we met at her father's farm stand, to the last in that wheat field.

"You loved her," Gray said softly.

At this, I pulled back and opened my eyes to meet her gaze. There was no jealousy there. Only empathy.

There was a time when that look in her eyes would've sent me into a rage. When *no one* got behind my walls without a fight.

But who the fuck was I kidding? This woman had crashed through those barriers the very first night she sat across from me at her own kitchen table, slinging the cards that revealed my nature to her.

I looked into her eyes, losing myself in their twilight blue depths. "Yeah. I loved her, Gray. I loved her, and then I killed her."

My throat tightened, barely keeping the tears at bay. The guilt.

"I never even got the chance to tell her I was sorry. To go to her funeral. To tell her father what had happened, man to man. My parents whisked me away in the middle of the night, forbidding me to talk about her. To this day, I'm sure her father thought she'd run away." The tears gathered, then spilled. Hastily, I scrubbed a hand across my eyes. "That was the worst of it. The man hadn't even known his daughter had died."

Gray took my face in her hands. "It's not your fault, Asher. You didn't even know what you were."

"Neither did she. So why am I the one still walking around? Still breathing and eating and drinking and fighting and fucking… Falling in love. I just…" I closed my eyes, reining it in. "She doesn't get a do-over, Gray."

"No, and that's not fair. Really. But Ash, even if she'd never met you, right now? Tonight? She would've already been dead for centuries."

"If you've got a point, Cupcake, I'd appreciate you getting to it."

In a voice so soft it nearly broke me, she said, "Why are you still carrying her on your shoulders?"

I felt another tear slide down my cheek, hot and bitter, and willed myself to end this. To change conversations, get us back onto neutral territory. Back to fake Tarot readings and teasing and kissing.

But Gray wouldn't let me. And in so many ways, I didn't want her to.

I loved her. With my whole fucking heart. With my soul, however tarnished and tattered it was.

So this part of me, this deep dark well of regret and pain… I had to let her see it. The worst of me. The best of me. All of it.

"I can't put her down," I whispered. "Carrying her, remembering that moment, watching the life leave her eyes… That's my punishment. My penance."

"That's just torture. You're torturing yourself."

"What else can I do?"

"Forgive yourself, for starters."

I grabbed her hands, pulled them against my chest, pleading with my eyes for her to understand. Why was this so fucking hard?

"Ash, you have to—"

"I can't, Gray. I just can't."

Gray shook her head, her own eyes reflecting my pain. My anguish. "I love you. That means you don't get to carry this burden by yourself anymore. You say Carina doesn't get a do-over, and you're right. But you *do*. Every day you wake up alive, it's a do-over. You decide every minute, every second. *You* choose. So if you can tell me that you're honestly not ready to put her down, or that you're not quite sure how to forgive yourself, I will accept that, and I'll do my best to help you through it any way I can." She reached for my face again, her eyes blazing with new fire. "But you don't get to say 'can't.' Not anymore. Not about this."

"Good advice, Doc. So how's that grandma of yours? You ready to forgive her yet?"

It was a low blow, a desperate move to get off the topic of Carina, and I regretted it the instant the words fell out of my big, dumb mouth.

Gray didn't take the bait, though. Instead, she just shrugged. "A traitor, a dark witch, and goddamn liar. The devil's playmate. I'm still on the fence about whether she's evil incarnate or not, but I'll keep you posted."

"Gray, you can't—"

"What did I just say about that word?" She leaned forward,

stealing a kiss I was all too eager to give her anyway. Beneath the heat of her thighs, my cock stiffened again, ready to pick up right where we'd left off.

When she pulled back again, she said, "You know what? Let's not talk about our fucked-up families for the rest of the night. Deal?"

Gray and I had both cut a little too damn deep—I knew she sensed it, too—and it seemed we'd both had enough soul-baring for one night. It would've been so easy to give in to her touch, to laugh at her joke, to let her soothe the ache that tore through my heart, just as I would do for her.

But I was done taking the easy way out. There was something I needed her to know, and it went beyond the love I felt for her, beyond the guilt and shame I'd felt about Carina, beyond the rage I still felt toward my parents.

One thing all of that had taught me was that standing around with your dick in your hand when you should've been telling someone how you truly felt was a one-way ticket to endless regret.

Immortal or not, none of us ever knew how long we truly had.

"Gray, listen to me." I slid my hands into her hair, fisting it, holding her steady. I'd never seen anyone so beautiful, so fucking incredible, and the fact that she loved me—that she'd continued to stand by me night after night—that blew my fucking mind. "The people who gave birth to me? They aren't my family. Darius, Ronan, Emilio, Spooky? *They're* my family." I pressed a kiss to the corner of her mouth, whispering close. "*You* are my family, Gray. The one I choose, every day I wake up alive."

The admission felt big, important, more vulnerable than anything I'd ever admitted to another being. Family—the kind I was talking about? It was so much more than being in love. Yeah, that was part of it for me and Gray. But it was friendship. It was respect. It was calling each other out on our bullshit, and holding each other close when everything got to be too much. It was being vulnerable and scared because you knew and trusted your heart was in good hands.

It was everything I never had growing up, and never dared to dream I'd have now. Not until the first time she'd told me she loved me.

A tear rolled down her cheek, and she smiled, her eyes twinkling. "You're my family, too, Asher. Always."

She kissed me then, deep and passionate and wild, and I wrapped her legs around my hips and rose from the kitchen chair, carrying her into the common room. The few witches who'd been hanging out in there vacated the moment they saw us coming, closing the French doors behind them, and now we had it to ourselves. I laid her on one of the couches and kissed my way down her throat, loosening the buttons on her shirt as I went, the fire roaring beside us.

I'd just unveiled her sexy-as-sin black lace bra when I sensed an unwelcome intruder standing over us.

"I thought I smelled fire," Darius said. "Apparently I was correct."

I tore my mouth away from Gray's silky-smooth skin and glared up at him. "So you're, what? Swooping in to dump some cold water on my nuts?"

Gray laughed. "You and your visuals."

"You've got two options here, bloodsucker," I said, repositioning myself between Gray's thighs. "One—turn around, go back to your coffin, and we'll all pretend this never happened."

He folded his arms across his chest, gracing us with his smug grin. "What's choice two?"

I cut my glance back to Gray, her eyes glittering like twin sapphires. The smile on her lips felt like a dare.

"Yeah, incubus," she teased, arching up against me until I was about ready to come right there. "What's option two?"

"Ladies choice," I said, giving it right back to her. I rolled my hips, grinding my thoroughly-hardened cock against her clit, wishing I'd thought to take her jeans off before the shirt. "You wanna play with fire, Cupcake? Be my guest."

"Oh, I do, and I will. Darius?" she called out, never taking her eyes off mine, her smile never slipping. "Get naked. *Now*."

The command in her voice made me weak in the best fucking way.

The vampire was naked in a heartbeat. By the time I flicked my gaze up to meet his, he was already hard as fuck, a slow grin sliding across his face.

"Alright, little vampire," he said, kneeling down beside us. "I'm here and at your service. Does this mean I'm well and truly forgiven for last night's oversight in the woods?"

"Hmm." She looked at him with a wicked gleam in her eye that told me we were both about to be in some serious trouble. "I'll let you know later. Now shut up and kiss me before I change my mind."

SEVENTEEN

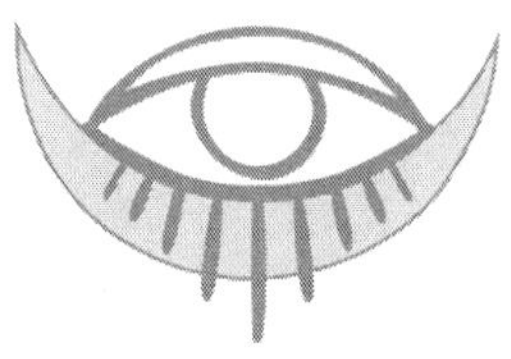

GRAY

The fire crackled before us, bathing my incubus and vampire in a flickering orange glow. They were naked, stretched out on their backs on the bearskin rug before the hearth, the French doors shut tight against intruders—including poor Sunshine and Sparkle, who'd been taking turns pressing their muzzles up against the glass as if they'd been utterly abandoned.

Ignoring the pang in my chest at locking my loyal beasts out, I knelt between Ash and Darius, one hand on each of their muscled chests. Outside, the icy wind was doing its damnedest to shatter the bay windows along the front wall, but nothing could break this moment between us.

"You're so beautiful," Asher said, his eyes glazed with emotion that belied the ever-present bad-boy smirk on his face.

Darius nodded his agreement, reaching up to stroke my thigh. "I'm not sure what we've done to deserve you in our lives, Gray Desario, but not a moment goes by that I don't thank the universe for you."

"I love you both," I said, emotion tightening my throat. We'd started this thing teasing each other, but now, seeing them together, both of them looking up at me like I'd painted every last star in the sky, I was overcome with gratitude. Asher was right—we were family in the true sense of the word. In the only sense that mattered. "More than you could possibly realize."

Before they could respond, I pressed my fingers against their lips. I didn't need to hear the words returned; I knew how they both felt. It was written in their eyes, glittering with the reflection of the firelight. It was laced through every touch, every kiss, every soft sigh I felt against my skin.

I'd once heard that the human body completely regenerates itself every seven to ten years. It sounded like myth to me, but in the last week alone, I'd already felt like I'd been through several iterations. I was a witch. I was a vampire. My blood contained that of the very fae we were hunting. Each revelation had unveiled countless others, until I no longer knew which way was up and which way was down.

Now here I was, a composite whole of all the various parts, sometimes breathing, sometimes not. Sometimes hungry, sometimes not. My heart never beat the same pattern for more than a few moments anymore. And each time I looked in the mirror, I found new facets, new scars, new shadows.

The only constant in my life now was this—my rebels. No matter how much I'd changed—physically, magically, emotionally—they'd stood by me through it all. Darius had asked what they'd done to deserve me in their lives, but I was the who'd been truly blessed.

Without their kindness, their loyalty, their bravery, their sacrifice, I'd still be a little lost girl shivering in a boat, floating in the harbor of a strange city she'd never even known was her home.

With tears in my eyes, I climbed on top of Asher, straddling him as Darius knelt behind me, kissing a slow, teasing path up my spine. My incubus was hard as steel, and I was wet and ready for him, lowering myself onto his length, taking him all the way in. Behind me, I felt the press of Darius's erection against my backside, just as eager, just as ready, but his turn would come later.

Unlike me, Darius had infinite patience.

Wrapping his hands around my hips, he guided me into a slow roll that had Asher fisting the rug at his sides, his breath catching in his throat.

"Fucking hell, woman," Asher groaned. "That's..."

"Bloody brilliant," Darius whispered, nipping my shoulder,

his fangs teasing my hyper-sensitive skin. I leaned my head to the side, exposing the tender flesh of my neck, inviting the bite I knew he was dying to give me.

"Are you certain?" he whispered, nipping my earlobe.

Bearing one of my most vulnerable spots to him was the ultimate sign of trust, and therefore, forgiveness. He knew what I was saying with that gesture, and it wasn't just about the exquisite pleasure I knew would follow.

"Yes," I breathed. "Absolutely certain."

As Asher's hands slid up to palm my breasts, Darius sunk his fangs into my flesh, and I let out a cry of pure ecstasy. Warmth pooled on my skin, and he licked it seductively, taking his time as he swirled his tongue over my super-sensitive flesh, every delicious stroke making my blood simmer.

Asher sat up, capturing my nipple between his lips, sucking me hard as his hand slid down between us, fingers brushing my aching clit.

The two of them played my body like an instrument they'd mastered together long ago, touching and teasing and caressing until my nerves were humming, my thighs aching, my core throbbing, and still, they gave me more.

I didn't want it to end, but I was quickly losing the capacity to hold back. I pushed Asher back down, hands on his shoulders, our eyes locked in a fiery gaze as I slowed my movements, rolling my hips, taking him in deeper and deeper until I brought him to the brink.

Clenching his teeth, he arched upward, driving in deeper, his hands gripping my thighs, fingers digging hard into my flesh.

"No," I commanded. "Not yet."

Asher blew out a breath, but I was in charge tonight, and I knew he wouldn't come. Not until I was ready to make him.

I leaned forward and captured his mouth in a deep kiss, slowly sliding off his cock. Inch by inch, I kissed my way down his body—his chin, his jaw, his collarbone, the impressive ridges of his abs, my tongue tracing lines along his tattoos as I went. When I finally reached my destination, I fisted the base of his cock and took him into my mouth, slowly teasing the tip with my tongue before taking him deeper.

I arched my backside, brushing against Darius's cock, an invitation as much as a demand. Without hesitation, Darius slid into me from behind, filling me as I took Asher deeper into my throat. Our connection was unbreakable; the pure pleasure of taking both of them inside me at the same time made me dizzy. It was all heat and fire and love and a perfect rhythm that drew me closer and closer to that pure, white-hot bliss.

I'd intended to tease Ash a little longer, but now I was the one who couldn't hold out. I sucked him harder, bobbing my head, bringing him right back to that razor-thin ledge I'd left him on as Darius brought me to the same place.

"Fuck, Gray. You're killing me." Asher slid his hand into my hair, fisting it, guiding me to take him in deeper, slower, then fast, then slow again. I loved the way he tried to grasp the very last vestige of control, even as he was absolutely losing it.

I couldn't hold out another second. Raking my nails down his thighs, I sucked him in deep once again, and he finally lost the battle, shuddering against my mouth, his moans of pleasure setting off my own orgasm. I arched back against Darius, who grabbed my hips and slammed into me harder, faster, chasing his own release and turning mine into an explosion of stars and fireworks that couldn't be contained.

The sounds that came out of my mouth… I was pretty sure I'd never heard anything quite like that before.

Finally, I crawled back up to rest my head on Asher's chest, collapsing in his arms as Darius collapsed on top of me, the three of us making the perfect sandwich, the echo of their heartbeats a beautiful song that I would carry with me for eternity.

* * *

"Are you cold?" Asher asked a little while later, rubbing my bare arm. The fire had faded to a soft glow, and a slight but icy draft snuck in around the windows.

"Not possible." I laughed. Curled up against his chest, with

Darius spooning me from behind, I was thoroughly cocooned, my body as hot as if we'd been lying out in the summer sun.

We'd gotten up to grab a quick shower and let the poor hounds in to sit by the fire, but other than that, we'd been tangled together on the bearskin rug for the last couple of hours.

I didn't want the sun to rise.

"You're shivering," Ash said.

"Your fault," I teased, tracing a circle around his nipple. His skin erupted in goosebumps. "Both of you make me lose control."

"It's a gift," Asher said.

"One that keeps on giving," Darius said, pressing a kiss to my bare shoulder.

"I'm just glad you finally gave in at all," I teased. Looking up at Asher, I told him about Darius's ridiculous demands about how our first time would be. "You should've heard him, Ash. 'It will be in *my* bed, blah blah blah.'"

Asher laughed. "I take it your first time didn't go as planned?"

"No. We were in the Shadowrealm, of all places. And I *still* haven't seen his actual bed."

"To be fair," Darius said, "we're dealing with extenuating circumstances. That aside, I assure you, I *would've* taken you in my bed. In fact, I still might."

"Whatever you need to tell yourself to get through the night," I said, earning myself a playful slap on the ass and a nip on the shoulder.

"So you really remember everything from before?" Asher asked Darius. A note of wonder echoed in his voice. "All of it?"

Sometimes, I still couldn't believe it myself. I'd tried to have faith, but for so long, I truly believed the old Darius was gone. That we'd have to rebuild everything we'd had from scratch, with no guarantee that it would turn out the same. I loved him; I was willing to try anything, even if it meant falling in love with him all over again, but I couldn't say I didn't miss the man I'd fallen for in the first place.

In the end, we didn't have to go down that road. Somehow, he'd come back to us.

I turned over onto my back and reached for his hand, lacing our fingers together.

"I do remember." Darius nuzzled the crook of my neck, his hand sliding across my belly. "Thanks to the tenaciousness of this crazy witch and her many blood spells."

"It wasn't just the blood spells," I corrected. "They definitely got the ball rolling, but the real magic was in the bite at the cemetery. I had no idea it would work like that."

"It was our blood bond," Darius said. "And you were the one who figured out blood was the key to—"

"Everything," I said suddenly, then I gasped, struck by a new realization. "Blood spells! Oh my God, that's it!" I turned on my hip to face my vampire, a smile stretching across my face. "Darius Beaumont, you're so brilliant I could kiss you."

"Allow me to save you the trouble, love." He claimed my mouth in a possessive kiss, and for a minute I almost lost myself again, a soft moan escaping my lips as heat rekindled in my core. Asher slid his palm over my hip, his fingers brushing across my belly, then down between my thighs. He was hard again, his cock thickening against my backside in a way that had me dreaming of all new ways for them to share me…

No. That particular pleasure would have to wait. I had work to do.

Disentangling from their embrace, I hopped up from the floor and hunted around the room in search of my clothes.

"Wait, what?" Ash laughed. "Why the fuck are you getting dressed? I was just getting warmed up again."

"Raincheck," I said. "I've got an idea, and it can't wait."

"Yeah," Ash said. "Obviously the worst one ever."

"Blame Darius," I said.

He turned to glare at the vampire, who held up his hands in mock innocence.

"Don't blame me, Asher. You heard the woman. She said I'm so brilliant she could kiss me."

"Maybe *she* could kiss you, bloodsucker," Ash sneered. "But *I* could kill you."

"You could try."

"Time and place, brother. Time and place."

"Simmer down, boys." I glanced around the room, exasperated. "Where the hell did my underwear end up?"

"Pretty sure the bloodsucker stashed them in his pants pocket," Ash said.

"What?" Darius blustered. "I did no such… Well, this is just preposterous. I demand a trial of my peers."

Glaring at Darius, I picked up his jeans from the couch, fishing my underwear from the back pocket. "You're incorrigible."

"Where are you going, Gray?" Ash stood up and grabbed my elbow, steadying me as I stepped into my underwear. "Seriously."

"First? The kitchen. I need supplies."

"Supplies?" he asked.

"Water, candles, crystals, salt, a glass bowl, and some herbs." Picking up my T-shirt, I answered his question, but I was mostly talking to myself, figuring it out as I went. "I'm thinking mugwort —it's good for clairvoyance and ancestor work. Maybe some wormwood as well. Oh, and something sharp and pointy."

"Mmm." Asher tugged the T-shirt out of my hands and dragged me back into his embrace, kissing his way up my neck, damn near convincing me to stay. "Kinky little witch, aren't you?"

"You don't… know the… half of it." I closed my eyes, temporarily sinking into the pleasure of his mouth on my flesh. Each kiss unlocked another image of the two of them inside me, a fantasy, maybe taking both of them in the same place at the same time…

Oh, God…

No. No, no, *no*. I *had* to concentrate.

"Pause button," I breathed. "I… I mean it. I need to find my… Oh, fuck. What was I even talking about?"

"No idea," Ash replied. "Do you remember, bloodsucker?"

"Funny, incubus. I seem to remember everything *but* that."

"Sisters!" I shouted, forcing myself to stay focused—a task that was growing more impossible by the second. Damn, Asher's mouth was something to behold. "You guys need to wake up my sisters and tell them to meet me in the kitchen."

"Why?" he asked. "I think we're doing just fine on our own."

I finally wriggled out of his embrace, yanked my shirt from his hands, and pulled it on over my head.

"Because as skilled as you guys are in the carnal arts," I said, grinning, "blood magic is not in your wheelhouse." I kissed each of them in turn, short and sweet, then called Sparkle and Sunshine and headed to the kitchen. "Don't wait up, boys. This might take a while."

EIGHTEEN

GRAY

The flames of a dozen candles flickered around us, throwing eerie shadows on the walls and illuminating my sisters' faces in the darkness. The three of us sat together inside the salt circle we'd drawn on the kitchen floor, grounding ourselves, tapping into the magic of the earth and air, fire and water, silently calling forth the elements to help us on our quest for answers.

Behind us, Darius, McKenna, and Verona stood guard, ensuring no one disturbed us—from within the lodge or from wherever our visions took us tonight. Verona had been especially concerned about outside interference, and had insisted we place black tourmaline, labradorite, and black obsidian in every corner to help shield us from psychic attacks, just like we'd done during the blood spell we'd performed on Darius.

That night, Haley and I had inadvertently tapped into a vision with Trinity and Georgie. It was short-lived, no more than a side effect of the blood magic intended to restore Darius's memories, and we hadn't even recognized what it was at the time. But my hope was that by doing the spell together, with the full intention of connecting with our mother and sister—our blood relatives—we could hold the vision long enough to get some solid information.

"And so we begin," Haley said, calling us back to the moment. Verona had prepared an incense of wormwood and mugwort, and

Haley lit it now, fanning the smoke with a raven's feather before setting the bowl to her left.

Unsheathing her athame, she glanced up at me. "Are you sure you're okay with this?"

"You're totally safe," I assured her. At Darius's insistence, I'd fed before we began the ritual. Neither of us believed I'd attack my sisters, but if I felt even a pang of thirst, there was a good chance I'd get distracted by freshly spilled blood and ruin the ritual.

Addie and I unsheathed our athames, following Haley's lead. At her direction, we all sliced our palms, then squeezed our blood into the glass bowl at the center of the circle, three crimson streams merging into one.

The tang of their blood filled my senses, making my mouth water. But I stayed focused, magic tingling inside, warming me.

Addie placed a piece of bloodstone inside the bowl, and I sprinkled African dream root powder on top.

Haley instructed us to touch our fingers to the rim, and then we recited the spell she'd crafted.

"Blood of Silversbane, blood of fae
On ancestors past we call today
Seeking your guidance, your wisdom, your love
Without and within, below and above
Bestow upon us the vision we seek
That we may hear the words they speak."

After our seventh incantation, we released the bowl and clasped hands, my skin tingling as our blood and magic connected and bound us. A sense of belonging washed over me, and though I was still getting to know Haley and had just met Addie, I felt the years of our separation melt away, leaving only the unbreakable bond of our sisterhood.

Blinking away tears, I glanced down at the bowl, the blood inside rapidly changing before my eyes.

Glowing brightly at first, it darkened to near-black, then, ever so slightly, began to swirl around the bloodstone. Entranced, I let my eyelids flutter closed, then followed the tug on my consciousness.

The sensation was similar to swimming in a calm, warm ocean —drifting along on gentle waves, weightless. But then the tide turned, an undertow sucking me further from the shore, pulling me down, down, down…

When I opened my eyes, I found myself standing in the center of a familiar home. I knew I'd been there before—recently, too— but I couldn't place it. There was no furniture, and though the room was freshly cleaned, it was also damaged. Floorboards were missing, walls bashed in, windows taped up.

"Norah's house," Haley said suddenly, and I turned to find her standing at my right side. Addie was on her other side, the three of us still holding hands.

It took me a beat to realize she was right. The last time I'd been here, the guys had basically destroyed the place fighting off a pack of rogue vampires while I saved Asher from a devil's trap in the attic.

"How did we get here?" I asked.

"It's just the vision," Haley said. "There must be something we need to see here."

"Is there anything that can see *us*?" Addie asked.

Haley shook her head. "We're basically in the astral realm. Come on."

We followed her into the dining room, where a lone woman sat at a large dining table with her back to us. Dark blue fingernails, manicured into sharp points, tapped impatiently against the table. Every few seconds, she glanced at her cell and sighed.

Creeping around to the side of the table, I turned to look at her from the front, gasping at the sight.

Too much eye-makeup. Dark hair pulled into a severe French twist. Lips pressed together in perpetual annoyance.

"It's you," I blurted out.

"She can't hear you," Haley said.

I turned toward my sisters. "It's her. Trinity."

Haley nodded. She'd seen her before, too—the night we'd done the blood spell for Darius. But Addie seemed shocked into silence, her mouth hanging open, her fingers wrapped so tightly around the back of one of the dining chairs, her knuckles had turned white.

I put a gentle hand on her forearm. "Addie?"

"That's our… She threw me into the creek." A tear slid down her cheek.

"You remember?" Haley asked.

Addie rubbed her forehead, her face pained. "Just flashes. Gray was begging her not to throw me in. Delly, you guys called me. 'Delly can't swim,' Gray kept saying. Over and over and over, and that woman just… She didn't even care. She wanted us gone."

Addie was shaking now, staring at Trinity with a mixture of fear and hatred.

"But you *did* swim, Addie," I said, rubbing her back. "You pulled yourself out of there, and you screamed your head off until a neighbor finally heard. You're the reason she didn't succeed."

"I can't believe it's her," she said absently.

I turned to stare at the woman who'd given birth to us. She was almost beautiful, and maybe had been at one time, but there was something off about her features. She reminded me of someone who'd had too much plastic surgery, and now tried to mask it with too much makeup. Parts of her skin drooped and sagged unnaturally, her brows and forehead unmoving. Her collarbone jutted out at an odd angle, as if it'd been broken and set improperly.

She reminded me of Jonathan, of the side effects of all the experiments he'd done on himself, constantly chasing the perfect hybrid combination that would make him strong and immortal. Trinity may have been immortal—she was a vampire now, after all—but something told me strength had eluded her. Her hands trembled, and her back hunched over as if it wasn't strong enough to hold her up.

It was hard to believe this woman had almost killed us.

It was even harder to believe she was our mother.

"She can't hurt us here," I said, turning back to Addie, offering what I hoped was a comforting smile.

"No, she can't." A calm steel edged into her voice, and now Addie moved to stand behind Trinity, attempting to wrap her hands around the woman's neck. They passed right through her, as if Addie were no more substantial than mist. "And we can't hurt her, either, which is a shame."

"Guys, someone's coming." Haley gestured for us to join her on the other side of the room, giving us a full view of the table and the entrance from the kitchen, through which four more figures emerged—three fae and one human male.

"That's gotta be Talia," I said, nodding toward the fae woman as she took the chair to Trinity's left. I recognized her wine-colored hair from Emilio's description. "She's on the Council. The fae dude with the scar on his cheek looks like a Darkwinter Knight." He was dressed in a black uniform, with a black-and-gold insignia on the armband. He took the chair on the other side of Trinity, spreading out a bunch of maps on the table before him.

I wondered if he was the soldier Jael's sister Kallayna had pretended to fall in love with.

I wondered if she was even still alive.

"Who do you suppose the other fae is?" Addie asked, nodding at the male settling in on Talia's other side. He was dressed in dark gray robes, with long, stark-white hair woven into several intricate braids. Whomever he was, he had an air of importance about him.

"If that's Talia," Haley said, "a hundred bucks says Mr. Self-Importance is Fenlos."

"Who the fuck is that?" Addie asked.

"He and Talia were higher-ups on the Council," she said. "Jael sensed their magic that night we got into that crash on the highway. They killed some poor truck driver."

I glared at the pair of them, wondering what it was going to take to kill them.

"And the human?" Addie asked, and I glanced to the opposite end of the table, where the human male was settling in and booting up a laptop. He was short and broad-shouldered, with a weathered face and a scraggly whitish beard.

Everything in me turned to stone, except for my heart, which pounded so hard it made my chest ache.

You and your kind will burn, witch…

The last time I'd seen him, that beard had been blond.

The last time I'd seen him, he'd slit Calla's throat before my eyes and ordered his son to kill me.

"Phillip Reese," I managed to choke out. "Jonathan's father. The hunter who murdered my mother. My *true* mother."

I felt my sisters seething beside me, our pain and anger shared. Each of us had been wronged by the people in that room. Each of us had scores to settle. If we could've lit that room on fire and butchered everyone in it, I'm certain we would have.

But we weren't really standing there in Norah's dining room. We weren't really standing *anywhere.* And so my sisters and I clasped hands, infusing each other with love and support, and allowed the meeting of our enemies to unfold before our eyes.

NINETEEN

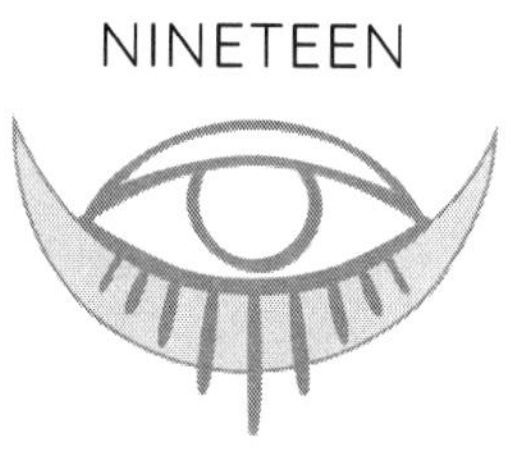

GRAY

"You're late. Again." Trinity glared at the doorway as the final attendee scampered in—another fae, dressed the same as the first guy, but with a lot more bling pinned to his shirt. Medals, no doubt, for all the witches he'd killed.

"Orendiel," Haley said. "The fae fucker in charge here. He and Phillip took over in the cave prisons when Jonathan went AWOL."

"The same fae fucker who killed Emilio at the warehouse raid." My fangs protruded, the magic inside me stirring. It was only the warmth of my sisters' hands that kept me still.

"Apologies, mistress." Orendiel offered a small bow before taking the chair to Phillip's left. "I was detained in the warehouse district. There was a small—"

Trinity cut him off with a single raised eyebrow. "Perhaps, Orendiel, you are under the false notion that my time is less valuable than yours."

"Quite the contrary, mistress." Orendiel lowered his eyes. "It won't happen again."

"See that it doesn't." Trinity finally tore her glacial gaze away from the fae and looked at Phillip, not thawing a bit. "The report, if you please, Phillip. Despite what you all seem to think, I'm not here this evening for my entertainment."

Phillip pulled up a file on his laptop, then began. "I've

received confirmation from our generals in each of our west coast targets that the teams are in position and awaiting the final order."

"Which cities, specifically?" Trinity asked.

"Seattle, Los Angeles, Portland, San Francisco, and San Diego, to start. We're expecting confirmation from Denver and Santa Fe by the week's end."

"Excellent," Trinity said. "And the east coast?"

"Our teams in Boston, New York, and Miami will begin roll-out as part of phase three," he continued. "We'll have more information in the coming weeks, along with reports on cities where we're still trying to establish a foothold."

"Do keep me informed," she said.

"Of course, mistress."

A chill ran down my spine. So many cities, with many more to come. So many people dead smack in the path of destruction. We'd already known that the shitstorm in Blackmoon Bay was merely a testing ground—that they'd planned to branch out, spreading their poison from sea to shining sea—but we had no idea that they were so organized, or that things had already progressed so far.

"They've been working on this a lot longer than we thought," I said. "Seems like Trinity's been running the show the whole time, too."

It jived with the info Asher and Ronan had uncovered in Trinity's office in the crypt. Trinity—our birthmother—truly was the mastermind behind all of this.

My stomach turned over, and I swallowed bile.

"And what's with the mistress shit?" Haley asked. "Why would they just allow her to take over the Council like that? This whole thing is giving me the creeps."

Addie opened her mouth to say something, but the other Darkwinter Knight was pointing something out on his map. From my vantage point, it looked like the area around Luna's Café.

"Blackmoon Bay is nearly ready to fall," he said, tapping the map. "Everything will branch out from this point here—ground zero. Once we've received confirmation that the operation was successful, we'll put the external teams on standby for imminent orders in each city."

"And local law enforcement?" Trinity asked

"We don't anticipate any issues," Phillip said. "Most of the local units have been fully infiltrated and replaced. The holdouts will be taken care of soon enough."

I glanced at my sisters. Holdouts? Was he talking about human cops? Shifters like Emilio's team, who'd remained loyal despite the Darkwinter invasion?

"How soon do you anticipate beginning operations on the east coast?" Trinity asked.

"After the successful completion of our objectives on the west coast, everything will begin to move at a much faster clip," Phillip said.

"Picture the whole country lined with dominoes, coast to coast," the other fae said. "Most of the work will take care of itself. It's merely a matter of knocking down the first one."

"Blackmoon Bay." Trinity smiled, her teeth gleaming, the heavy makeup cracking around her eyes. "What have we left to do here, then? As you can imagine, I'm anxious to remove myself from this festering city as soon as possible."

"The warehouse district is finally secured," Orendiel said, "Along with most of the residential neighborhoods. There are a few remaining strongholds in the Rockport area, but it won't be long before they surrender.

"Witches, I presume?" Trinity asked, her lip curling in disgust. "What, precisely, is the issue?"

At this, Fenlos gave a slight bow of his head. "They've been strangely resistant to the glamours, mistress. Furthermore, it seems the remaining witches in the area have banded together, making it nearly impossible for us to have any effect whatsoever."

I squeezed my sisters' hands, the first hopeful thing we'd heard yet. If witches remained in the Bay, and had gathered together to resist the invasion, they might be able to help us get inside.

I looked at Trinity, waiting for her to unleash her ire on Fenlos, but it never happened. She simply shook her head, clucking her tongue as though she could barely stand the weight of such disappointing news.

"Georgina really needs to work on gaining their trust," she said. "Where *is* that stupid girl?" She rolled her eyes, then shouted at the ceiling, "Georgina!"

My heart leaped. *Georgina.* She was here. Our sister was here, right upstairs.

That was two pieces of good news in the last minute alone.

At least, I hoped it would be good news. We still didn't know whose side Georgie was really on.

"Setting aside Georgina's oversights for the moment," Talia said, her tone even icier than Trinity's, "have you made any progress with her sisters?"

The three of us immediately tensed.

"I don't mean to question your authority, mistress," she continued, her tone suggesting that she'd meant to do *exactly* that. Unlike the men in the room, she did not appear to be the *least* bit enthralled with Trinity. "But you assured us the full cooperation of all four Silversbane witches. That was a condition of your appointment. This plan will not work without them—not in the long term."

"There's no cause for agitation, Talia." Trinity lowered her eyes, her fingernails running along a crack in the table.

Was she actually nervous?

"I'm getting closer to them each day," she said.

Like hell you are.

"So you've said," Talia replied, glancing at Fenlos as if to say, *see what I mean?* "At every meeting this month, you've made your empty promises. Yet we've seen no evidence that you've even *attempted* to reach the others, let alone gotten closer."

"Georgina knows. Ask her." Trinity glanced at the ceiling, as if my sister would apparate from thin air. "Georgina! Get down here! Now! You're—"

"Trinity," Fenlos said, calm and steely, "How can you be so certain they'll follow you?"

Trinity looked at the man as if that were the dumbest question ever uttered. "I'm their *mother,* Fenlos. Of course they'll follow me."

At this, Orendiel finally spoke up. "Forgive me, mistress, but I'm not so certain we should presume their loyalty just yet."

Yeah? Good call there, glitter dick.

Trinity folded her hands on the table in front of her, her eyelid twitching. She looked about three minutes away from core meltdown.

"What was that, Orendiel?" she asked, her lips stretching into a menacing smile.

Orendiel shifted uncomfortably in his chair and lowered his eyes, but he didn't back down. He simply cleared his throat and began again. "From my limited observation, Morgan and Serena are *extremely* loyal—not just to each other, but to the demons, the vampire, and the wolf. Somehow this motley assortment has convinced a great many others to join their cause—primarily witches—and after the losses we suffered at the cemetery, it's my opinion that we are underestimating their strengths, their numbers, and their ability to pose a serious challenge to our plans."

Morgan and Serena. Me and Haley. How the hell did everyone at this table seem to know so much about us?

How long had they been watching? How long had they been planning, plotting, killing?

"My understanding," Orendiel went on, "was that your daughters were removed from your care at a young age, raised in separate homes with no knowledge of you or each other. There's no guarantee they will even *remember* you, let alone agree to follow you into a cause that flies directly in the face of everything they now stand for."

"Agreed," Fenlos said, and Talia smiled at Trinity, vicious and vindictive.

"A mother's love for her children is a bond that cannot be broken," Trinity snapped, and again I tried not to puke, but she was just getting warmed up. "Not by time or by distance," she ranted on, "not by magic or rumors or lies, and most *certainly* not by creatures so vile as demons, vampires, and shifters. Yes, my daughters and I have some things to work through, as any family would after a prolonged estrangement. But as I've said countless times before, I'm confident that once we clear up those misunderstandings, we will be united again as a family."

"Tell me they're not buying this crap," Addie said, but for now, it seemed they were doing just that. Talia and Fenlos had settled back in their chairs, and if any of the others thought to challenge Trinity, none of them said it out loud.

I could barely believe my eyes and ears. Could our birthmother really be that delusional? Clearly, she'd been drinking her own Kool-Aid for far too long.

The question was… How the fuck had she convinced the others sitting around this table to drink from the same damn jug?

Commotion at the front door snagged my attention, and all three of us turned to see someone enter the house in a frenzied rush, her dark brown hair windblown across pink cheeks, glasses askew on her face.

Georgie.

My eyes misted. In that moment, I didn't care whose side she was on. I loved her instantly, and I suspected Haley and Addie felt the exact same way.

"We have to help her," I said.

"There's nothing we can do here," Haley said. "Let's just see what we can find out, then we'll go back home and make a plan."

"But she's—"

"Gray." Haley nodded at the table. "Shh. Just listen."

"Sorry," Georgie panted, rushing into the dining room, tracking snow through the house. "I was in Rockport trying to figure things out with the witches. I tried to get home faster, but this weather is insane."

Trinity arched an eyebrow, spearing our sister with her patented frosty glare. "Tell me you've made progress on that front, or you may turn around, march right back out the way you came, and try again."

Georgie removed her snow-crusted winter coat and draped it over one of the empty chairs, then flopped into the seat, her shoulders slumping. In a small, watery voice, she said, "It's not that easy, Mom. They don't trust me."

"And who's fault is that, Georgina?" Trinity asked.

Desperation crept into Georgie's eyes. "I tried to tell you before, but—"

"Enough!" Trinity silenced her with a raised hand, making her flinch.

The unknown fae started rambling on about maps and coordinates and supplies, but I barely heard him. I was so focused on Georgie, so shocked that she was here, right in front of us, alive and whole and beautiful and just… real.

And now, I knew without a doubt she was *not* here by choice. I could sense it in her reactions, in her movements around Trinity. And there, beneath the fear and desperation, a flicker of the fighting spirit I sensed in all of my sisters. In myself.

However Trinity had found her, whatever she had done or said to convince her to follow her, Georgie was a prisoner now. Again, I felt the anger rise inside me, the rage so close to the edge I could taste it.

Rage at my mother, who'd tried to murder us. Rage at Deirdre, who'd signed away my soul and separated me from my sisters. Somehow, she'd believed that if we were never reunited, the prophecy could never come to fruition. That the four of swords could never rise and fulfill our true destiny. That breaking up our family—our sisterhood—would somehow keep us safe.

I thought of all the witches back at the lodge, and all the witches here in Blackmoon Bay, and all the witches across the entire world who'd been forced to endure the same tortures, and I knew that we would *never* be safe. Not until every witch was free to live the life she chose, without the constant threat of hunters, dark fae, and power-hungry monsters like the woman sitting at the head of this table, desperate to claim what was never hers.

"Gray," Haley whispered, her hand on my lower back. "You need to calm down and pay attention. We need this intel."

I nodded, shaking out of the funk and re-focusing on the conversation. Haley was right. Already we'd learned more in fifteen minutes of spying than we'd managed to piece together over the last few weeks with the guys.

"What of the Grinaldi vampire?" The Darkwinter Knight asked.

"He's talking about Fiona," I said to Haley and Addie. She turned out to be a surprising ally, and was presently recovering back at the lodge with the others we'd rescued from the crypt.

Phillip waved away the question. "Useless to us now. As I suspected, her loyalty to Jonathan was thin at best. Sources tell us she's now firmly entrenched with the enemy."

"We can't just forget about her," Orendiel said. "She knows too much about Jonathan's plans—*our* plans."

"I will personally deal with her if and when it becomes necessary," Phillip said. "Our immediate concern is launching the operation here in the Bay, then relocating our core team to the permanent base in Seattle."

"And what of the units in Europe and Asia?" Trinity asked.

"Once the United States is converted and fully within our control," Phillip said, "it will only be a matter of time before the other countries fall."

Fear and frustration simmered in my gut.

"When?" I shouted, slamming my hand into the back of one of the chairs, but of course my touch passed right through. I could no more cause a physical action here than I could make the monsters sitting around the table answer me.

Still, I didn't know what else to do. If we had any hope of preventing whatever horrors they'd planned to unleash upon the world, we needed a damn timeframe

"When?" I shouted again. "When the fuck is—"

"When?" Georgie asked suddenly, and I gasped, my eyes darting back to her.

She was looking straight at me

"Georgie?" I asked.

"She can't see or hear us," Haley said.

I waved my hands. Georgie didn't blink.

But she didn't look away either.

"She heard me," I said. "I know she did. Guys, she knows we're here."

"What did you say, Georgina?" Trinity asked, her voice barely audible, yet shaking with rage.

Georgie's face was ashen.

She broke our gaze and looked back at Trinity, then lowered her eyes. "I just… I was just wondering when we… When you thought we would be leaving Blackman Bay?"

Good girl, Georgie. That's what we need to know.

"Do you have urgent business elsewhere?" Trinity asked.

"No, mother."

The fake smile came back out. A shark's smile. "A date, perhaps? With a boy?"

"Of course not," Georgie said, her cheeks darkening. But despite her obvious fear, she persisted. "I just wanted to know when we'd be heading up to Seattle."

"Our target date is in three weeks," Phillip replied. "But that's assuming—"

"That's enough, Philip." Trinity turned those dagger eyes back on my little sister. I wondered if she was using her vampire influence, but Georgie didn't flinch. Didn't blink. I sensed the tremble in her body, but she held her chin high, her shoulders squared.

Fucking fight her, little sister. You're a Silversbane witch. You've got this, and we've got you.

"It's a simple question, mother," Georgie said.

It happened so fast, none of us even realized it until my sister was already bleeding.

Georgie gasped, tears springing to her eyes. She pressed her fingers to the fresh gash on her cheek, wet with blood.

The same blood dripping from Trinity's dark blue fingernails.

Georgie met my eyes again.

"I'm sorry," she said, and I knew in my gut her apology was meant for us.

I no longer had control over my body—I no longer cared. All I saw was Georgie's blood dripping from Trinity's nails, and I was in motion, launching myself across the table, gunning for the bitch who called herself our mother.

"Gray, stop!" Addie shouted, and then it was like someone had hit us with a sonic wave. I was falling, spinning, sucked through time and space, everything around me disintegrating…

When I opened my eyes, I was pinned to the kitchen floor back at the lodge, Darius and Emilio trying to steady my thrashing limbs.

"She's awake," Emilio said. "She's okay. Gray? Gray, can you hear me?"

I nodded, blinking away my confusion and trying to sit up.

"That's it, love," Darius said, helping me up. "Nice and easy."

My sisters were standing in front of us, still inside the salt circle that I'd managed to break through, taking several candles down with me.

"What happened?" I asked. "How did we get out?"

"We didn't *get* out," Haley said. "Someone pushed us."

"Georgie," I said, adamant. "She knew we were there. I'm telling you, she could hear me. She knew we needed a timeline. That's why she asked. She pushed us out to protect us."

"Let's hope it was her. Because if Trinity or any of the others knew we were in there, then everything we've just seen is useless, and they're going to double their efforts to shield themselves now."

"I'm sorry," I said. "I know I shouldn't have blown up like that. I just… I saw Georgie bleeding, and then *all* I saw was red. I wanted to claw that bitch's eyes out."

"Your protective instincts are strong, Gray," Darius said. "That's not something to apologize for."

"No, it isn't." Haley offered a smile, but it quickly melted, and she knelt down to blow out the remaining candles. "It wouldn't have done any good, though. We were there on the astral. Georgie might've sensed us—I'll give you that. But that's about it."

"Only it *isn't* it. Not by a long shot." I held out my hand, unfurling my fist to reveal a chunk of Trinity's dark hair.

TWENTY

GRAY

In so many ways, it felt as if an entire year had passed since I last stood in the common room to rally the witches for a battle they never should've had to fight.

An entire year since I'd asked them for their support against an enemy bent on our complete annihilation.

An entire year since they'd given it freely.

In truth, it had been less than two weeks.

And now, the night after Haley's blood spell had given us a glimpse into the darkest corners of our enemies' minds, I found myself standing in the same spot at the front of the same room, looking out at a familiar sight.

The crowd was larger now—including the new friends and allies we'd rescued from the crypt and several more Raven's Cape area witches Verona and her people had rallied to the cause—but everything else about this moment felt exactly the same.

A room full of friends and allies gathered before the fireplace, some huddled on the couches, others standing near the fire, all of us trying to find a moment's warmth in an otherwise inescapable winter.

The men I loved, wordlessly sending me their unwavering support. My sisters standing by my side.

And in my shirt pocket, close to my heart, the objects I'd taken to carrying as gentle reminders of those who'd gone before me—

those who were with me still: the Page of Cups card for Sophie, the High Priestess for Calla, and the granite heart Liam had given me, carved with the raven's feather that would always remind me of Death, my teacher, my guide.

Borrowing their strength, I steadied myself for the task ahead.

The fire popped, and a heavy silence descended on the room.

It was time.

"We have some news about our enemies in the Bay," I began. "Before we get into specifics, let's just rip off the Band-Aid." I paced in front of them, trying to meet each and every person eye-to-eye. I wanted them to know we were in this together, no matter what. "Ten nights from tonight, whether we're ready or not, we are going to war."

A murmur rippled through the group, the tension in the room rising. I could feel the spike of their heart rates, smell the hit of adrenaline that flooded their bloodstreams as soon as I'd said the words.

But the sharp, pungent scent of fear? Completely absent. Two weeks ago, a month ago, three months ago, we had no idea what was coming for us, and that fear of the unknown was enough to drive a person mad.

Knowledge was ammunition, and now, we had a stockpile.

"You guys followed me into hell once before," I said. "Some of you are still recovering from that night at the crypt—and others never will. You put everything on the line that night, and now, I'm going to ask you to do it all over again."

"You don't have to ask us *shit*," McKenna said from the back of the room. "We've got your back, girl. No question."

The others quickly voiced their agreement, and I smiled, grateful for the boost.

"The same caveat we established before still applies," I said anyway, just in case. "And this goes for new friends, too. Anyone who wants to tap out can do so, no questions asked. You will always have a home here, so long as the rest of us are able to provide and protect it. But I have to be honest with you, guys. This is a balls-to-the-wall, all-hands-on-deck kind of situation. If ever we needed the numbers, it's now."

"We're here for you, Gray." This from the yellow-eyed witch who'd been imprisoned in the caves with Haley and McKenna. "We're here for each other. I know I speak for everyone in this room when I say that. This is family now. *You're* family."

"Here, here," came another call, and a few witches let out a whistle, showing their support.

"I… I feel the same," I said, emotion threatening to cut off my words. I swallowed past the tightness in my throat, then continued. "The fight at the cemetery was hard-won—for those on the front lines as well as for the brave souls who'd been imprisoned there. But from the enemy's perspective, the cemetery was just a minor outpost. Blackmoon Bay is ground zero for their entire operation, and it's no longer simply the home we're trying to take back. It's the spark that will eventually set the whole world on fire.

"I know we talked about this last time, but it bears repeating: this is not just about our own lives, but the lives of everyone we've ever loved. If we fail, we will *all* die. Witches, shifters, vampires, demons, fae, *and* humankind. None will be left standing. Not one soul but the few who've masterminded the entire collapse."

Haley and Addie joined me at the front of the room, and together we passed along all of the pertinent intelligence we'd gathered from the blood spell vision. Emilio, Elena, and detectives Lansky and Hobb shared their thoughts on the likely scenarios we'd face once we got past the fae's magical borders and into the city proper, assuming we could get in at all. And those who'd been imprisoned shed more light on the types of hybrids they'd encountered inside, along with details about the fucked-up weaponry both Jonathan and his father had been working on.

"Well," I finally said, certain the picture we'd painted couldn't get any bleaker, "I'm afraid that's all the good news we've got for you tonight."

Everyone laughed, breaking the tension just a fraction.

"If that's the good news, what's the bad?" Detective Hobb asked.

"We're outta booze and the roads are fucked," Asher said,

inspiring a chorus of groans and more laughter from the crowd. "That's about as bad as it gets in my book."

Taking advantage of the levity, I closed my eyes and took a moment to reset. Again, I thought about all of the people gathered here before me, all the people counting on me. I thought of my two sisters standing beside me, strong and beautiful women who I'd only just found again after two decades of separation. I thought of Georgie, trapped by a delusional, dangerous psychopath. I thought of the men that I loved, the men that I wanted to build a life with.

My heart expanded in my chest.

When the noise died down again, I opened my eyes to find the entire room looking at me, their smiles encouraging, their gazes serious but hopeful. No doubt they were thinking about their own loved ones, their own dreams of the future, their own reasons for fighting against these nearly impossible odds.

They were counting on me—each and every one of them. In that moment, amidst the laughter and the tears, the darkness and the light, I felt the weight of their collective hope settle firmly on my shoulders. It was, I realized now, mine to carry.

But it wasn't a burden.

It was an honor. I would die for them. Not just the men I loved, not just my sisters. But every one of the witches and allies gathered in this room.

And I suspected they felt the same way. Darkness had brought us together, but through that togetherness, we would fight our way back to the light.

I blinked away tears before anyone saw them fall. When it came to translating messages from the heart, words were a limited medium.

But I had to try.

"Despite what the Silversbane prophecy says about leadership and uniting covens and all that stuff…" I shook my head, those limited words crashing into each other and getting stuck on the way out. "Guys, I'm not really one for big speeches. I just want you to know that I appreciate each and everyone of you so much. I know what we're facing, and I know it won't be easy. I don't really have any big inspirational words or battle cries, but I can tell you what always helps me keep the monsters at bay. It's pretty simple, really." I looked at each of my men in turn and smiled. "You just remember the ones you love, and know that everything you're doing is for them. And if you're on your own right now, then I want you to look in the mirror tonight before you go to bed. Take a good look. Truly *see* that woman looking back at you. Memorize the color of her eyes, the shape of her face, the sound of her laughter. When things get dark out there, when things are at their most hopeless and bleak, know that whatever demons we face, whatever bombs are dropped at our feet, whatever evil befalls us tonight or tomorrow or ten years from now, that woman is *always* worth fighting for."

TWENTY-ONE

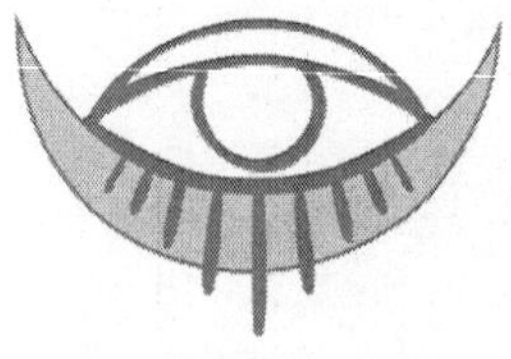

GRAY

From that moment forward, we went hard and fast on all fronts, pushing each other and ourselves to our absolute limits.

Potions and poisons. Protective amulets and charms. Darkwinter lore. Combat training. Mental acuity and shielding. Cardio. Strength-training. Weapons—God, so many weapons—all of them lethal, and not just to our enemies. Asher's fae swords would do a lot of damage against the Darkwinter Knights—the right hit would kill them on contact. But they would also decimate the shifters, as Emilio could attest to first hand. I'd grown particularly fond of a fae staff Ronan had taken from the crypts, but using the staff meant giving up the sword. Ash was immune to devil's traps, but Ronan could easily fall prey; we had no idea whether Jon's original devil's trap nanotech was just a prototype or if it'd been replicated on a larger scale. Darius and I, along with the other vampires we'd liberated from the crypts, could only fight at night, and we had to be particularly careful around fire and sharp swords. On the most basic physical level, the witches and Liam—the humans among us—were at the greatest risk, but all of us had weak points.

It was a lot to account for, and we had very little time to plan. If the intel we'd gathered was accurate, and the enemy's plans were still on track, we had about two weeks before all hell broke loose. The only way we were going to survive this, reclaim our home, and save the rest of—well, existence—was by working together, sticking together through the shit of it, and seeing it through to the very end.

Despite the risks, there was excitement in the air, a crackling charge I could feel everywhere I went. Though we'd only just learned about Trinity's plans, this battle has been a long time coming, and there was something to be said for knowing the end was on the horizon.

No matter what that end would bring.

We might very well be slaughtered in Blackmoon Bay, but after being forced into hiding for thousands of years, we were damn well ready to fight—and fight hard.

Fuck *anyone* who thought we'd go out quietly.

A few nights after our training had begun in earnest, Ronan and I took a break from sparring with Elena and Emilio to take the hounds for a walk along the shoreline, sneaking in some long overdue alone time.

We walked in silence for a while, keeping as close together as our curse would allow. It was our new normal—the "almost" we'd adapted to, almost without realizing it. He could *almost* brush a lock of hair behind my ear. I could *almost* lean up on my toes and kiss a path along his beard. He could *almost* wrap me in his arms, push me against the wall, and…

"Ronan, we can't wait any longer."

He nodded without meeting my eyes, knowing exactly where my mind had gone. Where it *had* been, ever since the blood spell.

The moment I realized I'd yanked Trinity's hair out of the astral plane and into our reality—that I'd captured physical proof that we knew of her whereabouts—the wheels began to turn.

We had leverage now. A new bargaining chip to offer Sebastian.

"We're heading into the Bay in six days," I said. "This needs to be settled up before then."

Ronan nodded, but didn't respond.

I stopped, turning to meet his eyes. "I need to see him. It's our best shot."

Ronan held my gaze for only a moment before cutting away,

his eyes roaming the dark, choppy sea, a stiff wind blowing the hair in front of his eyes. When he finally turned to look at me again, he said simply, "We."

"We what?"

"*We* need to see him. We're doing it together, Gray, or not at all."

I bit back a smile, toeing the ice with my boot. "So that's how it's gonna be, huh Vacarro?"

"That's how it *is*, Desario." He shot me another quick glance, catching my smile, his own crooked grin making me dizzy. A hundred, a thousand, a million years from now, I had no doubt he'd still have the same effect on me.

"So tell me something," he said, continuing our walk. "Once the Prince of Hell lets you out of your deal, what's your endgame?"

"Ronan, he's not going to let me out of the deal. Not even for Trinity." I swallowed my disappointment, stopping our forward motion and meeting his eyes once again. "Do you… Do you really think that's what this is about?"

Ronan sighed, raking a hand through his hair. "No. Just had to be sure. It's a big risk, Gray."

I looked deep into his eyes, so familiar, yet still so mysterious. There was so much more I wanted to know about Ronan—about his past, his human life, all the times and places our lives had intersected.

Before all of this started, some part of me assumed that no matter what had happened between us, we would always be friends. That we'd grow old together in Blackmoon Bay, even though Ronan wouldn't age. It was a nice fairytale picture, one that used to get me through the dark days.

But that felt like a million years ago. Now, I was immortal, too.

Now, I knew what dark days really were.

"You were born for this, Gray," Ronan said, once again sensing the direction of my thoughts. "I've always known it."

But I didn't want to talk about the war we'd yet to face, about the witches back at the lodge, about all the crazy shit still brewing on the horizon.

"I was born for *you*," I said. "Born to fall in love with you. Born to build a life with you. Born to… to *touch* you." I reached for his face, the wind blowing the tips of his hair against my fingers—an all-to-brief tease that made my heart ache even as it strengthened my resolve.

If Sebastian accepted my counter-offer, I would never take Ronan's touch for granted again. Never push him away. Never shut him out.

It didn't matter whether we had days, weeks, or a thousand years together. I would never let him go.

I closed my eyes, the frozen sea mist coating my lashes, the truth settling deep in my heart. Even if Sebastian refused, and our curse remained for the rest of our immortal days, that wouldn't change the way I felt. Ronan was mine, and I was his.

"What are you thinking?" he asked softly, and I opened my eyes to look at him again.

The moonlight glittered in his eyes, a sad smile pulling at the corners of his mouth. I could taste the depth of his ache, the loss we both shared each time we looked at each other.

"I want to spend the rest of my life with you," I said.

He reached for my face, but stopped short, just as I had, tracing the shape of my jaw a hair's breadth from my skin. "And you will."

"Let's just hope the rest of our lives last more than—"

"Hey." He touched a finger to my lips, ever so briefly. Heat sparked, but didn't ignite. "Shhh. Right now, in this moment, we have an eternity."

His hazel eyes blazed bright, calling to my heart, to that place deep inside where my love for him burned.

There were no words for it. All I knew was that I'd never wanted his kiss as badly as I had in that moment, and I wanted him to know it. Closing my eyes, I let my influence gently touch his mind. He dropped his guard immediately, and I sent him an image of my desire, real and passionate and all-consuming. Enough to melt all the ice from the shoreline and chase away this eternal winter for good.

Ronan leaned in close and whispered against the shell of my ear. "Me too, Gray. Always."

I nodded, offering him another smile. "I'll spare you the rest of that vision tonight. But as soon as we get back, you're getting the director's cut."

"I'd better." Ronan laughed, but eventually, his smile faded, and he turned away to watch Sparkle and Sunshine, who were trying to outrun the frigid waves about a quarter-mile down the shore. When he turned back and caught my eye again, he said simply, "I've already summoned Sebastian. He'll be here tomorrow night."

I nodded once, grateful. I should've known Ronan was already on it.

"We'll have five minutes to convince him," he said, "so let's make it count."

"I always do, Vacarro." I sent him a quick flash—a sneak peek of just what I had in store for him if we could entice Sebastian to take the deal. "Just in case you needed evidence of my commitment to breaking this damn deal."

Ronan groaned, then glanced down at his jeans, now bulging. "And now you've got evidence of mine, too."

I cracked up, wishing we could play this game all night, because I definitely would've won. But back in the direction of the lodge, a figure had emerged from the mist, running toward us. The breeze carried the sound of my name.

"Who is that?" Ronan asked.

"I think it's McKenna." I called the hounds back from their chase, and the four of us made our way back toward home.

"Gray," McKenna said when we'd caught up, her cheeks red from the cold, her eyes bright. "Okay, don't freak out, but we've got a *slight* problem."

"Define slight and define problem," I said.

"It's… It's probably best if you come see for yourself."

TWENTY-TWO

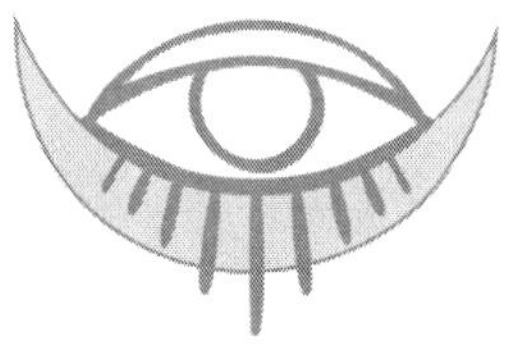

LIAM

Gray stood at my bedside, her face inscrutable, though her anger was quite palpable. Even my comparatively dull human senses could discern as much; her energy was so fierce, I feared my bed would ignite, with me in it.

"A concussion?" she demanded. "You got a *head injury*?"

"The pain is not unbearable," I said, which was only partially untrue. "To be fair, McKenna doesn't believe it's a concussion. We just have to ensure I don't fall asleep for a prolonged period tonight, but that is merely a precaution. In most of these cases, I'm told the patient—"

Gray held up her hand, silencing me. "What happened? The short version, if you don't mind."

"Your sisters were sparring with the detectives, trying to learn the best techniques for defending against shifter attacks. Were you aware that most shifter communities follow complex hierarchical structures that dictate—"

"Liam. What is it about the phrase 'short version' that's so unclear?"

"Right. Of course." My cheeks warmed under her scrutiny, but I pressed on. "Detective Hobb, in his wolf form, had set up on one side of the beach, with Haley and Bex on the other. He'd been alternating between them, charging straight for them while Detective Lansky instructed the women on defensive maneuvers. On this particular turn, Lansky wanted Haley to run straight at the wolf instead of waiting for him, but as she did so, she twisted her ankle. Down she went."

"Oh, shit," Gray said. "Is she okay?"

"Your sister is completely fine," I assured her. "As for me, well… I'd been timing them on the sidelines, taking notes and making observations, as I do. But the moment I saw her go down, instinct took over. I leaped in front of Hobb to prevent the inevitable collision, and…" I shrugged, knocking lightly on my head.

"You jumped in front of a charging wolf?" Gray nearly exploded. I'd never seen her so upset, so worried. "You're lucky you're still alive! You can't do things like that anymore, Liam. You're human. Understand? Not Death. Not the Great Transformation. Not a bird or a bat or a wisp of cloud on the breeze. You are a *man,* with breakable bones and spillable blood and a head that could crack open like a melon if you hit it too hard."

Shame burned a hot path up my spine and I turned my head, unable to hold her gaze. "As much as I appreciate the detailed enumeration of my many weaknesses, I assure you, I'm fine. So if that's all, I'd like to be alone now if you don't mind."

Undeterred, Gray waltzed over to the other side of the bed, once again capturing me in her gaze. From those twilight eyes, I could no more look away than I could've defended myself against the inertia of the rapidly charging wolf.

But now, her eyes were soft. Wounded. Gentle. "That's… that's what you think this is about?"

"It matters not what I think. These are merely facts, Gray. I can no longer protect you or any of the people I've come to care about. Not the way the others can. I am a liability in the truest sense of the word." I gestured toward the window, against which the wind sang winter's incessant song. "Despite the fact that I've brought much of this chaos to your doorstep, I am no longer in a position to help you defend against it. Despite the shame in my heart, I've lost the ability to right those wrongs or any of the—"

"Stop. Just… stop." She took my face between her hands, her thumbs sweeping over my cheeks. Tears shone in her eyes, and when she finally spoke again, her voice had lost all of its anger, though none of its ferocity. "It's about losing you, Liam. I can't… I told you that night at the cemetery—you're family. Losing you is not an option."

Family. The word echoed in my mind, suddenly bigger, grander, greater than it'd ever been. In truth, I'd wanted nothing more than what she was offering, but now, I felt as if I were the runt of the litter, the one who'd constantly need looking after while the others risked their lives to keep me safe.

But Gray was having none of my self-pity. She stripped down to nothing but her T-shirt and undergarments, then gestured for me to move over.

"What is this?" I asked. "Not that I'm complaining, mind you. It's just… a bit unexpected."

"As it should be." She flashed me a quick wink, then climbed into the bed beside me, sliding beneath the blankets, her bare legs tangling with mine.

The brush of her soft skin against mine was a balm for all that pained me, physically as well as emotionally.

We lay on our sides, face-to-face, and there we remained for many long moments. There was a time, however briefly it'd lasted, when it felt as though I could read the thoughts swimming in the depths of her eyes. But tonight, whether it was the loss of my greater powers or merely the shifter-induced scrambling of my soft human brain, I could no longer anticipate the direction of her mind's many wanderings.

"Please tell me what you're thinking," I finally said, my voice breaking, though I couldn't have said why. Some strange, uncomfortable emotion had climbed into my chest and taken hold of my heart, making it skitter and stall.

I hated that I'd disappointed her.

Gray ran her fingers through my hair, and I closed my eyes, settling into the comfort of her gentle caress.

"You're not weak, Liam," she said softly. "You are brave and strong and wise beyond measure. But you are accustomed to immortality. *Eternal* immortality. You don't have that self-protective instinct that humans develop. Your instinct is always to protect those you care about, and I appreciate that more than I can even express. But you have to balance that with common sense. What happened today with Detective Hobb… What if something like that happens in the Bay? What if it's not friendly shifters next time? What if you're not surrounded by witches with healing magic?"

I opened my eyes to meet hers once again. "Then I shall do my best to outwit them."

"That's not good enough."

"I will not allow you to fight these battles while I cower in the shadows. That is not up for debate, little witch."

"I'm not asking you to sit this one out, Liam. I'm just asking you to know yourself. Not as Death, but as a mortal man."

She was right, of course, and I promised her I would do as she asked. This seemed to appease her, and she drew closer to me, the crease between her eyes smoothing once again.

I traced an infinity symbol on her forehead, and she sighed, her eyelids fluttering closed.

"Tell me what you're thinking *now*," I said.

"Just that I miss our philosophical talks." Then, opening her eyes again and turning a bright smile my way, "But that just means we'll have lots more to talk about when all of this is over, and we can finally breathe again."

"I am looking forward to that day more than you know." I traced my thumb around the curves of her mouth. "I love you, Gray Desario."

She parted her lips to reply, but I cut her off with a kiss, drawing her closer, hoping she could feel just how much I'd meant those words. I would've been quite content to kiss her for the rest of the evening, but Gray pulled back.

"That day on the beach," she said, "when we first kissed? Do you remember?"

"I remember everything about that day. About you."

"You told me you'd never done anything like this before. Does that mean you haven't…" Her words trailed off, but her intense gaze didn't waver, and I knew exactly what she was asking about.

Again, heat flooded my cheeks, and I found myself babbling in the wake of her question.

"I... I have studied human anatomy as well as that of the animal kingdoms of several realms, and I'm quite knowledgeable about the physical mechanics of—"

"Liam. That's not what I meant, and you know it. But if you'd rather not talk about—"

"No, it's okay. It's just... I'm not exactly sure how to answer your question. Presumably, you're wondering as to whether I have ever engaged in sexual intercourse."

Gray's tender smile made my heart flutter. "I probably would have chosen to word the question differently," she said, "but yes, that is what I'm asking."

I considered her question, uncertainty creeping into my chest. But with Gray, there was no need for shame or nervousness. I'd betrayed her, and somehow she'd seen fit to forgive me. To welcome me back into her life, into her arms. From now on, I would only be open with her. Honest, no matter the topic.

"Perhaps my vessel has," I said. "And perhaps I, as a human all those eons ago, engaged in such pleasures. The truth is, Gray, I cannot recall much of that time. For all intents and purposes, I suppose I'm what you might consider... inexperienced."

She trailed her fingers down my arm, her touch sending electric tingles throughout my entire body. In a gentle voice, she asked, "Is that an experience you might like to have? With me, I mean?"

I swallowed hard, my heart trying its best to climb into my throat. "Is that something *you* might like? With me, I mean?"

Gray bit her bottom lip and nodded, her cheeks darkening.

I cleared my throat. "How would we... I mean, do we just... I'm sorry. This is... I suppose I am a bit out of my element." I offered her what I suspected was a rather awkward smile. For all I knew about human anatomy, for all I knew about a great many subjects both large and small, nothing had prepared me for this moment.

"Let's just figure it out as we go," she said, wriggling beside me as she stripped away her remaining clothing, and I did the same.

She shifted closer, our bodies touching. A brilliant warmth radiated from deep inside her, the complex magic pulsing like a second heartbeat, calling to me as it always had.

I was instantly erect.

I touched her face, capturing her mouth in another kiss as I shifted to lie on top of her. Gray parted her thighs and arched her hips, reaching for me, guiding me, and suddenly I was inside her, sliding into her wet heat, the feel of it unlocking ripples of pure, exquisite pleasure.

I gasped, unable to hold back, and instinctually, my body moved, faster, deeper, desperate for more of her. For all of her.

"Slow," she whispered, smiling up at me. "Let's go slow."

I did as she suggested and forced myself to slow my movements, though everything inside me was screaming to push harder, faster, to chase this feeling of pure bliss until it exploded inside me like a newborn galaxy.

"Breathe, Liam," she whispered, the touch of her palm against my cheek bringing my attention back to the moment. Back to my breath, which I now realized I'd been holding for far too long. I exhaled slowly, and I looked into her eyes, letting my gaze wander down the slope of her nose, across the planes of her cheeks, down to her dark pink lips.

I'd seen the sun rise and set upon every country in this realm. I'd seen the very bottom of the deepest part of the sea, and followed the winds across the highest mountain peaks. I'd watched the stars die and be reborn.

Yet I'd ever seen anything so beautiful as the look upon her face as I made love to her.

It was almost too much to bear—the warm silk of her skin, the sweet taste of her kiss, the soft moans escaping her lips, all of it creating a symphony of sensations that conspired to stop my heart. No matter; if this was to be my final hour in this mortal vessel, I could think of no better way to depart from this realm.

Eventually, I relaxed into the rhythm of this divine act, and just as Gray had suggested, we figured it out. Soon I sensed a shift in her demeanor, her hips arching, her own movements quickening.

"We can go fast now?" I asked, hope rising inside.

Gray laughed, soft and sweet, her cheeks flush, her eyes sparkling. "Yes, Liam. We can go fast."

At her words, I quickened my movements, my body taking over, bringing us closer and closer to the final act in this seductive dance. In so many ways I wanted to prolong that inevitable ending, but the mere idea of it felt like standing in the ocean and trying to hold back the waves with your bare hands.

"Liam," Gray breathed, her eyelids fluttering closed. I sensed she wanted to be touched, and I slid my hand between us, fingers seeking her most sensitive flesh, knowing we were both mere moments away from letting go.

She moaned softly at my touch, then gasped, her body clenching me in a grip so tight, so perfect, it made the stars dance before my eyes.

No, not the stars, I realized then, but Gray's eyes, open once again, locking fiercely with mine, her gaze full of love and passion that mirrored my own.

And then, as she shuddered beneath me, my name no more than a sigh on her breath, I finally lost the tenuous hold on my own control.

I kissed her, everything inside me exploding in pure, white-hot pleasure as the world crashed out of orbit, sending me spiraling into another galaxy, another time, another universe.

And through it all, we looked deeply into each other's eyes, a connection so deep and intimate it stole my breath.

There were tears in her eyes, and when she looked up at me and smiled, my heart was utterly full.

* * *

"How do you feel?" she asked later. Minutes, hours, I could not have said. In those precious moments in her arms, time had lost all meaning for me.

"It's not an exaggeration to say that I now understand why humans have gone to war for such a thing."

Gray laughed softly, a sound that made my heart sing. "Hmm. And this was just our first time."

"You mean… We get to do that again?"

Now, her laugh turned hearty, so full it made our bed tremble. "I love you, Liam Colebrook. You know that, right?"

"You've left no doubts, little witch." I cupped her breast, stroking her nipple with my thumb. In the span of a single heartbeat, I was hard for her again.

"About that whole 'doing it again' bit," I said, pulling her on top of me, "do you think we might…"

"Yes, Liam." She lowered her head, her lips alighting on mine as the dragonfly alights upon the lotus. Then, with a wicked gleam in her eye, she smiled and said, "I think we might."

TWENTY-THREE

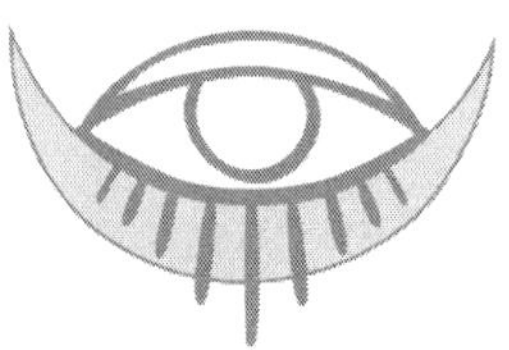

RONAN

In all the time I've been with Gray, from the moment I was assigned as her guardian to this moment right now, I'd been dreaming of the day when I'd have leverage over Sebastian—just enough to break his hold on Gray. Just enough to loosen the binds of her contract. Just enough to let us find that final, indisputable loophole.

All the fucking wishes and dreams in the world, yet in my mind, they'd always ended the same way.

Sebastian, laughing me out of his office, reminding me to remember my place.

Sebastian, threatening me with eternal banishment, with harming Gray, with assigning her a new guardian, with finding crueler and more heartbreaking ways to keep us apart.

He was a monster, and we were his prey.

Until tonight.

"What is so urgent," Sebastian demanded, "that I had to take time away from running my operations to come see you in person?"

It was the night after our walk on the beach, and one hour after our agreed-upon meeting time, he'd simply appeared at the kitchen table, where he now sat with his arms folded across his chest, his face pinched in annoyance.

I glanced at Gray, who was standing next to me, and she nodded once.

I tossed a paper bag onto the table in front of him.

"What's this?" he asked, barely glancing at it.

"A new deal," Gray said.

The D-word piqued his interest, as it always had. Keeping his eyes locked on Gray, he opened up the bag, fishing out the chunk of hair she'd yanked from Trinity's head, along with the passports we'd discovered in her crypt office.

Sebastian's eyes glowed red with rage.

I took a step closer to Gray.

"How did you come by this?" he demanded, pressing the hair to his nose and taking a deep whiff. "Answer me!"

As it had so many times before, Sebastian's total lack of emotional restraint gave him away, and for the first time since I'd traded away the ability to touch the woman I loved for a chance at keeping her safe, a spark of hope flickered to life inside my gut.

Hope that the Prince of Hell might actually agree to this.

Hope that tonight, rather than sleeping next to Ash as he touched her, rather than listening to her soft moans and Darius and Emilio brought her to the edge, rather than seeing her shy smile and swollen lips as she crept out of Liam's bedroom just before sunrise, rather than dousing myself with icy showers as I replayed the images she'd implanted in my mind, I might be able to share her bed again without burning her alive.

"How we came by it is irrelevant," Gray said. "What's important is what we're offering—*if* you're willing to negotiate."

Sebastian placed the items back inside the bag and set it on the table, feigning indifference, but it was too late for that. He couldn't hide the desperate desire smoldering in his eyes.

"You're bargaining with me, Silversbane?" he asked.

"There's nothing in my contract that prevents it," she said. "Besides, aren't you the king of the deal?"

"Get to the point."

"Ronan and I share a deep love you couldn't even *begin* to understand," she said, surprising me. I hadn't expected her to get so personal there, but Gray was on a mission, and wherever the hell she was going with this, I trusted her. "You had no right to take that from us."

"Oh, but I did," Sebastian said, condescension dripping from his voice. "It's all there in black and white. Ronan agreed to my terms, no tricks, no take-backs."

"You left him no other options, and you did it all for sport," she said. "You gain absolutely nothing by keeping us apart—nothing but your own sick amusement."

"What you call 'sick amusement,' Silversbane, I call managing my assets, which I'm free to do as I see fit." Sebastian folded his hands over his belly, offering a smug grin, assuming he'd gotten the upper hand.

But Gray wasn't done yet. Not even close.

"When I first met you," she continued, "I thought you'd never loved anyone in your life. How else could you be so cruel? So casual about destroying *our* love?"

Sebastian rolled his eyes. "In case you haven't noticed, girl, I'm the Prince of Hell. Love is not my primary motivator."

"It was once though, wasn't it?" she asked, her tone softening. "A young witch at the crossroads, a favor here, a favor there, and before you realized it, you'd given away your heart."

Bullseye.

I'd never seen the Prince of Hell turn so white. Gray had hit him right where it hurt.

Sebastian exploded, jumping to his feet in a rage. "I didn't come here to be manipulated and cajoled by—"

"Ronan and I know of Trinity's whereabouts," Gray dead-panned, once again hitting her target.

Sebastian's mouth dropped open. He tried to recover, reclaiming his seat and smoothing his hands over his pants, but once again, she'd tricked him into showing his hand.

"We know where she's been hiding," Gray continued. "We know who's been protecting her, we know who's given her an army, and we know about her plans for a major power grab that—if successful—will leave you unemployed and homeless."

"Are you suggesting she has the power to claim hell?" he asked, incredulous.

"Oh, I'm not suggesting it, Sebastian. I'm straight-up *telling* you. But if you'd rather bury your head in the sand and pretend your power and position come with an immortal guarantee, be my guest."

I coughed into my hand to hide my damn smile.

Fucking Desario. She had him by the balls, and all three of us knew it. I'd never been so proud of her.

When he didn't respond, she pressed on.

"My team and I intend to capture Trinity, decimate her army, and return her to your care, at which time you may deal with her as you wish."

He narrowed his eyes, but it was clear Gray wasn't bluffing, and he damn well knew it.

"And in exchange?" he asked.

"It's simple," Gray said. "I want to be able to touch the man I love. To take him in my arms—in my bed—whenever I damn well please. I want you to break that wretched curse, and I want you to do it right now."

"Now? But how do I know you'll uphold your end of the bargain? How do I know you'll succeed?"

"You don't, but those are my terms." Gray leaned across the table until her face was just inches from Sebastian's, her blue eyes blazing like midnight fire. "Stop interfering in our relationship, demon. We both know you have bigger things to focus on, as do we."

He glared right back at her, but just when I thought he'd explode in another fit, his gaze softened. It was only for a split second, but I saw it—a brief flicker of humanity in his otherwise cunning, cutting eyes.

"You remind me of her," he said to Gray, his voice so soft and tender I actually thought his vessel had been possessed by some other demon.

For her part, Gray looked absolutely stricken. "Trinity? I'm nothing like—"

"No—your grandmother," Sebastian corrected. "Deirdre."

If Gray felt one way or another about the comparison, she didn't show it. "And?"

"*And,*" he said, "I haven't yet decided if that's endearing... or a liability."

"Maybe a little of both," she said.

"Maybe." A crooked smile touched the bastard's greasy lips. "Don't disappoint me, Silversbane."

And then he was gone.

TWENTY-FOUR

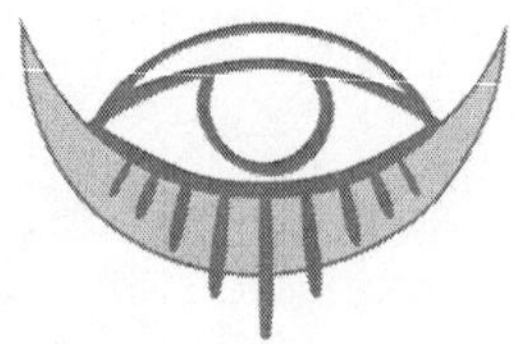

GRAY

I dropped into a kitchen chair and blew out a breath, the relief instant. Sebastian's presence had sucked up all the air in the room.

"Gray." Ronan knelt before me, his eyes glazed with emotion. "Did he…?"

"I don't know," I whispered. My heart hammered in my chest, my magic tingling inside.

Tentatively, Ronan reached for my face, stopping just short of touching me.

"Well, there's only one way to find out." He sighed, but didn't move any closer. "I don't want it to hurt."

"It's not too bad if it's just a quick burn," I said.

Ronan closed his eyes. "It's not the burn I'm worried about."

He was right. A burn would be nothing compared to the agony we'd feel if Sebastian had walked without granting my request. And so we hesitated, floating together inside this fragile, bubble-thin moment where hope still existed, where there was still a chance.

"You have to touch me," I finally whispered, the words aching in my throat. "We have to know."

Opening his eyes, Ronan sighed again, his warm breath teasing my skin. Slowly, he brought his fingers close to my lips.

"I love you," he whispered. "No matter what."

And then, swallowing hard, he touched me.

Quickly at first, then again, and then once more to be certain. This last touch lingered, and he held his breath as we both waited for the sizzle that never came.

Beneath his fingers, my lips stretched into a grin, tears spilling down my cheeks.

Ronan pulled back and glanced at his fingers, a gasp escaping his throat. He looked back at me for half-a-second, his beautiful leaves-in-autumn eyes the last thing I saw clearly before he crashed against my mouth.

Our kiss was endless, all-consuming, a vortex of relief and laughter and passion and love into which I gladly fell. Ronan could barely breathe, so intent was he on keeping his mouth on me at all times.

"Just so you know," I finally managed, panting between his increasingly demanding kisses, "if you ever… make another deal with him… like that again… I'll…"

"I know."

"We have to find other ways… to protect… each other. Ways that don't involve..."

"I know."

He scooped me into his arms and got to his feet, lifting me with him, still devouring me with kisses.

"And Ronan, you can't—"

"I *know*, Gray. I know." He shut me up for good with a searing kiss that I felt all the way in my toes, igniting a fire inside me that —for the first time in far too long—had nothing to do with hell's curses.

Ignoring the glances of everyone in the common room as Ronan carried me past, we headed upstairs and locked ourselves away in my bedroom, giving ourselves permission to forget the rest of the world for just a little while.

Still kissing, we stripped out of our clothes and tumbled onto the bed, touching each other everywhere at once, skin on skin, lips on lips, our breath mingling as we entwined beneath the sheets.

Ronan pushed the hair from my face and kissed my forehead, my eyelids, my cheeks, the tip of my nose. His eager mouth finally found its way back to mine, and there he lingered, his tongue exploring every soft curve of my mouth as if he were experiencing it all for the first time.

In so many ways, he was.

"I missed the taste of you," he finally breathed.

A tear slid down my cheek, and I pulled back, taking his face between my hands. The touch of his beard tickled my palms, and I closed my eyes and memorized the feeling, the shape, the texture. "I missed the *everything* of you."

"Nothing will ever come between us again," he said. A proclamation. A promise. "I mean it, Desario. The whole fucking world can burn for all I care, as long as you're still with me—you and the guys. That's who matters now. Call me selfish, but there it is."

I wouldn't—*couldn't*—call him selfish, because I felt the exact same way. My rebels and I were soul mates in the truest sense of the word, a single bright soul divided into six beings, always meant to find our way to one another, always meant to be together, in this realm and the next.

With no more promises to be made, I parted my thighs and pulled him on top of me, arching my hips up to meet him as he sank blissfully inside me.

Beneath my touch, the muscles in his shoulders and back rippled, and Ronan shivered, rolling his hips and sliding in deeper, filling me completely.

My body took over, and I matched his stride, eager for more. Harder. Faster.

"No," he said, stilling inside me, rubbing his thumb across my lower lip. "We've got all night, Gray, and I intend to take advantage of every last minute of it."

"But the training, and the others—"

"Can wait." He flashed the crooked grin I'd fallen in love with. "World burning, selfish demon, misses his woman—remember?"

Laughing, I gave in to his demands, relaxing my muscles, both of us easing our way back in.

Ronan kissed my shoulder, my collarbone, slowly making his way to my breasts. Each brush of his lips set my skin ablaze, and though we'd both agreed to take things slow, the physical sensations proved too much, too intense, too perfect.

I felt him trying his best to hold back, to make this reunion last, but it was a losing battle for us both.

"Ronan," I breathed, sliding my hands into his silky hair, "we don't need all night. We've got the rest of eternity now."

He nodded, running his nose down along my neck, tracing a new path with his tongue as his hips rocked forward, his body brushing my clit. He pulled out slowly, then slid back inside, and that was all it took to unravel the very last of my control. I dug my nails into his shoulders and arched my back to meet his final thrust, taking him in fully, sending him over the edge. He came in a white-hot rush as my own orgasm exploded inside me, and I cried out in pleasure, in relief, in bliss.

In that moment, the world very well could have burned, and neither of us would've known about it until we walked outside later and saw the ashes.

Ronan rolled onto his back, pulling me on top of him, my head nestling against his chest. I found the familiar, steady beat of his heart and followed it home, back to where he and I had begun, and a sense of rightness wrapped around us like a warm blanket,

We were meant for this love, this passion, this friendship. We were meant for this moment, and everything that had come before, and everything that would come after.

"Welcome back, Ronan Vacarro," I whispered, and he ran his hand down my bare back and sighed, content and happy.

I wanted nothing more than to spend the rest of the night in his arms, but the truth was, the world really *was* in danger of burning down, and we really *did* have a responsibility to try to prevent it. So, after another slow, lingering session, we reluctantly showered and headed back downstairs to see what else needed to be done, who else needed help, what other potions could be mixed, which weapons could be sharpened, what intel could be pieced together.

But as we descended the stairs, our fingers interlaced, our smiles still firmly in place, the sight in the common room stopped me dead in my tracks.

"Jael!" I bolted down the remaining stairs and basically launched myself at him, yanking him into an impossibly tight hug. I hadn't seen him since the night I'd been turned, and seeing him here tonight, safe, knowing he'd risked so much to protect my soul… I didn't have the words for the emotion suddenly swirling inside.

"It's so good to see you," I said, pulling back to meet his cat-like yellow eyes.

Jael offered a thin but genuine smile, the skin around his eyes crinkling, those fine lines a bit deeper than I'd remembered. "You as well, Gray." Then, glancing at Ronan, he gave a brief nod. "Both of you."

"Thank you for… With the moonglass," I said, not sure what exactly to say. He'd saved my soul, risking his own life in the process.

"Seeing you healthy and well is all the thanks I need," he said. "Vampire looks good on you."

"Thanks. I'm still getting used to it." I watched him a moment longer before I finally realized Ronan and I had interrupted a meeting already in progress. Verona, McKenna, and several of the other witches had gathered around the couches, with Elena and Emilio standing beside the fire.

No one was smiling.

"What's going on?" I asked. "What did we miss?"

Jael clasped his hands in front of his body, the last vestiges of his smile finally fading. "My sister was able to get a message to me last night," he said. "I'm here with news from home."

"Good news?" I asked, but deep down, I already knew the answer. I could see it in the way the witches sat hunched, knees drawn to chests. I could read it in the bend of Emilio's shoulders, in the heavy sadness on Elena's sigh.

Jael shook his head, looking at me with the pale, haunted eyes of a man who'd seen the future and witnessed the very end of our days. "Blackmoon Bay is burning, Gray."

TWENTY-FIVE

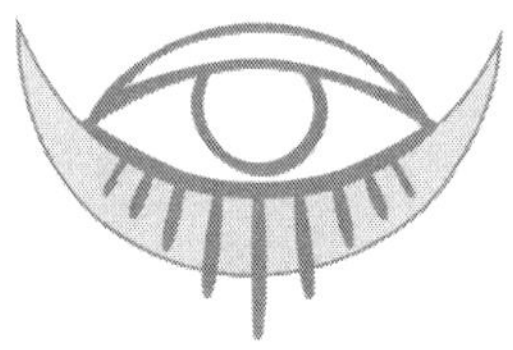

EMILIO

Blackmoon Bay had been many things to me. An escape when I had nowhere else to go. A refuge and a haven. The home I'd made, the community I'd served and protected.

Then, later, it became the place where I'd connected with the guys. Through Ronan, I'd met Asher and Darius, and finally, Gray. Years later, I'd come back into her life there following the murder of her best friend.

Blackmoon Bay was the place where I'd fallen in love. Where I'd begun my family.

And now, our home was nearly in ruins.

Luna's Café. Illuminae. The historic buildings that housed the police precinct and other government offices. The harbor. Johnny's Seaside Pizza. Bloodstone Park. Every neighborhood and every location, every home, every street corner bore the mark of Orendiel's dark army.

According to Kallayna, it wasn't the result of the coordinated, full-scale attack we'd been expecting—the one Gray and her sisters had learned about during their blood spell.

No, this destruction was born of the resistance.

Somehow, the witches remaining in the Bay had hooked up with the few remaining supernaturals who hadn't fallen prey to Darkwinter's mind games, and together they'd executed one hell of a sneak attack, stealthily killing several hunters and a handful of fae knights, saving a few additional witches who'd been captured and imprisoned by Phillip Reese.

But Phillip did not take the attack lightly. He retaliated immediately, sending in his armies, decimating anyone who even *looked* like he or she may be sympathetic to the witches' cause.

Jael told us that the hunters and fae had swept through the city like wildfire, slashing and burning, putting down the resistance with a show of force like nothing we'd seen before. Like nothing we'd predicted.

Jael had no idea how many survivors were left in the city overall, and whose side those survivors might be fighting on now—his sister's message was cut short before any additional details could be shared. At this point, he wasn't even sure Kallayna had survived the night.

But as far as I was concerned, even if there was just one soul, one heartbeat, one being still clinging to life and hope in our city, we would find them. We would protect them. We would help them rebuild.

Gray wouldn't have it any other way. None of us would.

Not long after Jael's visit, I found her on the upper balcony of the lodge, looking out across the winter-ravaged sea. The twisted fae magic had altered the climate conditions again, and waves of solid ice rose high above the shore, only to shatter and crash back down in a rain of glass.

Again. Again. Again.

By sight and by sound, it was as terrifying as it was beautiful.

I approached her slowly, not wanting to disturb her from whatever thoughts had taken up residence in her mind. Her face was turned down, her eyes focused on a Tarot card in her hand. After a beat, I cleared my throat to let her know I was near, but she didn't move at first.

Then, with a deep sigh, she finally tucked the card into her back pocket and turned to me, offering a sad smile.

"Can't sleep?" I asked, then shook my head, realizing my mistake. Gray slept during the daylight hours now, if she slept at all. "Sorry. Still getting used to your new routines."

"Me too." She leaned into my embrace, tilting her face up to meet my eyes. "I still climb into bed at the same time every night, only to remember I'm supposed to sleep during the day now."

"You always were a night owl, though," I said, brushing my lips across her forehead. "So it shouldn't be too much of a hardship."

She smiled again, but it didn't quite reach her eyes. "No brownies tonight, huh?"

I raised my hands in surrender. "It's not my fault—I swear. We're out of chocolate, if you can believe that."

"House full of witches? Yeah, I believe it."

"I brought you something else, though."

A gust of icy wind lashed us both, blowing her hair into her face. She swept her loose curls back, gathering them together at the base of her neck.

Steadying myself for any number of possible reactions, I retrieved the envelope from my shirt pocket, opening it up and tipping the contents into my hand. "This belongs to you, *mi querida*."

Gray gasped at the sight of it, her eyes glistening with tears.

"Elena was able to retrieve it from the station," I explained. "They've closed the case on the Landes murder, naming Jonathan as the primary suspect, officially believed deceased."

She reached for my hand, slowly closing her fingers around the crescent-moon amulet. "Thank you," she whispered, pressing her hand to her chest.

"Would you like me to put it on you?"

She nodded, handing it back so I could fasten the delicate chain around her neck. The crescent moon came to rest just beneath her collarbone, glowing faintly against her skin.

I smiled. "It seems Calla is still with you."

"Always," she whispered, fishing the Tarot card from her back pocket. "I asked for a message just before I came out here. Some sign that we'd be okay, that we were on the right path."

She turned the card so I could see it. It was the High Priestess, a woman dressed in blue robes, surrounded by tiny butterflies.

"This card always shows up when I'm thinking of my mother. My *real* mother," she amended. "Calla."

"I remember it from the night we dug up your book of shadows," I said. "It slipped out when you opened it for the first time."

Gray nodded, her smile softening. "I don't see or hear her like I do with Sophie sometimes, but I sense her in other ways. Namely through the card. Sometimes I'll dream of her, though, and then I wake up and smell her perfume."

"I sense my parents, too. More lately, since Elena and I have started to reconnect." I tucked her hair behind her ear, my hand lingering on her cheek. I had Gray to thank for bringing my sister back into my life. It was just one more thing I loved about her, one more thing that made my heart feel full every time I looked into her eyes.

"I love your sister," she said. "She doesn't take any shit from you."

"She loves you, too." I pulled her close again, inhaling her scent, her familiar sweetness mixed with the salty tang of the crisp ocean air. In my mind, an image danced through unbidden—my sister, crying tears of joy, helping Gray make adjustments to her wedding dress. The image was so startling I nearly gasped, but it felt comfortable, too. Inevitable. The thought warmed me.

"Do you think they're really with us?" she asked. "Watching over us or something like that? Or is it just wishful thinking?"

"I don't know, Gray." I sighed, pressing my lips to the top of her head. "That sounds like a question for Spooky."

Gray laughed, but it trailed off quickly, and she pulled out of my embrace to look into my eyes once more. The amulet around her neck still gave off a subtle white light.

"We have to send Reva in tomorrow night to see if there are survivors," she said. "For all we know, Trinity is still planning the full-on attack. I don't want to wait another day."

I nodded, totally in agreement. "She's ready for it, Gray. Liam's been working hard with her."

"Oh, she's totally ready. I just..." She sighed, looking out again over the white sea. "I guess I just wanted her to have a shot at normal. The shot the rest of us never got."

"She will, Gray. You've given her that."

"Letting her be our eyes and ears on this… We have no idea what she'll see once she gets in. But I do know that whatever it is, Emilio, she'll never be able to un-see."

Gray was right, and there was nothing I could say to ease her mind.

"When this is over," she continued, "I was hoping she might want to live with us. I mean, if you're all cool with that. I just thought…" She trailed off, finally turning to meet my gaze again. Her eyes were full of love. Hope, however fragile in this moment, the relative calm before the storm.

"Gray, there's no question, *querida*. Reva is family. *Everyone* here is family, and we take care of each other."

This got a smile—a real one—and she drew me close again. "Yeah, but just so we're clear? *Not* everyone here gets an open invitation to our house."

"Our house," I echoed. "I like the sound of that."

"Do you think it will happen?"

The wind kicked up again, bringing with it a wet, icy blast of slush, coating us both. But neither of us flinched, and I held her gaze, my heart pounding fiercely, the words fighting their way out against the onslaught of weather.

"I love you so much it scares me," I said.

"I'd tell you not to be afraid, but I feel the same way." She shivered in my arms, then laughed. "In a good way."

"In the *best* way." I dipped my head to kiss her, sighing against her lips. "I know you usually sleep during the daylight hours, but I was wondering if you might do your favorite wolf shifter a favor tonight?"

"What are you asking me, wolf?"

"Come to bed with me. Just the two of us tonight."

Wearing matching conspiratorial smiles, we snuck back into the lodge and found a small, windowless bedroom currently being used to store dried herbs and a few other bulk supplies. It wasn't pretty, but it was warm and quiet, tucked away from the main bedrooms, unlikely to be disturbed or even noticed.

As surreptitiously as I could, I retrieved a couple of extra blankets from the other bedroom closets, then returned to roll out a makeshift mattress for us. We stripped out of our wet clothes, and there in the quiet darkness of our secret room, I made love to her, soft and slow, savoring each tender touch and kiss, each smile and sigh.

We spent the next few hours talking about our dreams, about the future, about what our someday house would look like. She told me about the herb garden she wanted to plant, and I told her about all the different recipes I wanted to try, and on and on we chatted, until one by one, the others found their way into our little hovel.

Asher first, who could always sense whenever someone in the vicinity was getting intimate. He curled up on the other side of Gray, nuzzling the back of her neck. The three of us had just gotten comfortable when Darius appeared, staking out a patch of blanket behind me. Liam and Ronan came in last, neither saying a word. Like the others, they simply found their place among us. Their place in our family. There, in that tiny windowless room on our last night before our military operation began in earnest.

It felt right. It felt familiar. It felt real. And I allowed myself to hope, for the briefest moment, that it would be. That when all of this was done, we'd find that house Gray and I had painted in our minds, and the six of us—seven, if Reva accepted Gray's invitation—would make it our own.

As the others slowly dropped off to sleep, I forced myself to stay awake, wanting to watch over them, especially Gray. She may have been a powerful vampire, a prophesied witch, heir to an ancient fae legacy that she and her sisters were still struggling to accept. But there in my arms, her eyes closed, her lips red and puffy from my kisses, she was just a woman. The woman I'd fallen madly in love with. The one who'd made me believe—no, who'd made me *know*—that as long as we all held on to one another, as long as our family stuck together, we'd find a way through this darkness.

"We will survive this," I whispered into her hair, a promise for us all as I finally drifted off to sleep.

TWENTY-SIX

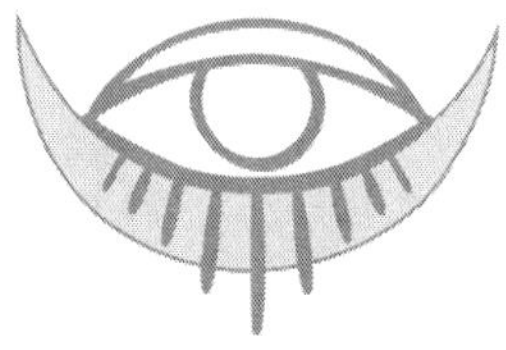

LIAM

More than anything, I wished I could take Reva's place. Or Gray's, or Haley's, or any one of the witches gearing up to invade Blackmoon Bay in the coming hours.

But I was human now. My strengths, my magics came in other forms. An encouraging smile, a hug, a touch. Information passed on from one generation to the next. A whispered promise against the bare flesh of the woman who'd made me remember what it meant to be human. To love, completely and with abandon.

To believe in something greater than one's own ends.

"I'm worried about her," Gray said now, doing a final check of the potions Verona had issued her. It was the night after the six of us had fallen asleep together, and now she and I were alone in the kitchen, the others doing final weapons checks and strategic planning and many other things that had to be fast-tracked as a result of the riots in the Bay and our now-shortened attack timeline.

Though none of us had dared to move from the peaceful serenity of that room until well after sunset this evening, we all knew ours had been a momentary peace. A bubble made of moonglass, destined to shatter at the first onset of our reality.

That reality was now upon us. In thirty minutes, Reva would be traveling amongst the shadows of Blackmoon Bay, searching for survivors. Searching for a way in. After that, the rest of us would make our move together, hoping that by sheer number and combined magics, we might overpower their fae cloaking spells—as well as the armies themselves.

Many of us would not survive to see the sunrise of another day.

"I know she's powerful," Gray continued, "and determined, and probably braver than any of us." Her smile softened. "But she's still just a kid. A witch who would do anything to protect us, not even realizing she was putting her own life at risk."

I couldn't help but laugh at that. "I think it's fair to say we've all done just that, and we'll all *continue* to do just that, as often and for as long as any of our loved ones are in danger. To expect anything less from Reva is frankly a bit naive."

Gray smiled softly. "Touché, Liam."

"And there's something else you need to know about Reva," I said. For the past few days, I'd grappled with the best way to reveal this information, but now seemed as good a time as any other. "Reva is not just a kid, as you say. She is a Shadowborn, Gray. Like you."

I watched her eyes, certain that through them I could read the thoughts dancing in her mind, all the little moments replaying, all the puzzle pieces about Reva that were now adding up to the complete whole.

"She will likely come into her full powers in the next year or so," I explained, "simply because she's been nurturing her connection with magic for years."

"Reva," she whispered, then nodded, the final pieces clicking into place. Her eyes twinkled with something that looked an awful lot like pride.

"So what does this mean for her?" she asked. "Who will train her now that you're no longer Death?"

"I must train her still," I said. "To the extent that my human limitations allow, anyway. I may not be able to travel with her to the Shadowrealm or interact with the remaining soul ferriers, but there is a great deal of knowledge I shall endeavor to impart upon her. And none of us truly knows what her unique powers will be, nor what her role will be in the absence of Death, where souls cannot readily pass on through the realm as they once might have."

"Does she know?" Gray asked.

"I haven't discussed it with her yet, no. I've yet to find an appropriate time, and I don't want her to be overly concerned about her future, particularly now, when she needs to focus on getting into and out of Blackmoon Bay undetected. As you might recall, learning that you have the power to influence death and manipulate soul energy is not always an easy thing to process and accept."

A smile curved her lips. "You mean, I wasn't all in with your whacky theories from the start?"

"If by 'all in' you mean refusing my many invitations at every turn, causing trouble wherever you went, and generally upheaving the universal order, then yes. Of course you were all in, Gray."

Gray laughed in earnest, but before she could ask any more questions, Reva entered the kitchen, her mouth set in a grim line, her shoulders squared.

"When am I going in?" she asked.

Gray closed her eyes, cursing under her breath. But then she, too, squared her shoulders, and by the time she turned to face Reva, her eyes were once again shining with pride.

"You ready?" she asked.

Reva gave her a thumbs-up.

"Come here," Gray said. "There's something I need to give you first."

Reva did as she asked, and Gray unclasped the amulet from around her neck, fastening it around Reva's instead. She pressed her fingers against the crescent moon and whispered a protective spell that made the charm glow brightly.

"Reva, I know you can do this," Gray said, once the amulet had dimmed again. "I wouldn't send you in there otherwise. But there's no shame in retreating. The goal of connecting with any remaining Bay witches and sussing out the situation? That's our second priority tonight. *You* are our first. The minute you feel scared or uncomfortable, the minute you get even the *slightest* vibe that something isn't right, you pull back. Got it?"

"I will. I promise."

Reva turned her bright eyes my way, and I put my hands on her shoulders, kneeling down before her, again wishing I could protect her with magic or sheer force of will.

But all I had now were words, and I offered them freely.

"Remember everything we talked about," I told her. "The shadows are your domain. You are not bound by physical constraints, by the natural laws of the universe. But while your astral body cannot be harmed in the way that your physical body can, fae magic is treacherous, and could very easily sever the cord that connects the two. You must avoid Darkwinter at all costs—their traps, their servants, their spies. You must keep to the shadows and avoid being seen by anyone but the witches and known allies."

"I remember," she said. "I won't let you down. Either of you."

At this, Gray pulled the girl to her chest, capturing her in a fierce hug. "You could never let us down, Reva. No matter what. Just come back to us."

We brought Reva into the common room, where Verona had blessed the space and set up protective charms and crystals throughout the room. Reva took a position before the fireplace, and all around her, the witches formed a half-circle, joining hands, whispering more protective chants and Reva stared into the fire.

All of us watched as she slipped into a trance-like state, her eyelids fluttering closed, her shoulders drooping as her consciousness departed her physical body.

As the witches continued their protective whispering, I stood to the side with Asher, Darius, Emilio, Ronan, Jael, Emilio, and Elena, all of us exchanging glances, no one daring to speak.

Other than the witches, none of us made a sound, though I was certain the vampires in the room could hear the frantic thumping of my heart, the fraying of my nerves. I felt as if I'd stopped breathing, and wouldn't dare to start again until Reva was wholly returned, her astral and physical selves united and safe.

An hour passed. Two. And then, just before the passing of the third, when I was certain one more minute would have us all charging blindly into the Bay to right whatever wrongs had most certainly been committed against her, Reva emerged.

Her face was as blue-white as the full moon shining on the snow.

"Reva," Gray said gently, kneeling beside her in front of the flames. "Are you okay?"

Reva blinked rapidly, then turned to look at Gray, her eyes going wide with shock. "I… I couldn't stay," she said. "Not more than a day."

Gray nodded, deciding not to tell the child that she hadn't even been gone three hours by our reckoning. Another trick of the fae magic.

"Why couldn't you stay?" Gray asked.

"There weren't enough shadows."

"What do you mean?"

At this, Reva looked up and met my eyes, her own clearing a bit as the shock receded. "It's morning there. All the time now. There's no snow, no fires, no armies, no darkness. There are flowers blooming on every street, and birds singing, and warm breezes coming in off the Bay… It's like… It's like this weird, twisted paradise."

"What of the people?" I asked. "Did you see anyone?"

"I saw everyone," she whispered. "Witches, vampires, humans. Everyone was smiling. Happy. Chatting with their neighbors, riding bikes through the park. But the thing is, something felt off about their smiles. They seem kind of like zombies. Well, not the kind that eat people. Just the spaced-out kind. I tried to talk to one of the witches and tell her we were coming, but the woman just kept asking me if I was lost, over and over again, even when I told her I lived in the neighborhood."

"Are you sure you traveled to Blackmoon Bay and not to another location by mistake?" I asked her.

"Yes. I saw Norah's old house, and the café where she used to take me for peppermint mochas sometimes. Not Luna's—the other place."

"Covington's Cup," Haley said. "It's around the corner from Norah's."

Reva nodded. "It was definitely home. Just… super messed up. And not in the way Jael said. I swear, you'd take one look at it and think that nothing bad had *ever* happened there."

"It must be glamoured," Jael said, "and heavily at that. Kallayna didn't mention it during our last conversation, so I presume it's a relatively new situation—one that makes our endeavors that much more challenging."

"Can you undo it?" Gray asked. "We really need an accurate picture if we've got any hope at sorting out friend from foe."

"I won't know until we're in there and I get a sense for the complexity of the spell weave," he said.

Gray got to her feet, turning to face the crowd. The collective energy in the room rose considerably, the air suddenly electrified.

We all knew what was coming next.

"Alright, guys," she said, meeting each of our gazes in turn. Then, with a resolute nod of her head, "Let's move out."

TWENTY-SEVEN

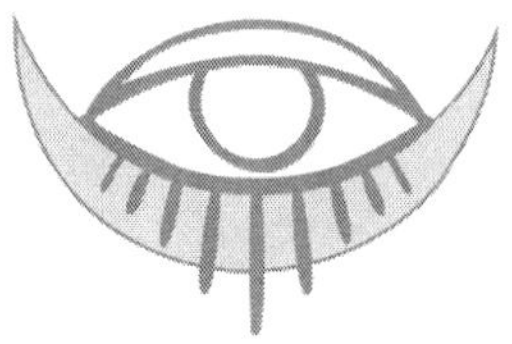

ASHER

Gray wasn't out for power. Hell, she'd had a hard time accepting her own magic, let alone trying to control anyone else's. World domination? It just wasn't her style.

But seeing her take charge of the troops, unflinchingly directing us into the Bay where we'd face our ultimate enemies... She had truly come into her own. She was, as Ronan had always believed, born for this.

Our girl was a total badass, and truth be told, I was kind of fucking turned on.

Unfortunately, I'd have to stash that thought for later.

On this night, there would be no sneak attack. No standing around in the snow with our thumbs up our asses, waiting for the signal. No more planning, no more plotting, and no more talking.

There would only be doing.

All of us were out for blood.

From the moment Gray ordered us to move out, we were in motion, loading into the emergency vehicles Elena had commandeered from the RCPD, caravanning east to Blackmoon Bay.

Gray had been confident that with so many witches concentrating their power and intention to a single outcome, we'd be able to override the fae cloaking spells that would otherwise send us in circles.

Her theory proved correct. After a tense drive, we found

ourselves driving across a bridge that led straight into the center of the warehouse district.

Ground zero.

We met no resistance. Not on the drive over, and not as we pulled in behind an abandoned warehouse, stashing the vans down a narrow alleyway.

The vampires had ridden in a van with tinted windows, uncertain as to how the Bay's perpetual sunlight would affect them. Now, I watched as Gray and Darius stepped out first, gingerly stretching their hands into a patch of sunlight.

Nothing happened.

"Remember, it's glamoured," Jael said. "None of this is real. Not even the sun. But that also means that when the real sun rises, we won't necessarily know it until it's too late. You all need to keep a very close eye on the time."

Gray glanced at her phone. "It's nine p.m. now. That means we've got a good ten hours until sunrise, but I don't want to take any chances. Vampires, we all need to be back here or seek other appropriate shelter by six a.m."

"Clear," Darius said, and Fiona nodded.

Gray and I checked all the vans, making sure everyone had their weapons and whatever magical items the witches needed. We made a formidable force—witches, vampires, shifters, demons, and our resident human, Spooky. Even Reva was in line, carrying a short blade, her blue eyes wild.

No one had stayed behind, and no one was unprepared.

"That's everyone," I said, giving Reva a fist-bump.

We moved quickly after that, the whole crew slipping inside the warehouse for cover. This part of the district had always been a ghost town, and so far, we hadn't spotted any people—human or super—but we weren't taking any chances.

Certain we were all secure inside, Gray turned back to Jael. "So, can you undo the glamour?"

"I need an hour, but yes, I can do it. Just remember, Gray—the moment I break the spell weave, they'll know we're here. Not necessarily where we are, but they will eventually find us."

"Or," she said, flashing a sly, ready-for-anything grin, "we'll make it easy on them."

"How do you mean?" he asked.

There was a fae sword strapped to her back, but in her hand, she gripped the staff she'd been favoring during the training. Raising it before us, she looked us over, taking our measure—her dark rebels, her fighters, her friends, her lovers, her hellhounds—and her magic crackled to life, arcing along the wood.

"Let's show these motherfuckers who's coming home tonight."

TWENTY-EIGHT

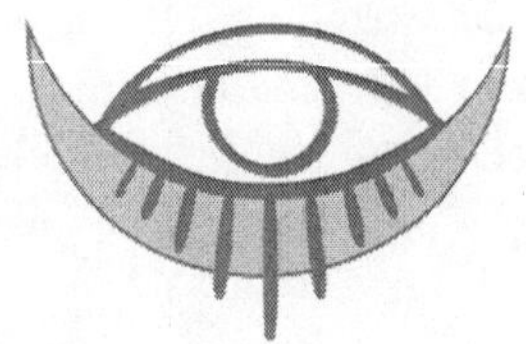

GRAY

Blackmoon Bay is burning…

Jael's earlier warnings echoed, but they had not done the situation justice.

As the fae glamour fell away, taking with it the sunshine and the birds and the bright, cloudless sky, my whole body froze in sheer horror as I took in the scene.

The *real* scene.

Our home, as we'd known it, was well and truly gone.

Luna's café had been leveled, leaving no more than a smoking husk in its place. The magical boundary that had protected it had clearly evaporated. I thought of Ella, the cute fox shifter I'd last seen behind the counter, how she'd always saved the last chocolate macadamia cookies for me. I hoped she'd gotten out alive.

The boats that hadn't been blasted ashore were frozen in the icy bay, smashed and sticking up at odd angles, unmoving. They were so still, it looked like a photograph.

The warehouse around the corner that had served as the base of operations for Waldrich's Imports, the black-market employer Ronan and I had shared, was little more than a steel frame now. The Waldrich's van I used to drive—the same one the guys and I had driven to Norah's house to rescue Asher—was tipped on its side in the middle of the street, all of the windows smashed.

Everywhere we turned, destruction and chaos reigned

supreme. Fires were still smoldering. Buildings we'd visited and passed by thousands of times had been reduced to rubble and ash. Stores and homes and restaurants, parks and plazas, trees, all of the places that had made Blackmoon Bay something more than a name on a map…

I swallowed the tightness in my throat. Those places no longer existed.

But the most frightening sight of all wasn't the burned-out husks of buildings or the rows of decimated houses.

It was the people.

Human and supernatural alike, they walked the streets in the same glassy-eyed daze as Reva had described. The same as when everything had still looked shiny and new, as though the glamour had so thoroughly transfixed them, they'd never again be able to see things as they truly were.

One of them passed by me now, brushing against my arm as if she hadn't even noticed me—a woman in a bright green sundress, her arms loaded up with flyers, the bare skin of her legs black with frostbite she didn't seem to feel. I reached out and took her hand, stopping her forward momentum.

At this, she finally turned around, her glassy eyes fixating on me as if she were waiting for me to cue up her lines.

"Are you okay?" I asked. Stupid question with an obvious answer, but in that moment, I couldn't form a logical thought.

She cocked her head, her smile unbroken. "Would you like to come to our meeting? Please bring a dish to pass." She handed me a flyer from the stack in her arms, then moseyed along, disappearing around the corner.

I glanced down at the paper, my heart twisting.

> Unhappy with your lot in life?
> Wishing things could be better?
> WITCHES ARE THE PROBLEM.
> The good news? Problems can be solved.
> But only by taking ACTION.
> A better, happier, richer life can be yours.
> Find out how!

There was an address and phone number, followed by a lengthy, small-print essay delineating all of the awful, terrible, very bad things witches had allegedly caused—everything from unemployment and economic crashes to STDs and the brainwashing of our nation's youth.

I didn't have the heart to tell the woman she, too, was a witch, just like me.

She, too, was part of the alleged "problem."

I crumpled the paper and tossed it onto a burning pile of trash, resolute.

No, this crazy disaster area wasn't the Blackmoon Bay of memory. But it was still home. *Our* home. These aimlessly wandering people, however bespelled in the moment, were our neighbors.

And when I turned and looked back at the guys, at the witches, at all the living, breathing, passionate, loving souls who'd followed me into this hell, I knew we were all thinking the exact same thing.

We're not giving up on our home.

I met Darius's eyes, and he nodded once. It was time.

I brought my hands up and closed my eyes, calling up the magic of home, the magic of my birthplace, the magic of the city we loved. It was still there, pulsing beneath the burning streets with a fire all its own, ready to be channeled, ready to consume anything in its path.

I drew it up into myself, then pushed it out into my staff, where it connected instantly with the weapon's fae magic, twining into a bright blue arc twice as powerful as anything I'd ever called upon, anything I'd ever wielded.

I pointed it at the warehouse on the corner across from us, a storage facility owned by the marina operators that was typically stocked with marine fuel and all kinds of other flammable shit.

And then I let loose my magic.

The warehouse exploded on contact, lighting up the docks and sending out a beacon bright enough to be seen from space.

The message was clear.

The Silversbane witch was here—right fucking *here*—and

she'd brought an army of witches and rebels who weren't going down without a fight.

Scratch that. We weren't going down at all.

I tightened my grip on the staff and looked back at my guys one more time, my lips stretching into a grin as I felt the drumbeat of a hundred enemy boots hitting the docks, finally barreling toward us.

It was time to take out the trash.

TWENTY-NINE

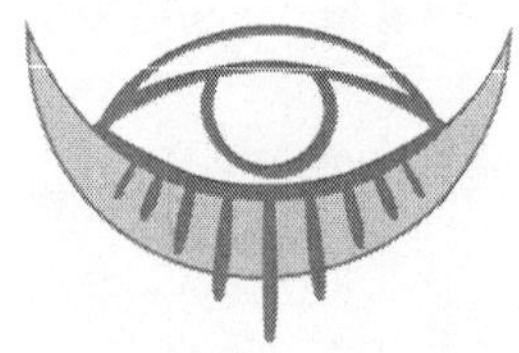

GRAY

Hunters and dark fae, hybrid shifters, rogue vampires… Every foul beast we'd ever faced now converged before us, their teeth sharp, eyes bright with menace.

Together with my rebels, my sisters, my hounds, and all the witches and supernaturals who'd come to fight at our side, we broke upon their army like a wave crashing against the shore.

All around me, the colorful explosions of different magics lit up the snowy night, including the familiar yellow-orange signature I knew belonged to Deirdre. She hadn't traveled here with us —I hadn't even spoken with her since I'd sent her away. But she'd shown up when it counted, and for that, I was grateful.

The fae forced the hunters to lead the charge against us. Eager for the kill, Sparkle and Sunshine cleared a path right through them, mauling their prey without a second thought. Blood ran red in the gutters as I blurred into action behind them, slicing through my enemies as though my staff were a hot blade and their bodies no more substantial than butter.

Against the deadly combination of my vampire speed and the magic, the hunters and even the hybrids were no match for me.

The fae, on the other hand, posed more of a threat, as did the vampires, and after I'd taken out almost as many hunters as my hounds had, I found myself surrounded by much more formidable opponents. All around me, I saw my rebels facing their own battles, the demons teaming up on other fae, Darius leading the RCPD shifters against the hybrids, the witches grappling with the remaining hunters.

I was on my own, but I wasn't alone. I took strength from them, just as they took it from me.

Steeling myself as the enemy closed ranks around me, I raised my staff, infusing it with the magic that hummed inside me.

"You're gonna die slow," one of the vamps said, but before he could pop off another useless threat, I swung hard, sending a burst of magic into the staff just as it connected with his head.

Blue flames ignited, quickly engulfing him. It'd happened so fast he hadn't even had time to scream.

The others lunged for me all at once, but I was faster than them, faster than Darius, faster than any vamp we'd ever come upon. They were no more than smudges in my peripheral vision as I darted and danced, keeping them at bay with the threat of blue fire.

One of the fae soldiers lunged for me with his blade, but I dodged easily. As his momentum carried him past me, I spun around fast and swung for his head, connecting hard. The force of the blow reverberated into my hands, jarring me for a brief moment before he dropped to the ground, dead weight.

The other fae watched me in shock.

Fae weapons were powerful in their creators' hands, but I had fae blood running through my veins, too.

"Take her down!" one of the soldiers ordered an unseen assailant behind me, and instinctively I dropped to the ground. A sharp pain bit into the top of my shoulder, but I'd dodged a deadlier thrust, and now I used my position to my advantage, grabbing the soldier by the knees and knocking his feet out from under him.

He hit the ground with a thud, and I leaped to my feet and bashed his skull in with the tip of my staff.

The two Darkwinter Knights remaining quickly turned tail, charging into another skirmish that had broken out behind us, hoping for an easier target with the witches.

Obviously, they'd never seen witches fight.

I scanned the crowd for my sisters, catching sight of Haley just as she sliced open her hand. She was on her knees, and now she pressed her bleeding palm to the concrete, calling forth a line of yellow fire that separated the witches from the hunters and fae who'd been attacking. The enemy leaped backward to avoid the path of that blood magic, but it had distracted them just enough to give the witches another advantage. Channeling their active powers, the group fighting with Haley pummeled the soldiers with a coordinated magical attack, lighting up the darkness.

"Gray! You good?" Ronan appeared at my side, his eyes black, a gash across his forehead, but otherwise unharmed. He eyed my blood-soaked shirt, but the wound at my shoulder had already knitted back together.

"Vampire healing for the motherfucking win," I said, and he nodded once, then charged back into the fray. I was close on his heels, taking out two hybrid panthers who'd tried to double up on him from behind.

Together, Ronan and I fought our way through a tangle of hunters, easily dodging their comparatively weak human attacks. I'd just turned around to get a read on the rest of the group when I saw six vamps circling a couple of witches, herding them down an alley away from the rest of the fighting.

Away from anyone who might protect them.

"Ronan!" I shouted, but I didn't wait to see if he'd heard me. I was already racing toward the vampires, unwilling to consider any outcome but their immediate destruction.

They had Verona and my sister, Addie. There was no way they were going to survive this.

Charging in at vampire speed, I slammed into the first one from behind, bashing the front of his skull against the brick exterior. He spun around, grappling for me even as blood streamed into his eyes, but I was faster, my staff already igniting.

Without a word, I touched it to his chest, lighting him up.

Movement just behind me, and I slid the staff backward, catching another vamp hard in the groin. He dropped to his knees, and I spun around, swinging. The staff cut through his neck, melting away muscle and bone, thoroughly decapitating him.

Four left, and two of them were taunting Verona and Addie, but the witches were holding their own, defending themselves with a combination of Verona's potions and the hawthorn stakes Addie had brought. I saw her slam one into an attacker's chest just as the other two grabbed me.

My staff clattered to the ground.

I twisted out of their grasp, but these two were relentless, coming at me again and again, both of them stronger than me, nearly matched on speed. One of them finally got his hands around my upper arms, and then the other grabbed a fistful of my hair, wrenching my head backward.

Behind them, I caught a glimpse of Ronan charging down the alley, fire in his eyes, fire in his steps. But just before he reached me, he stopped and smiled, and a Darkwinter Knight stepped out of the shadows, shoving his blade right through Ronan's heart.

It was Emilio's death at the warehouse all over again, and I screamed in horror as Ronan went down. He dropped to his knees, his blood spilling on the street before him, his eyes going vacant.

He caught my gaze for the briefest moment, then fell forward.

Dead.

It had happened in an instant.

Fear and grief overwhelmed me, twin serpents that slithered around my chest and threatened to choke the life out of me.

But… *no*. It wasn't real. It *couldn't* be real. I blinked rapidly, feeling the logical part of my mind trying to claw its way through a sticky haze. Ronan wouldn't have been caught unaware like that, wouldn't have stopped to smile, leaving himself exposed. He'd fought too many battles, lived too many lifetimes to make such a rookie mistake, especially after he'd seen Orendiel take out Emilio with the same dirty trick.

My instincts kicked in fully, and every last one of Darius's lessons on shielding came flooding back.

These bloodsuckers are fucking influencing me.

I blinked away the image of Ronan lying face down in a pool

of his own blood, and I ground out a string of curses, forcing the rogue vamp out of my head. I shook with the effort—he'd already embedded his poison quite deeply by the time I'd realized what was happening—but eventually, my thoughts became my own once again.

Ronan's lifeless body, no more than a figment of my vamp-infiltrated imagination, vanished.

Rage-induced magic surged into my limbs, and I wrenched myself from their vicious grip, slipping out from between them. I had just enough time to grab the fae sword I'd strapped to my back before they were coming at me again, but this time, neither would lay a hand on me.

I blurred out of their reach, then doubled back, swinging at the first one with all I had.

His head dropped to the ground with a wet thud.

I felt the invasive touch of the other vamp's influence again, and I forced my eyes to go glassy, a fake whimper escaping my lips. Standing perfectly still, I let him approach. Let him get cocky. Let him scent my fear.

And then I smiled, shoving my sword through his throat.

He choked and gasped, dropping to his knees. I yanked the sword back out and swung again, serving him the same fate as his buddy.

The other two vamps were still engaged with Verona and Addie, and now I crept behind them, taking down one in the same grizzly manner while Addie and Verona staked the other once again, then lit his bloodsucking ass on fire.

"Everyone okay?" I asked.

Verona and Addie were panting from the effort, blood and sweat and grime coating their faces, but they smiled now, nodding briefly and squeezing my hands before they took off in the direction of the main fight still unfolding in the streets.

I had just finished re-securing my blade on my back and grabbing my staff when new movement at the end of the alley caught my eye. Now, Ronan did appear there, he and Asher fighting off a pair of Darkwinter Knights. Sparkle was in the mix, too, her muzzle dripping with blood as she tore chunks of flesh from one of the fae's leg.

I tightened my grip on the staff and darted toward them, eager to help dispatch the two fae. But there was another figure behind them now, emerging from the swirling snow.

The sight of his white beard stopped me cold.

Even at a distance, I could see the eager glint in his eye. Casually, he raised his arm and took aim, and the moment played out before me like a slow-motion horror movie I was powerless to stop.

Phillip pulled the trigger.

This time, when I saw Ronan go down, I knew it *was* real.

Just as I knew Phillip's gun wasn't just a regular gun with regular bullets.

"No!" I screamed, but it was too late. Ronan was on his knees, leaving Asher to grapple with the Darkwinter Knights.

Phillip had already vanished.

I charged toward Asher, my staff raised and hungry for death. I cracked one of the soldier's skulls wide open just as Ash had gotten a hold of the other guy's head, giving it a sharp twist.

Both soldiers dropped.

Asher and I exchanged a quick horrified glance, then got to our knees, both of us reaching for Ronan.

"Devil's trap nano," he managed. "In the bullets… Smart."

The poison was already working its way through his bloodstream, sapping his strength, wringing the life from him before our eyes.

"Fucking hell!" Asher shouted.

"Listen to me," I said to Ash, shoving my fear into a tiny little box and burying it deep inside. Ronan didn't have much time; there was no room for anything but action. "Your blood… It's in your blood. You can fix this. You're immune to the devil's traps."

Asher immediately got my meaning, and without wasting another heartbeat, he scooped Ronan into his arms and got to his feet.

"Get him somewhere safe and find one of the witches with

healing magic," I said. "They'll figure out a way to make an infusion from your blood."

Asher nodded, and I took Ronan's face between my hands, staring deep into his eyes. They were shifting back and forth from hazel to black, his body convulsing.

"I love you," I said. "And if you don't come back to me, I swear to Sebastian himself I'm going straight back to Hell to hunt your ass down. So don't you pull any shit, Vacarro."

Asher lowered his head, capturing my attention. I saw the promise in the depths of his ocean-blue eyes even before he said the words. "I got this, Gray. Go find that filthy hunter and fucking butcher him."

I pressed my mouth to his and stole a kiss. "You can count on it."

THIRTY

EMILIO

The dark fae were absolutely everywhere, skittering across the streets like cockroaches, clashing with our witches and shifters as we all fought to reclaim the city.

Some of Elena's men and the witches had already been injured, but Liam had set up triage in an abandoned restaurant, and he and the witches with healing magic were doing their best to keep our people safe.

Twenty minutes in, and everyone was already bloody and exhausted, but I knew no one would give up. This was too important, too real. I was certain Gray's earlier words weighed heavy on all of our hearts.

Blackmoon Bay is ground zero for their entire operation, and it's no longer simply the home we're trying to take back. It's the spark that will eventually set the whole world on fire…

This is not just about our own lives, but the lives of everyone we've ever loved. If we fail, we will all die. Witches, shifters, vampires, demons, fae, and humankind…

And so we fought, holding true to the bond that had brought us all together, fighting for our lives and the lives of anyone and anything that ever mattered. Witches lit up the streets, vampires blurring in and out of sight, shifters and hounds tearing flesh and breaking bone.

And still, more came. More fae. More hybrids. More rogues.

But then, a light in the brutal darkness, more witches arrived.

Three dozen at least, charging up the street in formation, their steps quick and determined, their magic at the ready.

They needed no introduction. These were the witches of Blackmoon Bay, and they were ready to take back their freedom.

Side-by-side, they fought with our witches, all of them united in this purpose, in this singular mission. With their help, our side quickly regained our advantage, and slowly but surely, the enemy's numbers began to thin.

In the midst of the battle, my sister and I were a team in the truest sense of the word, never leaving each other's sides as we fought our way through hunters and hybrids alike, dodging the fae and their deadly silver weapons at every turn.

But there was one Darkwinter Knight we couldn't—*wouldn't* —avoid.

Elena and I had a score to settle, and the moment we caught sight of him, we were on the move.

"There!" she said now, nodding her head toward an alley at the end of the street. "He's down there. Three other fae are with him."

"You sure?" I asked.

Elena nodded. "I'll never forget Orendiel's face."

Checking to make sure the others were holding their own, we broke away from the main battle and headed in the direction she'd last seen the general, keeping our eyes peeled for any would-be ambushes.

By the time we reached the entrance to the alley, the sounds of clashing blades and the cries of the fallen had softened to a din behind us, and we leaned our backs against the exterior bricks, taking a quick moment to regroup. I knew this section of town; this was the First American Bank, and the alley cut through to Hodge Street on the other side.

The fae could be anywhere. Still, we had to try.

My sister had gone quiet, slipping into the darkness of her own mind. I didn't like that one bit.

"Talk to me, Lainey," I whispered, nudging her elbow. "What's on your mind?"

"Just that I'm… I'm glad it's you," she said. "If I have to die tonight, I want it to be fighting side-by-side with my brother."

"You always were a drama queen." I grinned at her and rolled my eyes, needing the levity as much as I knew she did. "*No* Alvarezes are dying tonight. Not on my watch."

"From your lips to all the saints in the sky."

"You ready?"

Elena blew out a breath, then nodded, and together we stepped into the alley, ready to end it, one way or another.

The strip was empty, but a commotion at the other end of Hodge caught our attention. More fighting, fae blades clashing, magic lighting up the wintry mist.

"It's Jael!" I said, quickening my pace. He was fighting alongside two women—one I recognized as his sister, Kallayna. The other looked just like them, but slightly older. Not so much by physical age, the way a human might, but by stature. By wisdom.

She was, I realized in an instant, their mother. Queen Sheyah.

Whether they'd asked for her help or she'd simply arrived, I didn't care. What mattered now was that she knew how to swing a sword, and she and her children made a formidable force against the tangle of fae enemies gathered before them.

Not waiting for an invite, Elena and I shifted into wolf form, leaping into the battle, taking down two Darkwinter Knights before anyone had even realized what'd happened.

The Queen swung a blade like a seasoned warrior, icing two soldiers in one shot, then pivoting to catch another in the chest. Her blade melted through their armor, eating down to the bone like acid.

I'd never seen anyone fight so ferociously. So calmly. I wondered how many battles she'd fought.

Together with the fae on our side, Elena and I continued to tear through the enemy, dodging their weapons, spilling their blood.

And then, backing away from the melee, a defector. A traitor to his own blood. A fucking coward wearing the uniform of a general, turning tail and trying to make his escape.

"Go," Sheyah ordered, taking down another soldier, and Elena and I were off at a good clip.

I reached him first, launching myself onto his back and slamming him to the concrete. He struggled to reach his weapon, and just as his fist tightened around the pommel, I sank my wolf fangs into his forearm, his scream of agony washing over me like a symphony.

Elena bit his shoulder, but despite his cowardice, Orendiel was not easy prey. He fought hard and scrappy, beating us back with his boot, with a rock he'd picked up, with anything he could.

He managed to get to his feet, once again reaching for the deadly blade at his side.

But Elena was having none of it. She shifted back into her human form, the sudden appearance of her nude, powerful body distracting Orendiel just long enough for us to get the upper hand.

Elena grinned at him. As if I could read my sister's mind, I locked my jaws around his ankle, biting until I heard the bone snap. Just before he dropped in agony, she swiped his sword.

Orendiel hit the ground, blood pouring from his wounds.

I pinned his legs with my massive form, and without hesitation, Elena shoved the fae blade into his throat.

"That's for my brother, asshole."

Certain he was no longer a threat, I shifted back into my human form, and together my sister and I loomed over the body as his skin melted away, the magic of the sword eating straight through. He writhed in agony, and I watched him burn, knowing full well the pain of that particular wound.

I couldn't say I was sorry.

After several long moments, Orendiel finally stilled, his eyes dimming, the white mist of his breath disappearing into the night.

I felt nothing but relief.

We made our way back toward Queen Sheyah, Jael, and Kallayna, who were fending off the last of the soldiers. Several lay dead at our feet, and Elena and I—still nude from the shift—stripped off some of their clothing, quickly covering ourselves.

We rejoined the fight just in time to watch Kallayna behead the last fae standing.

In the momentary calm that followed, the five of us stood silent, almost reverent, taking in the scene. Fae corpses littered Hodge Street, blood pooling and running in rivulets down the pavement.

"Thank you, your Highness," I finally managed, breaking the silence and offering a slight bow of gratitude. "I don't know how you came to join us here, but I'm beyond grateful."

"The Council has rotted from the inside," she said, her voice laced with a sorrow that surprised me. I did not take her for an emotional woman, but she sounded truly regretful. "It was not supposed to be this way. I am here to right that wrong."

I bowed again, then introduced my sister to the Queen and Kallayna.

"I'm glad to see you safe," I said to Kallayna.

"Me too," she replied, then squeezed her brother's hand. Jael's eyes were misty with unshed tears.

"This war is just beginning," Queen Sheyah said now. "Dark fae are crawling through your cities like rats."

"And we've just killed the biggest rat of them all," I said.

The Queen nodded. "Orendiel should not have risen to such heights unnoticed. Like the Council's darkness, I simply refused to see it. I assure you, that will not happen again."

I nodded, knowing she meant every word.

Gathering her children at her side, the Queen led them back toward the main battle, leaving me a moment alone with my sister.

"The fae gear looks kind of badass on you," I said.

"I know, right?" Elena started to laugh, but her smile quickly fell, her face crumpling into a look of abject horror as the events of the last few moments finally caught up with her.

She glanced down at her bloody hands and gasped, and I gathered her into my arms, rubbing her back, whispering promises into her hair like I'd done so many times before.

But this time, when I told her the worst was over, when I told her we'd survive this, when I told her I *knew* we'd be okay, I wasn't feeding her platitudes or trying to find the right words to make up for past mistakes.

I was laying the foundation for our future. For our family.

And this time, when her tears finally dried and she'd come back to herself, she looked up into my eyes and smiled, saying the words that for two decades, I hadn't even realized I'd needed to hear.

"I love you, Meelo. Just so you know."

THIRTY-ONE

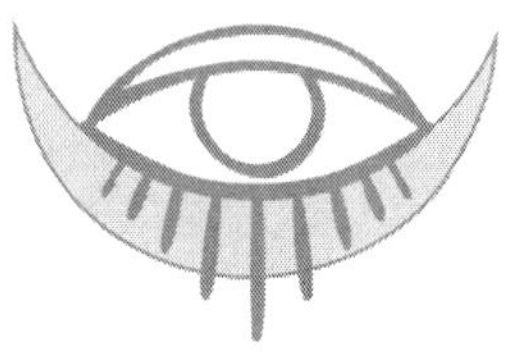

GRAY

The instant I was back in the crush of the battle, I found Dirty Beard, shouting orders at his hunters to attack the triage area Liam had set up.

Grabbing Darius along the way, I sped toward the group, both of us barreling into them at top speed, knocking them down like bowling pins. I pinned one to the ground, baring my fangs and tearing out his throat.

The touch of his foul blood on my lips sparked an ancient instinct, and this time, rather than repressing it, I welcomed the bloodlust, letting it fuel me. I destroyed two more filthy hunters in the same manner, looking up just in time to see Darius tearing into another.

In minutes, we cleared through the lot of them, leaving only Phillip alive, gaping at us with wide eyes.

He turned to bolt out of there, but Phillip and I?

We were just beginning.

You no longer need your weapon, Phillip Reese. Lower your arm, and surrender it to the woman standing before you. She will know what to do.

I focused my will and intent on sending him that message, my influence pulsing through his mind, already making him question his own instincts.

He turned back around slowly, confused, as if he'd just run into a room and forgotten what for.

That's it. Nice and easy. That weapon is dangerous, Phillip. It's best to turn it over.

Phillip nodded, then finally handed over the weapon, and I shoved it into the back of my waistband.

In his cloudy haze, Phillip had lost all common sense, and now he allowed Darius to approach him, totally unchallenged.

Without ceremony, Darius drove a fae sword into the man's gut, bringing the bastard to his knees.

But Phillip wasn't dead yet. Just bleeding.

Darius yanked out the sword and lifted it overhead, intending to finish the job with a clean swipe—a quick and painless decapitation.

But *this* job was mine, and there would be nothing quick or painless about it.

That was a promise.

I glanced up at my vampire, our gazes locked in a fierce battle of wills. Logically, I knew it didn't matter who killed Phillip, or any of our enemies, so long as it got done and we stopped their ultimate plans.

But I couldn't let Darius take the man who'd murdered my mother. Who'd set our home on fire, trying to burn me down inside. Who'd shot the man I love with a devil's trap his own twisted son had invented.

Darius read my thoughts, finally lowering his sword. "Whatever you need to do, Gray, make it quick."

I nodded. My mouth was already full of hunter blood, but there was another whose blood I'd taste tonight. Another whose blood needed to be spilled by my hand.

I knelt down beside Phillip and sank my fangs into his neck, taking exactly what I needed—not a drop more.

Phillip choked and sputtered, his body failing.

"Are you afraid?" I asked him.

No response.

I leaned in close, whispering in his ear. "Good. You should be." Then, glancing up at Darius, "I'll be right back."

* * *

The blue runes carved into the gates of the Shadowrealm pulsed brightly, its stone archway looming overhead. Here in my realm, the night sky was cloudless, glittering with stars.

It seemed fitting that he would die here—die by my hand, by my power. Die in a place he and all hunters feared—a place of a witch's true power.

"Do it," he hissed, kneeling before the rune gate, writhing beneath my grip on his shoulder. But his efforts were weak. He'd already lost too much blood. All he had now were his nasty words, his filthy lies.

He was going to choke on them.

"Do it!" he tried again, but I shook my head, a sense of rightness and calm washing over me.

This man, if I could even bring myself to call him that, had murdered my mother. I was also holding him at least partly accountable for Sophie's death, considering that his passionate hatred of witches ultimately drove his son mad. Phillip's torments had set Jonathan on a fruitless, lifelong quest to prove himself by any means necessary.

"You cut my mother's throat," I said plainly, "and you set our home on fire."

"Your mother was the devil's whore," he spat, "just like you."

Ignoring this, I said, "I watched her blood spill. I watched her bones turn to ash. I pissed myself waiting for you to come back and light me on fire next, but you never did."

"That woman needed to burn, and *you* will, too. Maybe not tonight, but soon enough."

"For more than a decade," I continued, still calm, still serene, "I've seen that moment in my nightmares, in my waking hours, in the bitter darkness. It took me years to accept that it wasn't my fault. That there was nothing I could've done to save her, just as there's nothing I can do now to bring her back. But there *is* something I can do to get that image out of my mind—for a little while, at least."

Phillip coughed up blood, but his eyes still burned with vicious hatred. "How do you plan to do that, sorceress?"

I smiled.

Then I removed the dagger from my boot, grabbed a fistful of his hair, and cut his throat. Not too deep. More of a nick, just like Ronan had shown me how to do. It was an art, really, getting it just right. Just deep enough to watch his artery pump out his blood, slow and steady, but not so deep he bled out too quickly.

I wanted him conscious for this.

Phillip growled at the fresh pain, his taunts quickly turning into moans of agony.

I took a step back, looking down on him and meeting his gaze.

"This is for my mother, Calla, and all the other witches you've tortured and killed. This is for Sophie, my best friend and the bravest witch I know. And this is for every witch and every woman who's ever had to hide her truth, her heart, her soul from the world because of men like you."

Then I reached into my pocket, pulled out a lighter, and lit him on fire.

There were no words for the sounds that came out of his mouth then. No words to describe the smell of his burning flesh.

From the moment I'd brought him here, I thought I'd want to watch, to wait until the flames consumed his body, until the very last smoldering ember died. I thought I'd want to spit on the ashes of his bones.

But hearing his screams? That was enough.

I took one more glance at his burning body, his twitching limbs engulfed, then turned my back on him.

And there before me, gaping at the burning mass of the former king of the hunters, was his son.

Half beast, half something else entirely, the hunter formerly known as Jonathan dragged himself closer, his eyes full of inexplicable agony.

He fell to the ground before the fire, keening, the sound making the hairs on the back of my neck stand on end.

That Jonathan would grieve for the man who'd ruined him

was a testament to the power of manipulation, the weaponization of love by those completely incapable of feeling it.

It was tragic. Logically, I knew that. And maybe there was a time when I would've felt bad at how things had ended for them. For Jonathan, the first boy I'd ever loved.

But I had no compassion left for the Reese family. The best I could offer Jonathan now was a quick death. And this time, I'd be sure it stuck.

"You're the last of your line, hunter," I said to his back. "And this is the end of yours."

Jonathan didn't move. I grabbed his head and twisted hard. Fast. Bone snapped, but a broken neck was only a setback for Jonathan. He was, after all, a vampire now, however mutated.

I retrieved the sword from my back. Gripping it tightly, I swung hard and true, decapitating him instantly.

As Jonathan's blood dripped from my blade, I watched just long enough for the flames to lick across the grass and catch his body, swallowing him in the inferno, the blaze burning father and son out of existence.

Feeling lighter than I had in years, I walked back along my path, taking in the whole of my realm—the black skeleton trees, silver eyes glittering from the branches. The scents of lilac and lavender. The rolling meadow, and the lake that seemed to appear and disappear at will.

I loved this place. It had brought me back to my magic when I was certain I'd never feel its warm touch again.

But now, it was time to say goodbye.

I sat down on the path, digging my fingers into the dirt, and closed my eyes, slowly releasing my hold, slowly letting it go.

When I opened my eyes, I was back on the material plane with Darius, right where I'd left him. It was clear that only moments had passed here, just as I'd intended.

He pulled me into his arms, pressing a kiss to the top of my head.

"Ronan?" I asked. "Have you seen him?"

Darius shook his head. "Let's go find him, shall we?"

We headed back to the side of the street where another skirmish had broken out, weaving through a cluster of witches and hybrids, helping them take out the last few enemy shifters.

We dispatched them quickly, and I was ready to be on my way again. But a flash of movement in the shadows in the alley beside us caught my eye, and I turned just in time to see her.

Alive. In person. Real.

The woman who'd once called herself my mother.

Her eyes locked on mine, gleaming with pure, unadulterated hatred.

"You *die*, Shadowborn filth," she announced.

But in that terrible, soul-wrenching instant, I realized it wasn't me she was after tonight. Not yet, anyway.

She charged toward us in a blur, plucking a witch from the group and sinking her fangs into her neck. It was over in an instant. She dropped the witch like a rag doll, sparing me a quick, bloodstained smile before blurring out of sight.

My heart shattered, exploding in a million tiny shards inside my chest.

I couldn't feel my legs, my lungs, my face. Nothing was working. Nothing would ever work properly again.

Because the witch lying broken on the street, blood leaking from her artery as she sputtered and gasped for her final breaths, was Reva.

THIRTY-TWO

LIAM

Darius charged after Trinity, disappearing around the corner as Gray dropped to her knees beside us.

Her heartbreak mirrored my own, and as she wept for the child that'd become like a fourth sister to her, I felt the weight of her impending loss bearing down on us both.

It stole the very breath from my lungs.

"I love you, Gray," Reva choked out. "You're… You're my sister in all the ways that… that count."

"Reva, don't talk." Gray held the girl's hands, pressing them to her heart as if she could bring Reva back from the brink with the force of her love alone. "Save your strength. We'll fix this. We have to fix this."

"It's too late," Reva said. "Don't—"

"If you say I'm your sister, then you have to listen to what I say," Gray snapped. "And right now, I say it *isn't* too late." She scanned the street in both directions, frantic. "Damn it. Where is McKenna? We need healing, now. Liam, find—"

"Gray, I… I need to talk to Liam alone." Reva's voice was faint, but her eyes were calm and clear. Resigned.

"Shh," Gray said. "Just be still."

"You have to let me go." A tear tracked down Reva's cheek, and Gray gasped, sensing the end was near.

"It doesn't have to be this way," Gray said. "I can… I can fix this." She closed her eyes, then shook her head, as if she were talking herself out of something terrible.

Or, more likely, *into* something terrible.

Immediately I sensed the direction of her thoughts, and I placed a hand on her shoulder, bringing her back from the darkness.

"No, Gray," I said softly. Gently. "Your heart is in the right place, but you mustn't act on it."

We both knew Reva wouldn't want Gray to turn her into a vampire, or to manipulate her soul energy, even if it meant saving her life. Even as Gray's skills had improved immeasurably, there could never be a resurrection without loss.

Reva would certainly lose something—some part of herself, some memory, something crucial that made her the Reva we all knew and loved.

"I can't just leave her like this!" Gray shouted, but I saw the resignation in her eyes, and tried not to show the relief in mine.

Reva was going to die. We both knew it. All that we had left was a precious moment in which to say goodbye.

I knew from my long tenure as Death that even a single moment was more than most people got, and my heart swelled, grateful for the gift that it was. Grateful for the gift that Reva *herself* had been, shining her light into our lives, however briefly.

"We're not leaving you," Gray told her, stroking her cheek. "We'll be right here the whole time."

Reva shook her head. "I want… I need to be alone with Liam. Please, Gray."

Gray bit her lip, shaking her head, but again I saw the resignation in her eyes. She would grant Reva this last wish, despite her own wishes on the matter.

"Are you sure?" she finally asked.

Reva nodded.

Tears spilled down Gray's face, and she bent down and pressed a kiss to Reva's forehead, her shoulders shaking. I placed my hand on her back, wishing I had the power to take her pain, that I could carry it for eternity.

But I also knew that I *wouldn't* take it, even if I'd had that magic. The pain itself was a blessing; it meant that she'd truly loved Reva, and from the depths of that ache, her love would continue to bloom, blossoming anew with every shared memory, every gentle reminder.

"Find Trinity," Reva whispered. "End her."

Gray kissed her once more, sealing the promise. Then, reluctantly, she released Reva's hands and got to her feet.

Her pain fell away, leaving only a steely determination in its place.

"I need to find Trinity," she said.

"I know, Little Witch."

"Look after her," she whispered. And then she was gone, blurring around the corner in the direction Darius had gone only moments before.

The instant we were alone, Reva's brave mask evaporated, and she began to cry in earnest.

"I'm scared," she said, her eyes wide and child-like.

"Me too," I admitted. It wasn't a lie. I was terrified—terrified to lose her. Terrified Gray would never survive the pain of this death. Terrified that I'd caused so much irreparable damage to the people I'd come to love—that I should've been able to find some way to prevent this tragedy.

Terrified that when we woke up tomorrow after all the dust had settled, we'd realize what fools we'd been—how hopeless our cause really was.

But in the end, my fear was no match for my faith, and as Reva took a deep, shuddering breath, steadying herself once again, I knew she would find her path in the Shadowrealm, despite the brokenness of the natural order.

Like Gray, this one was a fighter.

"Liam, I need to tell…" She coughed once, her body going still, even as the light shone bright in her eyes. "I know. I already *know*."

In that single moment, she'd aged a lifetime, and I knew immediately what she was referring to.

"How?" I asked.

"Being Shadowborn... It explains so much. It just... Everything makes sense."

I smiled, knowing she was holding back. "That's all? You just did the math, sketched it out on a napkin, and figured it all out?"

Her eyes glinted with mischief. "Well I... I heard you talking to Gray about it." A smile touched her lips, then faded, her gaze turning serious and ancient once again.

"Yes, Reva," I said. "You are indeed Shadowborn."

There was no point in denying it, though I wished now that I'd spoken with her about it sooner. Would it have changed this outcome? Given her some other advantage, some other path?

"Then you have to do it," she said, her voice faint, but totally clear. Her body was no longer struggling, leaving her mind to focus on this last request. "You have to sac—"

"*No.*" I was resolute. Reva may have surprised me with this new direction, but my instinct to protect her was as sharp as ever.

She wanted to take on the Death mantle. To allow me to sacrifice her to that end, just as the Old One had instructed. A Shadowborn witch, they'd said. That was the only way to undo the chaos of my banishment. The curse.

"It's the only way to fix this." She blinked the snowflakes from her dark lashes, even as more continued to gather. Her eyes were bright blue in the night. Half-wild now.

"I've already accepted the terms of my punishment," I said, "and I will deal with the consequences, however terrible they are. It's not your burden to carry, little one." I touched my hand to her cheek. "I can't ask you to make such a sacrifice."

"Hello?" She rolled her eyes, her playful spark undimmed. "I'm dying. It's not much of a sacrifice."

I shook my head. She was so, so wrong. Taking on the mantle of Death was a greater burden than she could ever imagine, a fate many would find worse than experiencing death itself.

But she was undeterred. And just as she'd been able to convince Gray to leave her, now, she was already slipping in past my defenses.

"Please, Liam," she said, her voice so soft now I had to lean in close to hear it. "I had a dream about this a long time ago, before I ever met you. You appeared as a black raven, and you showed me this moment, right here. I saw the snow falling on my face from above. You said I would know what to do when the time came."

I could only stare, open-mouthed. Reva had never mentioned this to me, not in all our lessons and conversations.

"When I woke up the next morning," she continued, "it was like this great sense of purpose and belonging fell over me, and I knew. I just knew." She closed her eyes, her skin so pale she was nearly translucent. "Let me do this. For Gray. For Haley. For all of the witches who came here today. It's truly what I want. What I was meant for."

Tears rolled down her cheeks, and my own eyes blurred.

Reva sounded so much like Gray in that moment, I could only smile.

She was nearly gone now, but in these final moments, she had won me over.

"Are you certain?" I asked.

Reva smiled, and my heart melted, knowing it would be the last I would ever see it.

Gently I placed my hand over her eyes and bowed my head, whispering the incantation given to me by the Old One, the last and only power I'd been left with. The one I'd sworn I'd never use.

When she opened her eyes again, they were electric, holding the wisdom of a thousand stars, the depths of the ancient oceans, the timelessness of the entire universe.

She opened her mouth to speak, but I would never know her final thoughts. Her body convulsed, then shifted before my eyes, the sight as awesome as it was beautiful.

A sleek, white raven flapped its great wings, hovering before me for a single heartbeat.

Fresh tears glazed my eyes, and I blinked them away.

All at once, the snow ceased.

Reva disappeared.

And there, in the place where she'd lain dying, was a single white feather.

THIRTY-THREE

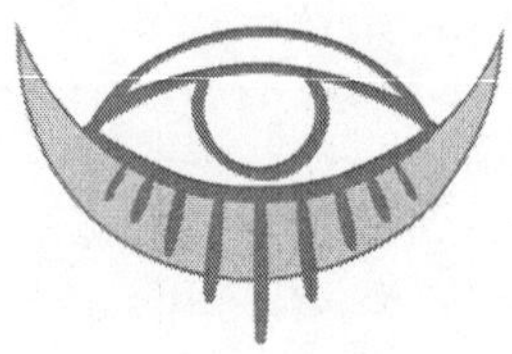

GRAY

There were no comforting words, no promises, nothing anyone could say to make this right.

Reva had been stolen from us by the very woman who'd attempted to snuff out my life when I was a baby. The woman who'd attempted to kill us all. The woman who thought she could take over *our* home, *our* country, *our* world, bending it to her will.

And now, for me, there was only darkness, powerful and all-consuming. Only hatred.

It fused with my magic, black and powerful, pushing me through the crowds of fighters in search of my sisters.

I found Haley first, and she took one look at my face and knew some serious shit was about to go down. Without a word, she followed me, and in a matter of minutes, we found Addie.

"Trinity is here," I said, sparing them the news about Reva. They'd hear about it soon enough, but right now, I needed them to be strong. Focused.

"Where?" Addie asked, and Haley double-checked her weapons. Where seconds ago they'd been exhausted and battle-weary, my words had infused them with new life. New purpose.

Trinity was the head of the snake. And that bitch needed to go down.

I picked up on Darius's scent, and led my sisters in the direction he'd gone, hoping that he'd already found her. Hoping that he'd kept her alive.

Minutes later, we crossed the abandoned railroad yard, and found ourselves standing in front of a small cathedral, one of the few structures that seemed to have escaped the riots and battles unscathed.

"In there?" Addie asked, narrowing her eyes. "Are you sure?"

"Darius tracked her here. Come on." I led them up a set of stone steps and into the cathedral proper. The scent faded under the heavy smell of incense and candle wax, but I picked it up again quickly, following it down the aisle between rows of pews, to a small set of stairs at the back. Ronan and I had taken a historical tour here once, and now I remembered that the stairs led down to a long, underground chamber that was once used by the town's founders to hide alcohol during prohibition.

Silently, we crept down the stairs into the cold, dank tunnel below. It was deep underground, with high vaulted ceilings and pillars that stretched up to the darkness above.

Of the three of us, I was the only one who could see clearly. But there was nothing but empty darkness, a sense of gloom weighing heavier with each step.

Suddenly, I caught a fresh whiff of Darius's scent, and I darted ahead, turning down another corridor that branched off the end, my sisters close behind.

The moment I reached the end, torchlight illuminated the space, throwing eerie shadows on the wall.

No, not shadows, I realized. A vampire. *My* vampire.

"Darius!" I gasped, taking in the sight of him. He was chained to the wall, blood dripping from his mouth. Four hawthorn stakes protruded from his body. In his eyes I could read a thousand thoughts—*I'm sorry, I love you, run…*

"Gray, we need to get help," Addie said, but I knew it was already too late.

"Oh, I'm sorry," a cruel voice cooed, and I spun on my heel, coming face to face with Trinity.

"Is he yours?" she asked, stepping into the light. "You really should housebreak him, Morgan. Vampires can be rather dangerous."

Fear threatened to overwhelm me, but just as I'd had to do with Ronan, I shoved that fear into a box and locked it away inside. Darius would survive this. All of us would survive this, but only if I kept my wits.

"What do you want, Trinity?" I asked, keeping my sisters close behind me. Of the three of us, I had the most active power, so if Trinity was going to blow, I wanted her to make me the primary target.

"There's no need for hostilities, Morgan. We're all family here. Isn't that right, Georgina?" Her eyes shifted behind me, and I glanced over my shoulder just as Georgie stumbled into the light.

Her face was pale, her eyes bloodshot. One of them was bruised. Blood crusted over a gash in her forehead, a matching wound slicing across her chin.

"What have you done to her?" I demanded.

"Oh, that? Just a little fall." She waved off my concerns. Then, to Georgie, "Georgie! Don't be rude. Come say hello to your sisters."

Inside, my magic roiled, but I kept it in check, not wanting to show my hand just yet. I needed to know Trinity's endgame.

"Trinity," I said, softer now, hoping to catch her off guard. "Really. What is it that you want? We're all here now. Just tell us."

She looked at me as if I were the dumbest person on the planet.

"*That* is what I want. For us all to be here. Together. A real family again."

I couldn't believe my ears. It was just like the shit we'd overheard in the meeting during the blood spell. She was completely delusional.

"If you wanted a family so bad," Addie piped up, "why did you try to kill us?"

Trinity pressed her lips together, hands on her hips, her eyes blazing with new fire.

Behind me, Georgie trembled.

"Why?" Addie pressed.

Why. For so long, I thought I'd wanted the answer to that question, too. I thought I'd wanted to hear her excuses. Hear her tell me why she'd tried to murder her own babies. Why she thought magic and power were more important than her children. More important than the so-called "real family" she kept espousing.

But staring into her eyes now, I saw only emptiness. Madness. Whatever my birthmother had endured in her life, it had broken her beyond redemption.

There was nothing she could say to me to convince me otherwise. No answer would eradicate the pain of what she'd done.

Raising my staff, I pointed it at her and ordered her to step back against the wall.

"What is the meaning of this aggression?" she asked, still feigning innocence, even now. When I continued to glare at her, staff raised, she rolled her eyes and said, "Oh, for the love of all that is wicked."

She snapped her fingers, and Georgie let out a small yelp.

Seconds later, shapes emerged from the darkness behind Trinity.

Shifters. Hybrids. The same awful monsters we'd fought in the crypts.

"Georgie!" I shouted. "Get back!" I had no idea whether she could fight, but something told me Trinity hadn't trained her to defend herself.

Haley, Addie, and I sprang into action, meeting the monsters in the center of the chamber. I blurred out of their reach, drawing upon my magic and the power of my staff to take down two in a single shot.

"Gray! Help!" Haley shouted, and I was by her side in an instant, launching myself at the beast, knocking him to the floor just before he sank his fangs into her throat. I dropped my staff and grabbed the sword at my back, taking his head clean off before he could even get to his feet.

There were about a dozen of them, but there was no way they were touching my sisters. No way they were touching Darius again. Clearly, my mother preferred not to fight her own battles; she'd much rather use her vampire power on teenaged girls.

The thought of Reva brought tears to my eyes, but no. I wouldn't go down that road. Not yet.

Fueled by rage and adrenaline and magic and hatred, I whirled through the chamber, decimating my birthmother's army in a bloody, chaotic battle that left me exhausted, but ultimately, victorious.

When the last hybrid dropped to his knees, I cut off his head, sending an arc of blood splattering across my mother's face.

"I gave birth to you!" she shouted, as if that had any meaning to me now. I raised my staff, ready for whatever she decided to throw at me next.

Movement in the shadow of the first chamber, and from the corner of my eye, I saw four figures charge forth out of the darkness.

Not hybrids. Not rogue vamps. Not fae soldiers.

Just rebels.

Liam.

Emilio.

Asher.

Sunshine and Sparkle.

And then, bringing up the rear, with demon-black eyes and a seriously pissed off scowl, Ronan.

He was alive. He was okay.

And they were all here.

Hope surged anew.

I glared at Trinity, the magic inside me so desperate for a target, it singed my fingertips. "In case you haven't noticed, *bitch*, I've been reborn."

Without another thought, I unleashed my magic through the staff, slamming a bolt of energy into the column closest to her, bringing down a pile of blasted concrete. It barely missed her head, but her lower body was completely pinned.

"Georgie!" she shouted. "Do something!"

But Georgie was looking at me. At Addie. At Haley. After a

beat, she finally smiled, her eyes glazing with tears. She knew us. She *felt* us.

Cutting her gaze back to Trinity, she shook her head, finding her voice. "You're on your own now, you crazy bitch."

"You can't mean that!" Trinity shouted.

Saying nothing, Georgie came and stood beside me, her arms folded over her chest. As far as Trinity was concerned, Georgie wasn't budging.

Relief washed over me in waves. "Sunshine," I called, gesturing at the pile of rubble. "Sparkle."

The hounds charged forward, taking point on each side of Trinity, growling in warning. Vampire strength or not, that woman wasn't going *anywhere*.

I raised my staff, pointing it at her face. "You've caused enough damage in your lifetime to last a thousand eternities. You're done now. It's over."

"Kill me, then!" Trinity shouted, completely unraveling. "If I can't be with my babies, then just kill me!"

Her eyes filled with fear, with hatred, with a self-loathing so endless it nearly sucked me down with her. Trinity truly wanted to die.

But I wouldn't kill her. Wouldn't give her that gift.

She had wronged us. She had robbed us of our childhood, of each other, of our chance to grow together and come into our powers. She had ushered in the destruction of the home I loved. She had killed and harmed people I cared about. She had masterminded a plot to eradicate most of the world's witches and supernaturals and humans alike.

She was pure evil. A monster in the truest sense.

When I looked into her eyes, I felt nothing now. Not even a vague recognition, not even a flicker of compassion or regret.

She deserved to die.

But I could not—*would* not give her that escape.

I set down my staff. Stripped off my sword and my daggers.

After all the blood I'd spilled tonight, I was done killing.

It was time to stand with my sisters. It was time for the four to rise.

Instinctively, we all joined hands, with Georgie on my right, her grip warm and solid inside mine, her smile broad, her eyes determined.

Sisters.

Reunited.

Rejoined.

All of us had so much catching up to do, so much to reflect on and plan for, to laugh and cry, to learn and get to know each other. But that would come later. I knew it now with a certainty that wouldn't be broken.

For now, we had other business to finish.

As the guys helped Darius down and removed the hawthorn stakes, my sisters and I flowed into a seamless chant, our unique magics combining into a powerful spell.

"Bane of Silver, blood of fae
We call upon your aid today
The powers she's stolen, the powers she's schemed
Reveal what is real, and not what is seemed
Above and below, by stars, moon, and sun
We bind her eternally, as four become one."

"What are you doing?" Trinity seethed, her eyes wide with fear and revulsion. "I'll kill you! I'll kill each and every last one of you! The legacy is mine. It was always mine!"

Her eyes bulged from her face, blood pooling in the corners of her mouth, but my sisters and I were undeterred. We repeated the spell, chanting until our voices were hoarse, and soon other voices chimed in. The witches we'd fought with in the streets had followed the guys here, and now they all gathered behind us, lending their voices to our chorus.

Deirdre was at the front of the group, her eyes shining with pride. With love.

I looked to her and nodded, making the tiniest space in my heart for forgiveness. Not today, but someday.

Every witch in the room was chanting the spell, slowly

leaching the stolen power from Trinity's body, binding her so that she could never again hurt another soul.

And in that moment of complete solidarity, I realized that this was it. What it was always supposed to be.

It wasn't our weapons or our fighting skills or even our magic. It was our loyalty. Our love. Our friendship. The bond of sisterhood that would never again be broken—not by a twisted hunter, not by minions driven mad by someone else's cause. Not by words or fire or blade.

I felt it in my fucking heart, my bones, all of me. *This* was the fruition of the Silversbane Prophecy, the four swords rising as one, uniting the others to overcome our enemies.

It wasn't about dominating or saving or asserting our will through sheer force.

It was about coming together.

It was, I realized now, about forging a new path forward—many new paths, in whichever direction each witch chose for herself.

When the spell was completed, when we'd tapped almost all of our magic, my sisters and I finally unclasped hands.

It was done.

Trinity sat motionless, bloody tears tracking through the makeup and grime on her face.

The witch was all out of words. All out of power. All out of hope.

Turning to Ronan, I placed my hand against his chest, grateful to feel the steady beat of his heart once more.

Then I nodded, steeling myself for what came next.

"It's time," I said. "Summon him."

THIRTY-FOUR

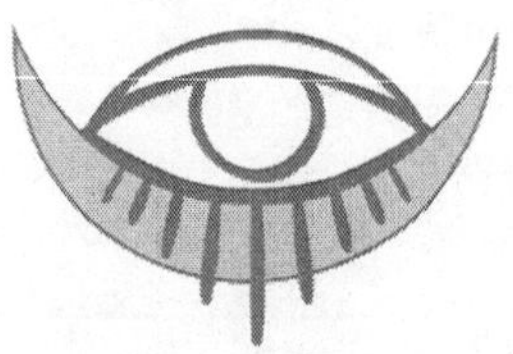

GRAY

"Where is she?" Sebastian's voice slithered into my ears, and this time, I didn't bother to hide my disgust.

Moonlight filtered in through the stained glass windows on the main level of the cathedral. I stepped into the colored light, showing myself.

Standing on the altar fifteen feet in front of me, the Prince of Hell spread his arms and smiled wide, a greeting that normally would've sent chills skittering down my spine.

But tonight, everything had changed. Tonight, I was in charge.

"Ah, Silversbane," he said. "For a moment there, I thought you were going to stand me up."

"I've told you a hundred times, Sebastian. I don't back out of my promises." I took a few steps closer. "But you? You're not exactly a model business partner, are you?"

At this, he narrowed his beady eyes.

"You've made us bow," I said. "You've made us beg. And for centuries, my friends and I have done just that."

His faux-friendly demeanor was all but gone, and when he spoke again, there was ice in his voice. "As you should, witch. I am the Prince of Hell—a fact you seem to keep forgetting."

"Oh, I remember that fact, Sebastian. But now that you mention it, there is something I *had* forgotten until just this very minute."

He coughed out a laugh. "What's that?"

"At the end of the day, you're still a demon, *Prince*." I raised the gun and pulled the trigger, hitting him in the shoulder. His greasy smile evaporated as he stumbled backward, crashing against the wall at the back of the alter, sliding down to the floor.

I looked at the gun in my hand and smiled. It was nothing if not efficient. Before Sebastian could even find the words to sputter at me, the devil's trap was already working its way into his bloodstream.

I took aim again, fired off another round. It hit his other shoulder.

"No wonder the hunters love this thing so much," I said. "Effective, right? You don't even have to be a good shot. You just... Oops!" I squeezed off another round, hitting him square in the chest. "Sorry! Sensitive trigger, I guess. Who knew?"

His eyes glowed demon red, but Sebastian could barely hold up his own head.

For the first time in our long and twisted relationship, it seemed the Prince of Hell finally knew the score.

"So that's it, then?" he raged, his words beginning to slur. "You're just going to smoke me like a stuck pig?"

"You deserve it."

"Maybe I do, maybe I don't, but are you prepared to deal with the demon who takes my place?"

I shrugged, letting him stew in the silence for a bit. Then, quickly bored of the game, I rolled my eyes and said, "Who said I wanted to kill you?"

"Kill, obliterate, what's the difference?"

"Are you always this dramatic? God, how did you get so far up the ranks with an attitude like that?" I stepped up onto the altar and crouched down in front of him, enjoying the view of his pathetic body crumpling in a heap. Meeting his gaze, I said, "I don't need to obliterate you, Sebastian. I just need you to know that I *could* have. I need you to remember it. To think about it every day for the rest of your wretched existence. For all your machinations, your tortures, your power games—at the end of the day, it was a witch who put your balls in a jar. A witch whose soul you once thought you could buy."

Sebastian lowered his eyes. He had nothing to say to that. There was nothing he *could* say.

"I'm officially taking myself off the market," I announced, getting back to my feet. "As of right now, I'm no longer for sale—for you or anyone else."

Reluctantly, painfully, he nodded.

"Say it," I ordered.

"You're… You're not for sale, Silversbane."

"Neither is Ronan."

His eyes blazed with fresh anger, but before he got another word out, I pointed the gun at his balls.

"Say it. Ronan is not for sale."

"But his parents bargained away his soul in a fair—"

"There is nothing fair about someone trading the eternal life of a child to further their own greedy ends, and you fucking know it, asshole."

Sebastian unleashed a scream of frustration, but he'd lost, and he knew it. Resigned, he could only glare at me now. "What are you asking me, witch? Be specific. You know I relish in the fine print."

"Release Ronan from his contract," I said. "From all connection to you. And just so we're clear, I'm *not* asking you." I pressed the toe of my boot against his balls, making him squirm. "I'm telling you."

Sebastian's face turned purple with anger, but eventually, he nodded. "You and Ronan are both released from your agreements. My claim on your souls is hereby relinquished."

"That wasn't so hard, was it?" I took a step backward and lowered the gun. "Hey, don't look so glum. Lucky for you, I *do* honor my own agreements."

"Trinity?" he asked, perking up.

I nodded. "But before I release her to you, and release *you* back to hell, there's one thing I need to know."

"What's that?"

"Why her?" I asked, genuinely curious. "What was so special

about Trinity's deal that you spent all these decades trying to find her?"

For a long while, I didn't think he was going to answer. But then he finally sighed, and said, "It was never about her deal, Silversbane. Trinity O'Leary murdered your father. Do you have any idea what that did to your grandmother? To know that her daughter-in-law murdered her only son? Her only child?"

My mouth hung open, my eyes wide with shock. "You wanted to bring her to justice for what she'd done to my family?"

"No. I wanted to bring her to justice to give your grandmother the peace she deserved. Sadly, I was never able to do that for her."

His voice was so human in that moment, so broken, I almost forgot he was the Prince of Hell.

"You can do that for her now," I said, allowing him a one-time moment of my compassion. "But Trinity won't do you much good if you don't survive the night."

"Speak plainly, Silversbane. I may not have that much longer to stay and chat."

"I have the power to save your life," I said, folding my arms across my chest. "But I've got some terms of my own. And no, Sebastian—I won't be negotiating."

He nodded for me to continue, helpless to do anything but.

"I expect Ronan to be fully released from his contract, as I've already mentioned. He will never again be subject to your demands. Trinity will be handed over to you to do with as you please, so long as she is never released, and never returned to the earthly realm, in any form. You will also relocate your primary place of business back to hell, also never to operate from our realm again."

"But I love Las Vegas!" he whined. "That's where—"

"Furthermore," I continued, "At a minimum of twice per year, or more if I deem necessary, you and I will meet on neutral territory to review the current conditions in both the supernatural communities as well as the demonic realms as part of an ongoing effort to maintain balance and ensure no one faction grows too strong again."

"That is a *big* ask," he said, nearly panting now. "I can't just—"

I held up my hand, cutting him off. "The hounds stay with me as well. They're no longer your possessions, but my companions."

Sebastian seethed, but he knew he had no choice. Not if he wanted to walk out of here tonight.

"And in return?" he asked. "How do you propose to spare my life, now that you've shot me full of poison?"

I saw the resignation in his eyes, and in that moment, I knew I'd finally won.

Sebastian would agree to every last one of my demands.

I was finally free of him.

I retrieved a vial of Asher's blood and a syringe from my jacket pocket, holding it before his eyes.

"What is this?" he asked.

"It's the only possible antidote for what ails you."

Hope flickered in his eyes, but then dimmed. "Possible? You're asking me to wager my life and business and future on a mere *possibility*?"

"Nothing is guaranteed, Sebastian. In this life or the next, above or below. But you know what I've learned?" I set the vial and needle before him, then turned and walked away, leaving him with one last thought to ponder. "Some things are worth taking a chance on, aren't they?"

THIRTY-FIVE

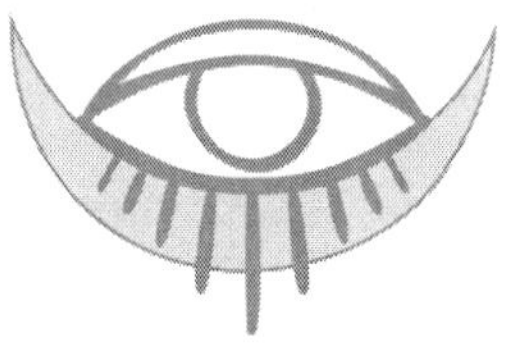

GRAY

After the snow stopped falling, after the blood stopped running in the streets, after the wounded had been treated, after the fires stopped burning, after the final clash of swords faded into the night, I stood in the middle of the warehouse district and took stock of my people. My home.

Blackmoon Bay was ours again. Everything we'd fought for. Everything we'd finally reclaimed.

But as we'd learned time and again, nothing came without a cost.

The city we loved, the city we'd saved… It had been gutted. Rebuilding would take months. Years. Not just the physical construction, but the slow, painstaking resurrection of trust among neighbors, supernatural and human alike.

We'd lost Reva. Two witches from the Bay had been killed by hunters. A fae soldier had taken down one of Elena's shifters—a rookie cop I'd just met last week. Bex, one of Verona's witches, was mauled to death by a hybrid shifter. And McKenna, perhaps most tragically of all, was wounded in a magical explosion caused by the Bay witches. None of them had known she was in the vicinity. By the time anyone realized she was missing, it was too late.

Every one of those souls had fought for me. For their sisters. For freedom. For all of us.

Every one of those souls was gone.

And still, the fight wasn't truly over. We'd taken out the leadership, the base, but there were still sleeper cells in other cities that would need to be eradicated.

It was so much to consider. So much to mourn.

I hadn't even begun to process these losses. To allow myself to truly feel them.

Yet now I stood before Sheyah, the Queen of the Summer Court, guardian of my soul, wondering what news would befall us next.

"Queen Sheyah," I said reverently, forcing myself to stay strong for just a little longer. Later, back in the arms of my rebels, I could fall apart. But not now. Not yet.

"You and your people have fought bravely," she said. "As I told Mr. Alvarez, I am deeply sorry that it had to come to this at all. I am especially sorry for the losses you have personally suffered."

I choked back a sob and lowered my eyes. "As am I, your Highness. Thank you for your kindness."

"I wanted you to know that I have disbanded the Fae Council. Talia and Fenlos were captured trying to leave the city. They will be escorted back to my realm as prisoners, where they will be dealt with according to our laws. The Council shall be replaced with a new group comprised of representatives from each of the supernatural races, as well as three witches. As guardians of earth's magic, we thought your people should be better represented." She paused to let it sink in, then asked the question I knew was coming next. "Would you consider serving on such a council?"

I was honored by the Queen's faith, but in truth, I had no interest in a government job. My place was here in the Bay, rebuilding my home, however long that took.

As diplomatically as I could manage, I said, "Regretfully, I must pass on the opportunity, though it is quite an honor. I'm wondering if you might consider my sister, Addie." Addie was a natural peacemaker. I knew she'd be perfect for the role, and she'd enjoy it, too.

The Queen gave a small bow of her head. "If she is willing, then it shall be our honor to have her serve."

"Thank you," I said.

At this, the queen took my hands, surprising me with her touch. "There is one more matter I wish to discuss with you, and it is one of great importance."

I nodded, my stomach fizzing. It could only be about one thing.

My soul. My eternal fate.

"I have come with a blessing from the Old One," she said, her voice taking on an official tone that was as intimidating as it was regal. In that moment, I was grateful we were on the same side.

"You, heir of Silversbane," she continued, "daughter of Darkwinter, daughter of the first witches, daughter of the night, shall not be damned."

Before I could even ask what she'd meant, she released my hands and retrieved a glowing sphere from her cloak.

I gasped. The moonglass.

Without warning, she smashed the glass on the ground, and I watched with tears in my eyes as my soul swirled before me, floating back home, filling me completely.

"Thank you," I whispered, feeling whole and right for the first time in years. In decades. "I don't know what to say. I'm…"

I trailed off, but when I looked up to meet her eyes, the Queen was already gone, leaving nothing but mist and memory in her wake.

* * *

Goodbye was the most painful word in the English language, and I'd already had to say it way too many times in this life.

Calla, the mother I loved and missed every single day.

My life in Phoenicia, the home she and I had shared there.

Sophie.

Reva.

McKenna.

All the others I had only just begun to know, their names still fresh on my lips from the very first time I'd ever uttered them.

The accounting made my heart ache.

After everything we had endured, I thought the universe might hit the pause button, give me a chance to catch my breath. To heal my heart.

But it turns out there was one final goodbye on my horizon.

And no matter how many times she tried to explain it, my brain refused to accept her words.

"We've all made deals to keep each other safe," Haley said. We were back by the vans now, taking stock of what was left, trying to figure out accommodations for the next few nights, and she leaned against the side of the one with the tinted windows, her eyes imploring me to understand. "There was no other way."

"What are you talking about?" I asked.

"By her grace, I was able to stay and fight, Gray. To see this through with you—to fight by your side as my sister and as my best friend. And I've never felt more proud or honored. But now it's over. We did what we set out to do. And I have to pay the price for that grace."

Her grace…

Realization suddenly dawned, and I remembered Haley in the crypts, performing the blood spell that would ultimately save us from the hybrids.

The spell echoed in my memory.

Blood of hell, blood of night
I call on the darkness to show us the light
May evil and malice and violence intended
Return to its hosts uprooted, upended
Dark Goddess I bend, Dark Goddess I bow
Hear my petition, and thusly I vow
My service is yours, by blood and by blade
Until my last breath shall deem it unmade.

"You pledged her your service," I said, remembering. I closed my eyes as the word hung between us, burning through my heart.

Pledged…

"I have been called to her court to meet with her elite guard. She has an assignment for me, possibly training. I don't know the details."

"So you're just, what?" I asked. "At her beck and call?"

"That's kind of how it works. She's a goddess. I invoked her, and she heeded my call. We… We would have died otherwise."

A shadow darkened her eyes, and for the first time since I'd met her, Haley seemed to have lost her sparkle.

"I love you, Gray," she said now. "I just need you to know that."

"Then why does this feel like a permanent goodbye?"

"It's not—I promise you that. But it might be a while before I can see you again. Take care of Addie and Georgie for me, okay?"

"You aren't going to tell them?"

At this, her face crumpled, her voice dropping to a whisper. "I can't."

I hugged her close, feeling the tremble of her sobs in my arms. I tried as hard as I could to hold on tight, to make her stay, to undo the spell that had bound her to this fate.

But in the end, like so many others who'd come before her, I just had to let her go.

THIRTY-SIX

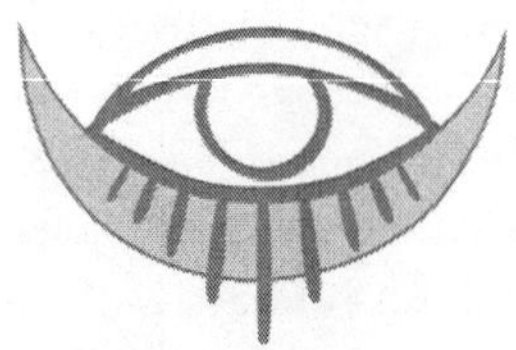

GRAY

After more time and broken hearts than we could count, my rebels and I finally returned to the place we'd once called home. The place we'd decided, somewhere between the end of the Battle for Blackmoon Bay and the showers and naps at the Kingston hotel and the long drive into these woods on the outskirts of town, to call home for good.

The safe house was neglected from our long absence and partially damaged from the storms, but it was still standing, untouched by the violence that had decimated the city.

Inside, we wandered in silence, the only sounds the click-clack of the hounds' nails against the hardwood floors as we tried to get our bearings again, each of us coping with our own pain, our own losses.

Back in one of the bedrooms, I found my old book of shadows. It was cold to the touch, no magic sparking.

I closed my eyes, a feeling of loneliness threatening to suck me out to sea.

But then a familiar scent—leather and whiskey—followed a firm touch on my shoulders.

"Don't suffer in silence, love," Darius whispered from behind, his lips brushing my ear.

Seconds later, his scent mingled with Asher's spicy cinnamon, followed by Ronan's cloves and campfire, and the woodsy vanilla that could only belong to Emilio. Liam came last, bringing with him the ocean and the memories of our first kiss.

Slowly, they coaxed me back into the living room, where Asher started a fire in the fireplace and Ronan put on some mellow music. Emilio rummaged through the kitchen, finding enough non-perishables to put together a small feast. From his old room in the basement, Darius retrieved a few bottles of fancy French wine he'd been saving for a special occasion, knowing that this moment of togetherness, of aliveness, of love was more special than any occasion we could possibly celebrate.

Tonight, there were no battles to fight. No plans to make. No enemies to track. No blood to spill. And as we sat together to enjoy our makeshift dinner, I looked around the table and knew that in that moment, all of us were grateful for this peace.

Finishing our meal, the last bottle of wine empty, we all seemed to sense the shift in energy. Wordlessly, we rose from the table and made our way to the living room, the demons moving aside the furniture, making room in front of the fireplace for the mattresses and blankets Darius and Emilio were dragging out of the bedrooms.

Until we got a proper ginormous bed, it was the only way we could all fit together comfortably. The only way we could do all the things we wanted to do.

To feel.

To love.

To be.

It was the first time I'd ever been with all of them at the same time, and though I was nervous, I was excited, too. Happy. It felt right, all of us like this. It felt like home—a reminder of everything we'd fought for.

The fire crackled and popped, bathing the room in a soft orange glow, and I looked at my men and smiled, slowly stripping out of my clothes and kneeling before the flames.

I was about to invite them to join me when Liam cleared his throat, raising his hand in an adorably awkward gesture. "I just wanted to say that I've completed my research and feel much more prepared."

"What research?" I asked, and poor Liam's cheeks turned the color of apples.

"There were some... films..." he stammered, scratching the back of his head. "It was suggested that I might watch and take notes..."

He trailed off, and I looked at the rest of the guys, trying not to laugh.

"You made him watch *porn*?" I asked.

"Made him?" Ronan said. "That's not exactly how I'd describe it."

"I can't believe you guys!"

"To be fair," Emilio said, "he did ask for our help."

I looked to Liam for confirmation.

He gave me a sheepish smile, the tips of his ears turning bright red to match his cheeks. "I thought perhaps they could direct me toward learning different... different skills."

"By watching porn?"

He ducked his head, clearly mortified. "My understanding was that watching such... films... I thought it was tradition for males on the earthly plane to prepare for events such as these."

I glared at Asher, knowing full well he was the ringleader in all of this. The incubus was covering his mouth, his shoulders shaking with the laugh he could barely contain. He refused to meet my eyes.

"Liam," I called, gesturing for him to disrobe and join me by the fireplace. He did as I asked, more nervous about admitting to watching porn than stripping naked in front of four other dudes. As he knelt beside me, I pulled him in for a kiss, then glanced up at Asher. "Since you boys like watching so much, that's exactly what you're going to do."

They unleashed a chorus of groans, but I was unfazed. Gazing into Liam's ancient blue eyes, I took his face between my hands, tracing the line of his jaw with my fingertips, making him shiver.

"Liam, you are amazing," I said. "The way you touched me that night... I've been fantasizing about it ever since."

"You... You have?"

I bit my lower lip, nodding.

"Thinking about you now, knowing you want to touch me again..." I grabbed his hand and guided it between my legs, letting him feel how wet I was. How turned on. How incredibly powerful his touch really was.

He let out a low moan, his fingers sliding into a perfect rhythm. It didn't matter that he was inexperienced, or that he didn't remember doing this before he became Death. He was in tune with my body on a level that went far beyond the physical, and he knew instinctively how to touch me, how to bring us both to the very brink of insanity.

"I still feel sparks when you touch me," I whispered, and he increased the pressure, hitting me just right. "So the next time you want to prepare or practice," I breathed, stealing a kiss, then pulling back, "come find me, because no matter how many so-called films you watch, there's no substitute for the real thing."

Without warning, Liam thrust deeper, his thumb brushing my clit, and I lost it, gasping as the orgasm grabbed hold of me.

Unable to stay on the sidelines another moment, the rest of the guys stripped out of their clothes in record time, joining us on our giant mattress by the fire.

I pushed Liam onto his back, sliding down to take him into my mouth, sucking him slowly, wanting him to feel every sensation. Behind me, I felt Ronan shift into position, his hands wrapping around my hips as he guided himself inside me.

It wasn't long before we all switched positions, and I straddled Asher, taking him in deep, reaching for Emilio and Darius, stroking them as I had that night in Elena's closet.

There were so many possibilities, so many positions, so many kisses and touches and tender caresses, so many sensitive spots to explore. But this was our first night back, the first of many, and right now, I was just happy to be with them, no matter how long it took us to find our rhythm, to chase our beautiful finish.

I was on my back again, Darius's face between my thighs, Ronan teasing my nipples with his hot, wet mouth. Darius grazed my tender flesh with his fangs, and then he shifted, Liam settling in his place, sliding inside me in a deep, perfect stroke that pushed me right over the edge.

I came with a shuddering cry, a gasp, a moan of pleasure so intense and so deep, it felt like I'd traveled to another realm.

When my legs finally stopped trembling and I came back to myself, tears slid down my cheeks unbidden, but the smile on my face was big and bright, all-consuming.

This was what we'd fought for. What we'd *keep* fighting for. Love and passion and life and laughter and family—the family we chose, the family we made.

I took Emilio next, then Asher, then Darius, all of them taking turns. We carried on for hours, well into the night, until we were certain every last one of us had been satisfied multiple times and exhaustion finally set in completely.

We collapsed in a pile at the center of the mattresses, still touching each other, still sharing stories and dreams, making plans for the rest of the evening, the rest of the week, the rest of our lives.

By the glow of the fire, I closed my eyes, letting myself drift along on the warm current of their voices, their heartbeats, their laughter. A sense of pure contentment and peace washed over me, and I sent a silent prayer of thanks to the universe, to my friends, to my sisters, to my ancestors.

I was here with my rebels. I was safe. I was alive. I was loved.

And for the first time in my life, I was truly home.

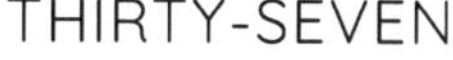

THIRTY-SEVEN

GRAY

Four Months Later…

I'd never climbed a mountain at night before.

Come to think of it, I'd never climbed a mountain, period. But it was something Sophie and I had talked about doing.

Some day.

One day.

Another day.

And that day had never come.

But now, I could give her this gift, taking the Colorado trip I knew she'd always wanted to do.

Thanks to Reva's sacrifice, winter had finally released her icy grip, and spring had emerged with renewed ferocity across the United States. Here in Colorado, wildflowers had exploded across the landscape, the aspen leaves so bright green they nearly hurt to look at.

Sophie would've loved it.

Excited to reach the summit, I pushed ahead, forcing myself not to run up the mountain at vampire speed. I wanted to enjoy the view, the sights and sounds of Colorado at night.

"How is everyone holding up?" I called back, pausing at a large boulder to wait for them to catch up.

"Just… give me a moment." Liam slumped against the boulder

when he reached me, one hand pressed to his chest as he tried in vain to catch his breath. "It's like… breathing through… a cocktail straw."

"Oh, it's not that bad," I teased.

"Easy for you to say, Little Witch. You don't require oxygen, of which there is precious little at this altitude." He pulled a water bottle from the pack on his back, then took a swig. "Things were so much easier when I could take avian forms."

"Do you want to turn back?" I asked.

"And take a nap," Ash said, patting Liam's back, "maybe get a little room service, have someone rub your delicate feet and—"

"Not on your life, incubus."

"That's the spirit, Spooky." Asher laughed and elbowed him in the ribs, but when we got moving again, Ash hung back, keeping Liam company the rest of the trek up.

An hour later, we were at the top, just me and the guys.

The summit of Mt. Elbert was Colorado's highest peak. At over 14,000 feet above sea level, we were standing three miles up into the sky, each of us taking a moment to ourselves to take in the vast beauty glittering before us.

It was breathtaking.

I waited until the moment felt right, and then I removed the pack from my back, retrieving the items I'd brought with me.

A letter from Haley to Sophie, that I now tucked beneath a large rock on the eastern side of the summit.

Several palm-sized stones, each one painted with Sophie's mandala designs and written with messages of love and the names of each of the witches who'd given their lives in Blackmoon Bay. Addie had helped me paint them, and now I placed them together on the southern side of the summit, whispering a few words for the ones we'd lost.

In some ways, I felt like I should be saying a few words for Reva, too. Losing her had been hard on all of us, and remembering her now sent a fresh bolt of pain through my heart. But Liam had assured us that we hadn't seen the last of her. That she'd be back in one form or another as soon as she completed her training.

Apparently, she'd given the Old One a real piece of her mind, and they were—to quote Liam—"implementing some changes for the betterment of all" in their recruiting and training process. Liam hadn't been privy to the details, but I smiled now, knowing that Reva had come into her own, trusting that she'd find a way to carve out her path, just as we all had.

Then, it was finally time.

I looked across the summit and gestured for Ronan to join me. The other guys gathered behind us, silent and respectful.

Sophie had been Ronan's friend as much as she'd been mine, and though we still hadn't been ready to talk about her, to share the good memories, we were getting there.

And I was so, so grateful he was here with me now, helping me to finally set her free.

"Thank you," I whispered to him, and he nodded, reaching for the urn that held Sophie's remains. With each of us taking one side, we tipped the urn and scattered her ashes, watching them spin and dance in the night sky, shimmering like the stars above until they finally winked out and disappeared.

Ronan stepped back with the others to give me some space, and I let out a soft breath, but I didn't cry for her. This wasn't a goodbye. Sophie had been with me through all of it, and even if I couldn't see or hold her again, I knew she'd be with me through all the days and nights to come.

"I thought you should know," I told her, "we re-formed Bay Coven. We've got a lot more members now, including Verona, who makes the trip out every new moon for the meetings." I laughed, knowing what Sophie would say. "Yeah," I replied, as if she'd said it out loud. "I said *we*. I'm a founding member, so you finally got your wish. Crazy, right? My sisters are members, too. Addie and Georgie… You would've loved them."

I closed my eyes, reaching out for her once more, knowing I didn't need to say the words out loud anymore.

Of course she was there. She'd always be there.

Even now, I could feel her presence, her smile, her light. She lived in my heart. She lived in the ocean at Raven's Cape, as wild as it had ever been. She lived in the sky. She lived on this mountain. She lived anywhere love and light were found.

Behind me, I felt the strong, calming presence of my men washing over me, soothing me.

Asher, my fiery incubus, who'd never stop making me laugh, even as he set my insides on fire. Darius, my commanding, intense vampire, who still didn't know how to turn on his cell phone, but never failed to make me feel safe and desired. Emilio, my sweet, brownie-baking, swoon-worthy wolf shifter, strong and powerful, gentle and kind, who'd made it his mission to know and care for the softest parts of my heart. Liam, the man who'd already taught me so much, my intrepid explorer, my passionate lover, a man I couldn't wait to see the world with, to know each place through his eyes.

And Ronan, my crossroads demon finally freed, the first real man I'd ever loved. My best friend, my rock, my love, now and forever and always.

I took a deep breath of mountain air, memorizing this moment. This feeling. This peace.

With the bright moonlight soft on my face, my heart full of love and gratitude and wonder, I dashed the tears from my eyes and turned to them with a smile as broad as the horizon stretching out before us.

"Take me home, boys. I'm ready."

* * *

Happy sigh!

Thank you so much for reading The Witch's Rebels series! After six books, it's so hard to believe it's over, but I know I left Gray and her guys in the best possible place, eager to rebuild their home, strengthen their city, and live a long and beautiful life together!

But Wait! What About Haley?

You didn't think I'd leave our girl hanging after all that crazy Dark Goddess stuff, right? No way! Haley's got her own reverse harem series, filled with a bunch of dark and twisty monsters who are more than ready to be tamed by this fierce witch!

The Witch's Monsters kicks off with a bang in book one, Blood and Midnight.

Three sexy-but-psycho monsters. One fiery, determined witch. And a high-stakes heist about to go *very* wrong...

I've made some pretty questionable choices in the name of my witchcraft—dabbling in necromancy, double-crossing vampires—but summoning the dark goddess? *That* was just plain stupid.

Now I'm in her debt, and goddesses don't exactly do payment plans. She wants the blood of the dark fae warlord of Midnight, a realm of exiles where the sun never rises and torture is a competitive sport. It's a death trap only three men have ever escaped—my newly appointed escorts.

Jax, a terrifying demon whose icy touch leaves me trembling in more ways than one. Hudson, a hulking, fiercely loyal shifter hiding secrets so painful he barely speaks. And Elian, a cocky fae prick with eyes like molten silver and a heart full of vengeance—a heart that once belonged to me.

I'll do anything to settle my debts and get back home, even if it means teaming up with my infuriating ex and the other sinfully hot psychos for the most dangerous blood heist in history.

But when it comes to the cruel fae warlord, not even my monsters can protect me…

Especially when we discover why the dark goddess *really* sent us to Midnight.

* * *

Read on for an excerpt, and grab your copy of Blood and Midnight now!

SNEAK PEEK: BLOOD AND MIDNIGHT

PROLOGUE

HALEY

There's an old adage about the difference between falling in love with a hero and falling in love with a villain. Go for the latter, it says, because a hero would ultimately sacrifice you to save the world, but a villain? He'd burn down the world just to save *you*.

Sounds pretty epic, right? And let's be honest—who doesn't love a bad boy?

The thing about villains, though… Ultimately, they're just the heroes of their own stories. Still fighting for a cause. Still trying to prove something to the world.

Trust me, I've fallen for both. And those assholes? They broke my heart every damn time.

So now I've got a new saying:

Screw the heroes and villains.

I want the *monsters*.

Dark. Vicious. Depraved. The men who slide into your heart like a surgical blade, so sharp you don't even feel it until you're on your knees, trembling and soaked in blood.

A monster won't try to woo you with roses and chocolates, with sweet promises whispered across satin pillowcases. He'll kick down a fucking door to get to you, though. Snap a man's neck just for leering. One threat against you, and he'll tear out the guy's throat with his teeth, then kiss you with a mouth full of blood, no apologies.

A monster's got nothing to prove and nothing left to lose.

And in bed?

Damn.

He'll *own* you, pushing until he finds the very edge of your limits, then smashing right through them. And oh, how you'll *beg* him for it—beg him to break you, again and again and again. To absolutely ruin you for anything less than a life of obsession and fire.

And while the hero slays his dragons and the villain burns down the world for the woman he loves, the monster will simply hand you the matches and gasoline, step aside, and smile as you burn it down yourself.

Because all along, the monster always knew you could.

He just had to make sure you knew it too.

ONE

HALEY

The blood on my boots was still wet when I stepped inside.

My weapons needed a good cleaning too, but the novitiate asked me to leave the daggers and stakes at the entrance, and I obliged.

The Temple of the Dark Moon, she reminded me, was a holy place.

Right.

Appropriately chastised, I nodded and followed the swish of her long black robes across the threshold, my eyes widening as the interior came into view.

The temple had probably been beautiful once, but now it lay in ruins. Half the ceiling had caved in, and broken pillars of onyx and moonstone flanked the inner sanctuary, several of them reduced to rubble. Deep, angry gouges scored the masonry as if some feral god-beast had been locked up inside.

Everything smelled like rot and death.

What the hell happened here?

Hoping whatever it was had already been dealt with, I lowered my eyes and quickened the pace.

"Yours?" the novitiate asked from beneath her dark hood, and I knew she meant the blood I'd tracked across the chipped marble floor. I wondered if she'd be the one mopping it up later or if that would be my job now—one of the many menial tasks the Goddess surely had in store for me.

"No." I scraped the toe of my boot along the floor and left another smear, which was about all the acknowledgment the previous owner of the blood deserved. "Listen, I'm sorry about the mess, but I was summoned here kind of last-minute and I didn't really have time to... I mean... Should I bathe before I meet her?" I dragged the back of my hand across my forehead, skin gritty with dirt and sweat and probably more blood. "Maybe do a purifying juice cleanse or... something?"

With a serene smile, the novitiate lowered her hood and said, "The Goddess Melantha does not require purity of body. Only purity of intent."

She looked younger than I expected—only a teenager—and she wasn't a witch. Just a regular human girl. I wondered what she'd done to end up a servant in the realm of the Dark Goddess, a place you couldn't even access without being summoned by the deity herself, then portaled in by her magick. Ruined or not, this temple was more than just a holy place—it existed in a liminal space all its own, nothing but stars and darkness as far as the eye could see.

Didn't the girl have parents? Friends? *Someone* missing her on the other side?

A sharp pain lanced my heart, but I breathed through it. I had no idea how long the girl had been here, but this was merely day one for me, and I had a long road ahead. I needed to stay grounded. Committed.

"How will she know my intentions are pure?" I asked. "Is there a test?"

"Fear not, Daughter of Darkwinter. I'm certain Her Holiness will be quite impressed with your offering."

Ignoring the Darkwinter bit, I forced a smile and scratched the back of my neck, sneaking a covert whiff of my armpit.

Let's hope her Holiness is impressed with Eau de Urban Warfare, because that's about all I'm offering at the moment...

"Come. She's expecting you." Still wearing a look of pure

serenity, she continued on through a doorway at the back of the temple sanctuary, gesturing for me to follow.

The antechamber was small and intimate, much less imposing than the main temple. The warm glow of hundreds of candles flickered across plain mud walls and a low ceiling, the ground nothing but bare earth. My boots sank into it with every step, and as the scents of candle wax and dirt washed over me, I let out a sigh of relief.

This room, at least, had remained untouched by whatever monster had gone batshit crazy in the sanctuary.

My eyes adjusted to the candlelight, my gaze drifting to the stone altar in the center of the room—a large slab covered in fresh flowers and bowls of fruit, ringed by votive candles in red glass orbs.

Offerings, I assumed. For the…

Oh, shit.

I gasped as I finally spotted the boy, no more than ten or eleven, lying in repose on the altar. His skin was milk-white, the robe they'd dressed him in much too large, as if it was borrowed in haste from someone much older.

Someone much closer to death than this child should've been.

"How did he pass?" I whispered.

"He didn't." The novitiate frowned. "Melantha's son is very much alive."

"Her *son*?" I couldn't hide my shock. The Dark Goddess was tens of thousands of years old—probably older. Lots of witches prayed to her, worshipped her, wrote volumes about her history and magick. I'd never once heard of a child. "How long has he been like this?"

"Six months." She sighed, running her fingers through the sweep of dark hair across his forehead. "He was cursed by a dark fae warlord called Keradoc. A vicious monster who punishes children for the sins of their parents."

An icy shiver ran down my spine. Dark fae were powerful, but Melantha was a dark *goddess*. *The* dark goddess. How could a fae warlord have gotten anywhere *near* her child? And what sin could she have committed to provoke such terrible retribution?

"He's alive," the novitiate continued, "but his soul is trapped in moonglass." She retrieved a small wooden chest from the offerings at his side, opening it to reveal a glass-like sphere as delicate as a soap bubble. At her gentle touch, it glowed with a bright, pearlescent sheen. "It's made from pure moonlight, cast with dark fae magick that's been banned for thousands of years."

"Because it's a prison," I said, disgust churning inside. It wasn't the first time I'd encountered moonglass. According to legend, the very first fae created it by deceiving the moon into lending the fae her light, then forging the magickal globes to trap the souls of their enemies. Eventually, they'd release those souls into the most hostile fae realms, sentencing them to an eternity of torment. "How did this happen?"

She met my eyes, but her serene smile was gone, replaced now with a look of grim determination. "What matters, Daughter of Darkwinter, is that you alone can free him."

"Me? But… how?"

"Breaking the curse requires the blood of the one who cast it."

"Keradoc. Of course." I blew out a breath, the tightness in my muscles loosening as the pieces clicked into place. I was a blood witch—a damned good one at that. Melantha needed me to do some sort of spell to help the child. "So, when do we start?"

"You will travel to his realm as soon as possible," she replied. "Once you've extracted the blood, you'll return to the Temple of the Dark Moon to perform the spell with Melantha, breaking the curse and—"

"Wait. Did you just…" I blinked at her, my mind racing to keep up. "You don't have his blood? Then how can I do the spell?"

"As I said, once you return to the Temple—"

"Her Holiness expects me to hunt this guy down? Some psychotic warlord from a realm I've never been to?"

She arched an eyebrow, as if in warning. "Her Holiness granted you untold strength and power in your time of need, for which you so eagerly pledged your service."

Tension simmered in the air as she glared at me, making my skin hot and itchy.

"I know. It's just..." I took a breath, trying to regroup. Who *was* this girl, anyway? Where were the other novitiates? Melantha's soldiers? "Forgive me, but when Her Holiness summoned me, I was under the impression I'd be meeting with her elite guard."

"Elite? Hardly." A bitter laugh rang out through the small chamber. "No honor among them. No fortitude. I'm sorry, but the Guard of the Dark Moon is no more."

A prickle of unease tingled at the back of my mind. What the hell did "no more" mean?

Fired? Furloughed? Executed?

Crushed to death by falling pillars?

None of this made any sense.

I paced before the altar, my sudden movement snuffing out a few of the votives. "The guards are gone, so now it's on *me* to assassinate some creepy warlord?"

"Not assassinate, no. If Keradoc dies before we perform the spell, the blood will be useless." She grabbed a taper candle and touched it to one of the votives, reigniting the flame. "You must retrieve the blood without harming him—without so much as *alerting* him—or all will be for naught."

"Are you serious? You just said he's a warlord!"

"And you're a formidable blood witch, are you not? One with access to spells and magick you're only just beginning to tap into."

"I'm good at what I do, sure. But dark fae warlords? I'm not... Look, you seem... knowledgeable. Clearly, you're fond of the boy." I smiled, fighting to keep the desperation from my voice. "Maybe you should go instead? I'll stay here and keep an eye on things until you get back." I took the taper from her hand and lit the remaining votives. "See? Already getting the hang of it."

She pinched one of the flames between her thumb and forefinger, the frustration in her eyes finally boiling over. "One candle remains unlit to honor the darkness that exists in all of us, without which we can never know the light."

"Right." I raised my hands in surrender. "I should've known

that, but I didn't. That's what I'm trying to tell you. I'm not the witch for the job. I'll do anything else she asks of me, but—"

"*This* is the quest the Goddess has set out for you," she snapped. The girl was unraveling, her eyes blazing, her voice nearly trembling. "Are you reneging on your sacred vow?"

"No, of course not. I just think we should look at all the options. I'm sure if we put our heads together, we can—"

"How *dare* you question the will of the Goddess!" she bellowed, the force of it making the ground rumble. Her eyes turned a fiery red, two hot embers smoldering in a shadow-dark face. Flames crackled suddenly at her feet, the inferno rising higher and higher until she was completely engulfed.

The mud walls cracked and bubbled around us, and I watched in mute horror as her robes burned away to reveal a body as black as the night sky, pale white serpents slithering around her thighs and torso. Her limbs elongated before my eyes, twisting like those of an ancient tree, hands and feet curling into monstrous talons. Two massive black wings burst from her back and smashed through the walls of the antechamber, each feather dripping with blood.

The altar remained untouched, the boy undisturbed.

I stumbled backward, my heart slamming against my ribs.

The novitiate.

All along, it was her. Melantha.

And this was her true form. Dark and magnificent. Hideous and terrifying.

I dropped to my knees, half-tripping, half awed, and bowed my head. "Forgive me, Your Holiness. I was wrong to question you."

Sharp claws pierced the underside of my chin, forcing me to look up and meet her fearsome gaze. I blinked through the pain, ignoring the warm blood trickling down my neck.

"Daughter of Darkwinter," she said, her voice echoing across the night like a death knell. "If you value the lives of the sisters you fought so bravely to protect in Blackmoon Bay, you *will* achieve this task. By blood and by blade, as you have promised."

By blood and by blade.

The words of my spell echoed as clearly as they had the night I'd first spoken them.

Blood of hell, blood of night
I call on the darkness to show us the light
May evil and malice and violence intended
Return to its hosts uprooted, upended
Dark Goddess I bend, Dark Goddess I bow
Hear my petition, and thusly I vow
My service is yours, by blood and by blade
Until my last breath shall deem it unmade.

That night, my allies and I—my sisters among them—had been trapped in a prison compound hidden in the Olympic National Forest. We'd managed to free the prisoners—dozens of witches and other supernaturals captured by human hunters and the corrupt fae they were working for—but soon our enemies surrounded us, outgunning us four to one. They were hybrids—nearly unstoppable beasts with the combined powers of vampires, shifters, and genetically altered super-monsters we couldn't even identify.

Even with our own formidable team of supernatural heavy-hitters, there was no way we could've survived their relentless attack.

In a last, desperate move, I petitioned Melantha for the strength and magick to turn the tides. She answered my call at once, and thanks to her, we earned our victory—first retaking the compound, then finishing the job last night at the Battle of Blackmoon Bay.

The battle for our lives and our home. For everything we held dear.

I glanced down at my boots, the last of the blood soaking into the dirt, along with any hope I had of avoiding this disastrous mission.

If I refused her, everything I was able to accomplish through the spell would be undone. The city of Blackmoon Bay would fall.

My sisters—the family I'd only just discovered—would die. And everything we'd fought so hard to save would just...

It would end.

A surge of renewed strength shot through my limbs, my blood simmering with magick. *My* magick.

"My service is yours," I said now, repeating the vow I'd made that night. "By blood and by blade. Until my last breath shall deem it unmade."

"Rise, Daughter of Darkwinter."

I got to my feet and met her gaze once more, hoping like hell we were done with the Big Goddess Energy show. I'd seen enough of her scary magnificence to fill my nightmares for the next decade, thanks.

Her dark wings fluttered in the breeze, and the same rot and ruin I'd smelled in the sanctuary assaulted my senses. I tried not to recoil.

"Are you prepared to accept this task?" she asked. "To see it through by any means necessary?"

"I am," I said firmly. I was in it to win it now, no going back. With what I hoped was a confident smile, I asked, "What must I do?"

Melantha extended her arms. One claw held my weapons. The other clutched a glass vial about the size of a tube of lipstick.

After re-securing my stakes and blades, I took the vial and peered inside. Magick swirled beneath the glass, red smoke shot through with threads of black and gold. It was oddly mesmerizing.

"Keradoc dwells in the dark fae realm of Midnight," she said. "This portal spell will take you there, but you won't survive it alone. There's a man in your home realm—also fae—one rumored to have escaped Midnight alive. You must ask for his assistance."

My heart stalled. All the confidence I'd conjured up evaporated in an instant.

The ground spun out from beneath my feet, and I fell back to my knees, my lungs struggling to suck in air.

Deep inside, beneath all the magick and fire, behind all the parts of myself I'd sharpened into weapons and hardened into shields, a tiny box lay hidden, bolted with iron chains and encased in cement. That box held my darkest, most private pain. All the ghosts that had the power to eat through my very soul.

I'd sealed them away years ago, vowing to never open that box again, no matter how often it called to me. And though it still rattled inside on occasion, for the most part, I'd kept it on strict lockdown.

Until now.

The dark fae realm of Midnight… One rumored to have escaped… Ask for his assistance…

Her words were the bolt-cutters on those iron chains, unleashing all the pain I'd so diligently buried. It seeped into my heart, burning it like hot acid, taunting me from across the long years as if no time had passed at all.

Midnight. The most treacherous realm in the universe, controlled by the darkest of the dark fae. A place where the sun never rose and so much blood had been spilled upon its war-torn lands, the lakes and rivers ran red. Melantha was right—there was no way I'd survive it alone.

And the fae who had?

There was no way I'd survive *him*, either.

Not again.

"I will return you to the mortal plane," the Goddess continued, as if I wasn't falling apart before her eyes. "To the city of—"

"New Orleans," I whispered, and she nodded, sealing my fate.

A tear slipped down my cheek.

New Orleans. The one place I swore I'd never, ever go. A place that terrified me even more than Midnight.

No, not because of the ghosts that haunted the city's many cemeteries and historic landmarks.

Because of the ghosts that haunted my heart. The ones she'd just set loose.

"And this… this *fae*," I said, still unable to speak his name out loud, even after all these years. "If he refuses to help me?"

Her black lips twisted into a cruel grin, her wings spreading to their full, terrifying span. The ground rumbled beneath her feet, but instead of flames, skulls rose from the dirt, a dead army blooming at her command.

Behind me, a portal opened, ready to ferry me to New Orleans.

To him.

"Convince him, Darkwinter," Melantha hissed. "Or the ones you claim to love will suffer the consequences of your failure."

I nodded and took a deep breath.

Fought off an onslaught of memories—strong hands sliding into my hair. Eyes the color of molten silver. Promises whispered, promises broken. The salty taste of tears and the dull ache of wounds that never fully healed.

I took a step backward, then another.

Closed my eyes.

And tumbled, ass over teakettle, into my own private hell.

TWO

HALEY

Two years.

That's how long I'd spent convincing myself this place didn't exist. Convincing myself that Elian's return from captivity in Midnight and the subsequent launching of a whole new life in New Orleans—one that *didn't* include me—was just a rumor.

Now, standing before the entrance to his exclusive French Quarter club, I could no longer deny the truth.

Saints and Sinners, the sign read. To humans, it was just another abandoned cathedral with blown-out windows and crumbling spires, complete with a hulking gargoyle perched above the main archway.

But for those of us who could see past the illusion of the fae glamour, a set of glowing silver doors awaited—an invitation I still couldn't bring myself to answer.

There were no bouncers or velvet ropes, no demands for the secret password. Just the ancient gargoyle and the doors and a small plaque reminding me this was hallowed ground, so could I please check my weapons at the armory inside the narthex?

I practically snorted.

Fat fucking chance.

This was no Temple of the Dark Moon. Just because Elian's den of supernatural sin was housed in an old church, that didn't make it hallowed ground any more than it made him a priest.

No one showed up in a place like this looking for redemption, anyway.

They showed up looking for an escape.

Or in my case—to beg.

Damn it. The thought of even *facing* that prick again—let alone asking him for help—tied me up in knots. But what choice did I have? My sisters' lives depended on me seeing this all the way through, and Elian truly was my best shot at surviving the horrors of Midnight.

Probably my *only* shot.

So, decked out in a new lace dress the color of the stars and thigh-high leather boots I'd picked out just to make him suffer, strapped from hip to ankle with weapons that would finish the job if the outfit failed, I pushed open the doors and stepped inside.

And immediately fell under its spell.

Everything about the place was designed to hypnotize, from the rich, blood-red walls to the restored stained-glass windows that pulsed with magick. Suspended in gilded cages from the ceiling, painted fae couples performed dances so erotic, I was already wishing for a cold shower. Semi-private candlelit alcoves lined both sides of the former cathedral, and the pews had been removed from the nave, the flooring replaced with black marble that glittered with tiny silver points.

It looked as if the club's many revelers were dancing across the night sky.

I was relieved not to spot Elian among them. Despite the fever-inducing performances of the fae dancers, five years' worth of resentment and abandonment issues still simmered inside, and one look into his entrancing silver eyes would set it all ablaze.

Not a fire I wanted to face while sober.

Chin raised, shoulders squared, I beelined for the bar and slid into an empty barstool at the end, trying to spot any potential threats. Hunters were always my first concern, but we'd taken a pretty big bite out of their organization during the Battle at Blackmoon Bay. Those who remained loyal to their fucked-up cause would likely be licking their wounds for a good long while.

Here at Saints and Sinners, vampires and fae made up the majority of the clientele, all of them rich, well-dressed, and predatory. The fae were even more refined than the bloodsuckers, their otherworldly beauty as mesmerizing as it was dangerous.

The bartender, though… He didn't fit the profile. Demon. Rough around the edges. A head of messy, jet-black hair and a mouth so sultry it was almost a crime to look at. He wore a white dress shirt and dark slacks but no tie, his sleeves rolled up to reveal muscular forearms mapped with scars.

My own scars practically tingled in response.

As he finished up with one of his vampire customers, I studied him. Another sexy scar ran the full length of his face, slicing through his eyebrow and ending in the dark stubble along his jaw. A black patch covered the injured eye.

When he finally made his way over to me, he nodded and set a coaster on the bar, but didn't smile or say hello. Just waited, arms crossed over his broad chest, one blue eye glowering at me like he was daring me to ask about the missing one.

What I *really* wanted to ask was what time he got off work and how soon he'd like to get started on becoming my next ex-boyfriend, but…

"Drinking or leaving, new girl?" he asked, smooth and cold as ice. "You're holding up the line."

I took a deep breath, trying to re-focus on the mission.

Midnight.

Begging.

Elian.

"Drinking. Definitely drinking. I'll have… I don't know." I offered a flirty smile. "Whatever you think I'll like."

He leaned in close, his demonic scent enveloping me. It reminded me of the smoke that lingered in your hair when you spent too much time by the fire, a hint of lemon simmering beneath it, and holy *hell* did I want to jump across the bar and—

"I need a bit more to go on," he said, then shot me an icy grin to match his voice. "If it's not too much trouble for you."

"Fine. Let's do something with a kick, but nothing boring or predictable. That rules out whisky, vodka, and tequila. I'm not a huge fan of bubbles either, and I don't like anything too milky. Sweet's good, but not *too* sweet, and a little fruit is fine, but nothing *super* fruity, unless it's—"

"Sorry I asked." Without waiting for me to finish, he wiped his hands on the towel draped over his shoulder, selected a martini glass from the rack overhead, and turned toward the multi-colored bottles lined up behind him.

Before I could offer any more helpful pointers, a wave of vertigo hit, alerting me to the presence of a vampire. One getting way too close and personal.

"Did it hurt?" A husky voice breathed in my ear.

I turned to meet his gaze, resting bitch face locked and loaded. "Excuse me?"

"When you fell from Heaven?" He spread his arms and grinned as if I might find the whole package so charming I'd leap into his embrace, wrap my thighs around him, and ride him all the way home.

"Not as much as it did when they cut off my horns and tail," I said. "Anyway, I'm all set here, so… Have a good night."

"Can I at least buy you a drink, beautiful?"

"No, thank you. I'm not interested."

His face fell, then twisted into a scowl. "You don't have to be such a bitch."

"Actually, I do. Because otherwise bloodsuckers like you assume a smile or a kind word is a full-on invitation to Pussy-town, and I promise you, friend. *That's* an exclusive ticket."

"Check the guest list again." He reached over and touched my hair, bringing a lock to his lips before dropping his hand to my thigh and giving it a possessive squeeze. "Pretty sure I'm on it."

Pretty sure you're going to regret touching me, but ooh-kay…

"Well, since you're so persistent," I cooed, "maybe I *should* check." With a faux-seductive smile, I slid my fingers into the top of my boot, seeking that cold, comforting piece of wood I never left home without.

One minute, the hawthorn stake was minding its own business in the boot holster. The next, it was jammed into the back of the fucker's hand.

Such was the beauty of my sharp and pointy friend.

He jerked back with a howl, the hawthorn poison already paralyzing his fingers. I yanked the stake free, spun it in my palm, and shoved it against his crotch, stopping just short of inflicting a more serious injury.

"Touch me again, bloodsucker," I hissed, "and your hand won't be the only thing going limp."

"Go… go fuck yourself, bitch."

"I'd return the sentiment, but I'm pretty sure that hand won't be up for the job any time soon." I laughed. "Get it? Hand? Job?"

He bared his fangs, then stumbled away like a wounded, dejected bird.

"First drink is on me," the bartender said. "That was the best thing I've seen in months."

I reached forward and yanked the towel off his shoulder, then wiped the blood from my stake. "Thanks for the assist, demon."

"You had it handled. Be grateful I don't toss your ass out for smuggling in that stake."

"This teeny tiny little thing?" I finished cleaning it off, then slipped it back into the holster. "It's not like it was going to kill him."

Wooden stakes could poison the fuckers—hawthorn was especially good at interfering with their healing abilities, and a well-placed stake to the chest would knock them out for hours—but still, that was just a temporary fix. Killing vampires required decapitation or burning, and I wasn't about to ruin my new outfit with all *that* mess.

"In any case, best not to draw too much attention." The bartender set down the martini glass, now brimming with pale amber liquid. A single mint leaf floated on top.

"What is it?"

The barest hint of a smile quirked his lips. "It's called a Fallen Angel."

It was the smile that saved him. *Asshole.*

Hiding my return grin behind the rim of the glass, I took a sip, then another.

Damn, that Fallen Angel concoction was good—good enough

to savor over a long conversation laced with innuendo. A conversation that on any other night might've led to a kiss and maybe even an orgasm or two.

But tonight?

I tipped back the glass and chugged it all down. Then, before I could talk myself out of it, I said, "I'm looking for Elian."

THREE

HALEY

I blew out a breath, seriously impressed with my ability to say the bastard's name without crying and/or breaking something.

Progress!

The sexy bartender, however, was *not* impressed. Quite the opposite, actually.

"Elian," he said flatly, folding his arms over his chest again, and I swear the temperature dropped ten degrees.

It didn't feel like jealousy. Aside from a little teasing, he wasn't exactly putting out any "let's take this back to my place" vibes. So why did he clam up when I asked about Elian?

"Is he in tonight?" I pressed.

The guy sized me up with his singularly intense blue eye, which apparently found me lacking. When his gaze finally made its way back to mine, he scowled as if I'd just threatened *his* dick with the stake. "Who the *fuck* wants to know?"

"Pro-tip, buddy. Usually, when a person straight-up tells you they're looking for someone? Dead giveaway right there."

Glaring. He had it down to a science. The eye, the ticking jaw muscle, the flex of those pin-me-down forearms.

I tried to glare right back at him, but when it came to squaring off with intimidating, hot-as-hell demons, I was out of practice. "You *do* realize the size of your tip is inversely proportional to your bullshit, right?"

"What do you want with... *Elian*?" His lip curled when he said the name—a reaction I understood all too well.

"I need to speak with him. It's private and it's important. So if you could just fix me another drink for the road and point me in the right direction, I'll gladly—"

"Are you a dancer?"

A dancer? Was this demon for real?

I reached for my stake again. It wouldn't take much. I could probably put it through his good eye before another insult had time to fall out of that sexy mouth.

The thought calmed me almost as much as the booze.

"I'm more of a stabby, pokey kinda girl," I said. "With a little magick thrown in for fun."

"Well, we're all set on security detail and spell casters, so unless you can work that stabby, pokey bit into a cage dance, we're not hiring."

"You think I'm here about a job?"

"Not sure I care enough to give it much more thought, honestly." He grinned, but I could tell he didn't mean it. Something about all this had gotten under his skin. Something about Elian.

I opened my mouth to push him on it, but before I could utter another word, he flicked his hand to shoo me away, already turning to the next customer.

"Enjoy your evening, *angel*," he said over his shoulder.

Enjoy my *evening*?

It'd taken me two years and the threats of a scary-ass goddess to work up the nerve to set foot in this city, a killer outfit to walk through those silver doors, and a good dose of booze just to say Elian's name without a string of curses attached.

And this demon thought I was *done*?

I was on a hot streak—no way was I bowing out now.

I waited until he finished up with his other customers, then tapped my empty glass. "Still needing that second drink, friend."

He watched me for a beat, then muttered something inaudible before clearing away the empty glass and reaching for another. "Shall I start a tab, then?"

"I'm not staying long enough for that." I opened up the black hole otherwise known as my purse, emptying its contents onto the bar as I searched for my money.

Cell phone, lipstick, lip gloss, a vial of shifter blood.

Hand sanitizer, emergency tampons, emergency black tourmaline, breath mints.

Three vampire fangs, black eyeliner, a stun potion leftover from the Blackmoon Bay fight, Melantha's portal spell, a hair tie, and…

Aha! Sweet, shiny credit card of questionable remaining balance. After today's shopping spree in the Big Easy, I wasn't too sure how much farther it would get me, but hey. Hope sprang eternal.

"Let's give this one a whirl." I held out the card, but the demon didn't take it.

His gaze was on the glass vial from the goddess, utterly transfixed. The blood-red smoke roiled inside, its black and gold threads shimmering.

He glanced up at me again, and I braced for another argument. A brush-off. Anything but what flashed through that stone-cold eye.

Recognition.

The demon *knew* that particular magick. Which meant…

Holy shit. Had he been to Midnight too? Was that how he knew Elian?

He reached across the bar and covered the vial with his hand, his voice turning dark. "Put it out of sight. Now."

I did as he asked, too stunned to do anything else.

"Wait here," he said in that same deadly tone. "Do *not* leave this bar."

"Okay, but what about my—" *Damn.* He was already gone. "Drink," I said with a sigh. I was just about to hop behind the bar and make something myself when the vertigo hit me again, this wave so strong it nearly knocked me off my barstool.

I fisted my stake and palmed the stun potion, slowly turning to face the newcomers—three of them this time.

My wounded bird was flanked by two of his friends, each one more despicable than the last. Whatever supernatural genetics made most vampires hot as fuck and impossible to resist? Clearly skipped this lot.

A quick scan of my surroundings and my heart sunk. No sign of the demon, and the other patrons in the vicinity were too wrapped up in their own flirtations and petty skirmishes to pay any attention to mine.

Shit.

"Sorry, boys," I said as the vampires crowded in close. "You really *aren't* on the guest list."

"It's not pussy we're after tonight, witch," my original stalker said, ever the romantic. His hand hung limp at his side, the skin black and blistering. "We're here for—"

I shoved the stake into his chest, taking him down for the count, then hurled the stun potion at the second vamp's feet. It exploded in a bright yellow starburst, freezing him on contact, but the third one wasn't close enough to the blast to feel its effects. I tried to reach for one of my daggers, but he was too fast, too strong, and too smart.

He was on me in a heartbeat, hauling me out of the stool and locking me in a vise grip, my back against his chest.

"Got any more tricks, witch?" he growled in my ear.

I struggled against his hold, but it was no use. My arms were pinned at my sides, my feet no longer touching the ground, and I had maybe a minute before the stun potion wore off on the other vamp. "Let me go and I'll show you all *sorts* of magick."

"I don't think so, pretty girl." With a sick groan of pleasure, he clamped down hard on my neck, fangs piercing the skin. Before I could even cry out, he'd drained enough blood to make my world spin.

I fought to remain conscious, to reach the dagger in my boot, to do something other than let this asshole finish me off. The temporarily stunned vamp was already on his feet again, stumbling toward me with rage in his eyes, fangs bared, mouth practically foaming for a taste…

Someone slammed into us from behind, breaking me out of my captor's relentless hold and knocking me to the ground as another man—the bartender, I realized—staked my two attackers in quick succession.

Guess I'm not the only one good with the stabby, pokey bit...

I caught his gaze and managed a quick smile of thanks, then turned my attention to the guy who'd knocked me down.

The *fae* who'd knocked me down. Half-vampire too, I realized, dressed in a three-piece black Nehru suit that perfectly hugged his leanly muscled frame.

My mind spun.

How was this possible?

He was partially on top of me from the fall, one hand cradling the back of my head, lips muttering my name like a prayer. His long hair brushed across my face, a fall of silver waves and intricate braids I itched to run my fingers through.

Only the strongest magick could erase time, and there was no magick more powerful than scent for yanking you right back into the past. It washed over me like a dark curse—the particular mix of bergamot and rain that could only belong to him.

Butterflies danced through my insides, my heartbeat quickening.

When I finally found the courage to meet his eyes, my breath hitched, and not just because his weight was half-crushing my lungs.

Five years ago, he walked out of my life without so much as a goodbye... and crushed my fucking heart.

"Elian," I whispered.

Accidentally.

Shit.

His molten silver gaze swept down to my lips, then back to my eyes. A cocky grin curved his mouth, tugging slightly higher on the left.

It did things to me, that crooked grin. Always had. Bad things. Stupid things. And before I knew it, I was grinning right back at him.

Elian brushed his thumb across my lower lip, eyes sparkling, his touch making me shiver. "Still dreaming of me, little sparrow?"

"I am," I admitted.

Then, just to prove it, I did something I'd been *dreaming* about every day for the last five years.

I punched that sexy, silver-eyed fae-hole right in the mouth.

* * *

Ready for more of Haley and her smokin' hot monsters? Grab your copy of Blood and Midnight now!

ABOUT SARAH PIPER

Sarah Piper is a Kindle All-Star winning urban fantasy and paranormal romance author. Through her signature brew of dark magic, heart-pounding suspense, and steamy romance, Sarah promises a sexy, supernatural escape into a world where the magic is real, the monsters are sinfully hot, and the witches always get their magically-ever-afters.

Her recent works include the newly released Vampire Royals of New York series, the Tarot Academy series, and The Witch's Rebels, a fan-favorite reverse harem urban fantasy series readers have dubbed "super sexy," "imaginative and original," "off-the-walls good," and "delightfully wicked in the best ways," a quote Sarah hopes will appear on her tombstone.

Originally from New York, Sarah now makes her home in northern Colorado with her husband (though that changes frequently) (the location, not the husband), where she spends her days sleeping like a vampire and her nights writing books, casting spells, gazing at the moon, playing with her ever-expanding collection of Tarot cards, binge-watching Supernatural (Team Dean!), and obsessing over the best way to brew a cup of tea.

You can find her online at SarahPiperBooks.com and in her Facebook readers group, Sarah Piper's Sassy Witches! If you're sassy, or if you need a little *more* sass in your life, or if you need more Dean Winchester gifs in your life (who doesn't?), come hang out!